Oathtaker

PATRICIA REDING

unfolds a world full of mystery, majesty, yet simple humanity . . . [She] parts the mists and introduces us to a flesh and blood human being . . . who anyone could immediately identify with . . . [Reding's] prime concern is to tell a gripping human story . . .
    —*Joshua Grasso, Associate Professor of English Literature*

From the very beginning I was pulled into this story. The author writes with clarity and creativity. She successfully created characters with such great depth that the issues of commitment, honor and integrity were skillfully woven throughout the story. I loved the fantasy world I found myself immersed in, and the thrilling ride that the characters took me on. This was a great read! I will definitely look for more books from this author.
    —*Lori Stevic-Rust, a Goodreads author*

When you pick up this book be prepared to fall in love with Mara as she battles her way through the maze of evil and magic . . . This story contains adventure, intrigue, battles to the death and, of course, love . . . Reding is truly a gifted storyteller. This is not a book to miss. I am anxiously waiting . . . *Select* the next book in this series.
    —*Mary A. Adair, a Goodreads author* and *Readers' Favorite 5-star rated author*

This is a wonderful adventure filled with believable characters, plenty of twists, and an enthralling storyline. This is a fantastic book for a new author and I would read more in this series. Highly recommended to fans of fantasy fiction.
    —*E.B. Brown, a Goodreads author*

I have never been able to get into a fantasy book before BUT . . . Reding opened by eyes to a brand new world! I found myself falling in love with the characters . . . I spent so many late nights reading because I couldn't put my Kindle down . . . I am looking forward to reading more from this author in the future. To me it goes on my top 10 books of the year . . . !
    —*Anne*

Oathtaker is a beautiful and fantastic epic adventure filled with all the things I love most — a captivating storyline, edge-of-your-seat suspense, thought-provoking characters, and never-ending twists and turns . . . Reding has created a wonderfully enjoyable story filled with a spectacular array of characters that are so rich and vivid that you will wonder if you can still hear them talking to you even after you have finished reading this book . . . Reding is a marvelous new author that you simply have to discover for yourself!
    —*Amber*

What an awesome story. Best fantasy I've read in ages . . . It's a masterful work . . . There is a world created . . . that makes me want more . . . This book makes me want to read the next one, and the one after that, and so on and so on . . . I wanted a saga, a story I could sink into and read for hours and not put down. I got exactly that. The plot was superbly executed, very detailed and an adventure at every page turn. Be prepared to put down every other book you own when you pick this one up.

    —Naomi

Fantasy is not a genre that I usually read, but I think *Oathtaker* may have changed that . . . Also, I just wanted to say, Mara and Dixon are adorable. I cried at some points . . . I've decided to call them Mixon.

    —Kenna

An Epic book deserves an Epic review! . . . Reding weaves this story that just sucks you in. Two thumbs up . . . two very big thumbs up!

    —Kel

Oathtaker kept me busy at nights under my blankets with a light, in the car, and pretty much everywhere else I could smuggle a book. I would definitely recommend this book . . . and I can't wait until *Select* comes out . . . I almost cried when the story came to an end . . .

    —Kerrisa

Oathtaker . . . immediately grabbed my attention and pulled me into its alternate world. I became intrigued by the characters, their history and the land they inhabited . . . I felt personally invested in the story . . . Battles between good and evil, the struggle to meet a challenge you never imagined you could face, not backing away from an oath no matter what the sacrifice – being there, side-by-side with the characters in *Oathtaker*, I came away feeling challenged and emboldened in my own life.

    —Sharon

A beautifully crafted epic fantasy adventure . . . masterfully written prose . . . I would definitely recommend this one . . .

    —Kerry

It's time for me to lose the notion that I don't care for fantasy novels . . . I recently tore through . . . Reding's *Oathtaker*. It is a perfectly paced story . . . I thought about the characters when I wasn't reading and couldn't wait to get back to them . . . The plot kept me reading longer and later at night than I normally can stay awake for . . . The best thing about *Oathtaker* is that there's more! It's the first in a series . . . I look forward to the next book . . . I guess I really am a reader of fantasy.

    —Tammy

A satisfying glow accompanies the final chapter of *Oathtaker* and leaves me begging for more with the same excitement that comes with receiving a . . . present. A new kind of magic laces this book, not with typical wands and wizards, but a . . . magic that is as unique as the characters that sit in the pages. My heart aches that they are not sitting at my kitchen table sharing stories . . . Reding truly earns herself her first Readers' Favorite Award with *Oathtaker* . . . impossible to put down . . . I give *Oathtaker* five stars and beg for sequels, prequels and spin offs!

    —Annie

I couldn't stand it anymore and had to read the last 120 pages in one night. I laughed, cried, and even yelled . . . a few times. I'd call *Oathtaker* a magnificent adventure story that lures you in from the very beginning . . . I loved this book so much I gave it to my kids' teachers, friends, and family members . . .

    —Deanna

I am in awe of the author's descriptive, clever and imaginative writing . . .

    —Charlene

What an awesome storyline! This novel can be enjoyed by a broad range of readers, including the younger . . . This . . . is definitely a "5 star." I am anxiously awaiting Part II . . .

    —Jean

This book is fantastic and beautifully written! I love everything about it . . .

    —Brianna

I felt like I was transported to another realm. I . . . am looking forward to reading her next book as well. I would definitely recommend this . . . to others . . .

    —Deb

I loved this book . . . I . . . enjoy it when an author puts her heart and soul into a story that compels you to turn the page . . . I can't wait for the next . . .

    —Raymond

Oathtaker

The Oathtaker Series: Volume One

PATRICIA REDING

Scripta Manent Publishing
WRITTEN WORDS REMAIN

BOOKS BY PATRICIA REDING

The Oathtaker Series
Oathtaker
Select
Ephemeral and Fleeting

DEDICATION

To my family, with a special reminder to my children, Andrew, and his lovely bride, Desireé, Madeline and Isabelle: always aim high.

Acknowledgements

A special thanks to my early readers, especially to Denny who let me tell my own story; Madeline who hovered over my shoulder for each new chapter, then evolved into an editor extraordinaire; Isabelle who just kept smiling; Kim whose keen insight saved me from what could have been some embarrassing errors; Jodi for her constant encouragement, vision, and for keeping me on track; and Katie who has been converted—she has become a fan of fantasy.

Time and Place

Again the people turned from Ehyeh, the Good One, and His decrees, and became evil in their ways. Each person was a law unto himself. Chaos reigned. One small remnant, however, remained faithful, carrying Ehyeh's ways and words through the ages and to the world. They were Ehyeh's special people, the *Select*. Others grew envious of them and eventually, enslaved them. Even so, they remained faithful.

The Good One's heart was moved. From among those who had turned to Him, He sought people who would agree to protect the Select. He commissioned them the *Oathtakers*. Each chose to become a member of the group and to willingly undergo the rigorous training required. When Ehyeh called upon one to aid a member of the Select, the Oathtaker could choose to swear a voluntary life oath for the protection of that person. If he did, that Select became his charge.

When an Oathtaker completed his training, he was awarded an Oathtaker's blade, a weapon infused with magic that would exist for so long as he lived. Upon swearing an oath for the protection of one of the Select, Ehyeh granted the Oathtaker two additional weapons. The first was attendant magic—unique abilities that would assist the Oathtaker in his endeavors. Second, Ehyeh granted the Oathtaker continued youth for so long as his charge lived. A special rule applied to one whose charge was seventh-born: he would remain forever youthful.

Upon the death of his charge, an Oathtaker could begin his life anew, but in the meantime he could not bind himself to another. An Oathtaker could not have divided loyalties; he could not be unequally yoked.

With the assistance of their Oathtakers, the Select gained their freedom. Then together, they moved to the lands known as Oosa, where they built a strong, free and thriving nation.

But once again, the times have changed . . .

Chapter One

Mara stopped abruptly in her tracks. Moments ago, there had been the sounds of crickets, an occasional bird chirping, the giggling sass of chattering squirrels as they scurried from tree to tree, branch to branch. Suddenly, all was quiet. The breeze whispering its secrets through the foliage, giving relief from the heat of the day, stilled.

Stepping off the path, Mara had the niggling sensation that someone watched or followed her. Catching a glimpse of something out of the corner of her eye, she glanced in that direction, but saw nothing unusual. Trying unsuccessfully to shrug off the disconcerting feeling, she cautiously placed one foot ahead of the other. Trained to move stealthily, no gravel moved under her step, no leaf rustled. Step by step, she returned to the pathway that led to the river. The distant song of slowly moving water was all she heard.

Then as suddenly as the quiet had descended, there came a great howling. It sounded like a pack of dogs or wolves, but it was louder, more grating to the ears, more ominous. It had a spooky, hair-raising quality.

A shiver ran down her spine. She stopped midstride. "Grut?" she wondered aloud. *Surely, not,* she thought, *but could it be?*

Few grut, the dreaded beasts of Sinespe—the world under, the world of the hopeless and dead—had been seen in the area for some time, as few of the Select they were sent to pursue and to destroy, remained. Still, the cacophony was unlike any she'd encountered before.

As though in response to her query, the screeching, howling lament increased in volume.

In an instant, the smell of the air changed. Earlier, an intense, almost floral-like scent had piqued Mara's curiosity, driving her to follow this particular wooded path to find the source of the fragrance. It compelled her to follow her nose, though it took her far from her intended track. But now there came a pervading stench. It reeked of danger, was rank like decay, like death.

For a moment she thought she could make out the smell of blood, but a survey of the trail around her revealed none. Intensely alert, she recalled an instructor having surmised that blood was red because the color screamed *danger!* Big on colors and smells, he encouraged his students to give careful consideration to them. "Smelling danger in advance," he lectured, "can be an important skill, as it may serve to keep one from coming upon it casually or unaware."

Mara fleetingly contemplated turning back, but her training as an Oathtaker caused her to brush the thought aside. She could feel the emotional tugging, the urge to respond to the call, that an Oathtaker felt when encountering perilous circumstances.

Her heart racing, she continued toward the sound. It became more insistent with each passing breath. She eased her way through the brush toward the screaming chorus. A thorny branch caught at her tunic. She pulled herself free, tearing a small patch from her clothing, then approached a giant oak.

Though the heat had lessened from the peak afternoon hours, a sheen of perspiration covered her. She wiped her brow with the back of her hand as she took a quick mental inventory of the things she carried: weapons, supplies, wits. She gave a nervous inward laugh over that last one.

The screaming continued, unrelenting.

She crouched low behind the oak, its branches bent nearly to the ground. Its full summer shroud already displayed a dry fuscous brown cast. She grasped hold of a low hanging branch, found a notch in the trunk for her leather-booted foot, and boosted herself up. Dressed in simple free flowing garb, she easily melded into her hiding place. She glanced out.

"Great Creovita!" she muttered. *Grut. There must be an entire pack of them!* A shiver ran down her spine. Her heart raced. Her hands shook and her stomach clenched. A single scratch from a grut claw, fang, or tail, would infect, causing a painful death within hours. The victim's skin would begin to burn away and his—*or her*—throat would close. She watched below.

Ten or more muscle-bound beasts paced outside a small wayfarers' hut. At first glance they resembled wolves, but they were larger, nearly four feet high at the shoulder, covered with hair, smoky black in color and coarse as wire. Each sported a spiky spine and a razor sharp tail. Their bulging red eyes oozed thick black mucus. As they howled, the beasts' three rows of teeth, curved slightly inward, became visible. *Like a snake*, Mara thought.

As though to punctuate the truth of their nature, the grut emanated the unmistakable odor for which they were known: the smell of death, the smell of Sinespe.

She struggled to breathe as the air became more putrid. Feeling assaulted by the odor, she covered her nose briefly with a portion of her tunic.

The wayfarers' hut stood at a distance of about twenty long strides. Branches of the great oak in which she sat reached out and over the hut, which was old and nearly hidden among the surrounding brush and trees. Something over ten-foot square and about as high, the building sported a dilapidated exterior. Its lower walls were made of mottled red-brown river rock packed together with clay from the nearby riverbed. Moss covered, it had begun to decay from a combination of age, weather, and neglect. Ivy surrounded the structure, holding to it tenaciously, as though it intentionally, maliciously, pursued the building's demise.

The hut had no windows, only a small opening near the roof that served to allow smoke and heat an escape, and a single low door, rounded at the top, likely barred from the inside. Though wayfarers traditionally used such huts in days past, few of the cabins remained standing. This one had withstood the test of time—if only barely.

Nearby, lumbering between the surrounding brush, sting weed and rock, several grut spread out in a ring around a fine russet gelding, imprisoning the animal. Repeatedly darting and withdrawing, teasing and taunting, the grut toyed with their captive. Its eyes wide in terror, it snorted, then screamed. Coming up on its back legs, it dropped down upon the beasts, but they continued their attack. They tore at the equine's flesh, hideously delighting in their torture. In short order, a killing grasp brought the animal to its knees. It went still.

Pulling and ripping, the grut quickly consumed the gelding's remains, leaving only scattered bloody bones and tufts of hair that drifted in the air, then settled down upon a few travelers' bags of coarse burlap that littered the ground, their contents tossed aside.

The smell of blood filled the air.

Mara took count. *One, two, three . . . seven, eight.* Noting a group coming from around the backside of the hut, she continued: *Nine . . . twelve, thirteen. Dear Good One! Thirteen?* A single such beast was a formidable foe; a full pack was extreme.

A path ran between her hiding place and the hut. The underworld beasts filled the space, pacing, panting, howling, with the gelding's blood sprayed across their backs and saliva the color of urine running from their fangs.

"My lucky day, thirteen grut," Mara muttered. She pondered how she might get around or through the pack and to the hut.

Notwithstanding the pervading foul odor, the Oathtaker could make out, now and again, the same sweet scent she'd noticed earlier. It reminded her of an exotic combination of jasmine, sandalwood and heliotrope. She wondered if it could be the fragrance of one of the Select. Although trained for their protection, she'd never encountered one of Ehyeh's chosen, each of whom, after reaching the age of accountability and having found the Good One's favor, began to emanate his own unique and exquisite aroma. As the scent made for an easy trail to follow, it left the Select open and vulnerable to pursuers.

Now and again, through a break in the gruts' screaming, Mara thought she heard moaning coming from inside the hut. She had to hurry.

She opened her bag to check on her supplies: a rope, hooks, a torch, some dried food, and various herbs suited for an assortment of purposes—from healing, to sleeping, to killing. Also, she carried small utensils, a sack of gold coin good in any of Oosa's seven provinces, blankets, and extra clothing. Two canteens hung from her belt, as did a hatchet and two blades. Attached to the inside of her boot was a third blade. On her back, she sported a bow and a dozen arrows. Finally, and of course in its carefully hidden sheath at the back of her neck, she carried Spira, her Oathtaker's blade, the physical sign of her training, a blade infused with magic that would live for so long as she did.

The Oathtaker climbed higher, scratching her knees and forearms along the way. From this height she had a better view of the hut. Weather had worn through the roofing in some places.

I could hang my rope from a branch and drop in. Maybe?

She contemplated. No, that wouldn't work. She'd need space to maneuver. Also, she'd need to escape the hut eventually, and she might need to help someone else to get away as well.

Trained for emergencies and dangerous situations, Mara willed herself to breathe slowly and steadily, to take in all of the features of the problem before her, to concentrate, and to formulate a solid plan. Even so, it was becoming increasingly apparent that she'd have to act quickly.

The beasts grew more insistent. Those that had been gnawing on the dead gelding's bones lost interest in their pursuit and resumed pacing with the rest of the pack. Occasionally one snarled or snapped at another.

She was grateful she'd taken along that morning, her bow and a quiver of arrows. Of course, to bring the beasts down, she'd have to hit the grut in any one of three small, but particular targets: the space right behind the grut's ear to go straight to the beast's brain, the center of the grut's chest to reach the place where its heart would be—if indeed it had one, or the grut's eye to take out its link to the underworld, although in that case, death might not be instant.

Although considered a sure shot, target practice on a warm summer day was an entirely different matter from her taking aim under the pressure of a pack of stalking, growling beasts. She had to take her time and use care. When her dozen arrows were spent, she would use her hatchet and knives, though she preferred not to use Spira unless absolutely necessary. Removing it from a grut—even a dead one—could expose her to the beast's deadly poisonous blood or saliva.

Mara climbed to a position high enough that no beast could reach her, but low enough to get a clear view of the vulnerable targets she sought. She checked her balance. Nocking her first arrow, she whispered, "Ehyeh, Lifegiver, let my aim be true. Help me to bring destruction to these minions of the underworld." She looked at the howling mass below.

There, that one that just turned to the side.

She loosed her arrow. It sang through the air, moving straight to her intended target behind an ear of one of the grut. On impact, the beast stopped short in its tracks, howled, and then fell. Instantly, and to the Oathtaker's surprise, it went up in flames—and disappeared.

That's curious.

The stench of sulfur infused the air. She tried to rid her nose of it.

Her second arrow nocked, she took careful aim, then loosed it. Another perfect shot, this one to the center of the beast's chest. A flash of fire and smoke, and the second grut vanished.

The next four shots were just as true.

Six down, seven to go, with six arrows remaining . . .

The young Oathtaker's kills agitated the remaining grut. They stalked warily, hauntingly.

She readied her seventh arrow and shot. "Blast!" she muttered. "Missed." Now only five arrows remained while seven beasts prowled.

Steady.

She took aim for the eighth time. She loosed the arrow. It hit her intended target. The seventh grut disappeared.

The next three shots also found their mark.

One arrow to go and three grut standing . . .

Mara paused, watching the manner in which the remaining beasts paced. She took her time. She found an opening. She aimed. She fired. Another grut went up in flames.

With her arrows spent and two grut standing, she reached for one of her three knives.

Each grut's disappearance reduced the noisy wailing. Now more consistently, but still only sporadically, came the sounds of moaning from inside the cabin. She hoped the grut had not touched someone or surely, he would die.

She tested the weight of her knife, then scooted further out in an effort to get a closer shot. Momentarily off balance, she paused to steady herself, wiped her brow of sweat, shifted her weight, and then took in a few calming breaths.

As she turned her attention back to the grut, one turned and looked directly at her. She loosed her knife. It spun through the air, end over end, and landed— nearly as intended—not straight in the beast's eye, but right between its eyes. Imbedded deeply, the weapon looked like a horn protruding from the creature's face. The grut yelped and pawed at it. Then it let out a shrill whine and dropped to the ground, raising a cloud of dust. The wound attracted the attention of the other remaining grut. It stopped screaming and approached its injured pack mate.

Is the burning away of each grut intended to keep the others from being lured away from the target they were sent to destroy?

Seeing an opening, she readied the second of her knives, took aim, and then let it fly.

Curse it. Another miss.

Finding the as yet uninjured grut in a position that made for a perfect target, the Oathtaker grasped the last of her three blades, took aim, and then threw it. It was a good shot, but not the best. It stuck between the grut's shoulders, full to its hilt. The beast howled and bolted.

The grut wounded between the eyes staggered toward its pack mate and pounced. The two beasts snapped and snarled, each seeking the jugular of the other. With teeth gnashing, each sought to shred its adversary. Tails lashed, leaving bloody gashes. The grut struggled and screamed in their battle.

Shortly, the grut wounded between the shoulders dealt a fatal blow to the other. It burst into flame and vanished in a flash.

One grut remained. It was wounded, but not ready to give up the battle. It tottered, panting. Its scream became an intermittent, monotonous whine. Its coat was mottled with blood, black and thick as pitch. Its yellow saliva ran to the ground.

Pant . . . Pant . . . Pant . . .

Seemingly with a second wind and a renewed commitment to destroy, it approached the hut. Dust spiraled upwards behind its every step. It stood on its haunches, then threw itself against the cabin door. Again, the beast rose. Again, it fell. On the grut's third attempt, the door shook in its frame.

It's about to give!

Quickly Mara scrambled down. As her feet hit the ground, the grut looked her way, then turned back. It resumed its pouncing . . . pouncing. Splinters around the latch broke away.

The door could withstand little more. If Mara didn't kill the creature and do so quickly, it would be inside the cabin in seconds. Rushing forward, she stumbled on a root. The grut glanced at her as though considering whether to pursue her instead of whoever was in the hut, as though daring her to come nearer, to attack.

Dear Good One, don't let it pounce!

Catching herself before falling fully to the ground, the Oathtaker continued toward the wounded beast.

It turned away, once again rising up on its haunches and dropping down on the door. Its feet back on the ground, it staggered, it heaved, it stumbled, but it did not stop.

Near death but with furious intensity, the beast focused its final efforts on its intended target.

It would only take a touch, a single drop of blood . . .

Another pounce rattled the door. Wood splintered, then cracked. The door swung open. It hung barely on its hinges.

Again the grut glanced at Mara. It seemed to laugh at her feeble efforts. Wheezing, it raised one foot, preparing to step inside.

A scream from within rent the air.

Mara sprinted forward as the grut's foot landed on the threshold. Just as the beast prepared to take another step, she threw her hatchet. But for Spira, it was her last weapon. It slammed into the center of the back of the grut's head.

The beast went still.

Mara jumped back.

The grut's legs gave way. It shuddered, it shook, then flames consumed it. The blast of heat singed the hair on the Oathtaker's forearms as she instinctively covered her face. A second later, the fire was gone and with it, the last of the thirteen grut and all trace of their ever having been. No hair, no blood, no saliva remained.

She staggered, breathless. Tears stung her eyes. When she reached the doorway, she leaned against its frame and peered inside.

The rotting stench and the burning smell of sulfur disappeared with the grut. In its place, Mara again could make out the same sweet floral scent that had first moved her to follow the forest path she'd taken. She breathed in the heady perfume, closing her eyes for a moment to delight in its luxurious depth, then entered the hut and closed the door behind herself as well as she could, given its condition. She sought to be cautious against another possible grut attack, or from an assault by a stalker of any other sort. She glanced about, quickly taking in her surrounds.

On the cabin's walls hung shelves upon which sat simple earthenware jugs with faded, pocked exteriors. Likely they were for carrying water in from the river that ran behind the building, its gurgling once again audible. The surface of the simple dirt floor, packed down over many years, was smooth and shiny in spots. Scattered about were piles of dry decomposing leaves, various shredded linens, and a cape of the whitest, softest cashmere—a clear sign of extravagant wealth. Mara assumed the items belonged to the woman she found before her.

Great with child, she lay on the floor, a tattered moss green blanket mottled with grime beneath her. Blood spotted her clothing. Of an undetermined age— past the start of her third decade, but clearly not having seen the dawn of the first day marking her fourth—she boasted exquisitely flawless skin. It gave her an almost unearthly quality, though so wan, it nearly matched the white of the cape. Her face showed signs of great strain. Her breathing came short and perspiration stood out on her face and throat.

Fear in her brilliant green eyes, she turned her head to the side, waving her hand weakly, as though resigned to take whatever might come. Then she cast a furtive glance toward the door before settling her gaze back on the Oathtaker, a question in her eyes.

Mara edged closer, bending down, hands forward. "I'm an Oathtaker. I killed the grut, but I see I arrived too late. I'm so dreadfully sorry that they harmed you."

She hung her head. "You know, there's nothing I can do now—except perhaps ease your pain and bring some comfort to your last hours. I'm so, so very sorry." She reached down and touched the woman, seeking to console her. "Here, I have some herbs with me and—"

"No," she whispered softly.

"No?"

"Not the grut." She placed her hand upon her midsection as her body tensed. She was in labor.

Trained to assist with injuries and illnesses, Mara had attended numerous birthings in the past. But what she saw before her now was unlike any birthing room she'd ever seen before. Quickly, she turned businesslike.

"What's your name?" She seemed to know instinctively that the woman needed to rely on another so that she could concentrate her efforts on the birth of her child. Mara's arrival, if it had been any later, would have been to no avail. As it was, she could only hope to save one of them—the mother or her child.

"I am," she began. Her voice broke. She gasped as another contraction took hold. When it passed, she continued, "Rowena."

"Good, Rowena. I'm Mara. I can help. Just relax. You're going to be fine. Now, let me take a look here." She removed Rowena's coverings, then touched her tentatively. "Just relax now, you're safe." She examined her. "The child is near. I need to go to the river for water, to get some supplies, and—"

"No," Rowena interrupted. "Please, listen . . . carefully." She struggled with each word, each breath.

"I'm listening. Take some steady breaths. That's it. Relax."

"I . . . will not survive this birth."

"Hush! Hush, now. Don't you say such a thing."

"I must tell you . . . Please, listen," she sputtered out between chokes and gasps. She grew ever more agitated. Though weak, she grasped Mara's wrist with urgency.

"What is it? You tell me, and then we'll see to this new gift from Creovita, the life giver."

Rowena loosened her grip. "I am a . . ." She winced with the pain of another contraction. "I am . . ." She cried out. Tears spilled. "A se—" She struggled to catch her breath. "I am a—"

"You are what?"

"Se—seven."

"You are seven. Seven what? Leagues from home? That's not so far. I'll help you to get there afterwards, or to get word to whomever you like if you can't make the journey right away. That needn't concern you. Now let me see what I can do here."

She shook her head again. "This child is—" She sucked in a breath. "This child—"

"Surely, this can wait. Yes? You need to save your strength. We have some work to do here." Mara pressed her hands against her shoulders to lay her back again.

She rested for a moment, then her eyes opened large. "Listen, I haven't much time. I'm a . . . seventh. She is a seventh."

"A seventh? *A seventh!* But that can't be!" The Oathtaker pulled back. She thought for a moment, then looked at Rowena closely, her eyes narrowed. "Oh, dear Good One, are you *the* Rowena? *Rowena Vala?* The ranking member of the Select?"

She nodded.

"Goodness! But . . . who's 'she?' Was there another seventh with you? Are there *two* of you?" Mara glanced about. Nothing indicated that anyone else had been there.

Rowena struggled as a powerful contraction bit. She clenched her teeth. "I'm a seventh," she continued when the contraction ended, her voice steady and clear for the first time. "A seventh daughter. This child, my daughter, will be a seventh daughter of a seventh daughter, and the ranking member of the first family. You must save her. Take her. Run. Promise me, I—" She choked down a sob. "I can trust you. Yes? You're an Oathtaker." She sucked in a breath. "I'm counting on you. Please . . . tell me I can trust you."

"Dear Good One! Rowena, your child could be my assignment—my charge!" The Oathtaker's eyes lit up. "Oh, I'll help you! But first we have to get you through this labor. Oh, if this child is a girl—"

"It is a girl. Help . . . me."

Mara picked up a nearby cloth and wet it with water from a canteen hanging at her waist. She placed the cloth on Rowena's forehead, then retrieved a blanket from her pack to cover her against the chills that had come with her loss of blood. Once done, she examined her again. The child's head would soon crown. Mara hoped a few strong pushes would do it, as Rowena had little strength remaining.

After pouring water into a cup from her sack, she rummaged through her dried herbs to find a relaxing, pain-numbing tea blend. When she tore it open, the smell of green permeated the air. She could not brew a tea without a fire, but it would steep at least some in the tepid water.

"Here, drink this." She helped Rowena lean forward, then put the cup to her lips.

She drank, then turned her face away as another contraction took hold.

A small mark behind Rowena's right ear drew Mara's attention. It looked like a tattoo of the numeral seven, in a rosy color. "So this your sign, yes? This mark here?"

Rowena nodded.

Gingerly, the Oathtaker brushed her thumb across the mark. She'd studied for so long and finally she was face to face with one of the Select. *Beautiful.* Setting the tea aside, she took another look at how the birthing progressed.

"The child has crowned. With this next contraction, I want you to bear down with all your strength. Try to focus your energy. Don't scream or cry if you can help yourself." In an effort to lighten the intensity of the mood, she chuckled quietly and leaned in as though sharing a secret. "My grandmother always said a woman wasted good energy during a birthing when she cried out. Now I don't know if there's any truth to that, but if she was right, it would be wise to follow her advice. You've no extra strength to spare."

She lightly patted Rowena's arm in encouragement. "Oh, here it comes. You feel that contraction building? Yes, that's it. Now bear down and focus. Good . . . good. Well done. I see it's almost— Yes . . . here comes another. Right now. Push. Push!"

Rowena did not shed a tear. She bore down with astounding energy given her circumstances. Then, spent, she fell back. A single tear rolled down her cheek.

Some minutes passed and with them, several more contractions. Mara spoke gently, encouragingly. Then with one final push, the infant was born.

"That's it! Rowena, look. You have a beautiful baby . . . girl. Oh, you've done it." The Oathtaker wiped the child's face and cleared its nose, then took some heavy string from her pack and tied the cord off as needed. Once done, she used Spira to cut the cord. She felt a tingling and almost instantly, a new scent, clean and sweet, filled the air. She breathed in deeply of its mind jarring, almost mesmerizing and complicated combination of orange, violet, iris and jasmine, accompanied by cedar, sandalwood and oak moss. For a moment, she wished she could drown in the fragrance.

Briskly she rubbed the infant's back, encouraging the little one to breathe. The child gulped in her first breath, but did not cry. Mara laughed with relief. *She's all right!* She wiped the infant down, stopping to take note of a birthmark behind her right ear. Of a light blush color, it looked like two numeral sevens, the second intersecting halfway down the vertical line of the first. She marveled at it, touching it softly, then wrapped the child in a clean soft cloth.

"Rowena, look here." She placed the infant at her breast. "She is so beautiful. What's her name?"

"Reigna."

"That's a lovely choice. And she looks like a 'Reigna.' She is regal. Surely she will reign in this life as would any queen."

Suddenly, Rowena's eyes opened wide. She grasped the Oathtaker's arm and pulled her close. "Mara!" she exclaimed, her voice soft but firm.

"What? What is it?"

"Another—"

"Another? Another what?"

"Mara," she repeated, as a contraction bit deeply.

The Oathtaker took another look. "Oh, goodness, there's another!" This was indeed a miracle. No Select had ever before born twins—not one, not ever. "Easy, Rowena, you can do this." Half giddy, Mara fought to hold down her grin.

A tear rolled down Rowena's face as another contraction took hold.

"Almost there," Mara encouraged. "Almost there."

After a couple minutes, a final contraction gripped the woman. When it released, the Oathtaker held up another child. She tied off the cord and cut it. Once again she felt a tingling sensation, then the infant's heavenly scent momentarily overtook her. Although this child looked identical to her sister, her fragrance, a combination of bergamot, jasmine, and orange, with hints of warm musk, differed. Like her sister, the infant took in a gulp of air, but she did not cry.

Mara rummaged for something in which to wrap her. Once done, she looked for the infant's sign. It differed from her sister's. She studied it for a moment before she could make it out, but then it seemed completely clear. It consisted of two squares. When looking at them as touching side to side, the top horizontal line of the one on the left was in a darker pink color. From its upper right corner came a downward stroke, again in the darker color. This line divided the two squares. Then, on the square to the right, only the right side vertical line was darker from the rest of the mark. Together the darker portions denoted the numerals "seven" and "one." But when considering the mark from the other angle—as one square atop the other—the mark looked like a straight-sided numeral eight.

She turned her attention back to business. "Rowena, look." She placed the infant next to her mother. "What will you call her?"

Her eyes rolled briefly, then refocused. "The seventh seventh 'who is but . . . is not,'" she whispered.

"What's that?"

"She is a seventh, but she is not."

Mara didn't understand, so she simply nodded. "What's her name?"

She pulled in a shallow breath. "Eden."

"Eden. Paradise." The Oathtaker pulled the blanket up over mother and children to keep them warm. Then she focused her attention back on Rowena. She placed her hands upon her, praying for healing, but sensed no change. "I'm so sorry I can't do more. I—" Hot tears welled in her eyes. She wiped them away brusquely. "Is there anything I can do to ease your pain?"

"Mmmm . . . no." Rowena breathed shallowly. "Thank you," she whispered. Her eyes rolled upward, then closed. Then she said softly, "I have . . . done it."

A minute passed in silence. Mara sat quietly stroking the woman's face and brushing back her auburn hair.

Suddenly Rowena's eyes shot open. She grabbed a handful of Mara's tunic. "You must run—quickly. Take them . . . to safety." Her words grew softer as her grip loosened and her eyes closed.

"I promised I'd help you and I promise I'll help them. I accept your daughters as my charge. I swear to you and to Ehyeh, who is above all, that I would give my life for them. I will be their Oathtaker for so long as they live."

At that very moment, the ground shook. A sense of power, unlike any other, filled the Oathtaker. It was as a welling of emotion, a filling of needy places in her heart, a song bursting. This was the confirmation—the Good One's acknowledgement of her oath. She now owed Reigna and Eden protection for so long as they lived. She'd never heard of an Oathtaker with more than a single charge before, that was true, but then she'd never heard of a Select bearing twins, either. It had felt right to swear to protect them both. However could she have chosen between them?

"I am . . ." Rowena shuddered, suddenly overtaken with chills.

Once again Mara's eyes welled with tears. Then she remembered. *Oh, great Ehyeh!* "Listen. Listen to me!" She slapped Rowena's face, first lightly, then more firmly. She knew she couldn't save her, but she also knew that it was too soon to let her go. "Rowena, release your power. Release your power, now!" If she did not, her children would not carry her power forward.

Slowly, laggardly, Rowena's eyes opened and refocused. Mara's words jarred her back fully, if for only a moment. She fought for a breath as she struggled to speak.

"Now!"

The woman whispered three simple words slowly but succinctly: "Restore . . . and . . . revive." With that, her eyes rolled up and back, her body shuddered violently, and she exhaled the last of her breath.

In that same instant, the earth shook. The trees around the hut swayed. Blinding lightning burst and crackled causing a deafening, exploding thunder. The sky, visible through the hole in the roof, turned momentarily blood red. The children let out their first cries—

And the door of the hut burst open.

Mara's eyes flashed upward.

There stood the most fearsome looking man she had ever laid eyes upon.

Just over six foot tall, he stood lean, but strong. A man in his prime, he'd taken on all of the bulk and muscle of a life of discipline. Bent forward in a fighting stance, his feet slightly apart, his breathing came rapid and deep, like that of a bull whose space had been invaded. In a single glance his piercing blue eyes inventoried all of the details of the cabin's interior. Glaring, they flickered past Mara, rested on Rowena's face for the briefest moment, then turned back to the Oathtaker. He reached up and back.

His eyes held a look of murderous intent. Fearing she and the babies were in danger, Mara reached for Spira, her only remaining weapon. Even had it not been so, it would have been her weapon of choice, as an Oathtaker's blade never misses its mark. Grasping it firmly, she slipped Spira from its sheath and let it fly. The weapon sped through the air straight toward the heart of the threatening intruder.

As she released Spira, the man loosed a nearly identical blade. In that moment, they both knew that the other was an Oathtaker.

The blades stopped and hovered in mid-air, each just inches from its intended target, for while an Oathtaker's blade will never miss its mark, it will never harm an Oathtaker—with one exception: were an Oathtaker's blade to be used against its owner, his death would be instant.

Mara and the stranger looked at one another's blades and then, simultaneously, they glanced up. Their eyes met.

The newcomer spoke first. "An Oathtaker?"

"Yes, as I see, are you. I'm Mara. Mara Richmond."

"Hmmm," was his curt reply. Then he said simply, "Dixon." He grasped Spira as Mara clasped his blade. Each offered the weapon of the other to its owner and then both returned them to their sheaths.

Dixon moved forward. "Rowena. Rowena, I'm here." Gently, he shook her.

Mara watched, her eyes riveted, expectant.

Upon touching the woman, Dixon's eyes turned quickly from the soft glance he'd given her, to a kind of madness. He jumped up and glared. "What have you done?" he hissed.

"What have *I* done?" Mara crouched down, pulled away the blanket that covered Rowena, then carefully took into her arms first Reigna, then Eden. She stood back up, holding herself as tall as she could. She glared. "What have *I* done? Oh, nothing! Oh, well that is, except—ahhh . . . well . . . let me think here . . ."

She hesitated, playacting. "Oh, yes, I remember now. I took down a full pack of grut, helped Rowena birth these beautiful children, accepted them as my charge, saw to it that she released her power with her *dying* breath, comforted her in her last moments . . . Shall I go on?" She took a deep breath. "What have *I* done? Who are you to accuse me of anything? I have done my duty!"

"I am her Oathtaker. That's who I am!"

"Were," Mara snapped. "You *were* her Oathtaker. She's dead. Or did I forget to mention that? So I might ask—what have *you* done? Where were *you* when she so clearly needed you? The truth is, if I hadn't arrived when I did, I expect we would have lost them all!" Her eyes remained fixed on him.

After some seconds, he looked away. "Dead," he whispered.

She couldn't tell if he was stating the fact, or asking if it was true. Considering the shock he must be feeling, she decided that arguing with him would not be in anyone's best interests. She recalled that above all, she must get the girls to safety quickly.

"I'm sorry, I did all I could. Rowena had lost too much blood before I arrived. She was a fighter, I know."

He didn't take his eyes from his former charge. He dropped to his knees at her side. Taking her hand into his own, he lifted it to his cheek and closed his eyes. His breathing slowed. His jaw set. Mara sensed he fought back tears. Slowly, he leaned forward to stroke the woman's cheek, then her hair. Finally, he bowed his head and audibly exhaled.

Mara watched his easy touch, saw his shoulders sag, and his eyes pressed closed. She knew that look.

"You loved her." She hadn't intended to speak the words out loud, but there they were—hanging in the air.

"Well," he said, clearing his throat, obviously restraining himself, "of course I cared deeply for her. She was my charge. She's been my charge . . . for some time now. I've forgotten what life is without her."

"No, that's not all. You . . . loved her. I can see it in your eyes, in your touch, in—"

"She was my charge!" He held Mara's gaze, as though daring her to challenge him further.

She said nothing. Perhaps he was trying to convince himself, but she wondered.

"You do understand the significance of the oath you just swore?" he asked, scornfully.

Of course she did. An Oathtaker's vow came with commitments. Mara hadn't given it much thought earlier, but when she swore her oath, she had sealed the deal. Her word bound her to the twins for so long as they lived. She could no longer follow another path. In the moment she took her vow, Ehyeh bestowed gifts upon her, attendant magic and continued youth. She would not physically age until the death of her charge. Only then could she begin her life anew, follow other dreams. The same had been true for Dixon while his charge lived. But what did his denial mean? What was he trying to imply? That because he'd sworn to accept Rowena as his charge, he'd not still been vulnerable to his own feelings, longings, desires? Had he been one who'd fallen into the state of pain that came with loving someone while subject to his oath?

"Of course I do," she confirmed.

He folded Rowena's arms across her breast, then brought the coverings up to her shoulders, as though to keep her from getting chilled. His trembling hands stopped every few moments to stroke her hair. Mara could see he warred with himself—wondering whether to keep his former charge in sight, or to cover her, or to look away so that he could deny to himself the reality of her death.

Not wanting to further interrupt him in his grief, Mara stepped out of the hut with the infants. She found a private space behind some shrubbery where she quickly changed out of her now bloodied garb.

On the ground nearby, she found a basket. She picked it up and examined it. Although worn, it was sturdy. She placed Eden inside, then removed the last of her blankets from her bag. With it, she wrapped Reigna up to her front side, and then grasped the basket's handle, leaving one hand free.

Stepping back inside the hut, she picked up Rowena's things scattered about. She examined each item briefly: a beautiful silver compact, a hairpin studded with small crystals in various colors, and the shawl. She placed them in her bag.

"I have to go. Rowena thought her children would be in great danger and I suspect she was right. I don't believe there's been a seventh seventh for . . . What? A couple hundred years or more? Reigna is likely the child we've all been waiting for. And that says nothing for Eden. Twins . . . It's never been heard of—a Select bearing twins," she whispered. "In any case, I promised I'd take the girls to safety at once."

"Reigna? Her name is Reigna?" Dixon raised grief-stricken eyes. "And Eden?"

Suddenly Mara felt deeply sorry for her fellow Oathtaker, and badly for having lashed out earlier. She looked away. His pain was too real. It made her feel as though she eavesdropped.

"Yes," she finally said, "the eldest is Reigna, the youngest Eden. Rowena named them herself. I took my oath while she still lived, and I intend to abide by it. So, I have to go. These babies will wake soon, and they'll wake hungry. My first order of business is to find milk for them—perhaps a wet nurse." She made her way to the door.

"Wait! I'll go with you." He sprang forward and grasped her arm. When she tried to pull away, he loosed his grip. "Listen, Mara. It's Mara, right?"

She frowned, then nodded, her brow raised.

"Listen, Mara, you're right about Reigna. She's the first seventh seventh in ages. Many have awaited her birth for . . . a very long time. Rowena and her friends planned her very existence. As to Eden, I can only guess at the significance of her birth." He hesitated. "Look, I can help you to carry out your charge. You need me. That is I . . . I—" He lowered his gaze. "Please. Please, let me come with you."

She considered his words. She could use some help. "Very well then, but we'd best be on our way and quickly. Just one thing though—and don't forget it. The girls? Reigna and Eden? They're *my* charge." She stepped out of the hut.

"Stop! Mara . . . stop. Rowena's releasing her power may have bought us— bought you," he quickly corrected himself, "a bit of time. But someone trailed us for months and they won't stop now. We need to erase whatever signs we can of what happened here."

She recalled the teachings of her local unit of the Oathtakers' Guild, her hood. When the ranking member of the Select released her power to her offspring, a unique magic allowed for a short window of time during which no one could track the new ranking member. Its origins had long since been forgotten, but stories told of the event having been witnessed more than once before.

"How much time do you think we have?"

"It's hard to say." He dropped his pack outside the door.

"Could you venture a guess?" She found his behavior encouraging her natural tendency toward sarcasm.

He gazed into the distance. "About two sun downs."

"Well then, I suppose leaving Rowena's body here would tell a great deal. You're right. It won't take that long to dig a grave. We don't want it too shallow, but we need to be quick and—"

"Think," he said condescendingly. "If we bury her body, those thugs following us could still find it. More likely, they *would* find it. Then they'd know she gave birth. We should burn this hut with," he hesitated, "her body. Then if those cretins find any sign we were here, or if they find her remains, they'll still have no evidence of the twins or of what happened here. With any luck, they'll think their chase has come to a close."

"Yes, I guess it's not likely they'd give up if they were responsible for the pack of grut that tried to take Rowena down. When they realize the beasts were destroyed, they'll have good reason to think someone survived."

"Hmmm."

"Well then, let's get moving." She exited.

"Where are you going?"

"To get some wood so that when this hut goes up in flames, there's plenty of fuel to keep it burning hot and for a good long time. The less evidence the better. Isn't that what you just said?"

Leaving him, Mara went into the woods. She kept Reigna tied to her front side and walked about carrying Eden's basket. It left her but one hand to work with, so she selected large branches that she could drag back to the hut.

After some time, having seen no sign of Dixon, she grew irritated that he wasn't assisting her. Finally, breathless, she stepped back inside the hut. She found him kneeling at Rowena's side.

"Dixon, finish your 'good-byes' so we can get out of here."

Her voice jolted him back to the present. He unclasped a locket from around the dead woman's neck and placed it in his breast pocket, then slipped a ring from her finger. Finally, he pulled the blanket up over her face.

Mara wasn't certain, but she thought she heard him tell Rowena to "sleep well." Perhaps it was not such a good idea to take him along. She couldn't allow his mourning to hold them up. Shrugging, she went to gather more wood.

Dixon joined her efforts, but several minutes later, was nowhere in sight. Mara looked around. There, at the other side of the hut, he had squatted down. He brushed sand away from something on the ground. His head cocked to one side, then the other.

She approached.

"What's this?" He moved small twigs and fallen leaves aside revealing several sharp, triangular-shaped items of an uncertain gray, thick and curved, each about the size of his thumb.

She put Eden's basket down, then dropped to her knees for a closer look. She picked up one of the objects and turned it over. "Could they be . . . grut teeth?"

"Then there really were grut here," he murmured.

"I beg your pardon? Of course there were grut here. I said as much, didn't I?" She got back to her feet.

"Hmmm." He shrugged and looked away, as though embarrassed for having been so tactless. "Well, we'd best take them along. They contain powerful magic."

"Magic!"

"What are they teaching in the hood around here anyway?" he muttered. "Yes, they contain very powerful magic. They're the only part of a grut that might remain after its destruction . . . which is why they're extremely rare. The beasts can't attack one who holds a grut tooth." He looked at her. "Of course the wearer could fall to any number of other weapons, but a grut couldn't harm him . . . or her."

Saying nothing more, she collected a total of twelve teeth. After placing eleven of them in a small leather bag tied to her belt, she approached Dixon who'd gone back to hauling wood. She held out one of the teeth.

He put his hand out to accept it, though he refused to meet her eyes. After pocketing it, he resumed his task.

Once they collected enough wood to keep the cabin burning long and hot, Dixon reached forward, his hand in a fist. With a flick of his fingers, a fire burst forth.

Mara sprang back in surprise. "Well then," she said after catching her breath, "I guess we'd best get going. I have a lot of questions for you. I suppose, since my training has been so abysmal, so appallingly lacking, I'll need to draw on your expertise for a time. If you're willing, of course."

He shrugged.

Just then a howl carried through the air. Though well in the distance, it made Mara edgy. "Let's go."

Dixon turned away and entered the forest.

CHAPTER TWO

A sudden storm caught the small and ragged group of men unaware. Thunder and lightning rattled. Rain pelted. On horseback, they slogged through until their mounts resisted, then dropped camp near the edge of the forest.

Gadon, leader of the motley crew, wore pants and a tunic of a dull brown wool mottled with the filth of dust and food stains accumulated over many days. His nearly black hair fell past his shoulders in stringy, oily twists. His skin was light, his piercing eyes small and black. He appeared angry about everything, content with nothing, and cared for by no one.

"Bruce!" he shouted. He stood with his hands on his hips, scowling at the poor recipient of his attentions.

"Yes, sir, master Gadon, sir," came the ready reply, as out from behind the horses, a young man skittered forward. His dark eyes darted about, like flies flitting at offal. One wandered, making it difficult to ascertain the subject of his gaze. He licked his chapped lips repeatedly. Angry pustules covered his face and neck, interrupted only by a scar that ran down his left cheek from just below his eye to his chin.

Holding a bag of oats, he pulled on its ties to close it. Shaking in his nervousness, the ties instead slipped from his hand. Down went the bag. Oats now covered his already manure-slogged shoes. His hands jittered as his focus skipped to Gadon.

"Idiot!" The man stepped toward the cowering youth and delivered a blow with the back of his hand, knocking Bruce from his feet. "Isn't that right? You're an idiot."

"Yes sir, master Gadon, sir." Bruce's voice quivered. He scrambled back to his feet. Rainwater dripped from his hair, and mud now accompanied the former filth of his attire, running the various stains and grunge together into a mottled frenzy of foulness.

"Call Simon for me, then get the others and finish with those horses."

As the young man scurried away, Gadon entered his tent. Inside, upon a makeshift table, sat a map of Oosa, a burning lamp, and dinner, which consisted of dried meat, cheese, stale bread, and nuts. An old stump he'd dragged in from the nearby forest, served as a stool. Breaking a nut open with his teeth, he unfolded the map, its crinkling sounds filling the air.

Odd were the circumstances behind this mission. Gadon had worked at the palace in Shimeron for some years. He'd been an officer in charge of a legion, but over time his sympathies changed. He slacked in his work and drank to excess. Eventually, his superiors demoted him. So, when seeking a scapegoat for his troubles, he fixed his resentment on the Select. He reasoned that they sought to rule the lives of all men, whereas people just wanted to do as they pleased.

One day while on duty in the palace gardens, he saw a woman, a beauty beyond compare. She had porcelain smooth skin. Her silken hair hung over her shoulders. Her lips, painted scarlet, nearly matched her blood red satin dress. Her scarves played in the breeze sending about her, the high, thick, sweet, overpowering scent of rose and lily.

The woman approached Gadon much as a snake might slither upon its dinner. Cocking her head, she looked at him from the outside corner of her eye, then ran a fingernail down his chest.

"Hmmmm," she purred. "What have we here? A big, strong soldier." Eyelashes went closed, paused, then opened again, as she graced him with the slightest of smiles. And so began the seduction of Gadon.

Over the next months he became more involved with the woman, and less concerned about any consequences. The two met regularly in a hidden alcove in the palace gardens where they sought their delight in one another. Over time the woman gained greater and greater control over him, his desires, and his thoughts.

After some time, Gadon's ladylove recruited him to keep his eye on a certain Select. "She'll be the ruin of us all if left to her own devices," she cooed. "I need you to watch her for me. Can you do that?" She moved in closer, her lips just inches from his.

He couldn't tear his eyes from the fullness, the promise of that mouth. He could feel her, smell her, taste her with each breath she exhaled.

"That child simply must be destroyed," she whispered. "If not, Rowena will stop at nothing to bring it to power one day."

He simply nodded. He would agree to anything. The woman had bewitched him, and he cared not.

"Rowena has heard rumors that she's in danger here. She's growing ever more fearful. She plans to leave the palace tonight. I need you to follow her and to make sure that the child she carries never sees the light of day. Don't come back until you've accomplished that."

After leaving their trysting place, a gentleman overtook him. Tall and slim of build, the man had melded into the shadows. "I have something for you," he said as he grabbed Gadon's shirt, slammed him up against the courtyard wall, and then held a knife to his throat. "If you say anything, I'll kill you," he snarled.

True to form, Gadon simply nodded. Independent thought had become foreign to him.

The man sheathed his knife, then reached into a bag tied to the waistband of his black wool pants. He pulled something out, then handed the object to Gadon.

"Take this. It's a call for the grut. Only use it when you know you're very near Rowena. We don't want undue attention drawn to this mission now, do we?" He chuckled. "But whatever you do, destroy her before she bears her child. Do not fail," he added as he released Gadon with a shove, then disappeared into the night.

Immediately, Gadon recruited a group of men who'd run into difficulties with their palace duties. Once done, he and his recruits left the palace grounds. Now, months later, their search continued.

Turning his attention back to the present, he fumbled at the grut whistle in his pocket. Always so close—she was always so close—but she was never close enough.

He thought about the route he'd taken since leaving the palace. Despite traveling day and night whenever possible, practically sleeping in the saddle and eating on the run, Rowena always managed to stay one step ahead. She traveled with a single companion, her Oathtaker, Dixon. Together, the two were quick and shrewd, though recently Gadon had caught a sighting of them. His prey was heavy with child. His window of opportunity grew very short indeed.

The flap of the tent opened and Simon entered. "You called for me?"

For a time, the men studied their whereabouts, contemplating where their quarry headed, as they made their plans for the morrow.

"Tomorrow, Simon. I feel it. Tomorrow we get her." Gadon held the grut whistle in his fist. "Set up the round of watches and awaken me at first light."

With morning came a sun that beat down, promising a blistering day. Hurriedly, the men packed their foodstuffs, tents, and packs.

"Let's go," Gadon ordered.

The air became more humid as the day wore on. Waves of heat quivered in the distant air. Flies buzzed overhead, awaiting their opportunity to rest upon a sweat slicked body to feast.

The men remained quiet; they had little to say. This was just one more day in an endless chase.

Periodically Gadon called a halt to look for tracks in the grasses and shrubbery to the sides of the well-worn path. He surmised that Rowena and Dixon stayed off of it so that they could take cover more quickly if the need should arise. Occasionally, in their wake, they left broken twigs and flattened grass where they walked, or hoof prints where they rode.

"Here . . . and here . . . and here. See that?" Gadon pointed out footprints in the sand. "And look here. They stopped for a time. This must be where they spent the night." He scouted further. "Wait— What's this? Blood? Hmmmm. Maybe. Looks like." He touched the spot, then brought his fingers to his nose. "Smells like." He wiped the sweat from his brow with the back of his hand. "Heri!"

A man stepped forward. His lack of discipline was evident in his slouched stature. His scraggly, thinning hair hung in his eyes. "Yes, sir," he said, smiling to reveal crooked, ill-kept teeth.

"Ride ahead. Stay in line with that path." Gadon pointed. "See there? As it enters the forest?"

"Yes, sir." Spittle hung from Heri's lips.

"Ride hard. If you see them, prepare to signal us. We'll enter over there." He showed the man his intentions. "We'll catch up soon enough, so don't try to take them alone. If you don't see us within a few hours, then stop and wait."

Heri nodded his understanding, then rode off.

As Gadon muddled over the tracks, he determined that this might be his best opportunity to take Rowena down. They were in an isolated place, and she was close. She had to have left her tracks late the previous night, after the rain had ceased.

Yes, my patience has run out.

He took the grut whistle from his pocket, placed it to his lips, and then blew.

A shriek cut through the air. The men covered their ears to stop the excruciatingly painful sound.

The ground burst open. Dirt and debris flew into the air. With a blast of wind as from the pits of the underworld, a pack of grut emerged, panting and screaming. Their tongues hung out and their eyes took in their surrounds. Their wiry hair stood on end.

The explosion threw Gadon from his feet. He landed on his back, the wind knocked from his lungs. He struggled to pull in a breath, then rolled over and onto his hands and knees. He stood, staggering and stumbling.

Simon fell and hit the side of his head on a boulder. Blood ran down through his hair and muddied his eyes.

Bruce, who'd stood on the very spot that opened to the grut, flew through the air. His arms and legs thrashed about. When he hit the ground, he was knocked unconscious. Blanketed in debris, he looked like a corpse in a shallow grave.

The grut shot out toward the forest ahead.

Another of the men, Petron, approached Bruce, brushed aside the dirt, then helped the youth to sit up. Bruce's eyes were glossed over, one seemingly focused on the hole in the ground, while the other—his wandering eye—appeared to watch the grut streaking off into the distance.

"There!" Gadon cried as the last of the grut entered the forest. "We'll give them a head start, then follow, but not too closely." He wiped at a stream of blood running down his face while he paced anxiously. A few minutes later, he turned and mounted.

Just as the men prepared to move out, something whizzed above them. Gadon ducked, then looked behind. Again came the sound, this time to his left.

"Under fire, sir!" Simon shouted.

Gadon quickly dismounted, dropped into a ball, then rolled forward. He crouched behind a boulder. "Down, Petron, down! Bruce, damn it!"

As the men sought cover, another arrow came in just over their heads.

Staying low and behind trees and boulders, they sought to determine the sniper's whereabouts.

A couple additional arrows flew overhead. Then, the shooting stopped.

A few minutes passed. Then, as Gadon rose to his feet, the siege began again, this time from a new direction. One arrow pierced though his cloak at his shoulder, then continued down to the ground, lifting a tuft of grass before coming to rest. He dropped down.

Then, just as suddenly as it began, the shooting stopped again.

He surveyed the forest line, but couldn't make out any movement. "Anyone see anything?"

"Negative," Simon said.

"I can't tell where the shots are coming from," Bruce quipped.

"Idiot," Gadon mumbled.

Once again, after a few still minutes, the firing resumed, this time from yet another place at the forest edge. This went on several more times. Each interval brought only a few arrows. Finally, came a lull that lasted for some time.

Gadon poked his head around the boulder that shielded him. He waved Simon forward. "You thinking what I'm thinking?"

"That there's only one shooter and that it might be over? It's been a while now since the last shots."

"Exactly. We're losing time. The grut are already an hour and more ahead of us. I'll make my way—there," Gadon pointed. "Petron, that way," he ordered, designating another spot.

"I'll stay here with the others to cover you," Simon offered.

As the men moved toward their designated destinations, the earth shook suddenly and violently. The trees swayed wildly. Bending with the wind, some snapped like twigs. Lightning burst in sudden, blinding blasts, and deafening thunder pounded. The sky turned a deep bloody red for a moment, then to a silvery, ashen gray.

"Damn it," Gadon cursed.

Chapter Three

The Oathtakers headed to the river, its waters lowered from a long hot season. Mara mimicked Dixon, snapping off a goodly portion of a nearby bush to brush the ground behind so as to leave no obvious tracks for their pursuers. Upon reaching the riverbank, they dropped their branches.

He stepped into the water and walked upstream.

"We'd best leave as little to track from the area as possible," he said without looking back.

They continued in silence for some time as the sun raced for the horizon. Soon everything appeared the same nondescript, drab, brown-gray color.

Reigna cried. Mara picked up her pace. When she caught up to Dixon, she grasped his arm, bringing him to a halt.

"We have to find food for the girls soon," she said, breathing heavily, "or all of Oosa will know our whereabouts."

"There's a goat farm up the river another hour or so. We could get milk there. I'd rather not have to stop for aid and attract any attention, but we've not much choice."

"If we walk along the bank, perhaps we could make better time."

He stepped to it. Water sloshed from his boots. He started off, clearing a path as necessary.

Reigna and Eden were slight children, but Mara found it difficult to carry them both and all of her gear. At times her feet failed to respond to her command. She nearly tripped, righted herself, then walked on. Finding a sturdy branch, she adopted it for a walking stick. Every so often she stopped to catch her breath. She never saw Dixon look back.

A distant howl carried through the air. Crickets chirped and frogs croaked. Birds swooped down toward the forest interior to find their warm beds for the night.

When Reigna cried again, Mara stopped. She crooked her finger to let the child suck. The gesture satisfied her, but the Oathtaker couldn't walk this way and carry Eden's basket at the same time.

She set out again, having fallen considerably behind. She could just make out

Dixon's silhouette ahead in the fading light. With a renewed commitment, she increased her gait. Finally, she reached him.

He moved aside a branch blocking their view. Wild herbs and grasses spotted the rocky pasture ahead. The fresh scent of creeping thyme filled the air.

"Where are we?"

He motioned toward a small building. "There's the place I mentioned. The old man and his wife are faithful followers of the Good One. I'm sure they'll help us."

The twins both cried out in earnest. Doubting she could quiet them again, Mara took the lead.

Full darkness descended, leaving for light only a sliver of the first of the three moons and scattered stars in the night sky.

In her impatience, she tripped on a stone. Dixon's hand at her elbow to steady her, surprised her. With no attempt to get her permission, he slipped Eden's basket from her grasp.

"Go ahead, lead on," she said, then followed him to the farm.

The small thatched cottage showed signs of wear. It leaned slightly to one side as though it had grown weary of holding its own weight and rested on one hip. Planters at its windows sported scented violas, while a large flowerpot at the steps provided an assortment of herbs at the ready for kitchen use. The citrusy scent of lemon thyme, the clean smell of lavender, the earthy scent of oregano, the freshness of mint, and the piney aroma of rosemary, filled the air.

Upon the cleanly swept porch sat a full rain bucket near the front door. A dipper hung over its side.

Dixon approached, but didn't knock. "Drake!" he called out over the infants' cries. "It's your old friend, Dixon. Dixon Townsend. Are you in?"

Mara started. "Dixon Townsend!" she whispered. "Townsend? Like of the Brecken Townsends?"

He shrugged off the query. "Drake!"

She remembered hearing stories about the Townsends at her local hood. There was something about their having served as Oathtakers to some of the more famous Select in years past, and of their having assisted with Oosa's governing Council. *Was there some kind of scandal, too?* Yes, there was something, but just what, she couldn't recall.

The door cracked open. The light of an interior lamp made a silhouette of Drake's frame. His wild gray hair stood up as though it had somewhere it would rather be going. His ears, somewhat pointed, made him appear almost elfish. When he turned, the light caught his face. Time had begun to tell its story there. It was the tale of a man who loved to laugh.

"Dixon, old friend! May the Good One bless and keep you. What brings you out on a night like this?"

"Oh, just helping a friend to make her way back home. We ran into a bit of trouble and I'm afraid we're in need of a hand. We hoped you'd be willing to sell us some milk for her girls here, and perhaps allow us to rest in your barn for the night."

"Sell! Barn!" The old man shook his head. "Don't be ridiculous, Dixon. Come in. Come in!" he urged. "Maggie," he called out in a voice bigger than he, "we've company!"

Making her way into the kitchen in response to Drake's call came the shortest full-grown woman Mara had ever seen. *She's almost as round as she is tall!*

Maggie's bright blue eyes sparkled as she greeted Dixon with a full embrace. "How very good to see you. It's been too long." Quickly, she drew for her visitors, sturdy ladderback chairs with braided rag cushions. Mara found the woman, like her husband, instantly likable.

"Oh my," Maggie cried when Mara unwrapped the girls. "What beautiful children! Why, Dixon, what a surprise! We had no id—"

"No, no, Maggie!" he interrupted, shaking his head emphatically.

Is he blushing? For the first time, Mara saw him smile. She was startled at how handsome he was. He'd only had scowls for her. Realizing her mouth hung open in astonishment, she quickly closed it when he turned her way.

"This is Mara, a . . . friend of mine."

"Mara Richmond," she said by way of completing the introduction.

"I'm helping her get back home. It's a long story. I'm sure you wouldn't want to be bored with the details," Dixon said, waving his hand. "In any case, her girls are very hungry—as you can hear."

Maggie gazed at Mara. "Milk hasn't come in yet, huh hon'?"

The Oathtaker's mouth dropped open. *Now am I blushing?*

"Well never you mind," the old woman said, wagging her head, her gray hair bouncing. "Sometimes it takes a day or two. When my oldest was born, why I thought it would never come and worried myself near to sick. Then wouldn't you know, when it finally did, I had enough to feed my poor neighbor's twins when she took ill and dried up." She laughed at her own story. "I have some nice fresh goat milk right here. It's still good and warm."

Mara asked how she could assist, but Maggie assured her she had all well in hand. She made a bottle out of a clean spongy cloth and an old, small blue glass bottle. Together, they fed the infants. The girls suckled greedily.

With the twins fed, Maggie served her visitors warm bread just from the oven, fresh goat cheese, thin slices of ham, and apple pie. While they ate, she fussed over the twins. So round and soft, the girls nuzzled close to her and soon fell asleep. She offered to set up a cradle.

"Please, don't go to any trouble," Mara protested.

"No trouble! It's my pleasure. You just sit there and rest. I'll have things ready for the little dears in no time." Maggie handed the girls off.

Dixon held Eden. He snuggled her closely and firmly, while he and Drake enjoyed their ales. "Mara is fearful. She thinks she may need a wet nurse. I guess her sister had the same problem."

Now, I know I'm blushing!

Drake turned her way, frowning in his sympathy for her imagined plight.

"So I was wondering if you knew where we might go for such help."

"A wet nurse, huh?"

Her blush grew, its heat intensified. She wasn't accustomed to being the center of such personal discussions. She glanced Dixon's way and found him smirking mischievously, apparently enjoying his playacting at her expense.

"Well, there's the mission home the Oathtakers at Polesk set up. I understand they've taken in a number of refugees."

"Refugees!" Mara exclaimed.

"From Chiran, yes." Drake pulled a pipe and tobacco from his front frayed pocket. With a gesture, he inquired whether she minded. She did not. Turning to Dixon, he offered the pouch. Dixon refused with a shake of his head.

"Why are there refugees from Chiran here in Oosa?" Mara asked.

Maggie made her way back into the kitchen. She sat down with a sigh. "We don't know the full story, but we've heard rumor. For some reason, young women are leaving Chiran for Oosa. They claim they're in danger there. So the hood in Polesk takes them in and allows them to stay there until they can make it on their own. We take contributions at our local sanctuary to help with the expenses."

"From what we've gathered," Drake added, "the women often arrive pregnant or with newborns."

"That's odd," Dixon said.

"That's what we thought," Maggie agreed, "but we know one of the members of that hood. Ted . . . Ted . . . What's his name Drake? You know, we met him once here in the village?"

"Baker."

"Not Ted Baker," Dixon said. "Really? Why, he and I go way back. He worked with my father. He is a very special man." He patted his knee. "I didn't know he'd settled in Polesk."

"I believe his family originally came from there," Maggie said.

"You've spoken to this—Ted Baker?" Mara asked.

"Yes," Drake responded, exhaling pipe smoke.

"What did he say?"

"Not much. He's still sorting out the fact from the fiction. But in any case, Polesk sounds like the place for you."

For the first time in hours, Mara relaxed. She motioned for Dixon to hand Eden to her, then closed her eyes, cuddling the infants. She listened as the others talked, their voices soft and low, about the hood in Polesk, as well as of more mundane matters. When their voices grew quieter, she opened her eyes and looked at the girls. As they gazed back, she hummed softly. To her surprise, words to an old lullaby she thought she'd long since forgotten, tripped from her lips:

Hush, hush, close your eyes;
Feel the slowly passing time.
Hush, hush, from above,
Come dreams of peace, dreams of love.

Hush, hush—

She stopped short. The room was silent. Drake sat, his head on the table, his eyes closed, his breathing steady, as a faint snore escaped Maggie's lips. Turning Dixon's way, Mara caught a look of surprise in his eyes before they slowly closed.

As the infants too, fell asleep, Mara wondered if being an Oathtaker, if having accepted a charge, had been right for her. Could she do this? Her oath meant, at least for now, that she'd given up the pleasures of a family of her own.

Yes, it was right! Don't go back there. Don't remember. Besides, it's too late to turn back now. She warred with herself about whether or not to go down memory lane, in the end deciding she'd best not. It would do little to serve her now. Even so, she couldn't help wishing that she could stay put in this simple farmhouse with these good people. She smiled weakly and then, she was out.

"Mara . . ." Dixon shook her arm. "Mara."

Her eyes flashed open. Momentarily confused, she focused on her surroundings, then yawned and stretched her arms over her head.

"The sun will rise in an hour. We need to go."

She stood. The chair had been her resting place for the night. When she'd awakened briefly in the deep hours, she'd placed the girls in the cradle that Maggie had prepared. Then she'd fallen promptly back to sleep and the girls hadn't awakened her to feed. She rubbed her stiff neck.

The twins stirred. Reigna wore a newborn's smile. Eden twitched.

"I'll need to feed them. Do you know where they keep the goat milk?"

"Here." Dixon handed her a cup of milk. "There's a cooling cellar beneath the front step. I took enough for a few more feedings, and a chunk of ice. We'll have to be careful if it's to last the day."

She put some milk to warm in a small pan over the hearth fire. She took her time soaking in the heat, as the morning was a cool one. Then she tended to the children.

By the time Eden finished eating, Drake and Maggie were awake and the Oathtakers were ready to go.

"Take this." Maggie handed Mara a package of fresh bread, meat and cheese. "It'll be some time before you find a village of any size. You're sure to get hungry on the way."

Mara received the food with thanks.

Dixon shook Drake's hand. "I can't thank you enough."

"Don't mention it." The old man's hair, if possible, was in even greater disarray than the evening before. "We were delighted to have you. We don't often get visitors in these parts. Now don't be a stranger. We'll look to see you around again soon. And you," he said to Mara, "take good care of those little ones."

"Thank you, Drake, for everything," she said.

"Now don't forget what I said about your milk coming in," Maggie whispered to Mara. "You just relax and everything will be fine."

The Oathtaker nodded. There was no need to correct the woman's mistake. It might be better if people believed the girls were her own. There would be fewer explanations to make that way. "Thank you, Maggie, I will." She approached Dixon. "Do you think they'll be in any danger because of our stopping here?" she asked quietly.

He tipped his head in the affirmative.

"Is there anything we can do? It seems poor recompense for their kindness."

"No."

She frowned.

"Welcome to the life of an Oathtaker. Sometimes we do what we have to do."

A hot breeze blew steadily. The sun, past its zenith, burned strong. With a long day of traveling already behind them, Mara's back ached from carrying Reigna strapped to her front side, as well as Eden's basket.

She slumped to the ground at the edge of the trail and leaned against a small cottonwood, its leaves shimmering in the faint breeze. She needed to get off her feet, if only for a short time, and to cool down.

Dixon, who'd gone ahead as usual, turned around as he rarely but at least occasionally did. He turned back.

"We'll need more milk for the girls soon. They're going through what we got from Drake and Maggie quickly," she said as he approached.

"Hmmm."

"So we're headed to Polesk, right?" she asked, in an attempt to open a conversation. He'd said next to nothing all day.

"Mmhmmm."

She sighed. His reluctance to speak frustrated her.

"We'll need to make camp soon," he finally offered. "Early tomorrow we'll reach a village where we can get horses and more milk."

"Good. By then, according to your best guess, our window of protection will have nearly expired. Is that right?"

"Mmhmmm."

She shook her head, struggling not to be annoyed.

"I've been thinking about what Drake and Maggie said. I've been on the run and keeping a low profile for some time, but even then I've heard some troubling things."

His speaking surprised her. "Such as?" she asked.

He fumbled through his pack for their foodstuffs. He broke off a piece of bread and ate it. When Mara held her hand open, he tore some off and handed it to her. She was gratified that he looked embarrassed for not having offered on his own. Then he motioned for her to help herself to the rest of the food.

"And?" she urged again.

"I don't know how much you know about—shall we say, politics—in these parts, but for some years Oosa has kept a close eye on the goings on in Chiran. Zarek, the leader there, has made it quite clear that he intends to expand his sphere of influence. He means, some would say, to 'take over the world.'"

"Good work if you can get it, I suppose."

"Hmmm."

No laugh. Has he no sense of humor? Or did he just not find that amusing? "So what do the plans of this—Zarek—have to do with our finding a wet nurse for the girls?" It was frustrating having to drag information from him bit by bit . . . by bit.

He shrugged. "Word is that he's building himself an army in an unconventional manner. He's been supportive . . . No, that's not quite right. He's been instrumental in the cause to 'rid the world' of the Select. Zarek encourages the birth of all Chiranian boys. He gives gold and other favors to the parents of them. Not so for girls. As a result, there's been mass infanticide of girls born in Chiran."

"I'd actually heard things to that effect, but I found them too awful to believe."

"Let that be a lesson to you," he chided. "Wanting or not wanting something to be so, doesn't make it so, any more than repeating a lie makes it the truth."

"Yes of course, Dixon, I'm well aware of that." *Goodness, he's exasperating!* "I misspoke." She paused, annoyed. "What I meant to say was that the plan sounds so awful, it's difficult to believe anyone would agree to it."

"Make no mistake. Zarek keeps much truth from the Chiranians. They do as their 'great leader' says for fear of losing their own lives if they don't. He's convinced them that the Select are the scourge of the world, responsible for all their ills. Some say he's added Oathtakers, and even simple believers, to the list of infidels he tells his people he must rid the world of." He scowled.

Mara nibbled at her bread. "So you were saying how this relates to our finding help for the girls."

Just then, as on cue, Reigna fussed. Soon it turned to full out crying. Mara offered her some milk. The infant suckled hungrily, then turned her face away and cried again. After several more efforts to get her to eat, she did, greedily.

Dixon waited for the infant to quiet down, all the while watching the trail ahead.

Farmland surrounded them in sections of green and gold. An occasional lone oak spotted the scenery, stretching its mighty arms toward the sun as though trying to catch it. Along the pathway, intersecting the jumble of fields and outlining the way forward, trees and berry bushes, haystacks and fencing, stood out.

"Go on," Mara urged after quieting the infant.

He drank warm water from his canteen with a grimace. "Zarek encourages the death of infant girls. While most Chiranians buy into his plans, some refuse. I suspect that those who refuse include young women who have daughters, or who fear they will, so they escape Chiran."

"Very brave of them."

"Hmmm." He collected the remaining food, wrapped it back up and placed it in his pack, then stood and paced.

Mara finished with Reigna, then fed Eden. Sounds of the child's suckling carried through the air.

"I'm not quite sure what killing infant girls has to do with raising an army," she finally said, breaking the silence.

"Zarek wants a large army—and a hungry one. An army hungry for anything can be troublesome, but one clamoring for the things, including the women that only its leader can provide through successful warfare, can be awesome in its strength. I believe Zarek thinks it will make the men more pliable, that they'll make better warriors." He urged Mara by his actions to prepare to move out.

"So?"

Sighing, he responded. "So I suspect he intends the women of the places he conquers will be 'spoils of war' for his men."

"Uggghhh!"

"Hmmm, right." He took another drink.

"Have you wondered at all if—well, if it's wise to trust the girls to a Chiranian?"

"One who's shown she rejects all Zarek offers? I think so. In the end, I suppose there might be some danger with such a woman, but we'd know by her actions at least, that she seems to be in agreement with our cause."

"Our cause?"

"The cause of life and of freedom of course, which essentially is the cause of Ehyeh, the Good One."

"Maybe you're right." She put Eden into her basket and strapped Reigna back to her front side. "All right then, let's go."

Dixon helped her up, then took her bag and Eden's basket. To her great relief, she now carried only Reigna's extra weight tied to her front side in a makeshift baby-carrier.

CHAPTER FOUR

"I don't know what that force was that wouldn't allow us to pass earlier," Gadon said. "I've never experienced anything like it. Must've been some kind of black magic. And two days lost to this foolishness!"

He and his men bustled through the underbrush, leading their mounts. They stepped around a patch of poison ivy. Flies buzzed around their heads as the sun beat down, adding to their discomfort.

Gadon's leather creaked. "Now that the barrier's down, we need to move quickly. Hopefully we'll come upon her—or even better, her remains—soon. With any kind of luck, the beasts got to her in time."

The storm, complete with winds, thunder, and lightning, but without rain, had come upon the men two days earlier. In its wake, it left limbs of trees torn down and a pathway littered with debris. Now, hot and still, the air hung heavy and humid.

The men stopped periodically to check for tracks, but found nothing. Where earlier they'd followed a path, albeit a sketchy one, none existed now, and they found no sign of either Rowena or the grut.

"There . . . just ahead," Simon said, pointing. "Something burned down over there."

They trudged on to the place Simon indicated. There they found the remains of a fairly large fire. Smoke rose from it in tufts and streams, lending a heavy acrid smell to the air. Nearby, some bones from a horse were strewn about.

Petron stepped up to the fire's edge. He rubbed his eyes to clear them of the thick smoke drawn his way. He crouched down and poked a stick through the coals. Ashes flurried upward. Small flames erupted from hotspots within the bed of rock and embers. "What's this?" he asked, pushing out to the perimeter a large solid object.

Gadon got down on one knee. He reached for the stick Petron held, then moved things around, shoving some additional larger solid pieces to the side.

"Looks like bone. Human bone, I'd say," Simon said.

"Damn," Gadon swore. "There's no way to identify who this was. But the trail did lead this way."

"'Spose it's hers?" Bruce asked.

Gadon scowled. "Damn it. Do I look like I can identify one of the Select—or anyone else for that matter—by their burned up remains?"

"Now what?" Petron asked.

Just then, a voice cried out. "Hello!"

Collectively, the men turned toward the sound as someone neared.

"Heri," Gadon called, "where've you been?"

"After you sent me ahead, out of nowhere, a storm of sorts erupted. Lightning struck all around me. I thought I was a goner."

"Yeah," Bruce said, "we was caught in the storm too."

"Shut up," Gadon scolded with a forceful slap to the young man's head. "Then what?" he asked Heri.

The man shuffled his feet as though embarrassed. "It was odd, sir. I couldn't take a single step forward. It was as though a wall blocked my path." He looked up to catch his leader's reaction, apparently fearing ridicule.

"Yeah, we experienced the same thing. So what did you do?"

Heri smiled weakly, his dirty, crooked teeth making the expression more of a grimace. "I just waited. Then as suddenly as it came, the barrier disappeared about an hour or so ago."

"So you've seen no sign of Rowena or her Oathtaker?"

"None. When I could get through, I came straight this way hoping to intercept you."

"All right, then. Simon!" Gadon shouted.

"Yes, sir."

"We need to search the area. The fire may have been a ruse."

"Yes, sir."

In ever widening circles, the men searched. Cockleburs caught at their pants. Horseflies buzzed around their heads and bit their sweaty arms and necks.

"What's this?" Heri called out. Standing not far from a great oak, he held forth a small frayed swatch of cloth.

Gadon hurried to his side. He took the ragged piece of linen and inspected it. "Where'd you find it?"

"Here, in the brush."

"Looks like it was torn from someone's clothing." Gadon ordered Heri and Petron to continue to search for any additional tracks or other clues, then turned to Simon. "Let's take another look through the remains of the fire."

They sifted through the coals, finding only a few more charred bones.

"I'd guess that's a leg bone," Gadon commented.

"And I'd say these here are from an arm. Given their size, I think these are a woman's remains," Simon suggested.

"Right. But what woman? This could have been anyone."

Gadon called for his men. When they assembled, he gave his orders.

"Simon, you take Wayne and head downriver. Don't spend more than an hour or two. If you see nothing, return here. If we don't see you by nightfall, we'll expect you've found something and we'll make our way back to you come morning."

They nodded their understanding and moved out.

"Heri," Gadon continued, "my instincts tell me that Rowena would expect us to expect her to go downriver. That would make traveling easier for her. That means she probably did the opposite and went up river. You go that way at a good clip. If you find anything significant, stay on the trail unless it's safe to head back to report. We'll follow behind and search more thoroughly. If Simon and Wayne find anything, I'll send someone for you."

Heri mounted up and rode off.

"All right then, let's get started."

"Did you hear that?" Maggie patted Drake's arm.

"What?" he responded sleepily.

"That." She hesitated. Long seconds passed. "There. Hear that?"

"That scratching sound? Probably just mice." He rolled to his side and punched lightly at his pillow, then laid down his head.

"Shhh. There's someone at the door," she whispered. She sat up and nudged him.

He pulled his tired feet to the floor. Worn from a long day of gardening and goat keeping, the old couple had retired early, but Drake knew there'd be no sleep until he put his beloved's fears to rest. He grabbed his pants, thrown over a chair at the side of the bed, and slipped them on. He strained to hear the sounds he now agreed came from outside the door.

"Shhh," Maggie whispered again, pulling up on the quilt.

"I'm sh-shhhing." He lit a lamp. It cast a soft yellow glow.

The door burst open. A group of savage looking men exploded into the room. One rushed toward Drake, a knife in his hand. His black eyes narrowed. His breathing came hard and fast. "Where are they?" he demanded to know.

Maggie trembled. "Who? Where's who?" Her voice shook.

"You know who! We tracked them here. Where are they?"

"Slow down. Slow down." Drake motioned with his hands. He nodded at Maggie in an attempt to comfort her, then looked back at the intruders.

The leader addressed one of his men. "Hold him, Simon."

"Got it, Gadon." He held Drake from behind.

A knife sat on the table. Gadon picked it up and handed it off to one of his men, then grabbed the front of Drake's nightshirt, staring at him, so near that Drake could smell the intruder's sour breath.

"Where are they?" Saliva flew as the man shouted.

"Sir, we have many visitors here at the edge of the glen. If you'll tell us who you're looking for, perhaps we can help you."

"Wayne, over there." Gadon gestured toward Maggie who now stood trembling, her fingers fretting with the ties at her neckline. "If we can't get the old man to talk, perhaps his woman will do as well." He grinned menacingly.

"Please sir, just say who you're looking for and we'll help you," Drake pleaded.

Wayne pulled one of Maggie's arms tightly behind her back, then placed a knife at her throat. Its steel glimmered in the dim light. When he added pressure to the tip, a drop of blood spilled down her throat. He laughed when she froze in fear and her eyes widened in terror.

Drake tried to pull free from his captor.

"That's right, you'll tell us if you want to save your woman here." Placing the point of his blade below Maggie's eye, Wayne drew the knife down with just enough pressure to break her skin. Blood flowed freely across her face and neck, then dripped down and onto her nightdress creating a grotesque crimson spiderweb design.

Gadon watched on. "Show them, Wayne. Show them what happens to those who don't cooperate."

Wayne placed the tip of his knife at the base of Maggie's throat. Clearly, if he did not get what he sought, he would plunge it into the soft tissue.

"Drake!" she cried. Her tears spilled.

The old man pulled at his restraints. "No!"

"I'm only going to ask you one more time. I'm out of patience," Gadon threatened. "Keep stalling and your woman will die. Where'd they go?"

"Who? Who, sir?" Maggie stuttered.

"Leave her alone! We'll tell you what we know. Who are you talking about? We'll cooperate." Drake felt helpless, weak, and older than ever before.

"That damned Select whore and her Oathtaker companion!"

Drake and Maggie looked at one another. His brow dropped.

"We don't know who you're talking about," she cried. "We haven't seen any Select. If we had, we'd tell you."

"Is that right?" Gadon asked, one brow raised, having seen the old couple communicate with their shared look.

"Those filthy Select are responsible for— If it weren't for their money grubbing ways, we might not live in such poverty. They—"

"Maggie!" her husband cried.

"That's enough." Gadon approached the old man, knife in hand. "So you didn't see any Select with her companion, huh?" He leaned in closer. "Well, I don't believe you," he whispered. "Perhaps you'll see better with only one eye."

"Please, sir, we don't know who you mean."

Simon locked Drake's head in the curve of his arm.

Gadon pointed his knife at the old man's eye. "Last chance," he said.

"I don't know who you mean!"

Gadon drove his knife into Drake's eye.

The old man's body convulsed, throwing him back. Then he shifted his weight and started falling forward. He shrieked in pain. Blood flowed, splattered.

Simon let go his hold and Drake tumbled into the bedside table, then fell to the floor. When his face made contact, his lip broke open.

The table rocked. A drinking glass that sat upon it spilled to the floor in a crescendo of broken bits of glass.

Maggie screamed and fought against her abductor. The blood dripping from her face splattered across the wall.

Gadon stepped over the old man and made his way to her. "So," he sneered, "do you see better with two eyes than your husband did?" He grabbed her chin.

She shook her head from side to side, but couldn't free herself from his grip. "All right! All right, I'll tell you. Just leave him be."

Drake, now on his hands and knees, labored to reclaim his feet. He gasped for breath. His blood streamed into and blinded his remaining eye. "No, Maggie!" He breathed in heavy sobs.

"They were here!"

"When?" Gadon asked.

"Two days ago."

"Where did they go?"

"They—they—"

"Maggie, no," Drake pleaded between gulps and sobs.

"They left for Polesk. The woman couldn't nurse."

"A child!" Gadon exclaimed.

"Maggie!" her husband cried again, a warning in his plea.

"Newborn." She did not mention that there were two children.

Gadon stood up straight. "Heri!"

"Yes, sir."

"Head for Polesk. Go quickly. We'll try to meet up with you before that Select whore and her Oathtaker reach the city. If you come upon them, keep them in sight. We'll stop for a rest, then search more thoroughly in the daylight in the event you miss them, but I don't expect we'll be more than a full day behind you."

Heri turned on his heel, then retreated.

Gadon turned back to the drama playing out before him. He grabbed the back of Drake's nightshirt and pulled him to his feet. "So you didn't see anyone, huh? Don't know anything, huh?" He shook the old man like a rag doll.

Drake tried to focus his remaining eye through his thick blood.

Gadon released his hold. "Finish them off," he ordered as he stormed from the once peaceful abode.

Maggie screamed. "No, don't hurt him! No!"

Drake stared at Simon, determined he'd make the thug look him in the eye when the final blow was struck, so he didn't witness Wayne slide his knife across Maggie's exposed throat, then loosen his hold. Her eyes flew open. She clawed at her throat, unable to release her scream. Wayne pushed her down, then kicked her violently.

Blood pooled on the floor, showing crimson in the flickering candlelight. Drake felt its warm wetness on his bare feet. He looked down. "No!" he cried, then hurriedly, he fixed his eye back on Simon. He willed himself to hold the man's gaze, not to look to his beloved Maggie. She was life and goodness and caring and joy. He would not see her otherwise.

"Say 'goodbye' old man," Simon growled as, pulling Drake forward, he thrust his blade.

Chapter Five

On their second day of traveling, the Oathtakers stopped in a small village for supplies. They haggled over the price for a couple horses, settling on a russet mare for Mara by the name of Cheryl, and on Sherman, a roan gelding for Dixon. From a local artisan, to replace some of the weapons Mara had lost, they purchased two sturdy blades. Near the outskirts of the village, they found a goat farm. As luck would have it, the farmer kept ice in his cellar, so they purchased some of that as well.

Early on this, their third day, they'd stopped once again for milk and ice. Now, as the sun neared the western horizon, they led their weary horses, hoping to make a bit more distance, but not wanting to risk their own safety or that of their mounts by riding the beasts past their point of exhaustion.

Dixon walked ahead with Sherman and Cheryl, his silhouette just visible. As Mara slowed to catch her breath, he turned to look back. She couldn't see the expression on his face in the fading light, but suddenly, he dashed madly her way. He jumped over rocks, moved branches from before himself, and twisted around obstacles, advancing at an amazing speed.

From behind, a footstep rustled in the dry grass. Carefully Mara set down Eden's basket, then turned toward the sound, reaching for Spira. Just as she grasped her weapon's handle, Dixon brushed against her arm.

"No, Mara, no!" he cried.

By the time her eyes focused on the intruder, Dixon had slammed full force into the man, knocking him to the ground and pinning him down. He held him by the throat with a single hand, then patted him down, pulling out and throwing aside, the intruder's sword, and a half dozen knives.

While Dixon struggled with his quarry, Mara looked for others, but saw no one.

"Who are you?" Dixon shouted, only inches from the man's face.

The intruder tried to pry off the Oathtaker's chokehold.

Dixon lifted him and slammed him back against a large boulder.

"What are you doing?" Mara cried. "I had Spira at the ready. I could have stopped him."

"I'm getting some answers!" Dixon didn't relax in the slightest, his grip on his captive. His eyes were afire. His jaw clenched and his muscles flexed. He slammed the man against the rock once again. "Who are you?"

He shook his head and pointed at his throat.

Dixon loosened his grip just enough for him to take in a breath. "Who sent you here? You'd best talk, or—or I'll kill you."

"Dixon, I'm not sure that's the best way to get what we need," Mara interrupted.

He turned to her, wrath on his face, determination in his bearing. "Open your eyes!" he exclaimed. "You're in a war! This man was sent to kill Rowena and he would kill Reigna and Eden in a heartbeat. And make no mistake about it, he'll kill you if given the opportunity." He took in a deep breath. "Your job is to protect the girls—no matter what. With your life if you must."

"I know that. I'm prepared to pay with my life if I must." She glared at him.

"Yes, well," he growled, "sometimes the best way to make sure you don't have to pay with your life—to see to it that you can continue to protect your charge— is to make sure that those who seek to harm you, pay with theirs." He turned back to his captive. "Who sent you?"

The man's eyes bulged.

Dixon pulled him away from the rock, spun him around, and then held him from behind with a knife at his throat. "Start talking."

He shook his head and held his lips tight.

"Tough guy, huh?"

The intruder stared straight ahead, silent.

Dixon placed the tip of his knife below the man's left ear and growled, "I'll kill you. Now, talk. What's your name? Who sent you? And why?"

Mara had never before seen anyone as intent as was Dixon at this moment. She considered his words, and she felt foolish. Of course, he was right. There were real dangers to the twins. Dying in her service to them would be terrible, but failing to take the action necessary to keep them safe, would be worse. She was startled to realize that she could face the possibility of her own death more easily than that she might have to take the life of another in order to protect herself and the girls. She hadn't previously considered that fact. It shocked and troubled her. What good would she be as an Oathtaker if she couldn't take the action necessary to protect her charge?

"Dixon," she said, her voice calm.

"I've got this."

"I was just going to say that perhaps I could be of some help."

He scowled as his prisoner, with beads of sweat dotting his forehead and his eyes pleading for help, looked her way. "I said to stay out of this."

She persisted. "It's just that I think I know how best to reach him, how to get the answers we need."

"Mara—" Dixon's voice was heavy with warning.

"You see," she continued, "I think your threats are not as effective as they might be."

"Mara," he warned again, more insistently this time.

She wouldn't be stopped. She read the fear in the man, and it was not the fear of death. In that instant, she was sure she knew how to get the answers they required and vowed she'd do whatever was necessary to protect the girls.

"Like I said, I mean to help. You see," she said, not giving Dixon the opportunity to cut her off, "I know that there are things some men fear even more than death." She went quiet for a moment, carefully watching the intruder's eyes. "Some men fear pain more than death, for example."

He smirked.

"And some fear maiming more than they fear pain, or death. More in fact, than anything else."

His eyes opened wide.

Dixon, seeing the reaction, looked to Mara. "What are you saying?"

"I'm saying that I've studied the healing arts and I've learned a great deal. I've learned about places that when injured, can cause extraordinary pain. More important, there are injuries that will not—cannot—wholly heal. Well, at least not without the power of Ehyeh. Like right here," she said as she reached down and touched the back and side of her knee. "The right kind of cut—rrrright herrrre—will cripple a man for life." She hung on her words for added emphasis, intentionally meeting the stranger's eyes.

Dixon stared at her, then turned his attention back to his prisoner, whose eyes revealed his fear.

Sheathing Spira, Mara removed a knife from inside her boot. She stepped forward. The eyes of her would-be assailant followed her every move. "Something tells me that you're one of those men." She watched closely for his reaction. "Aren't you?" She raised a brow. "You fear crippling more than anything." She leaned forward. "Huh? More than death," she finished in a whisper.

He struggled and then, as she took another step forward, shouted, "Heri! My name's Heri!"

"Are you alone?"

"Yes. Yes!"

"Who sent you?" Dixon asked.

"Gadon. Gadon!" Heri cried through his crooked teeth.

"Who's Gadon and who sent him?"

The man closed his eyes and took short, shallow breaths. "He—that is we— were with the palace guard."

"The palace at Shimeron?"

"Yes!"

"Who sent Gadon?"

"I don't know. I don't know! Gadon recruited me to go with him. I don't know who sent him."

"Where is he now?"

"I left him and the others last night."

Mara quickly calculated. Heri had caught up with them amazingly quickly. "Left them where?" she asked.

"I don't know the name of the place."

"Where was it?"

Heri struggled, but couldn't escape Dixon's hold.

"Where did you leave the others?"

He shook his head. "I don't know."

Mara stepped closer, moving her knife from one hand to the other and back again.

His eyes followed her. "At a small farm on the edge of the glen."

"Drake and Maggie's?"

"Yes. No. I don't know. It was just some old couple."

"What happened to them? Are they all right?"

He went still. He seemed to have no fight left in him. "I don't know. Gadon probably had them killed."

"Is he coming this way?"

"Yes."

"When do you expect him?" Dixon asked.

"Not before sunset tomorrow, at the earliest. He's making a thorough search for signs and tracks."

The Oathtakers exchanged a glance.

"What were your orders?" Dixon asked.

Heri shook his head.

"What were your orders?"

"There's also a wonderful little spot right . . . here." Mara pointed to the center of the back of her hand, speaking through gritted teeth, after confirming that she had Heri's attention. "Hurts like nothing else to be stabbed in the back of the hand." As he nervously licked his lips, she continued, "And of course, if done correctly—you know, if you twisssst the knife around good—the hand will never work quite the same again." She shook her head. "A pity really."

She held his gaze, a faint smile upon her lips. Anger consumed her. She felt no pity for the monster. He and his companions threatened the twins and had harmed those who'd helped her.

Tears welled in his eyes. "We were," he said, his crooked teeth clenched, "we were sent to kill Rowena and her child. That's all I know."

"By whom?" she asked calmly.

"I swear, I don't know."

She looked at Dixon. "He speaks truth." She didn't know how she knew, but she knew.

Still holding his captive from behind, Dixon pulled his knife across Heri's throat in one smooth move. As the life left the thug's body, the Oathtaker pushed it aside. It landed with a thud in a thicket of brush. Without another word, or another look at Mara, he marched off.

"I thought maybe you'd have left the honors to me," she said to his back.

Dixon strode back toward where Sherman and Cheryl grazed.

Mara could think of nothing to say. He'd done the right thing, she knew. She felt both cheated of the opportunity to execute the righteous judgment Heri had so deserved, and grateful Dixon had spared her that act. She followed him.

After some time, he slowed.

A grove of trees surrounded them. A creek ran nearby. It was a good place to set up camp and to get some much-needed rest.

"Thank you, Dixon. I hadn't heard him coming."

"Hmmm."

"You did the right thing."

"I know." He turned and walked away.

She dropped the subject.

While she unpacked their foodstuffs, he set a snare, tended their horses, and then gathered up fallen branches. When he'd accumulated a sizable pile, he reached out, and with a flick of his fingers, started their campfire. Once again his magic caught Mara off guard, just as when he'd lit the wayfarers' hut on fire.

Dixon headed to the creek where he took a quick dunk to wash away the dirt and sweat of the day. Afterward he checked his snare. He'd made a catch. Quietly he skinned and gutted the hare, then skewered it on a small green branch from a nearby fruit tree. He set it over the shimmering center coals of the fire.

Meanwhile, Mara took the twins to the creek. With rags from her pack, she wiped them clean. Then after laying them down on the edge of the bank, she slipped off her dress and dipped in the pool. The water invigorated her. When refreshed and dressed again, she returned to the campsite.

The air was heavy, both with the Oathtakers' silence, and with the aroma of roasting meat.

Dixon pulled the sizzling hare from the edge of the coals. He dropped the hot dinner into a bowl and tore the meat apart, blowing on his fingers to cool them from time to time.

Mara sat nearby on a blanket. The girls slept soundly at her side.

With the sun now down, only the fire lit their camp.

From the edge of the pond came the mesmerizing sounds of frogs and crickets. An occasional lightfly flitted by, its iridescent wings twinkling in the firelight.

"Are we making good time do you think?" she asked, finally breaking the silence.

"Hmmm."

She shrugged and set her lips tightly. He annoyed her. They'd traveled for days and he'd said next to nothing to her. His manner was entirely different with the townspeople when they'd purchased their horses and other supplies. Chatting it up with the local innkeeper, Dixon had made fast friends, and even got a particularly good deal on their mounts. But while personable, even friendly, with others, with her he was continually brusque, habitually curt.

"Fairly good, considering how often we need to stop," he finally deigned to respond. "We certainly can't afford to stay here long." He sat down, then handed her a portion of the roast hare.

The smell made Mara's stomach growl. She ate quickly, finishing up as Reigna awakened.

"Funny baby," she cooed. "It seems you know just when it's time to eat, huh?" She kissed her forehead. "Such a funny baby. Such a squishy forehead," she whispered and laughed.

"What did you say?" Dixon asked, scowling.

She looked at him, still smiling. "Have you ever noticed that a baby's softest part is its forehead? I feel my lips could sink right in." She took a couple of the infant's fingers into her mouth and sucked on them gently. She'd fallen completely under the girls' spell.

His brow furrowed. He shook his head as though attempting to rid himself of a nuisance. He stirred the fire, then added some larger branches to it. The waltzing flames reflected in his eyes. "Glad you can take this all so seriously," he murmured.

Mara laid Reigna down. "You know," she said, "I have had about enough. You are so rude. Frankly, your derision is more than I can bear. Come morning, why don't you just make your own way? I appreciate your help with that Heri character and all, but from here on, I'd prefer to go it alone. The girls and I'll make it to Polesk just fine on our own. I don't want you around anymore."

She stood, threw her dinner scraps into the fire, and then walked away.

He jumped to his feet. "What? What? I don't understand! What's your problem?"

"My problem? What's *my* problem?" She turned back to face him. "I've no problem, Dixon, *you* do." She pointed at him. "You're surly and belligerent at every turn. It's not my fault you weren't where you needed to be when you needed to be there to protect the love of your life." She turned away. "So . . . go. And take your blame with you!"

Tears burned her eyes, but she wasn't about to let him see her weakness. She didn't want him to think she was frightened to go on without him, or was concerned about how she'd protect the girls. She was just angry. She didn't need him.

She returned to the infants to change Reigna's wet things. Fearing her anger would make her touch too firm, she took in a couple deep breaths to calm down before continuing.

Dixon watched on, his mouth half open.

As she stole an occasional glance his way, she thought he must be accustomed to having his own way about everything. He expected others to concede at every turn to his authority. He probably thought she needed him. Well, she thought not.

The nighttime sounds became steadily louder. The hoot of an owl added a tenor to the bass of the bullfrogs and the soprano of the crickets singing through the night air. Far away, a dog barked, adding an offbeat percussion instrument to the mix.

When through with Reigna's change, Mara tended to Eden. Then she pulled a blanket from her sack and wrapped it over her shoulders. She picked up the twins and headed to a large oak a few feet away, sat down, and leaned against it.

Several minutes passed as she fought to contain her anger. She closed her eyes. "I take it we'll need to put the fire out shortly to avoid attracting any further attention. I'll take second watch—if you don't mind. It's likely the girls will have me up by then anyway." She situated one portion of the blanket to act as a pillow, then rested her head.

"You're right," he finally said, softly. His shoulders slumped.

She opened her eyes, filled with stinging tears again. She wiped them with the back of her hand. Her frustration renewed, she simply stared at him.

He looked down and shuffled his feet, then glanced off into the distance. "You're right. I've blamed you and I've resented that you were there when I couldn't be. I . . . had no choice. A—about being elsewhere, I mean."

"Right. And neither did I—have any choice—about doing what had to be done," she said quietly, but firmly. "We both did what we had to do. Now rather than explain myself further, I'm through with you." She turned away again and closed her eyes. *End of discussion.*

Dixon stepped nearer. He squatted down and reached toward her, then pulled his hand back. He waited a few moments. "I'm . . . sorry. I shouldn't have blamed you. I had no right to, and no reason to. You're right—about most things anyway. I'm at fault. I failed Rowena." He took in a deep breath. "But I swear, if you don't send me away, I'll not fail Reigna and Eden."

Mara turned back.

His eyes rose to meet hers. "And I won't fail you. I promise. Please," he whispered, repeating his plea. "Please, I want to help. I *need* to help."

She closed her eyes and exhaled slowly. She was tired. It was so frustrating trying to keep peace with this difficult man. Every moment with him was demanding, exhausting.

She looked toward the fire, now reduced to shimmering coals. "I don't know, Dixon. I admit I could use some help, but I'm not going to deal with your moodiness and blame."

"Please. Please, I swear I would—" He swallowed hard. "I would do anything for those girls. Anything! I would . . . I would lay my life down for them."

At that very moment, the ground shook.

Dixon teetered.

Mara felt the same sense of power and fullness as when she'd received the confirmation of her oath. Stunned, mouth agape, she gasped and then looked up.

Dixon appeared equally shocked. "I thought you said you—"

"I did!" she interrupted.

"But then, how could—"

"This be? I don't know. But I swore an oath for the girls' protection and I received a confirmation. Just now, when you swore to protect them, I had the same feeling as when I gave my oath."

"Can you describe it?"

"Well," she said, her hand to her throat, "it feels like I'm full of emotions—of all kinds. Happiness, sadness, fear, longing, desire . . . I want to sit silently, jump in joy, sing praises. I . . ."

"Yes?" he prompted.

She exhaled audibly, struggling to find the right words to convey her feelings. Tears welled in her eyes. "I feel I've been filled in places I didn't know were empty. It's like music just broke open within me."

"Yes, that's right."

"And you? What are you feeling now? How can this be if I've already been called as Oathtaker to the girls? If I've already sworn an oath for their protection?"

He frowned. "I know what the confirmation feels like, Mara. I've experienced it. You've described it beautifully . . . and accurately. Just now, I felt the earth shake, but I didn't get those same sensations."

"But what does this mean?"

"I don't know. If I had to guess, I'd say the Good One acknowledged my promise, but not as the girls' assigned Oathtaker. From what you just said, from the description you gave, there's no question. *You* are their Oathtaker."

She got to her feet and went back to the campfire, Dixon following. She sat down, cradling the babies. "Well there certainly are a lot of questions to be answered. Even so, I can't go on like this. I feel I'm always walking on eggshells around you and . . . I refuse to do it any longer." She pursed her lips and shook her head. "If you really want to help, if you really think you can do this, then something has got to change."

He nodded.

"Perhaps if you told your story, you could put your demons at bay. Then maybe, just maybe, we can call a truce. *I* am not your enemy."

He moved as though to speak, then hesitated. "Fair enough," he finally said. He was quiet for a minute. "Goodness, where do I begin?" he asked with a sheepish grin.

"How about at the beginning? I usually find that to be a good place."

He sat down near the fire, then reclined on his side, just feet away from her. "Well," he said as he sat up again, "I'll try to keep this short so as not to bore you." He chuckled softly.

Mara thought she saw, by the glow of the burning embers, the welling of tears in his eyes, but she still appreciated how that smile, slight though it was, replaced the scowl that had been on his face for most of the time since they'd met. "Just don't leave out anything important."

Their eyes met. They both grinned.

"See? That wasn't so bad, was it?"

Dixon's entire persona changed when he smiled. Instead of surly, he appeared friendly; instead of condescending, he appeared companionable. It made him very, very attractive. Surprised by that discovery, Mara sought to dismiss the thought as quickly as it had arisen.

"Well," he said, "when . . ." He glanced up. "The beginning? Really?"

"The beginning."

"Well then, I guess the story really starts when I left my family in the hinterlands to go to train as an Oathtaker. My father had been one and then, after the death of his charge, served as an advisor to the Council in the City of Light. He was always busy and often away from home. In many ways my mother acted as a single parent raising my two brothers and me.

"We lived in a small town with good friends nearby. My best friend, Edmond, was also the son of an Oathtaker. His father, Madden Chantray, had been in the service, but . . . Well, he'd become a traitor to the cause."

Dixon crossed his legs and leaned in to stir the remaining coals, as though in doing so his thoughts and remembrances might also be stirred and thereby rise to the surface.

"Madden's betrayal devastated my father. He'd known him well, had worked with him for years. My father was especially pained when the Council assigned to him, the prosecution of the case. In the end, Madden was put to death for his crimes. Because my father felt responsible somehow, he frequently invited Edmond to stay with us, sometimes for weeks at a time. I didn't hear the whole story until my father was on his deathbed. I think he wanted to save Edmond from the scandal."

A quiet minute passed. The occasional bullfrog croaked, marking the passing time.

"The hinterlands you say?" Mara finally asked, bringing Dixon back to the moment.

"Mmhmmm."

"So your family . . . Are you one of the Brecken Townsends?"

"That's right."

"Nice to have friends in high places." Dixon's story was bringing back some of the details she'd tried to recall earlier. It must have been the Madden Chantray scandal that had triggered her memories.

Dixon smirked.

"Where are your brothers now?"

"They live in the hinterlands. They care for my mother."

"And Edmond?"

"He wanted to join the Oathtakers, but couldn't pass the final exams. I know the Guild didn't hold his father's treason against him. They just don't work that way. With the Oathtakers, every man or woman stands alone. It's unfortunate he couldn't be one, though. I think he would have made a good one."

"Where is he now?"

"He's an advisor to the Council and a regular at the palace of the Select at Shimeron."

"Sounds like he landed on his feet pretty well."

Dixon nodded.

"Do you stay in touch?"

"With Edmond? Oh, yes, he's like a brother to me. In some ways he's closer than my own brothers. We see each other fairly regularly. In fact, he may be just the person to help us to find a safe place for the twins."

Mara held the infants closely as they slept contentedly. "Then you agree with what Rowena said—that we need to disappear somewhere with the girls."

"Most definitely. Someone tracked her for a reason. I hope to find out who and why. And when I do . . ." He fell silent. Moments later, he changed positions again.

When the attention was on him, he tended to behave like a child who couldn't focus.

As he stirred the coals again, sparks flew up.

"Go on," Mara pressed, sensing he was lost in thought.

"Oh yes, as I was saying, I trained to be an Oathtaker. I got my first assignment—a fourth—about a year after my final exams. But she died in a tragic accident only a year later."

"A fourth born of a Select—one instrumental in laying new foundations for the cause," Mara said. "Let's see. They open new areas and organize events to educate the people about Ehyeh so as to recruit new believers."

"That's right."

"And they establish sanctuaries where others can study the Good One and His ways."

"Right again. Of course, like all Select, few fourths remain today." He stopped to take a bite of cheese that remained from their dinner.

"Did this fourth have a name?"

"Judith." He went silent for a moment. "Judith Jenkins." He bit his lower lip. "But like I said, she died in a tragic accident. While riding out one day to a new sanctuary she'd established, her horse bolted. She was thrown to her death." He paused in thought. "Actually, Edmond was along on that trip. We could never determine what caused her horse to bolt. It was tough going after that for a time, but I was cleared of any wrongdoing.

"Not long after that, I was out one day when I felt the calling. I was traveling back to the hinterlands to visit my mother when I came upon Rowena. She was making a quick getaway from a group of assassins sent out for any Select they could find. Her Oathtaker died in the battle. His sacrifice ensured her safety, but only for a short time. When I arrived, I immediately accepted her as my charge." Dixon stretched his shoulders. "And the rest, as they say, is history," he said with a smile.

"Oh no," Mara laughed, "you won't get off that easily!" His smile mesmerized her. "Tell me about Rowena."

He looked away. "Well, as you probably figured out, she is—*was*," he corrected himself, then swallowed hard, "the ranking member of the first family of the Select."

"I had picked up on that, yes."

"Her mother, Mae, was a third. Mae wanted to see the old days return. She had six children—six daughters. Then a number of years passed. Finally she became pregnant with Rowena.

"Rowena took her role, her position, both as the ranking member of the first family and the only living seventh, very seriously. She planned for her own seven daughters. Well, I guess that's seven *plus one* daughters. Her husband, Grant, was not of the Select. But of course—"

"Being a member of the Select follows the mother's line. So the twins are Select."

"Yes, that's right." He ran his fingers through his hair. "Anyway he, Grant that is, died just after Rowena got pregnant with the girls."

"What of?"

"We were never sure."

"No one could heal him?"

"No. Well maybe they could have, but no healer made it to him in time."

"Poor Rowena. She must have been devastated."

"Yes, she loved him very much." He closed his eyes in his reverie.

Mara watched him closely. Had it been hard on him to know that Rowena loved another?

"Are her parents still living? Mae and—what was his name? And what of her sisters?"

"Her parents, Max and Mae, are both deceased. Three of Rowena's sisters: Eve, a first; Dianna, a second; and Therese, a third; have fallen to assassins. But the others: Janine, a fourth; Sally, a fifth; and Lilith, a sixth, are still living. They're at the palace in Shimeron."

He was quiet for a minute. "Rowena studied history and prophecy. She believed, as many do, that a seventh daughter of a seventh daughter would one day be born, and that she would be the best hope for bringing back the 'golden days' of the Select and restoring Ehyeh's ways. She believed evil forces were at work in the world. She thought the people had moved too far from the beliefs and standards of Oosa's founders."

"How did you end up here?"

Dixon sat with one elbow on his knee and with his chin resting in his palm. "Rowena heard rumors of plans, perhaps among those close to her, to destroy her. So we left Shimeron shortly after Grant died. That was about six months ago. We have . . . that is, we *had*, been on the run ever since."

They sat quietly as the fire crackled and crickets sang.

"So," Mara finally prodded, "then what?"

"Like I said, we were on the run. Rowena had a destination in mind, but didn't want to lead anyone to it. The day the twins were born, we knew our pursuers were close. A mountain lion attacked one of our horses just days prior. It slowed us down. She was very frightened."

He stoked up the coals. "I think the fear may have caused her to go into labor early. That, and I suppose she was likely to anyway, given that there were two children and not just the one anticipated." He looked at Mara. "Two children! It's unheard of among the Select."

She nodded and motioned with her hand for him to continue.

"In any case, I found her a safe place—or what I thought was a safe place—then turned back to where the assassins trailed us. I guess they'd called upon the powers of Sinespe for the grut, but I didn't know that when I left her side."

He told about how he'd shot at the men. "I was really too far away to get in a good shot and they took refuge behind rocks and boulders, but at a minimum, I hoped to confuse them as to our whereabouts." He paused, his eyes closed. "I didn't think I'd been gone long . . . Maybe a couple of hours or so? Then I returned."

"And?" Mara asked gently after a minute or so.

"Suddenly, the earth shook. The sky changed color. I didn't connect in that moment that its turning red meant that the ranking member of the Select had . . . I just thought that Rowena must've given birth and released her power. I found it puzzling because the ranking Select usually doesn't do that until after his or her youngest has reached adulthood and found favor with Ehyeh. That way they know their children are ready to take on their responsibilities.

"But I figured that maybe she released her magic so she could put a cocoon of safety around herself and her infant for a time." He looked up. "What I didn't expect was that she would have had twins, or that I'd find you and that you would already have accepted them as your charge." His eyes glistened with unshed tears. "In the end, I failed her," he whispered.

"No, Dixon. Without your distracting those men, Rowena could not have born the girls. As it was, the grut nearly got to her. We all just did what we had to do."

She snuggled Eden nearer. "I like to think that Ehyeh, the great giver of life, is in charge of us all, and that things turn out as He intends—that when we're obedient to His ways in our efforts to further life and freedom, we're following His plan for us." For the first time in days, Mara's tears ran freely.

"Just as you committed your life to Judith, and later to Rowena, Rowena committed her life to the Select and to the people of Oosa, and I've committed my life to these children. We've each done what we believed the Good One called us to do. Ehyeh couldn't ask for more. Neither then, should you."

He allowed for a moment of silence. "Now may I ask you a question?"

"I suppossssse," she drawled.

"No fooling now. Was there really a full pack of grut?"

"Really."

"Really and truly?"

"Truly, a full pack."

He shook his head and laughed. "Honest to the Good One?"

"Honest to the Good One!"

Still shaking his head and grinning, he stood. He glanced into the darkness, then back her way. "Why don't you get some rest now. I'll keep watch."

Dixon walked the perimeter of the campsite, then positioned himself outside the fading light of the coals. Bullfrogs belched in the pond and bats squeaked overhead, but for the most part, his vigil was a quiet one. He was glad for the calm that gave him some time for introspection.

He'd been so busy being angry, of feeling jealous of Mara and of her having been in attendance at Rowena's last moments, that initially, he'd failed to take a good look at her. But her smile held a kindness, a sincerity he'd not encountered for some time.

He was weary of others using him, especially those who wanted something from Rowena. It had been so long since he'd been able to trust someone. He fervently hoped that he could trust Mara. Being an Oathtaker was a lonely business. So few understood its demands and limitations.

Goodness, but she was beautiful, as well. He found the light sprinkling of freckles across her nose amusing, attractive.

Perhaps best of all though, she was strong and spirited. Imagine a newly assigned Oathtaker telling him to take a hike. Then there was the way she handled Heri. That was genius, really. She was impressive, gutsy—and she'd been right. He had unfairly blamed her for his own failing. Ehyeh did use all things for good. The world did operate according to His design. Had Mara not been there, the twins might never have lived to see the light of day. He shuddered to think it.

He was certain she still believed that he'd loved Rowena. It was true, there had been a time, but of course it was impossible—for so many reasons. He was under oath and therefore, not free. She was married and therefore, not free. Though it had taken some time, eventually he'd come to appreciate that it wouldn't have worked anyway. Rowena did not return his sentiments.

In the early days, it had been painful to love without love in return, but he never acted on his feelings, strove never to allow any vestige of them to be known to others.

Over time, his love changed. Rowena became like a sister to him and the very best of friends. He supported and helped her in every way possible. He was willing to go, and would have gone, to the grave to protect her, just as he'd sworn he would do.

Yes, he had loved Rowena, but not as Mara thought. So why hadn't he corrected her misunderstanding?

Maybe because it keeps a distance between us.

One of the babies cried out. Mara awakened and prepared a feeding. In that moment, he was immensely grateful she was allowing him to share in this experience.

An owl hooted in the distance. He turned toward the sound and caught, at the edge of his line of vision, the splendor of a shooting star. *Luck is with me tonight.*

He walked the perimeter of the camp again. He relived some of the better times with Rowena in his thoughts: her laughing and teasing him about his apprehension over having accepted a seventh as his charge, the births of her children, and of how she'd placed her newborns in the care of Oathtakers she trusted while she continued on her mission.

She had called her supporters her *inner circle*—and what a group they made.

She was a rare one. Dear Good One, great Ehyeh, I miss her so much already.

CHAPTER SIX

Reigna cried. Out of milk, Mara cuddled her closely and gave her a knuckle to suck on. For the moment the infant seemed satisfied, but Mara couldn't help but notice that between the twins, Eden was easier to keep quiet. Already they displayed little glimpses into their base, and different, personalities.

The travelers had stopped to eat and to fill their canteens, but rest time was over.

"Just over that ridge there, is Polesk," Dixon said as he placed his hand on her shoulder and pointed through the trees. "So, not much longer. I'll lead the horses over the rocky ledge just ahead. They could use more of a break."

"Thank you." She strapped Reigna to her front side, then stretched her arms and shoulders. She grasped the handle of Eden's basket, but before she could lift it, Dixon gently brushed her hand away.

"I've got her."

"Let's trudge on then," she said.

The trail ahead, narrow and rocky, ran along the edge of a dry streambed. When they came upon thorny brambles and brush, Dixon placed Eden's basket down and handed the horses' reins to Mara.

Using a long scythe-like knife he'd picked up earlier, he cut a clearing. Occasionally, he waved his arm to break up the spiders' webs running across his intended path. Wild blackberry bushes nestling in the dappled shady areas snagged at his pants as he passed by.

When through, he returned to Mara's side, took her hand to lead her though the brambles, then went back for their horses.

Step. Step. Step. Will it never end? The added weight of carrying Reigna, or Eden, or both at times, took its toll. Mara's feet and back ached and her muscles protested against the unaccustomed riding. She envied Dixon's strength and stamina, but then offered a silent prayer of gratitude for his assistance.

When she tired, she asked him to take the lead. Occasionally he stopped and turned toward the flutter of wings, or the buzz of insects, his senses clearly on high alert, as he continually surveyed the landscape.

After a distance, with the horses somewhat rested, and the rocky patches behind them, the Oathtakers rode again, each with one of the twins.

Small farms dotted the landscape. Fields of oats and wheat, fully ripened and golden in the sunlight, waved in the light breeze as if greeting passersby. Dogs barked and donkeys brayed in the distance. The rhythmic clipping of Sherman and Cheryl's hooves sounded out when they passed over rocky surfaces.

Just when Mara thought she could take no more, they reached the top of a ridge. "Welcome to Polesk," Dixon said with a wave.

"Whew!" Mara looked out at the largest city she'd ever seen. People on horseback and traveling in carriages moved through, giving life to the surroundings like blood through arteries. Houses at the fringes sported small vegetable gardens where scratching chickens milled about. Farther in were larger buildings. Each seemed to rise higher than the one before, as though in a silent contest to determine which was the tallest. In the city's center stood the largest and highest of them all.

"Sanctuary," he said, following her gaze and answering her unasked question.

"It's huge!" Even from this distance, she could make out its grounds, like a park in the midst of which sanctuary stood like a beacon to all who sought refuge from worldly cares. Made of white brick, it sported a towering spire that rose up, and up, and up into the air.

"Polesk has a reputation for being a worldly, cosmopolitan city. People come from all over Oosa to study at, or simply to visit, sanctuary. As a result, political and religious thought and argument ran rampant, as do education, the arts, and the inevitable crime and graft that money and power attract," he told her.

Before long they made their way to the outskirts of the city. Its sounds and smells nearly assaulted them. People bustled. The smell of cooking food wafted through the air.

Dixon's stomach rumbled in hunger. Mara slapped his arm lightly with the back of her hand, caught his eye, and then joined with him in a good laugh.

As they rode on in silence for a time, they both kept a close look out so that no detail would escape their attention.

"Really and truly, Dixon. Honest to the Good One. A full pack," she interrupted his musings some time later.

His head snapped to meet her gaze. "What did you say?"

"You asked if there was really a full pack of grut. Yes, again I say, there was a full pack. Honest to Ehyeh!"

His eyes bore deeply into hers. "I didn't ask you anything."

"Of course you did." Her brow dropped. Her expression turned serious. "Just now, you asked me—again—if there really was a full pack of grut the day . . . Well, you know, the day Rowena . . . died," her voice fell off to a whisper.

"I didn't ask anything." He shook his head. Then suddenly, he smiled. His entire face lit up. "Mara! Your attendant magic!"

"What are you talking about?"

"Your magic. Your magic!"

"Magic! I just answered your question was all."

He grasped her arm. "Mara, didn't you know? When you accept your charge, you take on attendant magic. It's to help you to fulfill your duties. Apparently your magic is, or at least it includes, the ability to read thoughts."

Her mouth dropped open. She was befuddled. "Well of course I know about attendant magic. But that can't be it. I'm sure you spoke out loud."

He shook his head.

"Are you sure? It's not that unusual for someone deep in thought to speak out without knowing it."

"No, I did not speak out loud. I was just pondering over your story about the beasts. It's just so amazing. You heard me, but you didn't hear me speak. You heard what I thought."

"Hmmm. Well if that's true, then think something else and we'll see if I can do it again."

"We can try, but it may not work."

"Why?"

"Well, an Oathtaker's attendant magic is not generally 'magic on demand.' Not initially anyway. It takes practice before it becomes second nature. So you should test it however and whenever possible. But sometimes, especially in the beginning, it manifests itself in small ways, simply to alert you of its existence."

He turned his gaze to the increased flow of horses and carriages. With a wave, he directed her off the main route.

"You'll need to be careful with this," he whispered. "You don't want anyone to know about this ability."

She stared at him, her brow lowered. "What did you mean when you said my magic is, or at least includes, this ability?"

"Considering that Reigna is a seventh and that Eden is— Well, I don't rightly know what she is. Anyway, in light of their position, you're likely to be graced with significant power. Your magic is just coming into being. Be on your guard for anything out of the ordinary."

"Such as?"

He thought for a moment. "Actually, now that I think about it, we may already have seen your magic operating a couple of times without having been aware of it."

"I don't understand."

"Well, like the night you sang everyone to sleep."

She laughed. "That's ridiculous. I sang the girls a lullaby. You others were just sleepy." She lowered her gaze. "Oh, Dixon, I can't bear to think what happened to Drake and Maggie. I feel so responsible. Still, I'm sure you're mistaken—about this lullaby business."

He grinned, raising a brow.

"You're not serious."

"Completely. Actually, I wondered about it at the time. I was tired, but when you sang, I was completely unable to keep from falling asleep. I just never gave it another thought." He hesitated. "And about Drake and Maggie," his demeanor turned serious, "I know how you feel. But you should never take on responsibility for the evil deeds of others."

Mara recollected the night with Dixon's friends and the strange look in his eyes before he fell asleep. "But . . . what does singing others to slumber mean? What possible use would such attendant magic, if it's true my song had such power, serve?"

He shrugged. "Not sure. Maybe just that you can help others sleep. But it might be something much greater."

"Such as?"

"Well, such as being able to bring about specific actions, intentions—to be able to strongly influence others if you set your desires to song."

She stared at him. His expression was solemn. "You're really serious."

"Deadly." He grinned. "Then again, it may be nothing significant at all."

"What else? You said we might have seen my powers a couple of times."

"Mara, when that Heri thug attacked us, you seemed to know just how to get the information that we needed. Quite easily, really. And then you told me he spoke truth. Did you guess what would work best to get him to talk? Did you guess he was telling the truth? Or did you, somehow, know those things?"

"I can't explain it, but I can tell you that I knew—with certainty."

"Hmmm."

"So, you think maybe I have the power to identify truth from falsehood?"

"Perhaps. It's possible, though that is a rare power."

"What else? What other kinds of attendant magic powers do you know of?"

"Well . . . it could be the power to do something like being able to hear things, conversations even, from great distances. Or to see beyond a normal range, or even through solid objects. To . . . understand an animal's thoughts, or to influence others' thoughts. To infuse objects with magic power. To heal. To take on the pain of another. To speak or to understand languages previously unknown to you. To change the physical form of something. To create illusions, or . . . to move things by thought, or . . . to run or move very quickly, or—"

"Like you," she interrupted.

"What's that?"

"You know—like when you ran toward me to cut off Heri's attack. I've never seen anyone move so fast in all my life! It was as though my eyes couldn't take it all in as quickly as it was happening."

"That's right—that's part of my attendant magic."

"What other powers do you know of?"

"Hmmm, let's think." He paused. "Oh, I know. It could include something such as being a perfect shot."

"I am a perfect shot."

He chuckled softly.

"Really, I'm a perfect shot!" she argued. "Well in target practice anyway." She scowled. "I did miss a couple of tries at the grut that day."

He said nothing, just grinned.

She frowned at him. "I'm telling you the truth. I'm considered a very good shot. I hit almost every target, almost every time. How else could I have taken down that pack of grut?"

He held her gaze. "Perhaps that's why Ehyeh called on you when Rowena needed help."

Dust rose in the air from the passing wagons, distracting their attention.

"We'll need to talk more about this, Dixon, but right now we need to see to the girls."

"Right you are." Urging Sherman forward, he grasped Mara's arm again. "Just remember what I said. Be on the lookout for anything—anything out of the ordinary. Once you identify a power, it's good to practice it so that it'll be there for you when you need it. Having said that, don't forget that your powers are for the benefit of your charge, not simply to make life easier for you."

She thought over the events of the past days. She couldn't recall having noticed anything else out of the ordinary. "What is your attendant magic? I mean—aside from being able to move very, very quickly?"

"Several things. I received attendant magic with Judith, and of course with Rowena, I got additional powers. For example, I can go long periods with little or no sleep—when I condition myself for that, and . . . other things."

"Such as? Wait! No, don't tell me. Such as the power to light a fire with the flick of your fingers!"

"You caught me," he said, smirking, "but that's pretty simple. I'm sure you'll be able to do that. There are some things all Oathtakers can do."

"Huh. So what other powers do you have?" She glanced out at the crowds.

"Well, let's see here. The . . . the power to charm," he said, with a lift of his chin.

She jerked her head back his way. She thought he was joking, but he hadn't cracked a grin. His jaw was set as firm as ever.

"Charm?" Her mouth dropped open. "Oh, dear Good One, that is rich!" She tried to hold back her mirth, then burst out laughing. Though he was now fully frowning at her, she laughed until tears rolled down her face. "Charm!" she repeated. She held her stomach, it hurt from laughing so hard. "But of course!"

Scowling, Dixon turned to face her. Then the infection caught, and he too burst into raucous laughter.

A small boy played with a large black and white dog. The animal yipped and spun around, chasing its tail, then ran after a stick the boy threw.

The Oathtakers rode toward him. When they neared, Dixon dismounted. "Lo, there!" he called as he helped Mara to the ground.

The boy turned and smiled. "Hello!"

"I wondered, could you direct us to the nearest Oathtakers' quarters?"

"Sure! My dad, he knows some Oathtakers. And my brother is one. Course he doesn't have a charge yet, but he'll be a great Oathtaker some day! He's big and strong. I want to be just like him when I get tall."

Dixon chuckled at the boy's way of identifying adulthood with one's height. "Your brother's an Oathtaker, huh?"

"Who's there?" came a voice from off to the side.

"That's my dad there," the child said, pointing. He threw his stick again, then jumped with glee as his pet shot out to retrieve it. "Go get it, Bear!"

"Bear! Now, that's a funny name for a dog," Mara said to him.

Dixon left her with the boy and went to meet his father. The man sported simple garb. His short sandy brown hair accentuated his bold chin and prominent nose. His smile was friendly and quick.

Coming within easy speaking distance, Dixon greeted him. "Good day. We're just making our way into town and could use some directions."

Mara and the child drew near.

"Patrick," the man said with a grin, ruffling his son's hair, "I see you've made fast friends again." Then he introduced himself. "I'm Francis."

"Nice to meet you, Francis. I'm Dixon, and this is Mara. We're traveling and have found ourselves in some need. Your boy tells us you know some Oathtakers."

"That's right."

"I have a good friend who I hear is with the hood here in Polesk. 'Ted' is his name. Ted Baker."

"Ted! Ted Baker? Well isn't that something? I was just on my way to see him at the Oathtakers' mission home. My mother, Faith, lives and works there."

"We understand that the hood hosts some . . . unusual guests."

"Yes, that's right. Of course Ted would be the one to give you the full account, but I'm happy to take you there with me."

"Oh, that's so kind of you," Mara said.

"My pleasure." Francis took his hands from his pockets and with a wave, summoned Patrick who had wandered away, back to his side, as Bear jumped and yipped excitedly over the visitors.

"Patrick, run and tell your mother we'll be gone for a few minutes. Leave Bear inside, and then you can come along with us—if you promise to be well behaved."

"Oh, I'm bein' haved, Dad! I'm bein' haved!" the boy cried as he ran toward the house, Bear leading the way.

When Patrick returned, the group set out. Mara and Dixon led their horses. Wagons loaded with goods passed them in both directions, their drivers calling out to people in the streets to clear the way.

Stands scattered along the roadway became more frequent. Their offerings were rich and varied: handmade silver jewelry; pastries; sausages by the foot; goat cheeses; rice pudding sprinkled with cinnamon, its sweet aroma wafting in the light breeze; hats; gloves; patterned handbags; scarves and shawls dyed to every color imaginable, and portraying diverse designs, scenes, and patterns; handmade soaps boasting by their fragrances, their fresh herbal ingredients; flowers of every hue and scent; books, both new and used; stationery; and more.

One station caught Mara's attention with its array of exotic feathers for decorating hats, or for use as quills, canes with hand carved eagles and other wildlife on their handles, various trinkets claiming to hold magical powers, perfumery, and other assorted gewgaw and frippery.

"We appreciate your willingness to help us," Dixon said. "We just came from Mara's sister's place." He glanced her way. "Her sister died tragically bearing the little ones here." He gestured toward the infants.

"Yes, I promised Cecile I'd care for them. It's just that they're not taking well to goat milk. So, we asked around. We heard about the home the Oathtakers run here and thought perhaps . . . Well, we're hoping to find a young woman who could be of assistance."

"It's possible." Francis walked on, hands in and out of his pockets in a sort of nervous gesture. His long stride kept the company moving forward at a brisk pace.

"So it's true the Oathtakers keep a home for refugees from Chiran?" Dixon asked. "Amazing, isn't it? Anyway, we're hoping one might join us. We could help her to make a new life here in Oosa."

"I'd be ever so grateful," Mara said.

Just then, a stand displaying knives with beautifully carved handles caught her attention. She stopped mid-stride. She surveyed the table of goods, then picked up a blade to examine the intricate pattern on its scrimshaw handle. It depicted, in minutest detail, the form of a hawk, its eyes piercing, the vanes and barbs of its feathers exquisitely complex and detailed. She placed the knife back down as the attendant made his way to assist her.

"Lovely blade, Miss, lovely," he said as he lifted another for her to see.

She looked at the item he presented, then put it back down. Again she picked up the knife with the scrimshaw handle, testing its weight and balance. "How much?"

"Oh, that one is a beauty. A rare one. Yes, indeed. But luck is with you. We have a great sale today. Just two gold marks."

She turned the blade in her hands. "One and a half."

"I don't know. That one's special. The blade comes from Sugu. They're famous for their fine workmanship."

"One and a half gold marks," she repeated, looking the vendor in the eyes as confirmation of her final offer.

He wiped his hand through his hair. "Well, all right, it's a deal." He slipped the weapon into a simple leather sheath and handed it to her.

She paid the merchant.

"Might I interest you in anything more? We have these lovely—"

She waved her hand. "Thank you, no."

Patrick, who stood at her side, reached toward the knives. Fearing he'd harm himself, she grabbed his hand. "Careful, little man, those aren't toys."

"Patrick," Francis cautioned.

"I'm bein' haved, Dad! Look, no knife!" The boy released Mara's grasp and held his hands up, palms out, grinning broadly.

Francis took his son's hand, then picked up the conversation where they'd left off. "As a matter of fact," he said, "there may be just the person for you at the home. 'Nina' is her name. She's just arrived, so she's not had time to make this her home or to make any friends here yet. She's grieving terribly."

He pulled Patrick, who found the sights alluring, back to his side. "She had a child of her own, but the poor thing was born as she was escaping Chiran and it didn't survive. She was very near the border at the time. I believe it all happened just a few days ago."

"Oh, how very sad," Mara said. "Do you think she might be willing to join us when we return home to—"

"Princhon," Dixon interrupted. "We're headed back to Mara's family home.

"That's right," she continued, taking in a long breath. "I hope my mother will find some peace in having Cecile's children with her." She looked back to Francis, tears welled in her eyes. "We would be ever so grateful if you could put in a good word for us." She wiped at her eyes as though embarrassed for having allowed her emotions to show. Glancing at Dixon, she noted his surprise. It seemed he hadn't expected her to be so convincing an actress. She nearly grinned in response, but held herself in check.

"Well, you look to be good folks. I don't suppose either of you is a trained Oathtaker?"

Instinctively, Mara reached for where Spira rested. The light cloak draped over her shoulders concealed her weapon. She said nothing.

"I am, as a matter of fact," Dixon said. "That's one of the reasons we thought to check in with the local hood."

"Have you no charge either?" Francis asked.

Dixon hesitated. "No, I . . . I've no charge." He swallowed hard.

"It's a shame what's happened to the Select, don't you think? I fear for Oosa," Francis said.

After some minutes the group arrived at a large oak beam house in the midst of town. The dwelling was worn, but sturdy. The walkway leading to the front door was void of all vegetation but for a few scraggly weeds that had found purchase along the edges of the house. Clothing hung on lines running from the side of the building to poles in the yard where a handful of children played. Chickens rambled aimlessly, pecking at the grain and gravel on the ground near an outbuilding behind the house.

Francis stepped inside. An array of sandals on the floor and shawls hanging from pegs, greeted him. Two young women sat before him, one discreetly nursing an infant, a lightweight blanket draped over her shoulder.

A large tabby watched the party as it entered. It flicked the end of its tail. Mara stroked the feline behind its ears. It lifted its head, pushing back toward her as though to ask for more, then purred raucously.

"Hey!" shouted Francis. "Hey, Ma?"

A woman stepped into view. Her wavy graying hair was in a bit of a fuss. Her eyes, the color of a mid-summer sky, lit up. Her smile warmed her face, softening her otherwise sharp features. She grabbed a cloth from the waist of her white apron, which sported clear signs that dinner was in process. Flour dusted its surface along with various smudges and stains. Wiping her hands and walking with a slight limp, she made her way to his side.

"Francis! Wherever have you been?" She placed her arm around him and nudged him. "Shame on you for staying away so long."

"Ah, Ma, stop. You saw me just last week." He ruffled her hair just as he'd earlier done to Patrick's. "I suppose, next thing, you'll accuse me of keeping you from your grandson."

"Oh, have no fear. Nothing can keep me from my boy. Isn't that right, Patrick?" She squatted down beside the child and embraced him. She flicked and fluffed at his hair.

Mara grinned at the family resemblances in both looks and mannerisms.

As though noticing for the first time that Francis and Patrick were not alone, the woman stood again and looked at her guests. Seeing the infant in Mara's arms and hearing it whimpering, she reached out. "May I?"

Mara handed over the fussing child. "Plenty to go around you might say," she said as she reached inside the basket that Dixon held to uncover the as yet silent Eden.

"Goodness!" The woman turned her attention to the babe in her arms. "My, my, what a beauty. Who have we here?"

"This is my mother, Faith," Francis said, then completed the introductions.

"Mara's sister died bearing that little beauty you're holding and her sister."

As though on cue, Reigna cried loudly. Seconds later, Eden fidgeted, displaying signs of distress as well.

"They wondered if we might know of someone willing to accompany them back to Mara's home and . . . Well, they're looking for someone for the long term, a wet nurse for the twins."

"What? Have the little ones no names?" Faith asked.

"That's Reigna you're holding, and this is Eden," Mara said. "Do you think you could help us?"

Faith and Francis glanced at one another. He raised his brow in question.

"By golly, I think you're right," she said as though she'd read his mind. She looked back to her visitors. "A young woman came to us just a couple days ago. She escaped Chiran, bearing her child on the way. Unfortunately, her daughter did not make it. Of course, Nina is devastated."

Francis patted his mother's shoulder. "I mentioned her to them."

Just then, a slight young woman in a light blue cotton dress and wearing tattered sandals, walked into the room. Her skin was bronze, her hair so black and shiny that it had an almost purple cast. It lay long and straight down her back. Her eyes, dark as night, were red and puffy from crying.

Faith waved the newcomer forward. "Come, Nina. Come here, child. I'd like you to meet some new friends of ours." She introduced her visitors.

Nina nodded with each introduction, but the sight of the twins distracted her. The longing and suffering in her eyes was palpable.

Faith cocked her head and raised her brow, gazing at Mara. She was leaving it to her visitors to speak to the young woman.

Mara reached her hands out. Palms up, her eyes meeting Nina's, she invited the young woman to place her hands there. Understanding the invitation, Nina did. She looked down, back up at Mara briefly, then down again.

"Nina, we've come for help. Francis and Faith, may Ehyeh bless them, suggested that you may be the answer to our prayer. You see the girls here? This is Reigna." Mara stroked the infant's cheek. "And this," she continued, gesturing toward the basket, "is Eden. The girls' mother died a couple days ago. I need a nurse for them. That is, I need someone who can help me to mother them. You know, to nurse them when they're hungry, to comfort them when they're sad, to . . . Well, I'm sure you understand. In any case, I was wondering, would you be willing?"

The young woman burst into tears. She clasped Mara's hands tightly, then showered them with kisses. "Oh, you answer my prayers," she said between her kissing and crying. "Two babies. Two! Oh, which first?"

She released Mara and reached for Reigna. Faith placed the swaddled, fussing infant into her arms. Nina then took up Eden's basket.

Spotting a chair that caught her fancy, she went to it, then sat down. She took a lightweight blanket from the back of the chair, placed it over her shoulder, and commenced nursing Reigna. In that moment, her entire persona changed. Like the tabby sitting next to the front door that had purred at Mara's touch, her eyes closed as she rocked, humming ever so lightly, the faintest of smiles upon her face.

Faith led her guests to the kitchen and offered them something to eat. After assuring them there was nothing they could do to assist, she set out bread fresh from the oven slathered with butter, and warm lamb stew. A jar of orange infused honey sat on the table, along with various cheeses and large red strawberries.

Dixon leaned back in his chair, crossing his feet at his ankles, then moments later, sat forward drumming a beat with his hand to his thigh.

"Ma, Dixon is a friend of Ted's. Are you expecting him back soon?"

"Should be here any minute. He was at sanctuary and intended to stop back for a late lunch."

The front door opened.

"I'm back!"

"Why, that's him now." Faith placed her honeyed bread down and stood. The table wobbled. The plates and cups jiggled.

"No, let me," Dixon said, his hand on her arm, urging her to stay put. He went to the doorway facing the front entrance.

"Well, as I live and breathe!" Ted exclaimed from the next room. When he reached Dixon, he embraced him and clapped him on the back.

"Ted, my dear friend, it's so good to see you."

"Whatever are you doing here?" Ted's eyes glistened.

Dressed in his Oathtaker's garb, which was unlike that generally worn by those in training, in that it sported a series of decorations depicting his training and rank, he stood with his arm around Dixon's shoulders, smiling.

"How is Rowena? Never mind that," he continued as he glanced about, "*where* is Rowena? Why, I haven't seen you two since . . . When? A couple years ago or so, right? Certainly not since I came back here to Polesk."

Dixon's smile fell. His eyes welled with tears.

Ted stopped cold. "What's going on?"

Mara thought how quickly she'd become devoted to the girls and found herself, perhaps for the first time, truly empathizing with Dixon over his loss. Tears suddenly and unexpectedly sprang to her eyes.

"We need to talk, Ted."

Ted looked around the room. Francis's eyes held a question. There was confusion on Faith's face. His gaze shifted to Mara. He nodded at her. Turning back to his old friend, he said, "Let's go, then. I know just the place."

Dixon glanced at Mara, who tipped her head in response. She was fine now that the girls were nursing well.

"Take your time now. We'll have a bite for you when you get back," Faith called out.

Ted moved a basket of clean laundry to the side, straightened out a rug at his feet, then opened the back screen door. It squealed in protest. He gestured for Dixon to take the lead.

Mara stepped to the door as they walked away, grateful Dixon would be able to speak openly with someone he clearly trusted and held in high regard.

Sitting on a park bench a short walk from the mission home, they'd not spoken since leaving the house. Dixon leaned forward, his elbows on his knees, hands at the sides of his face. He appreciated his friend's presence. His own father had mentored Ted, and Ted in turn had ushered Dixon into manhood after his father died. He trusted the man implicitly.

He knew he would have to speak first; Ted would give him whatever time he needed. Lost in thought, he suddenly became aware of the sounds around him: laughter floating through the air, the tintinnabulation of sanctuary bells, the clip-clopping of a horse and buggy, the peal of a child's laughter.

He hung his head. How could everyone go on as though nothing had changed, as though things had not gone awry? Didn't they know the world had stopped when Rowena died? Or so it seemed at times.

With some regret, he finally broke the silence. "Rowena . . . died."

Ted watched as Dixon brushed his foot across the sand at his feet.

"About six months ago she discovered that she was pregnant with her seventh. Shortly afterward, Grant died. Then one day she insisted we leave the palace immediately and in the dark of night." Dixon kept his eyes downcast. "Someone was after her—someone close."

He told Ted of their journey, how distressed Rowena had become, and of how she'd gone into labor with their pursuers so close.

"So what happened?" Ted asked, reading Dixon's behavior as an invitation to speak.

"I found her a wayfarer's hut, then went back to do what I could about those chasing us."

"Yes?"

Dixon told how he'd shot at the men in pursuit. "I'd been gone, I don't know . . . A couple hours? Just before I arrived back at the hut, the earth shook. Then, I found Rowena . . . dead." He wiped at his eyes brusquely.

"And the child?"

Dixon smiled. His face lit up. "Child? Children! You didn't get to meet them."

"*Them*?"

"Twins. Reigna, the firstborn, and Eden. They're with Mara back at the house."

"Is that the woman who was with you?"

"Mmhmm. They are her charge. Or 'charges' if you like."

"Mara's charge? She's an Oathtaker?"

"A new and very inexperienced one." Dixon told about how Mara had been led to the hut when it was under attack by the grut.

Ted whistled. "An entire pack?"

"That's what she says. Says she's a perfect shot." Dixon grinned. "I believe her, though. I couldn't be there. Ehyeh knew that, so He sent the right person. They say He always does." He went back to brushing sand with the toe of his boot.

"When I burst into the hut it was . . . Well, we had a difficult start." He chuckled softly. "But I think we've worked through it now. I promised her I'd do anything to assist her. The problem is—I don't know who was after Rowena. Who wanted her dead? Who would send a pack of grut to do the deed?"

He patted his thigh, as though keeping beat to some unheard music, then stopped abruptly. "But having already lost two charges of my own . . . Well, I worry I may bring her more harm than good."

"No, you'll not do more harm than good. You believe in the Good One and in the great admonition. If you gave Mara your promise, the Good One will help you to fulfill it. She'll need help—a great deal of it, I'm sure."

"You don't know the half of it. The things she doesn't know." Dixon stared out.

"Go on."

"Well as I said, we had a rough start."

"Yes?"

Dixon told his friend about how Mara had told him to go his own way. "Said she wouldn't put up with me."

Ted grinned. "Seems maybe she knows you pretty well."

On seeing the man's smile, Dixon knew Ted was teasing. He laughed easily. "Yes, well, I told her I would do anything—anything to help her to keep the twins safe. I felt I owed at least that much to Rowena. So I swore an oath to protect them. And that's when the most amazing thing happened!"

"What's that?"

"The earth shook."

"You received a confirmation? But you said Mara was—"

"Well—yes, of sorts. And that's just it, you see," Dixon interrupted. "The earth shook as though Ehyeh had acknowledged my words even though the twins already had their Oathtaker, but it was Mara who felt the emotions that accompany a confirmation." Once again he beat a rhythm with his hand on his thigh. "What do you suppose that means?"

"I can't say, but I can look into it for you. Maybe sevenths are different. Seventh sevenths anyway. It's been so long since there were any."

"Thank you, my friend."

"I'm here to help." Ted's countenance turned serious. "Listen, Dixon, I'm dreadfully sorry for your loss. I know you loved Rowena dearly. I'll do whatever I can to help, but we need to get Mara in on this conversation. We need to consider where the girls might be safe. They are prime targets after all. Perhaps that's why your sworn allegiance had such an effect." He drew in a deep breath, then exhaled slowly. "Twins, you say." He shook his head. "It's never happened before."

"Yes, I've been thinking about that. With the number of Select so low, and with more marriages between them and those not born Select, maybe that had something to do with it."

"Maybe." Ted paused. "It would help to know what Mara's attendant magic is, and who she knows and where. Also, we need to sleuth out the facts about who ordered the hit on Rowena."

The two old friends sat quietly watching the park visitors.

"I should tell you that we weren't entirely honest when we arrived," Dixon finally said. "We didn't know exactly what we'd find, so we told the others that the girls are Mara's nieces."

"I don't see any harm in that. I'll set the record straight with them all. I'm sure they'll understand."

"Well, we were also in desperate need of someone to nurse the twins. I hope this is all right with you . . . A young woman living at the house who lost her child—"

"Nina?"

"Right, Nina. We asked her if she'd be willing to go with us to help with the girls. I'm sorry to say we hadn't had the opportunity to share all of the facts with her in advance."

"Sometimes an Oathtaker has to do—"

"What he has to do," Dixon completed Ted's sentence. The two smiled sadly, knowingly, at one another.

"I don't think anything would have stopped Nina from helping with those girls. Ehyeh directed you here. He directed her here as well. It was a good thing to do—to ask her to help you."

"Yes, but was it the *right* thing?" Ted had often reminded Dixon that doing a good thing, was not the same as doing the right thing.

Ted smiled. "I believe so." He brushed his hand against a rosemary shrub at the side of the bench. Its piney scent filled the air. "Listen, I say we head back to the house and then the three of us will have a good long talk."

Dixon stood. He was relieved to have been able to share some of the burden he'd been carrying. Combing his fingers through his hair, he responded. "Let's do it."

Chapter Seven

The young women at the Oathtakers' mission home retired for the night with their little ones. The children cried softly and whimpered as their mothers nursed and tucked them in. A gentle voice sang the melody of a traditional lullaby, while others whispered softly. Eventually, the household stilled.

Mara, Dixon, and Ted, gathered in the parlor. Faith set out tea and sugar, biscuits and cream, then closed the pocket doors to grant privacy to the little gathering.

The smell of blueberry, like a whisper through the air, rose up from the still warm biscuits to join the apple scent of the chamomile tea. Together they created a fruity perfume, both invigorating and calming at the same time.

Dixon poured cream into his tea. He untied his boots and loosened the laces. "Now that things are quiet, we can begin. I guess the question is: *where?*"

Mara caught his eye and smirked. "As you know, I like to start at the beginning." They shared a smile, recollecting how she'd asked him to tell his story.

"Mara," Ted said, "Dixon filled me in on what happened with Rowena and how the two of you made it here with the girls. He told me something of the danger Rowena had been in. I think we should try to come up with a plan for the girls' safety. I'll do whatever I can to assist."

"I'm sure Dixon told you that I'm very new to this. I was in training until recently, but with so few Select remaining, and so few instructors having actually worked with them . . . Well, I'm afraid my training was very sketchy indeed."

She wore a loose house frock and slippers borrowed from Faith that she kicked off her feet. Then she curled her legs to the side and put her hands in her pockets. "I appreciate your help."

"I like your idea. I too like to 'begin at the beginning.' So, could you fill us in on what are your skills? Also, what attendant magic have you identified? I expect it's still coming into play, but some may already made itself known."

She refreshed her tea, then sipped at it. "Well, my skills include instruction in the history of Oosa, the Select, and the Oathtakers. Of course I'm also trained in general defense, and I have some skill at healing."

"Mara," Dixon interrupted, "it might help to know that we're all of the same understanding. What do you mean when you say that you're skilled at healing?"

"I mean things I've been taught, such as how to set a broken bone, or to mend a cut, how to guard against infection, how to assist in childbirth . . . That sort of thing."

The three sat quietly for a minute.

Finally, Mara sighed. "Honestly, I'm feeling a bit over my head. I can't understand why I was called to aid Rowena, but I can tell you that I responded to something beyond my ability to define or to, I don't know—refuse?"

Ted nodded. "That's a good way to describe the call."

"But why me?" She frowned. "I worry I may not be right for this." *And I should be honest. I worry I'll fail to live up to my oath.* She cast the thought aside as quickly as it had arisen.

Dixon patted her arm. "That's my fault. We had a bad start and it was my doing. But rest assured, the Good One knows what's best. I had no right to second-guess Him, or you. And really, you shouldn't either."

"That's right," Ted agreed.

"Well, thank you, but there's just so much to learn in the actual practice of being an Oathtaker with a charge. Where do I go from here?"

"Hold on. You said it yourself. We start at the beginning."

She nodded. Ted's presence reassured her, made her feel supported.

He sat to the front of his chair. When the house cat rubbed up against his legs, he scratched it behind its ears. "All right then, how about your attendant magic?"

She tilted her head and narrowed her eyes. "I can't say I've seen anything yet, but—"

"She hears thoughts," Dixon interrupted.

She frowned. "I don't know about that."

"Take my word for it, Ted, it's true. She's picked up on my thoughts already. It wasn't about anything particularly important. I expect the Good One granted the 'hearing' as a means of informing her of the power."

"I don't know," she repeated.

"Trust me, you did. And about something you could have had no inkling I was thinking at the time."

"Anything else you've noticed?" Ted asked.

"She might have some attendant power related to her voice."

"What do you mean?"

"Let's just say it's a good thing she didn't sing the lullaby we heard earlier tonight, or we'd all be snoring now."

"Dixon," Mara chided, wincing.

"No, really! Ted, the other night she sang to the girls and put the whole room to sleep in mere moments."

She shook her head at him.

"Is that true?" Ted asked.

"We were all so tired. It was late. I think everyone just nodded off and it happened to be when I sang."

"Well, that's one to keep in mind."

"Supposing it's true, what use could that serve?"

"Perhaps you aren't fully appreciating the value of sleep." Ted grinned.

"What do you mean?"

"Well, even if all you can do is to sing someone to sleep quickly and easily, that could prove helpful—particularly to someone in need of it for healing." He paused. "Anything else?"

"Yes. Someone who'd been in the group that pursued Rowena and me, surprised us the other night," Dixon said.

"You didn't mention that earlier." Ted sat up, clearly alarmed. "What happened?"

Dixon told his friend about Heri.

"Did you learn anything from him?"

"That's just it. Mara seemed to know just how to get him to give us the information we needed."

"What did you find out?"

"Only that before joining the group tracking Rowena, he was with the palace guard. He said someone sent them out to kill Rowena. He didn't know who."

"Hmmm. What did you do?"

"Killed him," Dixon responded without hesitation.

"Good. Better him than any of you."

"It wasn't like we could take him along."

"In any case, we'd best keep you all as far from the palace and anyone associated with it as possible," Ted suggested.

"I agree."

Just then, Mara jumped up. "Oh! Oh my! Oh my!" she cried, flapping her hands and stomping her feet as in a frenzied rain dance.

"What is it?" Dixon shot to his feet.

Ted followed suit.

"I don't know!" she cried. "I feel this strange . . . buzzing. It's like a— Oh! Oh!" She slapped at herself and then, tentatively, reached into her pocket where earlier she'd placed the silver compact she'd found at the hut along with Rowena's scattered belongings. She touched it, flinched, then pulled her fingers back. Slowly she reached into her pocket again, grabbed the compact, then pulled it out and dropped it into her chair.

"What? What is it?" Dixon asked again.

"That thing!" she cried, pointing to the compact. "That thing buzzed or—or something! Oh, dear Good One!" she exclaimed, breathing heavily. She put her hands to her face, trembling.

He picked up the compact. It vibrated, visibly. He took Mara's hand and placed it in her palm.

It tickled. She looked at it, then back up at him.

He scrunched up his shoulders. "I don't know what's happening, Mara. I've never seen it do that before."

Ted took the trinket. It went still. "Where's this from?"

"It was Rowena's," Dixon said.

Ted placed the compact back into Mara's hand. Again, it vibrated. "Does it hurt?" he asked.

"Noooo."

The three stood, transfixed.

Ted scratched the back of his head. "You game to opening it?"

Mara placed her fingers on the clasp. Slowly, she opened it. When she looked inside, she shrieked, then sent the compact flying.

The tabby, arching its back, rubbed against Dixon's legs. Standing just to Mara's side, he held her elbow to steady her from falling. Ted, standing to her other side, held her other arm. She panted, chest and shoulders heaving, eyes wide, fingers and hands jittering. She licked her lips and closed her eyes tight.

"Rowena?"

The three exchanged glances, their mouths all open in surprise.

"Rowena?"

Mara took her arm from Ted's grip. She pointed at the compact on the rug under the table.

Ted and Dixon moved the table aside. The cat jumped at the compact and batted at it with its paws.

"Who's there? Rowena? Is that you? Are you all right?"

As the feline played with its new toy, Mara squatted. She caught a glimpse of a face in the mirror. She stopped the mewing tabby's tussling. "It's coming from there," she whispered. "It's like there's someone inside of it." She nudged the trinket and then, still shaking, picked it up and placed it on the table, directing it forward so that she could see inside.

There in the mirror, was the visage of a woman of perhaps thirty or so. Her face was round, cherubic even, complete with light blue eyes, rosy cheeks, and lips the color of a tea rose. As Mara peered into the mirror, the woman's demeanor changed.

"You're not Rowena. Who are you? And what are you doing with her compact?"

Mara's mouth gaped open. "Ahhh . . . ahhh," she stuttered. Taken so by surprise, finding the talking mirror so astounding, she couldn't collect her thoughts.

The woman's brow rose. Her head cocked to the side. "I asked, 'who are you?'" This time it was more than a question—it was a demand for information.

"I, ahhh . . . Well, that is, I . . ."

Dixon squatted down and peered into the mirror. "Lucy? Is that you?"

The woman turned her gaze his way. "Dixon," she said, obviously perturbed, "what is the meaning of this?"

"You know that woman?" Mara stared at him, pointing to the mirror.

"*What* is going on here?" Ted asked.

"I asked, 'do you know that woman?'"

Dixon scrunched his shoulders. "Yes, I—I do."

"You might have told me she'd show up in Rowena's mirror!" Mara scolded. "Scared me half to death."

"But I had no idea! I—"

"Look," interrupted Lucy, "I was expecting Rowena. Where is she?"

"Excuse me . . . ahhh . . . Lucy," Ted said, "but we have a few things to resolve here. Would you just be patient with us for a minute?"

She scowled. "Who are you? What are you doing with Rowena's compact? What's going on there? I want answers!"

"We'll get right back to you," Ted said.

"I don't care what you all do or how many minutes you take, I'm checking in with Rowena as usual and I demand to know where she is." Lucy's gaze moved from Dixon, to Mara, to Ted, the faces of all three now visible to her. "Now!"

"Like I said, ma'am, we need a minute." Ted motioned toward the other side of the room, then grasped Dixon's arm on his one side, and Mara's on his other. Retreating, he directed his question to his old friend. "Who is that woman?"

Dixon shook his head in disbelief. "That's Lucy Haven, a dear friend and confidante of Rowena's. She's probably the only living person other than me who's known all of Rowena's plans. She was instrumental in them. And she knows the whereabouts of Rowena's other six daughters." He rubbed his head. "This explains so much. I just wish Rowena had told me. I don't understand why she wouldn't have."

"What does this explain?" Mara asked.

"I always wondered how she got her information or decided on her next destination. Lucy just said she was 'checking in with Rowena as usual.' I never saw her use her compact to make contact with Lucy, but she must have. I'm just so . . . surprised."

"Can she be trusted?" Ted asked.

"Implicitly. She leads a group of Rowena's friends who helped her these many years. They know important things and people, and they possess incredibly powerful magic, both individually and collectively. Rowena referred to them as her 'inner circle.'"

"Meaning?"

"Meaning she knew there were always dangers ahead of her and that they went beyond the usual for the Select. Her enemies crossed all lines. The inner circle used various means to gather information. The one place they'd not been particularly successful, however, was at the palace itself."

"Why?" Mara asked.

"I can't say for certain. They just couldn't break through to the truth there. It was one reason we left."

Mara tightened the belt of her house frock and then, brushing her hair away from her face, said, "We'd best hear what she has to say."

Ted caught Dixon's arm. "What do we tell her about Rowena?"

"I think we have to tell her the truth. We have to trust her. We can trust her. To be of help to us, she'll need all the facts."

The three looked to one another and nodded agreement, then turned back to where the compact sat.

Mara took a deep breath and picked it up. It no longer vibrated in her hand; the vibrations had ceased when she'd opened it. Gesturing to her friends to attend to her either side, she sat down.

"Well?" Lucy asked, with a huff.

"Well, Lucy, it seems we have much to discuss," Mara said.

"First, tell me why you have Rowena's compact and how it is that you were able to answer my call."

"I don't know what you mean by 'answering your call,' but I can tell you how I came to possess the compact."

"Go on then."

Mara took a deep breath. "I'm very sorry to have to tell you this, Lucy." She hesitated. "Rowena is . . . dead."

"What? Dixon? Dixon! Oh, dear Ehyeh," Lucy moaned.

"It's true. It happened just days ago. I am so dreadfully sorry," he said.

Her eyes closed. She moaned. "Dear Good One, it was all for naught! Oh, how awful. Oh, dear, what do we do now?" she lamented. She looked up, her eyes closed, as though in prayer.

"Not all is lost, Lucy," he said.

Her eyes flashed open. She glared at him. "After all we've been through? To bring about the seventh seventh told about—prophesied about . . . waited for . . . longed for?" She shook her head, then moaned. "And to have lost all when the plan was so near to fruition? Oh, this is so devastating. Oh!" she wailed. Her tears flowed. "Oh, all is lost."

"Not all is lost, Lucy. The child lives."

She sucked in her breath. She blinked hard and wiped away her tears. Her mouth dropped open as she searched for words.

"The child lives," he repeated.

"Oh, dear merciful Good One!" She turned her gaze to Mara. "Dixon," she then said, "who is this woman? And what's she doing with Rowena's things?"

"Slow down," Mara interrupted, "and we'll tell you everything. Dixon told us about you and Rowena's inner circle."

Lucy's eyes narrowed. "You told them about me?" she asked him.

"I told them you were one of Rowena's most trusted advisors. You'll understand why in a minute."

"Very well," she finally said, tersely, "go on then." She wiped her eyes again and turned her attention back to Mara.

"I'm Mara. Mara Richmond. I was with Rowena when she gave birth to not one—but to *two*—girls. Their names are Reigna and Eden. I am their Oathtaker."

"*Two? Two!* Two infants?" Lucy shook her head. "Reigna, you say? And Eden? What lovely names, but . . . *two?* Are you certain?"

"Hardly something I could mistake."

"Yes, of course. Hmmm . . . two babies. Which was firstborn?"

"Reigna," Dixon said. "She is the seventh seventh."

"How appropriate. Yes, 'Reigna' is the right name." Lucy looked at Mara. "So you're her Oathtaker?"

"And Eden's too, yes."

"A single Oathtaker for two Select? Is that even possible?"

"I suppose it's as possible as Rowena having birthed twins. Beyond that, I've no idea. But it is so."

"Well that explains some things," Lucy muttered, as though to herself.

"What do you mean?" Dixon asked.

"Well, no one but Rowena or one with specific attendant magic could have felt my call or could have answered it. To anyone else, Rowena's compact was just that—a compact."

"Any idea why she didn't mention it to me?"

"I suppose I'm to blame for that."

He raised his brow. "What? You encouraged Rowena to keep something this important from her Oathtaker? Don't you think it might have been helpful for me to know this? It was purely accidental that Mara found the compact and took it along with her. What if it had gotten into the wrong hands? Or—"

"It was simply out of an abundance of caution," Lucy interrupted. "I thought the less said about it, the less it would be discussed, the less the chance it would be discovered. It couldn't be used by another, but I did go through great pains to create it, and you're right—it would have been a great loss had you not taken it with you."

"Are there any other 'cautions' you took that I—that Mara—should know about? So we don't accidentally leave something else behind?" he asked, his voice laced with anger.

She lowered her gaze. "Noooo." Then she looked back his way. "If it's any consolation, Rowena didn't like keeping the secret from you. The last time we spoke, she said she was going to tell you."

"Wait a minute," Mara said. "What did you mean? That you 'went through great pains to create it.' The compact, I mean."

"It's part of Lucy's attendant magic," Dixon said. "She can infuse objects with magic so they can be used for other than their ordinary purposes. Like the compact here is used to communicate. Or so it seems," he said, glaring at Lucy.

Mara nodded. "All right, Lucy. Shall I continue?"

The woman took in a deep breath and exhaled slowly, as though trying to rid herself of the knowledge that Dixon was angry with her. "Please, do."

Mara relayed the story of the past few days.

Lucy listened carefully, asking for specifics from time to time. "So Rowena released her power?"

"Yes."

"Thank the Good One for that. Her children's line will go on to lead the Select. And you're sure you weren't followed?"

"No, we're not," Dixon said. "We did our best to hide our trail, and of course Rowena's release of her power gave us a head start. But someone intercepted us once already." He told her all about Heri.

"We came here to Polesk because we needed a wet nurse for the girls," Mara said. "We've found a lovely young woman here at the Oathtakers' mission home for Chiranian refugees who's willing to go along with us to care for the girls."

"And the other gentleman there with you?"

"Ted Baker. Also an Oathtaker," Ted said.

"Baker . . . Baker," Lucy repeated, as though trying to conjure any information or recollection.

"He has my full endorsement," Dixon said.

"Well, no matter," she continued with a wave, as though Dixon hadn't spoken.

"Maybe you could help us," Mara said. "We were just discussing where we should go from here when you—what do you say—'called?'"

For the first time, Lucy laughed. It was a delightful sound. "Yes, that's right. This means of communication does come in handy. We'll be able to get information to you quickly this way, now that the twins are your charge and your attendant magic allows for it."

"Have you any suggestions for us?"

The woman pursed her lips and tilted her head. "It would be best for you to come here. It's where Rowena was headed after all. We just didn't want her to unintentionally lead someone right into the camp. I'll need to contact the others in the field to find out what they know, then get back to you. In the meantime, keep the compact handy, but don't ever answer my call unless you're certain no one can see or hear you."

"All right. We'll do as you say."

"Good. I'll get back to you with an update soon." Lucy hesitated. "Where did you say all this happened?"

"Just south of Parkton," Dixon said. "There was a small wayfarer's hut along the old messenger's route between there and Lentontown."

"I know the place. I'll send some folks out to see what they can learn. In the meantime, be prepared to move at a moment's notice. Keep the infants close, your bags packed, and your horses rested."

"Thank you," Mara said.

"Oh yes, what of the young woman? A Chiranian, you say?"

Briefly, Ted informed Lucy of Nina's predicament.

"She's positively taken with the girls," Mara added. "She wouldn't allow harm to come to so much as a hair on their heads."

"Good. Oh, one more thing. If you need to reach me before I get back to you, use the compact to communicate."

"How?"

"You can leave a message. Just open it and speak. I'll retrieve it when I can. Remember, be discreet."

"Just curious, Lucy," Dixon interrupted, "is Mara the only one with sufficient attendant power to make use of the compact?"

Lucy avoided his gaze. "No, Dixon. In that you were Oathtaker to a seventh, you certainly can and may use it." She paused. "I'm sorry. It was wrong of me."

He said nothing, though his scowl spoke volumes.

Suddenly, her expression turned grim. "You're awfully young for all of this, aren't you?" she asked Mara, her voice laced with accusation.

"None of that," Dixon said, his voice was firm. "Have no fear. The Good One sent the right person for the job. Don't try to second guess Him."

Lucy sighed. "Yes, I suppose you're right." She smiled at Mara. "Welcome then, little sister. Welcome to the inner circle."

Chapter Eight

Mara opened the door to a gentle knocking. "Come on in if you like while I get the last of my things together."

"Nina," Dixon said as he stepped inside, "good morning. You're looking well today."

"The babies make me very happy."

"Good." He paused. "You know, I was thinking, it would help us tremendously if we knew your story. For safety sake, I mean. What with your having escaped from Chiran, it could prove difficult if someone came looking for you."

Nina's smiled dropped away. Her face turned ashen.

"Dixon," Mara chided. "Do you really think this is necessary? And now? The poor girl has been through so much."

"Please, sir," Nina said, "don't make me speak of Chiran." Her eyes welled with tears.

"Nina, of course we won't make you tell us anything you don't want to," Mara assured her.

The young Chiranian brushed away her tears. "I understand the girls are special Select so I'll tell you anything that could help you to keep them safe."

The Oathtakers looked at one another in surprise.

"I've seen the girls' signs," Nina offered by way of explanation.

"But how is it you're familiar with the signs of the Select?" Dixon asked.

"Many years ago, my mother worked for a family of Select. That was before things changed in Chiran—before Zarek." She closed her eyes, as though reliving the memories in her mind's eye. "When I was just a child, she told me how to identify one. 'Look for the sign they each wear,' she said. You know, like the girls have."

"It's imperative you keep silent about this," Dixon said. "If word gets out, the girls could be in grave danger." He shook his head and frowned. "Actually, I suppose it's really only fair we tell you that, even now, danger pursues us. Perhaps we should have told you all of this up front, but—"

She looked at Mara.

"I'm sorry, Nina, we should have told you earlier, but it's true. We're looking for a safe place to take the girls. Our mission is very dangerous."

"It wouldn't have made any difference. I think I've known all along, what with the way you two have behaved. But I don't care. I accept it as the price of being close to the girls. I won't say or do anything that could harm them."

Gently, the young woman stroked Eden's cheek, then reassembled her bodice and removed the blanket she'd used to maintain her modesty while nursing. She turned her attention back to the Oathtakers. "I swear, Mara, I would . . . give my life for these girls."

At that very moment, the earth shook.

Mara's eyes opened wide. She stumbled, then dropped onto the nearby bed, as trinkets on the table and shelves rattled, and dust rained down from the ceiling. "Gracious Good One!" she cried.

Dixon stumbled, then regained his balance with a hand to the wall.

"What is it? What's happening?" Nina cried.

The floor stilled. The rattle of knickknacks and trinkets stopped.

"Nina, you're an Oathtaker!" Mara exclaimed.

"No! What's going on? I meant no harm, I swear!" The young woman's hands jittered. "Here, take her!" she exclaimed, handing Eden off. She returned to the edge of the bed and sat with her arms held tightly around herself, her knees up, in a sort of quasi-fetal position.

Ted called from down the stairs.

"I'll see to Ted and Faith," Dixon said.

"It's all right, Nina, you haven't done anything wrong. We just . . . Well, as you no doubt figured out, Dixon and I are Oathtakers." Mara knelt down and gently pressed Eden back into the young woman's arms. "When you swore to protect the girls, the earth shook much as it does when an Oathtaker accepts his charge." She searched Nina's face. "Did you feel anything else?"

"You mean fear? I thought the house would fall down."

Mara chuckled. "Anything else?"

"No, I don't think so."

"Believe me, you'd know if you'd felt anything like what an Oathtaker feels."

"Are you and Dixon Oathtakers to the twins?"

"I'm Oathtaker to both of them. But Dixon swore the same oath that you just did—and with the same results."

Dixon returned.

"When we get a chance, we'll discuss this further," Mara said.

"Ahhh . . . I had to do a little explaining, there. Ted and Faith both wondered what happened."

"What did they say?"

"Only that they're as confused as we are. I'd told Ted yesterday about what happened when I asked you to let me help with the girls. But now, with Nina getting such a response to her vow . . . Well, it's all very confusing. Anyway, he agrees this deserves a closer look, but for now, he'd like to take us to sanctuary. It would be nice to stop there for a short time. What do you think?"

"Yes, I'd like to take a few minutes to offer my thanksgiving," she said, "but we should get moving quickly, so let's bring our belongings along and be on our way from there. Agreed?"

"Yes," he said.

"Have you any thought about which direction we should head in from here? Without knowing what Lucy thinks, and since we don't know who might be seeking our whereabouts, I feel lost."

He pulled out a chair and sat down. He placed his elbows on his knees and his chin in the palm of his hand. "Rowena and I mostly stayed on the move, but that would be much more difficult now with the girls. It would be nice to stay in one place, at least for a time, but we can't head to Lucy's until she clears us for that. Still, the Good One will guide us if we keep our minds open and listen for His direction . . . I suppose there's always the City of Light. I know a lot of people there—including some Rowena trusted and greatly respected. Besides, getting lost in a crowd could be just the thing."

He glanced at Mara, a question in his eye. "Or we could head to the hinterlands. No," he then said, "never mind that. If anyone is hoping to find Rowena through me, they might have sent spies ahead thinking that my childhood home would be a natural place for me to go."

Mara sat next to him. She tapped on the table. "I trust your instincts."

"We'll talk more about this on the way then." He stood to take his leave. "We should set out within the hour."

"I'm finished here. You coming, Nina?"

"If you'll take Reigna, I'll get my things and be down with Eden in just a minute."

Faith greeted Mara and Dixon when they made their way into the kitchen. With the house so full, she was serving breakfast in shifts. Francis and Patrick sat at one end of the table, Ted at the other.

"'Mornin' again, Dixon. 'Mornin' to you too, Mara. A lot of commotion already today, huh? Well, I hope you two rested well." Ted slapped Dixon lightly on the back, directing him to an open chair, then guided Mara to another. "A couple more hungry mouths here!" he called out. "Let's get some more of that great breakfast over this way."

"Let me help," Dixon offered before taking his seat.

Faith jostled him. "No, I wouldn't hear of it. There's only so much room in here and you'd just be in my way."

"Well, if you're sure—"

"Sit. Sit," she ordered, gently pushing him aside and pointing to his chair.

Dixon sat.

Mara smiled at how malleable he was in Faith's capable hands.

Faith set out dishes for everyone, then refilled plates and bowls of eggs, scrambled and sprinkled with cheese and chives, crispy bacon, slices of sweet melons and pears sprinkled with finely chopped rosemary, and crusty bread.

Nina arrived with Eden. Then they all ate, enjoying breakfast over small talk.

"We're ever so grateful, Ted, Faith, Francis, for everything," Mara said when they were through, "but we should go."

Dixon stood. "We'd like to stop briefly at sanctuary, but we'll not stay long. We need to get underway while the day is still fresh."

"Very well then," Ted said. "What about you, Francis?"

"I have to go to sanctuary, Patrick," Francis told the boy. "You can stay here or go along with me and Grandma Faith—*if* you're not naughty."

"I wanna go with you, Dad! And I amn't naughty, Dad, I amn't!" the boy responded.

The kitchen erupted in laughter.

"He's adorable," Mara said.

"Yes," Faith agreed, "he certainly keeps us on our toes." Then she turned to Patrick. "Bear can't go into sanctuary, so you'll have to leave him here."

"Say, Ted, since we're leaving directly from sanctuary, what do you recommend? That we ride or lead our horses?" Dixon asked.

"I'll follow and take them along with Patrick, while you all visit," Francis offered.

"Excellent, thank you."

They headed to sanctuary. Francis and Patrick led Sherman, Cheryl, and Spot, a horse Ted provided for Nina, so named because of a single white patch on its forehead.

As they walked and visited, the day came alive. People scurried past, children laughed and ran, buggies clattered, roosters crowed, and dogs barked. Several townspeople greeted them. It was clear by their smiles and waves that Ted and Faith were neighborhood favorites.

"Faith here," Ted said, putting an arm around her, "was quite the Oathtaker back in the day, and is a great healer. People come from all around to see her when they need things. I bet she's birthed—what, Faith, about a hundred babies?" He pulled her closer and smiled at her.

"I suppose that's about right. With Polesk having swelled so terrifically in size in the last years, and now with the mission home up and running, my skills are called upon fairly frequently."

"How long since you—" Mara began.

"Were an active Oathtaker?" Faith completed the question. "My charge died of natural causes about forty years ago. Shortly after that I met my husband and had my family and now— Well, just think, now I have grandchildren!"

Before long the group came to sanctuary, situated at the top of a hill. The main building was larger by several times than anything else in the vicinity. Made of white brick, it reached up and up, then sported a tower that surpassed the height of even the tallest trees.

Gardens, benches, alcoves and statues covered sanctuary grounds. Even at this early hour, hundreds of people milled about. Families wandered around, hand in hand. The more business minded stood in groups, in quiet conversation. Gaggles of young people, dressed in the carefree common manner of students, were engaged in animated discussions.

"It's beautiful," Mara said. "I've never seen anything like this."

"It was the first here in Oosa," Ted said. "When the Select came to these lands, this was the first building they and their Oathtakers, built. You might say it was the center of their new venture. As you probably know from your childhood history lessons, others exploited and used the Select in their old country. Their service to Ehyeh made them prosper. Those envious of the blessings the Good One bestowed upon them, enslaved them.

"Eventually the Select fought for and won their freedom. They wanted a new life for themselves and their children. This land became their sanctuary, and they built the main building here as thanks to the Good One. They intended for it to represent the covenant between Ehyeh and the Select, and to serve as a continual reminder that the people should serve Him and follow in His ways."

"It looks like sanctuary in the City of Light," said Dixon.

"Yes, sanctuary in the City of Light was modeled after this one. It's larger to be sure, but its designers based it on this campus right here. And of course, contrary to popular thought, this is the only one that was built with magic."

"Magic!" Mara exclaimed.

"Yes, I'm afraid much of the history has been lost, but many old writings indicate that this sanctuary was built with magic."

The group followed a footpath to the front of the main building. Gravel crunched under their feet. Overhead the leaves of massive trees fluttered in the soft morning breeze. For the most part, the dew had burnt off, yet small glistening droplets still clung to the grass in the dappled shade beneath the trees. Pillars of night blooming jasmine, their blossoms just closing, their light, fruity aroma filling the air, grew near the entrance to the main building.

"What lovely gardens," Mara said. "Who sees to them? That can't be a small job."

"That's one of my many duties," Ted said. "Francis assists me. It's such a joy to work at sanctuary. Until I get a new charge, this is the closest I can imagine to being and doing as the Good One would have."

"What do you mean?"

"Well, I figure the Good One is responsible for all life and all good things. He made the world and all that's in it. That's where the name Creovita comes from—'give life.' Being creative is the best way I know to be like Him. Really, I think people have an innate longing to create, and that they are happiest when doing so. Fortunately, I get to satisfy my own such desires." He hesitated. "Does that make sense?"

"It certainly does."

Enjoying the heady scent of the jasmine, Mara approached sanctuary's front entrance, Nina at her side. The infants both rested contentedly. Reigna wriggled, then stretched her little hands and made them into fists. Mara grasped one and kissed it.

Just then, Francis and Patrick arrived with the horses. Francis motioned that he'd bring them to the back of the building.

"Right this way," Ted then said as he led the group inside.

Seven windows wrapped around the entryway, three to the right, three to the left, and one front and center. Each ran from floor to ceiling, upwards of twenty feet high, and each depicted a different scene. From the top of the windows rose a round domed ceiling made up of seven more windows that collectively, replicated a night sky of a deep azure blue with assorted stars, constellations, and other heavenly bodies.

Sunlight passed through the windows, all made of small crystals pieced together into mosaics. Each multi-faceted crystal caused the incoming light to refract many times over. As the breeze moved the leaves on the trees outside, colored reflections moved about, inside. The dancing, spinning speckles touched on and flitted across the walls, floors, and objects on display.

"Over there," Ted pointed, "hallways lead to the inner sanctuary—what you might call the prayer room, and classrooms and libraries. This sanctuary boasts the largest collection of original works of our forebears. Although Polesk itself is not the largest of Oosa's cities today, many people come here to study and to visit this sanctuary. That accounts for many of the people you see here today."

"What do they study?" Mara asked.

"Mostly history, economics, and social issues." Ted paused. "The Select who settled here sought above all, the freedom to serve Ehyeh. They also wanted to be free to work for themselves and to choose the type of work they would do. They wanted to be free to give help to others, or to refuse it when others did not contribute to their own welfare. They wanted to be free to come and go as they chose, and to speak their minds unfettered.

"The first settlers determined that the best way to ensure the freedoms they valued for themselves, was to support those freedoms for newcomers to the land.

They felt that so long as the community lived according to the great admonition, they could afford to acknowledge the same rights for everyone in Oosa. So, when people from other places settled here, they too practiced their own ways."

"We studied some of the history in our hood back home," Mara said. "We were taught that our forebears started what had never been done before. One professor told us that the story of world history was one of murder, oppression, and slavery. He said Oosa, which stood in opposition to that history, was the first and is still the only place of its kind."

"Freedom," Nina whispered, as though transfixed by the concept.

"That's right. Let me show you the story this sanctuary tells. We'll start there." Ted pointed toward the front of the room and to his right.

Taking Mara's elbow, he directed her to the window he'd indicated, the first of the three on that side. "This, as you can probably make out, depicts the first of the Select. The first signify new beginnings and birth."

"A seed just coming to life," she said. "It's lovely."

"Yes. Firsts are responsible for protecting life in all its forms. Of course, there are always more firstborns than any other, and as you probably know, if a family is blessed with more than seven children, the count begins anew. So the next born child—the eighth—is also considered a first."

The window depicted a yellow-green seedling with healthy roots branching downwards, water droplets surrounding it. Mara reached toward it. The refracted lights danced off her hands and arms.

After surveying it for some time, they all moved right, to the next window.

"Unity," Mara said. "The sign of the second of the Select."

"Exactly," Ted said. "Seconds govern the unity of person to person, most notably that of husband and wife to one another, second only to that of parent to child. Seconds encourage, support, and protect families and family relationships, without which life, a stable community, healthy children, and a safe future, eventually would cease. With fewer Select, these relationships have suffered."

The window portrayed the simple rendition of a man and woman. They stood, face to face, their hands clasped together at their sides.

"What treasures!" Mara exclaimed.

They moved to the third window. It displayed a simple geometric rendition of three interwoven golden rings.

"The sign of the third," Mara commented. "The whole."

"The third of the Select signify the fragile but strong relationship between serving the Good One in body, mind, and spirit," Dixon offered. "The three rings signify the Select's commitment to follow in Ehyeh's ways."

"Yes," Ted said, "and as I'm sure you can appreciate, today we see signs of a kind of malady among the people. When any of the three components of a balanced life gets out of order, the entire being suffers. So, as the Select have been reduced, people have found it more difficult to keep these three areas of their lives in order."

Faith, after having made her way around a group of visitors, joined the conversation. "Many think the balance of these parts to life isn't important. They argue that the Good One selfishly demands mankind's service. But I was taught that He wants people to be balanced for their own benefit."

"Well put," said Ted.

The simplicity of the picture that portrayed such a sound but fundamental principle, struck Mara.

Moving back around the main entrance, they made their way to the other side of the room. They waited until after a group of students with their instructor moved away before stepping toward the fourth window. It depicted a building in outline, with an emphasis upon its cornerstone.

"Here is the sign of the fourth of the Select," said Faith as she approached Mara's side. "The fourth signify the foundational institutions upon which society depends."

"Sanctuary, family, community, government," Dixon commented. "Fourths are sovereign over organizations and institutions necessary for a civil society."

"That's right, Judith was a fourth, wasn't she?" Mara commented as she glanced his way.

He nodded.

"Dixon is right," said Faith. "As the numbers of the Select get higher, so too do the responsibilities associated with them. When the Select are out of proportion, the people are hurt because societal institutions are no longer in accord with one another, or with the people.

"Over the last years, that balance has suffered. Sanctuary has lost significance. Few people find value in holding to traditions that support and hold individuals accountable for their own actions. Likewise, families suffer because people put their personal interests above the interests of those for whom they are responsible. Because families suffer, so too do the communities they make.

"Only one earthly entity can make up the difference, and that is government. But as our forebears knew, and as we see more all the time, when government takes on too much, it becomes too powerful. When the people rely upon it to do and to provide what they should do and provide for themselves, the sanctity of sanctuary and family suffer even more. It is like a spiral that continues to move downward, ever more quickly."

The group moved to the fifth window. It depicted a majestic wilderness. From the simplest earthworm to the lions of the savannah, to the birds of the air, to the fish of the sea, a noisy scene played out.

Mara imagined the patter of paws, the rush of wings in flight, the ripple of water. "And this," she said, "is the sign of the fifth—nature."

"That's right," Ted said. "The domain of the fifth is of nature in its many forms. This includes animal life, the forests, and waterways. It includes the living, whether underground, above ground, or in the sky, as well as the land itself, and the air we breathe. Fifths are endowed with keeping these areas healthy, because without a healthy environment, mankind cannot go on."

"I hear a 'but,'" Mara said.

Faith laughed. An easy, mirthful sound, it quickly died away to a sort of a sigh. "Yes, there is a 'but' as you say. You see, life depends upon these things and so we are all responsible for them. But we're not to worship the earth or the things of it. Our first concern should be to the highest life form—human life—though we should deal with no other form idly.

"When we care for our world responsibly, we protect all living things. While we care for the lesser creatures, the life of a dog, or a bird, or a lizard, will never equal that of a person." She paused, frowning. "It's sad, but today many place a greater weight on those things than they do on human beings. We believe that this is why people are behaving strangely in these areas."

"In what way?"

"Well, we're finding many willing to sacrifice their own children in exchange for leading lives of ease. Often women don't want the inconvenience and responsibility. Sometimes they abandon their young ones when they're difficult to care for or to support. Do you know, some cities report that dozens of people have left their children to live in the streets?" Faith shook her head. "It's tragic. And then there are the men who leave the wives of their youth and the children they begat to lives of poverty, in order to follow their own selfish desires.

"No one seems to bat an eye at these absurdities. They say people should be free to do as they please. And so they are—and so they should be. But society also should hold them responsible for their actions. You know, we've seen circumstances where mobs have attacked someone for stealing a beast's eggs, while they've left another unmolested for harming a child. We don't suggest the actions of the first are acceptable. We simply believe that the balance regarding the importance of life is, shall we say, off kilter."

"Hmmm, I see what you mean."

Moving on, the group came to the sixth window. It showed a multitude of faces of every skin color, hair color, eye color, shape, size and age.

"The sixth," Dixon said.

"That's right," Ted said. "The sixth oversee humankind at all stages and in all its varieties."

Mara marveled at how the complexity of the forms compared to the countless different people in the world. "So what happens when the sixth are out of balance?" she asked, directing her inquiry to Ted.

His eyes remained on the window. His shoulders sagged. "When the sixth are out of balance, people behave as though they can and should do whatever they wish, whenever they want, to whomever they choose. Each person acts as though he is a law unto himself."

"And then," Dixon said, "chaos reigns."

They all stood quietly, each processing the horrors that could exist in such a world. Then after some minutes, they moved on.

"And here," Ted said as they approached the seventh and final window, "is the sign of the seventh. The seventh signify completion and order. They are teachers and prophets. Their gifts enable them to educate others about the value of a life in balance. That balance is simple, but profound. Care first for yourself and those for whom you're responsible. Do not be a burden to others."

"And," added Dixon, "cause no harm, except or unless it is necessary to protect yourself or others. You are never obligated to allow another to steal your freedom, your time, or your labor. You are never asked to be a slave to the whims of others."

"The great admonition," Mara whispered.

The seventh window depicted a woman in simple attire. Signs of the other symbols of the Select—a seed, a couple in outline, three adjoining rings, a cornerstone, an animal, and a human face—surrounded her.

"Completion," Mara said. "Let me summarize this one. The seventh signify a reign over life in general, life in order, life lived fully, justly, and well. The seventh bring wisdom—that being the knowledge of all of the six underlying principles, how they interact, and how to apply those principles to daily circumstances. With the seventh properly in place, life goes forward in peace and prosperity, with the fullest of blessings."

"Well put," Dixon said.

When she looked at him, he winked. She smiled and blushed at his compliment.

The group made its way toward the center of the room. There sat a statue they could not have missed upon first entering the building. Now they examined it more closely. The lights from the surrounding windows and ceiling all converged at this place. Their continued waltzing played upon the outlines of the majestic rendition of a very old woman holding a perfect, an exquisite, newborn.

"How incredibly beautiful!" Nina exclaimed.

"This statue signifies the life we have through the Good One," Faith explained. "We are to value all life, from the earliest moment to the last. Ehyeh commissioned the Oathtakers to protect the Select because it is they who have carried this message through the ages and from place to place. There is nothing more important or precious than life and freedom. We guard it because it is the Good One's gift to us."

"Which again explains the great admonition, our creed," Dixon added.

"Exactly," Faith said. "The Good One has but two requirements for us: take care and responsibility for yourself, those to whom you are responsible and those unable to care for themselves, and cause no harm to others unless they threaten your life or liberty, or the life or liberty of others."

Mara stepped closer to the statue. The old woman was the visual representation of a life fully lived. Her skin was weathered and wrinkled, her hair thinning, her eyes wilted. A woman of strength, though well past her prime, she appeared content.

The statue was so lifelike, Mara half expected its subject to inhale. The artist had captured each wrinkle on her knuckles, the finest details of her ears, her toes, her lips, and even her tired arteries. By contrast, the infant was the depiction of perfect, robust, newborn health.

The old woman held the child with one hand placed high in the middle of its back and with one finger extended to steady its head. Her other, slightly curved hand, held the child's bottom. Arms and legs bent, fingers held in little fists, and chubby toes curled, the child slept the peaceful slumber of one nourished and protected.

Dixon stepped to Mara's side, arms folded.

They watched the fluttering colored lights dance on the statue.

"This is amazing," she said. "It's so like my dream," she then muttered, as though to herself. "Or nightmare, more like . . ."

He turned a hawk-like glare at her. "What did you say?"

"I said it reminds me of my dream—or my nightmare. But not this part. This is so like— Yes, I'd say it is exactly as I—"

He grabbed her elbow and pulled her away from their friends and some lingering visitors. He glared. "What dream?"

She pulled her arm from his grip. "What's the problem, Dixon? So I had a dream. The statue just brought it back to my recollection, that's all."

"Mara, tell me—right now. What did you dream?"

He spoke so quickly, he flustered her. Still, she couldn't help but notice the look in his eyes. Was it worry? Or perhaps, fear?

"I had a dream last night. Someone was chasing us. Actually, there were so many things from the past couple of days in it that . . . Well, I guess this statue was new, but . . . Well you were in it, and me, and Ted, and Faith, and Nina and the girls. And . . . someone else. Someone I didn't recognize. She was beautiful. That is she *looked* beautiful. But she seemed . . . confused . . . and I think she was a danger to the girls."

Dixon became more agitated. His eyes darted around the room. He pulled at her arm again. "Mara, tell me what happened. Who was the woman? This is important."

"All right. All right." Again she pulled free of his grasp. "It was a nightmare, that's all. This woman approached us by a statue just like this one. She led us out of the building and then she took Reigna and Eden."

His face went ashen. "Mara, we've got to get out of here right now!"

"What? It was just a dream."

"No, it wasn't just a dream! Seeing something like this in real life after having first seen it in your dream is almost certainly a sign. It's some kind of attendant power at work. A message from Ehyeh. He was trying to warn you! And now that it took so long before you mentioned this—"

"I didn't know!"

"Oh, I'm sorry. I just— Look, we've got to get out of here. Quickly! Head for that door! It leads to the back of the building where Francis left our horses. Take Nina. Now—go!" he urged, pointing to the exit. "I'll be right behind you. Just ride northeast as hard and fast as you can. Go! Go! Go!" He touched her low on her back and gently pushed her toward the door.

She grasped Nina's hand and then dashed away.

Dixon approached his friend who'd watched the exchange. "Ted," he said, his voice low, "we have to go—now. I'll explain everything as soon as I can. For now, I thank you and—"

"What is it?"

"There's trouble coming. I'll get back to you as quickly as possible, I promise. I—"

"Well, well, well," came a voice from the main entrance, "if it isn't Dixon Townsend."

<hr>

Dixon took in a deep breath, cautioning himself to relax his expression before turning around. As he did, a band of men barged into the front door. Noise and confusion accompanied them. Sanctuary guests spread out and backed toward the walls. Dixon looked to the woman who'd spoken as her eyes moved to the men. She exchanged a long glance with their leader.

In that moment, Dixon knew. He knew the source of danger. He knew it was *these* men who had pursued Rowena. He knew it was *this* woman who'd sent them. He *knew*.

He willed himself to remain calm. He couldn't let on about what he'd concluded. "Lilith," he finally said, "how good to see you." He stepped toward the woman. Then turning to the men who'd rushed into sanctuary behind her, he addressed them. "Excuse me, gentlemen, but this is sanctuary."

"Here, here, gentlemen," Ted said, "you are most welcome. Of course we must ask you to leave your weapons there, at the door. They'll be safe, I assure you." He turned and caught the attention of another Oathtaker. "Robert," he called, "please stand guard for these men over their . . . things."

"Yes, you should know better," Lilith scolded. Her eyes bore into the men. Then she turned her attention back to Dixon, a smile fixed upon her lips, her head tilted. "Dixon, so good to see you, too."

She glided toward him, her red silken skirts flirting about her. She was stunning, with hair like gilded gold, eyes of a deep green, and lips red and glossy. An almost sickeningly sweet scent, reminiscent of roses and lilies, surrounded her.

Dixon desperately wanted to see the reactions of the men to whom she'd spoken, but he dared not give her any inkling of his suspicions. Keeping his eyes fixed on her, he grasped just above her wrists to best keep her at a distance.

He turned to Ted and Faith. With Lilith unable to see his expression, he caught the eye of each of his friends for a moment, his brow raised by way of warning.

"Lilith," he said as he turned back to her, "let me introduce you to some friends of mine. Ted," he began, as he stepped aside.

Lilith approached Ted. Accustomed to having great power over men, her every movement was choreographed for maximum effect, for conquest: eyes narrowed, but not too much; lips pursed, but not too much; chest breathing hard—but not too much.

Ted shook her hand. Covering his with her own, she ever so slightly caressed it . . . but not too much.

Ted glanced at Dixon, who surmised his friend had read Lilith expertly, then looked back at her. "Pleased to meet you." He bowed slightly.

"No. No, it's my pleasure," she responded, holding out on the word "pleasure."

"Faith," Dixon said, "let me introduce you to Rowena's sister, Lilith, a sixth."

As Lilith greeted Faith, he looked at Ted, and with quiet gestures, filled him in on what he'd just discovered. His eyes moved quickly to Lilith, then to the men who'd barged into sanctuary behind her, then back again.

With a nod, Ted communicated his understanding. "Please excuse me," he said, "I must see to my duties." He exited sanctuary from the back door.

"Dixon," Lilith purred, "this is all very nice. I'm always happy to meet your friends. But where is Rowena?" She held his arm, pressing against him.

He wanted to take his time, to drag things out. He wanted to give Mara as much time as possible to get as far away as possible.

"Well," he finally drawled, "that's a long story and . . . not a happy one, I'm sorry to say."

"Oh, Dixon!" she said, leaning even more closely, brushing her breast against him. It was a mannerism she'd practiced to perfection. "You always talk in riddles!" Her laughter bubbled, but there was no sincerity to it.

"Truly," he continued as he gently, but not too obviously, tried to extricate himself from her grasp, "I'm afraid my news is not . . . good news."

"And what news would that be?"

He breathed slowly. He paused and looked to the ground. He had to buy time, to drag things out. "I'm so very sorry to tell you that Rowena . . . is . . . dead," he finally said, looking up.

Lilith's eyes flashed toward the men still loosely assembled near the door. He followed the look. The leader opened his mouth as though to speak, then closed it. Quickly, Dixon averted his gaze so she wouldn't know that he'd witnessed the exchange.

Turning back to him, she continued, her voice hard, "Really, Dixon, it's not nice to tell falsehoods—and such cruel ones. I would not have thought you capable of that. Now, where is Rowena, really? I haven't seen her in some time."

"I told you, Lilith, she is dead."

Her eyes narrowed. The smile on her face froze. It failed to meet her eyes. "Dixon, I want the truth."

"That is the truth. Why would I be false with you? Rowena died in childbirth."

Lilith glanced around the room, her eyes stopping for a moment on the men near the door. She seemed confused by what they tried to communicate to her.

"Well, how very . . . unfortunate. The family will be . . . devastated, of course. You must come with me back to Shimeron and tell your story first hand. I expect the Council will want a full accounting as well."

"Really, Lilith, that isn't necessary. I could hardly save Rowena from childbirth now, could I? What's to investigate? I'll just submit my report and then— Well actually, I'm thinking about taking some time to visit my family."

She studied him intently. "Really, I insist you come with me."

"Lilith—"

"No, Dixon, I simply won't take 'no' for an answer."

Her public insistence left him in a difficult spot. His refusal would only serve to offend her, and potentially to embarrass her.

"Lilith," he tried again.

"Come, Dixon, I want to return home immediately." She held his arm tightly.

He couldn't escape her clutches without making a scene. Moreover, he feared if he were to do so, that she might suspect there was more to his story. For now it was best to keep her close to himself, and as far as possible from Mara.

Ted approached. "Pardon me, Dixon, I don't mean to interrupt, but I wanted you to know that I sent Robert out to prepare your horse for you." He tipped his head toward the front of the building.

Dixon understood. Mara had left from the back, so Ted had asked Robert to bring his belongings to the front of the building.

"I expected Lilith would want to get the news of Rowena home as quickly as possible, and I didn't want anything to inconvenience or to delay you."

"Thank you so much, for everything."

"Certainly. You're welcome any time." Ted turned to Lilith. "It was a pleasure to meet you, ma'am."

"All mine, I'm sure."

"I'm sorry to see you leave so quickly," Faith said. "Are you sure we can't convince you to stay? After all, something must have brought you here to Polesk, to sanctuary?"

"I . . . Well," Lilith stammered. "I just planned a trip to visit a number of the sanctuaries in Oosa. I haven't been to Polesk now for several years. I thought the people should see that we still work in their interests. Since this is one of the closest sanctuaries to Shimeron, naturally, it was my first stop."

"Yes, of course."

"Even so, with news like this, I couldn't possibly continue on. It's imperative I return home immediately. This is all so . . . shocking."

"But you will come back, won't you?" Ted asked.

Lilith smiled at him. As usual, the expression didn't quite reach her eyes.

"We'll look forward to your next visit."

She took Dixon's arm and made her way to the door. As they retreated, she placed a bracelet around his wrist.

"Oh, no," Ted whispered to Faith, "she's taken him captive!"

Within moments after they exited, the men who'd burst in behind Lilith, took up their weapons and made their way out.

Chapter Nine

Lilith rode at Dixon's side. Her presence unnerved him. She'd always been insincere, but now he knew that she was also a traitor to her own kind. He pondered why she'd do such a thing.

He knew the leader of the first family, upon reaching her full power, needed to solidify her standing with her siblings if things were to run smoothly. Unfortunately, once Rowena had accomplished that—or at least thought she had—she'd largely ignored the others. She'd been so involved with her plan for her daughters that she left the affairs of her larger family unattended. But when a leader did not function successfully as the head of the family, the other members could get out of line. Apparently Lilith had done just that.

Dixon was surprised that he and Rowena had missed the signs, but then she never wanted to think badly of anyone. Still, Lilith was a typical sixth. Bent on having her way, she was driven by things of the flesh. She took the idea of freedom to its ultimate. To her, true freedom meant the liberty to do as she pleased. She epitomized selfishness. If one were to speak to her about the needs of others, her response would not be: "What others?" Rather, it would be: "There are others?" To Lilith, the only thing of importance—was Lilith.

She rambled on about something. Dixon, lost in thought, didn't want to listen to her, but neither could he be rude. He needed to get along with her for the time being, though he really wanted to squeeze the life out of the woman. The only good thing for now was the only thing that mattered: Mara had escaped.

"I'm sorry, what did you say? I can't seem to concentrate with this ridiculous band you put on me." He held his arm up, showing the bracelet of magic she'd placed there—a bracelet that could only be removed by Lilith herself, since she'd placed it there, or by her Oathtaker, or by an Oathtaker who ranked higher than Dixon—which left only Mara since her charge included a seventh seventh, or by the Council if its members unanimously agreed to its removal.

He fussed with the band, but of course, it was as one with his skin. A stranger would take it for a permanent body painting. "You know this is not necessary."

"Dixon, you really need to pay better attention," she pouted. "I said Pompom is going to have puppies! Won't that be so much fun? Can't you just see all the little

Pompoms running and playing?" She tittered and giggled.

She looked ridiculous behaving as she did. He recognized it as her way of keeping people off balance. She might be despicable, but Ehyeh knew she was no fool.

He'd have to be careful with her. But how long did she intend for him to stay at Shimeron? How long would she keep him banded? He wanted to get back to Mara and the twins as quickly as possible, but in the meantime, he'd glean what information he could from the palace staff. *Blast! How could Rowena and I have missed this?*

". . . and so I told her that— Dixon. Dixon! Are you listening to me?"

"I'm sorry, I seem to be lost in thought today."

"Well I must say, you generally pay better attention to me. Something on your mind?"

"This band, for one."

"Oh, never mind. It's nothing." She waved her hand in dismissal.

"It is not nothing, Lilith. It means you don't trust me. How could you do this?"

"You know you must answer to the Council. I'm just making sure I can deliver you to them, as is necessary. When you're cleared of any wrongdoing, the band will come off, of course."

"I've done nothing wrong."

She looked at him, still sulking. "Nothing wrong! But you're not even paying attention to me!"

He sighed. He couldn't stand this for long. "Just missing Rowena, I suppose."

"Terribly sad, yes." Lilith didn't sound in the least like someone who'd suffered a loss. Portraying grief went beyond her acting skills.

"Really, it's not important that I go to Shimeron. I want to see my family. I haven't been home for a long time. I could check in with the Council on my way."

"I insist you accompany me. I want to be there when the Council meets to hear the whole story, and to congratulate you when they find you without fault. Besides, I want you to help to keep me safe now that you don't have to watch out for Rowena."

"That's not my job. Marshall is your Oathtaker. He takes good care of you. What's more, as you well know, I can't use any of my attendant magic so long as I'm banded."

"Well Marshall is just . . . boring, that's what! He's not at all like you. I want you to be my Oathtaker, Dixon."

"I can't, Lilith. You know that."

"Well that's what I want."

He turned to face her. He took hold of her reins and brought her mount to a halt.

"That is horrible of you to say. Marshall puts his life on the line for you every day, and you don't make things easy for him. He answered the Good One's call and accepted you as his charge. You should have more respect for him."

Dropping her reins with a flick of his wrist, he urged Sherman forward. He might have to accompany her until he could get the accursed band off, but he didn't have to be near her or to listen to her every word.

She rode back up to his side. "Of course you're right, Dixon. It's just that," she fluttered her eyelashes, "I so enjoy your company. I—"

"Stop it." He set his jaw tight. Refusing to listen to any more, he rode ahead to accompany the most forward members of her escort.

Fields of long grasses spread out as far as the eye could see. A hawk flew overhead, its wings caught in a warm air current. Meadowlarks sang from unseen perches, accelerating their melodies, dropping into jumbling whistles, then moving back again into new songs. A marsh to the side of the roadway boasted cattails reaching up, their seeds just beginning to break free, looking as though they were begging for someone to pet them.

"Hello, I'm Dixon," he said to the head guard as he reached the man's side.

"Dixon," the man repeated with a nod, "Miles." He was dressed, as were all of the members of the palace guard, in dark gray pants and jacket, with black polished boots.

"I don't remember meeting you at the palace before."

"No. Just moved up in rank recently."

"How long have you been on the road, Miles?"

"We left long before dawn."

"What prompted the trip?"

"A rider arrived at the palace in the wee hours, demanding to see Lilith. He carried a message for her eyes only. She was awakened and met with him. Minutes later, she ordered us to get her things ready to leave immediately."

Dixon mulled this over. Likely, the men at sanctuary were the same ones who'd questioned Drake and Maggie. Had those men sent word ahead? Had his old friends told the men about Polesk? If so, he couldn't fault them. He just felt terrible for having put them in danger in the first place. So, what might they have found out? If they were decent trackers, or depending upon what Drake and Maggie had told them, Lilith might know, or might soon discover, that he'd not been traveling alone.

"And you rode straight to Polesk?"

"That's right. Lilith insisted we move quickly. We didn't stop at all on the way."

The horses' gait kept a steady rhythm. Their earthy, sweaty smell filled the air. Ears alert, tails swishing, they raised dust that now covered the entire retinue.

Dixon rode side by side with Miles in silence, pondering what Lilith might be planning. He might not be safe with her. Then again, if she thought he had any information, she wouldn't want him harmed. Still, he'd best be on guard. The woman wasn't to be trusted.

Well into the evening hours, the travelers neared Shimeron. Miles halted the group, then turned to Dixon. "It's time to take your place in the carriage."

"What? Why?"

"You'll see."

Dixon dismounted, handed over Sherman's reins, then made his way to the carriage and stepped inside. As he settled in, the entourage proceeded.

Soon, from outside, came shouting. He couldn't make out the words. He turned to Lilith and broke his silence. "What's going on?"

"Oh, you'll see soon enough," she replied, her lips pursed.

From out of the darkness, the shouting became clearer. He looked out the window. A few dozen people stood near the gates to the palace grounds. Some marched. Their voices grew louder as the carriage approached. "Death to the Select!" they called out. Then, "Kill the Select!"

His mouth dropped open. He turned back to Lilith, who sat stone-faced. "What is going on here?"

"Well, Dixon," she responded, condescension dripping, "if you and Rowena had stayed here where you were needed, perhaps this wouldn't be happening."

"I don't understand. What *is* happening?"

Some of the protesters carried torches. Others carried signs hastily scrawled upon in letters of red, as though in blood, bearing slogans: "Down with the Select!" "The Select are Trouble!" "We didn't Select them!" They pressed in toward the travelers. "Death to the Select!" they shouted.

Something hit the carriage door, then came a thud overhead. Dixon flinched, even as the guardsmen closed in tightly around the carriage. Steel rang in the night air as they drew their swords. They pushed the crowd back with their threats of steel.

A scream rent the air.

"Back! Back, or you'll be next!" a guard ordered.

Dixon feared the carriage wouldn't make it to the gates before the guards harmed more members of the crowd.

After more scuffling and shouting, the carriage halted. Lilith sat, braced in her seat, Marshall at her side, his face expressionless. He held a sword in one hand, his Oathtaker's blade in the other.

"What has been going on here since we've been away?" Dixon asked of no one in particular.

Lilith held Pompom close to her heaving breast. "It's just the local rebels. Nothing to concern yourself about," she spat. "The Good One knows you haven't concerned yourself until now."

"That's ridiculous. Rowena was not responsible for this, nor am I. I don't know what's going on here, Lilith, but I won't allow you to press the blame that belongs to others, on me."

Men approached from the direction of the palace to open the gates. Shortly afterward, the procession advanced. Once inside, the guards escorted the carriage to the front of the white marble palace. It glistened in the moonlight. Wide steps rose up to the front doors. The flags topping the turrets flapped in the evening breeze.

Marshall rose as the carriage door opened. He stepped out, then turned to assist Lilith. She made her way to the ground and then with a nod, dismissed her escort.

Stable boys helped the guards with their mounts.

The carriage, of light pearl gray, with a variety of intricate painted designs depicting leaves and vines set forth in greens and yellows, was festooned with the remains of what the crowd had thrown: eggs, tomatoes, and other rotting goods unidentifiable by sight or by their nausea inducing intermingled odors. Assistants arrived to clean and inspect it.

Dixon hadn't missed anything about the palace. He dreaded its endless protocol. Walking just behind Lilith and Marshall, he felt like a prisoner. *I am a prisoner, banded like this.*

Up the long staircase they climbed as a staff member lit torches along the way. Flowerpots cast in designs of birds and animals flanked the edges of the steps. In the middle of the landing at the top, sat a fountain. Around it was room to lounge, provided one did not mind getting damp from the mist in the air. When they reached it, Dixon called out, "I'll see you tomorrow."

"Dixon, do come in. It's late, and that crowd can't be trusted," Lilith said. "You're a guest here and you'll soon discover that those discontents out there don't hold to finding any differences between the Select and other palace visitors—including Oathtakers."

He held up his banded forearm and glared. "A guest, you say? *Banded?* More like a prisoner. Or what, Lilith, a criminal?"

She frowned. "Don't be ridiculous. It's for your own protection."

"Let me get this straight. You band me, and in doing so shut me from the very powers I would use to protect myself or others. Then with a straight face, you tell me it's for my own good." He shook his head. "Really, if you can't be honest with yourself, you could at least be honest with me."

"Like I said, you're being ridiculous. There are plenty of people who might not think too kindly of you, what with Rowena's death and all."

"Judging by the welcome of the crowd out there," he said, pointing toward the gate, "you've managed to please the locals so well that I'd be considered a hero if they believed me responsible for her death."

Lilith huffed. "Come in now."

"I'll be in shortly."

She didn't want to leave him unattended. She tried to convince Marshall to stay behind, but he refused with a curt shake of his head; his duty was to her. In a flurry, she proceeded to the front door as someone opened it from within. So perfect was the timing of the palace staff that she didn't miss a beat with her steps.

Dixon looked down at the band he wore. Either Lilith had concluded that he was in little danger from the mob, or she intended to leave him at a disadvantage if trouble came. Still, it would likely be only moments before she assigned someone to keep an eye on him. Not prepared to go inside as yet, he paced around the fountain.

"Hello there, Dixon."

"I see Lilith wasted no time in sending someone to watch over me."

He wondered what she was telling the palace staff. *The truth? That I am here against my will and at her demand? That she banded me as she would a common criminal or a traitor?*

He turned around. The burning torches gave off a smell of pitch that tickled his nose. They flickered in the breeze and made popping, crackling noises. "Oh, Bernard, hello."

Bernard, a doorman, had served at the palace for many years. He knew everyone, and nearly everything about them. A small man, slightly stooped at the shoulder, he was well into the fall of his life. As with the earthly seasons, his autumn was accompanied with the loss of things: hair, a bit of hearing, his formerly acute eyesight, energy, patience, and time. People tended to overlook him, but Dixon knew better.

Bernard held a wealth of information about the comings and goings of everyone at the palace. Although his perspective seemed somewhat naïve at times, in that he always looked for the best in everyone, when you needed information, he was often of assistance. Dixon was certain the man was not losing, with advancing age, his ability to observe, his memory, or his unfailing pursuit to do the right and proper thing.

"Lilith said you'd just returned."

"Mmhmmm."

"So, where's Rowena? We've missed her. By the mob outside the gates, I suppose you can see how much." The doorman placed a hand on the bench and slowly lowered himself to sit down.

"Lilith didn't tell you?"

"She just said you'd come home with her. I expected to find Rowena out here with you. Where is she?"

Dixon looked at the old man, then back at the pool of water before him. How many more times could he go through with telling the news? He dipped his hand into the cool water, then sat down. "I'm sorry." He paused, then shared his news.

"No!"

"Yes, just days ago. And now it seems Lilith finds it necessary to band me." The Oathtaker lifted up his arm.

"I'm so sorry. Rowena was so very special. I remember her from the time she was just a babe. Always so full of life, so full of mischief. The good kind, I mean. You know? She'll be sorely missed."

"Well, by some anyway," Dixon murmured.

"You mean Lilith?" The doorman lowered his voice. "She's harmless, don't you think?

"Harmless? Do you really think so?"

"She is terribly self-centered, of course. But that is the way of a sixth."

"There are always excuses for her."

The two sat quietly for a few minutes. The sound and smell of the burning torches filled the air and time.

"She died in childbirth, you say?"

Dixon nodded.

"Goodness, such a tragedy. It seems we may never find our way back," Bernard said. "I worry so for Oosa. The things we've always stood for, always believed in, are . . . disappearing. There doesn't seem to be any order any more. There's little honor . . . little caring. There are no heroes to speak of. No one knows what 'loyalty' means, and few seem to care. Every man is like a law unto himself.

"I'd hoped Rowena's child might grow to be a great leader, the kind that could bring us back to our roots." He hung his head. "And now she's gone and you're . . . banded. None of it makes any sense."

"Yes, well apparently Lilith thinks I'm a flight risk or something." Dixon stood and stretched. "I suppose she asked you to keep an eye on me?"

"Well, she did, but I thought she just wanted to be certain you were properly welcomed. But you? A traitor? Bah! That's ridiculous. I've never known anyone more faithful to Ehyeh's ways. I've watched you. I saw you care for Rowena. I—"

"Thank you. That means a lot to me."

"Ah, truly, she just asked me to be certain you had no need of anything." Bernard paused. "I don't understand. What's going on between the two of you?"

"Oh nothing really. It's just that she insisted in a very public way that I come here with her. So, here I am." Dixon shuffled his feet.

"Understood." The doorman leaned in. "Well, you tell me if you need anything. You know Lilith. She's just asserting her authority so she can have her way. She's always been partial to you."

"Ha! I mean no offense, but that is incredibly naïve of you."

Bernard's brow furrowed. "You don't think she fancies you?"

"No more than she fancies anyone else she can't control."

"Yes, I see what you mean. Well, if you like, I could see if she'd listen to me about removing the band."

"Absolutely not. Thank you, but I don't want you to have anything to do with any of this."

"Sure. Sure. You're just going to wait it out then?"

Dixon nodded. He brushed at his nose to clear away the scent of the burning torches. He grimaced when it was ineffective. "It'll be fine, I'm sure."

"Well, let's get you settled in for the night."

"I don't know. I'd like to stay out for a while just to spite Lilith."

Bernard laughed.

"You're right. No sense behaving as childishly as she does."

Chapter Ten

In some ways returning to the palace was like returning home. Dixon had resided there whenever Rowena had been in attendance over the past years. He looked about his familiar room. It sported a blue theme that ran from the rugs scattered on the dark stained oak floor, to the bedspread, to the curtains, to the towels and the pitcher of water and bowl left for cleaning up. An assortment of black and white chalk sketches, in frames of pewter, hung on the walls. A vase with an assortment of white lilies and blue irises sat on the table near the balcony. The orange patches on the flowers' petals lent a splash of unexpected color to the surroundings. Two chairs flanked the table upon which sat paper, a quill, and an inkwell.

Having awakened with the sun, he listened to the muffled voices of kitchen staff welling up from somewhere below his window. Delivery wagons rattled as they neared the stockrooms. A cock crowed in the distance, and nearby, mourning doves cooed.

A quiet tap came at his door. He ignored it. Palace etiquette held that if he didn't respond to the first muffled knocking, the visitor would wait a good while before returning.

He splashed water across his face and neck. After glancing in the mirror, noting he needed a shave, he retrieved his tools from his backpack. Once done, he dressed in clean clothing stacked in the armoire.

Again came a knock at the door. It was odd, given that it couldn't have been more than a quarter hour since the last attempt to rouse him. Again he ignored the beckoning. He didn't want to see anyone—least of all Lilith if, the Good One forbid, it was she at his door.

He stepped out on the balcony and looked out at the low mist covering the grounds. Droplets of dew sparkled on the lawn. He ran his fingers though his hair, then scowled at the band on his arm. Lilith's use of it was an extreme measure. She had no reason to suspect him of any wrongdoing. He'd always faithfully protected the Select.

Before she'd banded him, he'd been able to feel Mara's presence, as part of his attendant magic enabled him to find other Select and Oathtakers whom he sought. He sighed, longing to return to her and the girls.

Once more, came a knock at his door.

It startled him, interrupting his thoughts. With a huff, he surmised that someone must have a particularly pressing need. He answered the door.

"Edmond!" he exclaimed. "Am I ever glad to see you!"

"Dixon." Edmond threw his arms around his friend and clapped him on the back. He was a few inches shorter than Dixon, and slimmer. His dark hair and brown eyes gave him something of a secretive look. He was dressed the same as always, in tight black pants and a shirt open at the neck, and shiny black boots that came just short of his knees. His style lent him an air of nonchalance. He appeared to be just what he was: part of the established power. He took his position and rank for granted, and it showed in his countenance, which others could easily misconstrue as haughty.

"What are you doing here? I expected you'd be busy with Council duties in the City of Light." Dixon beamed. It was so good to find a friendly face.

"I was deployed to the palace as an envoy of the Council. I arrived some time ago. I understand it was about the time you left with Rowena."

Dixon gestured toward a chair. Edmond pulled up on his pant legs to provide room for movement, then sat.

"I can't tell you how good it is to see you. It's been a long time."

"I heard you came in with Lilith last night."

The Oathtaker held up his arm, displaying the band.

"Whew!" Edmond whistled. "What's that all about?"

"Lilith being Lilith."

"I don't understand."

"She found me at sanctuary in Polesk yesterday and insisted I return to Shimeron with her. Wouldn't take 'no' for an answer."

"What happened?"

"Rowena . . . died." Dixon swallowed hard.

"I heard that, yes." Edmond bowed his head. "I'm so sorry."

"Lilith thinks it necessary to band me to be certain I attend a Council hearing to explain what happened." Dixon leaned forward, crooked one finger so his knuckle pointed out, and said, "I am innocent of any wrongdoing."

"Of course!" Edmond eased his hand down and then, mirroring his body movements, leaned in. "Why would Lilith think otherwise? She knows you."

"Yes, and I know Lilith."

"Again, I don't understand."

"Oh, it's nothing. It's just that she has her ways. Nothing is of any importance unless it's about 'Lilith.'"

Edmond chuckled. "Yes, you know her."

"How long did you say you've been here?"

"Long enough to know you speak truth. I just try to keep her humored so I can go about my business with limited interference."

"I have to get this band removed."

"Why not just go along with her wishes? Surely, you've nothing to hide. It'll come off soon enough."

Dixon scowled. "Of course I've nothing to hide." He paced, then took in a cleansing breath. "Can you talk to her for me? Put some sense in her head?"

"You know I'd do anything for you, but maybe you should just do as she says and take care of this business first."

The Oathtaker looked into his friend's eyes. He considered telling him of his need to get back to Mara and the girls, then decided against it. If he left the palace, he didn't want Edmond to have foreknowledge so that he might feel compelled, or out of some sense of duty, feel the need, to inform anyone of the facts.

"Maybe. Or maybe I'll just wait until evening and be on my way. I'd rather be free and banded than be a prisoner and banded." He frowned. "Dear Ehyeh, being separated from my magic is uncomfortable."

A knock came at the door. Dixon answered it.

Bernard held a note in his white-gloved hand. "Good morning, Dixon. This is for you," he said.

"Don't tell me. I suppose Lilith requests the honor of my presence—"

"Now, now, Dixon," the doorman chuckled. Then, noting Edmond's presence, his expression became suddenly serious.

The Oathtaker glanced at his friend, then looked back at Bernard. He understood the man's discomfort. He never wanted to appear out of character with palace guests.

Having resumed his stoic countenance, Bernard handed the note over. Then he bowed and turned away.

"Well, I'm at your service, Dixon," Edmond said. "Why don't we spend the day walking the grounds? Maybe take in some hunting? I'm sure you'll feel better after you have a chance to see that Lilith may be right about setting the record straight sooner rather than later."

Dixon nodded his agreement, then opened the note.

"Anything important?"

"Only that I am to be certain to join the family for dinner this evening."

Darkness descended as palace residents and guests gathered for dinner, all dressed grandly for the occasion. Lilith had left the staff with orders to seat Dixon at her left, Edmond to her right.

Dixon was disappointed that Marshall would occupy the position directly across the table, as he would like to have spoken with the man. Now he couldn't do so without speaking before Lilith.

Farther down the table, Rowena's sisters, Sally and Janine, sat near their Oathtakers, Ronald and Gisele. A number of other palace regulars filled the remaining places.

Dixon had had no time to himself all day. Edmond, with him unceasingly, suggested one activity after another: a hike, target shooting, even ales before dinner. Dixon was getting the uneasy feeling that Lilith had called upon his friend to keep an eye on him. He knew Edmond was concerned for his welfare, but felt it insincere of him to do Lilith's bidding without first apprising him of the details. And if all that wasn't enough, now he had to sit through a stuffy, pretentious dinner.

Lilith had sent out a public notice earlier providing that the rank of leader of the first family had reverted back to Rowena's siblings. More specifically, it had reverted to her. Accordingly, she was to be last to enter the dining room.

Only a few empty seats remained. In his frustration, Dixon leaned back and closed his eyes. He kept his hands clasped behind his head. He tried to breathe easily and to remain calm, but it was difficult, knowing that Lilith was taking Rowena's place, and of course, he could tell no one the truth—that Lilith was not the ranking member of the first family—without also disclosing the truth about Reigna and Eden.

Minutes later, Lilith arrived. Guests pushed back their chairs, got to their feet and quietly applauded. Dixon huffed, then joined them. He didn't care that he was the last to do so. He clapped once . . . twice.

She stood in the doorway, her right arm resting on Marshall's, her left cuddled around Pompom. Her red dress—for Lilith always wore red—made her look as though she'd bathed in someone's blood. It shone in the lamplight, spraying sparkles around the room. Cut to expose a great deal of flesh, it hugged her body like a second skin.

She sauntered toward the dining table, stopping momentarily to hand her pet off to an attendant. Pompom barked her discontent.

When Lilith arrived at her seat, she simply stood. The applause died away.

A moment passed.

Another moment passed.

Then, suddenly and simultaneously, both Dixon and Edmond rushed to pull out her chair. Edmond won the tug of war. He assisted Lilith, then remained standing until both she and Dixon sat.

The Oathtaker scowled. His frustration building, he remained silent. He was tired of Lilith's games. He was tired of the band on his arm and the physical discomfort it caused by cutting him off from his magic. Strange how much more vivid something is when it's absent. But most of all, he was tired of his inability to leave the palace and return to Mara's side.

He wondered if his being cooperative and malleable was the right approach. It only seemed to encourage Lilith. Perhaps being surly would work better. He had nothing to lose in trying.

He glanced around the table. "Basha!" he exclaimed, surprised at finding a familiar face. "What are you doing here?" Apparently she, seated diagonally across from him, had arrived just moments before Lilith, while he'd been ignoring everyone.

Basha had changed some since he'd last seen her, although she still looked like she was in her late twenties or so. As an Oathtaker, she'd held her physical age for all the years Dixon had known her. But she seemed to have aged in some other way—spiritually perhaps, or maybe emotionally. It was as though her cares were too burdensome.

Her traditionally slim athletic build was somewhat rounder than when he'd last seen her. She wore her hair as always, cut straight around, just below her ears. It glittered like gold. Notwithstanding a difference in her countenance from days gone by, some overall sadness, her eyes still shone with the same genuineness and friendliness that he remembered from the past.

She looked him fully in the eyes. "Dixon, it is so very good to see you." Her voice was low, soft and comforting, like the sound of an old favored melody.

A waiter moved over Dixon's shoulder, filling his wine glass for the first course. Another followed behind with a crystal pitcher, to fill his water glass.

As the Oathtaker allowed the wait staff room to maneuver, his gaze held Basha's. He lifted his glass and tasted. Though not a great wine enthusiast, he could appreciate a good vintage at least as well as most.

"It does my heart good to see you, Basha. What has it been? Four? Five years?"

"Nearly five."

He looked down at the table, as did she. She cleared her throat, then looked back up, again meeting his eyes.

"Tell me, have you found the pain lessen any?"

She shrugged, then blinked repeatedly, as though holding tears at bay. "Some. Not entirely." She smiled weakly.

"That has been my experience as well." He raised his brow. "Even after the years that have passed, there just are no words, are there? I am so very sorry."

He remembered the day Basha had lost her charge as though it was yesterday. The first family of the Select, Rowena, Lilith, Sally, Janine, Therese, Dianna and Eve, along with Rowena's husband, Grant, Dianna's husband, Michael, and Eve's husband, Newland, were on an outing on the grounds far out from the palace. Their Oathtakers, Dixon, Marshall, Ronald, Gisele, Basha, Kenneth, and Marcel, accompanied them.

Assassinations of the Select in the surrounding communities had been increasing, but everyone believed they were safe on palace grounds. Even so, their children were not in attendance. Their parents had already sent them away to various places for their safety.

After an early hunt, the family made its way to a favorite picnic area near a cliff above the Mando River. The day had started with a fresh rain, but then gradually warmed, leaving the verdant green grasses begging for company. It was an appeal the family was all too happy to grant. They relaxed and visited, enjoying one another's company and freedom from duty for the day.

No one knew who shot the arrows that suddenly intruded upon their tranquility. When they realized they were under attack, Dixon and Marshall ran toward the source. The remaining Oathtakers surrounded the first family.

Basha and her charge, Therese, stood at the edge of a cliff a short distance from the others, overlooking a waterfall. When they heard screams over the surging water, Basha quickly calculated the risks of rushing her charge to safety with the others.

It was then that Therese staggered and fell down the cliff and into the water. Basha tried to catch her, but was a step too far away. No one knew if an arrow had hit Therese, but even if not, the likelihood of her surviving the fall was slim. Still, Basha demanded that a full guard accompany her to search the area and then to explore further downstream for several miles.

The hunt stretched out for days, but they never recovered Therese's body. She was the first of the first family to meet her demise. The event seemed to cause the family to start to unravel, stitch by stitch. All of Rowena's earlier work to bring them together, which had appeared to be taking hold, was coming apart.

His thoughts returned to the present. He was grateful to find Lilith engaged in small talk with Edmond. Indeed, she seemed to be ignoring everyone else, as waiters offered the diners roasted lamb in a red wine sauce, game hens with a pancetta, dried apricot, cashew and rosemary stuffing, and oven roasted potatoes and carrots with garlic and thyme.

Lilith laughed at Edmond's comments, touching him from time to time, first his arm, then his hand, then his knee. The two seemed quite comfortable with one another. Dixon was surprised that his friend tolerated the woman so easily, but then most men did fall under her spell.

"Is that true, Dixon?"

"Excuse me? I'm sorry, Lilith." He put his glass down. "Is what true?"

She turned to Edmond, pouting. "You see? It's like I said. Dixon ignores me."

"It's not possible to ignore you, Lilith," Edmond replied. His eyes were glued to her—or more accurately, to her cleavage.

Dixon glanced at Basha. He had to exercise great discipline to keep from rolling his eyes. With superb timing from his vantage, a waiter stepped between him and Lilith, offering a plate of steamed asparagus in a lemon butter sauce, lightly sprinkled with sea salt and fresh cracked black pepper. Lilith allowed the waiter to place some on her plate, after which he moved on.

"I'm not ignoring you, Lilith. I just have other things on my mind and I was enjoying Basha's unexpected presence."

"What other things?" She glanced at Basha with a grimace she made no effort to conceal.

"When you're around, Lilith, there are no 'other things,'" Edmond said.

Dixon cleared his throat. Glancing over Lilith's shoulder, he saw his friend shrug at him, his brow raised. So, Edmond was just playing to her ego, keeping her engaged, satisfied. He should be grateful—at least it kept her attention away from him.

"It's like I said, Lilith, I have other things on my mind. I was thinking about how I want this band off so I can go home. There was no cause for this."

"No cause!"

"Yes," Basha interrupted, "surely the band is unnecessary, Lilith."

Lilith sneered at her. "A lot you would know about an Oathtaker's duty," she spat. "No Select would be safe in your company."

Basha looked down.

Lilith glanced around the room. She tilted her head and smiled at her guests who'd stopped to watch the exchange as it had grown more heated.

When the diners turned back to their own meals and conversations, she turned back to Dixon. Her fingers touched her necklace, then slowly moved back and forth across her décolletage, as a hypnotist might do when trying to make his subject fall under his spell.

He did not succumb to her attempts at seduction. His eyes remained fixed on hers. "You're out of line, Lilith, and you know it. Basha deserves your undying respect and gratitude."

She glared. "Dixon. Be reasonable. Rowena is dead. Surely you can understand that it will be necessary for you to speak to the Council." She pursed her lips.

"Lilith. Be reasonable," he mimicked, his expression hard, resolute. "You know I always served Rowena faithfully. I'm not a miracle worker. I told you how she died. Of course I'll check in with the Council to inform them of the facts, but no reasonable person could find fault here."

"Oh, really? Well, I certainly have a lot of questions. Like . . . Where were you? And why were you there and not here at the palace where Rowena would have been safe? And . . . did you get assistance for her? And—well, many other things." Her jaw set.

"The palace isn't always safe," Basha said.

Dixon contemplated what both women said. For the first time since leaving Polesk, he felt genuine cause for concern. He was confident he knew Lilith was responsible for Rowena's death, but now he feared he understood why she'd banded him. She meant for him to be the scapegoat. She meant to keep inquiries about Rowena's travels at bay by keeping the focus on his supposed dereliction of duty.

He stared at Lilith.

She boldly stared back.

He refused to be the first to back down, to show any doubt, or to display any weakness upon which she would prey.

Finally, she looked away. "So you see, Dixon," she said, as though there'd been no showdown, "I had you banded so we could travel to the City of Light together. I've sent word ahead that we'll be there soon. In the meantime," she looked back at him, "the band stays."

His gaze met Basha's, then he looked toward Edmond. He had hoped his friend would speak for him, but the man refused to even look his way. "Suddenly I'm not so hungry."

He stood and dropped his napkin on his plate. With all eyes on him, he marched from the dining room, catching from out of the corner of his eye, Basha rising to her feet.

He made his way toward the foyer where two grand staircases rose, one flanking each side. He took the stairs two at a time, then strode down the hallway to his room. He was breathing hard when he arrived, not from physical exertion, but from frustration and a nagging fear that was taking hold: Lilith meant him harm.

Dixon entered his chambers and grabbed his backpack. Hastily, he removed his dress clothes, exchanging them for garments for traveling. Then he gathered his personal items.

He'd go to the Council this very night, before Lilith could further damage his reputation, before she could call his loyalty into question. Without her accusations and influence, the Council would understand. They would remove the band.

A tap came at his door. He surmised it was Basha. He didn't want her mixed up in this. He considered ignoring the summons, but the knocking came again, more insistently. He placed his pack down and out of view, then answered the door.

"Dixon," Basha said, "we have to talk."

"I'm tired of talking."

"To me?"

He sighed. His fight drained away. He slumped down at the edge of his bed. With one elbow on his knee, he dropped his head into his hand and shook it. "No, of course not. Not to you. I'm sorry."

She sat down and put her hand on his shoulder. "Dixon, this is serious. I must speak with you."

He looked at her, unsure what he saw. Was it fear, dread, worry—or perhaps it was . . . hope? "What is it?"

"We need to talk," she mouthed without sound. She cupped a hand around her ear, then placed a finger over her lips, motioning that they should not speak out loud.

He cocked his head and raised his hands in question.

She pointed to the door. Then she held up one hand, waving toward it.

He took the sign to mean that she would meet him somewhere, shortly. He mouthed his question: "Where?"

She looked away. She bit her lip, then took his hand and led him toward the balcony. Speaking out loud she said, "Dixon, I know you're angry, but . . . well, maybe Lilith is right after all. You know it's important you speak with the Council. You'll be cleared, I'm sure of it. It's all just a formality." She pointed to a well-known destination: the falls, where Therese had been lost.

He nodded. "Fine, Basha, I'll play along with her." He hesitated and then, so as to lend credibility to his words, said, "But I don't have to like it." He turned back to his room and sat down again at the edge of the bed.

"That's better, Dixon," she said as she sat beside him. "It's for your own good. You'll see. And it'll help to keep the peace around here. For now, it would be best for you to cool down. You need some time to process all of what has transpired. I understand."

"But it's all just so—"

"No, Dixon," she interrupted as she stood. "Tomorrow. We'll breakfast. Maybe after a good night's rest you'll see things more clearly. I'd like to go to the Council with you, but only if you agree to Lilith's terms. She is the leader of the family now."

He gestured toward his pack. Should he take it along?

She shook her head.

"Thank you, Basha. I'll see you in the morning then. You're probably right." He walked her to the door. "Good night."

After she left, he waited. When he felt the requisite time had passed, he snapped up his cape and opened the door.

"Going somewhere?"

❦

"Bernard! You startled me."

"Sorry, Dixon." The doorman entered with slow shuffling steps. He placed a stack of clean towels on the bureau. "Be careful," he said quietly as he made his way back to the door, opened it, then looked down the hall.

"Sure thing, Bernard. Thanks."

"See you in the morning then."

"Right. Good night. Thanks for the fresh towels."

The doorman waited, as though considering whether to say more, then softly made his way out.

If anyone was listening in, Dixon might have company on his trip. He didn't want to take that risk. He went to the balcony. A branch from a nearby oak reached toward his room, as though in invitation. He decided he would accept.

Rummaging through his backpack, he removed a rope, then confirmed that his Oathtaker's blade, Verity, was in its sheath. Its power wouldn't work while the band blocked his attendant magic, but it could still serve as a useful weapon.

He grabbed hold of the tree branch, then made his way to the ground. Guards at the gates to the east walked their beat. When the way was clear, he sprinted across the lawn, finding refuge behind statuary, trees, and shrubs, along the way. Upon reaching the south end of the lawn, he surveyed the area once again. Finding it clear, he dashed into the night.

Though he knew the palace grounds well, it was always riskier to move speedily in muted light. Fortunately, the sky was overcast, softening and spreading out the light of the two current moons. Still, his jaunt would have been much easier if the band didn't restrict his magic. Without it he had to move more slowly and use greater care.

When he reached the area near where Basha had instructed him to go, he slowed. He moved out from behind a tree. *There she is.* He raised his hand to catch her attention.

She placed a finger over her pursed lips, cautioning him to silence. Then she motioned him forward. When he reached her side, she clasped his arm and walked toward the falls.

Shortly, they came upon a pile of smooth boulders hidden among the branches of a willow. They sat. The rush of the falls thundered off to the side.

"Did anyone see you leave?"

"I don't think so."

"Good. I don't want anyone to overhear us. I chose this place with background noise so that any magic that might enhance someone's hearing would be of little use."

He nodded. "Are you all right, Basha? Lilith said some terrible things at dinner."

"Welcome home, Dixon," she joked.

He laughed easily.

She pursed her lips in thought. "Dixon, things are amiss at the palace."

"You think?"

The two shared another laugh before her demeanor became serious. "Dixon, there are so many things I need to tell you. So many questions I have. I'm troubled and I'm confused. Thank you for speaking with me. I'm so grateful to have found a friend here." Just as when Therese had fallen from the cliff, Basha seemed visibly shaken.

"What is it?"

She stood and paced a couple steps forward, then a couple back. Sitting back down, she grasped his hands. "Dixon, I fear for you. Lilith is . . . She is—"

"Not right?"

"Yes." Basha smiled. "Oh, how I've missed your easy ways. Even in the midst of trouble you can always make me laugh!"

"I guess it's just my charm, huh?"

She laughed wholeheartedly. "Oh, Dixon," she said as her voice softened, "I know this is a sad thing losing Rowena, and likely you're not ready to think about this now, but . . . Well, after your grieving, you might find you want to share your life with someone. Perhaps she's out there, even now, looking for you. Who knows? Maybe she's already found you and you just don't know it yet."

He chuckled. "Oh, I rather doubt that." He hung his head and shook it, still smiling. "You remember, huh?"

"Remember! How could I forget? What a funny story."

"And to think my own mother told you."

"Yes. So funny! She told me you were such a moody teenager, always cranky and scowling. She could never get you to ease up. 'One day, I told him,' she said to me, 'one day I told him that if he ever finds a woman who thinks he's charming, he'll be sure to know he's found his future wife!' Goodness, it's still just as funny today as it was back then."

"Yes, well it became a habit for me, you know? Before I took my first oath, I told every engaging woman I met that I had the gift of charm. None of them seemed to believe me!" He grinned, then became serious. "Maybe that's why I found it so easy to swear an oath first for Judith, and later for Rowena." He paused. "Figured no one else would have me."

"Not true, Dixon." Basha shook her head. "Not true at all." She smiled at him. "Why there will be many women who would be honored to know that in you they've found a man willing to swear an oath—a man who's shown himself able to live up to what it means." She paused. "Why, if I were a few years younger myself . . ."

He caught her eye and together they laughed again.

"Really, you might consider starting to ask the question again."

He smirked, but then became somber. What was it that had prompted him to tell Mara that he had the gift of charm? It was ridiculous. She had a charge. Even though he was now free, she was not. It was absurd, really. He turned to Basha. "Why don't you tell me what's going on? Why are you at the palace? I thought you'd gone back to—"

"I had—gone back to my hometown in Anka—yes," she interrupted, "but I missed the palace so. And . . . oh, never mind. You'll think I'm crazy." She turned away.

He placed his hand on her back. "I could never think you're crazy. Believe me. I've seen crazy. I've met crazy!" He paused for effect and then said, "Her name is Lilith."

Basha chuckled.

"Really, why do you say I would think badly of you? What's going on?"

She stood again, fidgeting. Her mouth would open to speak, then she'd place her fingers over her lips, then she'd try again. Back and forth she went.

"Basha, sit." He took her hand. "I won't think you're crazy. I promise. I know you and you're . . . Well, you're not the 'crazy' type!"

From a few feet off came a rustle in the underbrush.

"Shhh," Dixon cautioned, his finger to his lips. He reached for a knife.

Basha went still, then relaxed when a small hare jumped out from behind the brush.

"Never mind, just a hare," he said.

She nodded as she gathered her thoughts. "Dixon, what would you say if I told you that—well, that—"

"Go on," he urged.

"What would you say if I told you that I think Therese still lives? There, I've said it." She leaned back and waited for his reaction.

"Therese is alive?"

"I believe so."

"Wait—" He held his hands up. "Why would you say that? We searched for days for her after she fell. What would make you think she still lives?"

"I haven't seen her, but . . . I believe she's alive."

"Why? How?"

"Dixon, would you know if Judith was alive? Or Rowena? I mean—what if you didn't know for certain that either of them had died? What if you'd never seen their lifeless bodies? What if—"

He shook his head. "It's not possible, Basha. We searched for days, weeks even."

"But it is. It is! Don't you see? You'd know."

"I don't understand."

"Dixon, think about it. Suppose you hadn't seen Rowena after her death. What one thing might make you believe . . ." She shook her head. "No, what one thing would tell you with certainty that she lived?"

The cool evening breeze, filled with mist, brushed against his skin. Hesitating, he listening to the rushing falls. Over the surging water, came an owl's hoot.

"Well, I suppose there'd be only one way."

"And that would be?"

"The bond."

"Exactly," she whispered.

He stood and paced, then returned to her side. "You feel your bond with Therese?"

"Sometimes."

"Are you sure it's the bond and not just some . . . I don't know, some—"

"Longing?"

"Yes."

"No. No, Dixon, it's not just some longing. It's the bond. I know it. But it's very . . . odd. It . . . comes and goes."

"Comes and goes?"

"Yes. Sometimes it's so strong I find myself on a path to meet with her. I've gone days out of my way, only to have the pull disappear as suddenly as it first began."

Dixon didn't want to falsely encourage his friend, but he knew the bond was an unmistakable draw. An Oathtaker would drop anything to respond to it. "Go on," he said.

"I knew it. I shouldn't have said anything."

"No, I trust you. I've seen some unusual things with oaths and bonds of late. I don't believe you could mistake anything else for your bond, unless . . . Well unless . . ."

"Unless?"

"I've never heard of it happening, but could someone have bewitched you somehow? Could someone be trying to order your steps?"

She shrugged. "I don't know. I only know that it's happened on numerous occasions. Sometimes it lasts for days and is highly intense. Then it just . . . dies. Each time, I feel I've lost her all over again."

"Oh, Basha, I am so sorry. How awful. I don't know what to say." He played a drumbeat on his thigh. "So, what do you want to do about it?"

"I want to accompany you to the City of Light. That's the direction from which it seems to pull me each time. If Therese is there, maybe I'll find her. If she's alive, then she needs me."

"But why wouldn't she come to you then?"

Basha chewed on her lower lip. "I'd like to think it was because she couldn't, and not because she wouldn't."

"Maybe the Council would have some answers, or maybe scholars at the sanctuary library could help shed some light on this."

"Maybe."

He sat quietly for a minute, then turned his attention back to his own concerns. "What do you make of Lilith's behavior?"

Basha grew thoughtful. "Lilith is . . . She is . . . broken."

"Broken?"

"Yes. Rowena had finally managed to bring the family together, only to have everything disrupted when Therese died. Well, when we *think* she died. Lilith became lost. She resorted to her old selfish ways. Only now her behavior is many times worse."

"She's beginning to frighten me."

"Me too. That's another reason I want to accompany you. There have been rumors around the palace. I've stayed here on and off—mostly on—since shortly after you and Rowena left. It feels like there's a cloak of secrecy over the place. Meanwhile, Lilith has become more and more out of control."

"What kind of rumors?"

Basha sighed. "Dixon, some say she was behind Therese, Dianna, and Eve's, deaths. Some even say she may have meant Rowena harm."

"And Sally and Janine? They and Lilith are the only ones remaining of Rowena's sisters. Why would Lilith be behind the deaths of the first, second, and third, while leaving the fourth and fifth unharmed?"

"I don't know. Sally and Janine both stay here at the palace at all times. Lilith gives them free reign to do as they please. Sally uses her leadership as a fifth to . . . Oh, I don't know how to describe it. Let's just say that she encourages unusual things within her jurisdiction."

"Such as?"

Basha tapped her finger to her chin. "Oh, I know! Recently she encouraged new laws that forbid people from cutting wood from the public forests to burn for heating their homes."

"That doesn't make sense."

"She says 'the trees have feelings too.' She says if people want to burn wood for heat, they'll just have to get it elsewhere. And that's true even though the authorities only ever allowed the people to take out the deadwood, or to cut from certain areas so that if a forest fire broke out, it wouldn't burn out of control for miles on end. It's all so contrary to Ehyeh's ways."

"What does Lilith say?"

"She just laughs and says that's the price others pay for being 'commoners.'"

"Commoners! And Janine?"

"Oh, she does the most ridiculous things! People can't use medicines they prefer because *she* thinks they're bad for them. People can't teach their own children their skills, because *she* thinks children should be free to decide those things when they become adults. Do you know she's trying to restrict the kinds of weapons people keep for self-defense because *she* thinks they could be used to harm others?"

"It sounds like she just wants to control how others live."

"Yes, that's right. There's little rhyme or reason to most of what she does. The requirements are just extra burdens for the people, or could leave them vulnerable to harm."

"And I suppose Lilith reacts the same way with Janine?"

"To Lilith, the two of them can do no wrong."

Dixon pondered. "But why would she have intended harm to Dianna, or Eve? Or to Therese?"

Basha tilted her head right to left, then back again. "I know it sounds ridiculous, but it's the only explanation that makes any sense, the only one supported by all of the evidence."

"And that is?"

"They're trying to keep the people from being strong in their homes, families and convictions. When outside frustrations constantly harass the people, they're easier to control." She shrugged. "That's just a theory."

For a minute, Dixon considered telling Basha that he thought Lilith was responsible for Rowena's death as well, but he decided against it—at least for now. He didn't want to put any extra pressure on her should anyone discover he'd spoken with her.

They talked late into the night, contemplating the changes at the palace and in Oosa in general. When the first rays of morning light graced the sky, Dixon parted his friend's company and returned to the palace.

CHAPTER ELEVEN

Mara and Nina rode hard for two days. Each night they took refuge in a barn for a few hours. One kept watch while the other slept. Mara allowed Nina as much rest as possible so as to keep up her strength for attending the girls' needs. Now, dusty from their travels and exhausted, they arrived in a sizable city.

It was just after midday and the thoroughfare bustled. Buggies hurried past them, carrying both the mundane and the fashionable around the market square. Busy hawkers' voices carried through the warm air of the overcast day, as did those peddling the daily news from various street corners.

Reasoning that the most difficult things to find are often those hiding in plain sight, Mara chose an upscale inn in the busiest part of town. The building boasted a welcome sign informing visitors that they'd arrived at *The King's Court.*

An attendant provided her a stepping block. She dismounted, then waited as he assisted Nina down from Spot.

The steps to the front door creaked beneath their feet. The Oathtaker gazed back the way from whence they'd come. What was keeping Dixon? His delay concerned her. Grasping Nina's elbow, she guided her around a cluster of guests visiting near the entrance.

The doorman stood at attention. He wore khaki pants, a dark navy double-breasted jacket, and a white shirt and gloves. He gestured toward the reception desk.

The establishment had a homey appeal. The lobby was papered in robin's egg blue silk. Heavy damask white and yellow curtains hung at the windows that looked out over gardens offering discerning guests a variety of nooks and crannies for their leisure.

People walked briskly by. Waitresses carried trays of cool drinks from bar to table. Hotel staff rushed about, anxious to do the bidding of the guests and to avoid a scolding from the chief lobby attendant who kept an eye, like that of a vulture, on the goings on of his staff.

"Two guests?" asked the clerk.

"Well actually, my husband may already have checked us in." Mara hadn't given much advance thought to needing a story for traveling alone or for her current state of dress, but she could see by the clerk's expression that she'd need to answer some unasked questions.

"Ah . . . Frank. Frank . . . Portman. That's my husband. He would have checked us in as 'Frank and Mara Portman' along with our guest, Nina . . . Spink," she added, making up a surname for Nina on the spot. "Is he here yet?"

The clerk reviewed his list of guests, then shook his head.

She turned to Nina. "Didn't I tell you?" She clapped her hands like a spoiled girl and giggled, then looked back at the clerk. His expression was unchanged.

"You see, my husband has been very busy. We planned a trip to the city, but he canceled. So we reset the date and—wouldn't you know? He bowed out yet again. I told him I was going anyway, and I bet him that I could make it here on my own. I said I'd see how long it took him to catch up. And I did! I got here first. Isn't that funny?"

The clerk nodded, his brow raised.

The Oathtaker leaned in as though sharing a secret. "Men. They're too busy and have too many excuses until a woman just forces their hand."

He smiled as though he'd heard the same story before.

"I suppose, since Frank's not here, I'll just check in with my friend for the evening. We'll see how long it takes him to get here. Unless of course he sends a message to inform me of yet another delay."

The clerk handed over a key. "Please sign here." He waited as Mara did. "Room one-fourteen. Go down the hallway there to your right. It's the last door on the left. Have you stayed with us before?"

"No, but I've been told that this is *the* place to visit in the city." She smiled graciously, then turned away.

He commented that such a lovely young woman shouldn't be kept waiting, nor should her man allow her to travel alone. Surprised, she turned back, only to find the clerk absorbed in his books. After a moment, she realized she'd heard his thoughts. Pleased her story had convinced him, she guided Nina down the hall.

Upon entering their room, the Oathtaker dropped her sack near the door and untied Reigna from her front side. Moments later, a maid knocked at the door. She inquired whether they were in need of anything. Mara asked for drinks, which the maid assured her she would deliver shortly.

Nina sat quietly, taking her boots off. "This is luxurious."

"Mmhmmm."

"How long do you expect to stay?"

"Maybe just the night. I'm surprised Dixon hasn't met up with us yet. I don't want to get too far ahead of him and I'm not altogether sure where to go from here."

"What do you suppose happened?"

"I've no idea."

Another rapping came at the door. Mara answered it.

"For our two newest guests," the chambermaid said, "a treat on the house. Freshly squeezed lemonade on ice, sweetened with pure maple syrup, and sprinkled with just a touch of cayenne. I think you'll find it very refreshing."

"Thank you."

The maid put the tray down. "Is there anything more I can do for you? Schedule a table for you for dinner, perhaps?"

"Yes. Let's say . . . in an hour?"

"I'll inform the kitchen staff. I'm confident you'll be delighted with the meal this evening."

As she was leaving, Mara called out, "Excuse me?"

"Yes?"

"Do you have a local flier?"

"Certainly. Actually, there are three fliers here in Settleton. *The Vixen*, *The Messenbeck* and *The Seamen*. They each have morning and evening editions. Also, the criers are stationed in the town square most of the day."

The maid leaned in conspiratorially. "I noticed today's headlines about the big news out of Shimeron. Seems an Oathtaker was derelict in his duties. He may have committed treason! There's to be a hearing in the City of Light." She turned to go. "Would you like this morning's fliers or the evening editions later?"

"We'll get copies later, thank you." Mara frowned and bit her lower lip.

The maid left, closing the door softly behind.

"Is there a problem?" Nina asked.

"No, it's just that it's always troubling when an Oathtaker is accused of wrongdoing."

After cleaning up, they made their way to the dining room. Mara requested a table near the exit that would allow her to sit with her back to the wall. She surveyed the room looking for any sign of trouble.

At the table to their right sat what appeared to be a family of five, the three children all in their teens. Just ahead sat a couple, likely newlyweds. At the table to their left was a woman in a simple gown of royal purple, with canary yellow cuffs and neckline. She glanced repeatedly at Mara. There was something very familiar about her, but the Oathtaker couldn't place just what. A young man sat to each side of the woman. Both dressed in blue, they could well have been her grown sons.

The waiter arrived with the house dinner: freshwater trout in a hazelnut crust, wild rice pilaf, and fresh green beans with bacon bits. Mara and Nina both inhaled deeply, then laughed softly.

"A little hungry are we?" Nina asked.

Mara nodded. Turning to the waiter, she placed her hand on his forearm. "Thank you. Now I wondered if I might trouble you?"

"Anything, Madam! What may I do for you?"

"Have you copies of the local evening fliers?"

"But of course. I will procure them for you." Leaning in, he commented, "It is a most curious story about Mr. Townsend, is it not?"

The color drained from her face. Her grip tightened. "Did you say Mr.—Townsend?"

"Yes, that's right, Dixon Townsend. From all I hear the City of Light is about to witness a real circus with a hearing for him. Just imagine, one of the Townsends!"

She patted his arm. "Yes, I'm sure. Ahhh . . . thank you. A copy of each of the fliers would be most helpful. Please put the expense on my tab."

"Certainly. Room one-fourteen."

She felt someone's eyes upon her. She turned to the table to her left where sat the woman who looked familiar. Mara avoided making eye contact. "Let's enjoy, but not linger," she whispered to Nina.

When they returned to their chambers, the Oathtaker sat with her feet up on the bed, perusing *The Vixen*, the first of the three fliers the waiter had given her. Quietly, she read aloud:

The Official Council has been informed of possible wrongdoing by Dixon Townsend, Oathtaker to the former ranking member of the first family of the Select, Rowena Vala, a seventh.

Rowena's sister, Lilith, a sixth, brought the information to the Council after Townsend, who had acted as Oathtaker to Rowena for nearly a decade, informed Lilith of Rowena's death. Rowena had been pregnant at the time with her seventh child. In light of her premature and unexpected demise, Lilith informed the Council that she now acts as the current ranking member of the first family and of the Select.

While no charges have as yet been filed against Townsend, Lilith, in her new official capacity, has demanded a hearing into the matter.

Word is that Townsend, of the Brecken Townsends, insists he engaged in no wrongdoing and looks forward to answering all of the Council's questions.

Townsend is the son of Brent and Francesca Townsend, well known for their history of service to Oosa.

Townsend's late father, Brent Townsend, served many years as an Oathtaker. When no longer under oath, he returned to his hometown in the hinterlands where he married. He served as an advisor to the Council and is perhaps best known for his efforts in bringing the traitor, Madden Chantray, to justice. It was his role as prosecutor for the Council in the course of those hearings that made the Townsend name famous.

Francesca Townsend is well known and immensely popular among the people of Oosa for her programs to support Oosa's working people by keeping taxes low and restrictions on their personal freedoms minimal.

The Council issued a public statement, insisting that a fair hearing will be held. 'The Townsends have a long and honorable history in Oosa. Rest assured, Dixon Townsend will receive a full and fair hearing.'

The Oathtakers' Guild published a statement providing that, based on Townsend's history, it supports him unless or until the evidence should prove otherwise.

Others are not so supportive. Those related to The Citizens for Nonintervention, long opposed to the Select and the Oathtakers at any level, insist Townsend should be found guilty of treason not because of Rowena's death or due to any part he may have played in the events leading to it, but simply by virtue of his role as an Oathtaker and his relationship with the Select over the years.

Lilith and her entourage will escort Townsend to the City of Light where even now, plans are being set in place for the hearing. Security is likely to be at its highest.

"The Citizens for Nonintervention. I've heard of them, but I had no idea they were opposed to the Select and Oathtakers 'at every level.'" Mara frowned. "Interesting." She put the flier down and took up *The Messenbeck*. "Let's see," she said, looking it over. "All right, here it is." She read to Nina:

Dixon Townsend, former Oathtaker to Rowena Vala, the now-deceased ranking member of the Select, is in hot water yet again! Townsend, brought up on charges of wrongdoing, has been required to testify before the Council in the past.

Years ago, Townsend acted as Oathtaker to Judith Jenkins, a fourth of the Select, but not a member of the first family. Following her death, in what Townsend claimed was a riding accident, questions were raised about his behavior. Many believed his special relationship to members of the Council kept him from paying the ultimate price for treason to the Select at that time.

It comes as no surprise that the Guild supports Townsend. Even so, the Council plans to conduct a hearing into the matter in the City of Light.

This reporter notes that historically, the Select and their Oathtakers have repeatedly overreached at every turn.

Some years ago, after centuries of consistent and methodical intrusion into the affairs of the people of Oosa, the Select agreed to govern Oosa in part with the use of a Council that would represent various interests and factions. Notwithstanding, by maintaining control over those who would sit on the Council and by insisting on keeping the identity of the members confidential, the Select have managed to continually and systematically impress their ways upon the people of Oosa.

The Oathtaker looked up. "This is ridiculous. Oosa has gone nowhere but downhill since the Select gave the people what they purportedly wanted. I can't believe this!" She shook her head. "And what's this about 'consistent and methodical intrusion?' Who believes this stuff? All of Oosa was founded on the ways and teachings of the Select."

"What does the last one say?" Nina asked.

"Oh, let me see." Mara scanned *The Seaman*. "More of the same, really. Its a little less helpful than the account in *The Vixen*, but . . . Well, I guess if you read between the lines, it sounds more like *The Messenbeck*. Dear Good One, I had no idea people read such things. This is ghastly. Don't they know their history?" She threw the fliers down.

"Now what?"

Mara shrugged. "I don't know. I wonder if we ought to go to the City of Light. I could speak to the Council on Dixon's behalf."

Busily nursing Reigna, Nina raised her brow. "What if it's a trap to get the girls there?"

"Actually, the thought had occurred to me."

The Oathtaker picked the fliers back up, then slapped them back down again. She didn't think Dixon had engaged in any wrongdoing. She'd seen his reaction upon Rowena's death. He was devastated.

She remembered the look on his face, the slump of his shoulders, his near incoherence, the way he'd spoken his final farewell to his charge. She didn't know much about his history with Rowena, but she was certain he was innocent of any wrongdoing relating to the woman's death. Still, if she went to the City of Light, she couldn't approach the Council or assist him in any meaningful way without disclosing the facts about the girls—and the fewer who knew of their existence, the safer they'd remain.

"Sometimes staying out of things is the hardest," Nina said.

Mara nodded.

"When I was in Chiran, there were many times I wanted to take action, but I couldn't because of the danger it could bring to others. In the end I left, but my daughter paid for that. She paid with her life."

"Will you tell me about Chiran, Nina?"

"I was brought up in a small village outside the largest city, Fallique, where the emperor's palace is located." Nina poured herself a glass of wine, propped some pillows up, then reclined.

"My parents were very poor. The emperor, Zarek, cares nothing for the people. He lives in luxury while they suffer. If he desires anything, he sends raiders into Fallique, or out to the surrounding countryside. They take whatever he orders. They plunder the villages." She sipped at her wine.

"I was one of six children. Unfortunately, for my parents, four of us were girls.

In Chiran, girls are a liability, an expense to a family. The cost can be devastating to a poor one."

"I've heard that in Chiran, some people destroy their infant daughters and keep only their sons," Mara commented.

"That is so today. But things were a bit different when I was a child." Nina hesitated as footsteps came down the hall, passed the door, then grew quiet.

"As I said, there were six of us. Every winter grew a little harder as our stomachs grew a little larger.

"My brothers helped my father farm, but my parents feared for us girls. They knew Zarek's men could come at any time and that they raped the land and the women, taking whatever they wanted from whomever they chose." She swallowed hard. "My family tried to protect us, but eventually the pressure became too great."

"What happened?" Mara pulled her chair closer.

"Zarek's men caught my oldest sister, Marise, on her way to the well one afternoon. They . . . enjoyed . . . themselves with her for the remainder of the day." Nina's eyes spilled great tears. "They left her a shell of her former self. Worse—they also left her with child."

"Oh, I am so sorry."

"She was never the same again. But now we had yet another mouth to feed—and wouldn't you know it—another girl at that. My parents were desperate."

The young woman took another taste of her wine. The flavor she might have savored at any other time was bitter now as her story unfolded. She put the glass down, leaned her head back, and closed her eyes.

"Our circumstances were dire. We didn't have enough food for the approaching winter. There hadn't been much to begin with, and then Zarek's men raided what little stores we'd accumulated.

"About that time, Zarek put new policies into place. He decreed that he'd pay families who had sons an annual royalty, while he'd charge those with daughters double the amount as a penalty.

"So my parents were to receive two royalties for my two brothers, but were to pay ten penalties for my three sisters, my sister's child, and me. We were going to starve." Her body tensed as she recalled her memories.

"And then?" Mara prompted.

Nina bit her lip. "Then a handler came to my parent's farm."

"A handler?"

"Yes. Zarek sent handlers out to purchase servants for his palace and women for his troops."

"No."

"Yes," Nina whispered. "The handler explained to my parents that they would pay enough for a single one of their daughters for them to make it through the winter."

She closed her eyes. "I cannot imagine the horror they must have felt. Still, they thought they might save five children and a grandchild, by sacrificing one of us.

"When the handler returned a few weeks later, my parents offered Marise. She'd become nothing more than a mouth to feed. But the handlers refused her. So my parents offered Erin. She didn't know they'd sold her. She thought the handlers were taking her to Fallique to work so that she could send money back home.

"My parents told the rest of us nothing more at the time. I imagine it must have been very painful for them."

"I'm sure."

Now that Nina's story had begun, the telling was becoming easier. Even so, she wept.

"The second year they sold my next eldest sister, Yanny. Then the third year approached. Things had continued to spiral down. I was the only one remaining that could bring my parents a suitable price. It was only later I learned that I was considered something of a beauty, so the handlers were willing to pay more for me than they had for my sisters.

"I still have to believe my parents thought they were selling me into service for the palace as a servant, but in fact," she said in a voice now devoid of any emotion, "I was sold to the palace as a whore for Zarek's men."

"Oh, how awful." Mara stroked the young woman's arm.

Nina nodded, acknowledging the sympathies. Taking a deep breath, she bore on. "I served . . . Well, I guess it would be more accurate to say that I 'serviced' Zarek's men for about a year when I became pregnant. Whenever that happened to one of the girls, the authorities sent them away for the last few months. Most returned later, and they all told the same story. If the child was a boy, he was taken away. We believed Zarek made arrangements for them to be raised as future soldiers. The girls—" She choked back a sob. "The girls they . . . killed."

"No!"

"In front of their own mothers' eyes. Immediately upon birth, if the child is a girl, the attending midwife calls for a guard. When he arrives, he bludgeons the child to death." Nina, sobbing, dropped her head into her hands.

Mara sat beside her and held her in her arms, rocking her gently and rubbing her shoulder softly. "I'm so, so sorry."

After some minutes, the young woman's crying subsided.

"So that's why you escaped. Right? So they wouldn't harm your child?"

"Not right away."

"But you lost your child on your journey to Oosa."

"No. I lost my *third* child on my journey."

"Your *third?*"

"Yes."

Mara filled Nina's glass and handed it to her, urging her to drink. "Tell me of your first child. Was it a boy or a girl?"

"Oh," Nina cried, "I had a beautiful boy! A boy I'd recognize to this day if I saw him, and I hope one day that I will. It doesn't matter that his father was a beast. He's my flesh and blood."

"How would you recognize him?"

"By his birthmark."

"Oh?"

Nina smiled and closed her eyes for a moment, bringing back the memory. "He had a birthmark on his left temple. Right here," she said as she pointed to the place on her face. "It was only about this big," she made a circle with her thumb and pointer finger, "except that it wasn't exactly round. I'd recognize my boy by that sign in a heartbeat. Anytime. Anywhere."

"So they took him away," Mara said after a moment of silence.

Nina cleared her throat. "Yes. About a year and a half later, I became pregnant again. I was so afraid. I started making plans to escape, but . . . it was not to be."

"You bore your second child?"

"A beautiful baby girl." The young woman's body shook. "She was just minutes old. The guards . . . slaughtered her." She gulped back tears.

"The midwife told me it was my own fault for having had a girl and that the next time, if I wanted to see my child survive, I'd best bear a son."

Nina was quiet for a minute, lost in her thoughts. "A year or so passed," she finally said.

"And then?"

She took another taste of her wine. "Shortly before I became pregnant for the third time, I was chosen to attend a special event in honor of some of Zarek's prized soldiers." She closed her eyes and lost herself in her story.

The house matron called out the names of those who would attend the evening's event for the emperor and his men, a dinner to celebrate Zarek's latest success in battle and to honor his warriors. She'd already chosen several women. Nina dreaded the prospect of hearing her own name called.

The matron was an elderly buxom woman with a sadistic streak. In charge of the house in which the slave women lived, she saw to their basic needs. In exchange, she expected no grumbling, and no trouble. The slaves knew the price for misbehaving: death. Their fear kept them docile.

"Tamara!" she called.

A young woman of exquisite beauty stepped forward. Her smoldering black eyes maintained their blank expression. Dressed in the standard robe that was all any of the women had to wear when not working an event or called for by one of Zarek's men, she was regal, notwithstanding her surroundings.

"Nina!"

She made her way to the fore. The matron told the women it was a great honor when someone specifically requested them, but Nina found no glory in being a whore to the emperor and his vile henchmen. She hid her disdain.

"Mandy!" the matron shouted.

A young woman stepped forward.

"That will be all."

As those not chosen filed out of the room, the matron turned to the dozen women before her. She looked them over, walking from one end of the line to the other.

Satisfied, she gave her instructions. Her assistants would take them to be bathed, and for hair and makeup, then would provide them gowns for the evening. "Any questions?" she asked as she ran her finger over her light mustache.

No one moved.

"In that case, you are dismissed."

As the afternoon wore on, assistants processed the women. The matron had selected a gown of exquisite bright blue silk for Nina who thought the dress must be beautiful, but she could no longer see it as such. To her, it was nothing more than a visual representation of the chains, the bonds, that held her to a life of slavery.

When it was her turn, she approached the makeup station to which the matron directed her. Before her, on a dark wooden table, sat a tray of eye shadows, rouge, and lipstick, and on the wall, a mirror.

She gazed at her reflection. Looking back was the empty shell of a person. Her looks had changed. Once her countenance had held signs of life and interest, but no longer.

The face of the young woman who was to assist her came into the mirror.

Nina froze. "Erin!" she gasped.

The assistant looked at her with pure disdain. "And you would be?"

"Erin, it's me, Nina."

"I know no one by that name."

Nina was shocked. She turned back to the mirror. Her own sister wouldn't even acknowledge her. Tears welled in her eyes, but she dared not cry. The matron wanted the women to be beautiful. Red and puffy eyes would never do.

"It's not what you think."

Erin refused to look her sister in the eye, either directly or in the mirror. She selected the product she intended to use.

"Erin," Nina tried again, "I'm so glad to see you. I've thought of you so many times and have worried for you."

"I said I don't know you."

Though hurt and angry, Nina held her tongue.

When Erin completed her task, she turned away. "You're free to go."

Nina stood, then grasped her sister's arm. She tried to get away, but Nina held fast, pulling her forward.

"Oh, I see how it is," she seethed. "You're a slave to the great emperor's house and have no say in what your superiors demand of you, but you think, while you prepare his whores for his bidding, that you bear no moral responsibility for your actions, whereas I am to be held accountable for mine. You may not have to lie down for those dogs, but you're every bit as much a whore as I am. You do what you must to survive, as do I. Don't think for one minute that if they demanded you do as they've forced me, you wouldn't do the same as I have. You sicken me."

She loosed her sister's arm roughly, then marched from the room.

She saw Erin several more times over the next months, but whenever it seemed she might be called to her table, she changed places in the line up. After avoiding her sister for some time, Nina was unable to do so one evening. She approached the station and sat down, ignoring Erin's presence as best she could.

Erin's hands trembled. "I am so sorry," she whispered. "I had no right to say those hurtful things."

Nina looked up. She fluttered her eyes in an effort to hold back her tears, then smiled weakly. "I'm sorry too. I love you, my sister."

After that night, the two talked whenever they could. They filled one another in on the details of their lives as Zarek's slaves. While they dared not let others know of their relationship to one another, they each took comfort in the presence of the other. Eventually they spoke of the possibility of escape.

Erin's work with the slave women was just one of her many duties. During the daytime she ran one of the emperor's private kitchens. The position required that she prepare orders for food, kitchen utensils, linens, decorations, and other assorted goods. Non-slaves oversaw all of her work.

It would be difficult to collect items on the sly or to order shipments not deemed reasonable. Still, a plan slowly took shape. She would order product from select vendors whose enterprises were located well outside of Fallique. When a delivery from one of them was due in, and if Nina was to attend that evening's event, they would steal away with the departing vendor.

Erin stole three long blades that they could hide in their skirts while making their escape. Also, on the sly, she rummaged through items palace visitors threw away, eventually piecing together sufficient clothing for her sister.

Meanwhile, Nina became adept at lifting coins and jewelry that the men thoughtlessly laid about. Whenever possible, she left them with Erin. She'd place them in her sandals, then pass them on when getting a pedicure.

Then one day, a problem arose: Nina's third pregnancy. For the first few months, she successfully kept it hidden. As she entered her second trimester, she urged her sister to move up the expected date. Erin added more items to her request list—items that only one of her select vendors could deliver.

Just when Nina had lost all hope, as the authorities had sent her away for the remainder of her pregnancy, the matron called on her to serve at an event. One of Zarek's men preferred his women in her condition. Now, well into her sixth month, she could claim she was ill, but she dared not let the opportunity to escape pass her by.

On the day of the event, Nina made her way to her sister's table without raising suspicions. The Good One must be looking out for them, Erin said, for a vendor was due that very afternoon. She directed Nina to feign illness, then to go to the medical area reserved for the women. Erin would follow as soon as possible.

Nina found the clothing her sister had hidden for her—clothing that only a free woman would wear—in a hamper. She changed quickly.

Erin collected the coins and stolen jewelry she kept in an old flour bag in the back of a cupboard, then found Nina.

Together, they made their way to the kitchen.

The vendor was unloading his goods. Erin spoke to him and while she diverted his attention, directed her sister into his wagon.

Nina climbed up. She made her way to the back, found a crawl space behind some wooden boxes, and sat.

Erin offered the vendor the bag she placed in his hand to take her away from the palace. She didn't mention her sister's presence.

The bag jingled as he peeked inside. He agreed to the plan, then dropped the purse into a hole in the canvas covering the back of the wagon.

"Krippet!" someone called out.

Nina stiffened. The voice was very near.

"Is there a problem here?"

"Oh, no sir, no problem," the vendor responded.

"Is this slave bothering you?"

"No, sir. Not at all, sir. She was merely thanking me for the fine product I delivered."

Nina placed a hand over her mouth, closed her eyes tightly, and held her breath.

"Very well," the guard said. "Woman!" he then shouted.

Nina flinched.

"Off you go!" he ordered.

Tears welled in Nina's eyes as she imagined her sister returning to the kitchen.

Footsteps approached the back of the wagon. "Let me help you with those last crates."

Nina wanted to shout, she wanted to cry, but she dared not let so much as a squeak escape her lips. She feared her life was forfeit. Her hands shook. She thought she might choke, it was so hard to breathe. She willed herself to listen for more.

"Not for delivery?"

"No, thank you, sir," Krippet said. "The rest is for delivery in Mansk."

"Mansk, you say?"

"Just down the road an hour or so south."

"Make your way out quickly then," the guard ordered as he walked away. Then, just as Nina was about to take a breath, his footsteps pivoted back toward the wagon. "And next time, don't let me catch you loitering or chatting it up with any of the slaves again. You got that?"

"Right, sir. Absolutely, sir. I understand, sir."

"Be off then!"

After what seemed an eternity, the cart moved forward.

Nina's hands flew from her face as she gasped for air. Shaking, she opened her eyes. There, just inches away, sat the bag of riches she'd pilfered.

She knew then what she must do.

CHAPTER TWELVE

Rain fell, pit, pat, drip, drop. Guests ran inside as it grew heavier. The flash of far off lightning momentarily shone through the window, then abruptly died away.

"So Erin didn't make it?"

Nina shook her head. A tear fell down her check. "No. I had to get away for the sake of my child, so I went without her—and I'll never be able to forgive myself for that."

Mara shook her head. "It's not your fault."

"I guess it doesn't matter much. I escaped, then lost my child anyway."

"You did the right thing. You sought your freedom—and you got it."

"All right."

"No, I mean it. *You* have a purpose—with *me* now. With *us*. Reigna and Eden need you."

Nina pulled herself up from the softness of the goose down bed and made her way to the window. She pulled the curtain aside and peeked out. The rain came down in a torrent.

"I had no use for the jewels, so I left them, but I took about half the coins, leaving the others for Krippet," she said. "I reasoned that if he should return to Zarek's palace with another load on another day, and if Erin could steal away with him, he still would have been paid handsomely for his help. If not, he was certainly well paid for mine."

She dropped the curtain and turned back. "I knew he was headed toward Mansk. At least that was nearer the border with Oosa, not further inward. I thought he might get curious when he was far enough from the palace to see what the purse held, so I wrapped the remaining coins up tightly, moved to the back of the wagon, and awaited a good time to make my escape."

Reigna started to fuss. Nina lifted the infant and breathed in deeply of her heady fragrance. It was a complicated, consuming scent.

"When the wagon slowed sufficiently, I meant to jump," she said as she sat back down, "but I was six months pregnant. I couldn't jump far or run terribly fast. Some time later, Krippet stopped at a small inn in Mansk. When I heard him making his way down, I quickly made my escape. I don't believe he ever saw me, and I never looked back."

"You must have been very frightened."

"Actually, 'petrified' would be a more accurate word." The young woman smiled tenuously. "There isn't much else. I used the coins for a change of clothing and foodstuffs, then purchased rides on carts moving through the countryside when I could. As I got closer to the border of Oosa, I discovered more soldiers, so I hiked the remaining distance, keeping hidden. My journey took me nearly six weeks."

She cuddled Reigna closely. The infant buried her face into her breast, communicating her hunger, which Nina was ready and able to assuage.

"As you know, the Nix River and mountain range border parts of Chiran and Oosa. It was just after I crossed the mountains, on the last leg of my journey, that I lost my child."

"I'm so sorry."

"Stillborn." Nina looked away. "She was stillborn."

A flash of lightning peeked through the curtains. Thunder now mingled with it, rather than following several heartbeats behind.

Neither of the women spoke for several minutes.

Mara stood and stretched, then took in a deep cleansing breath. She cocked her head. "What is that?"

"What?"

"That . . . smell." The Oathtaker's brow furrowed.

"I don't smell anything."

"Can't you smell that?" Mara sniffed. The scent grew stronger by the moment.

"What does it smell like?"

"I don't know. I guess it smells like . . . hmmm . . . it smells like—purple."

"*Purple?*"

"Yes, purple."

"What exactly does purple smell like? Grapes? Eggplant?" Nina smirked.

Mara scowled. Then she touched her lip with the tip of her tongue. "I can taste it too."

"You can taste purple."

"Yes."

"Really. What does it taste like?"

"Ahhhh . . . Well, I don't know how to describe it."

"Wine? Plums?"

"Stop it, I'm serious."

"All right. So what does it taste like?"

"I don't know. It tastes . . . rich. Yes, that's it. It tastes *rich*. That's the only way to describe it."

Nina shook her head. "Mara, I think you need some rest."

"Maybe." The Oathtaker walked around the room, then toward the door. Whispering now, she said, "Come here."

The bed squeaked. Nina approached.

"There. Smell that?"

The young woman sniffed a few times, then inhaled deeply. "I don't smell anything. What do you think it is?"

Mara drew closer to the door, then turned back. "It's just as I said—I smell purple."

Nina giggled. "Mmhmmm, I know. But it makes no more sense this time than the last time you said it."

"No, listen, it's true. And I smell and taste yellow too. It's very faint . . . it's not nearly as strong as the purple."

"Really, what are you talking about?"

Mara's expression turned serious. "I know it sounds ridiculous, but it's true."

"What does the yellow taste like? Banana? Lemon?"

"No, it's more like . . . light." The Oathtaker's head shot up. She looked toward the door, then back to her companion. "Remember that woman sitting at the table near us at dinner?"

"Yeeesss."

"She was wearing purple and yellow. The others with her were dressed in blue."

"Yeeesss."

"I smell blue as well."

Nina's eyes opened wide. "Mara—"

"Look, I'm not making this up. The blue tastes like . . . I don't know. Fresh air?"

Nina burst into quiet laughter. "I could have guessed that. Gosh, Mara, what do you think 'brown' tastes like? Dirt? Or perhaps—"

"Don't say it," Mara warned.

Nina giggled.

In spite of her frustration, the Oathtaker grinned. "I was hoping maybe—chocolate."

Nina laughed.

"And there's something else. It's a delicate scent. It's not a color."

"Maybe it is chocolate. Or 'brown,' I mean."

"Stop it. I'm serious. You know that woman at dinner? She kept looking at me. That's why I suggested we rush."

"But people do not smell color. And they don't taste it either."

"Well maybe Oathtakers do!" Mara growled in response.

Nina looked deeply into her eyes. "You really are serious."

"Of course I am."

"All right. So what does it mean?"

"I don't know. Oh, gracious Ehyeh, I wish Dixon was here. There's just too much I don't know, and I really could use his help."

"Here." Nina directed Mara to a chair, then sat next to her. "So, let's say it's true."

"It is true."

"All right, it's true. What does it mean?"

"It means the woman and the two young men who sat at the table near us at dinner are standing outside our door, that's what it means. And I don't know if they are friend or foe."

"All right then, let's think about this. What's the worst case scenario?"

"I take them out, I guess."

"Can you do that?"

"If I must."

"What do I do?"

"Stay here. I'm going to open the door. If they're there, I'll surprise them. If not—"

"What'll you do to surprise them?"

Mara grasped Spira, confirming it was in its sheath and was loose should she have need to use it; an Oathtaker's blade was an extraordinary weapon, not to be used lightly. Grabbing her pack, she found the blade she'd purchased in Polesk. Her fingers ran over its stunning scrimshaw.

"All right, I'm ready."

"Stop. What about me?"

"Put the girls down there," Mara pointed to the floor in the back corner, "and then arm yourself."

"I don't know if I can do this."

"You can. If it's you or them, you can. If it's the girls or them, you most certainly can."

"All right." Nina placed a blanket on the floor, then gently laid the twins on it. Then she pulled the blade Mara had given her after their escape from Polesk out from the place where she kept it hidden inside her boot. She held it tightly.

"You know how to use that thing?" Mara asked, her brow arched, as she watched her move the knife around in her hand.

Nina grimaced. "Stick it in the bad guy?"

The Oathtaker's eyes lit up with her smile. "That's right. Just make sure you use the right end."

"I think I've got it. Pointy end in. Right. Now, go!"

In spite of the possibility of danger, Mara chuckled. She held her knife in her left hand. Then she made her way to the door, walking lightly on the balls of her feet, and yanked it open. In a flash, she stepped back, crouched, and reached for Spira.

At the door stood the woman in purple and yellow. Flanking her each side, stood the two young men dressed in blue.

The woman's mouth opened wide in surprise. She stepped back. "You won't be needing your blade, Oathtaker."

Mara squinted. "Oh?"

She nodded. "You can put it away now."

"Is that right?" Mara grasped Spira more firmly.

"If I may." Slowly, she moved her hair behind her ear. Then she turned to the side revealing that she bore a sign of the Select—a third. She looked back at Mara.

"Who *are* you?" the Oathtaker asked as she rose.

"My name is Therese."

"Therese, you say?"

"Yes, that's right."

Mara's guest, moving with extraordinary grace, took a single step inside. Her dark mink brown hair was burnished with highlights of copper. Her skin, creamy with a hint of rose, was flawless, but for a small jagged scar across her forehead. She stood with her hands loose at her sides, exhibiting no fear.

Mara could still smell and taste, faintly, the colors purple, yellow, and blue. The lingering scents reminded her of cooking smells left hanging in a kitchen hours after a meal had been prepared therein. As they dissipated, she made out another— it was the one she'd earlier identified as delicate. It was a soft combination of water lily, apricot, amber, apple, guava, mandarin, wild tuberose, vanilla, tiare flowers and—yes, very vaguely—dark chocolate. It was the woman's scent of the Select.

In a glance, Therese's eyes took in the details of the room.

Again, Mara noticed something vaguely familiar about her.

The two young men remained at Therese's sides. They might at first glance have been mistaken for twins, due to their similar size and coloring. On closer examination, their features actually shared little in common.

The woman gestured to her right. "This is Jules."

He nodded. His sandy blond hair was cut short around his ears and was squared off at his neck. He sported a square jaw, a broad nose, and eyes the green of a peacock feather.

"And this is Samuel." She nodded to her left.

Samuel's deep brown eyes were flecked with gold. Like Jules, he wore his hair clipped short. His muscles tense, his jaw set, he nodded at Mara, then at Nina.

"What can I do for you, Therese?"

"I wondered if I might speak with you."

Mara hesitated. Meeting the woman's gaze, she said, "Go on, then."

"Jules, Samuel, I'll find you back at our rooms shortly. I think this young woman may feel more at ease without you in attendance, and I'm perfectly safe with her."

After a moment's hesitation, they left. Therese closed the door behind them, then turned back.

Mara gestured toward a chair. "May I interest you in a glass of wine?"

"Thank you, no. Not just now."

"So . . . you'd like to speak with me?"

"Yes."

"What's on your mind then?" Mara didn't intend to be impolite, but the woman made her uncomfortable.

"I noticed you and your companion," Therese said as she looked toward Nina, "and the infants," she continued as her eyes shifted toward the girls, "in the dining room this evening."

"Yes?"

She sat forward, elbows on the table, touching together the tips of her fingers. She tilted her head to the side. "I thought you might be a trained Oathtaker when I noticed how carefully you surveyed the room—how aware of everyone you seemed."

"Yes?"

"And," she hesitated, "I noticed your reaction to the news of Dixon Townsend." She leaned in. "Tell me. How is he?"

A knock came at the door. The chambermaid inquired whether there was anything further they would require for the evening.

"Would you mind asking for a fresh pot of tea?" Mara asked Nina.

"Not at all." Nina spoke with the maid. "It'll be sent over directly," she then said as she resumed her place on the edge of the bed.

"And your name is?" Therese asked Mara. "And hers?" she gestured toward Nina. "And the infants' names?"

"It seems to me, Therese, that your seeking me out is rather unusual. I understand you are Select, and you've rightly identified me as an Oathtaker, so you're aware I'm no threat to you. But that doesn't mean that I can trust you—or that I do trust you."

Mara placed her hands on the arms of her chair. "So, before I answer any of your questions, I have a few of my own."

"Fair enough."

"You say your name is 'Therese.'"

"That's right."

A sudden recollection of a dream from the night before startled Mara. It had seemed so real—the darkness of a woods, the mist from a waterfall, a skittering hare, hushed voices she could just make out from what felt like a hiding place behind a nearby tree, the almost tangible feel of danger. She'd thought little of it when she'd awakened. But now she closed her eyes for a moment, drawing forth the details. Then she looked back at her visitor.

"Tell me, Therese, where is your Oathtaker? I take it you are not the charge of either Jules or Samuel. They are bodyguards. Yes? Not Oathtakers."

She fidgeted.

"No, wait, I'll tell you," Mara continued as she held her hand up, palm out. "Basha is your Oathtaker," she whispered. "Currently she is at the palace in Shimeron, and she believes you to be dead."

Therese's mouth dropped open. She closed it, then pursed her lips.

"Rowena is—that is she *was*—your sister. You rather look like her, actually."

Therese said nothing.

"How am I doing so far?"

"How do you know these things?"

Mara held her hand up again. "Stop. First, would you care to explain why you'd leave Basha in the dark like this?"

Nina rose as the attendant called out that their order had arrived. She took the tray, closed the door, and then set the tea and fixings on the table. Then she poured three cups. The apple-like scent of chamomile filled the air. She gestured toward Therese, inviting the woman to help herself to the small cakes.

"It's a long story," Therese finally said.

"Yes, I imagine it is."

"How do you— How do you know about Basha?"

The Oathtaker shrugged. "Let's just say I have my sources. If your story rings true to what I know, then perhaps I can answer some of your questions."

If her dream had been true in the details Therese had just confirmed, then perhaps it was true in other respects as well. It had been so vivid, so real. It was less like Mara had summoned the thoughts while sleeping, and more like she'd physically experienced the place and events.

Therese tasted her tea, then added a spoonful of sugar. She stirred it in slowly. Tasting again, she nodded her approval.

"Well, you know some of the story. I'm Therese, a third. My Oathtaker was— I mean *is*—Basha." Her eyes locked on Mara's. "I miss her. She's been more than merely Oathtaker to me. She's family, sister, friend. I want to be with her, but . . . I can't just now."

"And why is that?" Mara blew gently on her tea to speed its cooling, watching her visitor over the edge of her cup.

"It's a long story, and a bit complicated."

The Oathtaker placed her cup back on its saucer. "I've got time." When Reigna stirred, she picked her up and placed her in Nina's arms. She never took her eyes from Therese.

"Is that your child?"

"No. No. No." Mara held her finger up, moving it back and forth with each word she spoke. "No questions from you as yet. I've given you the rules of our engagement. If you want answers from me, I'll first require answers from you."

"Sorry."

"So, you were saying?"

"It's a long story, but it really comes down to this: someone tried to kill me. The arrow didn't hit me, but it did cause me to fall from a cliff. When I landed, I must have hit my head on something. For a long while I didn't even know my own name." Therese closed her eyes, apparently calling forth her memories.

"I was washed a long way down a river and was later found by some kind people who nursed me back to health. When my memory returned, I wanted to go home—to the palace at Shimeron."

"But you didn't."

"No."

"Why?"

"Many among the people I met were Oathtakers. When they found me, they feared I'd been the target of an assassination attempt. They begged me to allow them to investigate the facts quietly. Together we worked to get people placed strategically in and around the palace in an effort to learn as much as we could."

"How dreadful," Nina said.

"Yes," Mara agreed. "Then what?"

"Some time passed. Eventually we learned that my sister, Rowena, and her Oathtaker, Dixon Townsend, left the palace. The popular story was that Rowena feared someone there."

"Anything else?"

"No, but we believed the stories that my sister was in danger, were true. The first family—my family—thought me dead. In the end, it seemed that whether Rowena had reason to fear someone at the palace or not, I was safer from the reach of an assassin if the story of my death remained. So as much as I miss Basha and my home, I took what seemed the most reasonable action and stayed away."

"That's all in keeping with what I've heard."

"May I ask where you got your information?" Therese asked. "You see, if you know about me, then I have to assume that I'm not as safe as I'd thought."

Her question was fair enough, but Mara wasn't ready to concede any information. "Well for now, I'll tell you that the source of my information doesn't know you still live. You're in no greater danger than you believed yourself to be in before I told you what I know."

Therese looked carefully at Mara, a question in her eyes. Stifling it, she resumed her story.

"As I said, some Oathtakers, and members of the Select, helped me. I learned they'd been working for a long while with Rowena, secretly, to prepare a safe place for her and the child she was expecting. But now, with the news of her death . . . Well, it looks as though their efforts were in vain." She sighed. "What a terrible, terrible loss."

"Is that why you asked after Dixon? Do you think him responsible for Rowena's death?"

"Oh no, it's not possible."

"What's not possible?"

"Dixon would never ever harm Rowena. I would stake my life on that." Therese sweetened her tea. A faint *ting* rang out as she set her spoon down on the saucer.

"That's not what the fliers say. I read the various accounts, and it seems some believe he may have been behind Rowena's death."

"Impossible."

"You are so sure?"

"I'm certain." Therese tore a teacake in half, then ate one piece. "I've known Dixon for years and I have the greatest respect for him. He would have done anything for Rowena—anything to keep her safe.

"Rowena was in regular contact with us—you know, with the group I mentioned. She didn't know about me. We thought it best to keep my presence a secret from everyone, even her. But she knew we prepared a place for her.

"She was trying to rendezvous with us, but had been unable to free herself from some thugs who were dogging her trail. She didn't want to risk leading her enemies right into what we were trying to create as a safe haven for her."

"How did you manage to keep Basha from knowing your whereabouts? Wouldn't she be drawn to you through her bond to you?"

Therese nodded. "Yes, well, the place we are preparing is . . . Suffice it to say, when I was there, the bond couldn't be felt."

"But whenever you left there, it could be."

"That's right."

"And you left there from time to time over the years."

Her eyes narrowed. "Yes, that's right."

"And you've been away from there now since sometime before Rowena's death?"

"That's right."

"And Dixon. Did he know you kept in contact with Rowena, or if so, how you did?" Mara reached into her pocket and grasped the compact she kept there.

"I don't know."

"And how did you all communicate with her?" The Oathtaker's fingers traced the engraved filigree design on the compact. The cool of the silver warmed to her touch.

"I can't really say." Therese fidgeted.

"Can you tell me who is in charge of your group of friends?"

"Ahhh . . . I can't really say." She looked carefully at Mara. She cocked her head. "Why do you ask?"

Everything Therese had told her so far fit with the facts as Mara believed them to be—based on her dream. Some small gamble might pay off big rewards.

"Tell you what, Therese, you tell me the name of the person in charge of your group, and I'll tell you how you all kept in contact with Rowena."

She sat up straighter. "I don't know." She started to her feet, then sank back down in response to Mara's hand held out in an unspoken demand that she remain seated.

"It's simple really. If you can answer my question, I'll know if I can trust the rest of your story. If you can be trusted, then I agree to tell you my story."

Therese looked deeply into the Oathtaker's eyes as though trying to assess her character. "I guess it's only right then that I should turn your own question back on you: Who *are* you?"

"Answer my question correctly and you'll find out." Mara grinned. "And Therese—you won't be disappointed."

⁂

"Well, I don't know."

"It's perfectly fine by me if you should choose to say nothing further."

"It's just . . . Well . . ."

"Go on," Mara encouraged after a moment of silence.

Therese glanced Nina's way, opened her mouth as though to speak, then stopped.

Mara followed her visitor's gaze. "You may speak freely."

Therese looked embarrassed to have had her thoughts studied. "Very well then. I'll chance you would bear our group no ill will, that you would take no risks with our safety." She paused as she warmed her tea. "Our leader is Lucy," she said as a flash of lightning shone through the curtained window. Shuddering thunder followed.

Mara smiled and turned to Nina. "Would you kindly step out for just a moment?"

She stood, handed Reigna off, then exited.

Mara reached into her pocket and clasped the compact. "This is how Lucy and the rest of you stayed in contact with Rowena," she said as she pulled her hand out and opened her fist.

Therese gasped. "Where did you get that? That belongs to Rowena!"

"*Belonged* to Rowena."

"Yes! But where— How did you come to possess it?"

Mara turned the compact in her hands, admiring again the beauty of the workmanship of the object. She returned it to her pocket. "I'd like to invite Nina to return. I only sent her out so that I could respond to your question."

"She doesn't know about it then?"

"No. It seemed best to keep this particular detail to myself—at least for now."

"How did you come by it? It's a most crucial, most secretive, most powerful item!"

"I'm aware of that."

"You've used it?"

"Yes."

"And . . . you've spoken with Lucy?"

"Yes."

"Again I ask, 'who *are* you?'"

"I'm Mara. I'm Oathtaker to this child and also to the other lying just there." She nodded toward Eden.

Therese looked at the infant. "Two charges? I've never heard of such a thing. And pray tell, who are these children?"

Mara took hold of the blanket swaddled around Reigna, then lifted away the portion covering her face.

"Therese," she said as she bowed first at Reigna, then at her visitor, "I would like you to meet your niece, Rowena's daughter, a seventh seventh, Reigna."

Her mouth dropped open. "Rowena's daugh— My niece! Oh!"

"But there's more."

"More?"

"Yes. You see, I also need to introduce you to another." Mara placed Reigna on the bed, then crouched down for Eden.

"Therese," she said as she moved the blanket from the child's face, "I'd also like to introduce you to another of your nieces, Eden. She is also Rowena's daughter and—and don't ask me what to call her!"

"I . . . I . . ." Therese stuttered. Her eyes darted from one of the children to the other.

"You seem to be at a loss for words."

"Why," she gasped, "I am!" She held her hand to her throat. "When I heard the news of Rowena's death, I guess I just assumed the child hadn't survived. Oh, but this is wonderful! *Two* babies. How is that even possible? Does Lucy know? How'd you get the compact? Did Rowena tell you of it? How well did you know her? Where did you meet her? When—"

"Stop!" Mara held her hand out. "I told you I'd fill you in, and I will. For now, let's just agree to say nothing further of our means of communicating with Lucy."

"Yes, of course."

"Fine. I'll have Nina return. Then I'll tell you my story—that is, the girls' story."

The Oathtaker invited Nina back into the room, then resumed her seat.

"Oh, they both are so beautiful!" Therese exclaimed.

"Would you like to hold them?"

Her eyes glossed with unshed tears. "Oh, may I?"

Mara placed Reigna in her aunt's arms.

Therese touched and petted the child. She inhaled deeply of her fragrance.

Mara then placed Eden in her other arm.

"They are both so lovely!"

"Yes."

"Oh, what I wouldn't do for these little ones! You have my word, Mara, I would do anything to protect them." Therese looked adoringly at the twins. "I swear, I would . . . I would die to protect these girls!"

Just as her words were spoken, the ground shook. The windows rattled and the lamplight flickered.

Her eyes opened wide. "What was that?"

"Well," Mara chuckled, "if I hadn't trusted you before, I would know I could trust you now. You've just taken an oath to protect them."

Therese's brow furrowed. "Of course I meant it, but—"

"But you're no Oathtaker, is that what you were going to say?" Nina asked.

She shot a look her way. "Exactly."

"I'm not either. Yet the Good One accepted my oath, just as he accepted yours."

Therese eyed Nina carefully, as though trying to discern the truthfulness of her words. "I've never heard of such a thing."

"Nor have I," Mara said. "But rest assured, you just witnessed the Good One's acceptance of your oath."

"I don't understand."

"Neither do I." Mara smiled. "But Reigna and Eden are gathering quite a little army of protectors."

"Who?"

"Well, I'm their official Oathtaker, but two others also have sworn their loyalty, and both experienced the same acceptance. Dixon, and Nina here."

Therese stared. "I don't know what to say. I've never heard of such a—"

"Yes, well, that's the truth of it."

"Tell me more. How long did you know Rowena? Where did you meet her? How did you come to be Oathtaker to the girls?"

"So many questions. Have you time for the whole story?"

"Certainly."

"Very well then." Mara began her story with the day she'd come upon Rowena in the wayfarers' hut. She told of her battle with the grut and of Rowena's last moments. Therese held the girls more closely as the story progressed.

Before long, Reigna let out a healthy wail. When Nina reached for Reigna to feed her, Therese reluctantly released her hold.

As Nina nursed the infant, Therese's eyes held a question.

"We found Nina in Polesk," Mara said. "Dixon and I headed there as quickly as possible after your sister died. The Good One chose me as the girls' Oathtaker, but he didn't provide me with the means to feed them." She laughed. "What is it they say? 'The Good One provides every bird his food, but He doesn't throw it into the nest?'"

"And that ended up being my blessing," Nina said.

Mara continued her story. As the rain abated, she told of how she and Nina had left Polesk.

Therese interrupted. "Who was the woman?"

"I didn't know then, but I think I know now. I believe it was your sister, Lilith."

"Hmmm. Did you believe yourself to be in danger?"

"Me? No. Reigna and Eden? Most definitely. My attendant magic seems to include some sort of powers relating to my dreams, and it's because of things learned in my dreams, and the reports in the local fliers, that I suspect her."

"How so?" Therese asked.

"I'd say the things I dream are very . . . real. In some cases, such as when the woman who I believe was Lilith came to Polesk, they seem to be visions of things to come. Other times . . . Well, it's almost as though I'm present in the same moment in which the events happen."

"Physically present, you mean?"

"It feels like it."

"Have you tested it?"

Mara was taken aback by the question. "What do you mean?"

"Just that I've heard of many different types of attendant magic. I've even studied some of the best writings on the subject in the official sanctuary library in the City of Light. You shouldn't be afraid to test the limits of your powers. They were given you for a reason—to use."

"I'll give that some thought."

"So then what happened? After you left Polesk?"

By the time Mara completed her story, Reigna and Eden were both satiated and asleep, and the storm had moved on.

"And that is everything," she concluded.

A knock came at the door.

"Who's there?" she asked.

"Samuel and Jules."

Therese handed Reigna back to Nina's waiting arms. She went to the door and stood there silently, then turned back to embrace Mara.

"Thank you. I am ever so grateful. I'm sorry Rowena didn't make it to a safe place, but I'd like to help you to see to the girls' safety. May I return tomorrow to discuss this with you further?"

"That would be good. We'd expected Dixon and I'd hoped he'd help walk me through these early days, but . . ."

"So you and Dixon made fast friends, huh?"

The Oathtaker shook her head slowly. "I wouldn't say 'fast friends,' exactly."
"Oh?"
Mara chuckled. "We had a rocky start. But we came to an understanding."
Therese grinned. "I'll be back then, come morning."

Chapter Thirteen

Nina, with the twins cradled near her, slept. She breathed softly. The smell of the last of the burning beeswax candles that Mara had just blown out, infused the still air with the sweet smell of honey and smoke. Slowly, the orange glow at the tip of the candlewick died away.

She laid her head back onto her goose down pillow. The richness of the bedding was not lost on her, particularly since she'd had so little sleep over the past days.

Spira sat on the bedside table just inches from her hand. With the door locked and a chair wedged beneath the doorknob, she felt fairly secure. She knew, above all, that she needed rest.

She had so many questions and felt such uncertainty. Her charge was utterly unique. Every Oathtaker's charge was important, that was true, but to have two, and for them both to be so very needy, was unprecedented.

The evening was remarkably quiet. The occasional raindrop, cradled in the leafy treetops, fell.

Mara closed her eyes. She willed herself to relax, first her neck, her face, and her brows. Then came her shoulders, arms, wrists, and fingers. Concentrating on breathing in and out, slowly and steadily, she felt her body slacken, her mind loosen up.

Colors began to prance and shimmer before her eyes, lazily changing hue, modifying and altering in intensity. Now and then she caught a whiff of one of them—now yellow, now mint, now indigo, now . . .

A moving picture took shape. The colors coalesced and melded into forms and shapes. With relaxed concentration, the Oathtaker sharpened her focus. Slowly the swirl of tint and hue, shade and tone, became a solid scene before her.

She found herself on the floor of a small room with walls of burnt orange. Sheer curtains covered its single window. No light came in, confirming that nighttime was underway. Three iron bars ran vertically from the window top to its sill.

There was a single small bed covered with a loosely knit blanket of muted earth tones. A rag rug lay on the floor. To Mara's right stood a three-paneled room divider. Over the top of it hung articles of men's clothing.

A lamp sat at a nearby table, its flame flickering sporadically. It shed inconsistent patterns of light, then shadow, around the room. On the wall near the door was a sconce, its candle unlit.

Mara got up. She looked around for anything by which she might identify her whereabouts. Hearing the shuffle of feet at the door, the springing whine as the handle turned, she quietly stepped behind the divider and then peeked through an opening between its sections. The door opened.

". . . to go in the morning," came a voice from outside the room as a man entered.

There was something familiar about his silhouette, but the light was insufficient and the subject too far away for Mara to identify him.

The door closed from the outside, following which came the sound of a key turning.

Am I asleep? Or awake? she wondered.

The man reached up toward the wall sconce and fumbled with a flint to light the candle. He turned her way.

"Dear Good One!" she gasped.

He crouched instantly in preparation of defending himself.

She stepped out from behind the divider, one hand at her throat, the other held up, palm out. "Dixon!"

His brow furrowed. "How did you get in here?" he whispered.

"I'm not exactly sure that I am here."

"What are you talking about? You're standing right in front of me."

"Are you sure? Really, I don't know." She held her head in her hands. "Gracious, I'm so confused!"

"Shhh." He held his finger to his lips.

Sounds of shuffling came from outside the door, then a solid knock. "Is everything all right in there?" came the same gruff voice that had sounded out earlier.

"Yes, all is well. I just . . . stubbed my toe." Dixon turned to Mara and whispered, "Keep your voice down."

Now it was her turn to scowl. "What's going on?"

His eyes opened wide. "You show up unexpectedly in my room and ask me what's going on? And the girls, entrusted to your safety, are nowhere to be seen? Huh! Now, I'm confused!"

He sat at the table and directed with a wave of his hand for her to sit next to him. He tapped the tabletop with his flint—once, twice, thrice.

She gazed around the room. "Where am I?" She hesitated. "Am I asleep? Or awake?"

A grin spread from his lips to his eyes. "If you don't beat all."

The mood was contagious. She smirked, then reached across the table and placed her hand atop his. "Can you feel that?"

Head again shaking, his smile now brought unto submission, he grew serious. "All right, what's going on? How'd you get here? And what do you mean, 'can I feel that?'"

"I'm sleeping."

He stared. "Great Ehyeh, now I've heard everything."

"No, it's true. Nina and I left Polesk like you said. We reached Settleton late today. We spent the evening learning some . . . interesting things. Now we're down for the night."

He stood. "I hate to break it to you, but you're here with me at the palace. They've—that is, Lilith—moved me from my original chambers and had me placed in this," he motioned around the room, "servant's room. I'm under house arrest. I can't go anywhere without an escort. No one can enter my room without the guard's permission. Yet you show up. What am I to make of this?"

She approached. She placed her hand on his upper arm. For the span of a breath, the feel of his strength distracted her.

His eyes dropped to her hand, acknowledging its presence.

"You really can feel that?" she asked.

He reached out and pinched her upper arm. "Can you feel that?" he snorted.

"Ouch!"

"Well, what a ridiculous question!"

"You don't understand, Dixon. I really am asleep. Or, at least I think I am . . . Only this feels so real!"

She rubbed the spot where he'd pinched her. "Remember when I told you about my dream at sanctuary in Polesk—that some woman would try to take the girls away from me there?"

"Yes, Lilith."

"So it was Lilith then."

"Yes," he said, "go on."

"Well, it seems there's another dimension to this attendant power."

"What's that?"

"I believe I'm moving from place to place in my dreams. Or, that is, I think I've done so."

"I don't know. I've never heard of such a thing."

She sat down. "Listen, I know it sounds ridiculous, but I think I can prove it. I'm not really here. Or maybe I am really here, but I'm also at an inn in Settleton, with Nina at my side, the babies cradled in her arms. Or maybe I'm here and I'm not also at an inn in Settleton—in which case, for the moment at least, the girls are without an Oathtaker's protection." Her brow furrowed.

Dixon resumed his seat. "I may be ready to believe just about anything because I can't think of any other way you could have made it into this room. What do you mean when you say you think you can prove it?"

She traced a design with her finger on the tabletop. "I believe you met with a woman named 'Basha' last night—here in Shimeron."

He sat up straighter, gesturing with his hands, urging her on with her story.

"Basha is Therese's Oathtaker. I listened in on your conversation from the place where my dreams took me."

He raised his brow.

"I wasn't eavesdropping or anything—at least not intentionally. I was just . . . there."

"Was," he said. Then reading the question in her eyes, he continued, "Basha *was* Therese's Oathtaker."

"No, Dixon, *is*. Basha *is* Therese's Oathtaker."

He studied Mara's expression. "If you heard our conversation, then you know Basha questions whether Therese lives. But I've thought about it. Surely you don't think it would make any sense for her to avoid her Oathtaker."

Mara tilted her head slowly right, then left. "I wouldn't say she's 'avoiding' her, exactly."

"What do you know about this?"

"I've met Therese."

Dixon's jaw dropped. "Really and truly? She lives?"

"Really and truly."

"Where?"

"At the inn here in Settleton. That is, I met her here in Settleton. Or is it . . . *there* in Settleton?" She shook her head. "This is all so confusing. Am I here? Or there? Or am I in two places at once? I—"

He shushed her again. "I'm not sure of the answers to your questions, but I can see and hear you in the flesh, right here and now. You may or may not also be in Settleton, asleep, I don't know. But if you're caught here . . . Well," he contemplated, "I don't know. Would you awaken in Settleton? Or here?"

She shook her head. "Stop! Dixon, I need answers, not more questions."

"One thing at a time. First, did you hear my entire conversation with Basha?"

"No. I only heard you discuss whether Therese might still live."

"How did you awaken?"

"Reigna cried."

"Oh." He hesitated. "Well, assuming you really are experiencing an attendant power and that you're here in your 'sleep,' let's not take the risk of your waking here since we don't know what would come of it."

"You really think this is real?"

He pinched her arm again.

"Ouch! Stop it, Dixon!" She slapped his hand away. Again she rubbed the spot where he'd pinched her. "Of course I feel it."

"So do I, and I'm not dreaming."

"But how can I test it? Wait! Maybe I have. Or, maybe I've begun to anyway."

"What do you mean?"

"When I met Therese, I quizzed her with facts I'd learned from your conversation with Basha. When she tested true, I revealed my identity and introduced her to the twins."

"You sure the woman you met is Therese? You think she can be trusted?"

"Absolutely. I mean, I might have wondered, but she took an oath."

He jerked his head back. "And it was confirmed?"

"The same as for you and Nina."

"Huh. Those little ones are gaining quite a following."

"Yes. And Dixon—she's been staying with Lucy."

"Lucy!"

A knock came at the door.

"Dixon!" a voice cried.

"Stop!" someone else shouted.

"What is it?" Dixon called. "I'm . . . ahhh not dressed. I'll be just a minute."

"Dixon, they won't let me in!"

"That's Basha," he whispered.

"Dixon!" she called again.

"You can't go in there!"

Mara gestured to Dixon that she would wait behind the divider while he answered the door. She stood, but as she stepped away, she suddenly felt lightheaded. She placed one hand on the table to steady herself, her fingers lighting upon his flint.

The room spun, the colors melded and fused.

She turned to Dixon. Her voice began with a whisper, then faded to nothingness so all he could make out at the end was the shape of her lips as she spoke: "Reigna wakes." Then, as mysteriously as she'd arrived, Mara vanished.

As he grasped the doorknob, he noticed the band on his wrist. *Blast! I should have thought to have her remove this!*

⚔

Mara gasped as she awakened to the sound of a baby's cries, her linens rustling beneath her.

"Is everything all right?" Nina asked.

"Yes. Why do you ask?"

"You jumped like you were startled."

"It's nothing." *What an odd dream!* She laid back, placing one hand beneath the pillow. There, she felt something unexpectedly. She grasped the object, then bolted upright. "Great Ehyeh!"

"What? What is it?"

Mara lit the lamp at her side. She waited for her eyes to adjust to the light, then stared at the item she held, her mouth gaping open.

"What is it? Are you all right?"

The Oathtaker reached toward Nina, a flint in her hand. "Have you seen this before?"

Nina took the item. She turned it over a couple of times. "No."

"It's Dixon's flint."

"So?"

Mara stared at it. "This is very odd, but I just dreamed of him."

Nina grinned. "Nice dream, huh?"

Mara felt herself blush. "No, that's not what I meant. I meant I was just in his room."

"Oh, it gets better. I've seen how you look at him."

"Stop it," Mara said, grinning good-naturedly. She sat at the edge of her bed. Nina's comments set her thinking. Was she attracted to Dixon? Was there something there? *No, of course not. And Dixon loved Rowena. Besides, I've taken an oath. End of subject.*

"So what's the problem?"

Mara went to the window and looked out.

"What's going on?" Nina prodded.

"I think I've just discovered another attendant power."

"Go on."

"It seems I can go elsewhere in my dreams. Not just in my mind, but . . . physically."

"I don't understand."

"That flint there? It's Dixon's. In my 'dream' I was with him, having a conversation that was every bit as real as the one I'm having with you now."

The Oathtaker returned to her bed and sat. She took the flint from Nina. "I took this as I was leaving there and awakening here."

"You really believe that?"

"Remember the colors?"

"Of course."

"And I was right, wasn't I? This is just more attendant magic, though I'm not sure what it's for or how to use it." She shook her head. "You know, in some ways these powers are frightening."

"Why is that?"

"Because . . . Well, take these dreams for instance. When I was with Dixon it was so real. That was when I realized this 'dream journey' wasn't the first time I'd gone elsewhere in my sleep." She told Nina about her dream of the falls and of Dixon's conversation with Basha.

Nina listened intently as she finished nursing Reigna, then handed the infant to Mara. "It seems you need to learn more about these powers. How do you think you can do that?"

"Therese said I should test them. Maybe that's what I was unconsciously doing when I took Dixon's flint. But you're right. I need to know more. Perhaps we might head to the City of Light. There are libraries full of information there."

The crisp bedding rustled beneath Nina as she laid her head down and put her arm around Eden. "Well, whatever you decide to do, I think you'd be wise to get some rest now."

"You're right. I'm sorry I awakened you."

"No, you didn't. Reigna did."

"Yes, that's right. Her cry brought me back." Mara cuddled the infant. She looked back at Nina. "Aren't you going to feed Eden now?"

The young woman groaned. "Not until she asks to be fed."

"Oh. Why wouldn't you feed them both at the same time?"

Nina pulled herself up on one elbow and opened her drowsy eyes. "Because she's not hungry. When she's hungry, she'll awaken. I'm not going to create a schedule that doesn't fit her." She put her head back down. "With any kind of luck, she'll start sleeping through the night soon." She snuggled nearer to Eden. Within moments, she was breathing steadily.

"Sleep well, Nina," Mara whispered. Then she got back into bed, snuggled Reigna, and turned out the light.

Chapter Fourteen

Candlelight flickered off the walls and mirrors of the grand bedchamber. Red damask drapery hung from ceiling to floor, shutting out all external light. Down pillows covered the canopied bed.

Lilith sat at her vanity, its mirror proclaiming her beauty. She admired herself as a young handmaiden combed her hair with a steady stroke. "Ouch!" she cried, turning around to slap the girl soundly.

"Sorry, ma'am." The maid rubbed her cheek to lighten the sting.

"You are worthless. I should have you expelled from the palace for all time."

"Sorry, ma'am."

"Just go away!"

The young woman limped off.

"Adele—"

The maid turned back. "Yes, ma'am?"

"Come."

She returned to Lilith's side.

Lilith placed her finger below the maid's chin, then tilted her head up.

Adele flinched. She'd been at the woman's mercies too many times to ignore the warning signs. Lilith could go into a rage at the slightest provocation—or at no provocation at all—and she didn't hesitate to employ her own form of "discipline."

"Look at me."

Adele raised her eyes. They sparkled with unshed tears.

"You know the rules."

"Yes, ma'am."

Lilith slapped her lightly on the cheek.

Adele closed her eyes, seemingly in anticipation of more to come.

"If I hear any rumor of what goes on in this room, I'll know you're the source."

"Yes, ma'am."

"Don't you forget it."

"No, ma'am."

"Be gone before I render the punishment you so rightly deserve for failing to attend to me to my satisfaction."

The maid turned to go.

"Adele."

She stopped in her tracks. "Yes, ma'am. Thank you, ma'am, for correcting me."

"That's better."

As the young woman left the chamber, a low chuckle came from behind the sheering-draped bed. "You sure know how to handle the help."

"Yes, I thought it best to remind her to keep her mouth shut. If she should speak of your presence here . . . But I needn't worry about that. I've warned her."

"Perhaps you should cut her tongue out." He laughed.

"Funny you should say that. That's exactly what I told her I'd do if she spoke out of turn."

"You didn't."

"I did! Rowena was too soft on them all. They need to learn their place. And can you imagine? Taking a cripple into the palace?" Lilith swung her hair back and folded her arms. "It's obscene."

He grabbed his pants from the floor. "Rowena was soft?"

"She was always preaching about how the Select were supposed to serve the masses." Lilith grimaced. "What utter bunk. It's the masses that should serve us. They need us. They need a *real* leader. They need me!"

"Well, it seems you know how to elicit the greatest loyalties from the people."

"Adele wouldn't dare say a word. Fear is the best means for instilling loyalty in those like her."

He stood behind Lilith, brushed her hair to the side, and then nuzzled at her neck. "Is that why you've placed Dixon under house arrest?"

She turned in his arms. "Exactly. Imagine him packing his bags to leave the palace. How dare he! I made it perfectly clear that I expected him to remain here. Oathtakers are intended to serve the Select and he's no exception."

She ran her finger along her guest's jaw line. "Now that I'm rid of Rowena *and* that ridiculous child, I can move forward. I'm in charge now and Dixon's trial will be the icing on the cake."

Extricating herself from her guest's embrace, she turned away. "I'd like to be alone now."

"When will I see you again?"

She pressed herself against him again. "Later tonight," she whispered, her lips flitting softly upon his. "After dinner. I need to see if Basha has been trying to visit with Dixon—though I've instructed the guards to forbid her entrance to his room."

"What's the harm? She can't remove his band. And she's not likely to make an issue of it. Had it been put there by anyone else, perhaps. But you're the ranking member now. She wouldn't challenge your authority."

"Right. Mmmm, I like the sounds of that. I am the ranking member! Things are looking up." Lilith stopped to pout. "Still, I don't trust Basha. She's behaving strangely. Why don't you see what more you can find out from Dixon?"

"My pleasure," he murmured as he indicated with a hand to her breast that he would in fact find his pleasure elsewhere.

Lilith nodded toward the door. It was time for him to leave. After some delay, he did.

She sighed, her hunger for all things physical, momentarily satiated. She sat at the vanity and turned the light down. A wisp of smoke drifted upwards.

Gazing into the mirror, she murmured softly. It was finally time to connect with her spirit guide. He would be pleased with her. Slowly she placed herself into a trance. Her eyes rolled up. Then, with a rush, her spirit moved as though transported elsewhere.

Like a blackened skull with decomposed flesh hanging, and with eyes like burning lava, a face slowly came into focus in the looking glass.

"Daeva, my guide," Lilith whispered, "nothing stands in our way now. I lead the Select!"

Fire burst forth.

Gasping, she stared at the malevolent countenance before her, stroking her cheek pained from the inferno.

Daeva sneered. "You have failed," he said, his voice heavy and thick.

"But Rowena has been removed!"

"Yesssss . . . but the child livessss."

"Ahhhhh!" she screamed, as she swept her hands across the vanity, propelling various items from its surface, to the floor.

※

"How could you have missssed the clear sign, Lilith? This newssss should come as no surprisssse to you." His voice, eerily quiet but unyielding, mocking, shook her. "You. Have. Failed. Me." With each word, he sent a jolt of pain out that racked through her being.

Her head snapped back. She fell to the floor, groaning, then stumbled back to her feet. "I don't understand! How could the child live? What sign?" She faltered. "How could I have known?"

He laughed, but there was no humor in it. "I fear I have given you too much. Promissssed you too much. Been too eeeeassssy on you. Perhapssss I should bide my time and choose another—a better woman—another day."

The air grew thick with smoke.

"I have waited too long to let you stand in my way. I cannot grant power and immortality to a failure. I cannot allow you to lead if you are inept."

Lilith struggled for air. "No, tell me! How could I have known?"

Daeva tilted his head. His red eyes burned into hers. "Think," he sneered. "Rowena was to die before she releassssed her power. What ssssign would accompany that change?" Each word he spoke was drawn out, the whole having the quality of a hissing snake.

She struggled for breath. She had to concentrate. *What was the sign to which he referred?* She fought for control over her thoughts. *What was the sign? What was the sign?* "Oh!" she cried. "Oh, no! How could I have missed it?"

"How indeed?" Again fire flashed from his eyes, narrowly missing her tangled hair. She pulled it back and wiped her stinging brow. "Sssso," he inquired, condescendingly, "what have you ssssurmissssed?"

"I would have received her magic power."

"Exxxxactly. We have planned this ever ssssince Rowena became the ranking member. Do you remember the day, my pet? Do you remember when you first turned to me?"

How could she forget? She'd been distraught over her sister's position. Finally, in desperation, she vowed she'd do anything to keep Rowena from successfully leading the Select. To her glorious surprise, Daeva had visited her. "Lilith," he'd purred. "Do you mean what you pray?"

At first his presence startled her, but she longed to believe her plea might be answered. "Are you asking if I'd do anything to keep Rowena from being successful? To become the ranking member myself? Yes. Anything!"

Daeva laid out his plan. Lilith could pretend to back Rowena, but she was to dispose of her sister before she released her power to her offspring. Then the power of the Select would revert to Lilith. Once done, Daeva would grant her even greater power—dark power.

Putting aside her reminiscing, she turned to him. "Yes, I remember."

"You knew Rowena vowed to wait until after she bore her sssseventh child to release her power—and you knew you needed to dessstroy her before that happened."

"Yes."

"Sssso, my pet, where issss that power? Hmmm? Where?"

She bowed. How could she have missed the obvious sign? In her excitement over her sister's death, she'd never given it a thought. "I didn't think," she whispered.

"Heh, heh, heh," he chortled mirthlessly. "I cannot support one so shortsssssighted." As if to emphasize his words, he increased the wave of searing pain.

"Ahhhhh!" she cried in agony.

"Had you 'thought,'" he continued, "you would have pressssed Dixon for information about the child when you found him in Polessssk. If you had done so, you might already have her in your grassssp."

"Yes, I failed. But I can do better. I beg you to give me another chance."

Again he increased the pain.

Lilith's back arched and her mouth opened in a silent scream. When he reduced the anguish, she slumped in relief.

"Perhapssss," he said, "perhapssss, there is a way."

"What can I do? I'll do anything!"

"Yessss, I know. You have sworn your allegianccce to me, my pet. You no longer have the option of exercisssing choicccce. You are mine," he whispered. "You will do whatever I assssk."

"Yes." *How could this have happened? How could I have lost control?* In her zeal for power, she had allowed Daeva to trick her, and now he would use her however he chose. Still, she would get what she wanted . . . eventually. "What can I do?"

"I have jusssst the plan. There is sssstill a way . . ."

"Yes?"

"Firsssst, you shall find out all that you can from Dixon."

"Yes!" He would pay.

"Then," Daeva continued, his voice dripping with venom, "you shall kill him."

"Gladly." She envisioned Dixon conceding information he hoped would save him from torture, begging for mercy, lying dead at her feet. *Oh, yes!* "But how will I accomplish this? I've no power over him except the power to band and to hold him."

"I shall endow you with sufficient power."

She smiled. An onlooker would have seen the resemblance between her smile and Daeva's own.

"When? When will I receive power?" She'd won him over. She was on the verge of becoming the most powerful leader of the Select ever to exist. *But this leader will not exercise the power of the Good One or pursue his simplistic goals for the people. No, this leader will use the power of Sinespe, the underworld.*

The sound of Daeva's laughter rippled about the room. "Now!" he said as the flame of his presence rushed upon her, invading and enveloping her.

Lilith dropped to the floor, panting, burning. The flames licked at her head, her mouth, her hands. Engulfed in a torrent of agony, her body steamed.

The screeching flames seared down her back and legs. She couldn't breathe. After what seemed an eternity, but could not have been more than mere moments, he reduced the torture.

Finally able to pull in some air, she gasped. "Stop! I'll be consumed!"

"But Lilith, my chossssen," he taunted, "you have already been consssssumed . . . by *me.*"

"I beg you to stop. I'll die!"

"You will not die, though you may wish you would." He pulled back most of the remaining pain.

"Take the rest away. Please, take it away!"

"Hah ha ha ha ha," he laughed. "The remaining pain will never go away."

"But why?"

"Becaussssse it will remind you of what I will do if you displeasssse me. What is more, it will be a consssstant reminder that I am now a part of you."

She sat up, one hip against the floor. "Please, Daeva . . ."

"Oh, Lilith, trussst me. You will come to appreciate it—to enjoy it even. It will drive you to do better. It will remind you of the goal you seek—because you have some detailssss to attend to. You musssst find that child. And then, here'ssss what you must do . . ."

Lilith rested on her plush chaise lounge, her anger assuaged, her energy spent. After Daeva left her, she'd ransacked her room. She glanced at the mess that Adele would have to clean.

Her tantrum left a brass hand mirror shattered, shards of glass scattered about, some ground to a dangerous dust. A broken tea service spilled into an open drawer, staining the silk scarves within. Feathers floated, landing on the bedding, the dresser top, the array of shoes, the hats, the carafe of wine, then were set to flying again with each movement to the air.

Perfume bottles splattered across the floor emitted the ghastly, overpowering smell of spices, flowers, and citrus. It was so strong it left a bitter, soapy taste in the mouth. Funny, she mused, how easily she could fool people into believing that whatever scent she wore was authentic confirmation of her having found Ehyeh's favor.

Rowena had done it again. She was always the favored, always a step ahead, always the *seventh*. Ever since she was born, she'd usurped all that should have been Lilith's own.

The youngest of six for some time, everyone believed Lilith was to become the leader of the first family. Her training would soon begin. Then to everyone's surprise, Mae became pregnant with her seventh, long after others believed it was still possible. She bore Rowena—the accident—the *seventh*.

"Come girls, look at the new baby!" Max had exclaimed.

Lilith could still recall every sight and smell of that day. Her mother lay exhausted after a difficult childbirth. Her chestnut hair, now sprinkled with gray, lay in tangles, her skin a ghostly pallor. A nursemaid wiped sweat from her brow. The attending physician had been concerned he might not be able to save both mother and child; the infant was breech and the mother stressed. But at the last minute, the infant turned. Both would survive after all.

"I don't want to see her," eight-year-old Lilith said as the others wrestled one another to hold and to coddle the infant, swooning ridiculously over her scent. It made her want to retch.

Her father turned to her. "Surely, you don't mean that. Come, meet your little sister. Just think, now you needn't worry about all of the responsibilities of being the youngest. All you need to do is help your sister to be the best leader possible."

"I don't want to help her. I want to be the youngest. I want to be the leader."

"Oh, you'll change your mind when you see how hard things will be for Rowena," her mother whispered. "Take it from me, it's difficult to lead the family."

Were they all stupid? What was so difficult? There were servants to take care of problems, people to order about. Lilith looked from one parent to the other, sneering. "I don't want to see her."

"Max," her mother said, "bring her to me."

Lilith's father approached. He reached for her hand.

She pulled hers away.

"Come," he said. This was no longer a request; it was a demand.

In that moment, she knew all had changed, and she vowed she'd do anything to turn things back to the way they'd been. She would lead the first family and no one, not even that screaming, smelly infant would change that fact.

Max guided Lilith toward the newborn. She squirmed under his touch. She looked at her sister, all pink and . . . pretty.

Her mother stroked the infant's cheek. "Isn't she pretty? And smell. It is the smell of Paradise. You smelled very like this yourself once, and you will again when you come of age and find favor with the Good One."

Lilith said nothing. She hated Rowena. She would always hate her.

By the time Rowena turned four, everyone was eating out of her hand. "Oh, look what a beautiful girl she is!" "Oh, see how quick she is to learn!" "Oh, what a great leader she'll make one day!" Everywhere Lilith turned, Rowena was the center of attention.

At twelve, Rowena's official training began. From then on, her parents and others constantly pressured Lilith. "Lilith, you know how important Rowena's leadership will be." "Lilith, you must support her in all things." "Lilith, isn't your sister wonderful?" "Lilith, doesn't your sister have great insight?" "Lilith, isn't it wonderful how your sister studies about the Good One? Surely, He will be favorable toward her."

When Rowena finally completed her training, Mae was making plans to transfer her power to her daughter. Illness forced her to do so sooner than she'd intended. Her death shortly afterward left a young Rowena in charge of a family that was in emotional shambles.

Now it was teachers, Oathtakers, even commoners, who would exclaim, chide, and cajole. "Lilith, you know your allegiance belongs to your sister." "Lilith, you must assist Rowena in her endeavors." "Lilith, what an honor it must be for you to be of service to her!"

It was always about Rowena. But would Lilith grant her allegiance to her sister, be of service to her? She would not.

A knock interrupted her thoughts, bringing her back to the present. "Come," she said.

Two middle-aged women entered. "Lilith!" the first exclaimed as she took in the wreckage. "What happened here?"

Lilith reclined with her arm bent over her eyes. She removed it and looked up, scowling. "Well, Sally, it seems I've had a tantrum of sorts."

Sally straightened a picture that hung askew. Slightly overweight, she was plain looking. She wore the front portion of her waist length yellow brown hair back and tied with a bow at the top of her head, just as she'd done since she was a child. Drifting feathers, newly disrupted by the gust of air that had accompanied her into the room, blew about. She brushed at those that landed upon her gray wool dress, causing yet another flurry, like snow falling while the wind blew.

"What is wrong?" asked the other visitor.

"You don't even want to know, Janine." Lilith buried her face in a pillow.

Janine, a near replica of Sally, but without the ever-present hair bow, frowned. "Maybe not, but this looks like trouble to me."

"Oh, Sally! Janine! Close the door."

Janine did. "Well?"

"That witch, Rowena, has done it again," Lilith growled, her anger newly agitated.

"I don't understand," said Janine. "She's dead. You're the leader now. What can she do? And you know Sally and I support you."

"We've got a problem."

"What is it?" Sally asked.

"In a word: Rowena."

"But she's dead," repeated Janine.

"Yes, well unfortunately, she left us with trouble."

"How?" asked Sally.

Lilith closed her eyes as though trying to shut out the truth. "The child lives," she muttered, "and Rowena released her power."

For a moment, there was silence. Then Janine cried, "No! That means—"

"That I'm *not* the ranking member," Lilith interrupted. "I am not the rightful leader. Well . . . not yet anyway," she mumbled.

"What'll we do?" Sally asked.

"We get Dixon to talk. We—"

"Dixon! What do you suppose he knows?"

"He can't lie to you Lilith," Janine said. "He owes his allegiance to the Select."

"Well, as I think on it, perhaps he didn't exactly lie to me. He told me of Rowena's death. I never inquired about the child." Lilith pouted. "Oh, it never occurred to me that the child might have survived. I don't know what I was thinking!" She stood and stomped her foot.

"But an infant can't lead the Select," Sally said.

"No, but her Oathtaker may act as her regent," Janine offered.

The three women exchanged glances.

Sally traced a design in some spilled powder on the vanity.

Janine bit the inside of her cheek.

"You suppose Dixon is the child's Oathtaker?" Sally finally asked.

"Possibly," Lilith responded. "No—probably. Which means he— Oh no, *he* could act as the ranking member. Then the band would be useless!"

"But where would he have put the child? And why would he let you believe the band was effective if the child is his charge?" Janine asked. She brushed broken items off a chair and sat. "I'm not about to go back to the way things were with Rowena. Without her around we were at least able to act in our own interests."

"For now, say nothing," Lilith said. "No one must know. Things do happen, you know. I'll deal with Dixon. I'll get him to talk."

"How?"

"Rest assured, he'll talk. I'm not without means of my own."

Sally and Janine looked at one another.

"Enough for now. As to Dixon, I'll do whatever it takes." Lilith's expression was grim.

"You wouldn't!" Janine exclaimed.

Lilith raised a brow in response.

"Would you?"

"Oh, you'd better believe I would," she growled as she ground shards of broken mirror beneath her boot.

CHAPTER FIFTEEN

She slammed the door closed. Bits of plaster came loose from the ceiling. They floated down like fresh snow. She strode up the carmine red carpet to her desk.

Gadon flinched. "Lilith, I—"

She struck him with all her force.

His head shook. His eyes opened wide. "But, Lilith, I—"

Again she struck. His head snapped to the side. His lip broke open. Blood trickled down his chin. He wiped it away with the back of his hand.

"You have failed me." She uttered the exact words Daeva had said to her.

"No ma'am, I—" He rubbed his stinging face.

Once more, she struck. "That wasn't a question. You have failed me!"

"Lil—"

"Stop. I've not given you permission to speak," she growled.

A knock came at the door. Marshall peeked inside. "Is everything all right in here?"

"Everything is just fine, Marshall," she said dismissively.

After a moment's hesitation, he retreated, then closed the door.

Gadon turned to Lilith. He opened his mouth as though to speak, then closed it again.

"That's better." She looked him over from head to foot. "First and foremost, don't you ever again call me by my given name," she fumed, her voice little more than a whisper. "I don't know what made me think that you—*you* could successfully stop Rowena."

"I—"

"Stop right there. I don't want to hear anything from you as yet. You'll speak when I say so and not before. Do you understand?"

He nodded.

She leaned against the back of her desk, glaring. "You have failed me."

He said nothing.

"You have failed me!" she screamed as though egging him on, as though expecting he would defend himself and give her cause to strike him yet again. Her red face matched the color of her dress. Her chest heaved with each breath. Her hands clenched into white knuckled fists.

Finally, her breathing slowed, though the force of her glare never waned. "So then, suppose we start at the beginning." She walked around her desk, pulled out her chair, and then sat.

He shuffled his feet.

"Now," she said, "you may speak. Tell me how you managed to miss her."

He relayed the story of his months on the run. He told about the pack of grut, coming under fire, and the barrier. He told of Drake and Maggie, and how they'd conceded that Rowena and Dixon had visited them with an infant.

"What did you do with them?"

"Killed them, of course. I knew you didn't want any loose ends."

"What sent you to Polesk?"

"The old folks told us that Dixon and Rowena were headed there. I knew it was time to be checking in with you again, so I sent you word that we were headed to sanctuary there—that I hoped to see you soon."

"By which I understood you to mean that you'd been successful and were on your way back." She glared as she chewed on her lip. "So why didn't you get word of these events to me after I saw you in Polesk?"

"I had no idea how to do that. I looked for you in the gardens where we used to meet. I wanted to tell you that I didn't think you had all the relevant facts."

"Oh, so this is my fault? How was I to know you could be so utterly incompetent?"

He was silent.

"Why didn't you stay in Polesk and continue your search from there?"

"I thought you had other plans to get Dixon to give up Rowena's whereabouts. I had no other leads to follow, so I came here. I expected you'd call for me immediately, but . . . you didn't. Now days have passed. If Rowena has escaped—"

"It's not Rowena that concerns me," she interrupted. "Rowena is dead."

"Then who was the woman with Dixon? And what of the child the old people talked about?"

"I don't know who the woman was, but the child was Rowena's own."

"So now what?"

Grimacing, Lilith approached. "Well, it seems I can't trust you to get the job done, so I no longer require your services."

He looked long and hard at her. "Very well. Am I excused?"

She held out her hand. "I'll take the grut call."

He handed it over.

She drew forward, her face inches from his, forcing him to meet her gaze. "You are excused, but don't get any ideas. If you or any of your men speak a word of this to anyone, you will regret it."

He turned on his heel and left, closing the door firmly behind.

Lilith paced. *What to do? What to do?*

Plush rugs covered the center of the wide palace hallway, muting the sounds of her steps. Portraits of former leaders of the Select hung on the walls. She stopped at the painting of her mother. She'd have to get someone to remove it. The constant reminder of the woman's betrayal in having given birth to Rowena was something Lilith could live without—and the sooner, the better.

Rounding a corner in her haste, she nearly knocked a potted plant from a pedestal. She looked up. In the room at her side, Adele swept the floor. "Adele!" she called.

The young woman visibly cringed as she turned.

"This needs cleaning up," Lilith said. She pushed the pedestal. The pot teetered for a moment, then fell, shattering on impact. As it rolled, soil covered the freshly swept floor.

Adele's mouth flew open.

Lilith flashed her humorless smile, the one derived from Daeva himself. "Right away."

"Yes, ma'am." Conditioned to the woman's rages, the maid immediately started in to her task. "Thank you, ma'am, for pointing that out to me."

Lilith stopped in her tracks and turned back. She grabbed Adele by the forearm and pulled her forward. "Are you mocking me?"

"No, ma'am."

Lilith pushed her. "See that you don't."

"Yes, ma'am. Thank you, ma'am."

When Lilith arrived at the servants' wing, she nodded to the man watching Dixon's room. She'd hoped that placing Dixon under house arrest would make him more amenable to assisting her. Now she had to break down his guard.

She considered whether she should try kindness first, or whether she should go straight to the torture. Along with the constant burning Daeva left within her, vibrations of his power ran down her spine, but she was leery about using that power, as Dixon would wonder at its source.

The guard opened the door. She stepped inside.

Dixon sat at a table, a book open before him, his lamp burning. He glanced her way, then turned back to his reading.

Was he dismissing her? *The audacity!* Even so, she'd first try a peaceful approach. She would try to enchant him. He was a man, after all. She would turn his head, his mind.

"Dixon," she said, sweetness dripping like tree sap, "how are they treating you?"

He turned to her and stared, one brow raised. His mouth dropped open. "How are *they* treating me? Hah! You can't be serious. Why the charade?"

"Oh, Dixon, you always were prone to the dramatic. May I?" she asked as she pulled out a chair.

He shrugged.

She sat, then leaned forward, causing the front of her crimson silk dress to drape open, revealing her cleavage. It was as though she'd practiced this very move in front of a mirror.

He averted his eyes.

She put her hand on his arm.

He drew away. "What do you want?"

"Can't I just want to see you?" she whined. "You were away for so long and . . . Well, Dixon," she said, now putting her hand on his knee, "I missed you."

"Don't be ridiculous." He removed her hand and placed it firmly on the table. He stood, his arms folded. "When are you going to unband me, Lilith? And when are you going to let me out of here?"

"I'm not."

"Then I've nothing to say to you."

She willed herself to stay calm. "Well, Dixon, I think you do have something to say. You see, I've received some rather dist—ahhh . . . interesting news."

"Oh? What's that?" His eyes narrowed.

"You said Rowena died in childbirth."

"That's right."

"So when were you going to tell me that the child lives?"

He blinked hard. "Wh—what are you talking about?"

"Oh, really, Dixon. I'm not stupid," she pouted. "All right, I was a bit slow—I admit it. I should have caught on right away. But now that I know—"

"Caught on?" He sat.

"Well of course—caught on. Rowena swore she wouldn't release her power until after her seventh was born. Had she not done so, her powers would have reverted to me." She crossed her legs. "But you see, they have not." She glared in open hostility.

"Are you sure?"

"Most certainly. So you see, that can only mean that she released her power—that she bore her child."

"Are you sure?"

"Completely. And that's why I need you to tell me about her. So, where is she, Dixon?"

"I don't know."

"So you admit it. The child lives."

He hesitated. "Suppose, for the sake of argument, that you're right. Why would you want the child anyway? You hate children." He got back to his feet and paced.

"I don't hate children."

"Sure you do."

"That's ridiculous."

"Oh, and that's why you were so good with your own that Rowena had to take him from you?"

"Stop trying to change the subject." Glowering at him, she exhaled slowly. "In any case, it's irrelevant."

"Irrelevant?"

"What I mean is that it's important we raise the child here. Rowena's sisters and I will see to her proper upbringing. How else will she learn of her role?"

"She?"

"Well of course, 'she.' Rowena used every trick there was to be certain she had only girls. So tell me, where is she? She needs to be here where we can instruct her, where we can help her to acquire the tools necessary to lead."

"The tools?"

"Yes, of course."

"What kind of tools?"

"Oh, never mind, Dixon, just tell me where the child is!"

"I don't know."

"Of course you do."

"I do not. And if I did, I wouldn't tell you." He crossed his arms.

"So you're saying the child does live, but you don't know where she is or who is to raise her."

He shrugged. "If you say so."

She came within inches of him. "There are ways to make you talk."

"Go ahead, Lilith, do your worst."

She raised her brow. "Oh, Dixon, you are going to be very, very sorry you said that."

He stepped back. "Fine. But you said yourself you're without power, and you're not the leader of the Select. So why not just let me go and leave Rowena's plans in place?"

"Who says I'm without power?" With that, and with a twist of her wrist, Lilith threw out a taste of Daeva's power. She gloried in the release of the heat that burned within her. Like a strike of lightning, the air snapped.

Dixon's body slammed against the wall. Blood dripped down to his ear and across his cheek. He tried to right himself, but then dropped forward, landing on his knees. His clothing burned, his skin blistered. Choking for breath, he stared at Lilith.

She smiled. For a moment, the freakish gaping grin of a long dead corpse stared back at him.

He made his way to his feet. He tottered, but held his ground.

She threw out more pain. "Is that not enough for you, Dixon?" she mocked, willing the heat to increase.

He staggered. He struggled for breath. "Stop—it," he finally managed to utter.

"Tell me what I need to know," she insisted. "Where is the child? Has she an Oathtaker? Is it you? Is it someone else? Who was the woman with you and the child?"

"I can't tell you what I don't know."

"Oh, I think you know quite a lot."

He gasped for air.

She drew back the pain. "Is that better?" She pressed against him. "I can make it go away, you know." She took his face in her hands, drew her finger through the blood that trickled down his cheek, then put her finger in her mouth and sucked on it.

"Mmmm," she moaned. "Shall I make it go away, Dixon? Shall I?" Her lips were just inches from his. "Just say the word." She ran her tongue up from his chin to his lips, licking at his blood.

"Stop it, Lilith," he demanded through gritted teeth.

"Tell me what I need to know," she whispered, "and I'll make the pain go away." Her lips touched his. "Then I'll kiss away all your troubles. Would you like that, Dixon? Would you?"

He pushed her away. "I told you, I don't know anything."

Again she increased the torture.

He fell to his knees. "Stop it, Lilith."

"I'm afraid I can't do that." She walked around him as he slumped to the floor. "Where is the child?"

He moaned and writhed.

Fearing he'd pass out, she again let up on the pressure. "Where is the child, Dixon? Where is she?"

He shook his head.

"Are you the child's Oathtaker?"

"No. No!"

"See," she sneered, "you do know something."

He panted, his eyes closed.

Sensing he wavered in his resistance, she persisted. "Who is the child's Oathtaker, Dixon?"

He strained against the pain. "Dear Ehyeh," he cried, looking upward. Then, as if in answer to his prayer, he lost all consciousness.

Chapter Sixteen

The air was dusty, as was often the case during the dog days of summer. Along the marsh at the edge of the road a multitude of cattails bent in the breeze like a throng of worshipers in obeisance to the glory of their god. Open water, spotted with algae, dotted the landscape. Red winged blackbirds perched on tall grasses showed off their colorful shoulder patches as they chirped their high squeaky song.

Mara rode with Reigna, Nina to her left with Eden, Therese to her right. Jules took the lead. He kept a constant vigil for anything out of the ordinary, while Samuel brought up the rear, guarding against possible ambush from behind.

After a two day rest at The King's Court, during which she'd not been able to repeat her sleep time travel, notwithstanding her efforts to do so, Mara agreed, at Therese's encouragement, to head with her to Lucy's. It would take weeks of dangerous travel over rough and unknown terrain for the small crew to cross the countryside. The journey would take them around the City of Light and then farther north.

Midday had come and gone. They would need to rest the horses soon, as they couldn't risk injury to the animals. Moreover, the twins would need to nurse. Already Reigna grew restless, as witnessed by her increased whimpering, although as usual, Eden seemed to go along with little complaint.

Jules vanished over a rise ahead. Minutes later, he reappeared. Approaching the others at an easy pace, his eyes continually scanned the countryside. The women halted when he neared. As like a chorus, their mounts nickered and blew, signifying that it was time to stop.

"There's a small wooded area just over that hill," Jules said pointing, directing his comments to Therese. "It's well concealed." He patted his horse's neck. "It's time to stop for a rest."

Within minutes they pulled into the resting place. Huge basswoods grew in clusters of a half dozen or more full-sized trunks. Their branches created a lacy canopy for things below. Their leaves, just beginning to wilt, attested to the fact that basswoods were among the first of the forest to lose their leaves in the autumn. Intermingled with them was the occasional oak and cherry tree.

Nina fed the girls while Mara and Therese prepared flat breads stuffed with cold meats and cheese.

After Samuel and Jules attended to the horses, watering two at a time at a nearby creek, they devoured their lunches quickly, then stood guard while the others ate.

"Any luck?" Therese asked Mara.

It was clear of what she spoke. Ever since traveling to Dixon, Mara had thought of little else. But the more she yearned to repeat her journey, the more difficult it was to sleep at all.

"No. The more I think on it, the harder it seems. I feel like the ability is almost there, it's almost as though I can touch it, then it just . . . disappears."

"Sometimes I find that the easiest way to accomplish something, is to take the pressure of possible success or failure from my mind. I just wait and let it happen."

"Maybe you're right."

The birds and beasts of the air and field fluttered and nagged. The horses flicked their ears and swished their tails as the local flies discovered their presence.

"I'm going to wash up," Mara said. "Maybe I'll stick my feet in the water. We'll get started again when everyone is through eating and the horses have cooled down."

She sauntered down to the creek. Sunshine sparkled on the slowly moving water. A small twig made its way downstream and then, just where she stood, got caught up in an eddy. It twisted and twirled and popped up and down in its fight to escape its prison.

She sat in the tall grasses at the bank and took off her boots. She wiggled her toes and dipped them in the water, luxuriating in its coolness. Once done, she found a flat spot and leaned her head back facing the sun. Its light created a swirl of colors behind her eyelids peculiarly similar to what she experienced during her magic traveling.

The past days had been a dizzying rush of wonder and fear. From the moment she'd discovered Rowena, Mara's life had changed. She'd been on her way to an Oathtakers' meeting that morning. Did they wonder of her whereabouts? Had they sent a posse to find her?

She reclined, then put her knees up, flattening her lower back. She rubbed her feet against the waxy blades of grass, curling and releasing her toes.

A squirrel chattering noisily in a nearby tree scolded her for lying in its intended path. She smiled at the bossiness of the inconsequential rodent, then listened to a meadowlark singing in a nearby field. *How lovely is his song.*

Her mind wandered. She didn't concentrate on where she was, or where she was going. She rode the wave of sound and light and heat and breeze and emptiness and color and . . .

Magic transported her. She was weightless, altered while simultaneously remaining unchanged.

She halted. All was silent. The sunlight's intensity was no more. A sudden chill swept over her. She opened her eyes.

The floor was damp and dirty. Moisture trickled down the walls. The stink of mildew made it hard to breath. She tried to rid her nose of the smell. She was elated she'd journeyed again, though she wasn't even asleep. She was simply at ease, relaxed, purposeful. She would have clapped her hands with joy, were it not so quiet.

She got to her knees, then glanced about.

Gracious Ehyeh, I'm not alone!

Several feet away lay a man who, it appeared, was sleeping. He was on his side, facing away. His form and size looked right. His build was right. The hair color, as well as Mara could tell in the light of the single burning candle nearby, was right. Could it be Dixon?

She placed a finger to her lips, then touched his arm.

He didn't move.

She leaned closer. His hair was matted with blood. He was so still. Was he even breathing? Yes, but very shallowly. Once again she touched his arm, this time more aggressively.

Still, he did not move.

She rolled him onto his back.

"Dixon!" Dried blood covered his face. His lip was split open and swollen. Bruises decorated his eyes, his jaw, and his chest. "Oh, Dixon!" she whispered, a hand to her mouth. "What's happened?"

A pitcher of water sat on the floor. Just as she reached for it, a sound came from behind. She spun around to find a door in the cramped space. It cracked open.

She stood and rushed to stand against the wall to its side. When it opened, it would hide her. Then, she reached for Spira. If the visitor intended harm, at least she'd have the advantage of surprise.

It was hard to make out the words coming from the other side of the door. Shaking with fear, she willed herself to breathe slowly. Her hands felt clammy. *Relax. Relax.*

"I told you, I'm going to see him," a woman said as the door opened farther, allowing more light to enter the room. "Just go back to your post."

That voice is familiar.

"But—"

"You heard me. Go back to your post."

"But what about—"

"I don't care what she says!" the woman cried as she stepped into the room and closed the door, then stood with her hands on it to hold it shut, her head bowed, and her eyes closed.

Mara stood just inches away.

The woman turned away. "Dixon!" she cried. She dropped down and leaned over him. She patted him gently on the cheek. "Wake up. I need to get you out of here. We'll use the tunnel. I swear I'll kill Lilith's guards if that's the only way around them. But, Dixon, I can't carry you." She wiped away a tear. "Please, please wake up," she urged.

Mara could just make out a portion of the woman's profile. Where had she seen her before? *And that voice. I know that voice. Ah yes, it's Basha.*

Basha ministered to Dixon. Her touch was gentle, her voice pleading. "Dixon, please wake up. We have to get you out of here. Oh, what'll we do? What'll—"

Mara's foot slipped.

Basha turned her way. Her eyes opened wide as she sucked in a breath.

"Shhhhhh!" Mara cautioned, her finger to her lips as she approached.

Basha held her hand up.

"I'm here to help," Mara whispered. She feared the woman might shout out and reveal her presence. She had only seconds to win her over. "Basha—"

"Who are you?"

"My name is Mara. I'm Dixon's friend."

"How did you—"

A sound at the door interrupted them.

"I'll only be a minute, I swear," came a young woman's voice. The door cracked open. A sliver of light entered the room. "I have to warn her. Let me go!" There was a scuffle outside the door. "I said, 'Let—me—go!'"

"You two have seconds to get out of there. If Lilith is on the way, you dare not let her catch you," a man responded.

The door swung open.

Mara jumped back.

"Adele!" Basha cried. Then her eyes flashed toward Mara just as she—vanished.

Mara transported. Once again on the banks of the creek, the sunlight stung her eyes and the sounds of the countryside invaded her senses. Startled, she sat upright.

"Oh!" Nina exclaimed. "Where did you come from?"

Mara looked up, squinting. "I've been here all along."

"You most certainly have not."

"Are you sure?"

"What do you mean, 'am I sure?' Of course I'm sure. We've all been looking for you. I'd best tell the others you're here."

"Oh, Nina, I did it! I traveled again." The Oathtaker jumped to her feet.

"That's great!"

"Yes, now tell me again. Were you right here before you saw me? Just now I mean?"

"I've been standing here for several minutes. When I first came to find you and couldn't, I informed the others you were missing. We split up to look for you. I came back here and I've been standing right in this spot, looking up and down the creek. I thought you might've walked downstream. Then suddenly, you appeared."

"Oh, you've just answered a question for me!" Mara, positively giddy, embraced the young woman.

"I don't understand."

"When I traveled before, I couldn't be sure I wasn't just traveling in my mind and I didn't know if I was 'here' or 'there.' You see?"

"I think so."

"Now I know that when I travel, I'm no longer 'here.'"

"Oh, yes I see."

"Thank the Good One, you saw me."

"Yes, but we'd best let the others know you're safe. They're concerned for you." The two returned to where they'd lunched.

Upon seeing Mara, Jules visibly relaxed.

"I apologize, Jules, for worrying you. Please let Samuel know all is well." She looked around. "Where is Therese?"

"I'm right here." Therese came out from behind some brush, holding Eden in one arm. Blood dripped from her free hand.

"Therese, where's all that blood from?" Mara rushed to her side. "Is Eden hurt? What happened? Are you all right?"

"Oh, it's nothing really, I just cut myself on a sharp rock over there."

"Let me see that," Mara insisted. She took the woman's hand.

"It's nothing."

"Nothing! This is very deep." Suddenly and unexpectedly, a stream of magic left the Oathtaker and entered into Therese. Both women gasped at the power of it, and at the sight of Therese's wound healing before their eyes. Moments later, only a light scar remained.

"Oh my!" she exclaimed as she brought her hand to her face and wiggled her fingers.

Mara stood with her mouth open. "Where did that come from? That healing power, I mean?"

"Seems your attendant powers keep coming."

"That was amazing!" Nina exclaimed.

"It sure was," Therese agreed. "Listen, Mara, not to make light of this or anything, because I appreciate it, I do. But where were you? You frightened me nearly to death."

"Oh, I did it!"

"You— Oh, you traveled again?"

"Yes!" Mara smiled, but then her countenance turned grim. "Oh, but I have to go back."

"Well, tell us all about it."

The Oathtaker explained where she'd gone, and what she'd seen.

"Dixon was hurt?' Nina asked.

"Terribly."

"And you saw Basha?" Therese asked.

"Yes, but as I said, when I left it seemed she might be in danger. A young woman was entering the . . . I don't know what it was. A cave? A prison? Anyway, she was explaining to . . . a guard I guess he must have been, that Lilith was coming. She meant to warn Basha. So Lilith must be the cause of Dixon's current state."

"Do you know who the woman was?"

"I think Basha called her by name. What was it again? Amelia? Alicia? No . . . Adele. Yes, that's right, Adele."

"Yes, I know her. A lovely young woman. Rowena adored her. But why would she risk Lilith's ire?"

"I don't know. But I have to go back. I have to do what I can to help Dixon."

"Mara, you know where your first responsibilities lie," Therese cautioned.

The Oathtaker nodded. "Yes, but there must be some reason I'm able to do this traveling. Maybe the Good One is trying to make it possible for me to . . . Wait . . . Wait a minute!"

"What?"

"Oh! How could I have missed it?"

"Missed what?" Nina asked.

"Oh, Nina! Therese! Don't you see? Remember the night I traveled to Dixon and spoke with him? I returned with his flint."

"Yeeessss," they said in unison.

"So, don't you see? If I can take something like a flint through my travels, maybe I can bring Dixon back to us."

"I don't know," Therese said. "You have to be very careful, Mara. If Lilith is responsible for the state he's in, you don't want to risk getting caught in her clutches."

"Yes, I've been thinking about that. I'm trying to put my finger on what it was that I did to travel there and back. I think I might have it."

"You think you can travel at will now?" Nina asked.

"I think so. Earlier my traveling was . . . I don't know. Almost an accident. But when I realized the danger there, I recreated the ability almost instantly."

"Do you think you could do it again?"

"I think so."

Therese stepped away, then turned back. "Here's the thing though, Mara. He may need your help, but the girls—"

"I know, I know," the Oathtaker interrupted. "I can't risk harm to them. Then again, if he could be instrumental in seeing to their safety, I can't risk failing to help him."

"So do you plan to return to his side now?"

"No, not immediately. It's likely Lilith is with him now. I don't want to walk into that situation. But I'm going to try again soon." Mara sighed. "I just hope she doesn't further harm him in the meantime."

"Very well then."

"Therese, try to understand. I'm acting as I believe Ehyeh is leading me. I know the dangers. I'll be careful."

"Well," Nina asked, "are we ready to move out then?"

"Yes, let's go," Mara said.

The women went to their horses. Suddenly, Mara stopped cold. "Therese?"

"Yes?"

"I've been thinking."

"Yes?"

"How did you come to know Samuel and Jules?"

"Why do you ask?" The woman untied her mount, Cloud.

"I just wonder. How is it you feel you—we—are safe with them as guards? I mean . . ."

Therese refastened the latch of her saddlebag. "Samuel and Jules have been entirely faithful to me. They don't have an Oathtaker's powers, but they've kept me safe for some time."

"But how do you know them? What do you know about them? Like you said yourself, I owe Reigna and Eden my first responsibility."

Therese made room for Nina to untie her mount. "Since you mention it, I think you should hear their story for yourself." Just then, the men came into sight. "Samuel! Jules!" she called. "I need you to tell Mara your story."

⚔

"What do you want to know?" Jules asked.

"In a nutshell, I want to know why Therese trusts you two so completely. How is it you're not Oathtakers, yet you've taken on the responsibility of keeping her safe?"

"That's rather a long story," he said as he and Samuel mounted up, then led the group out.

"Why don't you start at the beginning?" Mara asked, once again recollecting the night Dixon had told her his story. Her thoughts frequently turned to him.

"You ride with the women," Samuel said, "and I'll go ahead." Looking behind, he cautioned the others, "Just keep an eye on things. We're kicking up quite a dust."

Jules turned back to Mara. "Samuel and I are cousins. We both came from families that had many Oathtakers over the years. We both would've become Oathtakers ourselves, but there were no Select remaining back home."

"Where's home?" she asked.

"Near the intersection of the Rivers Modan and Costan in Anka."

"There are no Select at all there?"

"Very, very few."

"Why is that?"

"Pretty much the same reason their numbers have decreased throughout Oosa."

"Assassinations?"

"Exactly."

"So you chose not to become Oathtakers."

"That's right."

"Well, but I come from the Barten Lake area of Usta. We also have very few Select, yet—"

"Yet you chose to become an Oathtaker anyway."

"That's right."

"Well, we decided we could be of service to the Select and to Ehyeh, even if we weren't Oathtakers. So we set out to discover how to do that."

"And what did you find?"

"In a word, we found Lucy." He grinned.

"And?" Mara urged him on.

"Lucy is . . . Lucy is . . . unique."

Therese laughed.

The Oathtaker glanced at the woman, curious at her response. It was as though she and Jules shared some great secret. "What do you mean?" She slowed her mount, as it was getting anxious amongst the pack.

Jules searched for words. "Lucy is . . . Well, that is, she has a long history with the Select. She was Oathtaker to the last two female sevenths before Rowena."

"The last *two*? But that was ages ago!"

He rose up in his saddle and looked behind. As he settled back into his seat, he smiled. "Yes, it was."

"How long ago are we talking?"

He laughed. The sound was free and easy. "Well now, I guess that's why Lucy is so unique."

"So? How long?"

"A couple hundred years ago."

Mara's mouth dropped open. "But that's— That's im— How is that even possible?"

"Attendant magic," Therese said.

"What? Does she have nine lives, like a cat or something?" Nina asked.

Jules glanced at the young woman. He seemed surprised to find that she had a ready wit.

"Not exactly," Therese answered, "but Lucy has cheated death on more than one occasion."

Mara's brow furrowed. "She didn't appear that old to me," she mumbled.

"Yes," Therese said, "we should all look so good at that age."

They all laughed and then, as if in collective thought, scanned the landscape around them. They could just make out Samuel's presence ahead through the dust and heat wavering in the air that created a surreal look to the landscape.

Mara turned to Therese. "So, who was the first seventh who was Lucy's charge?"

"Selene, from a province near where Samuel and Jules grew up. Everyone was excited when she came of age. They hoped she might usher in the seventh seventh written about in prophecy."

"But?" Mara asked after a moment's silence.

"But Selene was never able to come to a full appreciation of who and what she was. In short, she didn't believe."

Mara brushed hair from her face. "You mean she didn't believe in the Select? She didn't believe in their cause? She didn't believe in Ehyeh? What?"

Therese tilted her head to the right, then left. "I guess you could say she didn't believe in herself."

"I don't understand."

"Well, everyone has a special calling—and none more or greater than a seventh. But a seventh who doesn't believe in herself, in her mission, is unable to bring others along in her pursuit. Does that make sense?"

"I guess so."

"In any case, Selene was unable to come to grips with the fact that there was a special call on, and of service for, her life."

"What happened to her?"

"Basically, she wasted her life away. She became a recluse. Of course Lucy continually urged her to an appreciation of her special place, but it never worked. Lucy was devastated. She spent years with her charge studying and preparing, and then one day, the young woman just . . . walked off."

"Never to be seen again?" Nina asked.

"No," Therese said, "she was seen again—just not alive."

"What happened?" Mara asked.

"No one ever really knew," Jules said. "Her body was found at the base of a cliff, days after she'd gone missing."

"She killed herself?" Nina shuddered. "How awful."

Therese wiped sweat from her brow. "Actually, no one knows. Was it an accident? Did she find her life useless? Was she frightened to face what was ahead? No one knew."

"Who was Lucy's other charge?" Mara asked.

"Some years later, on her way to the City of Light to report, Lucy felt the calling. Imagine her surprise to find she'd been called to serve *another* seventh-born daughter."

Nina glanced at Therese. "But I thought sevenths were so rare."

"Yes, that's true. But there were more of them in those days."

"Who was this second seventh that Lucy served?" Mara asked.

"Bridget," Jules said. "A seventh born in the City of Light."

"What was her story?"

He ran his fingers through his hair. "She was quite influential and of course, Lucy gained additional attendant powers when she accepted Bridget as her charge."

"More lives, no doubt," Nina muttered.

Jules eyed her again, chuckling.

"Actually, Mara," Therese interrupted, "you and Dixon also have some of the same attendant magic as Lucy."

"What do you mean?"

"Well, as you know, an Oathtaker doesn't physically age for so long as his charge lives. Right?"

"Yes."

"Well, there's one little difference for the Oathtaker of a seventh."

"What's that?"

Therese smiled. "Once you accept a seventh as your charge, you will never physically age again."

The Oathtaker's eyes widened. "Never?"

"Never ever."

Mara had not heard that before. So much had been lost over the years. *Oh, I have so much to learn!* She turned her attention back to Jules's story. "And Bridget? What of her?"

"Assassinated," he said.

"How dreadful." That word kept coming up. It dampened her spirits. Mara looked at Reigna slumbering in her arms and breathed in the infant's beautiful scent. "Assassinations must have been rather rare then."

"Yes," Therese responded, "they were."

"And Lucy has had no charge since then?" Nina asked.

"None," Jules said. "Well, that is, she's not been bound to any individual member of the Select."

Mara stared at him. "I don't understand."

"Well," Therese said, "since Bridget's death, and given the danger to the Select as a whole, Lucy's mission has been to protect all of the Select. She has hoped to live to usher in the prophesied seventh daughter of a seventh daughter who might bring restoration and revival to the Select and to Oosa."

"A self proclaimed mission?"

Therese tipped her head right to left, left to right. "Hmmm, not exactly."

"What do you mean?"

"As Lucy tells it," Jules said, "Ehyeh informed her of her mission."

"How?" Nina asked. "Did he just sit down and talk with her or something?"

Therese smirked. "Well now, that would be a question that you'd have to ask Lucy."

"Why is that?" Mara asked.

Once again, Jules glanced quickly behind. "She just says that when the right Select and the right Oathtaker come along, she'll be able to share all that she knows and how she came to learn it."

"And in the meantime?" Nina asked.

"In the meantime she works with anyone who wants to assist with the Select so that they can continue to pass Ehyeh's ways down through the ages."

"And that's where you come in," Mara said.

"Exactly."

"So, your story then is—what?"

"It's simple, really. Samuel and I met Lucy in the City of Light. We agreed to work with her and to follow her for the benefit of Ehyeh, the Select, and Oosa. We swore to do so."

"You mean you swore to all of the Select, as opposed to a particular member?"

"In a manner of speaking."

Mara pulled back on Cheryl's reins, leaving the rest of the group moving forward. A moment later, they halted. Their eyes darted about for any sign of an ambush.

Jules was the first to turn his horse around. He kicked dust up as he returned to Mara's side. In a flash, he covered her with his body. "What is it? What happened? What did you see?"

"Nothing. Nothing!" Her leg was cramped between their horses. She broke Jules's hold. "Nothing's wrong!" By this time, Therese and Nina hovered nearby.

"Is everything all right?" Therese asked.

"Yes," Mara said, "everything is fine."

Samuel approached. "What's happened?"

"Everything is fine," she repeated.

Therese reached toward the men, her palm extended, indicating that they should back away. She urged her horse closer to Mara. "We feared for you. One second you were there, the next, you weren't. I'm sure we all thought the same thing." She looked around. "We thought perhaps you'd been hit from somewhere—that we'd missed something."

The Oathtaker shook her head. "I'm sorry, I didn't mean to frighten any of you."

"So what is it?" Nina asked. "What made you stop?"

"I just . . . I just thought about you others who've sworn to protect the girls. You all received a confirmation. And it occurred to me what great peace of mind that's given me."

Jules looked at Samuel.

"Absolutely!" Samuel said as though his cousin had verbalized his question.

"You're right, Mara. We should have thought of this before. Samuel and I will swear oaths to protect the girls." Jules put his hand to his heart. "To put your mind at ease, I solemnly swear that I will protect Reigna and Eden with everything that I have and everything that I am. I would die for them if need be."

Just as Mara had hoped, the earth responded with a great shake. The leaves of the nearby trees quivered.

The young man's face radiated joy.

She turned to Samuel. Her brow rose. "Well? Are you game?"

"Mara, you need never doubt me. I solemnly swear that I will protect Reigna and Eden with my very life if need be."

The air seemed to pop. Rocks bordering the roadway broke loose their hold to the earth, then rolled away.

The travelers all broke out in quiet laughter and applause.

CHAPTER SEVENTEEN

Mara wanted to know more of Lucy, but for now was content to have time to think. She looked forward to her next opportunity to travel. As the hours passed, her concern for Dixon's wellbeing grew. Would she be too late, even if she could return to his side right this minute? And why was she so obsessed with him and his safety anyway, when she already had so much to handle with the twins?

As dusk neared, the temperature dropped. The air felt electric.

Jules had ridden ahead and was now on his way back. His gait easy, his face calm, he indicated that he sensed no danger ahead.

Nina watched him. She looked expectant, stimulated. *Happy?* Mara followed her gaze to Jules. "Nina?"

"Yes?"

"Do you want me to take Eden?"

"No, I'm fine. But they'll both need to eat soon. In fact, I'm surprised Reigna isn't fussing already."

The Oathtaker looked up. The sky was an odd mix of gray and green. "It looks like bad weather is coming."

Jules approached. His eyes rested momentarily on Nina before he turned his attention to Mara.

"Is everything all right?" she asked.

"I think we've got a storm brewing," Therese interrupted, as she rode up, Reigna in her arms.

"That's what I was just saying."

Things suddenly quieted. The air stilled. Everything had a green cast to it, including the travelers' faces.

"Did you see any possible shelter ahead?" the Oathtaker asked Jules.

His horse shuddered, jerked its head, and stomped its foot. The other mounts followed suit. Skittish, their eyes darted about. As though on cue, small bolts of lightning high in the sky flickered on and off.

"There's an old building not far from here that looks like a barn built into a hill. It has a chimney, so we should be able to stay warm and dry. I rode up and peeked inside a window. I didn't see anything—though I admit I didn't get a very good look. It appears abandoned, so it should be safe. In any case, I think it's our only option just now." As he finished speaking, another flash of lightning shot across the sky.

The hair on Mara's arms rose. "Let's go then. Be quick about it, but be careful. We need to get these horses out of this weather before one of them bolts. And besides, with all their gear, they're easy targets for lightning."

As Jules turned away, she called to him. "Wait, Jules—how far is it?"

"Shouldn't be more than a couple minutes," he said as a gust of wind suddenly blew.

"Let's go!" she ordered.

Raindrops fell sporadically, then increased as though they were grasping to catch a rhythm, a beat beyond the riders' abilities to hear.

Mara waved her hand, motioning for Nina to go next. "Go!"

The young woman urged her horse onward with her heels.

"Quickly! Quickly!" the Oathtaker exclaimed just as both infants cried out.

Within seconds, the wind became a howl. Rain pelted down, stinging the travelers' faces. It slapped at the dry ground, then splashed back up, quickly soaking them and their mounts.

Through the downfall, the outline of what looked like an old gray barn built into the side of a hill became visible. Some wood shingles from its roof broke free. They flipped and tossed through the air.

"Hurry!" Jules shouted to those behind.

Nina's horse stumbled. Fearing it would fall and roll, Mara urged her mount forward, preparing to pull the young woman toward herself if need be. Then the animal righted itself.

"Are you all right?" Mara shouted over the rushing wind.

She nodded, then looked toward the barn.

Jules dismounted. He ran to the door to slide it open upon its rail, but struggled with it. It wouldn't budge.

Oh, no, he can't open the door! It's locked! Mara bolted toward the barn, dismounted in a flash and tossed Cheryl's reins to him. She grasped Spira and then, with one deft move, the lock gave way.

He rolled the door open and seconds later, Nina rode inside.

Mara rushed to her side. "Are you all right?"

Therese with Reigna entered, followed by Samuel, who quickly closed the door, cutting off the storm's fury.

"I'm fine." Nina, teetering, handed the now wailing Eden, to Mara.

Jules grasped the young woman's hand and helped her to the ground. He hesitated before releasing her.

Her eyes fixed on him.

"Are you sure you're all right?" he asked.

"Yes," she pointed to her mount, "but I'm not so sure about Spot. He tripped and I thought we were going down. I feared he'd crush Eden and me." She looked at Mara. "Oh, I'm so sorry! Eden may have been hurt. Crushed!"

"It wasn't your fault. I should have watched the weather more closely. The storm surprised us is all. You're not to blame yourself."

A gust of wind slammed into the building. The windowpanes rattled and clattered when a small branch brushed against them.

Nina jumped. "Oh!"

Mara squatted down, chuckling. "It's all right now." She handed the infant back to her, then turned her attention to Therese. "Are you and Reigna all right?"

"Yes."

"Let's get some dry things for the girls then. Here," Mara handed her pack to Nina, "check my bag."

Samuel ran his hands over Spot's fetlock, then his knee.

"How is he?" the Oathtaker asked.

"I don't see anything wrong, but I want to keep a good eye on him." He patted the beast's neck as it reached for the carrot he held.

"I'm glad of that. We'll see how he is in the morning."

She turned away and looked around. The building consisted of one large room, its back carved deeply into the earth. A hearth graced one exterior wall. Upon the dirt floor, scattered piles of old riding tack, broken bottles and pottery, a few pails with holes, and bits of rope, laid about.

A ladder stood, leaning against a loft. She approached it to climb, but Jules intercepted her. He assured her he'd give the loft a thorough review.

She continued her survey. As she approached the window, hailstones rat-a-tat-tatted against it. A few jumped near the bottom of the door, like popcorn popping.

"What do you think of a fire?" she asked Samuel. "We could all get dry. I for one," she grabbed the bottom of her skirt and wrung it in her hands, causing a stream of water to run to the floor, "am soaked."

Just then, Jules came back down the ladder. "You see how this is built into the hill?" He pointed to the back of the building.

"Yes," Mara and Samuel responded in unison.

"The upper floor goes back even farther. I think we should check it out, make sure there are no hidden dangers."

"I'll go with you," Samuel said.

The men climbed the ladder, then disappeared from view.

Mara and Nina saw to the girls' needs while Therese tended the horses, removing their wet saddles and blankets and then brushing them down.

A few quiet minutes passed, punctuated now and then with a shudder from one of the horses and the howling wind.

"Mara! Therese! We may have trouble here," Jules said, his voice strained.

"Coming!" the Oathtaker cried.

"I'm not sure you should come up."

"I'm coming anyway. I'll send Samuel down to guard you all," she said to Therese.

When she reached the loft, she directed Samuel back down, then turned to Jules. "What is it?"

He nodded toward the back of the room. They walked for a couple minutes in silence.

"See how this keeps going back?" he asked. "We only came about this far. We thought we shouldn't go any further because— Well, do you smell that?"

A foul odor wafted out of the cavern. Mara put her hand over her nose, then stepped forward. "Oh, gracious!"

"What? What is it?"

"There!" she pointed.

Just ahead, a thick lead chain was attached to the wall. At its other end, was a grut.

The beast awakened. Its piercing red eyes oozed black mucus. It growled as it pulled itself up on its haunches. Thick yellow saliva dripped from its fangs.

"That explains the odor," she said.

"Back away, Mara."

She removed a knife from her boot, confident she could take it out. *After all, it can't hurt me. I carry a grut tooth.* She put her arm out to restrain Jules. "I'm going to kill it."

"You want me to do it?"

"No, really, it'll be my pleasure."

She turned back to the grut. Its wary red eyes followed her every move. Its growl turned to a low scream as it strained on its chain, its teeth bared, its tail swinging side to side. Chips of rock broke loose from the walls. Then, as though it could smell the protection the Oathtaker wore, the beast sat back on its haunches and whined.

"Watch this," Mara said as she threw her knife. Only then recollecting the blaze that would follow, she sprang back, pulling Jules with her.

The grut burst into flames.

Mara and Jules coughed. Moments later, they smiled at one another. The grut had vanished, along with the stench of Sinespe.

"Well done," he congratulated her.

"Thanks. I've had some practice."

"Did you know it would go up in flames like that?"

She chuckled. "Yes. Great, huh?"

He frowned, his brow lowered.

"Oh, sorry. I wasn't thinking about that before I threw my knife. You weren't hurt, were you?"

"No," he shook rubble from his hair, "I'm fine."

"Good. Let's keep going then."

A few minutes later, they found what appeared to be an altar. It emanated light in shimmering colors: the molten blue of a topaz, the clear purple of an amethyst, the deep and dreamy shades of an emerald, the bold crimson beauty of a ruby. Upon the altar sat a small, open book. Odd though the scene was, it was utterly breathtaking.

Ba bum, ba bum, ba bum . . . The sound came from the book.

Mara stepped on something. She glanced down. Human bones laid in awkward positions, as though someone had thrown them, or as though their once breathing owners had writhed in agony before finally succumbing to some greater power. A full skeleton near her feet, still clothed, held a sword in its hand.

"Fat lot of good that did him," the Oathtaker commented, gesturing toward the weapon.

"We should both turn away."

Mara contemplated the scene before her. She looked carefully at the book upon the altar. "It's as though it's breathing," she said. "Do you hear that sound?"

"Yes."

"There's something strange here."

"You think?"

She snickered, then turned serious. "Really now, look at the altar. It's like a shrine. And that book . . . It positively exudes life and beauty. Even the sound of it, like a heartbeat, is like a testimony to life."

"So?"

"So, I have to see what's there." She turned toward the altar. When Jules tried to restrain her, she brushed his hand away. "It's all right. I need to see what the book says."

"Careful."

"I'll be careful." She stepped forward, brushing remnants of an old skeleton from beneath her feet. Smaller bones crunched under her boot. As she got closer, the light from the shrine increased.

"What was that? Did you see the light change?" Jules asked.

"Mmhmmm."

"Be careful," he cautioned again.

"It's all right. I won't touch anything."

"I'll do it."

"Wait. Look." She leaned forward. The light increased. She leaned back. It faded. "You try."

Jules moved toward the book. The light dimmed and flickered. The sound from the shrine altered. Where it had been throbbing like a heartbeat, suddenly it seemed to skip a beat. Then it emitted a low, ominous sort of moaning, like a faint cry.

"Stand back," Mara said. "Something's not right when you get close."

He retreated.

Again she stepped forward. The light increased and the sound calmed back down to a steady heartbeat rhythm. She leaned in. The heady scents of smoky sandalwood and sweet vanilla filled the air. Startled, she drew back. The colored lights faded and the scents fainted away.

Again she leaned in. The light grew until it was so bright that it hurt her eyes, but little by little, they adjusted to it. Every detail of the page to which the book was opened, came to life. It was as though the words rose off the page and lifted toward her.

"I can read it," she whispered, glancing at Jules.

His hand covered his eyes, protecting them from the light. "Well?" he asked.

"Here it is," she said. Then she read: "'*Caution to anyone not called to these words of life and of succor. Proceed at your own risk.*'"

"All right, Mara, that's enough."

"No, wait, listen to this. It says: '*Here are the words of Ehyeh, the Good One, the Author and Creator of all. Here are the instructions for those who may bring restoration and revival, the seventh seventh waited upon, and the other, she who is but is not.*'"

"Can we just go now?"

"No, there's more. Listen to this: '*Only they or their Oathtaker—*'" She stopped, swallowed hard, then began again. "'*Only they or their Oathtaker may rescue these Words of Life. Death will come swiftly but surely to all else.*'"

She stepped back. The light dimmed. "Jules!" she cried. "What if this is for Reigna and Eden . . . and me?"

"How could you know that? What if it's a trap?"

She bit her lip. "Look, I know my duty is to the girls. They are my charge. But if these words are for us—for the girls and me, then—"

"And if they're not?"

"If they're not?" She fixed her gaze on him. "If they're not, then I guess that today, perhaps, I will die."

"Mara!"

"No, don't you see? If these words are for the girls and me, then I have to take them. I have to. If I refuse, I could be putting them in even greater danger. And who knows what this could mean for them?"

"But what makes you think this is for you? How did it get here? Who put it here? Why was the grut back there?"

"Exactly," she said. She paused to collect her thoughts. "It seems there are two ways to look at this. Who could know I'd stop here? Who could know I'd be immune from the grut—that I'd carry grut teeth—protection from the beasts? Who but the most powerful could chain a grut? If all that's true, then how could this be a trap? But even if some malevolent power chained the grut there, it must have done so to keep others away. Yet the Good One already provided me with a way to pass." She lifted the tooth that she wore on a string around her neck.

"Jules, some things can't be explained away as chance or coincidence. Some things could only be by the design, or at least by the allowance, of the Good One.

"I have to do this. If I'm wrong, I may end up with this pile of bones here, but at least I'd go knowing I did what I believed was right. And if I'm right but I refuse my duty, then I'd be responsible for any resulting danger to the twins that I could have avoided. I wouldn't have done my duty by them. And I'd always wonder whether my failure, my own fear or inability to make a decision or to take a risk, was responsible for added danger or harm to them. Better that I meet this head on. For Reigna. For Eden. Don't you see?"

He sighed. "Does it say anything else?"

She leaned toward the book again. "Yes. It says, '*These Words, these Gifts, are for those Long Awaited Ones.*'"

He shook his head in frustration. "At least let's ask Therese what she thinks," he finally said. "I mean, look around you. Others before you might have thought it was for them too and look where they ended up."

Her shoulders sagged. "I suppose you're right. Sometimes I act too quickly, I know. We'll discuss this with Therese, but I believe I have to see what's there."

"Fine."

The two backed out of the cavern and made their way down to the others.

"What is it?" Therese asked. "What's up there?"

Mara described the altar to her, the book that lay upon it, and its message.

"A shrine! An oracle!"

"An oracle? Yes, that must be what it is. But why here?"

"Sometimes the Good One communicates through an oracle. Oh, Mara, it could contain a divine revelation!"

The Oathtaker's eyes narrowed. "I think the message is for the girls—for me."

"What makes you say that?"

"Well, its words seem directed to us. It says it's for '*the seventh seventh waited upon, and the other, she who is but is not.*' I think I've heard those words before."

"They do sound vaguely familiar . . ."

Mara paced. Suddenly, she stopped. "Rowena said something very like that about Eden when she was born. She said something about her being a seventh, but . . . not."

"I don't understand," Therese said.

"How would you describe the child of a seventh pregnancy who is not seventh born?" the Oathtaker asked.

Understanding dawned on Therese's face.

"And," Mara said, "the book says it's for the seventh seventh and 'she who is but is not' and *their* Oathtaker. What other Oathtaker do we know who has more than a single charge?"

"I think you're right."

"It's decided, then. I'm going to go get it."

"But that doesn't explain why the grut was up there," Jules said.

"Grut!" Therese exclaimed as her eyes flickered toward him, then rested back on Mara. "You didn't say anything about a grut," she scowled.

Mara told of the beast chained to the wall and how she'd killed it.

"And what of all those bones? The skeletons?" Jules asked.

"Bones?" Therese grimaced. "What's this about bones?"

"Seems we weren't the first ones to come upon the shrine," he said. "The floor is covered with the bones of others who came before."

"Grut? And bones? I don't know, Mara," Therese said.

"You think the grut killed them?" Samuel asked.

"Maybe," Mara said, frowning. "Look, I know this is the right thing to do. I have to see what's there. I believe it's for me—for the girls and me."

"Therese?" Jules asked, turning to her.

She sighed. "I suppose Mara's right. Someone left the message for some purpose. If it's for her, it could be important."

"I'm going back up," the Oathtaker said.

"All right, we'll do things your way," Jules agreed.

"Jules," she swallowed hard, "if I'm wrong, please take good care of the girls until Ehyeh sends their new Oathtaker. Help Therese to get them safely to Lucy's."

He nodded.

"And take good care of Nina too. She's had a very difficult time."

He looked hard at her. His expression held a question, as though he tried to read whether she meant anything in particular by her comment.

"For me," she added, hoping she hadn't spoken out of turn.

"Sure."

"Very well then," she said as she breathed in deeply and turned toward the altar, "the leap of faith."

She reached forward, jittering, then grasped the book. A surge of power raced through her. Her being tingled, vibrated. She gasped with the glory of it, felt an energy course through her center, as the lights seemed to slip into her. She looked down at her hand. It glowed.

"Mara!" Jules called.

His voice seemed far off. She put her hand out, cautioning him not to come nearer. Then slowly, the colors and lights died away.

It was several moments before she caught her breath. She looked at her companion. "Well! It seems I'm not to die today."

He grinned. "You had me worried for a minute there."

Something startled her. She jumped. "Did you see that?"

"What?"

"Something just flitted by me." She brushed the top of her head and ducked. "What was that?"

"I didn't see anything." He looked about. "A bat maybe?"

"Ewwww, no, it wasn't a bat."

"What did it look like?"

"I didn't get a good look. It was just a flash of light. A shimmer. It was like it flitted out of the book and over my head."

He hesitated, then laughed, the tension finally released. "Don't tell me you believe in fairies now."

"Actually, I'm not sure anything is beyond belief anymore. Did you see what just happened?"

They laughed softly, as comrades who together had come through a difficult time, a battle, then watched as the altar shimmered and melted away. They looked down. The bones beneath their feet turned to dust.

"Whoa!" Mara exclaimed. "All right then, let's join the others. I think they've held off remarkably well."

When they reached the ground floor, Therese was waiting for them. "What happened?"

"Is everything under control?" Samuel asked, his eyes on Jules.

"All is well," Mara said. "We've just had a little—"

"Adventure," Jules interrupted.

Mara laughed. "Yes, an adventure."

"Well?" Therese asked.

"You go ahead," Jules waved at Mara, "I'm going to find scraps for a fire. We all need to dry off and warm up."

Mara and the others sat shivering, on stumps and old pails that Samuel and Therese had collected and placed in a semi-circle before the hearth. The cold wind had found its way inside through nooks and crannies in the exterior walls.

The Oathtaker filled her friends in on what had happened in the cavern.

Jules dropped off a load of wood and put some in the hearth, then walked away.

Mara reached out and flicked her fingers. Flames licked at the wood scraps. As if only then realizing what she'd done, she grinned. "I feel like those flames have been dying to get out!"

"Attendant magic?" Nina asked.

"I guess so." Mara chuckled, amazed at how quickly and easily she'd used those powers.

Turning back to their former conversation, Nina said, "Well anyway, I'm glad you're safe. We need you."

The Oathtaker looked at her, Therese, then Samuel, one at a time. "Look, we all need to get something straight here." The flames sparkled in her eyes. "My job is to protect the girls. I know that, and I can't begin to tell you all how much I appreciate your help, but," she hesitated, "I can't be handicapped with fear, and neither can you.

"I'll do what I think the Good One has called me to do, but if I'm wrong . . . Well, then I trust Ehyeh to come up with another plan for their protection. You'll all need to abide by your oaths to see to that. But *my* safety is not anyone's first concern. Is that understood?"

They sat quietly as Jules rejoined the group. Finally, Therese broke the silence. "You're right, Mara. Understood, everybody? We follow her lead here. Agreed?"

They all voiced their agreement. Only Nina was hesitant, but when Mara's eyes didn't leave the young woman, she finally relented.

"So what's in the book?" Therese asked.

"Let's take a look." Mara held it up. Its cover, made of old, soft brown leather, sported a design in gold of intricate swirls. On closer examination, she made out a crown, a sword, and a scepter. The design looked vaguely familiar. She opened the cover. As her companions all leaned in for a closer look, she turned the page.

There, was the single word, "Go."

"Go!" she exclaimed. "Go where?" She turned the page. Again in intricate script, was the single word, "Go." Again she turned the page. Again the same word appeared. Again and again, she turned pages. Each read identical to each of the others.

"Is that all it says?" Nina asked.

The Oathtaker finished flipping through the book. "They're all the same! But . . . go where? To . . . Dixon?"

"Maybe it just means you should go from here," Therese suggested.

"No, that doesn't feel right."

"Well, maybe it does mean you should go to Dixon. But we talked about this earlier. He's under Lilith's thumb. Your going back would—"

"I know. It would put me in danger. But there has to be some reason for this message. I think I need to go back."

"You mustn't!" Nina exclaimed.

"I must—and as quickly as possible."

"Then I'll go with you," Therese said. "Do you think I could?"

"No!" Samuel and Jules cried in unison.

"But she can keep me safe."

Jules shook his head. "I don't like it."

"Nor I," Samuel said.

"Mara?" Therese turned to her.

"Honestly, I don't know if I could take you along. What's more, I'd like to try to bring Dixon back here. What if I can't travel with you both? No, I have to do this on my own."

Samuel turned to Jules, worry in his eyes.

"Don't look at me," Jules said with an upraised hand. "I've learned not to try to stop her when she's made up her mind."

Smirking, Mara said, "Look, let's all eat now. Then I'm going to give it another try."

"But what if Lilith is there? With Dixon, I mean," Therese said. "What if she catches you there?"

"Then I guess I'll have to return quickly."

"Can you do that?" Nina asked.

"I think so."

"And if you're wrong?"

Mara grinned. "Jules, what if I'm wrong?"

"Well in that case," he frowned, "today might be your day to die."

"Jules," Nina jumped to her feet, "you take that back!"

Mara grabbed the young woman's arm and pulled her back into her seat. "He's just repeating what I told him up there," she pointed to the loft.

"Still." Nina frowned at him.

He looked as though her scolding pained him.

"Stop it, Nina. He's right. Don't you blame him for being truthful."

Their discussion over, they ate as they got warm and dry. Once done, they determined that, except for Nina, they'd take turns keeping watch. Then they all settled in for the night.

It had been a long day. Mara was grateful to close her eyes. As she reclined against her saddle, she listened to her companions. Samuel coughed. Nina cooed softly to one of the girls as she nursed her. Gravel crunched under Jules's feet as he walked the length of the door to the barn, back and forth, back and forth. Therese huffed, then bundled herself into her blanket. The horses whickered, whispering amongst themselves. Gradually the sounds dimmed and then, in an instant, her surrounds changed.

CHAPTER EIGHTEEN

Her confidence having increased with each of her journeys, Mara was more comfortable with the sense of traveling than previously. She felt the movement to, the change in, her surroundings. She concentrated on the colors before her. They were glorious, quieting. They filled her senses, empowering her to deal with whatever was ahead.

She came to a stop and opened her eyes.

Basha stared at her. "It's you again."

"Yes. How is it that you also are here again?"

"Fortunately, I got away earlier before Lilith arrived. I've only just returned now to see to Dixon." Basha's eyes never left Mara, as though she measured her every move. "How do you know who I am? And what's your connection to Dixon?"

"That doesn't matter now. I came to help him."

"Who are you?"

"I told you before. My name is Mara."

"How do I know I can trust you?"

"Look, I'm not here to harm Dixon, I'm here to try to help. Maybe even get him out of here."

Although wary, Basha allowed Mara to approach.

"Oh, gracious Ehyeh, look at him."

"I know, and I'm afraid what Lilith might do next—that she might be driven to even greater destruction." Basha's eyes welled with tears. "He's near death already."

"No!"

"Well, look at him! And I can't wake him or I could try taking him through the tunnel, but—"

"Tunnel?"

Basha gestured toward the door. "There's a back way out of here, but I can't carry him."

"He's blessed to have a friend like you."

"Blessed! Look at him!" Basha wiped a tear away, roughly. "And Lilith's not likely to stop until she gets what she wants."

"What is that?

"I don't know. She refuses to speak to any of us."

"Perhaps I can heal him."

"You're a healer?"

"Yes," Mara said, thinking back to when she'd healed Therese's wound. "I'm an Oathtaker and a healer."

"Is that how you're able to appear out of nowhere?"

"Attendant magic."

"Uh-huh. So your charge must be rather important."

Mara bit her lip as she met the woman's gaze. "You could say that."

"Who?"

"Not now. I'll do my best to fill you in, I promise. But for now, I need to concentrate on Dixon."

"Very well." Basha did not look pleased.

"I think he has some broken ribs."

"I believe so."

Mara put her hands on him. She concentrated on encouraging his body to heal. After a couple minutes, she sat back on her heels and sighed.

"I'm trying to get some power to him, but it just stops dead. Basha, I'm going to try to take him from here. I want to see if I can travel with him. Maybe it's this place."

"How do you plan to do that?"

"I'm not sure I can. But before he was in this . . . prison . . . I traveled to see him. Did he tell you about that?"

"No."

"When did you last speak with him?"

"I haven't spoken to him since the night after he arrived here. I tried the next evening, but the guards refused me entrance to—"

"At the falls you mean," Mara interrupted.

Basha stared. Her eyes narrowed. "What do you know about the falls?"

"Like I said, it's a long story. But since you haven't spoken to him since that night, you couldn't know about my earlier visit to him—before he was brought here. When I saw him, I was able to take something that belonged to him back with me."

"And you think that maybe you can take him with you this time?"

"I'm hoping so. By the way, where is 'here?'"

"We're in the bowels of the palace. Lilith turned it into a dungeon of sorts. Where did you come from?"

"No time now, Basha. I've got to try to take him away."

"I guess wherever you'd go couldn't be worse than this."

Sounds came from outside the door. The same voice Mara had heard the last time she'd found Dixon, called out.

"Who is that?" she asked.

"Adele. She's a maid to Lilith."

"She's got lousy timing."

"She hates Lilith. She's probably coming to warn me that she's on her way back here."

"Can you keep her from coming in?"

Basha went to the door and opened it a crack. "Adele," she said, "what is it?"

"Lilith is coming back."

"How long have I got?"

"Not very."

"All right. I'll leave as quickly as possible. And Adele, thank you."

"My pleasure, believe me."

"Run along then."

"I'll wait for you."

"Adele—"

"No, Basha, I know my way around here better than anyone. I'm staying here to wait for you in case you need help. I'll hide you if need be."

"Suit yourself." Basha closed the door and turned back. "You don't have long."

Mara nearly wept with frustration over not being able to heal Dixon. She wrapped her arms around him to travel, then tried to find her way. She felt the current she was to grasp, but couldn't move. Frustrated, she looked up. "It's not working."

"Hurry!"

"I don't understand. Nothing works. I can't heal him. I can't travel with him." Then Mara had an idea. Her eyes opened wide. "Basha, let me try to take you."

"Me!"

"Yes, you."

"But I need to be here for him if you're unable to take him away."

"I'm just trying to figure out if I can do this at all." Mara smiled, faintly. "Trust me. You'll be glad you did."

The woman's eyes narrowed and her head tilted. "Why would that be?"

"Hurry, Basha, decide. Will you travel with me?"

"Very well."

Mara stood. She put her hands out, palms up, inviting Basha to place hers on top. Once done, Mara wrapped her fingers around her hands. Almost instantly, she felt the current. She stepped into it in her mind and—

Her feet landed. She opened her eyes. "I did it! Basha, I did it!"

"Basha? Basha!" Therese cried, Mara's voice having awakened her. "Is that you?" She rustled up to a seated position, then jumped to her feet.

"Therese? Oh, dear Good One!" Basha turned to Mara. "You didn't tell me!" she exclaimed before rushing to her charge and embracing her.

"Surprise," Mara said with a grin. "Listen, I know you two have a homecoming to get to, but I need to go back. I just can't figure it out though. Why could I take you, Basha, and not Dixon? It doesn't make any sense."

Therese turned her gaze from her Oathtaker to Mara. "You tried to travel with him and couldn't?"

"No. I mean yes!" Mara was frustrated, angry. "I was able to travel with Basha, why not with Dixon? And I couldn't heal him either. Now Lilith is on her way back to him, I'm running out of time—and I don't think I'll get another chance. She might kill him this time!"

"Your magic just wouldn't work for him," Basha said, tearing her eyes from Therese.

"Exactly!" Mara exclaimed. She growled with frustration.

"Waaaaait a miiiiiinute," Basha cried, as understanding came to her. "I know why. Lilith banded him."

"Banded him!" Therese exclaimed.

"That's right."

"Mara, that's it! The band is blocking your magic," Therese said.

"Oh," Basha cried, "I'm so sorry. I should have thought of that sooner. The band cuts off all magic and you can't get past it."

"Yes, she can."

"But that's impossible. Lilith is the ranking Select and she banded Dixon. No one but Lilith or or her own Oathtaker can remove it—or one who ranks higher than Dixon. And Marshall won't help. He wouldn't risk her ire. So the only other option that leaves, is the Council, and . . . Well, that's not really an option now, is it?"

Nina, now awakened, stood behind Mara. She stepped forward, Reigna in one arm, Eden in the other. "No, she's not," she said.

"No, who's not what?" Basha's brow dropped low, as she looked her way.

"She's not the ranking Select."

"Of course she is—"

"Basha," Nina interrupted, "meet the ranking members of the Select." She held the infants forward.

The woman looked at the twins, then to Nina, to Mara, and finally to Therese. "I don't understand."

"Look," Mara said, "I know there's a lot to fill you in on, but for the moment I need to know what to do about the band." She turned to Therese. "What do I do?"

"It's simple, really. All you need to do is open it."

"You mean, just grab the band and it'll open?"

Therese nodded.

"But how do I get my fingers under it?"

"It will release at your touch."

"You sure?"

"Positive."

"Then I'm off!" Mara closed her eyes. She identified the current immediately. She jumped in mentally and moments later, found herself in Dixon's presence. She moved to his side.

The door burst open.

"Who are you?" a young woman demanded. She looked all around. "And where's Basha?"

"Shhhh," Mara cautioned. "You must be Adele." *The girl really does have the most abominable timing!*

"Yeeessss. Who are you?"

"My name's Mara. I've come to rescue Dixon." She reached for the band on his arm. Upon her touch, it slipped free.

"How'd you do that? Oh, I hear her now! Lilith is coming. You have to get out of here. She'll kill you!"

"I'm taking him with me."

"Taking him! Where to?"

"Adele, I don't have time. I've got to go. Quickly, before Lilith arrives, get away from here." Mara wrapped her arms around Dixon.

"Well, well, well," came Lilith's voice from the doorway. "What have we here?" She pushed Adele toward Mara and then stood, her back straight, glaring at the three of them.

Mara glanced at Dixon. She couldn't fail him now. She reached with her mind for her traveling stream.

"No!" Adele screamed.

Mara looked up as Lilith advanced.

Adele grasped Mara's arm, fell against her, then kicked out. "No, Lilith!"

Mara found the current. She prepared to jump in. She felt Dixon's added weight—and something more. Adele, holding her arm, was going to be caught up for the ride. Mara hoped that Lilith didn't reach them before they were all swept up into the traveling wave together. If so, she would deliver the woman right to the girls' hideaway.

She looked up and caught Lilith's eyes of fury, and in that instant she— vanished.

With a thump, she landed, Dixon beneath her. Worried she might crush his already damaged ribs even more, Mara quickly rolled to her side. As she did, another weight fell upon her. *The moment of reckoning! Did Lilith catch a ride along with Adele?*

Frantically, she pulled to her feet as she grasped Spira. This was one of those rare circumstances that would allow her to use a weapon against a member of the Select: the life of her charge, or her own life in the course of her protecting her charge, was in imminent danger.

She crouched, preparing to meet the threat. In a moment, Samuel and Jules were at her side. Each held a sword pointed at Adele thinking it was she against whom Mara intended to defend herself. Near the men stood Basha with her Oathtaker's blade in her hand.

Adele slumped to the floor.

"Stop!" Mara cried. "She's harmless!"

"Oh, it's Adele!" Basha exclaimed.

The young woman was on the floor, one leg stretched out, as though kicking something away. She sat up and shook herself, ruffling through her hair to shake loose the dirt from the floor. She glanced up to find a ring of onlookers. "What happened?" she asked.

"It looks like you came along for the ride," Mara said. "I hope you're not in a hurry to return to the palace anytime soon, because I have no intention of going back there."

Adele scrambled to her feet, tottering on her lame leg. She grasped Mara's hands, kissed them repeatedly, then fell to her knees. "Oh, may the Good One bless you!" she cried. "I've been trying to get away from there for . . . Well, ever since Rowena left." She looked around. "But where am I?"

"I'll let Basha and Therese explain things to you. I have to see to Dixon."

"Oh, Therese," Adele cried, "we all thought you were—"

"Dead. Yes, I know."

Mara knelt beside Dixon.

Jules approached. "Will he be all right?"

"I don't know," she said, her voice shaking. "He's in very bad shape."

Jules rolled Dixon over. "Gracious Ehyeh!" he exclaimed. "He's hardly breathing."

Mara laid her hands upon Dixon and summoned the force within her being. She needed all her knowledge of healing, and all the power of her attendant magic—and she needed it now.

She released magic into him. She moved her hands over his injuries, beginning with his ribs. She felt the knitting of his bones, the renewed strength of his breathing. She concentrated on the condition of his heart and lungs. His pulse quickened.

Methodically, she sought out his other injuries. Beneath her hands, her power seemed to light up within him, bringing healing to his bruises and the bleeding lacerations that criss-crossed his body.

She turned his face toward herself. His eyes were swollen shut, black and blue. She laid her hands upon them. Nearly spent of energy, tears rolled down her cheeks as she reached within herself for more power, more magic.

His eyes fluttered. He groaned.

"Shhhh, Dixon, shhhh. You'll be all right." *Dear Good One, heal him!*

"Mara?"

"Shhhh, Dixon."

"Mara, go. Lil—"

"It's all right, Dixon. You're safe now."

"Mara . . . run. Reigna. E—"

"Shhhh, Dixon. Sleep." She needed to settle him down. He was agitated and trying to get up. Then she remembered the night with Drake and Maggie. Dixon believed her singing had put them all to sleep, and later, Ted had hinted at the healing power of rest. Was it a foolish idea? *Oh well, no harm in trying.*

She placed her hands to the sides of Dixon's head and her lips near his ear. Then she hummed an old lullaby. Softly, sweetly, she encouraged him to sleep through her rendering of the ages old melody.

He took in a full cleansing breath and then fell into a deep, deep sleep.

It was then that Mara slumped to the floor.

CHAPTER NINETEEN

"Mara." The voice came from somewhere distant. "Mara, wake up now."

Her head was foggy, her thinking lethargic. She couldn't concentrate. *Is someone calling me?*

"Mara!"

Someone lightly slapped her face.

There was something on her forehead. It was heavy and cold. *Is that a damp cloth on my forehead? Whatever for?* She tried to fight through the fog. *Where am I? What's happening?*

"Mara," the voice urged again. It was insistent, growing louder.

Through her sluggishness, she wondered, *is there danger? What's all the fuss about? Oh, go away and let me sleep.*

Again the voice called out. Again someone slapped her face. "Wake up now, Mara. Can you wake up now?"

Slowly, she turned her head from side to side. She didn't want to awaken. She wanted to stay in the land of dreams.

Wait. Who is that? For a moment, she fought for clarity, but her dreams called her back. She smiled as she felt herself drifting away.

"Mara!"

It's that voice again. Who is that? I know that voice.

"Mara!"

She groaned.

"There she is. She's coming to now," someone whispered.

Another slap—a little harder this time.

Ouch! Is that absolutely necessary?

"Mara."

Frustrated with her inability to remain in that place of calm and quiet, she struggled to regain consciousness. *If I can just get through this fog.*

She pushed harder, concentrated more intensely. Finally, she felt the fog lifting. The sounds and smells around her grew louder and stronger. She heard voices, the shuffle of horse hooves, wind whistling, and a fire crackling. *Is that burning wood I smell? Yes, there must be a fire here. Mmmmm. Do I smell food?*

"Mara!"

She opened her eyes slowly, then closed them again. They were so heavy, but at least her grogginess was dissipating. She opened her eyes again. "Dixon?" she asked, in a whisper.

"Yes!"

He's smiling. He looks good. He's whole. He's healed! "Oh, Dixon," she breathed in deeply, "is it really you? Are you all right?" Her words tumbled out slowly.

"Yes, it's really me."

"Oh, I thought you were done for." She turned away and closed her eyes.

He put his hands to her face and turned it back toward himself. Seconds passed before she opened her eyes again. Smiling, he said, "I hear I have you to thank for saving my life."

She closed her eyes. "It was nothing," she mumbled.

"Right. That's what I told the others, but they insist I should be grateful to you."

Her eyes flashed open. *If that didn't beat all!* Then she saw it. He was teasing her.

He chuckled. "Well, I guess I know how to awaken you now."

"Really? How's that?" she asked, smiling in turn.

"Just appeal to your greater vanity."

"Charmer."

"Ha ha ha!" he laughed. "Well, I see you're back to your old self. But you had us frightened there for a time," he added, now serious.

She tried to sit up, but feeling very weak, gave up.

"Did I hear someone say you were charming, Dixon?" Basha asked. She stood near him, her hand on his shoulder, looking down at him. She smiled, though Mara could see it was an odd smile. It was sad, somehow.

"Pure flights of fantasy, I'm sure," he said.

Mara groaned. "But don't you know, Basha? He has the power of charm. Or so *he* says."

Basha's eyes held Dixon's. Once again, there was a touch of sadness in her expression.

He turned away.

"Well, all right then," Basha said. She turned to Mara. "I want to officially introduce myself and to thank you. I can't say how much I appreciate what you did to reunite Therese and me."

Mara waved away her words. "It was nothing."

"Are you feeling better?"

"I'm fine. I don't know what all the fuss is about. I'm just tired, I guess."

"That'll teach you to go on a magic binge," Dixon said.

"See what I mean, Basha? All charm, this one." Mara closed her eyes. A long moment passed. Then she looked out again. She blinked repeatedly, trying to gather her thoughts. "What are you talking about, Dixon?"

"You really need to use more care with your magic," he chided, still smiling.

"What do you mean?"

"It has a price. You could have killed yourself with all that magic. Traveling—with others. Healing. What were you thinking?"

He looks worried—like he cares. The thought startled her. She shrugged. "Just doing what I had to do."

"Yes, the others told me all about the oracle while you were out," he said. "I think you're right—about the reference to the girls as 'the seventh seventh and she who is but is not.' I'd never thought about it before. But, dear Good One, we thought you'd never awaken again."

She tried to shake off her lethargy. "How long was I out?"

Basha squatted down. Holding an apple, she took a bite.

Mara watched her closely. Her eyes narrowed. "Where'd you get that?"

Basha looked down at her apple, then pointed toward a bucket near where the horses stood. "Over there," she said. "Want one?"

Mara pulled herself up on one elbow. Without further thought, she reached forward and—

An apple flew to her hand. "Ah!" she exclaimed when she realized what she'd done. "What just happened?"

Dixon frowned. "Careful, Mara. You need to regain your strength. This is no time for magic."

"Sorry," she said, looking chagrined, "I wasn't thinking. Besides, I didn't know I could do that."

"Yes, well take it from one who knows," Basha said. "You don't want to make that a habit."

"What do you mean?"

"The ability to move things. It can be . . . addicting."

"She would know," Dixon said.

Mara's eyes flashed from him to Basha. "What?"

Basha tipped her head, her lips pursed. "It's part of my attendant magic, as well. I went through a spell—when I first discovered the power—of using it a bit too much."

"Too much?"

"Yes." Basha's expression turned serious. "It can make you lazy—and lazy means weak. Anyway, it's a good power to have, and you should practice it some. Just don't make it a habit."

"Hmmm. Here, help me up."

Dixon offered his arm. "Not too fast now. You're just coming off a . . . binge, and you've already started back into the magic. Take your time."

"That's right," Basha said. "You need to regain your strength. You've been out since you healed Dixon. That was . . . Well, you were out all of yesterday and all of last night and it's nearly midday now."

Mara took a bite of the apple. It was fresh and juicy. The sweet fruity smell filled her senses. "Mmmm. Good. I'm hungry." She stopped chewing. "You mean I slept all of yesterday?"

Basha nodded.

"And it's midday now?"

"Nearly, yes."

"I suppose we should be on our way." Mara tried to get up, but still weak, dropped back down.

Jules approached. "It's still raining. I think we should wait to see what tomorrow brings."

"And just wait around here? Doing nothing? Getting nowhere?"

"It would give us all a good chance to get fully rested. Dixon still isn't at his best," Basha said.

"Hey, hey, hey!" he responded in mock disagreement.

Mara shushed him. Her head hurt. "I suppose I could use some more rest. I feel like I've been drugged." She took another bite of her apple. Her strength was returning, little by little. "Oh, what's wrong with me?" she suddenly cried. "How are the girls?"

"They're both well," Nina said as she drew near. "We're all well, thanks to you. But we needed to wake you, to make sure that you were all right. You ran a fever most of yesterday and last night. We were very worried for you."

"Thanks, Nina."

"Samuel found a big old trough out back. We all helped drag it in and have taken turns bathing. I think you'd enjoy one."

"Baths? How'd you get enough water for baths?"

"A nearby spring."

"And you got it warm enough?"

"You can thank Basha and Dixon for that," Therese said as she neared.

Mara looked at Basha. "Attendant magic?"

"Comes in very handy."

"Sounds good. But right now—I just want to *eat*."

Her companions laughed. It was the sound of a great release.

"So is this all I get? A lousy apple?"

Still chuckling, Dixon went to the hearth, then returned with a plate of hot roasted hare and hash-browned potatoes.

With Basha's assistance, Mara sat up. She ate. Twice, she asked for more. Twice, Dixon refilled her plate.

"Gosh, Dixon, if you're any nicer to me, I might start believing those rumors you keep spreading about yourself," she said, her voice low.

"Oh, you mean about my being so charming and all?"

She looked at him, held his gaze. He actually did seem rather charming at the moment. "Right. Anyway, you're looking well."

"Mara, truly, I can't thank you enough. I—"

She patted his hand. "Forget it."

He nodded. "So, about this oracle . . ."

"What about it?"

"Therese tells me that you thought it was telling you to go to get me."

"We all did." She swallowed a mouthful. "Look for yourself. Every page says the same thing: 'Go.'"

"Funny thing is—it doesn't say anything now."

She bolted upright, nearly spilling her meal. "What do you mean?"

"He's right," Therese interrupted, having overheard. "The book is empty now."

"But you all saw what it said!"

"Yes, but it's blank now."

"Where is it?" Mara tried to get up, but a wave of weakness washed over her. She feared she might faint. With Dixon's help, she settled back down.

"I'll get it for you."

When Therese returned with the book, Mara opened it. She was astounded. Every page was blank. She closed it again and looked at Dixon. "I don't know what to say."

He took it, then ran his fingers over the design on its cover. "You recognize this?"

"Can't say that I— Wait a minute. It's familiar somehow, but I can't place it."

He leaned in closer. "The compact," he whispered.

"Of course!" She reached into the pocket of her tunic where she kept the compact, and stole a quick glance at it. Sure enough, the symbols were identical. "Is that significant somehow?"

"I have no idea."

"Oh, Dixon, there's just so much I don't know. That's why I knew I had to bring you back here. When I saw what Lilith had done the first time I was there— after she started torturing you—I was so frightened for you. I . . . I just knew the message meant that I had to go for you."

"We'll figure it out, Mara. We'll figure it all out."

She smiled in gratitude, then looked around at the others, all busy with one task or another. She was blessed to have this team. She looked back at Dixon. "So what did Lilith want from you?"

He patted his knee, a mannerism that told her that he was thinking. "She figured out that Rowena's child is alive."

"You mean children."

"No, I mean 'child.' She doesn't know there are two of them."

"How did she find out?"

"Well, Rowena had always said that she wouldn't release her power until she bore her seventh. But of course, she did release it. If she hadn't, the position of ranking member would have reverted to her siblings—to Lilith, the next in line. Then Lilith would've been endowed with the magic that goes with the position. But of course, she wasn't.

"Also, I suspect she spoke with the men who'd been dogging Rowena and me. They arrived in Polesk right after she found me at sanctuary. They must've learned enough from Drake and Maggie to pass word along to her that Rowena's *child* had been born."

"And you couldn't just tell her that she was wrong?"

"Like I said, she received no magic power upon Rowena's death. It passed to Reigna or Eden—or both, I don't know. Then of course, since the girls haven't reached the age of accountability and found favor with Ehyeh, *you* as their Oathtaker, possess that power, as well as the attendant magic that comes with your position as their Oathtaker."

"So—"

"So she was furious! She used some strange magic on me. It was awful." He closed his eyes, apparently recollecting the torment, and shuddered. "When that didn't work, she set her thugs on me and had me beaten."

"And you said nothing."

"I'd like to think I wouldn't have anyway, but I think I may have been protected from giving away your secret by the oath that I'd sworn to protect the girls."

"I don't understand."

"Well, as you know, when you take your oath for the protection of your charge, the Good One gives you strength to help you hold to it. Some say you can't breach your oath—that you can't intentionally do anything to harm your charge."

"Hmmm."

"Most anyone would succumb, sooner or later, to torture. But some believe an Oathtaker can't—if it would mean that he would betray his charge."

"You mean an Oathtaker would be tortured to death first?"

"I don't know for sure. But I believe Ehyeh protects us. If the only choice is betrayal, or death, I believe the Good One won't allow us to choose betrayal."

"An Oathtaker has to choose death."

"That's what I believe. There may have been a time when this was commonly known, but no longer, I'm afraid."

"But even if you're right, you're not the girls' Oathtaker."

"Maybe not, but I think the Good One held me to my vow just as He would have held you to yours."

"I'm sorry for all you suffered, Dixon. Truly. And I'm glad you're well now and back with us."

"That makes two of us." He chuckled. "But next time, take it easy on the magic."

Oh, why can't he just stop when he's ahead?

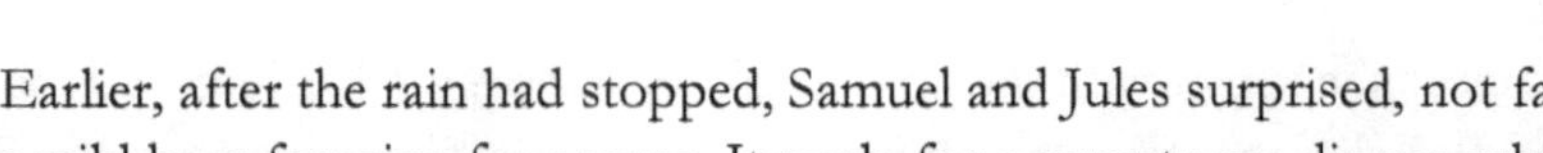

Earlier, after the rain had stopped, Samuel and Jules surprised, not far from camp, a wild boar foraging for acorns. It made for a sumptuous dinner, which Adele had prepared on the open fire, proving her willingness to be of assistance. Everyone seemed relaxed, as they all were now clean, dry, warm, rested—and fed.

Mara finished her dinner with a bite of the crunchy potato skins, savoring the steaming hot pulp. She watched Basha and Therese. It seemed that wherever one went, the other followed shortly behind. Their bond was very strong. Watching them, she got new insight into Dixon's pain from losing Rowena.

She looked down at Eden, in her arms, and contemplated what losing the girls might be like. She was startled at how completely she'd changed since becoming their Oathtaker. The very thought of losing one of them pained her greatly—and it brought back memories she did not want to probe. She shook her head to dispel them, then turned her attention back to the ongoing conversation of her friends.

"I simply don't know," Basha was saying. "It was as though she changed suddenly. She was always difficult, but then she seemed out of control. It reminded me of how she behaved back before Rowena took her son. You remember?"

"Her son!" Mara cried. "What son? What are you talking about?"

"Oh, it's a long story, but Lilith had a child—not long before we thought Therese had been assassinated. Rowena took him and . . . well, no one really knew why."

"She took him? Why would she do that?"

Dixon, having left the watch to Samuel, approached the group huddled in a semi-circle around the hearth. "For his safety," he said, "or at least that's my best guess."

"Lilith put her own son in jeopardy?"

He sat beside Mara and drummed a rhythm on his knee, then suddenly went still. "Rowena— Well, she always thought the best of everyone, so I can't say for sure. But some . . . odd things transpired, so she made arrangements for Lilith's son. All she told me was that she thought it better to be safe than sorry."

"What did Lilith say about that?"

"Now that's where it gets interesting."

"That's right," Basha interrupted. "Lilith never said a word. Never asked after him. Never asked for him. It was as though he'd never existed."

"Where is he now?" Mara asked.

"With Lucy," Therese said.

Dixon and Basha looked at her in surprise. This was news.

"Huh. Interesting," Mara said. "And his father?"

Dixon shook his head. "No one knows."

"Hmmm."

"Yes, well, as I was saying, Lilith is behaving strangely," Basha said. "I'm frightened of her."

Dixon looked down at the fire. "She's right. Lilith is operating under something different—something dark."

"Dark magic?" Nina asked.

He shrugged. "If I had to guess, I'd say so."

"But why?" Therese asked. "What could have happened to her? I mean, she always seemed to lack confidence, always wanted to be the center of attention. But to have gone to the dark side? To serve the master of Sinespe?"

"You think she lacked confidence?" Basha asked.

"Or maybe she lacked some sort of self esteem—like she wanted the best, but didn't think she was worthy, somehow."

"Self esteem!" Dixon exclaimed. "No, Therese, I'm sorry to say, you couldn't be more wrong. Lilith doesn't lack confidence or self esteem."

"But she was always trying to be something she wasn't," she argued. "It was obvious from the time Rowena was little that Lilith resented her. You know, I recall the day Rowena was born. In that moment, Lilith changed."

"Which proves my point exactly."

"And that is?"

Mara put her hand on his arm. "Let me see if I can do this." She glanced to the ground, noticed a stick someone had used to spread the fire earlier, then called it to herself by magic. When she looked up, Basha's eyes were on her.

"Practice, but be careful," she cautioned.

Mara smiled. She liked this particular attendant power, though Basha seemed so cautious about it. She would have to get the rest of that story someday. She looked back at Dixon.

He grinned at her. "Go ahead."

"The truth is," Mara said as she spread coals about, "that Lilith doesn't lack self esteem. The truth is that she esteems herself so highly that she thinks she should have—or should have had—Rowena's place. The truth is that Lilith would be willing to expend anyone or anything—other than herself—toward her cause."

"What do you mean?" Nina asked.

"Well, most evil comes from someone trying to be something they are not. Or from someone trying to do something they have no authority to do. Or from someone taking something they have no right to possess. That's how Lilith is.

"She doesn't lack self confidence or self esteem. She lacks self discipline and self control. And you can be sure she has bound herself to the powers of Sinespe.

I saw it in the look of her. She exuded evil. I could practically smell it." Mara shivered.

"I think she's right," Dixon said. "Lilith is very dangerous."

Everyone looked down or away.

Finally, Therese broke the silence. "So what do we do? I couldn't harm her. Evil or not, tied to the underworld or not, she's my sister. And you all," she said motioning at Dixon, Basha, then Mara, "are Oathtakers. You can't harm one of the Select—not unless it's in the course of protecting your charge."

"Who said anything about harming her?" Basha asked.

"No," Dixon said, "I think she's onto something."

"What do you mean?"

"I think we might have to go far away from here—at least for a time. Lilith will pursue the girls to the ends of the earth if she has to. And there's little we could do to stop her, particularly given the dark magic she now wields."

Mara sighed. "So we need to find our way to Lucy's."

"It seems the best course."

"Enough of this," she said. "We need to make plans. I say if it's not raining tomorrow, we move out—try to make time as quickly as possible. The farther we are from the palace and from Lilith, the better. It's going to take plenty enough time as it is. We've none to lose."

"I agree," Basha said.

"You know, Mara, you could just travel ahead with the girls. You probably don't really need any of us," Dixon remarked, his head down, as though he didn't want to see her reaction, didn't want to admit she'd done, and would likely continue to do, very well without his assistance.

She looked at her cohorts, each in turn. She bit her lower lip. "I had thought of that."

"So you see? It makes sense," he said, scrambling to his feet.

Mara put her hand out to stop him. "No, wait. I said I thought about it, but I don't like the idea." The expectant eyes of the others were upon her. "First, of course, I'm getting better at this traveling thing, but I'm not all that certain that I have much control over where I'm going—at least not yet. So how would I get to Lucy's? Second, I feel we're supposed to do this together. At a minimum, I need Nina to help with the girls. The truth is that this job is too big for any one person."

Nina caught Mara's eye and smiled. She appreciated the importance of her role.

"Still," said Basha, "Dixon's idea merits consideration."

"Let me finish," Mara interrupted. "Third, I've considered taking you all one or two at a time, but," she grinned, "I've learned my lesson, you might say, about overdosing on magic."

Basha laughed.

Dixon looked at Mara with a smile and a wink.

"And finally," she said, grinning, "you'd all simply miss me too much. I just couldn't do that to you!"

The sounds of laughter filled the air.

"Restrain yourself, Dixon," she said.

"What? What are you talking about?" he looked at her, clearly perplexed as to what she meant.

She laughed heartily. "I know, after all the troubles we've had, you'd find it a relief to be free of the worry I've brought."

He chewed on his lip, then responded. "It's not kind to read the thoughts of others when they are unaware."

Her eyes flashed wide. Her mouth dropped open.

"Ha ha ha! You have to admit, you set yourself up for that one!"

His mirth contagious, she joined him. "So it's agreed. We stick together if possible. Right?"

"Right," her friends responded unanimously.

"Anyway, there's a more immediate issue to attend to."

"What's that?" Nina asked.

Mara's looked at Adele. "Adele, do you want to stay with us?"

"Yes," the young woman's eyes narrowed. "Why?"

"Basha?" Mara turned her way.

"I wouldn't be anywhere else. I feel I've found my way home. Why?"

"Oh, I know!" Nina giggled, then covered her mouth.

Jules grinned at the sound of her mirth.

"What?" Adele and Basha both asked.

"Well," Mara said, "I'd like to have you stay with us, but I need to know where your loyalties lie."

"I'd do anything for the girls," Basha said.

"Me too," Adele agreed.

"Well if that's the case, you won't mind swearing to that. Of course if you do mind, that's not a problem. We'll simply accommodate your decision. Either way, I need to know where you stand."

"I realize you don't really know us, but is an oath necessary to assure you?" Basha didn't seem the least troubled by the prospect, more like she found it interesting.

Therese placed her hand on her Oathtaker's arm. "Prepare yourself for a grand surprise," she said.

"Can she do that, Mara?" Dixon asked.

She looked surprised. "You mean—"

"She's subject to her oath for Therese's benefit."

"Hmmm. I never thought of that. But then I swore an oath for the protection of two people—for both of the girls."

"Oh, I have no problem with swearing an oath if . . . Well, you don't mind, do you?" Basha asked Therese.

"Not in the least."

"It seems like the right thing to do. So, what do you want me to say?"

"It's simple, really," Mara said. "Just, if you want to, swear you'll protect the girls with your very life. If you mean it, that is. Above all, it must be a true and voluntary oath if you give it."

"No, of course I'll give an oath. You mean like the one I swore to protect Therese?"

"Exactly."

"Very well." Then without hesitation, Basha continued, "I swear to protect Reigna and Eden with my very life if need be."

The ground shook. The windowpanes rattled and dirt and debris from the ceiling rained down on the troop.

"Oh, Dear Good One!" she exclaimed.

Therese laughed. "I told you that you were in for a great surprise."

"But *she's* the girls' Oathtaker!" Basha pointed at Mara.

"Remember the night at the falls?" Dixon asked. "Remember I told you I'd seen strange things with the oath?"

"This is what you meant?"

He grinned. "Quite something, isn't it?"

Mara turned to Adele who was brushing fallen dust and rubble from her hair. "Are you up to this?"

She smiled. "I might know Lilith better than any of you right now. She's evil and cruel. I'd help the twins even if it didn't mean bringing her down. But the fact that it might only helps!"

Everyone laughed.

"Go on then," Mara encouraged, "if you like."

Adele got to her feet. She teetered for a moment on her crippled leg and then, bowing at the waist toward the girls, she said with theatric aplomb, "I am at your service dear Reigna and Eden. I swear on my life I will do all I can to protect you."

As Mara had come to expect, the earth trembled. The barn shuddered.

Dixon jumped to his feet to catch the young woman, as the shaking caused her to lose her balance. "Well done!" he exclaimed.

Mara looked at Basha, and then at Adele. Her eyes glistened with tears of appreciation. "Welcome to the girls' army," she said.

For a moment everyone was quiet. It was as though the oath gained new meaning each time someone swore to protect the infants.

"So," Jules said at last, "is everyone up for some intense traveling come morning?"

"I'm ready. I feel great," Mara said.

"Me too," Dixon added. "The truth is, I haven't felt this good in a long time." He turned to her. "You really are quite the healer," he said.

She rolled her eyes. "Charmer."

Chapter Twenty

The air crackled. Power emanated from the mirror.

Lilith stood her ground. She shook with unrestrained anger. Her features, which until recently had at least been beautiful when she was at repose, had grown repugnant with her unfettered lust for power and retribution.

She swayed on her feet, concentrating on the pain Daeva inflicted, willing herself to rise above the mere physical. To her sides knelt Sally and Janine, both of whom had sworn their loyalty to Daeva at her bidding.

Sally rocked to and fro, as waves of heat pelted down upon her. Smoke rose from her clothing.

Janine clutched at her throat, agonizing over each breath, her eyes wide in terror.

"You'll kill them!" Lilith cried.

"They should be sssso lucky." Daeva's visage pulsed with power. "How could you have failed me again?" His voice caused the floor to shake and pictures on the wall to rattle.

Lilith stood firm. "There was nothing I could do. Daeva, stop."

"Why, you pompoussss little she-devil."

"Daeva," she pleaded, "I've done all you've asked. I'm bringing others to you. Look! I brought my sisters. They've sworn to serve you faithfully. And I'll find the infant. I will!"

He pulled back on his power as Lilith gasped for air. Clearly, he loved to see her squirm and whimper, to beg for his mercy—and he with no mercy to extend.

"But you allowed Dixon to essssscape. This is twicccce now you have had the child nearly within your grasssssp, only to losssse your chance due to—ineptitude. Ah Lilith, my pet, what am I to do with you?" He shook his head. Red eyes punctuated his black skull. They seared into Lilith.

"Daeva," she cried, "I'll find her! I will. No one wants her more than I!"

"Well now, that is where you are wrong."

"I will find her," she repeated. She fell to her knees. She grasped her collar and pulled it loose in an attempt to get more air. She feared she would suffocate.

"How did Dixxxxon escape? I am beginning to think, my dear one, that you fanccccy him—that you never intended to do what you had to do to get the information from him that we require." He scowled. "Oh, you are sssso dissssappointing."

The room smelled of old smoke and sulfur. It made Lilith cough. "I don't know how he escaped," she said, "but I know he had outside help."

"Who?"

"I don't know. I'd never seen her before."

"Her?"

"Yes, 'her!'"

His eyes narrowed. "You're telling truth."

"Yes!"

"How did she get to him?"

Lilith shook her head. "I don't know."

"When did you last see Dixon?"

"Moments before he vanished."

"You ssssay this woman helped him. Was she with him when he—vanished—as you ssssay?"

"There were two people with him: Adele, a palace servant, and the woman I didn't recognize."

"Did you get a good look?"

"Fairly good."

Sally's dress burst into flames. Quickly, she grabbed a nearby shawl, wrapped it around herself, and then rolled, screaming all the while.

"So what, Lilith, my chossssen, do you intend to do about thissss?"

She glared at him. "Before or after I kill them all?"

He laughed. The eerie, grating sound made the hair on her arms rise. "That issss the ssssspirit. Perhapssss I was wrong about you. You might go far, after all. But I think it is time to call in the reservessss." He pulled back on his power.

The three sisters all gasped for air. They panted and heaved.

"What are you talking about?" Sally asked after catching her breath.

His eyes pulsed with heat. "You know Zarek, do you not? The emperor of Chiran?"

The women stared at Daeva. Of course they knew Zarek. Lilith was particularly familiar, having spent time with him a few years back.

"What of him?" Janine asked, her voice trembling.

"Like you, Zarek serves me. Perhaps it issss time you worked with him more directly. With his help, the army you will need will be available to you immediately." He looked at Lilith. "I take it you have a plan," he badgered.

"Oh, I have a plan."

"Pray tell, Lilith, what issss this grand plan of yours?" His voice dripped with ridicule.

"I plan to kill her."

"Yessss, sssso you ssssay. Had you rid yourself of Rowena before she released her power, you would have cut her line off at that point. But now, you musssst get to her child. You must sever that line of descent—and you know how. Yet the infant continues to esssscape your grassssp. You must do better than merely dessssire to kill the child. Oh, I admit, desire is a good start. But, Lilith, how will you see this plan to fruition?"

She pulled herself back to her feet and stood tall, then stared Daeva in the eyes. "If I can't find the single child I seek, then I'll kill them all," she said.

Sally gasped. "Lilith!"

Daeva grinned. "Yessss, you really are a woman after my own heart after all. I like it. Zarek will be of great assssistancccce to you. I'll ssssee that he lendssss you aid assss quickly assss possssible. Sssso, Lilith, when do you hope to put this plan in placccce?"

She sneered. "Is yesterday soon enough?"

Slowly, Daeva's visage dissipated, leaving behind only the sound of his cackling laughter, bouncing and echoing off the walls.

Chapter Twenty-One

The traveling army Zarek sent to the palace of the Select at Shimeron was not large by military standards, numbering only in the few thousands of men. But a small and highly trained group of soldiers could accomplish a great deal in a short time.

Hamm, the commander, rode in advance of the others. His black leathers and armor, complete with holes and dirt, melded into the color of his mount. A large man, his shaved head sported various scars. A particularly gruesome one ran from below his ear to his neck. His narrow black eyes glittered in the late summer sun.

With his principal men to his right and left, he held out his arm, patterned with tattoos of skulls and snakes, signaling a halt. The clanking of armor and squeaking of leather filled the air along with the smells of dirt, sweat, and horse.

From her place inside a wagon with the other slave women, all tied with strips of heavy leather to the wagon's frame, more fetters about their ankles, Erin looked up at the palace.

In stark contrast to her surroundings and state of hunger, bondage, and despair, its exterior glistened in the sun. Banners flew from its turrets high in the air. A beehive of activity covered the grounds: a carriage pulled up to the door, servants labored in the gardens, house staff cleaned the front entrance, and gardeners clipped topiary on the front steps.

Guards stood at the palace entrance and strategically about the grounds, clearly aware of Hamm and his men.

She reflected on her journey. Had she known what would happen, would she have assisted Nina to escape from Zarek's hold? Would she have cried out, revealing her sister's presence in the merchant's wagon that afternoon? If she'd not later confessed, would her masters have relegated her to the position in which she now found herself? In the end, it mattered not. She was grateful Nina had escaped and hoped she'd found freedom.

How wrong she'd been to deride her sister all those months ago. She could not have imagined then the horrors of living day in and day out, servicing Zarek's men. Now, she understood.

Erin realized that she'd lived her entire life from a place of weakness. Her parents must have known they burdened their daughters with shackles. Perhaps they believed their own lives were more important than their daughters' lives and freedom. Or perhaps they believed their actions were the only ones open to them. Now, though the actors differed and the stage props had been altered, Erin remained a slave. But she vowed, one day, she would live free.

She watched and listened as several of the men discussed how and when they would approach the palace where Lilith awaited them.

"Isn't he dreamy?" a nearby voice whispered.

Erin looked up at Genny, another slave. Soldiers had captured her near the boundary of Chiran and Oosa a few years back. Her shabby brown hair was matted and filthy, and her crooked yellow teeth were decaying.

Erin couldn't help but notice that, as compared to the generally accepted standards of beauty, Genny's nose was too hooked, her lips were too thin, and her eyes were too gray—and slightly crossed. Still, of all the slaves, she alone went unfettered because she never caused a problem. She looked at her position as one of opportunity.

In the quiet hours of the late nights, when the other women cried away their sufferings, Genny boasted of how she would find a soldier who would fall in love with her and take her from this life. She was the only one who didn't show her disdain at the men's forced advances, the only one who tried to engage them in conversation, the only one who laughed at their filthy language, the only one who welcomed their attentions. The idea sickened Erin. Still, Genny had made it possible . . .

"Don't you think?"

Erin followed the woman's gaze. It rested on Hamm. A shiver ran down her spine. Hamm was the most violent of Zarek's men. He delighted in the horrors he bestowed upon the women, the degradation they suffered, and the abuses they endured at his hand.

"I thought you were only cross eyed," Erin said, "now I see that in truth, you are blind."

Genny scowled. "It's because you say things like that that you remain in restraints."

"No, Genny, it's because of filth like that," Erin gestured toward Hamm, "that I am in restraints."

"Well I think he's dreamy."

Erin sighed. "Don't you ever want to be free of all of this?"

"It's not so bad."

"I suppose Hamm will be the soldier who falls madly in love with you and frees you from this life?"

"Maybe."

"More like, 'maybe not.' Really . . ." Erin stopped to scold herself for her unkindness. She should be grateful. If Genny hadn't found the tool for her, if she hadn't risked her own safety to help . . .

Erin closed her eyes to stop herself from crying. It didn't seem to matter how many times she told herself there'd been no choice but to abort her child. If they'd known, they would have killed her. The child put her life at risk. Still, she felt guilt—guilt that she'd taken its life to save her own.

What if she'd waited? What if something had intervened?

A new thought shocked her to her core. Were her actions so different from those her parents had taken? At least when she left their home, she was alive and breathing. Guilt drenched her anew.

Erin spent many days bleeding afterwards, shivering and feverish. It was then she knew, somehow in her spirit, that in the moment she took the life of her child, she had damaged herself beyond repair. In that moment in which she committed infanticide, she also committed a sort of matricide. It was not an act against her own mother, but rather, one against the potential mother that previously had lived within her. She knew she would never carry another.

The men made camp for the night. They scattered out in the field, destroying the crop in the process. They raised tents, started fires, fixed meals, and tended to their horses. Tattered and dirty, loud and gruff, they might have spent the evening improving their looks for the next morning. Instead, except for Hamm and his immediate assistants, they drank heavily and brawled as loudly.

As night wore on, the women kept silent, so as to draw no attention to themselves. Eventually the men retired. One by one, the women started breathing freely again, and one by one, they fell asleep. Only Erin remained awake.

She removed from the place where she kept it hidden, the tool Genny had given her. Just looking at it sickened her. With the sounds of sleep all about, she set out to break the leather bands that enslaved her.

The morning brought cooler weather. A light frost covered the grounds. The sun, which had risen shortly after the first of the men, shone with but little warmth. The horses, invigorated by the chill in the air, stomped and whickered while the men readied for their advance to the palace.

With great pomp, the army gathered together for Hamm's orders. He and his assistants, Yuri and Shurik, along with a few additional arms, would meet with Lilith while the others remained just outside the palace grounds.

Hamm was unconcerned with the men's behavior. He believed their wild ways would help to build an overall fear in the people of the land. It would work to his benefit, for where there was sufficient fear, he could meet his goals with limited effort.

Upon reaching the palace, a number of palace guards met Hamm's forward contingent. Both groups remained at attention, carefully eying one another.

Hamm, Yuri, and Shurik, followed by ten more vicious looking men, dismounted. When they approached the palace doors, Bernard met them. As he bowed to the Chiranians in greeting, Hamm pushed the doorman. Bernard lost his balance and slammed up hard against the wall. Before he could steady himself, the commander demanded to see Lilith without delay.

"Excuse me, sir. Who shall I say is calling?" The doorman tried to stand his ground, but the Chiranians would had to have been blind not to see him shake with fear, or deaf not to have heard the quiver in his voice.

"Just get Lilith. She's expecting us."

"Who is 'us?'" Marshall asked as he entered the palace foyer in response to the commotion. He had a commanding presence. His dress was easy, his strength obvious, and his confidence in the face of potential danger, unwavering. He approached.

Lilith's dog, Pompom, followed behind, yipping at his feet.

"Who's 'us?'" Hamm repeated. "Who're you?" He sneered.

Marshall took in the full measure of Hamm and his men. "Let's get a few things straight here. This," he said with a wave of his hand, "is the palace of the first family of the Select, and I, not that I owe you any explanation, am Oathtaker to Lilith, the ranking member of the first family. So again I ask, who are you?"

Pompom stood between the two men. Her high-pitched barking grated on their ears. *Yip yip yip! Yip yip yip!* With each yelp, the miniature canine drew closer to Hamm. When she reached him, she grabbed a portion of his pant leg in her needle sharp teeth.

Hamm smirked at the Oathtaker, paused for a moment, then tilted his head toward Yuri.

On cue, the man squatted down. Pompom tried to back away, but was not quick enough. The Chiranian grasped the animal with both hands, and— twisssssted—its neck. Then he dropped Pompom to the floor.

Behind Marshall stood several members of the palace guard. As he reached for his blade, they all drew swords. Like a dance carefully choreographed, Hamm and his men likewise reached for their weapons.

In that moment, Lilith came into view at the top of one of the stairways flanking the foyer. "Well, well, look who's here," she purred.

"You know these men?" Marshall asked, his question clearly directed to her, though his eyes never strayed from the Chiranians.

"Why, I believe I do," she said. She turned her attention to Hamm as she slowly made her way down the stairs. With each step, the skirts of her red silk dress flowed lazily, like the waters of a late summer stream. She looked the group over and scowled. "What took so long? And where is Zarek?"

"Zarek!" Hamm exclaimed. "Zarek couldn't be bothered with the likes of such a mission."

"Is that right?" Lilith was surprised to discover she'd been looking forward to seeing the Chiranian leader. With ceremony, she made it to the bottom of the stairs and approached the men.

When she neared, Marshall held his arm out to hold her back.

She scowled. It was then she noticed Pompom on the floor. "What's this?" she asked, pointing.

"That," her Oathtaker said, "is the work of that man." He gestured toward Yuri.

Lilith pursed her lips. She was angry at the state in which she found her pet—not because she felt anything for the animal, but because it belonged to her. Once again, she stepped forward, and once again, Marshall restrained her. She pushed his arm away.

"Lilith," he cautioned.

She glared at him. "If you can't be trusted to keep the likes of this filth from harming a small animal, how can I expect that you could keep him from harming me?"

He closed his eyes for a moment. He'd been at the end of Lilith's complaints many times. Still, he'd taken an oath. He couldn't merely walk away. "Lilith, I—"

"Enough!" she interrupted, glaring. "You know, Marshall, I've been giving it a lot of thought. And you know what I think?" She held his gaze. "Do you?"

He stood, mute.

"I think that I shall release you." She tilted her head back. "Yes," she continued, "that's exactly it. I hereby release you."

His mouth gaped open. He stared at her. An Oathtaker was deeply shamed if his charge released him. Yet in that moment, his countenance reflected an incredible release.

"Have you nothing to say?"

There was no arguing with her. He swallowed hard. "Shall I leave the grounds immediately?"

"Immediately."

"Very well then." He bowed and turned to go.

Lilith turned her attention to Yuri. "So this is your doing?"

"Damn thing wouldn't shut up."

"Well . . . you're right, she wouldn't stop yipping. Still," Lilith paused, "you all should know something." She reached toward him, her hand in a fist. She twisted it back and forth in the air. As she did, the man choked, and sputtered, and gasped for air.

Hamm stepped toward her.

"You'd best not," she cautioned, "unless of course, you want to be next."

He stepped back.

Yuri's face turned red. His eyes bulged. He sweated, as though in a great heat. His clothing smoked. He pulled at his cloak, grasping and clawing, trying to loosen it, to free his airways, to stop the burning.

"That's enough," Hamm said.

Lilith glared at him. "I'll say when it's 'enough,'" she snapped.

Yuri fell to the floor. He writhed and shook. His eyes pleaded with her.

"Well, well, look at that!" she exclaimed, pointing at him.

For a moment, everyone stared at her. Even Marshall, who'd stopped at the head of the stairs turned back to watch. Then they all looked at Yuri. Moments later, his body stilled.

Hamm's eyes glared. "You've killed him!"

"Quite right." She paused, then smiled. "And that, I should think, is 'enough' as you say."

He reached for his sword.

"Careful, now. Your sword is no defense against me. In case you are unaware, I'm in charge here, and you'll do exactly as I say." She stood mere inches from him. "Is that understood?"

Shaking with rage, he clenched his jaw.

"Is that understood?"

He dropped his gaze.

"Very well then. But have no fear. I'll give you plenty of opportunity to work out your frustrations."

She paced up and down the line of Chiranian soldiers, measuring each of them and their weapons. At one point she stopped in her review near a young man, handsome in his fierceness, a primitive look about him. His muscles bulged through his uniform. She ran her fingers down the sun-darkened skin of his hand.

He stared ahead, unmoving.

"Hmmm," she said softly, "this will be such fun." When she completed her review, she stopped before Hamm. "Send one of your men out to the rest of your troops. They are to lay down their arms and await further instructions."

He jerked his head toward one of his men who then followed the unspoken order immediately. His leathers creaked, his boots clicked on the marble floor, as he exited.

"The rest of you are to return your arms to their proper places and show your respect to the palace."

The men followed her orders without delay.

"Oh yes, and you," she said, catching the eye of one of the soldiers as she pointed at Yuri's remains, "clean up this mess. It's unsightly." Then she returned to the young man she had admired earlier.

His eyes met hers.

"What is your name?"

"Freeman."

Lilith laughed. She sounded like a schoolgirl giggling shyly, but then her words belied her true character. "Not anymore you're not."

She turned away. "Follow me," she instructed with a glance back at Hamm, then at the young soldier. She stopped to inform the captain of the palace guard to maintain control, then made her way down the hall to her office and followed the red rug to her desk.

"Well then," she said as she took her seat.

The men looked around for chairs.

"Oh, you'll not be seated today. Today you're here to take orders from me." When Hamm opened his mouth to respond, she interrupted him. "I caution you against speaking."

He closed his mouth.

"That's better." She made herself comfortable. "So Zarek couldn't be bothered to attend to me." She exhaled slowly. "I guess you'll have to do then."

Hamm nodded.

"Well, to business then." She paused, her lips pursed. "It seems we have a problem with some people trying to impose an imposter on the first family and thereby on Oosa. Specifically, they have a child they claim is a seventh seventh."

The men said nothing.

"Yes, well, I'm sure you can appreciate the difficulties this presents. So," she smiled, pleased at how easily she'd silenced the warriors, "we must find the child."

The men stood motionless.

"Would you like to know how we're going to accomplish this?" She was enjoying this new position as the bearer of Daeva's power. She could feel his presence with her, in her, even as it seemed to burn through her body and soul. "We need to get the people on our side—to get them to give the child up to us."

Hamm moved to speak, then apparently thinking better of it, closed his mouth. Lilith watched on. "You may speak."

"With all due respect, ma'am, how do you intend to do that?"

She laughed. "Oh, I thought you'd never ask. It's easy, really. We give them good reason to want to give the child to us."

"And that reason would be?"

"We begin our mission immediately. We'll ride into the towns and villages, the havens, farms and communities all across Oosa and . . . here's the best part," she said leaning forward, sneering, "we shall kill them all."

"Kill who all?"

"Why, all the infant girls, of course!"

The men exchanged a look.

"It's genius, don't you think? When word gets out that we seek a certain child—one others would perpetrate upon us as a fraud—and that we'll take the life of any in our search until she is delivered to me, the people will do anything to save their children."

"All the children?" Hamm asked.

"Hmmmm," Lilith pondered. "Well we know the child in question is a girl, only weeks old. So let's simplify this. Since the men will be unable to tell an infant's age, I'll direct them to kill any girl not old enough to speak. Any child that is, except for the specific one I seek. That one they must bring to me—unharmed. She'll be easy to identify by the sign of her birth, the sign of a seventh. If we move quickly and thoroughly through Oosa, we should resolve the problem in short order."

"Sign of her birth?" Hamm queried. "I thought you said the child was an imposter."

"Excuse me?" Her eyes glared.

"Ahhhh," he stammered.

"It's not yours to question. Just do as you're told."

Hamm nodded. Whether the child was a fraud or not was irrelevant to him. "And if we miss the child in question?"

"We won't miss her. It's like I said, the people will clamor to bring her to us when they learn the cost for failing to do so. We'll go house-to-house if need be. I expect we'll wrap this up in record time."

"And how will we know this child when we find her?"

"Like I said, she bears the sign of her birth. I will give a great reward for her." Lilith smiled. "I believe we'll find her with a man named Dixon, the former Oathtaker to my now deceased sister, Rowena. I also have reason to believe that another—a woman, likely an Oathtaker, accompanies the child. But that's all I know."

"Where will we begin?"

Lilith stood, then approached the window behind her desk and looked out at the palace grounds. She hadn't given much thought about where she'd begin her search. She knew only where it would end—with the death of Rowena's child. Then it came to her.

She turned back to the men. "We begin where she was last seen. We begin in Polesk."

Freeman shuffled.

She watched him, her eyes narrowed. "I suppose you're wondering what you're doing here?"

"Yes, ma'am," the young soldier spoke for the first time.

"You," she said, with a sticky sweetness to her voice, "shall accompany me."

Chapter Twenty-Two

Hattie smiled as she reminisced about the sacrifices she'd made since first learning she was to bear her own child. How she'd longed for her little one. For two decades she saw to the needs of the women in her neighborhood, nursing their injuries, healing their children, providing them food when needed, and assisting with their daily needs. Her body showed signs of wear, and still the Good One had not blessed her with a child of her own.

She clearly remembered the day she learned she was pregnant. It was a morning like any other, ushered in by the sounds and smells of the neighborhood. It was also the morning her dear Charles's heart gave out. Hattie still thought of him constantly.

Her back aching, she set out for home, her infant, Claire, in her arms. All day, her spirit had worried. She couldn't pinpoint the reason, but something caused her anxiety. She concentrated on the things around her, so as to be responsive to anything Ehyeh might try to communicate through events, or through others' words and actions, but as yet, she could make no sense of her feelings.

She looked forward to a calm evening with Claire, if only she could shake this odd feeling. She looked up to find a young woman running toward her.

"Hattie! Hattie, have you heard the news?"

"Slow down, Dora." The poor young woman worried Hattie as, inclined to act on impulse, she had two small children, no husband, and no prospects. Young men sought Dora out, but did not consider her seriously as a possible future bride. As such, she was constantly needy, and various social circles ostracized her. Hattie hoped her own influence might be helpful. She spoke wisdom and restraint into the young woman's life whenever possible.

Dora, carrying an infant in one arm, grasped Hattie's hand.

Upon noticing her bedraggled clothing, Hattie made a mental note to go through her own things to find something she might pass on to her. "What is it? And where is your other little one? Where's Larry?"

"Oh," Dora said with a wag of her head, "I left him at home so I could meet you."

"It is unwise to leave your small child unattended."

"It's only for a minute, Hattie. I can see our place from here." She pointed toward home. "Really, relax."

"No, child. You don't seem to understand how quickly things happen, but I do. One minute my Charles was alive and well. The next, his heart gave out and he left me for all time."

Dora pouted. "Don't be ridiculous. Larry's heart is not going to give out."

"Maybe not. But life is full of unforeseen dangers. Now, you run along and we'll catch up later."

"But I have news!"

"Very well then, child, but be quick about it. I'll not be responsible for your leaving Larry unattended."

Dora sighed. "I thought you'd want to know was all."

It had been a long day. Hattie was not up to playing games. Dora could tell her the news or she could move along. "You thought I'd want to know what?"

"Well," the young woman said, pulling a paper from her pocket, "did you see the fliers today?"

"No. Why? What's happening?"

"Oh, it's all so exciting! There's a small army making its way here. Imagine that. To Polesk! And they're nearly here. See, it says so in this." Dora waved a flier.

The hair on Hattie's arms rose. Was this what her spirit had been dreading all day? Was this the danger she'd been anticipating? "What army? What for?"

Dora smiled, clearly satisfied that she finally had Hattie's attention. "Lilith is with them. Or rather, they're with Lilith."

"Lilith! Of the first family?"

"The very one."

"Why are they coming here?"

"She's coming to bestow blessings on all of the infant girls."

Hattie's heart beat wildly. Something was not right. She stopped in her tracks. "Why?"

Dora laughed. "Oh, Hattie, I don't know why. But just imagine, an army! And I saw them. Earlier, I went out to take a look. Ooooh, they looked good." She closed her eyes and smiled.

Hattie scowled. "Dora, you cannot go gallivanting about. You have two small children. You need to be responsible for their sake."

"Oh, blah, blah, blah." The young woman didn't hide the fact that she didn't like Hattie scolding her. "I didn't say I was going to do anything."

"Very well then."

"So, do you want to go with me when I bring Leena for her blessing?"

"When?"

"Midday tomorrow. Lilith is going to be in the town square. The flier says she'll seek out any infants not brought to her. But I want to go. It'll be so exciting, don't you think? Will you go with me?"

"I'll think about it."

"Good. I'll come around for you tomorrow. We should leave early to get a place up close. Well, I've got to go now. I don't want to leave Larry unattended any longer, you know." She skipped away.

"Wait!"

Dora turned back.

"Be careful."

The young woman shook her head. "See you tomorrow, worry wart."

Chapter Twenty-Three

After the townsfolk discovered the army's presence in the vicinity, various messengers carried news from Lilith back to Polesk, announcing when she would arrive on the morrow. Lilith expected record attendance. After all, it wasn't every day a celebrity came to town.

She briefed the men on what would transpire come morning and cautioned them to control their behavior. She wanted the people of Polesk calm and unsuspecting. Already curiosity had spurred some townsfolk to come out to the grounds. The soldiers, under Lilith's threat, disregarded them. It was most difficult for them to ignore the women who lurked about, smiling coyly and gesturing suggestively of their availability. Still, if they engaged with them, Lilith would deliver swift and sure punishment.

The slave women, hidden from view, were grateful to be left alone for the evening after having spent the last night in near continual demand. While they'd hoped Lilith's presence might change their fate, they soon learned that she had no eye for them, no ear for them, no care for them. When they'd screamed out for help, she ignored their pleas. When that didn't work to quiet them, Lilith visited the women. She warned them that if she heard anything further, she would sentence them to an immediate death. With that, and their knowledge of her plans for Polesk—plans they learned when she addressed the men—they were certain she was without conscience or mercy. Thus, their pleas ceased.

The clear night sky displayed but a single sliver moon. The stars once again boasted of their heavenly splendor as the campfires burned out and the night grew old. Conversations lulled and eventually broke off altogether.

When Erin felt certain the others slept, she retrieved her tool. She'd come very close the night before to breaking through her leather tethers. So close in fact, that she had to tie a bandana over her bindings to hide her efforts from the others.

If she broke free tonight, she might make it to Polesk before Lilith and her army and find a safe place to hide. So, she set to work.

Mere minutes later, the last strands of her bonds gave way. She was free. Astonished and delighted, she crawled to the back of the wagon.

"Where are you going?" Genny asked. "You can't leave."

Erin turned, her finger to her lips. She considered lying, but doubted the woman would believe her. "I don't know, but please, don't turn me in. I beg you."

"Where are you going?"

"I don't know, but please, please don't try to stop me. Come with me."

"Why would I want to do that?"

"Genny, this place is no good. But you're not tethered! All you have to do is walk away. So, let's do it. Let's just walk away."

The woman said nothing. She appeared to be contemplating her options.

"Come with me," Erin pressed.

"I can't."

"Of course you can. We'll help each other. We can do it!"

"No, I want to stay here with Hamm."

"Hamm!"

"He's going to take me away from all of this."

Erin's mouth dropped open. "Genny, he lets his men use you, day after day. What makes you think he'll—" She sighed. "He won't, you know. If he cared for you, he'd take you away now."

"You don't understand. He can't do that now."

"He's lying to you." Erin's words were blunt, but true.

Genny's gaze burned. Then as quickly as her anger arose, it seemed to fizzle out. She turned away. "Just go."

"Genny—"

"I said, 'go.' Be careful. And take this," she added as she threw a wool shawl Erin's way.

Erin pulled aside the tarp. The camp was quiet. Even through the darkness she saw sentries making their rounds. She wrapped the shawl over her shoulders and jumped down, then stood motionless for a moment.

She sprinted to a large boulder, then looked about to find her next stopping point. In this way, from shrub to boulder, from boulder to shrub, she made her way to the outer circle of the camp. There, she hid in some brush.

As she was about to stand and make a mad dash, a sentry came her way. She stopped, scarcely breathing.

The man stood for several long minutes scanning the area. Finally, he moved on.

Erin waited a bit longer, then ran from the camp as fast as her legs could carry her.

Faint suggestions of light graced the sky to the east as Erin entered Polesk. She shuffled along in her exhaustion. Her shoeless feet bled. Her clothing was tattered from sparring with thorny bushes along her way. She was hungry, tired, and filthy.

Thinking she heard footsteps from behind, she pulled into a nearby door frame. A minute later, she peeked out. Seeing nothing, she continued on.

After wandering directionless for several minutes, she saw a woman step out of a house carrying what appeared to be an infant in her arms.

Repeatedly, the woman's eyes darted forward, then to the right, then to the left, then straight ahead. Occasionally, she stopped to look behind.

She must have heard about Lilith's plans, Erin reasoned. *That would explain why she's sneaking away with an infant.*

Erin followed, but stayed out of her line of vision. Finally, she came within yards of her.

The woman turned on her heels. In one arm, she held an infant. In her free hand, she held a knife. It was as though she intended to portray life and death in the same instant.

"What are you doing? Why are you following me?" she asked.

"Please, oh please, don't harm me." Erin held her hands up, palms out. "I mean you no harm."

She brought her knife up, clearly intending to use it if need be.

"I escaped from the army camped outside the city. I'm looking for a safe place. I thought, since you appear to be leaving the city, you might know somewhere to go."

"What were you doing with the army? Why is it coming here?"

"I thought you knew since you're leaving with your child." Erin stepped forward.

"Stop right there," the woman ordered. Then she said, "Come," as she motioned to an alley.

"Please, don't harm me."

"I'll not harm you unless you give me reason to. Who are you? Why were you with the army?"

"My name is Erin. I was a slave to Zarek's men."

"Zarek!"

"Yes."

"Of Chiran?"

"Yes."

"What's he doing in Oosa?"

Erin took in a deep breath. "He's not here, but some of his men are."

"What are they doing here?"

"They're with Lilith."

"Lilith. Of the first family?"

"Yes!"

The woman shook her head. "I don't understand. What would she be doing with Zarek's men?"

"They're on their way here—to Polesk. This is Polesk, isn't it?"

The woman nodded. "Why are they coming here?"

Erin closed her eyes and shook her head. "It's too terrible."

"What's terrible?"

"What Lilith is going to do!"

"The fliers say she's coming to bless the infants in the city."

"No, it's a lie! She spoke to the men two nights ago—before they all left the palace. She told them she seeks a child someone is trying to pass off as a seventh seventh."

"What? Why? I don't understand."

"Look," Erin said, "I'll tell you anything you want to know, but you're not safe here." She looked at the infant in her arms.

The woman pulled her child closer. "Why am I not safe here?"

"Well actually, you might be, but your child is in grave danger."

She shuddered. "Why?"

"Lilith told the soldiers that if the imposter child is not delivered to her, she will . . ."

"What? She will what?"

"She will kill all the infant girls."

Swaying, the woman's mouth dropped open. "Are you sure?"

"I heard her myself!"

The woman looked around the edge of the building. The city was awakening. A man walked down the street. A carriage rode by.

"You have to find a place of safety!" Erin cried.

"When is she coming?"

"She's starting her ceremony at midday."

"Here," the woman sheathed her knife, "come." She grasped Erin's arm.

"Where are we going?"

"To see an Oathtaker I know. He may know what to do. If what you say is true, we have to warn others."

Erin quickened her step.

"Lilith wants people to bring their children to her in the town square. She'll look for the child there. If she doesn't find her, the soldiers will slaughter the others. Then they'll search the city, house-by-house."

"Hurry. We need to find Ted."

"Ted?"

"The Oathtaker I mentioned."

"Will I be safe there?"

"As safe as anywhere in this city."

Erin sighed in relief. "Oh thank you! Thank you, ahhh . . . What's your name?"

"I'm Hattie. And you are?"

"Erin."

"Let's go, Erin."

"Bless you!" she cried.

"Bless *you*. Now hurry, Erin. Hurry!"

Chapter Twenty-Four

Hattie and Erin's rambling through the streets became both more conspicuous and somehow less so as the city came to life. As they rushed past, people caught glimpses of their shawls carried in the breeze behind them, of Erin's mangled feet, and of Hattie's distressed countenance.

Nearly an hour later, they arrived at the Oathtakers' mission home, just as the sun made its way fully over the eastern horizon.

Hattie knocked, not loudly, but insistently: *rap rap rap,* pause, *rap rap rap,* pause, *rap rap—*

The door opened. Faith stood inside, her eyes glowering at her unexpected guests. "What's the meaning of this ruckus? You beat upon the door as though death itself was chasing you!"

"It is!" Hattie exclaimed. "Faith, don't you recognize me?" She was panting. Portions of her long gray-streaked hair had escaped their confines. Although the morning was cool, her brow was moist from her exertions. She had her arm around Erin, who grimaced in pain.

Faith squinted. By her fussy hair, it appeared their knocking had awakened her. "Hattie, is that you?"

"Yes! Faith, quickly, where's Ted?"

"Come. Come in! What's this all about? And who's this with you?" Faith turned her attention to Erin, her eyes narrowed. "You look familiar. Do I know you?"

Erin shook her head. "No."

"Come in. Come in."

"Faith, where's Ted? This is an emergency!" Hattie cried.

Faith gestured for her guests to enter. They stepped over sandals and toys on their way. "Sit down," she urged. "Ted likes to get an early start. I expect him shortly. What's this all about?"

"Oh, Faith, have you heard? Lilith is coming to Polesk today."

"Yes, Ted and I talked about this last night. He was concerned because of our last run-in with her. He left last night to look into some things. He says the Select are bound by certain rules and—"

"Your last run in?" Hattie interrupted.

"Yes, just recently. Lilith arrived at sanctuary and insisted a dear friend of Ted's return with her to the palace. The next thing we heard, she planned to take him to the City of Light for a hearing. But the fliers and criers had it all wrong."

"You mean Dixon Townsend?"

"Yes. Do you know Dixon?"

"No." The stray strands of Hattie's hair fluttered about her head. "I read in the fliers about him, and the claims about what he'd done."

"Yes, well, don't believe everything you read."

"Trust me, I don't."

Hattie glanced at Claire, then back up. "Faith, I have to see Ted right away."

As though on cue, the front door opened and Ted entered.

Hattie rose to meet him.

"Hattie," he asked, smiling, "is that you?" He approached, then turned down the blanket covering Claire's face. "She's a beauty. But what are you doing here? And so early? Why it's barely daybreak."

"Ted, it's good to see you. I just wish it were under better circumstances. Oh Ted, we have a problem!"

He looked carefully at her, then at Erin. He cocked his head. "Do I know you, young woman?"

"No."

"Ted, this is Erin. Erin, Ted." Hattie covered Claire back up, then sat back down.

Erin hadn't moved. Dried blood surrounded the cracks and cuts on her feet. Scratches from brambles she'd forced her way through along the roadside covered her legs. The tabby cat jumped into her lap and rubbed itself against her hands and face, begging for attention.

"Look at your feet!" Faith exclaimed. "Why, they're all bloody and torn! What happened?"

Erin looked down. "I'm fine, thank you. There are more pressing matters."

Ted sat near Hattie. "What's going on?"

"Erin, tell them what you told me."

"About Lilith?"

"What about Lilith?" Ted asked.

Hattie sat forward in her chair. "Erin was a slave to Zarek's men. Some of them are coming here with Lilith." She turned to Erin. "Tell him. Tell him what you told me," she repeated.

"I escaped their camp last night and ran to the city. I found Hattie this morning. She said we should come to you for help."

"I don't understand," Ted said.

"You will in a minute." Hattie breathed in short gasps. "Tell him, Erin. Tell him why Lilith is coming to Polesk."

Erin told of how Zarek's men met up with Lilith at the palace and about how Lilith had spoken to the troops. "I couldn't believe my ears!" She closed her eyes and put her hands over them.

"What?" Ted asked. "The fliers say she's coming to offer some sort of blessing to the children of Polesk. Mind you, I've never heard of such a thing, but—"

"No," Erin cried, "she's not coming to bless them! She's coming to kill them!"

Ted sprang to his feet. "What?"

"So you see, Ted," Hattie interrupted, "I've got to get out of the city. I have to get Claire to safety. But I had to be sure you knew so that you could warn the people of Polesk."

"What did she tell her men?" Ted asked, his question pointed at Erin.

The young woman relayed everything she knew.

"Imposter child?" Faith interrupted. "I don't understand."

"She said someone is trying to pass a child off as a seventh seventh and that she'll do what she must to find the infant. She told the men how to identify her, and offered a great reward for her. She swore she'd kill all the infants in Oosa to get to her if necessary."

Faith's eyes met Ted's. They nodded at one another.

"What?" Hattie asked, looking from one of them to the other. "What do you know about this? My Claire is in danger. You have to tell me!"

"We'll do what we can, Hattie," Ted said. "Believe me, I've been looking into the problem of Lilith already. Something's not right with her. I believe she turned from the Good One. If what Erin says is true, then it's clear she no longer follows His ways."

"But an imposter! How could someone put all the children in danger for an imposter? Ted, if you know something, you have to speak up!"

"No, Hattie, I couldn't do anything that would put any child in danger. You know that. You wouldn't either. But I can tell you this much: The child Lilith seeks is no imposter."

"You mean there is such a child? A seventh seventh?"

Ted sat. "Rowena Vala's seventh born."

"Rowena's child? How do you know? Who told you? When—"

"Calm down," he interrupted. "I've seen her. She's real. She is what they claim."

"Oh!" Hattie sprang to her feet. "I have to get out of Polesk right away!"

"But Hattie, I've been thinking. I'm not sure there's anywhere for you to go," Erin said.

"What are you talking about? I can't stay here where Claire is in danger."

"Lilith said that Polesk is just her first stop because it was the place she thinks the child was last seen. She plans to cover all of Oosa if need be."

"Oh, great Ehyeh!" Faith exclaimed.

"Ted, what do I do?" Hattie asked.

Faith exited the room.

"Hattie," Ted said after a moment of silent contemplation, "I've been concerned about Lilith for some time now—since she was here last. If she's doing as Erin says, she's working against Ehyeh's interests. A Select who does so is one to whom we owe no duty."

"What does that mean?"

"The archives tell of past instances when members of the Select acted in ways that put Oosa's people in danger. You might say they were negligent. In other circumstances, worse circumstances, they knowingly acted against the interests of the people, or of others of the Select. Such acts are criminal. According to ancient writings, when a Select acts criminally, she removes herself from Ehyeh's protection."

"But what does that mean for us? For Claire?"

Faith returned with a basin of water, then got down on her knees and put Erin's feet in it. The young woman leaned back and closed her eyes.

"This sanctuary at Polesk is unique," Ted continued. "Ancient writings tell us that it was constructed with the magic of Oathtakers. It was intended to be a place of safety at all times and for all people. I believe Lilith didn't plan for her ceremony to be held at this sanctuary because she knows she can't do what she plans there."

"You mean the children will be safe at sanctuary?"

"If there's a safe place in all of Oosa, I believe that sanctuary here is it."

"Are you sure? What if she does go there?" Hattie brushed hair away from her face.

Ted got up for his shoulder bag. He rummaged inside of it, finally removing a small weathered book.

"What's that?" Faith asked, looking up from her ministrations.

Ted sat next to Hattie. "The libraries at sanctuary are some of the oldest and most complete in all of Oosa. I've spent a great deal of time studying what's there. One of the resources I've gone back to repeatedly over the years, is a study of the written accounts of divinations, vaticinations and prognostications."

"You mean—prophecies?" Hattie asked.

"Well," he tipped his head right, then left, "yes, in part. Sometimes they are prophecies—tellings of things to come. A true prophecy must come to pass, at least eventually. Sometimes they're merely forecasts or predictions of what might occur, or of the effect some event might have if it does occur. Sometimes they're explanations or insights into things past or present and how those events may touch upon things for the future."

"What's this got to do with Lilith, Ted? We need to act quickly."

"I'm getting there." He leaned in. "This little book," he said as he patted it, "is one I've referred to again and again over the years. I never dreamed my years of study would be so important one day." The small red leather book fit in his palm.

Its cover was cracked and dry, making a design that looked like veins on the back of a hand. Its corners were curled.

"What is it?"

"Perhaps the most important book in the entire library."

Faith turned from her task. "What is it Ted? Something's troubling you."

"You might say that."

"So what's the book, Ted?" Hattie asked.

"This," he said, waving the book with each turn of his wrist, "is *The Book of The Blood*."

Ted turned the aged pages absentmindedly. He ran his hands across them as though reading them by touch. "*The Book of the Blood* reiterates the most important history of Oosa, the Select, and of the Oathtakers. It also includes the most critical prophecies about Oosa's future. I believe it speaks directly of events currently unfolding."

"What does it say?" Hattie asked.

"What do you know of our history?"

"Not much, I'm afraid."

He nodded. "That seems to be the way of things these days, and this book shows some of the dangers that can come of that."

He proceeded to tell the others that the history of the earth was one full of slavery, viciousness and cruelty of man to man, and of how, when the people turned from Ehyeh and His decrees, chaos reigned. He told of the origins of the Select and of the Oathtakers and how they left their former lands of oppression and moved to Oosa.

"Upon arriving in Oosa, Ehyeh chose a leader for the people: Patience. She was a seventh daughter of a seventh daughter. Ehyeh granted her magic to help her to lead. He also set forth the means by which that power would pass to the person who would rule after her.

"The Good One provided decrees telling how the people should live. These He inscribed into a crown, a sword, and a scepter. He gave them to Patience to use and to hand down. The three great artifacts serve as evidence of His hand on Oosa and its people.

"Upon the sword Ehyeh inscribed the truths of life and the living. A man was not to take the life of another, except to protect himself or others, or to punish one who'd wrongfully taken someone's life. In other words, murder is wrong, but not every taking of life is murder. One may take the life of another when acting in self-defense or to protect others, sometimes even on a large scale, such as in the form of warfare.

"Upon the crown He inscribed decrees regarding the fair governance of the people. They are to be free to pursue their own ways and dreams, the fruits of their labor belong to them and no one else, they may speak as they choose, and they may follow Ehyeh or not, as they choose.

"Finally, upon the scepter, Ehyeh provided the principles of fairness for those in authority. They are never to use power simply because they are able, but only when necessary. The leader is always to consider what the people want, but recognize that granting something to the many, could harm the few."

Ted paused, collecting his thoughts. "Anyway, back to Patience. At the Good One's direction, Patience established protocol regarding the responsibilities of the first through the seventh born of the Select. These were to be the means by which the Select would participate in overseeing the interests of the community.

"Patience's line lives to this day. It is the line of the first family. Before the ranking member dies, he may release his power to his offspring. If he does, that line will lead Oosa. If he does not, the position of leader will be determined by going back to that ranking member's next older sibling and his or her line." He paused to take a breath.

"So Rowena was the ranking member of the first family. If she released her power before she died, the rank would fall to her children," Hattie said.

"That's right."

"And did she release her power?"

"She did."

"Thank goodness." Hattie rubbed her head in thought. "But wait. If she released her power and something happened to her last born, wouldn't it still remain with her other children? Wouldn't the power go to Rowena's next older child?"

"Yes," Ted said, "unless . . ."

"Unless?" Faith asked.

"Unless the entire line is cut off."

"How could that be?"

"Listen to this." Ted shuffled through and then read from *The Book of the Blood*. "'*Should the life of a Select be cut off by the blade of a living Oathtaker, neither that Select, nor anyone in his direct line, shall ever rule.*'" He shook his head. "It seems Ehyeh intended to insure that an unworthy Select would not be the ranking member, or that if that ever occurred, his or her progeny could not carry that taint forward."

"I don't understand," Faith said.

"Well, an Oathtaker may only use his blade against a member of the Select in the course of protecting his charge. Such an event could only happen if the line of that Select was tainted somehow and so, that line would be cut off from any possible future rule."

"So if someone killed Rowena's last born with an Oathtaker's blade, that line would be cut off," Faith ventured.

"That's right," Ted affirmed.

"Otherwise, the rank would remain with Rowena's children's line."

"Yes," Ted said, "unless the ranking member was the last of Rowena's children and had no progeny, or she did not release her power to her children."

"So if Lilith takes the life of Rowena's youngest, she'd still have to take the lives of Rowena's other children before the power would revert to her," Hattie said.

"Yes. Again, unless the life of the current ranking member—in this case Rowena's child," Ted said as he glanced meaningfully at Faith, "is taken with the blade of an Oathtaker.

"You see, Rowena's child is the rightful heir, but at this time, has no progeny of her own. For now, her 'line' consists of her, and her siblings. Once she has progeny, her siblings will no longer be in the direct line of rule. They would only be in the direct line again if that child and all her progeny died without children of their own, or if that child died without releasing her power to her children.

"So only if all Rowena's children die without leaving progeny to whom they release their power, would the rightful heir be determined by going back to Rowena's siblings—in this case, to Lilith. Do you see?"

"Goodness, it gets complicated," Faith said with a sigh.

"It certainly does. But I think we have to assume that Lilith intends to destroy all of Rowena's children—or otherwise to cut off their line."

"That's horrible," Hattie said.

"Yes." Ted sighed.

Erin stirred in her sleep. Faith looked from her to Ted. "She looks so familiar."

"That's what I thought." He turned to Hattie. "What do you know of her?"

"Only that she was a slave to Zarek's men."

"Hmmm. Well anyway, my studies have often directed me back to this book. I believe now that I know why. Especially given the news that you bring today."

"Why is that?"

"This book provides what I believe is crucial prophecy—prophecy about the new seventh seventh, and another."

"What does it say?"

"Listen to this." He opened *The Book of the Blood* again to a page marked with a black satin ribbon, then read: "'*Be wary, for in those days shall come she who is not a leader, yet having sold her soul, she shall seek to lead. Woe to the people, for there shall be much wailing and mourning for the infants lost by her. Run quickly to Sanctuary! For only there may you be saved.*'"

He turned the ancient page carefully. The fluttering sound of the paper broke the silence.

"And listen to this: '*The land shall move to mourning. Even so, a way has been provided, and you must pray that it shall come to pass, for a seventh seventh, and she who is but is not, may rise after a time of misery and fear. In their day, they may lead the people forth.*'"

"What does it mean?" Hattie asked.

"I've read and reread these pages so many times. They never made sense—until recently that is. There's much more here, but I think I know now what these passages mean.

"Lilith is not to lead, for she is not the rightful heir to that position. When Rowena died, the line of leadership moved to her children. Among them is a seventh daughter of a seventh daughter—the child we've witnessed and told you about. But here's the part that leads me to believe we're living in the dangerous days to which this prophecy speaks. Rowena bore a seventh, but she also bore 'she who is but is not.'"

"What? I don't understand."

"Oh, dear Good One!" Faith exclaimed, understanding having come to her.

Ted nodded at Faith. "Rowena bore twins," he said to Hattie. "She bore a seventh seventh, and a child by a seventh pregnancy who 'is a seventh' by virtue of that fact, but who also 'is not' because she was not the seventh born. She was the eighth. Which of course, by the rules of the Select, means she is a first. I believe the second born of the two is 'she who is but is not.'"

For a moment all were silent.

"And this prophecy never made sense before? Why was that?" Hattie asked.

"I suppose because no Select had ever before born twins. I never considered that among the Select, there could be a child of a seventh pregnancy who was not seventh born."

"So then what?" Faith asked.

"So the children of Oosa are in grave danger. We must encourage those we can to bring their children to sanctuary. You'll note that when *The Book of the Blood* was written, the only sanctuary in existence was the one here in Polesk. For that reason, I believe it's the only safe place for the children in all of Oosa."

Chapter Twenty-Five

Leaving Erin at the house to rest, Ted and Faith rushed to sanctuary. Upon arriving, midmorning just hours away, Ted called his temple assistants to his office. The young men and women, trained Oathtakers all, stood at attention.

Ted cleared his throat. He paced. His eyes betrayed his concern. "Thank you," he said, "for your regular and consistent efforts on behalf of sanctuary. I commend you all for your fine work." He took a deep breath. "I have a serious assignment for each of you—that is, for all of you. I believe the people of Polesk are in grave danger."

The young men and women remained at attention.

"I have much to explain to you, but for now, I must send you all out on a mission. Time is of the essence, so I ask that you follow through with my request with great haste. I know there's no way we'll see it through to a full and satisfactory result, but we must do what we can."

He focused on each Oathtaker for a few seconds before turning his gaze to the next. "As you may have heard, Lilith of the first family is on her way to Polesk. Sources tell us that she intends to hold an event in the town square just short of midday today.

"What I'm about to tell you may seem contrary to your understanding of the Select and of our duties to the first family. Rest assured, I don't take my responsibilities to them, nor to any of you, lightly."

The young men and women stole glances at one another.

"I'm not asking you to do anything directly contrary to the Select," Ted said as though having read their thoughts.

Heads nodded, eyes squinted, as the young people watched on.

"I have good reason to believe that Lilith is acting contrary to the interests of the people of Oosa."

The young Oathtakers became visibly agitated. Feet shuffled, heads tilted, and eyes narrowed.

"But whether or not I'm correct, I've decided that there are things we must do for the safety of the people at large. If I'm right in my expectations, you'll all know before the day is out. If I'm wrong—and I sincerely hope I am—there will have been no harm to the Select, to sanctuary, to the people of Oosa, or to you as Oathtakers."

The young men and women visibly relaxed.

"I have reason to believe the infant daughters of Oosa are in grave danger. Therefore, I'm sending you all out to bring every person you possibly can who has an infant daughter, back here to sanctuary with her child." Ted could see the questions on the faces of his audience. "Jack, you have a question."

"How old do you want the children to be?"

"Let's say . . . any infant girl too young to speak."

"We're to bring them here?" a young woman asked.

"Yes, Sarah, if possible."

"But there are hundreds. Perhaps thousands!" someone exclaimed.

Ted nodded. "That's right, Faye. I can only ask you to bring all those you are able."

"But all the city is in an uproar over Lilith's coming visit," another young man reasoned.

"Yes, I'm aware of that. We can't force the people to bring their daughters here, and I'm sorry, but we also can't say why we want them to do so."

"Excuse me, sir?" a young man interrupted.

"Yes, Ben."

"You said that you wanted us to act quickly. Shouldn't we know what this is all about?"

"I'm sorry, Ben, but the entire city could be in turmoil if my concerns are shared and I want to avoid spreading fear. So this is the plan. Begin with any Select of which you're aware. Once done, move on to the families of members of sanctuary." Ted shook his head. "I don't like to have to do things in this manner, but we have to have a plan of action and this is the one I've decided upon."

"What are we to tell them?"

"That's where it gets difficult. Tell them that we've planned a special event for them here because we're aware they can't all fit into the town square for the chance to meet with Lilith for the blessing that she supposedly will bestow."

"'Supposedly,' sir?"

"I know this is a difficult assignment, particularly considering you're all operating in the dark. Still, this is what we will do."

"So we're to bring or send all the people with infant daughters we can back to sanctuary for an event we can't describe, and we're to do so as quickly as possible." Sarah made this observation, but whether as a statement or a question was uncertain.

Ted nodded. "That's right."

"When do we begin?" Ben asked. As an unofficial leader amongst the young people, he clearly intended for his question to cut off the questioning so they could get started.

"Divide the city up into sections. Each of you cover one. Please, begin immediately. Consider this a mission of life and death, but do your best to avoid spreading fear. Go with my blessing and may Ehyeh in His infinite mercy and wisdom accompany you all."

"I said I'd do what I could for Dora, Hattie's neighbor," Faith told Ted, "so I'll go there first."

"No, I'd rather you assisted with the people as they arrive. Above all, try to keep them calm. I'll see to Hattie's neighbor."

The morning wore on as Ted and the young Oathtakers sought out city residents with infant daughters. They were surprised to find that among the Select and members of sanctuary, the people insisted they would seek out Lilith. The Oathtakers could not convince them to do otherwise. The remaining townspeople met the Oathtakers with complete disinterest.

Unsuccessful in getting Dora to join him, just short of midday, Ted retrieved Erin and the other young women from the mission home. No sooner had the small band returned to sanctuary grounds, than a number of armed men took up stations around its perimeter.

Ted rushed the young women inside and then closed the door. Within moments he discovered that all of the young Oathtakers had just returned. He was devastated to learn that they'd all met with the same results as had he. In the end, Hattie's daughter, Claire, was the sole infant girl under protection at sanctuary.

As the sun reached its zenith, Ted filled the young Oathtakers in on what he expected might transpire. "I'm sorry," he said. "I hope I'm wrong."

A piercing scream cut through the air, then another, and then another.

"And so it begins," Ted said as he closed his eyes, wishing he could shut out the horror that grew around him. The air filled with the sounds of women rushing from the town square.

Looking out a window, he watched helplessly as one tripped over her skirts, madly dashing down the street, her hair tangled about her face, her eyes wide in horror, blood running down her face. Behind her came another screaming woman. Soon came another. Their mourning and anguish filled the streets.

As the afternoon wore on, soldiers entered nearby houses. In some cases, within moments, women came running out, screaming and crying. They fell to the ground, clawing at their faces, pulling at their hair, and howling skyward.

Occasionally, the soldiers murdered a husband or father who tried to protect his own. They made the most public spectacles possible of the events. Ted shuddered as he watched the prophecy he'd read aloud earlier come to pass.

The city was in mourning.

Hours passed. Ted, Faith, Hattie with little Claire, Erin, the other young women who'd been at the mission home, and the young Oathtakers, all sat in silence.

When nighttime finally arrived, Ted made his way to the top reaches of the building's tower. Traditionally, sanctuary personnel kept the tower lamps lit at all times so that the broken, the weary, the hurt, the sad, the needy and the desperate, could always find their way to sanctuary. The lights identified it as a place of refuge.

He made his way around the tower, turning the lights out, one by one. It only seemed right, as he'd been unable to save anyone this day. The lamps, he thought, should reflect that failure, that grief.

Chapter Twenty-Six

The ragged little army supporting Mara and the twins had been on the road for weeks. The intensity of the summer heat had passed and cool autumn days had descended. Leaves covering the ground snapped and crackled beneath the horses' steps. Soon fall would give way to winter.

Mara wearied of riding. With an outstretched arm, she signaled a halt. At that same moment, Samuel, riding forward, looked back. She waved at him to draw near.

"Are we lost?" Adele asked.

Mara laughed. "Lost? Goodness, no! We're too far away from home to be lost."

Laughter rippled through the air.

"What do you mean?"

"We have no idea where we are, and little idea of where we're going, so how could we be lost?" Mara chuckled, then looked the group over.

"What's on your mind?" Dixon asked her.

She patted Cheryl's neck. "I've been thinking," she paused, "and I'm not sure you're going to like what I've come up with. I mean, I know we've discussed this and have been planning to travel straight around the city to Lucy's, but . . .."

She dismounted, then stretched and bent, trying to loosen up. Her friends all waited for her, having become familiar with her way of pausing before sharing her thoughts.

"I think that going to Lucy's directly might be a mistake," she finally said.

"Why is that?" Basha asked.

"There's just so much we don't know. I think we need to find some resources. I know you've advised against it, but I would very much like to visit the library at sanctuary in the City of Light."

"Perhaps you can take a trip there by magic," Nina suggested.

"I've tried . . . unsuccessfully. I get the feeling I'm not to visit the city without the twins. What's more, they're coming up on their forty-ninth day. They could be—they should be—dedicated at sanctuary. And for now, the one in the City of Light is the nearest."

"Mara, you know that could be dangerous," Dixon said.

"Perhaps. But might it not be more dangerous to pass by when what we need most is information?"

He nodded. "Still, maybe the idea of traveling en masse to the city isn't . . . wise. We don't want to attract undue attention."

"Yes, I thought about that."

"You've a proposal then?"

"Just this: I think we should divide into two groups. We could meet in the city, even stay at the same place, but if we travel in fewer numbers we would attract less attention."

"What is it you expect to find there?"

She hesitated. "I can't say. I just know that some of the uneasiness I'm feeling is about passing by without stopping." She looked around. "Therese, you know what I'm talking about. I can tell. I see it in your eyes."

The woman nodded. "I'm not fond of the city. There are too many people there. Too many who might know Dixon—or me, for that matter. I've traveled in and out of it regularly in the past years, but I always kept a low profile. Still, I've felt much as you do. These questions about Lilith concern me. And I'm feeling more anxious about the crown, the sword, and the scepter, by the day."

"Oh?" This was news. Mara hadn't given any thought to them.

"The last I knew, the three items were in three different places. The crown is supposed to be in the city. I think we should confirm that it's safe. I'd hate to see Lilith get her hands on it. What's more, it's been weeks since we've heard any real news. Lilith isn't about to give up looking for the girls. Maybe the city holds some clues."

Mara turned to Dixon. "Do you know if the crown is still in the city?"

He shrugged and cocked his brow. "So far as I know."

"Where?"

"At sanctuary."

"What about the scepter and the sword?"

"The scepter, unfortunately, is at the palace."

Mara grimaced. "And the sword?"

"With Lucy."

"Why did Rowena keep them separate?" Basha asked.

"The three items contain powerful magic and are intended for the leader of the Select," Dixon said. "Rowena knew she was in grave danger and feared someone might get them from her. So she had them split up. In fact, the more I think about it, the more I think Mara might be on to something. I can't imagine what would happen if Lilith got her hands on the items. Mind you, I'm not overly concerned, but it would be good to confirm that the crown is still where Rowena left it."

Mara remounted. "Here's my proposal. The city is already in view. I say Dixon, Nina, Adele, the girls and I, will set out first. The rest of you could follow a short distance behind. We would meet up later. Any idea where we might stay when we arrive?" she asked, directing her question to Dixon.

"I've an old friend, Ezra. He owns a place he calls—don't laugh—The Clandest Inn."

Notwithstanding his caution, laughter rippled through the group.

"The Clandest Inn? Sounds rather shady. Who is this friend and can he be trusted?" Basha asked.

"Infallibly. Oh, he looks rough enough, but that's mostly a disguise." Dixon grinned. "He's one of us. He treated Rowena like his own sister. He's a former Oathtaker. Now he runs the inn, but makes his living on information. He has an entire network of spies. Most of them are in the city, but Ezra also stations spies throughout Oosa. He buys and trades information. When I need to know something, he's always my first stop."

"And he wouldn't sell or trade information about us?" Mara asked.

"Not a chance."

"You said he was a former Oathtaker," Basha said. "What's the story there?"

"You'd never guess."

"Assassin?" Nina asked.

"No," Dixon grinned, "his charge died of pure, old fashioned, old age."

"Why, that's the first encouraging news I've heard in some time!" Therese jested.

"Very well then," Mara said, "are we all in accord?"

Her friends signified their agreement.

"Can we make it to the inn before nightfall? If not, we could camp the night and go in the morning."

Dixon looked into the distance. "We should be able to make it before dusk. We've traveled quite slowly today, so it shouldn't be necessary to stop again until this evening, and really, it's not far from here."

Once he informed the others how to find The Clandest Inn, Mara and Dixon set out. Along the way, they discussed what information they might find at sanctuary.

Mara wanted to know what could be done with a Select who'd turned her allegiance to the dark side. She felt in her heart that none of them owed Lilith any protection any longer, but the cost of an Oathtaker being wrong in such an assessment—of wrongfully taking the life of one of the Select, should it come to that—was death.

She was also curious about the artifacts, the crown, the sword, and the scepter. What was she to do with them until the girls came of age? Did they belong to both of the girls, or to only one? And if to only one, which? Should she take possession of them for safekeeping?

Gradually, the countryside changed. Where things had been quiet in the city's outskirts, the noises grew in volume. Along with them came the varied smells of a lively city and the shuffle of people and goods.

As the sky showed signs that dusk would soon approach, the travelers made their way to the innermost part of the city.

In their efforts to ensure that they could respond to danger quickly, Mara and Dixon rode on either side of Nina and Adele, each of whom carried one of the infants. Because Dixon wanted to keep his presence concealed, he kept the hood of his cloak up to hide his face.

Crowds sashayed this way and that, as daytime workers made their way home and nighttime laborers made their way to work. The city bustled with sounds: callers cried out the news, horses whinnied their dissent to orders from on high, chains rattled as they held dogs at bay, grinding carriages clickety-clacked through the dusty roads, hawkers plied their wares, and children cried for treats—or perhaps because they'd consumed too many.

The buildings on either side grew up, up, up. Mara's mouth dropped open. "I've never seen anything like this!" she cried. "And I thought Polesk was large."

Riding on, she shielded the light of the setting sun from her eyes with a hand to her forehead. The last rays of sunshine shone from an angle that caused sanctuary, suddenly coming into view, to glisten. Slowly, she drew her hand down.

"It's amazing!" she gasped.

Sanctuary's steeple, crowned with a globe, stood in stark contrast to its surroundings. While it signified longevity, continuation, consistency and perseverance, its immediate environs were a study in hustle, change, perhaps even mutiny, to things of old, whether they be systems, places, people, or things.

"Yes, I can feel it. There are answers here. Answers I want," she said.

Dixon nodded. "To the inn then?"

"To the inn," she responded resolutely.

Since the streets had narrowed, the travelers now rode two by two, with Mara and Nina in the lead. They made their way through the throng of people and traffic to a side street Dixon pointed out, then turned in.

News criers bracketed both ends of the street. They shouted out the headlines and accosted passersby to purchase their fliers. Dixon bought one, then pressed onward, keeping a tight grip on Adele's reins so that nothing could come between them.

When Mara turned back for further directions, Dixon pointed out a small weathered building at the end of the block. Unlike others nearby, it stood a mere two stories high, unattached to the buildings immediately to its sides. Aged, but well maintained, it sat back from the roadway. A stable stood behind it. Horses and carriages madly made their way in and out from the premises.

A young groomsman, just a boy really, small and string bean thin, ran out to assist the inn's newest arrivals. A middle-aged man followed him, shouting out orders more quickly than the boy could follow them. The man pointed and bullied, prodded and cajoled the youth to anticipate and to meet the every need of the inn's guests.

Dixon spoke briefly to the man in charge, explaining how he wanted their horses to be cared for and offering a tip to the stable boy for a job well done. Then, turning on his heel, he grasped Mara's elbow. "How many rooms?"

"I hadn't considered that." She thought for a moment. "Let's just make it two. One for you, Samuel and Jules. We women will make due with one . . . somehow. With any luck, perhaps we'll get a common joining space."

They entered the inn. It was a simple place, enlivened by a small pub at the front. Two young barmaids wound their way through the tables where customers sat talking and laughing with them like old friends.

One of the barmaids was plump and rosy, her ample bosom spilling out the top of her simple frock, her blonde hair tied back in a single braid that dropped down her back. The other was slight, delicate, with bronzed skin and chestnut hair that hung down and straight. Her dress fit her closely, covering her from neck to feet. Quieter than her coworker, she held the eye of many of the men in attendance, as she exuded a sensuality that defied what she wore.

Dixon removed the hood of his cloak. He looked around, briefly watching the barmaids and taking in the number and look of the guests.

He turned back to Mara to usher her toward the currently unattended reception desk, but before they reached it, the first of the barmaids made her way to his side. He turned abruptly as she caught his attention with a poke to his side.

"Nancy!" he said, clearly pleased.

"Dixon, it's so good to see you." She embraced him briefly. "Well, who have we here?" she continued, her arm still around his waist, as she turned and looked over Mara, Nina, Adele, and the infants. "Goodness, Dixon, you have been busy! No wonder we haven't seen you around here of late."

He laughed. "Ahhh, Nancy."

Mara watched the exchange, surprised that their lighthearted bantering bothered her. She tried to remove the frown from her face, but failed to do so before the barmaid turned her way.

"Not to worry, ma'am, Dixon and I go way back." She removed her arm from around him.

Mara's mouth dropped open in surprise. She was at a loss for words.

"Truly, you've nothing to fear from me," Nancy said, smiling.

Looking down, Dixon grinned and shook his head.

Mara's anger rose. That was all she needed—to have him assume this woman somehow bothered her.

The other barmaid approached. She slid near to Dixon, then reached up and tied her arms around his neck. She kissed his cheek. "Dixon," she cooed, her eyes glued to his. Her voice was quiet, though her words seemed to carry a deeper meaning coming from the exquisite creature. "So terribly, terribly sorry to hear about your loss."

He nodded his appreciation for her sentiments. As she dropped her hold on him, he turned to Mara. "Mara, meet Nancy," he said motioning to the first of the young women, "and Celestine," he continued, as he gave a slight squeeze to the exquisite dark creature still in his embrace.

Mara found herself at a loss for words and was troubled as to why that should be. *Celestine. 'Heavenly.' Figures. But why should that bother me?*

Celestine greeted Mara, who remained mute, while Dixon introduced the others. Once done, he promised the barmaids he'd catch up with them later.

At the reception desk sat a scruffy looking man. Mara surmised it must be Ezra, based on Dixon's earlier description. The man's hair was turning to gray. He wore a beard of a few days growth. There were the beginning signs of crow's feet at the outer corners of his eyes, and his shirt, opened at the top, revealed an incredibly hairy chest and toughened, bronze skin.

Mara, sensing power and kindness in the man's eyes, felt some of her concerns over safety, lessen.

"Dixon, how good to see you." Ezra embraced his friend, but then his expression turned serious. "It's been too long. I heard about—"

"Oh, Ezra, there's so much to fill you in on." Dixon's eyes held further meaning, which the innkeeper did not fail to read.

"Very well then. We'll have to catch up after you've had a chance to freshen up."

"Sure." Dixon introduced Mara and the others.

"Interesting company you keep," the innkeeper said to Mara, chuckling and motioning toward Dixon.

She grinned. "Tell me about it."

"He's a favorite around here."

"Yes, so I see." She was relieved to have regained her voice.

"He's just so very charming, you know. The women can't seem to stay away from him." Ezra's eyes twinkled.

"So he tells me."

He laughed. "I like you," he said. "We're going to get on famously, you and I."

"Well," Dixon interrupted, "if you two are through with your mutual admirations . . ."

"Relax, Dixon," Ezra said, "you've nothing to fear from me." His eyes quickly darted to Mara. He winked at her, signifying that he'd heard Nancy's earlier comment and had witnessed the discomfort it caused her.

Mara was delighted to find that Dixon seemed to be momentarily at a loss for words, but within seconds, he regained his composure. He asked Ezra if he thought they could stay without attracting any unwanted attention. The innkeeper assured him that they could. Dixon then told his friend that additional members of their group would arrive shortly. With that, Ezra led them to their rooms.

"I'll see you later then?"

Dixon nodded.

"I like her," Ezra said with a smile as he motioned toward Mara. "Be sure to bring her along."

She leaned over the washbasin and splashed her face with water.

Nina approached. "You shouldn't worry about it," she said, her hand on Mara's back.

The Oathtaker stood up and looked at Nina. Her eyes narrowed. "Worry about what?"

"Oh, you know, about Dixon's teasing you. He's just trying to rile you up."

Mara dried her face. "I don't know what you're talking about."

"Really, you've nothing to worry about."

"I'm not worried. About Dixon? Don't be ridiculous."

"He respects you enormously, you know."

Mara pursed her lips. She was at a loss for words.

"And," Nina continued, "he was jealous out there."

"Nina, there's nothing between Dixon and me. We have a job to do, that's all." She turned away.

"Now who's being ridiculous?" Nina murmured.

"Excuse me?" Mara turned back suddenly. She could hear herself, the frustration in her voice.

"I'm just saying—"

"Let it go." Mara would have to have a talk with the woman one day. She'd have to explain how impossible it was for her to be attached to Dixon—or to anyone for that matter—so long as she was subject to her oath.

She took Eden from Adele, then sat to cuddle the infant. She closed her eyes, confused. Nina had set her to thinking. Why had she kept Dixon with her anyway? Why had she been so insistent about getting him back from the palace? Was it because she needed him to help her to protect the girls? Or because she just wanted to have him near her?

Her thoughts wandered. She'd chosen to be an Oathtaker. She knew that upon taking her oath, she'd given up any chance of being connected to anyone, or of having her own family—possibly for a very long time. The rules did not permit it—and it was just as well. One time had been enough anyway. That one time, so long ago, had been enough.

She generally discouraged looking back, and since swearing her oath, she'd refused to do so, even for a minute. But today she found herself stepping back in time, into her memories, her hauntings, her pains.

As her past invaded her thoughts, she grew tense. Flashes of images ran through her mind, as vivid and intense emotions coursed through her body—feelings of longing, abandonment, betrayal, pain, loneliness, and confusion. She weakly attempted to hold them back, then succumbed to their power.

She'd been so young, so innocent, so trusting and naïve when Jack had come into her life—handsome, captivating, Jack, whose smile brought a twinkle to his eyes and dimples to his cheeks. She saw him so clearly in her mind. She could almost smell the ever-present scent of mint that he wore.

Just seventeen, she'd been ignorant of the ways of the world. Jack charged into her life, wooed her. He stirred emotions she'd never before experienced. She thought he'd be there always, that she was the only one for him, and that she need have no fear for the days to come. He would meet any troubles alongside her. She was moved by his presence, his power, his . . . charm. The thought made her frown.

But then . . .

Then, along came Jo; Jo, the youngest; Jo, Mother's favorite; Jo, who never did anything honorable, but whom Mother could never admit did any wrong.

It had taken Mara years to appreciate how that could be. Then one day, a revelation came to her: Jo was exactly like Mother. She epitomized everything Mother was, everything she believed deep inside herself, and everything she wanted to be, or to have been. Mother allowed Jo her every flaw because Jo's flaws were her own. The only difference was that Jo was willing to act on things Mother had only dreamed of doing.

Jo always wanted whatever belonged to Mara. So naturally, when she discovered Jack, she set her eyes upon him. Younger than Mara by just a year, Jo pursued him wherever he went. She seduced him with her smiles and her favors.

It was only afterward that Mara discovered what Jo had done.

Afterward. But, am I really at fault for abandoning the little one? Hadn't it been the only way? I wonder, where is he now? She saw his face in her mind. She counted his little fingers, his toes. She felt his smooth skin, the warmth of his rosy cheeks.

She didn't want to revisit these emotions. She didn't want to remember her failure. She didn't want to go back. She'd been with the girls for weeks now and had successfully managed not to reflect, not to remember.

"Mara?"

She jolted upright.

"Are you all right?"

She looked at Nina. She fought to bring herself under control, to put a figurative finger in the dam that would hold back her emotional journey. "Yes, of course."

"Are you crying? I'm so sorry. I didn't mean to—"

The Oathtaker wiped her eyes with the back of her hand. She hadn't meant to reveal her emotions. "No, of course not."

"Truly, I'm sorry. Really, I didn't mean—"

"Forget it, Nina. I'm not angry. I'm just tired, I guess. This journeying wears on a body."

"We're all right then? You and I?"

"Sure. Why wouldn't we be?"

"You know. What I said before?"

"Forget it, Nina. I have."

Someone knocked at the door.

"Care to tell me what color is on the other side?" the young woman asked, in an effort to lighten the mood.

Mara smirked. "I don't need to. I can hear what they're thinking."

"That works too," Nina chuckled, clearly relieved that the tension between them had dissipated.

"It's Therese and the others." Mara opened the door to them.

By the time everyone had cleaned up and changed clothes, it was getting late. They were all hungry—except for the twins, both of whom Nina had just nursed.

"Want to dine in?" Dixon asked.

"No, I think we should all go down. These quarters are going to feel cramped soon enough as it is," Mara said.

"Great. Do we all sit together? One big group?"

"Mmmm, no. I think we stay in the same two separate groups. That way, we can better observe whether anyone pays us any undue attention."

"I like it." He turned to Samuel and Jules. "We'll go now. You come along whenever you're comfortable."

As they made their way to the pub, he turned to Mara. "You know, Nancy was just having a bit of fun with us, right?"

"Sure. Of course." She kept her eyes forward. She was unsure of her own feelings and didn't want to give the wrong impression. Her trip down memory lane had momentarily weakened her.

"We go way back."

She stopped short. "Is there some reason you're telling me all this, Dixon?" She willed herself not to disclose her discomfort.

"No . . . I just didn't want you to get the wrong impression."

"I didn't get any kind of impression." She continued forward.

When they arrived at the pub, Ezra met them. "You look lovely," he said to Mara.

She grinned. "How very charming of you," she said as she nudged him.

Dixon looked on without expression.

Ezra directed them to a comfortable corner table. Near it was another empty one. Dixon motioned with a nod that the rest of their party would take it.

Nina and Adele sat against the wall with the girls. The Oathtakers glanced at one another. They both would have preferred sitting there, but they also wanted to be where they could best defend the infants. They'd have to rely upon Basha and the others to keep their eyes on their backs.

Celestine arrived with cold ales for them all. "On the house," she said. "We're serving roast beef this evening. I hope that will be all right with you all?"

Just then Ezra directed Basha and the others to their table. Once done, he returned to Mara's side. "May I?" he asked as he pulled out a chair.

"Certainly."

"Well, old friend, I am surprised to see you here," he said to Dixon.

"Oh? Why's that?"

"Weeeeelllll," Ezra drawled, "rumor has it that trouble follows you."

Dixon chuckled. "Some things never change, I guess."

"Really, are you safe in the city? There are those who would recognize you."

"But you said you weren't concerned for our safety here."

"Noooo, that's right. We're well covered."

"I figured if anyone would be, it would be you. Anyway, I suppose my being in the city isn't entirely safe, but it's necessary." Dixon took a long drink. "We've come for information, so naturally, I thought of you."

"What kind of information do you seek?"

The collective attention of the group turned to the bar where a scuffle was underway. Mason, Ezra's hired muscle, broke up the troublemakers and then ushered them to the door. Once done, the din of the room returned to its former level. Within moments guests lifted mugs and clinked silverware as they returned to business as usual.

Dixon turned back to his friend. "Lilith."

"What of her?" The innkeeper turned serious. His jaw muscles flexed.

"What are you hearing?"

Ezra motioned for Nancy. He pointed at Dixon's ale, then back to himself, directing her to bring another one. Then he leaned in. "It's odd. I've never seen this before."

"What's that?" Mara interrupted.

"What does she know about my enterprise?" he asked Dixon.

"The general stuff."

The innkeeper directed his next comment to Mara. "As Dixon no doubt told you, I have eyes and ears throughout Oosa. Oddly enough, I've gone blind and deaf over the past few weeks."

"I don't understand."

Nancy returned with Ezra's drink. Foam slid down the outside of the mug. He wiped it off, then dried his hand on his pant leg. He took a long, deep drink.

"Ahhh, that's good," he said, setting his mug down. "Just what I said," he then continued. "My people are unable to come up with any information. Well, not much anyway."

"They aren't checking in with you?" Dixon asked.

"No, that's just it. Most of them are reporting as usual. Although," the innkeeper frowned, "the numbers are down." He took another drink. "Of those that report, they just say they've no news."

"Nothing? But—"

"What I mean," Ezra interrupted, "is that I'm usually able to get solid information on what's going on at sanctuary, what's happening at—or at least around—the palace, what's going on with the first family, and so forth. But now the only news I get is that Lilith is looking for you. She says you're trying to escape justice."

"That's absurd," Mara said.

"I'm sure. Still, word is that she is on a mission to find him. The fliers are full of it every day."

"I saw that in the one that I purchased when we arrived," Dixon said, his eyes narrowed. "What else?"

"That's just it. There is nothing else."

Celestine approached. Ezra's dark eyes bore into her, as though challenging her for interrupting. She handed him a flier.

"This just in," she said. She waited as his eyes ran over it. When he was through, he scowled, then dismissed her with a nod.

"What is it?" Dixon asked.

At that moment, Nancy arrived with dinner. She slapped the plates down, each with a resounding smack. The smell of roast beef and gravy wafted over the table. After inquiring whether anyone required anything more, she retreated.

"This is ridiculous," Ezra said. "When I can't get information until it's in the fliers!" He slapped the item down on the table.

Mara took up the handbill. She read it, willing herself to remain calm. When she finished, she handed it to Dixon.

Quickly, his eyes scanned the print. His jaw set. "You've heard nothing of this?"

Ezra glanced at Nina holding Reigna, then at Adele holding Eden, then back to Dixon. "Nothing."

Dixon followed the man's gaze. "Perhaps we should leave." He pushed his chair back and stood.

Ezra put his hand on Dixon's forearm. "Sit down. Sit down. You're safe here." He looked toward the infants again. "You're all safe here."

Gradually, Dixon's tension released. "But—"

"There's no reason for you to leave now. You're here. You might as well see to what you came here to do."

"It's a lie," Dixon said.

"The child is not a fraud?"

Mara pursed her lips. She looked at Ezra and shook her head.

"The real thing?" The innkeeper's desire to believe was evident.

"One of them," she indicated with a nod toward the infants, "is what we claim she is."

"And the other?"

"We're not exactly sure what to call her. We believe she should rightly be known as 'she who is but is not,' of prophetic fame."

Confusion set in Ezra's eyes. "The seventh seventh 'who is but is not?'"

"They're Rowena's *twins*," Dixon said. "One is a seventh. The other is a seventh, but . . . is not."

"Whew! Rowena's *twins?* Why, that's amazing! And that prophecy is ancient. No one has ever been able to figure out what it means."

"Well, I think we know now. It fits."

The innkeeper shook his head. "You'll need to find a long-term place of safety for them. For all of you."

Mara put her hand on his arm. "Ezra, you'll pardon my concern, and it's not that I don't trust you . . ."

He grinned. "Have no fear, little lady, you're safe with me."

"It's not me I'm concerned about." She looked toward the infants.

His gaze followed. "I see." He fidgeted.

She studied him. Then she heard his thoughts as clearly as though he'd shouted them out loud. "You know, I think that's a great idea," she said, smiling.

"What? I didn't say anything."

"But you thought it," Dixon said.

Ezra looked at his friend. "How do you know that?"

"I don't." Dixon gestured, fork in hand, toward Mara. "She does."

The innkeeper looked carefully at her. "You're an Oathtaker?"

"I'm *their* Oathtaker."

"I thought you were," he said to Dixon.

"You thought wrong," Dixon said.

"Well, if that don't beat all! But why is Lilith after you then?"

"She heard Rowena's *child* lived, and I suppose she assumes that the infant is with me."

"I see. So, Lilith doesn't know there are two of them."

"No."

"Well?" Mara asked, directing her question to Ezra.

"Well what? Oh, you want me to swear an oath to protect the girls."

"Only if you're willing. If not, that's fine too. I just need to know where we stand."

"Well, like I said, you should have no fear. I can swear without reservation that I will do anything in my power to protect you all."

"Thank you, Ezra." It had not been a life oath, but she appreciated it anyway.

Ezra watched her, then leaned in. "Truly, Mara, I would do anything to protect those girls. I would . . . die for them. I swear it on my life."

As the group had come to expect, the earth shook. The walls of the room rattled. The overhead chandelier swung, causing the candles' flames to flicker. Silver rattled, glass tinkled, and people gasped. The pub's guests all stopped what they'd been doing. Some grabbed the edges of their tables for security. One young woman dashed beneath an empty one.

Ezra's mouth dropped open.

In the span of just a breath or so, the shuddering ceased. Slowly the workers and guests returned to their interests, which in some cases, included cleaning up spilled drinks.

"Goodness! What just happened?"

"Remarkable, isn't it?" Dixon grinned.

"I've never seen anything like it."

"Yes. Right?" Mara laughed.

"But you said you were their Oathtaker," Ezra said to her.

"And so I am. But you've just joined their first line of defense."

"You mean . . . the others?" He pointed toward those at Mara's table, then nodded toward Basha's group.

"Yes, they're soldiers in the girls' army as well."

"Amazing." Ezra sat quietly for a moment, shaking his head and smirking. "Truly amazing," he said. "So I hope your concerns have been put to rest."

She smiled. "Yes, thank you. As I said, I would never insist on such an oath. But you've certainly added to my sense of security knowing we might be here for a time."

"What if—" Dixon turned to the innkeeper, clearly excited. "What if we used your network to spread false information?"

Ezra's head shot up. "False information?"

"Yes! What if we used your agents, to spread stories about our whereabouts? Maybe then we could hold Lilith at bay."

"Dixon, that's brilliant!" Mara exclaimed.

He grinned at her, then turned back to Ezra. "Now that you're one of us, maybe we can use the system you already have in place to help us to protect the girls. Would you be willing? Do you think it could even work?" he asked.

"We can certainly give it a try!"

Ezra had suggested that when the little ones were down for the night, Mara and Dixon return for further discussion. Mara bowed out, but Dixon agreed to the meeting.

He entered the pub just as a young local son sang a favorite ditty to the guests' delight about a maiden pleased her true love was "as steady as a rushing river." Meanwhile, a traveling magician impressed the folks, showing off his talents at prestidigitation. He made cards fly through his fingers, coins vanish and reappear, and empty mugs levitate, all to the delight of the onlookers.

Nancy and Celestine bustled about, keeping the spirits of the guests up and their mugs filled.

Dixon sat with his back against the wall. The quiet figure of a man in the opposite corner caught his attention. A hooded cloak partially hid his face. Slowly nursing his drink, he seemed to watch every person's every move.

Ezra's eyes followed Dixon's gaze. He grinned. "One of mine," he said.

"And that one?" Dixon's eyes flashed to the opposite side of the room where a young woman sat alone. Though silent, her demeanor seemed to shout that her space was off limits. Even to a casual observer, she appeared ready to spring at any moment, at the slightest sign of danger.

"Yes, that one too." Ezra motioned for Celestine, then asked her to bring drinks.

Dixon refused with a shake of his head.

"Actually, Celestine will bring me tea, not ale. I never have more than two brews in an evening. She knows I mean to keep my wits about me."

"Very well then. I'll have one too."

After Celestine left, the innkeeper sat quietly, watching Dixon. "You miss her?" he finally asked.

"Rowena?"

"Mhmmm."

"Terribly." Dixon closed his eyes. "I keep thinking I hear her voice. I keep waiting for her to come around the corner. I—"

"You were still in love with her," Ezra interrupted.

Dixon started. "What?"

"Oh, come on, a man would have to have been blind not to have known."

"That was a long time ago." Dixon shook his head. "It was just the longing of a young man who should have known better. I was subject to my oath. She was married for goodness sake."

"I see. So now Mara's got your eye."

Celestine stopped with the tea.

"I don't know what you're talking about," Dixon said, looking down, after she walked away.

"So, she's fair game?"

Dixon's eyes shot up.

Ezra laughed. "That's what I thought." He shook his head. "She's a good woman."

"Among the best. But of course, she's committed now. And even if she wasn't, she wouldn't be interested in me—so there's no cause for concern."

"Now that's where you're wrong. Or perhaps you didn't see her reactions to Nancy and Celestine?" The innkeeper paused. "And that's why you have to be very careful."

Dixon was silent for a time. He patted his thigh. "I'm sure you're mistaken. We've been thrown together for the time being, for good or for bad, that's all."

Jules approached. "Mind if I join you?"

"Not at all. I'd appreciate your input." In part, Dixon was relieved that the subject of conversation would be changed. He turned to Ezra. "Mara's convinced there might be information at sanctuary for us," he paused, "or for *her*, that is. She wants to do some research. Since she couldn't leave the infants, at least for an extended time, to the care of others, she decided we'd all come to the city."

"What about your friends who arrived after you did? What about you?" Ezra asked Jules.

Dixon explained about Therese and Basha, allowing Jules to relay his and Samuel's history.

"And the two other young women? The ones who are tending the infants?"

"Nina is a Chiranian refugee. She lost her child while escaping to Oosa. We met her in Polesk and she agreed to join Mara to help with the girls."

"And the other young woman?"

"Adele?" Dixon chuckled. He explained how Mara had rescued him from Lilith's grip. "Adele came along for the ride rather unexpectedly."

"Traveling? Why, that is an extraordinary power."

"Yes, indeed."

"And you're all part of the girls' army?"

"Every last one of us," Jules said.

"You've all sworn an oath for their protection?"

"That's right," Dixon said.

"And you all received the same confirmation?"

"Yes. Isn't that amazing? Have you ever heard of anything like it?"

"No, I most certainly have not," the innkeeper said. He took a drink.

The three discussed the group's travels to date and their expectation of joining up with Lucy.

"Do you have contact with her?" Dixon asked.

"Occasionally. Now and again she sends someone to the city to leave, or to get, information."

"When did she last do that?"

Ezra brushed his hand against the whiskers below his chin as he thought. "Well now, let me see. I last had a guest from her camp a few months back."

"Any particular reason for the visit?"

"No. I believe she just wanted to know if we'd heard any news from out of the palace." Ezra looked around the room, then motioned to Celestine to see to a nearby table that was running dry. "How long do you think you'll be in the city?" he asked as he turned back.

"Don't know. A couple of weeks? Maybe longer. It'll be up to Mara."

"You plan to take the children to sanctuary?"

Dixon shrugged. "Actually, I can't think of a safer place for them. I don't know if Lilith would go there."

"If what you say about her is true—about her trying to usurp their position—then you can't be too careful. But your other idea merits some discussion as well."

"About passing out false information?"

"Yes."

"This sounds good," Jules said. "What's this all about?"

"Dixon thinks we might put my network to use." Ezra turned to him. "So what have you got in mind?"

"I'd rather hate to impose Lilith on anyone, but maybe we could pass out word that we've been seen in different places—places we haven't really been and have no intention of going."

Ezra chewed his lip. "You remember I told you how most of my agents were checking in but that some were . . . Well, I assume they're just late. It's unusual, but not unheard of."

"What's this?" Jules asked.

"Some of my agents haven't checked in with me as they usually do," the innkeeper said, scowling.

"Where are those people stationed?"

"Now that I think on it, they're all generally positioned between the palace at Shimeron and around the Polesk area."

"Polesk! That's where Lilith found me before taking me back to the palace," Dixon said.

"In any case, I say we put a plan together." Ezra said. "With luck, she'll follow the leads we plant."

"I like it," Jules said. "So, how do we pass this information?"

"The local inns and pubs. It's amazing what information one may glean from such places."

As the evening wore on, the men formulated a plan.

When the hour grew late, the locals made for home. It was then that one of Ezra's spies stumbled into the inn. Dirt covered his face. His clothing, torn and stained, showed the wear of long travel. He was a small man, built for quickness.

Nothing about him would catch the attention of others but for his crooked nose, a certain sign of one or more brawls in which he'd drawn the short end of the stick.

The innkeeper jumped up. "Lance, finally! We've been awaiting your arrival." He ushered the man toward a chair. "Steady. Are you all right? Have you any injuries?"

Lance shook his head. He put up a hand motioning that he needed to catch his breath. "I . . . I'm just a long time on the road. Three solid days since I've stopped for a proper rest." He paused. "Drink!" he exclaimed.

Nancy brought a full mug and a pitcher.

He tipped the mug up and drank until it was empty, then slammed it down on the table. "Ahhhh."

Ezra excused the barmaids for the evening, then locked the front door and turned out most of the lights. Once done, he turned his attention back to Lance. "You ready to talk now?"

He struggled for breath. "Rest," he murmured.

"Soon enough. Have you a report?"

"Not much to tell. I left Polesk weeks ago." The spy motioned to his mug for more.

Ezra filled it. The smell of yeast and hops filled the air. "What about Polesk? You're the first to report from that section for some time now."

"When I left, Lilith was due to arrive. The local fliers reported that she intended to hold a ceremony for the infants of the area."

"Yes, the fliers here say that she seeks someone who's trying to perpetrate a fraud upon the people with the false claim of a seventh seventh."

"But . . . a ceremony? For the infants?" Dixon asked.

"Something about 'bestowing a blessing' on them," Lance said.

"So then, you've no news of what happened during her visit?" Ezra asked.

"None. One of the others was to follow me within a day or two. Generally we keep a continuous relay coming and going from Polesk and some of the other larger cities, but I met up with trouble along the way. I expected that someone would have returned here long before I did."

"We've seen no one. What kind of trouble did you meet with?"

"Soldiers."

"Soldiers?"

"From among those Lilith brought with her to Polesk."

"The palace guard?"

"No," Lance shook his head, "not the palace guard."

"I don't understand," Dixon said.

"They were foreigners and they just came out of nowhere."

"Foreigners?"

"Yes. I thought I'd be well out of range by the time Lilith arrived. We all knew the event she was going to hold was out of the ordinary, so I wanted to report back here. But I met up with her soldiers every step of the way. Finally, caught with my back to the wall, I was forced to jump off a cliff—and I mean that literally, not figuratively," he added, glancing at Ezra. "Fortunately, I was met by the river." He took another drink. "I followed it for miles, far from my intended path, before I was clear of them."

"Then what?" Dixon asked.

"Then I came straight here." Lance shook his head. "I can't believe no one got here before me. Someone should have been here long ago."

"No, you're the first in some time," Ezra said.

"Hmmm. Well, all I can say for sure is that something definitely is not right."

Chapter Twenty-Seven

This being the forty-ninth day since the girls were born, and having rested for nearly a week since arriving at The Clandest Inn, Mara planned a trip to sanctuary with Nina, Adele, and the twins. Dixon wanted to accompany her to dedicate the girls. Concerned, however, that he would not go unnoticed there, and that if discovered, the authorities might take him into custody, she insisted he stay behind. Although reluctant to take anyone else along, she finally relented to his urgings, and allowed Jules to join her.

When they entered the grounds, a young man handed them all copies of *Tidings*, the traditional writings attributed as divine revelation of the Good One. "Compliments of the local Oathtakers," he said with a smile.

Several groups sat on the lawn in circles reasoning and discussing amongst themselves. Just off sanctuary grounds, picketers carried signs bearing slogans against the Select and their Oathtakers. Private troops of Oathtakers that served at sanctuary surrounded the area so as to keep the peace and to provide safety for sanctuary visitors.

The steps to the front door rose up before them. In the middle of each was an indentation testifying to the countless souls that had come and gone before. As the ball of Mara's foot met up with the smoothened groove in the step, she almost lost her balance. She righted herself, then offered a hand to Adele who followed behind.

When they entered sanctuary, they joined a group touring the campus.

In many ways the main building rivaled that of sanctuary in Polesk and in some ways even exceeded it. Paintings delighting in life events covered the walls. The ceiling of one room boasted a mural in the minutest of detail. As at Polesk, the windows depicted the meanings behind the firsts through the sevenths of the Select. Here, however, they were made from glass panes, not with the seemingly infinite number of small crystals as made up the windows at Polesk. Consequently, these windows did not refract light in the same manner as did the others.

The Oathtaker leading the tour brought the group to the area reserved for paying respects to Ehyeh. There, a number of people, many elderly, prayed. The sounds varied from the quietest whispers of gratitude, to full voiced supplications, to exclamatory songs of praise.

Mara inhaled deeply, recognizing the scent of some Select in attendance. As she did, she had the uncanny feeling someone watched her. She looked about. Seeing nothing, she shook off the sensation.

"Listen to those worshipers!" Nina whispered. "The hair on my arms is rising. Oh, I've so much to be grateful for. It makes me long to add my thanks."

Minutes later, the group moved on. The guide pointed out the library and research center located in a separate building accessible from the same walkway that led from the street to the main sanctuary. To the other side, he noted the training center and a dormitory used by students, guests, and sanctuary regulars. It was there, he explained, that young people spent years living and training, in an effort to earn their Oathtaker credentials. He returned the group, when his tour was complete, to the vestibule of the main building.

"I'd like to spent a few minutes in the worship hall first," Mara said. "Then we'll go to the research center."

"Lead on," Jules said.

Once inside the worship area, Mara took Reigna from Nina. She positioned the infant in the crook of one arm, then asked Adele to place Eden in her other arm.

Nodding at Jules, she silently entreated him to keep a close eye on things. Then she asked Nina and Adele to accompany her to the altar. Worshippers in fervent supplication surrounded it. She carefully laid the infants down, then took each of the young women by the hand.

Looking skyward, she spoke. "Ehyeh, dear Good One, I thank you for the opportunity to serve you. I thank you for the confidence you've placed in me with these little ones. Dear Good One, I dedicate these precious lives back to you and to your service. I pray you will use me, hone me, teach me, so I may best serve them, and in that way, may best serve your cause."

Tears welled in Nina and Adele's eyes. Mara smiled at them, then resumed her prayer. "Dear Good One, I pray strength for myself and for my friends and cohorts. Bless them all. Bless them for their care, their giving, and their sacrifices."

She looked to Jules and then added, "Bless them dear Good One for their strength of heart, mind, and body." Finally, she bowed her head. "Dear Good One, I commit these blessed infants to you and to your care and protection."

When she was through, Mara led her group to the rear of the chamber. "To the research center," she said.

As she turned to go, an old woman brushed past her. The veins in her arms and hands stood out like markings of blue delineating riverways on a map. Her arthritic fingers were curled and bent, as though in the act of grasping something for eternity. The moment she touched Mara, their eyes met.

The Oathtaker tensed.

The old woman's gray eyes boasted a streak of strength and perseverance that was ages old, but in no way tired or lacking. Her old, puckered mouth gaped into a smile. Putting a crumpled hand to her breast, she exclaimed, "Oh, dear Good One!"

At a loss, Mara looked around. Seeing no one, and realizing the woman's attention was on her, she reached for Spira. She didn't want to attract attention, but prepared herself to meet danger in any form.

"Don't be frightened," the old woman murmured, reaching out.

Mara pulled away before the woman could grasp her, then stepped back. She kept one hand on Spira. With the other, she directed her friends to retreat.

The woman smiled, startling Mara. While poor, disheveled, and generally untidy, her expression was genuine. She portrayed a sense of peace.

"I thought that was you there at the altar. Oh, how I've waited for you!" she exclaimed in a voice barely above a whisper. "The Good One promised I would meet you one day, and here you are, after all this time." Her fingers trembled. Her eyes glistened with unshed tears.

Mara's eyes narrowed. Quickly, she assessed the situation. There was no apparent danger, yet the Oathtaker remained alert.

Once again, the old woman stepped forward.

Once again, Mara stepped back.

The woman looked down at herself. She pouted, but then smiled wanly. "Don't believe everything you see," she chided. "My body, my strength and beauty, all are things of the past. But my heart remains pure for Ehyeh," she said, tapping her finger to her chest.

"Who are you? And what do you want of me?"

"I am Leala. The Good One changed my name to Leala when he saw my faithfulness."

Mara's brow rose. "What do you mean you've been waiting for me?"

"I've been here every day for sixty long years waiting for you. After my husband went to meet with the Good One, I came here to seek Him daily, and here I've remained ever since."

"Who is it you think I am? And how could you know I would come here? Even I didn't know until recently."

Leala smiled and shook her head. "No, it's not you exactly whom I've awaited." Her voice quivered with age.

"What do you mean?"

"We've been waiting for the little one."

"'We've?' Who is 'we've?' And the 'little one?'"

"Her!" Leala exclaimed as she pointed toward Reigna. Then she cocked her head to the side. Her brow furrowed. She turned her gray eyes from Nina, who held Reigna, to Adele, who held Eden. "Waaaait," she whispered, a question in her eyes. "Her?" she asked, nodding toward Reigna again. "Or . . . her?" she asked as her gaze moved to Eden.

Mara stepped forward. She grasped Leala by the forearm. "Explain yourself."

"I don't understand."

"You don't understand what?"

"I know you're the right Oathtaker, and that one of those infants is right, but . . . But I . . . Which—"

"What do you mean that I'm the right Oathtaker? What Oathtaker do you seek?"

"Why you, of course." The woman poked her finger at Mara.

"And what Oathtaker am I?"

Leala's smile moved from her lips to her cheeks and then landed in her old gray eyes, making them glisten. "The Oathtaker to the seventh seventh of course!"

Mara pursed her lips. "What do you know of a seventh seventh?"

The old woman looked at Nina and Reigna, Adele and Eden. Her gaze did not return to Mara until Jules stepped forward, cutting off her view.

"Now, that's where I'm confused," she said slowly. "I'm sure she's here, but I know not which . . ." She looked away, lost in thought for a moment. Then she exclaimed, "Oh, gracious Ehyeh!" Her eyes flashed wide, her face lit up. For a moment she looked twenty years younger. "The seventh seventh 'who is but is n—'"

"Shhhh!" Once again, the Oathtaker looked around the room. Fortunately, notwithstanding the old woman's apparent agitation, they'd not attracted any unwanted attention.

Leala could barely contain herself. She squirmed, a question in her eyes.

Mara glanced downward. "You are correct, Leala," she said, looking back up to meet her eyes, "but I'm sure you can appreciate that I will require your silence."

"Oh yes! Yes, of course. We won't say anything."

"'We!' Who is 'we?'" Mara asked for the second time. This time her voice sounded hard and demanding.

At just that moment, an elderly man approached. Dressed impeccably, he carried himself as a man of nobility, a man of means. His age-spotted shiny head reflected the candlelight in the room. His cheeks, clean and pink with good health, practically shone.

In anticipation of danger, Mara again reached for Spira. She was surprised to find Leala's hand upon her forearm urging her not to take action.

The old gentlemen stopped. He bowed from his waist. His cloak fell forward. When he stood back up, he moved it back behind his shoulders.

Mara regarded him silently for a moment. "Who are you?"

"He's—" Leala began.

Mara turned hardened eyes upon the woman. "I'm asking him," she gestured with a flick of her head.

The old man bowed again. "I am Fidel. At your service."

"Fidel, huh?"

A look of surprise crossed his face. "Yes, Fidel."

"And I suppose that you also were named by the Good One? Named for your faithfulness?"

"Why, yes, of course."

"Uh-huh. And what business have you with me, Fidel the faithful?"

He smiled softly. "Why, dear Oathtaker, my business is with you because you bring to us the seventh seventh."

"Fidel," Leala said.

Mara shushed the woman with a frown. "And how is it you've come to know of a seventh seventh?" she asked the old man.

"Why, the Good One promised I would live to see this day, of course. I've waited many long years for—"

"And what makes you think I know anything of this seventh seventh you seek?" she interrupted.

He scowled. "Why she's right there," he said pointing toward the young women and infants. "But . . ."

Leala fidgeted.

Mara shook her head at the woman, insisting she remain silent. "But what?"

"But . . . there's something more here," he continued, squinting.

"Yes?"

He dropped to his knees, then bowed so low his head met the floor.

"Get up!" Mara demanded quietly.

"Dear Oathtaker," he whispered, "may the Good One bless and keep you! You have brought to us the seventh seventh and she 'who is but is not!'"

"Get up!" she again demanded. "You're going to attract attention to us all."

Slowly, he made his way to his knees, and then with Mara's assistance, to his feet. He glanced around. A few onlookers had stopped, puzzled by the drama going on. He waved them away with a smile.

"Forgive me, dear one," he said turning back to her.

"Should I be watching out for more of the faithful?" Mara could hear the old sarcasm in her words and voice, a sarcasm that was ever present in moments of perceived danger.

He chuckled. "No, it's just me and old Leala."

"Old!" Leala exclaimed, grinning. "Speak for yourself, ancient one."

Mara dropped her head and shook it. "I'd hoped to keep our presence secret." She looked back at the oldtimers. Her expression softened. "So you've been waiting for the girls?"

"I've been waiting for years, as I said," Leala responded. "And I was only waiting for a seventh seventh. I never dreamed!"

"And you?" Mara asked, turning to Fidel.

Tears moistened his eyes. "I've been on my own for many years now. I've dedicated my life to others and to Ehyeh. Like Leala here, I've spent my days in service and in supplication. The Good One assured me that in exchange, one day, I would see the seventh seventh foretold of. But like Leala, I never dreamed of meeting 'she who is but is not.'"

Mara watched them both, then motioned for her companions to approach. "Would you like to meet them?"

"Would we!" they exclaimed simultaneously.

As Nina and Adele neared, Jules drew closer. Clearly, he was less than pleased. Even so, Mara presented the girls to Leala and Fidel. Their eyes welled with tears.

"Can we count on your silence?" she asked.

"Most certainly!" Leala assured her.

"And you?" Mara asked Fidel.

"My dear, I would—"

"Die for them," the two old ones said in unison.

At exactly that moment, the ground shook.

Some sanctuary guests ran for cover, while others cried in fear. Within moments, however, the shaking ceased and the people resumed their former activities with little loss of time.

Accompanied by the oldtimers, Mara and company gathered around a table on sanctuary grounds. She explained about their journey and their purpose for visiting sanctuary. In answer to their questions, she informed the old ones that the oath they'd each sworn was most serious, as the confirmation they received witnessed. Leala and Fidel assured her of their good intentions and expressed their desire to be of assistance.

"How many years did you say you'd been studying here?" Jules asked Leala.

"Years? Oh, my, more than sixty, for sure."

"You must have been a very young woman when you first arrived."

"Young! Oh, dear me, no."

"Not young?" Mara asked.

The old woman laughed. "No. No, I married my dear Jonathan when we both were just twenty. What a dear good man, may his blessed soul rest in peace. He died at near seventy and I've been here since."

"Wait," Nina said. "That makes you . . . What? About—"

"I'd say one hundred thirty or so. I must confess, I stopped keeping track some time ago," she whispered conspiratorially to the young woman.

"Whew!" Jules exclaimed. "And you, Fidel? How about you?"

"Oh, I'm just a young pup compared to Leala here."

"Young pup, my—"

"There, there, Leala," he said, patting her gnarled hand. "Young ears. Young ears about. Watch your language." He smiled broadly.

"Well?" Mara asked, struggling to keep her grin at bay. "How long?"

He leaned in. "If you must know," he said, then he turned to Leala. "Cover your ears old woman. This information is not for you."

"Ha ha ha! You're no spring chicken. I know that."

Mara smiled as she watched the old people banter like siblings. "Well?" she asked again.

Fidel looked at Leala and raised a brow. She sighed deeply, then covered her ears and rolled her eyes, clearly humoring him.

Once again, he leaned in. "Well now, don't let on about this to Leala." He turned to confirm she covered her ears and was not trying to read his lips. "She thinks I'm younger than she is," he whispered, "and the truth is, I like to let her think so. But," again a quick glance her way, "I'm three years her senior!"

Mara and her friends laughed.

"What? What's funny?" Leala removed her hands from her ears.

"Nothing, old woman," Fidel said. "They're just enjoying a good chuckle at my expense is all. They're clearly amazed at how a young man such as I, could be so brilliant."

"Huh! They're probably laughing at what a know-it-all you make yourself out to be."

"All right, so you've both been here for some time," Mara interrupted. "What I need to know is how you can help me. I don't think it's any mistake that you're both here. I believe you're here for this time and for a particular purpose."

"Well put," Fidel said.

"So?" the Oathtaker asked.

"Well," Leala said, "we've both studied here for years. My expertise is history."

"And mine," Fidel said, "is prophecy."

"Prophecy?" Jules asked.

"Indeed."

"Are you a prophet?"

"Oh, dear me, no. Simply a scholar."

"So, what do you know of the girls?" Mara asked.

"Well now," the old man said, "prophecy can be a difficult thing."

"How is that?"

He looked out across sanctuary grounds. "Before today I spent years studying prophecy, including that which tells of a seventh seventh 'and she who is but is not.' But not until the moment I saw the girls did I realize what it all meant."

"How is it that you knew when you saw them?"

He held the Oathtaker's gaze. "I saw that everything about them was alike and yet . . . different. I knew in that moment that they were twins. And suddenly, it all just . . . fit."

"Leala, Fidel," Mara said, looking to each in turn, "I have so many questions. Sometimes I feel I don't know where to begin."

"Perhaps at the beginning would be best," the old woman said.

"I often find the beginning to be the best place, yes," Fidel agreed.

Mara chuckled. "Good advice. I've been known to give it myself on occasion."

"So, what are your questions?" Leala asked.

"I guess when you get down to it, my questions are in three main areas. First, what is my position as Oathtaker to not one, but to two, of the Select, particularly given that they are infants and far from being able to take on the missions for which they are meant. And . . . what about the dangers of having both of them as my charge? Or is it, 'charges?' Either way," she said with a wave of her hand. "For example, what if my acting on behalf of one puts the other in danger? Sometimes I can't sleep at night considering these issues."

"I never thought of that," Jules said.

"Second, what of the crown, the sword and the scepter? Are they for just one of the girls? For both? Am I to keep them safe myself? Or are they better off left where they are? And what if they land in the hands of—"

"Whoa! Whoa!" Fidel interrupted. "That's a mouthful there."

"Yes, and there's more."

"That's not enough?" Nina asked.

The Oathtaker grinned. "No, there's more. Third, how do I keep the girls safe? May I leave them at any time in the care of others? Does it matter if it's someone who's sworn to protect them? Is there anywhere in Oosa safe for them?"

She turned to Jules, directing her next questions to him. "And what of Lucy? What about—"

"Lucy!" Leala exclaimed. "How do you know her?"

"You know Lucy?"

"Sure!"

"You too?" Mara asked Fidel.

"But of course."

Leala chimed in. "We're Lucy's eyes and ears here. Well, that is, I'm Lucy's eyes since nothing escapes my attention. Junior here," she said, her eyes rolling Fidel's way, "acts as her ears—when he's not too busy worshipping the sound of his own voice."

The old man frowned as the others laughed lightly.

"I don't understand," Jules said. "What's your connection to Lucy?"

"We've known her for a very long time," Leala said. "We met her here at sanctuary. She said she was waiting for a seventh seventh, working behind the scenes to help ensure that Oosa would have such a one some day. When she heard that we awaited the child as well, that the Good One had assured us we would meet her one day . . . Well, we all decided we'd keep one another informed."

"So if we'd said nothing more, you would have reported this information to Lucy?" Mara asked.

"Truth is, there was a time I might have," Leala said. "However, having given an oath to protect the twins, and having witnessed Ehyeh's confirmation of that oath, I feel it's outside my authority to take any action with respect to them."

"Well put, Leala," Fidel chimed in.

"You don't trust Lucy?" Jules asked.

"Oh no," the old woman said, "that's not it at all. I just appreciate that Mara must make these decisions. I'm no Oathtaker."

"I agree," Fidel said.

"So what now?" Nina asked Mara.

"That's just it. I'm overwhelmed. I don't know where to begin. Maybe I've come to depend on Dixon too much. I don't know."

"Did you say Dixon?" Leala asked. "Dixon Townsend?"

Mara eyed the old folks carefully. "Yes."

"What's he got to do with this?" Fidel asked.

"Why do you ask?"

"We've heard troubling things," Leala said.

"And?"

The old woman slapped the table. "And it just doesn't make sense. From all I've ever heard, there is not a more committed, more honorable, more honest and worthy man, than Dixon. And then we hear that he's some kind of traitor!"

"He's no traitor."

"But Lilith—"

"Lilith has turned to the dark side."

Fidel's head jerked up. "What's that you say?"

Mara explained the role Lilith had played to date.

"But of course, the girls are Rowena's."

"Yes."

"So that makes four categories of questions," he said.

"What's the fourth? You think I don't have enough on my plate already?"

He shook his head. "Oh, you have enough all right. But if what you say is true, there is much to determine about Lilith and about how to deal with her."

"Tell us something we don't know," Adele said, finally having something to add to the conversation.

Chapter Twenty-Eight

Mara called a meeting so that she could bring everyone up to date. She sent a note via a housemaid to Ezra. Would he be free to join them for the evening? He assured her he would be happy to assist in any way possible. He offered the group a back room, but requested they dine first, as he could not attend until later. Then Mara sent messengers to Leala and Fidel to ask if they would join her. Within the hour, the couriers returned with acceptances from them both.

When the two oldtimers arrived at the inn, Celestine ushered them into the room. Upon meeting Dixon, they offered their sympathies on the loss of Rowena. Mara thanked them for coming. As she did, she couldn't help but notice, out of the corner of her eye, Dixon lost in conversation with, his rapt attention upon, Celestine.

After dinner Mara surveyed the group before her, pleased it had grown. Even so, she had to face reality. Missing only Ted and Faith, everyone who knew of the girls and wanted to assist with keeping them safe, sat before her. Thus, her assistants included Dixon, Basha, and Therese, two "would be" Oathtakers, one cripple, one lactating woman who was hard to keep adequately fed and who was always slowed by the need to feed the infants, one very old woman, and one very, very old man. They all visited quietly, awaiting Ezra's arrival. *Oh yes, and one spy*, she added to her count.

A bustle came at the door. Mara, Dixon, and Basha, all jumped up at the same time.

"In there. Get him in there! Stop. Watch out!" Ezra shouted.

Mara reached for Spira. Her eyes darted to Dixon, who held his blade, Verity, and then to Basha who held her blade, Honora. Behind her, her friends pushed their chairs from the table. She surmised that Samuel and Jules prepared to jump into battle.

The innkeeper burst into the room. With Nancy's assistance, he held up a man. Behind him, two of his aids, Arne and Connell, dragged another man forward.

Having sheathed Verity, Dixon jumped toward them.

Nancy and Ezra placed the man they held into a nearby chair. He looked near death. Blood spotted his clothing. When he swayed to the side, nearly falling over, the barmaid aided him.

Ezra turned to Arne and Connell. Tattoos of flames covered the arms of the man they led in. When he tensed and contracted his biceps, the flames appeared to devour his flesh. He opened his dark eyes at half-mast and peeked out over his hooked nose, surveying the room menacingly.

Arne and Connell flanked their prisoner, holding him tightly, though they had bound him earlier with rope. Ezra stood before them, while Dixon remained to one side crouched to strike.

"Who are you?" the innkeeper asked.

The man lifted his chin and raised his brow. His eyes traveled down Ezra, then back up, as though sizing him up for battle. His sneer intensified, then he looked away.

"I asked, 'who are you?'"

The man took a deep breath in, then exhaled slowly as he rolled his eyes.

"He's coming to!" Nancy exclaimed.

Ezra shifted his attention to the man in the other chair. "Dooley!" he cried, placing his hand under the man's chin and lifting his head.

Dooley's eyes opened slowly, then closed again.

"Dooley, can you hear me?"

"He needs rest," Nancy said.

"We'll get him down shortly." The innkeeper turned his attention back to the stranger. "Are you going to speak or do we have to drag it out of you?"

"Where'd he come from?" Dixon asked.

"I stationed Arne and Connell near the city gates. They saw him following Dooley. They caught up with him shortly afterward, but by then he'd done his worst."

"Dooley doesn't look good."

"No, he doesn't. What did you want from him?" Ezra then asked the stranger. "Were you intending to rob him?"

The man refused to look at his questioner.

"He was not going to rob him," Mara said. "He planned to kill him."

For the first time, the dark man's gaze settled on Mara. She stepped forward. As she reached Dixon's side, he held an arm out to hold her back. She moved it away, then advanced.

"Tell me when I get off course," she said, contempt in her voice. "You came from the Polesk area where you were with the group that accompanied Lilith there."

The stranger's glare intensified. One eye squinted almost imperceptibly.

"And your errand was to keep Dooley from reaching his destination. So I assume you think he has information that Lilith doesn't want out."

He rolled his eyes.

After a pause, Ezra spoke. "You know what to do," he said to his hired muscle. "Take him down. We'll question him later."

"I'll question him," Mara said.

"Ma'am, it may not be safe. He's bound, to be sure, but very dangerous."

"Where is it you intend to take him? And what measures do you intend to use?"

The innkeeper looked about uneasily. He stepped closer. "I'd rather not say," he responded quietly as he leaned in.

She nodded. "Ezra, you may have to use strong methods to gain the information from him that we need." She looked about as though defying anyone to argue with her, or as though challenging the others to offer convincing argument to the contrary. "I understand under most circumstances, that force—or whatever other means you may have in mind—is not the preferred method for getting truthful information. Moreover, in general, it goes against what we believe."

He opened his mouth to speak, but Mara motioned to him with an upraised hand to say nothing. "However," she continued, "we have to consider what is at stake. Timing is everything. If we get the information we need, but we get it too late, it will of no value to us. This man knows something, and what he knows is information we need quickly. We can't afford to stall. If we don't use the most—"

"Indeed," Ezra interrupted. "I understand completely."

"Very well then." She turned away, then stopped in her tracks and looked back to the innkeeper. "Stop at nothing," she said in a voice barely above a whisper. She looked to the stranger, satisfied when a flash of fear crossed his eyes.

Arne and Connell shuffled out with the dark man in tow.

"I'll be there shortly," Ezra called after them.

The tension in the room released. Everyone seemed to take in a simultaneous breath.

"I don't know when we'll get anything from Dooley," Ezra said. "The truth is, he looks pretty bad. Still, you should know that I think you're right. He was stationed in Polesk. From what Lance told me, he expected Dooley back here some time ago." He glanced at his spy. "I can't tell the extent of his injuries. He's taken a beating and has been at the mercy of the elements for some time."

"I could help with the healing," Mara offered.

"No, thank you, I've got this one. Save your energy. We may need it yet."

"Just make it quick, Ezra. We need answers."

Basha stepped forward. "Mara, Ezra," she said looking from one to the other, "I can help with the questioning."

Mara's eyes narrowed. "You're an interrogator?"

"An excellent one," Dixon said. "She's well known for her skills."

Mara was pleased to learn of Basha's abilities. She still had so much to learn about the powers of those around her. "Questioning the stranger could prove difficult," she said.

"I've no scruples about doing what must be done to keep the twins safe." Basha placed her hand on Mara's arm. "You were right. Gaining the information we need too late would be as bad as not gaining it at all."

"Do as you please then."

"Very well." Basha turned to the innkeeper. "Can someone show me the way to where the prisoner was taken?"

"I'll show you myself as soon as we get Dooley to a room."

Dixon approached Mara's side. He wore a puzzled expression. He pointed to the door. "How did you know where he was from?" he asked her.

"I dreamed last night that a stranger came our way. He was from the army that accompanies Lilith. That's all I remember, and I didn't remember that much until I saw that man right here before us."

"Excuse me, ma'am?"

Mara turned to the voice. "Yes, Adele? What is it?"

"I ahhh . . . I had the same dream."

"Me too," Nina offered.

"And me," said Basha.

"Count me in," Therese quipped.

"Yes," Samuel and Jules added, in unison.

Mara's gaze rested on Dixon. He closed his eyes and nodded.

Ezra, exhausted from his efforts to heal Dooley, and from overseeing the questioning of the stranger, jumped as a knock came at the door. When Connell opened it, its squeaking hinges sounded eerily into the room.

"How is it going with Dooley?" Dixon asked as he stepped inside.

"He's resting."

"That's probably what you should be doing."

"Yes."

"Any information yet?"

"No, but I'm still hoping he'll have something for us when he awakens."

Dixon watched his friend closely. "Really, you should get some sleep. You look awful."

"Thanks. How's the questioning going?"

Dixon sat next to his friend. "We keep thinking he's breaking, but then . . . nothing."

"Nothing at all?"

"No. Hopefully soon. Mara insists Basha turn up the heat. It's difficult, but she's rising to the occasion. Therese is helping."

"How's Mara holding up?"

Dixon looked away. "I'm not sure. She's been . . . distant. Probably just feeling overwhelmed. I remember those early days. You?"

The innkeeper chuckled. "Yes, but maybe you should just tell her the truth about Celestine. I see the way she looks at her."

Dixon shook his head. "Don't read anything into it, Ezra. She's just feeling she's in over her head. Leala and Fidel are inundating her with information and resources. It's amazing how the education of Oathtakers has changed so quickly over just the past few years. I didn't realize how much they were no longer teaching. Besides, it's not like we—" He stopped short. "It's not like she could acknowledge . . . Well, she's committed. She's under oath. Even if . . ." He paused and drummed a beat upon his thigh. "Even if, as you seem to be implying, there was any interest on her part, it would probably be best to keep obstacles in the way."

Ezra watched his friend closely. "I can't say that I disagree with you. Even so, the two of you might be getting along better. We're all feeling the tension."

Dixon's brow rose.

Just then another knock came at the door. Once again, Connell answered it. Once again, its squeaking hinges sang their eerie tune. There stood Mara, looking wan and tired.

"We were just talking about you," Ezra said.

Her gaze shifted quickly from him to Dixon. "All good things, I hope."

"Most certainly. We were discussing how hard you've been studying."

"I feel my head's about to burst."

He motioned to a chair. "What's the news?"

"Basha just sent a message. She thinks he might talk soon."

"But she's gotten nothing yet?" Dixon asked.

"No, nothing yet." Mara brushed her hair from her face. "Well, that is, he gave Basha his name. It's Udaye. And he confirmed he was with the army in Polesk."

"Nothing about what they were doing there?"

"No." Mara turned to Ezra. "Have any more of your men made it back from that area?"

He shook his head. "No. I finally sent a few more that direction. They left last night. I arranged for them to put out false information about your whereabouts along the way."

"Good," Dixon said. "Where are they going to say we were seen?"

"I figured the farther away from here the better, so they'll say they've seen you in various villages in the highlands. That should make it sound like you're on the move."

"Sounds good."

"Ezra, are you sure your people can be trusted?" Mara asked. "I mean—"

"I understand your concerns, Mara, but short of requiring a life oath from each of them, all I can do is tell you that I chose each of them because of their skills and their personal histories. I trust them."

She sighed. "It just makes me wonder if we should move on. It seems to be getting harder and harder to keep the girls' existence a secret."

"You could try going to the Council."

"No, I don't know them, and I don't trust that Lilith hasn't already poisoned those waters." She sighed. "Besides, as you well know, I can't go making accusations against her without any specifics or proof. And really, what do I know? What proof do I have?"

The three discussed Mara's studies. She explained that Leala and Fidel strongly encouraged her to study a source called, *The Book of The Blood.*

"I read that years ago," Dixon said. "It was part of the standard reading for an Oathtaker's training."

"Me too," Ezra said. "We had to take a whole course dedicated to it."

"What do you remember?" Mara asked as she poured a glass of water.

"Not much," Dixon said.

"Me either," the innkeeper said. "But then, I was never very good at prophecy. What are you finding? Anything of interest?"

She sat quietly for a moment. "Fidel directed me to portions that are very thought provoking. They're prophecies about a seventh seventh and she 'who is but is not.'"

"And?" he urged.

She repeated the language she and Fidel found troubling, language she'd quickly memorized: "*'Be wary, for in those days shall come she who is not a leader, yet having sold her soul, she shall seek to lead. Woe to the people, for there shall be much crying and mourning for the infants lost by her. Run quickly to Sanctuary! For only there may you be saved.'*"

She shrugged. "I can't imagine what horrors it seems to imply will come. What does it mean when it says that infants will be 'lost by her?' Still, Fidel and I agree that the prophecy seems to refer to Lilith as the one who is not the legitimate leader who seeks to lead."

"Why is that?"

"Well, the prophecy goes on to say: '*The land shall move to mourning. Even so, a way has been provided, and you must pray that it shall come to pass, for a seventh seventh and she who is but is not, may rise after a time of misery and fear. In their day, they may lead the people forth.*'" Mara paused. "I think the prophecy applies now because it makes sense that Eden is 'she who is but is not.'"

Once again, came a knock at the door.

"There seems to be a constant stream of activity this morning," Ezra commented as Connell opened the door to Celestine who carried a tray of refreshments. Instantly, the smell of fresh crusty bread permeated the room.

"Here you go," she said. "You could all use some energy. You especially, Ezra," she admonished as she tapped him on the shoulder. "You know the cost that comes with healing. Anyway, we prepared warm sandwiches for you all."

"Sounds good," Dixon said.

"Your favorite." Celestine put the tray down. "Prosciutto, hard salami, aged provolone, super salty olives, and sweet grilled red pepper on crunchy bread. Oh yes, and with a drizzle of fruity, peppery olive oil."

"Mmmmm!" he moaned with anticipated pleasure.

Mara choked back a "harrumph."

"Your mother introduced these to us all, don't you remember?" the barmaid laughed as she ruffled Dixon's hair.

"I do," he said with a smile.

"You know his mother?" Mara finally trusted herself to speak.

"But of course! Aunt Francesca could make the most out of the least. She loved to cook and to teach us all."

Mara looked from Celestine to Dixon. Though her gaze remained on him for a long moment, he did not look up. "Aunt Francesca?" she asked as she turned her attention back to the barmaid.

"Yes, Dixon's mother."

"Dixon's mother is your aunt?"

Celestine laughed, a light rippling sound. "Not just my aunt, my favorite aunt and 'fill in' mother. I always envied my cousin Dixon here," she said nudging him, "for his good fortune in being her son."

Mara nodded. "And your mother is—"

The barmaid's smile vanished. "Well, I . . . That is, I never knew her."

"I'm sorry."

"Don't be. She abandoned me when I was an infant. I figure if she was the kind of woman who could leave her child to go off to live the wild life, then I was better off without her."

"That's very wise of you. Still—"

"Don't give it another thought," Celestine continued. "I was fortunate enough to be left to the care of her sister—Dixon's mother. And I got three big brothers in the bargain. It was the greatest good fortune." She grinned, then slowly her smile faded. "I thought you knew." She looked down at Dixon, then back to Mara. "Oh, goodness, what must you have thought!" she exclaimed with a hand to her mouth.

"Really, I didn't think anything," Mara said, having surmised the meaning behind the barmaid's words and glances. She looked at the spread of food before her and inhaled deeply. The sandwiches smelled wonderful. Small crispy fried potatoes, fresh fruit salad, and a chilled carafe of wine finished off the refection.

"Well, dig in," Celestine quipped as she turned away.

As they helped themselves, Mara noticed Ezra grinning. "Something funny?" she asked him.

His eyes shot up. "No. Nothing."

"Uh-huh." She bit into her sandwich. Her eyes widened. "Mmmm, these are . . . Mmmm!"

Dixon, too busy chewing to speak, winked at her. Caught off guard and momentarily flustered, she turned her attention back to her meal.

Moments later, Therese and Basha arrived.

"Sit down. Sit down," Ezra said. He pulled chairs out for them.

"No, thank you," Basha said. "Mara, I'm so sorry." She shook visibly.

Mara stopped chewing. She sensed Basha's fear and frustration. She swallowed hard as though in doing so, she would flush any unwanted information away at the same time. "Not getting anywhere?"

"It's worse than that," Therese said.

"How could it be worse?" Dixon asked. "We need information."

Therese slumped into a chair and directed Basha to the one next to her. "May as well get it over with."

"What? What is it?" Mara asked.

Basha looked to the floor. "I'm sorry, we . . . lost him."

"Lost him!" Mara jumped to her feet. When Dixon reached over, urging her back to her seat, she sat back down, hard. "What do you mean you lost him?"

Basha shook her head. "It was very strange. It was as though he'd been ensorcelled or something."

"What does that mean?"

"We got his name, and he confirmed he'd been with the army that accompanies Lilith," Therese said.

"I know that much."

"That was it," Basha said. "We pushed, but it was as though he was under a spell. Just as we thought he'd spill the information we sought, his eyes flashed open and he writhed as if from a source of pain we'd not authored."

"And?" Mara asked, sensing there was more.

"And he started to go up in smoke."

"Smoke!" Dixon exclaimed.

"What?" Mara cried.

"He literally burned to death on the spot," said Therese.

"Oh, dear Good One. Wh—wh—" Mara stammered for words. "How could this happen?"

"There was no way we could have anticipated this," Therese said. "I've never seen anything like it. It was as though he was on fire from the inside." She grimaced. "Oh, the smell!" She coughed and waved her hand before her face.

Mara threw her napkin down and jumped up again. "We need answers! We need to know what Lilith has been up to."

"We'll get answers," Dixon said in an effort to reassure her.

"How can you say that so calmly? How do you know? Oh, great Ehyeh!" she cried as she dropped her head into her hands.

He approached. Though at first she tried to move away from him, he put his arms around her gently, but firmly.

"I know because I serve Ehyeh, the Good One," he said, his voice low. "I know because *you* serve the Good One. I know because every breath I take assures me that it's right and good to be on the side of life, of freedom, of choice. I know because nothing Lilith does will stop us from seeing to that purpose—to the Good One's purpose. *Nothing.* We will get answers. We will prevail. No matter what she attempts to do through evil, Ehyeh will conquer through good."

CHAPTER TWENTY-NINE

The smell of snow filled the air. Some soldiers congregated around campfires while others waited in line near the meal wagon. From their midst, a fight broke out. Laughter rang out as a man fell back. Someone had extricated the food from his hands. He jumped at the mountainous offender, ready to brawl, fists raised. Moments later he fell to the ground, this time never to rise again. A knife protruded from his chest. More laughter erupted as others kicked away the body. Without hesitation, someone took the man's former place in line and proceeded as though nothing out of the ordinary had occurred.

Lilith sat inside her wagon watching the chaos. She'd been on the road for weeks now. Before entering an area, she ordered guards to ride ahead to cover all the roadways to her next destination. Once stationed, she moved in. On pretense of holding an event to bless the infants of the area, she first asked the locals to deliver the imposter child to her. When they did not, she oversaw the demise of hundreds of infants. For those townspeople who had not felt compelled to join in the event, Lilith sent her men out to search house-by-house. In her wake, she left a continuous trail of blood.

Once she accomplished her task in an area, Lilith left sufficient guards with orders not to allow anyone to leave the city after she moved on. They remained on the lookout for the child she sought, as well as for any others that may have escaped her wrath.

As a safeguard, Lilith had placed a spell over the men at the outset of her venture. Under no circumstances could they tell of the events that transpired. A soldier who tried to do so would literally burn to death from the inside out before he could reveal anything of importance.

Of late, she'd also sent small groups out all over Oosa, to scout for areas where she might later make camp.

She turned to Freeman. Her attention devoured his body. "I'm so tense," she purred.

He massaged her neck and shoulders.

Her eyes rolled up and she moaned. Just then came a scuffle outside the wagon. She scowled. "Get that."

Freeman went to the back of the wagon and pulled the tarp aside.

"Sir, we seek Lilith."

"Who is it?"

"Lilith!" a man's voice called. "It's me! Let go of me! She'll see me," he shouted.

She looked out. Two soldiers held another man tightly. She sighed audibly.

"Lilith!" he cried again.

She recognized him by his voice, his haughty bearing, even by the way he dressed, always in the same style, always in black, as though he was in uniform.

"What are you doing here? I told you to stay away."

He tried unsuccessfully, to pull free of his captors. With a sigh and a nod from Lilith, they released him.

"What are you doing here?" she asked again.

He elbowed the bulky, well-armed soldiers surrounding him. "May I speak with you?"

She motioned Freeman to disappear, then waved her hand at the guards to disperse. Turning back to her visitor, she nodded, then retreated into her wagon and sat at the edge of her bed.

The man entered. His eyes did not miss the rumpled bedding, the half empty bottle of wine on the table, the partially emptied wineglasses, and the lamp turned low.

"What do you want?" she asked.

"I wanted . . . Well, that is, I thought I'd see what I could do for you."

"I told you to wait at the palace."

"But what if I can help you to find Dixon? Maybe I could urge him out of hiding?"

"And how do you propose to do that?"

He motioned to a nearby chair. "May I?"

She nodded.

He sat, then tossed a bag of coins from one hand to the other. "I know Dixon. He trusts me."

"Where do you suppose he's to be found?" she asked, her voice laced with boredom.

"Well now, I've been thinking on that." He smiled. "The City of Light."

"That's not what we're hearing in the local pubs and meeting rooms."

"What are they saying?"

"Someone sighted him in the highlands. I'm heading there next."

"You must be getting false information. The City of Light is the obvious place for him to go."

"And why is that?"

"Dixon is well known in the city."

"It seems you've just given the best reason for him to avoid it." Lilith scowled.

"No, don't you see? Dixon always thinks everyone is on his side. He thinks he's everyone's favorite. It would be just like him to go there for aid and support."

She rose. "We'll make it to the city soon enough. If he's there, I'll find him."

"Right. But maybe I could help. I could check out the inns and some of his favorite haunts. Likely, it will take some time, but . . ."

Lilith sneered. "What exactly is it you propose?"

The man leaned in. He smiled, encouraging her to join him in his plans. "Dixon is a wily one. If he gets word of your nearing the city, he'll leave. But if I found him, I could keep him there." He hesitated. "Don't you see? I could make him feel secure there while keeping you informed of his whereabouts."

"You think he'd follow your advice?"

"Think! I know. He'll trust me. I'm sure of it."

"He travels with a woman. What of her?"

"I'll win her over."

She smirked. "You are so sure of yourself?"

"With women?" He laughed.

Lilith looked at him disdainfully.

"Well, I mean, with an average woman—which surely in comparison to you, she must be." He tossed his bag of coins again, back and forth, then stopped. "Yes, I'm sure of it. I can win her over."

"Very well then, see to it. If you discover Dixon's whereabouts, get word to me. For now, I plan to head to the highlands when we're through here. I'll put my guards on notice to be on the lookout for any messages you might send. If you find him, do what you can to keep him in one place."

He smiled. "When would you like for me to head for the city? In the morning maybe?" His voice, his glance, held an invitation.

She was not amused. "When? Why, immediately, of course." She tilted her head toward the back of the wagon, motioning for him to leave. "And be quick about it."

He got up and turned to go, then jumped down. Just as his feet touched the ground, she called out. "Oh, wait! Come back here."

He returned, smiling leeringly.

"I almost forgot. You're going to need protection against revealing your intentions.

"I don't understand."

"You don't need to understand." Lilith had to put him under the same spell she'd used on the soldiers who accompanied her. She could not risk his informing Dixon of her whereabouts, or that anyone might see through to his real intentions. She reached toward her guest. In a moment, he dropped to the floor and thrashed in pain.

CHAPTER THIRTY

The fire crackled. No one had spoken for some time.

"Mara," Dixon finally said, breaking the near silence.

"I said I'm going."

"But, Mara—"

"Look. Look here," she said, cutting him off. She held the oracle toward him and ruffled through its pages. "It says 'Go,' so I'm going." Her eyes, reflecting the fire in the grate, were hard on him. She took a deep breath and let it out slowly. "I probably shouldn't have waited this long to go."

"Mara," he said again, his voice soft, "maybe it means that you should go from here. You know, leave the City of Light. Or maybe it means you should go back to sanctuary for more resources. Or maybe . . ."

"No. It means I'm to go to Polesk to find out what Lilith was up to while there, and to learn anything else I can about what she—"

"How can you know that?" he interrupted. "What if—"

"I'm going, Dixon, like it or not."

He shook his head.

"Maybe she's onto something, Dixon," Basha said.

His eyes flashed her way. "How can you say that when you know it could be dangerous?"

"Dixon, we got nothing from Udaye, and all Dooley could tell us was that Polesk was in an uproar." Basha stood at Mara's side. "You know how it is. Sometimes there's no explaining the call, the demand. If Mara is so adamant about this, well then, I think we should support her." She turned to Mara. "I'll go with you, if you like."

"Basha—no," Dixon said, "your duty is to Therese now that you've been reunited, just as Mara's is to the girls."

"I know my duty, Dixon," Mara snapped.

"I know. I know. I just . . ." He shook his head. "Look, I'm sorry. That didn't come out the way I meant it. All right, so you insist on going. Leave Basha here. Take me along. I don't have a charge to attend to."

She set her lips tightly. "I don't know," she finally said before turning away.

He grasped her arm. Gently, he turned her back toward himself. "Take me along. We'll go to Ted's. If anyone will know what happened when Lilith was there, it'll be Ted."

"Maybe you should stay here to help with the girls."

"Of course we'd prefer you were both here, but we'll keep the girls safe," Basha offered.

"You think I should take Dixon?" Mara asked of her.

"Yes."

"Very well then." Mara glanced at him. "I need you to understand. I don't want to go. I *have* to go. I just . . . know it, and I can't explain it."

"Can you explain what you feel?" he asked. "I'm trying to get a handle on this."

"Peace."

"You mean you feel a sense of peace about going?"

"That's right. And I feel . . . discord, discontent, distress, about not going."

"You know how it is, Dixon," Basha said.

He sighed deeply, then smiled. "Yes, I know the feeling. So when do we leave?"

"Immediately. I hope we'll be back within hours—a day or two at the most," Mara then said to the others. "If we're not back within . . . let's say three days, take the girls and proceed to Lucy's safe house. If that happens, have Leala and Fidel send some resources so I can continue my studying when we meet back up with you. Understood?"

"Understood," they responded in unison.

"May I make a suggestion?" Dixon asked.

"Please, do."

"I recommend you leave someone in charge. If something should happen to you, the Good One will call a new Oathtaker for the girls, but in the meantime, there could be chaos. Fear can breed discord and indecision and with that could come added danger to everyone."

"I agree. Basha, you're in charge. Everyone will take their orders from you." Mara looked to Therese. "If that's acceptable to you."

"Certainly."

"Very well then. Keep the group together as much as possible." Mara turned to Dixon. "Anything else you can think of?"

"Just that we should grab some food and carry extra weapons."

She grinned weakly. "Done."

"Done?"

She pointed to two backpacks on the floor near her. "Nancy and Celestine put some things together earlier." She watched him closely. "Not to worry, there's enough for two."

"But— Who were you—"

"Planning to take with me? Why, you, of course."

He shook his head. "You drive a hard bargain."

"You notice I had to use my best powers of persuasion to get you to agree to accompany me."

He chuckled. "Right. Very persuasive."

"Nearly as persuasive as you are charming," she said as she reached down to put something into one of the backpacks. She stood back up and held his gaze. "Really, are you all right with accompanying me? You don't have to. I can go alone."

"If you believe it must be done, then I'm with you."

She turned to Adele who sat quietly near the fireplace. "The babies are resting?" she asked.

"Nina was just feeding them."

Mara approached the adjoining door, knocked lightly, then entered just as Nina placed Eden in her basket for the night. She went from one of the infants to the other, stroking each gently across the cheek and kissing each in turn. Then she turned away to hide the tears welled in her eyes. For a moment the bitter, nostalgic feeling of having left someone before, overwhelmed her. She tried to shake it off.

"Take good care of them, Nina. I'll be back soon."

"I'm counting on it."

"And Nina, thank you."

"It's my pleasure. Really."

"Well, thank you anyway. See you soon then." Mara left the room, her tears stinging her eyes. She'd not expected such pain on leaving the girls. When she looked up at Dixon, she could see a question in his expression. She blinked rapidly to hold her tears at bay. "Are you ready then?"

"Are you all right?"

"Fine. I'm fine."

He watched her closely. "All right. What's the plan then?"

"I need quiet. I haven't traveled for some time now." She looked at her other friends. "We'll leave from here if you don't mind."

"Take care, Mara, Dixon," Therese said as she, then Basha, embraced them each briefly.

Next came Samuel and Jules. Jules bowed slightly and wished them well. Samuel simply nodded his head, remaining mute, as was his custom. For a moment, Mara wondered if she would even recognize his voice, he spoke so rarely.

Finally, Adele stepped forward. "Watch out for that witch," she said.

"I intend to," Mara said.

The young woman turned to Dixon. "Don't let her catch you again."

He grinned. "Right. We'll be back soon. You just help care for the girls."

"It's just that I know how evil Lilith is."

"It's all right, Adele. We'll be all right," Mara tried to assure the young woman.

After everyone was gone, she handed a backpack to Dixon. "You have all the weapons you want?"

"Yes."

She pulled her pack over her shoulder as she looked toward the room where the infants slept. She feared going into the unknown, but even more, she feared remaining ignorant of what Lilith was doing.

"Here we go then." She grasped Dixon's forearms. When she looked up, their eyes met.

"Are you sure about this?" he asked.

She nodded.

"Have you a destination in mind?"

"I'm shooting for Ted's."

"Can you do that?"

She smiled. "We're about to find out. Here we go."

Landing with one foot upon a rock, Mara fell forward, only to have Dixon grasp her arm to steady her. "Are you all right?" he asked.

"Yes,"

"Whew! That was incredible!" he exclaimed.

She laughed. "I know. Indescribable, isn't it? Too bad it's over so quickly."

"Yes, I'm sorry I was unconscious through it the first time." He looked around. Leafless hardwood trees surrounded them. An inch or two of new fallen snow covered the ground. "Where are we?"

"I'm not sure. I was aiming for Polesk, but it seems . . . Well, needless to say, I'm still working on this particular talent."

The waning second moon cast limited light into the glen. The rustlings and babblings of the night creatures that stuck around for winter, sounded out. Mara jumped at the laughter of a skulk of fox, then wrapped her shawl more tightly around her shoulders and shivered, in part from the cold, and in part in response to the sound.

"Where to from here?" he asked.

"To wherever my nose leads us, I guess."

He laughed. "Picking up any scents?"

She shook her head, grinned, then headed for a trail she made out in the moonlight. Edging her way around a thorny bush, she pointed out to Dixon, so he would not misstep, a hole in the ground.

Soon, they reached the edge of a rocky ledge. Dixon moved aside the branch of an evergreen obstructing their view. The smell of pine permeated the air. He placed his hand on the small of Mara's back, directing her to take a look.

She inhaled deeply of the scent. "I know where we are. We passed through here on our way to Polesk. That's the city there."

"Right you are." His eyes scanned the horizon. "It's odd, though. Polesk isn't nearly as lit up as usual."

"How can you tell?"

Standing just behind and to her side, he moved the branch farther back to get a better look. He leaned in, his cheek nearly touching hers. With a nod, he directed her attention. "See there? Those lights?"

She couldn't help but notice his closeness, his hand on the small of her back. "Yes." She struggled to focus.

"See those lights just below the tower? Those are the Oathtakers' offices. It appears some lamps burn, but not as many as usual. And look," he continued, directing her attention higher, "above the offices, is sanctuary's steeple. Usually it's lit up right to the top. Mirrors surround the lamps in it. They multiply the light many times over. But they're all out now." He bit his lip. "In the past, when I've been through here at night, sanctuary has lit up the night sky."

"Why would the lights be out?"

"Not sure. Mourning, maybe?"

"Mourning?"

"Maybe they're still acknowledging the loss of Rowena. I don't know. But it's like the heart of the city has been shut out." He allowed the branch he'd been holding aside to fall back into place and then they retook the trail.

"You know, I can't help but note that Ehyeh brought you here rather than directly into the city, Mara. Maybe we shouldn't go there after all," Dixon said after several minutes of silence.

"Maybe. But for now, I feel led that way."

"So, why do you suppose we landed here?"

"I don't know. Maybe there's something He wants us to see."

In silence, they advanced, one lending a hand to the other when needed, one moving a branch aside for the other when needed, one pointing out a pitfall to the attention of the other as needed. They communicated with signs and gestures.

After an hour or so, they came upon a small thatched cottage. It was silent and dark. No smoke rose from its chimney. As they neared it, something drew Mara's attention to the ground. There she found dark splotches in the snow. She cocked her head, then crouched down and grasped a handful of the darkened snow. She smelled it.

"What is it?"

She looked up. The light of the moon shone in her eyes. "Blood."

He crouched down at her side. "Blood?"

"Look," she whispered as she grasped Spira, then pointed out a trail of scattered drops of blood, then larger pools, then more drops. Nearby shuffled footprints headed in no certain direction.

Dixon unsheathed Verity. "This way." He took her hand.

They followed the blood trail. "There!" Mara gasped.

His gaze followed her direction. There lay two bodies, silenced in death. Around them was a lake of frozen-over blood.

Mara drew nearer. Her eyes followed the outstretched arms of one of the dead. Several yards away, partially covered by brush, lay an infant stripped of all covering. "Oh, great Ehyeh!"

Dixon put his hands on her shoulders, then turned her toward himself and away from the scene.

"Why? Why would someone do such a thing? And to an innocent child!"

He drew her nearer. "There's no explanation but evil, and there is no explaining evil."

"Do you suppose they were Select?" she asked, tears pooled in her eyes.

"I don't know. But I can find out."

"How?"

"Upon death, an innocent Select will always show the sign of his birth. All infants are innocent." He stepped away.

"No, Dixon. No, let's just get out of here."

"But we should know."

She hesitated. "Yes, I suppose you're right. I can do it."

"I've got it," he said, motioning with an outstretched hand for her to stay put. He moved the infant's head to the side and looked where her sign would be if she had one. "No."

"She was not of the Select?"

"That's right."

"So this wasn't an assassination."

"No."

"Do we bury the bodies?"

"No, it would take too long."

For the next couple hours, they marched on, passing one quiet farm after another.

Dixon stopped short. "This is very odd. None of these homes show any signs of life at all."

"I was just thinking the same thing." Mara nodded toward a nearby farm. "Let's check out that place."

Not far from the front door, signs of death again greeted the Oathtakers. An entire family lay slain. They found the youngest, an infant girl, in the same state as they'd found the earlier child.

Mara examined the infant. "Not a Select," she said. "What is going on here, do you suppose?"

Dixon shrugged. "I don't know. But these bodies haven't been here long. A few hours at most, I'd say. Do you still want to go to Polesk?"

"I feel I have to. Maybe Ted knows something about all this."

Sometime later, near the city, they stopped in a ditch to watch and listen. Crouching, then pulling Dixon down to her side, Mara pointed. "See there?" she whispered. "It's a sentry."

"And there," he gestured, "is another."

"Is the city always guarded?"

"I've never seen this before. They're not locals." He stood and reached for her hand. "Let's get closer. Careful now." He grasped Verity, as she took up Spira.

A minute later they took cover again, this time behind a large boulder. They peeked out to find guards stationed on each street within their view. Then more men walked out from the city center.

"Relieving!" a nearby gruff voice called out.

"Relieved!" another responded. The relieved guard made his way back into the city while the new man remained.

Mara dropped back on her haunches. "Dixon," she whispered, "see that building? The balcony there on the second story?"

He leaned over her shoulder. "You want to enter the city from there?"

"Watch how the guards move. See there?" she asked, acutely aware of his nearness.

The guards all moved to their right. Upon reaching the station of the next post they each then moved to the left, back to their original position.

"We time our entry between their moves."

"Got it. Rope?"

"Here." She pulled a length of rope out from her pack.

"Should be enough. And a hook?"

"I don't think we'll need one. Look," she pointed. "See that corner post?"
He nodded.

"Using a hook might be too loud. We could just catch the rope on that post." She turned to him, his face just inches from her own. "Do you think?"

"Yes."

She handed the rope to him. She held his gaze, smirking. "All right, so here's the thing. I'm a great shot," she paused, "but I kind of suck at lassoing. I'm leaving that to you." She raised her brow.

He grinned, tied the rope so it could catch easily on the post, then set out, motioning for her to follow.

"Oh!" Mara dropped her hold on Dixon. "I thought we'd had it there for a minute."

He rolled over. "Not safe yet," he whispered. Looking down as a guard made his way toward them, he motioned for Mara to find cover. When something momentarily diverted the guard's attention, Dixon unlatched the rope from the deck post.

Mara pulled tight against the wall, as though willing herself to become a part of it. A woodpile partially hid her. It smelled sweet, almost wine-like.

As Dixon crouched down at her side, his hand brushed against something furry. He pulled away. A cat leapt out, screeching in fear, its back arched in protest. Wood crashed down from the top of the stack.

The guard turned back to the deck. He approached, stopped, and then shouted, "Who goes there?" He paused to listen, then jabbed his sword up through the balcony railings.

The cat jumped to the top of the railing and hissed.

The guard flinched. Then recognizing the beast for what it was, he relaxed. "Damn cat." He stood quietly, watching for further movement, listening for further sound. A long minute passed and then finally, he moved off.

Mara exhaled slowly, soundlessly.

Dixon grinned at her as he made his way to his feet. "Nothing like a little rush of fear to get the morning off to a good start, huh?" he joked, his voice hushed. He helped her up, then turned to a door against which he'd been resting. "Before the next guard comes by," he whispered.

She pulled on a loop of rusted wire that served as a makeshift handle. The hinges emitted a faint creaking as the door opened. She stepped inside, Spira at the ready, Dixon immediately behind.

The Oathtakers entered a room, nearly dark. Only weak rays of the rosy, emerging dawn's light entered it through cracks in its boarded up windows. It smelled musty and old. At first glance, Mara thought it empty, but then she saw a woman seated silently at a rickety table, rocking, her shapeless gray woolen garb melding into the background.

"Who are you?" the woman asked, turning vacant eyes on her visitors. She ceased rocking.

Mara quietly introduced herself and Dixon.

"Klynn," the woman tersely responded.

"We beg your pardon for intruding, Klynn. We mean you no harm. We merely sought a way into the city around the guards."

"Have you come to lend succor to the city?"

"I don't know what you mean."

"Whyever would you steal your way into the city while others seek to escape, unless you've come to lend aid to others?"

"We're Oathtakers," Mara said.

"We seek information," Dixon added.

"What is it you wish to know?"

Mara pointed toward the empty chairs at the table, a question in her eyes. Klynn nodded her assent. The aged seats creaked in protest as the Oathtakers sat.

Mara leaned forward. "We've just arrived in the area and . . . we've seen some disturbing things. We need to get to sanctuary to meet with a friend."

"Good luck."

"Why do you say that?" Dixon asked. "Is it unsafe to move about in the city?"

"I think the world is coming to an end."

"What?" Mara asked.

Klynn breathed in and out slowly, audibly. Suddenly, she cocked her head to the side, furrowing her brow as if in great concentration. Then she cocked her head to the other side. "Are they screaming again?" she finally asked, of no one in particular.

"Who? Is who screaming?"

"Why, all of them. All of those they've come after," she said, making a circular motion with her hand.

"Ahhhh, Klynn, we just arrived in Polesk. We don't know what you're talking about. Who was screaming? Who is after whom? We don't understand."

"So no one is screaming now?"

"No, no one is screaming now."

"I've wanted to stop them. Oh, merciful Ehyeh." Klynn dropped her head into her hands.

Patiently, the Oathtakers waited until it seemed she would say no more. Mara looked at Dixon, raising a brow and shrugging, silently inquiring as to whether he had any ideas.

He signaled that he would give the questioning a try. "Klynn, can you tell us who you were talking about? Who was screaming?"

Her dull gray eyes slowly moved his way. "Everyone. They run through the streets screaming, crying. I think it will never end." She rocked again.

"Why do they scream?"

"Why?" She stilled, then cocked her head again, as though picking up some distant sound. Moments later, she turned her attention back to him. "Wouldn't you scream if it was you?"

"I imagine if something terrible happened to me that I would scream, yes," he said. "Was that it? Did something terrible happen?"

"Terrible, yes. Horrific. Unspeakable."

"What?"

"So many dead. So many still dying."

"Who's dead?"

"So many."

"Excuse us, Klynn," Mara said. She stood, stepped away, and then motioned for Dixon to join her. "I can't tell what's wrong," she whispered. "Maybe she's not in her right mind, or maybe she's in shock. I don't think we'll get anything more from her. Perhaps we should—"

"Shock, yes," the woman spoke out, as though Mara's comments had been directed to her. "No," she then said with a shake of her head, "that's not right. It's just that I keep reliving it all and . . . it goes on and on." She held Mara's gaze. "I'm not crazy." She motioned for her guests to regain their seats. "It's just been so awful. They keep searching and finding and . . ."

"I'm sorry. I meant no offense," Mara said, "but we're short on time and we don't want to trouble you. Perhaps we should move on."

"Please, don't leave." Klynn grabbed Mara's forearm. "I'll tell you what happened. I think your coming here is good for me. I've not been myself for weeks now. But you're Oathtakers. You give me . . . hope." She glanced about, her eyes narrowed. "There is no screaming now," she said with conviction, "is there?"

"That's right." Mara said. "Tell us, what happened?"

"It sounds impossible. Had I not seen it, I would not have believed it myself. That dreadful woman. Who would have believed it of her? Oh, I should have done something! But what? What could *I* have done?"

"What dreadful woman? Who are you talking about?" Dixon asked.

"Lilith. That demon, Lilith!"

"Of the first family?" Mara asked.

The woman nodded.

"What about her? What's she done?"

Klynn relayed the story of how Lilith came to Polesk accompanied by an army of thugs from Chiran, how she deceived the parents of infants so as to murder their children, how the soldiers at her bidding went house-to-house seeking any child that might otherwise have escaped her wrath, and finally, how they now held the city and its surrounds captive.

"Oh dear, Klynn. How dreadful for you!" Mara exclaimed.

"The wailing, the lamenting. It has gone on for weeks now."

"And that's why you asked if there were people screaming."

"That's right."

"So, these Chiranian soldiers who remained behind are still killing people?" Dixon asked.

"Yes. They remain on guard for anyone who may have escaped Lilith's orders. They watch all entrance and exit points to ensure no one escapes the city. And they roam the surrounding lands to seek out any infants she may have missed. But you know, I think the worst part is seeing some people give away the whereabouts of those in hiding."

Dixon and Mara exchanged a meaningful glance. "This all must explain the bodies we saw last night," she said to him. "Why would Lilith not allow anyone to leave the city?" she then asked Klynn. "I don't understand."

"To be certain word does not get out."

"And if it did?"

"Oh, ma'am, she is only done in Polesk. Now she's making her way through all of Oosa, city by city, village by village."

"To do the same elsewhere!" Mara exclaimed.

"She said as much. She said that if the people did not deliver to her the child that she sought . . ."

"Do you know where she went from here?"

"No. I only know that she'll devour every city in her wake."

"Oh dear, Klynn," Mara said. "I'm terribly sorry for everything you've been through and we thank you, but we have to go now. We need to get to sanctuary."

"You still want to go there even though you've learned what you came to Polesk for?" Dixon asked.

"Yes. I want to see Ted. Maybe he can tell us more."

"I know the best ways through the city," Klynn said as she got to her feet, "and all the shortcuts and alternate routes. I feel you've brought me back from the brink of insanity and I'm so, so grateful. I'm going along to help you."

✦

Dixon stepped out of the alley. They'd followed the same pattern over the past couple hours, slowly making their way to sanctuary. Occasionally city residents passed them, all wearing faces of fear and defeat, like masks of sorrow. They went through the steps of living, but seemed to have lost their grasp on what transpired around them or were without the will to do anything about it.

No one smiled. No one chattered. Other than the soldiers who stopped to harass the people from time to time, the city was like a ghost town inhabited by breathing spooks.

Mara peeked around the corner, then gasped when Dixon nearly collided into her. "You frightened me!" she exclaimed quietly, a hand to her breast.

He put a finger to his lips, then motioned for her and Klynn to move back. They all stepped over odds and ends littering the ground: an old metal cup, now rusting and dented; a rug, weathered and threadbare; scraps of food waste, ground together and rotting; an old flower pot sporting a dead rosemary plant that someone might once have used to provide a quick addition to a recipe, or as a remedy for a headache; a tattered blanket; old boots with holes and sandals with missing ties; broken dishware; and an old rag doll that, if it could talk, would likely tell tales of great comfort and later, of painful neglect.

"More soldiers," he whispered. "We'll wait a minute. If they don't leave, we'll go the other way."

Nearby soldiers called out to one another and then, after some minutes, silence ensued.

"All right," Dixon said, "now remember, Klynn, if we get separated, get yourself to safety. Mara," he continued, a question in his eyes, "if that happens, I've got your word to return immediately to . . . you know . . . Right?"

She nodded.

He peeked around the building's edge, looked one way, then the other, then waved the women forward. "Remember, single file. Leave space between us. To the corner there," he said with a nod. "We're getting close now."

He stepped out. After some seconds passed, Mara, then Klynn, followed. The trio made their way to the end of the block without anyone molesting them. The women hid inside the framework of one deep doorway while Dixon hid within another. Again they repeated the pattern, and then again, as they neared sanctuary in fits and starts.

Once again stalling in an alleyway, they listened for sounds of trouble. Hearing nothing, Dixon pointed to the next stop, then stepped out.

Mara counted off the seconds. Just as she was about go, she heard someone cry out.

"Hey you! You there! Hey, I'm talkin' to you!"

She peeked out. A soldier shouted at Dixon, who kept his head down, behaving as though he assumed the man called out for someone else.

Mara looked toward Klynn, her eyes wide with fear.

Klynn ran out of the alley. She rushed toward the soldier.

What is she doing? She said she wanted to help. Had all of this just been a game on her part? Mara held her breath.

"Sir! Sir!" the woman cried as she approached the soldier, dragging one leg.

He pulled out his sword. The sound of steel rang in the air.

"Oh, sir, I've found one! You must rush there. Quickly! Quickly! Before they leave!"

His eyes narrowed. "What's that?"

She halted. "Sir, you must go quickly, before they find refuge elsewhere. Hurry, sir, hurry! I'll tell you where they are."

"What did you find?"

"A Select infant, sir! You missed her. Quickly!"

"Where? Take me."

"Oh, but look at me!" She stepped forward, pointing out her faux crippled leg. "I would detain you, sir. I'm sorry. But please, please don't let them get away."

"Where?"

She pointed away from where Mara waited. "There, sir. You'll find them that way. Go down a few blocks to a big red inn. I don't remember the name of it. Then turn east and go until you find a wide-open space on your left. Go down three more houses from there, and you'll find them. They're probably leaving even now, sir. You must hurry!"

Given that some city residents eagerly gave away the whereabouts of helpless infants that were, or at least were believed to be, Select, Klynn's behavior was not entirely unprecedented.

The soldier turned to Dixon. "It looks like today is your lucky day, but I wouldn't count on it to remain so. Get to where it is you intend to go and do it quickly. I don't want to find you wandering the streets when I return."

Dixon bobbed his head submissively.

The soldier repeated to Klynn the instructions she'd given him.

"That's right, sir. Hurry!"

He rushed away.

Mara looked out from her hiding place. Dixon, then Klynn, made their way to the next stopping place. Moments later, she joined them.

"Klynn!" she exclaimed. "How could you do that? Bring trouble to others?"

"She didn't," Dixon said.

"But—"

"There are no houses in the direction she sent the soldier."

Mara's mouth dropped open. "You mean you sent him on a wild goose chase?"

"I did. And I expect we haven't long before he figures it out and heads back this way."

"That was quick thinking, Klynn, thank you," Dixon said. He looked around the corner, then turned back. "Lucky for us, sanctuary is just ahead. Follow me."

Chapter Thirty-One

The three approached the front door to the main building. Mara tried to open it, but it wouldn't budge. She tried again. Still it did not move. She knocked. No one answered. She knocked again. Still no one answered. "You don't suppose they've all gone, do you?"

Dixon shrugged. "I can't imagine. And I've never seen sanctuary locked. Not any sanctuary."

She put her ear to the door. "There's someone in there. I can hear them." She knocked again. "Hello! Hello! Is anyone there?"

The door opened a crack. "Mara, is that you?"

"Yes, Faith, it's me and Dixon, and another visitor. Please, please let us in."

Faith opened the door. When they entered, she stood before them, her Oathtaker's blade from days gone by, in her hand. She sheathed her weapon.

"Oh Faith, you haven't locked sanctuary!"

"We have to keep an eye on anyone trying to enter." Pain shone in the woman's eyes.

"Are you all right?" Mara asked.

"Sure. Fine. I'm fine. Thank you for asking." Faith stepped back. Her eyes narrowed. "Where are— Oh, gracious Good One! Don't tell me that anything has happened to—"

"No! No, all is well. Not to worry."

"What are you doing here?"

Footsteps approached.

"Ted, it's good to see you!"

"Mara," he nodded in greeting, "Dixon." He patted his friend's shoulder. "I heard some commotion. What happened? What are the two of you doing here?"

"It's a long story, Ted," Dixon said, "but the crux of it is that we heard reports of something going on here in Polesk. Mara insisted we check it out."

"But the—"

"Everyone is well and safe," Mara interrupted.

"How did you get here?"

She grinned. "We'll fill you in on everything, but you should know that we won't be here long. We have to get back to Nina and . . . and the others."

It was clear by the look on Ted's face that he was confused, concerned.

Dixon clapped him on the shoulder. "Patience. We'll fill you in." He introduced Klynn to his friends. "How long have you been staying at sanctuary, Ted? We heard what happened."

The man dropped his head and shook it. "It has all been just horrible. We did what we could to save some, but in the end we didn't succeed."

"Except for Hattie's little one," Faith said.

"Yes, of course, Hattie's little one," he repeated. He turned to Dixon. "What's the matter with us? Are you hungry? Can we get you anything? We've made sanctuary a sort of home away from home while the soldiers still roam the city."

"Thank you," Mara said. "Actually, I could use something to eat. I hope it's not too much trouble."

"Just this way," Faith said.

"How long have you got?" Ted asked Dixon as they followed the women.

"That's up to Mara, but I expect she'll want to make this quick so we can get back. We met Klynn when we got into the city. She helped us to make our way here."

They entered a back room that traditionally served as a rest area for guest speakers. It sported a hearth, the space and tools necessary for cooking, and it had its own well-stocked larder.

"Right in here is where we set up our temporary home," Faith said. Several comfortable chairs nestled in one corner and a table and chairs occupied another. She held her hand out to Ted and her guests, signifying that they should stay there for a moment, then made her way toward a young woman who was busy preparing food and had a quiet word with her.

"Say, Faith," Ted called out.

She turned to him.

"What do you say we ask Erin to keep Klynn company while we get caught up with Dixon and Mara?"

"I think that's a wonderful idea." She motioned for Klynn to join her and the young woman with whom she'd been speaking. Then she escorted the two out of the room.

"She looks incredibly familiar," Mara said.

"Who?" Ted asked.

"The woman Faith was talking to."

"I thought the same thing," Dixon said.

Ted laughed. "She must have one of those faces. Both Faith and I said the same thing of her."

"Who is she?" Mara asked as she sat down. The smell of a hearty lamb stew wafted its way toward her. Her stomach growled.

The men sat to either side of her.

"I know who she looks like!" she suddenly exclaimed. She looked at Ted, her eyes narrowed. "What did you say her name was?"

"Erin."

"Oh, great Ehyeh! Is it possible?" She shook her head. "Where is she from?"

"What are you talking about?" Dixon asked.

"Where is she from, Ted?" Mara asked again.

"Chiran."

"And you said her name is '*Erin*?'"

"'Erin,' yes. Why?"

"What? What are you thinking?" Dixon asked.

"Ted! Dixon! Nina has a sister, Erin. That's who she looks like. Like Nina!"

Dixon sat straight up in his chair. "Right you are."

"Ted, is it possible?"

"I don't know. She escaped from the army that was with Lilith. If it hadn't been for that young woman, we wouldn't have known anything of Lilith's plans. She found Hattie—oh, we'll have to introduce Hattie to you—and told her of Lilith's plans. We sent all the local Oathtakers out, trying to get the people to bring their infants here instead of taking them to Lilith's gathering, but . . ." His voice dropped off to nothing.

Mara and Dixon waited quietly for him.

"I've never felt such a failure," Ted finally whispered. "Here we are at sanctuary," he waved his hand to designate his surroundings, "but we weren't able to provide actual sanctuary to the people when they most needed it."

"Is that why the lights in the steeple are out?" Dixon asked.

"It seems an appropriate sign of mourning."

"You can't blame yourself, Ted."

"I know. Still . . ."

Faith entered the room and headed toward the bucket of stew hanging at the hearth.

"Faith, what do you know about Erin?" Mara asked.

"Oh, not to worry. I've not told her anything. I assumed the same was true of Klynn. With them busy now, we can speak freely. We have a lot to fill you in on."

"No, I mean, what do you know about where she's from?"

"Mara thinks Erin might be Nina's sister," Dixon said.

"Oh! Is it possible, do you think?" Faith asked.

"We'll ask her when they return," Ted said. "In the meantime, we should catch up."

They visited for a time, occasionally interrupted by someone inquiring about sanctuary matters. Mara and Dixon told their friends everything that had transpired to date and of the girls' slowly growing group of supporters. In turn, Ted and Faith told all they knew about Lilith's venture.

Mara pushed away the now tepid cup of tea she'd been drinking. "I guess it's time we got back to the inn. I'd just like to meet Erin first."

Faith stood and gathered some of the dishes from the table. "I'll go get her now."

"How long do you plan to stay in the City of Light?" Ted asked.

"No idea," Mara said. "I'm just following what I think is the Good One's lead."

"And you've had no contact with Lucy since you left here?"

"Just once to let her know we were stopping in the city," Dixon responded.

"I'm thinking," Mara said, "that Lucy can get the word out about Lilith and save lives."

"It certainly would be worth a try," Ted said. "Perhaps she'll have better luck than we did." Once again, he dropped his head and shook it.

Mara touched his arm, stroking it gently, commiserating with him.

Footsteps *click-clacked* on the floor.

Mara stood as Faith entered, her hair in its typical flurry. Klynn and Erin followed her.

Mara looked closely at the young woman, then smiled.

Erin fidgeted uncomfortably. "Ma'am," she said softly.

"Erin, I've—that is *we've*—all commented on how very familiar you look. When I heard your name, I wondered . . . have you any sisters?"

"Yes, ma'am. That is, I had sisters. Why do you ask?"

"Because I know a young woman who you look very much like. I think you might be sisters. Her name is—"

"Nina! Oh, do you know Nina? So, she made it here? She survived her trip? Oh, where is she? Where is she?"

Mara laughed as she put her arm around Erin's shoulder. "I can assure you she's well."

"And what of her child? A boy? A girl? Oh, tell me!"

Mara slowly shook her head. "I'm sorry. Nina's child did not survive."

Erin's smile vanished. Her eyes pooled with tears.

Mara told her how Ted and Faith had aided Nina. "When Dixon and I first arrived here in Polesk, some weeks back, we needed help with . . . a newborn, and she was kind enough to agree to come with us."

"I want to see her."

"I don't think that's possible," Faith said.

"She's right," Ted said. "Nina is some distance away and I'm afraid we can't get you there just now."

Erin looked at each of the Oathtakers in turn. "I don't understand. If she's staying with you," she pointed at Mara, "and if you're here, then how could she be somewhere else?"

The others laughed. It was a healthy release of tension.

"I'm sorry, Erin. Dixon and I traveled here by . . . magic. We can't take you back with us. Not this time, anyway. But we'll be sure to let Nina know that you're well. She'll be happy to know you're in Ted and Faith's good hands." Mara turned to Dixon. "Well then, are you ready to go?"

"Yes." He embraced Ted, then Faith.

Mara followed suit.

Klynn stepped forward. "Good-bye, Mara, Dixon."

"Thank you, Klynn. I don't know what might have happened had it not been for your quick thinking back there."

"I'm sorry you didn't get a chance to meet Hattie, Mara. But for her, we wouldn't have Erin with us now," Faith said.

"Hattie. I love that name. My mother had a sister named Hattie. She was my favorite aunt. I used to wish . . . Well, next time."

Faith smiled. "Next time."

"Would you all mind terribly? Could we have just a minute of privacy?" Mara felt rather a spectacle.

"Oh, not at all," Ted said. He ushered the others out to a chorus of "so longs" and "see you soons."

Dixon handed Mara her pack, then pulled his own up over his shoulder.

She held his gaze for a long moment and grinned. "Here we go then," she said, clasping his hands. A moment later, they vanished.

The sights and sounds, the colors of their traveling once again took over as the Oathtakers entered into the stream of magic.

When they came to a stop, Mara opened her eyes. She loosened her hold on Dixon's hands. She expected he'd simply release her as well, but he did not. Instead, he tightened his grip.

"Mara, before I forget to say it—thank you. Thank you for allowing me to accompany you. It makes me feel useful when I can be of service to you and the twins."

"I appreciate your help." Again she tried to loosen her hands. Again he held tightly to one, freeing the other. She sensed he had no intention of letting go and found she quite liked it—though, truth to tell, she also feared it.

"Right on target," he said as he looked around.

She looked up. They'd arrived just outside the door to their suite. She shook her hand free. "I have to go!" She couldn't wait one more minute to lay her eyes on the girls.

Chapter Thirty-Two

The noises that the rummaging soldiers made played on Lilith's nerves. Although the burning pain of Daeva's presence within her had generally waned, it stirred up into a painful presence from time to time. She felt it most intensely when outside forces irritated her, or when she was in the midst of her most murderous acts. When irritated, the force was painful, but strangely, when in a murderous rage, it became somehow—pleasant.

The soldiers were out of order tonight. They'd spent the past several days picking off those infants they uncovered at farm sites and in small hamlets on their way, but now had time on their hands.

Lilith smiled as she considered her progress to date. Still, she'd best keep moving. The men required constant stimulus or they became surly and belligerent. It was then that they turned on one another. Their infighting often resulted in the loss of lives, and she couldn't afford to lose more of them.

She sat at a writing desk that she kept folded away when not in use. Mindlessly, she sorted through various notes that Sally and Janine had sent to her over the past weeks. The presence of the soldiers she'd left at the palace unnerved them, but her sisters' complaints lessened as she ordered more of the troops to meet up with her and the greater army.

She would have taken more with her at the outset, but in her haste to get started, she'd not considered that as she vacated each village, hamlet and city, she'd have to leave a small force behind. It was they who saw to any necessary cleanup and who locked down the areas so as to keep information from leaking out and making its way ahead of her venture.

Shouts from the soldiers, followed by a woman's screams, made their way to her consciousness. She frowned. The hoodlums were beginning to bore her. She started at the sound of a rapping at the rear of her wagon. "Who is it?"

The visitor moved back the tarp, allowing cold air to rush inside. "'Scuse, ma'am."

"What is it now?"

A low growl, followed by a high yapping, sounded out.

"Shush Pooch," Lilith scolded as she stroked the animal she'd chosen to replace her former pet, Pompom.

Once again, Pooch growled. The canine disliked Freeman, who now made his way into the wagon.

"The men are terribly unruly this evening," she said.

"They're bored, ma'am."

"Bored! They're here to be of service to me. Their boredom is not my concern."

More shrieks cut through the air.

"What is going on out there?"

Freeman shrugged. "Jus' the men havin' a bit o' sport with somma the wimmin they gathered up in Martinsville."

"I'm sure I don't want to know more."

"Prob'ly not. 'S not a pretty sight."

"So why are you bothering me with this? I assume that's why you're here?"

"Weeelll, seems one a the prisoners 's 'n Oathtaker." He watched Lilith's expression closely. "She's causin' a scuffle, she is. Thought ya'd wanna know."

"What possible difference could that make to me?"

"She's threatnin' the men, she is. Says she'll kill 'em." He shuffled his feet. "I tol' 'em I'd check wi' cha 'bout what tuh do."

Lilith sighed. She tried to think back to when the man's presence had begun to bore her. Maybe it was when he'd first opened his mouth to speak and proved himself such an idiot.

"Never mind." She extricated her shawl from under Pooch who sat upon it, as a king upon his throne. She placed it over her shoulders, then scooped up her pet, pulling him close to her bosom.

"Ya comin' 'long then?"

"Lead the way."

He jumped down, then assisted her. As her foot met the ground, Pooch snapped at the man's hand. He jerked it back, then grasped Lilith's elbow as the dog growled.

"Never mind, pet," she said, patting its head. "Well," she said turning to her escort, "where to?"

Freeman led her to the center of the camp. The cacophony of pounding boots, jingling chains, and the occasional captive's scream, covered the crunching sound of the light ground-covering snow beneath their feet.

Hollering and laughter filled the cold night air, which hid some, albeit some lesser, portion of the stink that typically accompanied the men. Mercifully, the smell of smoke and cooking dinners further concealed the hired thugs' stench.

A swarm of perhaps twenty thickset men, all covered in capes, gathered around someone.

"I said, 'stay back!'" a woman cried. "Stay back, or I'll kill you. Don't doubt me."

"Ha ha ha!" the men laughed. Notwithstanding their bravado, fear laced their voices.

"Mahlon," the woman said, "they're making sport of you. Can't you see that?"

Lilith elbowed between two men at the back of the group. Upon recognizing her, they shuffled their feet, then moved away, leaving others in her immediate presence.

"Put it down, Mahlon," the woman commanded. "Put it down and stay back."

"I will have you!" a man Lilith assumed to be Mahlon shouted back. His shaking defied the control he sought to portray, as did the jittering knife in his trembling hand.

"That's right, Mahlon," one of the soldiers mocked, "she's yours!"

"Like we said—next one's yours," said another.

"Go on, Mahlon. What's the matter? You scared?"

"You a coward, Mahlon? Huh?"

"Go for it, Mahlon!"

The daring, bold, clearly intoxicated men were having as much sport with Mahlon as with the woman they'd captured.

"There she is, Mahlon. Have at her!" laughed another, pushing the man toward his intended victim.

The woman jumped back. "Stop! I'm telling you—one more step and you die."

"Yeah, well if you kill me, *they'll* just have you." Mahlon sneered at the woman as he gestured toward the others. "What're ya gonna do? Hold the whole army off with that little blade of yours?" He glanced at his mates and smiled, seeking their approval.

"That's right, Mahlon. Once I use this blade, I may be as good as dead. I know that. I've no other weapon. But I promise you, if you don't stop right now, you'll beat me to the hereafter."

"What're ya gonna do? Kill us all?" he repeated, laughing nervously.

"No, Mahlon," she held his gaze intently, "just you." Despite her circumstances, she remained calm. Her voice did not waiver. She held her blade steady.

The men had dealt with similar circumstances before. Each time they eventually overcame the Oathtaker, but never without some cost to their ranks. If Mahlon didn't cease in his endeavors, he would go down. Depending upon the woman's skills, others might join him.

Mahlon stood on the balls of his feet, ready to spring forward at the slightest opportunity. In his indecision, and at least partial intoxication, he rocked unsteadily, then glanced at the surrounding gang. With words and hip thrusting gestures, they urged him on.

Lilith sighed and stepped forward. She should let them take what they had coming, but it wasn't worth losing more of the soldiers over such foolishness. Before she made her way to the front, Mahlon rushed the woman.

In a flash, she let loose her blade. It landed with a thud in his chest. He stopped in his tracks, then staggered back. He made to advance again, but before he could take another step, started falling.

The Oathtaker rushed forward, grasped her blade, yanked it out, then pushed his body away. The thud, as it hit, shook the ground. Blood splattered and within moments, started to pool around the dead man's body.

In little more than a heartbeat, the Oathtaker had armed herself once more. She hunched into a battle position. Her eyes darted around at her captors. Her head snapped from side to side. "Who's next?"

Lilith watched the men. One stepped forward, hesitated, then returned to his former position. With Mahlon's fall, the woman had checked their bravado, but oafs that they were, more would surely fall as they continued in their efforts to subdue their quarry. One more, two more, three more of them might die, but in the end, they would disarm the woman.

Lilith stepped out from the midst of the crowd, then turned and scowled at the men. They all pulled back upon recognizing her, shuffling their feet. She turned to the Oathtaker. "That will be quite enough."

The young woman looked intensely at the newcomer. She started to bring her weapon down, then jumped back into a fighting crouch when one of the thugs took another step toward her.

"I said, that will be quite enough," Lilith repeated, her voice raised.

The soldiers all looked downward as though suddenly enamored with whatever was at their feet.

"Be off with you."

They moved away, quiet at first, but their mumblings, oaths and curses rose in volume as their distance increased.

"And who might you be?"

The Oathtaker lowered her blade. "I was about to ask you the same thing." She pulled her dark auburn hair back.

Lilith crossed her arms, set her lips, and glared.

The Oathtaker's eyes narrowed. "Lilith? Are you Lilith?"

"Who else would I be?"

"But—but—"

"But what?"

"It's just that I'm . . . I didn't . . . That is—"

"You didn't expect me here?"

"Exactly! And with these—these—"

"Cretins?" Lilith completed the woman's sentence, disdain in her voice.

"Well, yes. That is—"

"They're here at my bidding. Have you a problem with that?"

"Oh, no!" The woman smiled, exposing a single small dimple on one side of her mouth. "I was just surprised, that's all."

"Well now that you know in whose presence you stand, perhaps you could fill me in on who you are and what you're doing here."

The young woman bowed. "Excuse me, Lilith, ma'am. I am Velia. Velia Bettina."

Lilith looked hard at the Oathtaker whose clear brown eyes flitted about, constantly surveying her surroundings. "Where's your charge, Velia?"

"Oh, I've no charge."

"No?"

"No, my charge is . . . deceased. I've not been called to serve again."

"Pray tell, Velia, what brings you here?"

The Oathtaker sheathed her blade. "I was taken prisoner."

Lilith smirked. "Prisoner. Surely you don't expect me to believe that. I've seen you in action."

"Nevertheless, it's true."

Lilith admired the young woman's gumption in the face of her superiors. "How could you be taken prisoner with an Oathtaker's blade at the ready?"

Velia grinned, once again flashing her dimple. "Well, like I said, it's true I was taken prisoner. It's just not . . . Well, it's not the whole truth."

Lilith waited. When the young woman said no more, she resumed her questioning. "And the rest of the truth would be?"

"Those men, those . . . thugs, entered our village. They took some of the women captive. I could have protected myself, but thought I'd go along to find out what they were doing. So I allowed them to take me with the others." As Velia spoke, the sound of a woman's scream pierced the air. She winced. "What's going on?"

"These men are here at my bidding, as I said."

"But what in the name of Ehyeh could you want with such—barbarians?"

"Not that it's any business of yours, Velia, but they're here to protect me."

"But what of your Oathtaker?"

"Again, that is none of your concern, but I've released him."

"Oh, gracious Ehyeh! Your Oathtaker failed in his duty? Has not another been called to your service?"

Lilith sighed. The young woman certainly was persistent. She considered what to do with her, then smiled weakly.

"I'm sorry, Lilith. I mean no disrespect."

"I wonder, Velia, if you could assist me."

The Oathtaker bowed. "Most certainly. I am at your service."

"Very well then." Lilith turned to Freeman. "See her to the wagon next to my own. Do not let any of the others near her—on pain of death." She turned back to the young woman. "Will those arrangements be satisfactory?"

Another scream carried through the night air.

"Certainly, Lilith, but—"

"But?"

"But what of the others? What of the women those thugs took captive?"

"What of them?"

The Oathtaker's mouth dropped open. She took a deep breath. Could she do this? Could she remain in this place that reeked of evil? Could she stand by while Lilith allowed the most criminal of acts to go on?

She squared her shoulders. "I understand, Lilith. I'm sure you have many things to consider in your position. Please, forgive me for questioning you."

"Oh, Velia, of course, there's nothing to forgive, I'm sure."

Velia stopped in her tracks, holding her breath. *Is that more screaming? Dear Ehyeh, will it never stop? What is Lilith up to?*

As was her pattern upon approaching a city, Lilith had ordered that Velia remain at camp with a few soldiers to "protect" her. On threat of death, the guards avoided interaction with her. Thus, try though she might, she'd gleaned no information from them. Still, she remained with Lilith's venture. She did not like what she saw, but with her attendant power to tell truth from falsehood, she hoped to learn more.

"Did you hear that?" she called out to one of her guards.

"What?" the man responded scurrilously.

Another scream sounded out.

"That," she said, sternly. "That scream."

"I didn't hear nothin'," he said. As his eyes met those of his cohort, he sneered. Then together, they chuckled.

Velia watched the exchange. Everything she saw and heard disgusted her. Every day she prayed the Good One would open her eyes and reveal the facts. They might be difficult to face, but better that than to continue in the dark. Every night she sought an opportunity to see Lilith, but the woman ignored her. If she could just question her, perhaps she could catch her in the lies that would reveal the truth. But Lilith only passed by occasionally and had no time for the Oathtaker.

Why would she want me here anyway? Why hasn't she just left me to the men as she's done with so many others? Why hasn't she just killed me?

"It sounded like a scream to me."

"Didn't hear nothin'," he repeated, glancing at her. "You'd best mind your own business or you might be next."

"So it was a scream."

His muscles tensed as though in warning, but she stood firm in the face of his threat. He shook his head, made a face at her, then turned away.

She closed the tarp, then pulled her hair back and tied it up. She started yet another mental inventory of the things she'd seen that confirmed that Lilith was no longer on the side of the Good One. Velia had never known a Select who'd released her Oathtaker and she'd never seen a Select without one. Still, she didn't feel moved to swear an oath for Lilith's protection—and the woman never suggested she do so. It all added up to no good.

More screams came to her attention. She had to get to the bottom of this. But what if she did? What would she do with the information anyway? Who would she tell? Who would believe her?

She decided to see what would happen if she left her wagon. When Lilith first confined her there, she said it was for Velia's safety. She accepted that explanation without question, at least outwardly. But after days turned into boring weeks, she concluded that Lilith was not concerned for her safety. The woman kept her prisoner for some other, unknown reason.

Velia grasped her shawl and unsheathed her Oathtaker's blade. Then she lifted the tarp and jumped down. The light snowy groundcover crunched under her boots.

"Stop right there," one of the guards said.

"Oh, really, and who's going to stop me?" She turned his way. "You?"

He nodded, a weak smirk on his face.

"I don't think so. Or have you forgotten about this weapon I carry?" She brandished her blade as she stepped forward.

The guard blocked her way. "You're not going anywhere."

"Well you might, if you don't let me pass. You might find your way straight to Sinespe."

"If you kill me, Lilith will have your life."

"Is that right? What makes you think she cares what happens to you?"

He sneered. "Nothing. What makes you think she cares what happens to *you*?"

Velia bit her lip. He had a point. "I just need to take a walk. I can't sit there any longer," she said, pointing to her wagon.

"Not now."

"Let me pass."

"No."

She sighed. "What will Lilith do to you if you allow me to pass? Really now, what harm could it cause?"

"She'd kill me, that's what."

"So let me get this straight. If you don't let me pass, I'll kill you. If you do let me pass, Lilith will kill you." She smiled. "I rather like the sounds of that."

The guard's smirk fell, but he stood firm.

Once again, she stepped forward.

He followed suit.

She raised her blade.

"What's this all about?" Someone approached from behind Velia's wagon.

The guard looked up and grimaced.

Velia turned. There stood Lilith. Clearly, the woman was not pleased.

"I asked," Lilith repeated, "what's all this?" She turned to the guard. "I told you not to allow her to leave."

"I didn't," he said. "I was just—"

"And you," she said turning to Velia. "I thought we had an understanding. I've left you under guard for your own protection."

Velia knew that what the woman said was false. She decided to take a chance. "Lilith, ma'am, I just can't stay cooped up like this. I need to get out. But he," she continued, gesturing toward the guard, "won't let me pass."

The woman was quiet for a long moment. "I think it's time we had a talk," she finally said. "Velia, was it?"

In frustration, the Oathtaker closed her eyes and inhaled slowly. Perhaps she held them closed a second too long.

"Something wrong?" Lilith asked.

"I'm sorry. I meant no offense. Yes, my name is Velia."

Lilith's expression did not change.

"It's just like I said, Lilith, I feel cooped up here. I'd hoped to be of some assistance to you, but it seems you've no use for me. So perhaps I should just be on my way."

Lilith's stared, silent.

"Or we could . . . talk . . . as you suggest?"

Lilith's eyes ran down Velia's form slowly, then made their way back up. She showed her obvious disdain with pursed lips and a raised brow. She turned away, calling over her shoulder, "Come with me."

"Your lucky day," Velia mocked the guard, quietly. "It looks like you won't die after all." Without waiting for his response, she followed Lilith.

The men had trampled upon everything in sight, leaving filth and scraps and excrement around every corner and creating a foulness to the air. Mangy dogs sniffed around and urinated on trees, tents, and wagon wheels.

Lilith never looked back. A guard assisted her into her wagon, then turned to Velia and leered. "One uh these days," he whispered, "we'll have tuh get together, huh? Just you an' me. You'll like it."

She spat on him.

He wiped the spittle from his face with the back of his hand. "Ya don't have to say nothin'. Just keep pretendin' you're not int'rested." He reached for her arm.

She shook his hand free. Still holding her weapon, she stared.

He stepped back.

"Are you coming?" Lilith called.

Velia stepped into the wagon. Upon entering, the headache inducing scent of roses and white lilies assaulted her. She could taste rosewater. It nearly made her gag. She swallowed hard. The scent was so unlike that of any other Select she'd ever known. After composing herself, she turned her attention to Lilith.

"Was he bothering you?" the woman asked in a tone that sounded deeply insincere. "Like I said, I have you under guard for your own protection."

"No, ma'am, he wasn't bothering me."

Lilith raised her chin. "Very well then, have a seat."

Velia sat. She held her hands clasped in her lap, in her most attentive pose.

"So, what can I do for you, Velia?"

The Oathtaker felt Lilith's eyes bore into her. "Well, ma'am," she said, "I'd like to be of service to you, but I don't see how I can be. Why must I stay behind when you're about your business? Why surround me with guards rather than allow me to be of service to you? And if I can't be of service, then why don't I just move on? I'm sorry, but I've just so many questions."

"Questions can prove dangerous."

Was that a threat? "Yes, ma'am, but how then am I to serve you?"

Lilith reached for Pooch and cradled the animal in her arms. "I don't know why I'm bothering to discuss this with you, but if it will keep you out of trouble . . ." She took in a deep breath, then let it out slowly. "Before you came to us, Velia, had you heard any rumor of a new seventh?"

"A new seventh? Why, no, ma'am. The only one I knew of was Rowena, but I'd heard that she . . . died." Velia hesitated. "I'm terribly sorry for your loss."

Lilith's expression remained unchanged.

"What's this of a new seventh?"

Lilith smiled insincerely. "There are those who would like to remove me from my place among the Select. They are jealous of me and of my position. They seek power for themselves and so, would foist a fraud upon the people."

"A fraud, ma'am?"

"There are those who claim to know of a new seventh." Lilith brushed crumbs off a nearby table, as though she was brushing away the claims.

Velia knew the woman spoke lies. But exactly what things were lies? Did Lilith's words mean there was no new seventh? Or that there were no people who claimed there was a new seventh? "I'm sorry," she said. "Who are these people?"

Lilith straightened her skirt. "Those who claim to have been friends of Rowena's."

True they *claimed* to be friends of Rowena's. But was it also true that they *were* friends of Rowena's? "Who, ma'am, if you don't mind my asking, that is?"

"Rowena's Oathtaker."

True. Rowena's Oathtaker made the claims. But was it also true that the claims were true? "Wasn't Dixon Townsend her Oathtaker?"

"Yes, that's right."

True. "And he was Rowena's friend as well as her Oathtaker?"

"Yes."

True again. Oh, how to ask the right questions so as to get the right information . . . Velia didn't want to know whether it was true or false that someone *claimed* something. She wanted to know if what the person claimed was true or false.

"A new seventh. But, Lilith, wouldn't that be wonderful?"

Lilith refused to meet the Oathtaker's eye. She said nothing.

"But of course, a fraud upon the people would be devastating." Velia hesitated, collecting her thoughts. "Lilith, I'm so sorry Dixon would lie about such a thing."

"Yes, well, he would and he did."

False. There is a new seventh. "I'm so sorry, Lilith." The Oathtaker took in a deep breath. "But why would he do such a thing?"

"He hates me. He always has. Ever since I refused him. Now he plans to mislead the people with this nonexistent new seventh."

False. False. False. And false. "So what can you do about it? How can I help?"

"Well, Velia, thank you, but there's really nothing you can do." Lilith turned away. "I'm just trying to find Dixon so I can put a stop to this nonsense."

Velia couldn't tell about the veracity of that statement. She recognized it as partially true and partially false. Was Lilith trying to find Dixon? Or was she trying to put a stop to the "nonsense?" Or was it just false that it was "nonsense?"

"I understand, Lilith. I understand completely." She glanced at the trinkets on the table at her side. She was momentarily surprised to find a bottle of rosewater. *Why would a Select try to cover her own heavenly scent? Or is Lilith merely trying to create the impression that she has one, that she's found favor with the Good One? That's it! There is further confirmation she's not following the Good One.* "Have you any idea where he might be? Perhaps I could help you to find him."

"No, I don't know where he is."

True. "No idea?"

"I've heard rumors in a number of places we've passed through. Some say he's been seen in the highlands. Someone else suggested he might have opted for the City of Light."

True and true. "But how will you put a stop to his plans?"

Lilith rose. "If I find the person he claims is the new seventh, I'll bring her to the Council for review."

False. In that moment, Velia knew that the woman planned to kill the new seventh. "Do you still want me to stay? Is there some way I can assist you?" She hoped Lilith would dismiss her. On the other hand, she did want to find out more.

Lilith resumed her seat. "I had hoped when the time came, Velia, that you might be of assistance. I mean, you must admit, it is rather odd for a Select to be without an Oathtaker."

Oh, gracious! Don't let her ask me to be her Oathtaker! After all this time, she wouldn't ask now, would she? What would I say? What could I say but that Ehyeh has not called me to swear an oath for her protection? Surely, she would understand that.

"It may help me to avoid unnecessary questions if I have an Oathtaker traveling with me."

"Even if you're not that Oathtaker's charge?"

Lilith waved her hand through the air. "Oh, I've had enough of all that. I don't want an Oathtaker. I don't need one. I just want to be recognized for what I am."

True that she doesn't want on Oathtaker. True that she doesn't need one. That's odd. False that she just wants others to recognize her for what she is. "I understand," Velia said as she rose to go. "Thank you, Lilith. I appreciate this."

"Sure. Just stay out of trouble now and stay out of the way of my guards."

"Yes, I will. Thank you again for your time." Velia turned to go.

"Oh, by the way . . ."

The Oathtaker turned back.

"What are your attendant powers?"

Velia blinked. She opened her mouth to speak. For a minute, she feared her voice would fail her. "Oh, nothing much," she said. "My charge was a mere first." *What a lie!* "Just simple things like lighting lamps, heating things quickly. Oh, and I can take on the pain of another." She paused. "And I have some limited power to communicate with animals."

"Animals?"

"Yes, but it's quite limited really."

"You should do well with these men then."

The Oathtaker grimaced as she turned away, but in acknowledgement of Lilith's comment, she laughed. "Yes."

She jumped down. On sight of the guard, she pulled out her blade and watched him as she passed by.

When she arrived at her wagon, she walked around to the back of it. She confirmed that no one watched her. Then she grasped its edge, pulled her hair back, leaned forward—and retched.

CHAPTER THIRTY-THREE

Nancy and Celestine set dinner out family style. The smells of wood roasted fowl, steamed vegetables, fresh bread, blueberry cobbler, and assorted side dishes, filled the air.

Dixon picked up the bowl of oven roasted potatoes, drizzled with olive oil and sprinkled with rosemary and sea salt. He inhaled deeply.

"Everyone pass to your left," he shouted over the din to the diners' delight. He put some on Mara's plate per her direction, as her hands were full with Reigna, before helping himself to a sizeable portion. He turned to Leala to assist her, then excusing himself, handed the bowl to Therese at the old woman's other side.

The group treated the back room that Ezra had provided for their convenience, as a sort of home away from home. They conversed, caught up, shared information, and generally enjoyed one another's company. Fidel and Leala spent significant time with them, as Mara rarely left the inn. The innkeeper joined in whenever his duties allowed.

Mara held Reigna tightly. The girls, having grown considerably, were awake a great deal more and paid more attention to their surroundings. Everyone enjoyed their smiles and coos. Often there was a near battle for who got to hold one of them next. Fortunately, they were both napping now.

Her eyes brimmed with tears. At her insistence, Nina sat with Eden at her other side. From time to time, Mara reached over to touch the child or leaned over to nuzzle her. She'd been nearly inseparable from the twins ever since she and Dixon had returned from Polesk.

He watched her closely. "They're safe," he said quietly as he leaned in. "We'll get what we need here and be on our way before Lilith arrives. Ezra has plenty of men in the field to keep us informed."

"It's not just that. I just don't want to have to leave them again."

"Sometimes it can't be helped. You were right when you insisted on going to Polesk. You're the only one who could have traveled there and back so quickly. And now we know."

"It's just the pain of being separated from them." She swallowed hard.

"Still, sometimes it's good to take a breather. That's why I asked you to go out for a walk with me this evening. What do you say? Come on," he urged, "don't say 'no' this time."

"I don't know."

"The fresh air would do you good. You've been cooped up too long, studying too hard."

She shrugged. "Maybe."

"I'd enjoy it." He nudged her shoulder. He reached out with little touches more and more frequently all the time.

"Yes, I would too. I just . . . I don't know."

"They'll be fine."

"But what of your being out? You might be recognized."

"We'll go after dark and stay away from the crowds. Come on, say you'll join me."

Dixon seemed genuinely concerned about her since their return from Polesk. It was almost frightening. Again and again she thought about her future—about Dixon. She couldn't involve herself with him in light of her oath, but she found it increasingly difficult not to be angry about it. Was it possible the Good One would have introduced her to the man she would come to love, the man she knew she wanted to spend her future with, just moments after she'd sworn her future to the lives and safety of others, just moments after Rowena's death had released him from his oath?

"Come on, humor me. Tell me I've sufficiently charmed you into agreeing," he whispered.

She smiled wanly. "Very well then, I'm charmed." She looked long into his eyes. "We'll go after the meeting." She glanced over at Eden and once again stroked the infant's face.

Dixon caught Basha's eye. She glanced at Mara and raised a brow, then looked back at him in question. He shrugged in response.

When dinner was complete, Nancy and Celestine removed the dirty dishes. They left behind a few carafes of wine, various finger-sized chocolates, and some tea.

Mara stood. She handed Reigna to Adele, then returned to the middle of the table. The room went quiet. All eyes were on her as she resumed her seat.

These meetings were intended to be all-inclusive, to encourage everyone to participate, to offer suggestions and to share what they learned in their studies. Mara knew that if she stayed on her feet, the others would be less likely to participate, that conversation would be stilted and cautious. In that event, their cause might suffer. She wanted all ideas on the table at all times.

"Thank you, all." She swallowed hard. "You all mean more to me than I can say."

Everyone watched her closely.

"Leala and Fidel," she said, "to pick up on our earlier conversation, you seem to think that this is a simple matter of my claiming my rightful position as the girls' regent to lead the Council, but—"

"You have that right," Leala interrupted, "and it would thwart Lilith's plans, stop her in her tracks."

"Certainly, she has the right," Basha said, "but forgive me for saying, Leala, that you don't know Lilith. Rest assured, the facts would not interrupt her. Who knows what influence she might already have had with the other Council members? What lies she may have told?" She turned to Therese. "I'm sorry, but I have to tell it like it is."

"No, you're right," Therese said. "I can't let the fact that she's my sister color the truth. If Lilith is willing to do as she's done when she knows full well she's not the rightful leader, then I'm sure she wouldn't let something like Mara's claims stop her. And I agree with you that we can't know what influence she may have had, or may even now be imposing, on the Council."

"I tend to agree," Dixon said. "There are serious repercussions if someone goes to the Council without sufficient evidence of the claims she makes there. What's more, as Mara has consistently pointed out, going to the Council could mean that she would disclose the girls' whereabouts."

"So then, Mara, you think it best to simply leave the city? To seek refuge elsewhere?" Fidel asked.

She nodded.

"What are your plans for now?" Therese asked.

"They haven't changed. We'll still meet up with Lucy when we leave here. But I've been thinking . . ."

Again, Basha questioned Dixon with a raised brow. He tipped his head in response, indicating that he didn't know what was troubling Mara.

"Excuse me, Mara," Basha said.

"Yes, I'm . . . sorry."

"Forgive me if I'm speaking out of turn."

Mara looked around at the others, only to find raised brows, pursed lips, and eyes that wouldn't meet her own. "What is it?" she asked. "What's wrong?"

"Actually, that's what I was going to ask you. Something seems to be bothering you. You know, maybe you should take a breather—get out for a bit. The girls would be fine with us for a time. You need some exercise and a change of scenery. Sometimes it's important. It can help you to regain focus."

Once again, Mara glanced around. No one's gaze met her own except those of the Oathtakers in the room: Basha, Dixon, and Ezra. She closed her eyes. "Whewwww," she breathed out heavily. "Actually, that's what's troubling me."

"What's that?" Basha asked.

"Leaving the girls." Mara blinked hard to keep the tears that welled in her eyes from falling. "I feel I have to leave them again for a time and it seems almost too much."

Dixon grasped a carafe of wine. He filled a glass, then lifted the bottle in silent offering to the others. One by one they looked his way, then each shook his head "no" or quietly waved away the offer. He moved the glass toward Mara. "Here," he said gently, "take this."

She twirled the liquid and breathed in the aroma, then slowly took a drink.

"What's on your mind?"

She took another swallow, then put the glass down. Her hands shook. "You know, we've concentrated on whether to leave the city, when to leave the city, where to go . . . We've discussed the possibility of taking the crown with us for safekeeping . . ."

"Go on."

"Well, Fidel and Leala, you say when I leave the city, I should take the crown."

"That's right," Fidel said. "It belongs to the girls by rights. You should take it to a place of safety."

"And the sword is with Lucy," Mara said, turning to Dixon.

"That's right."

"But the last any of you knew, the scepter was at the palace, yet we've never discussed it." She watched her cohorts shuffle. "You see, don't you? You see that I have to go to there to retrieve it before Lilith goes back there or sends someone there for it—assuming it's still at the palace at all."

"Mara," Basha said, "that could be very dangerous. No doubt Lilith has taken precautions with it. She might have taken it with her. What's more, everyone at the palace believes she's its rightful possessor."

"But she is not."

"No, she is not." Basha hesitated. "So you believe you're to go to the palace in search of it."

"Yes. And you, Basha, are to accompany me."

"Wait a minute!" Dixon exclaimed. "I—"

"No, Dixon," Mara interrupted. "Don't you see? They all think you've done something wrong. They all think Therese is dead and she's better off if they continue to believe that. They don't know anyone else here," she said, gesturing, "except for Adele. And she certainly can't return. Lilith probably told everyone she helped you to escape."

"I don't want to go back," Adele said.

"Don't worry," Nina assured her, "Mara wouldn't make you return to the palace."

"No, Adele, I wouldn't make anyone do anything they thought was not right. What's more, I've other plans for you. It wouldn't make any sense to take you with me. Basha knows her way around the palace and they trust her there."

"She's right," Therese spoke up.

"Therese—" Dixon said.

"What plans for me?" Adele asked.

"She's onto something," Ezra added.

"But what about—" Jules began.

"Stop, everyone!" Mara cried. "I'm sorry. Look, all your opinions are valuable and I want you all to be free to voice them—and also your objections. They're important. But please, one at a time."

Silence descended.

"Adele," Mara said, "in response to your question, my plans are that after Basha and I return, assuming we find the scepter, a small group of you will take it to Lucy's for safekeeping. So, you could start preparing things for that trip. The rest of us would follow in due time."

Adele grimaced, but said nothing.

"But, Mara," Dixon said, "I should go with you to the palace. Basha should stay with Therese. And what's this about splitting the group up? Why send the scepter ahead? Then it wouldn't be under your protection."

"No, Dixon, Mara's right. Basha should go," Therese said. "She's the best choice. She came and went from the palace regularly in the past, so it's unlikely anyone would question her return. She could bring Mara in openly, as a guest. Besides, Samuel and Jules are accustomed to assisting me. It all makes perfect sense."

"But that's assuming she should go at all," he argued.

"Dixon, you said it yourself earlier," Mara said, "about my leaving the girls. You said that sometimes it can't be helped, and that I'd been right about returning to Polesk. I believe I'm right about this also."

He patted his knee, thinking. "But before we went to Polesk, you thought the oracle supported that decision."

"And so it does now."

"Oh? And what cryptic message did it leave this time?"

She grinned. "You won't like it."

"Well?"

"Again, it just says, 'Go.'"

"And you take that as confirmation that you should go to the palace?"

"It's the only . . . It's the issue over which I've particularly struggled of late." She tried to banish the other issue she'd also wrestled with, the issue about her feelings for Dixon. "It's the only thing it could mean," she said, perhaps as much to convince herself as the others. But she wondered. Was the oracle actually suggesting she go on without Dixon?

"All right, so you go to the palace and you take Basha along. What's this about sending part of the group away with the scepter, if you get it, after your return?"

She twirled her half empty glass. "It just makes sense. I still need to learn whatever I can from sanctuary resources, but that's going to take time. I don't want to retrieve the crown until I have to. Why risk that when it goes missing, the city becomes subject to the authorities' searches? In the meantime, I might at least get the scepter to safety."

"She's right," Jules said. As per their usual behavior, he and Samuel had been quiet throughout. Perhaps it was their reluctance to offer comment during discussion that gave their conclusions such an air of authority when finally they voiced them.

"I agree," Samuel added.

"Are you sure I can't accompany you?" Dixon asked.

Mara looked at him and smiled. "Thank you, Dixon. I appreciate it. Really, I do. But I'm quite sure that I should take Basha. It makes sense. You have to admit that." She saw that he didn't seem pleased. "You'll just have to forego the pleasure of traveling by magic this time."

"Well, I guess I know when I'm beaten."

Chapter Thirty-Four

"I've got her, Mara."

"Oh, but just—"

"I've got her." Nina put her hand out. "It will do you good. Go, now. Get out for a walk. Dixon's waiting for you in the pub. You told him you'd go. Now don't keep him waiting."

"I'll be back soon. Just—"

"Just go," Nina interrupted, "and take your time."

"What was it Dixon said? 'I know when I'm beaten?'"

"They'll be fine. You have a good time."

Mara waved to Therese and Basha visiting in the common room, then brushed past Samuel and Jules standing guard in the hall. She mused about the girls having three levels of protection. That much was comforting at least.

She entered the pub. Guests laughed raucously and clapped their hands, delighted with the antics of the magician who was back to entertain them.

Dixon stood near the bar with Ezra. He looked at Mara as she entered the room. He waved her over, his eyes never leaving her, drinking in the sight of her.

"So you're going to catch some fresh air, huh? It's high time," Ezra said when she approached.

"So they tell me."

"It does a soul good, Mara. You're lucky to have friends like these."

"Right you are, Ezra."

"You kids have a good time now," the innkeeper said. Then he looked at Dixon. "Careful, now," he cautioned.

Dixon bit his lip and nodded.

When Mara reached the front door to the inn, he opened it for her. As she stepped ahead, he placed his hand on the small of her back. What is it about that gesture, she wondered, that feels so strong, so protective? Is it the guidance, the support it seems to offer? Or is it the unspoken, "I've got your back" that it suggests? Or perhaps it's just the touch, the intimacy of a moment . . .

She warred with her emotions, not wanting him to take his hand away, yet knowing that his closeness was becoming a greater danger to her emotional wellbeing all the time. She frowned.

"What?" he asked.

"Nothing, just . . . thinking."

"Anything you'd care to share?"

She shook her head. "No."

"Which way? Toward sanctuary? Or toward the river?"

"Toward the river, I think."

"Toward the river it is." He turned right. Once again, he guided her with a hand to the small of her back, to the inside of the walkway, away from the bustling traffic, leaving himself in the position of protector.

They walked in silence. It was an unseasonably warm winter evening. They passed busy taverns and inns. Coaches for hire rushed by.

They stopped outside an inn to watch a wedding celebration within. The partiers raised glasses, made toasts, laughed, and drank. The newlyweds' delight mesmerized Mara, yet left her heavyhearted at the same time. She tore her eyes away, willing herself to think of something else.

They left the busier streets to follow a path along the canal that ran through the city. Longboats quietly floated by. Now and again a ripple of laughter wafted through the still night air. Soft lamplight had replaced the light of day. Benches scattered along the pathway invited guests to stop to enjoy their surroundings.

The further they went, the slower Mara walked.

Occasionally Dixon glanced her way, but she didn't speak, so neither did he.

After several minutes, they passed by a fiddler. He played a sweet, soft melody that floated on the breeze. It was haunting, sad, doleful, mournful even. It seemed to urge, to beg listeners to entertain deep, hidden, emotions.

"You're mighty quiet," Dixon finally said. He glanced at Mara just as she stopped in her tracks and turned away, then grasped the back post of a nearby bench, leaned forward, and wept.

"What is it?" He reached for her and helped her to the seat. He turned her toward himself and wrapped his arms around her.

She sunk her face into his chest.

"What is it? What's troubling you?"

She shook her head.

"What is it, Mara?" He tightened his hold. "Do you have doubts about going? If so, you shouldn't go. You should trust yourself. I don't question you because I'm trying to be contrary. I'm just trying to help."

Again she shook her head. She cried as though her heart would break. Like the music that wafted on the breeze, she seemed to be in mourning.

"You think you should go?"

She nodded, her face hidden in his chest. *Oh, dear Good One. It feels so good. I don't ever want this moment to stop.*

"But you don't want to go."

She shook her head.

"All right. Why don't you want to go?"

She pushed against him and tried to turn away.

"On, no you don't," he said. He held her even more tightly. Then he whispered in her ear. "Please, Mara. Please . . . don't turn from me. Please don't make me . . . let go."

She sucked in her breath, then tried again to push away.

"Please. Please, don't. Tell me, what is it?"

She gave in to his embrace. She sobbed as he rocked her gently.

"It's all right. It's all right," he said over and over again.

After some minutes, her tears momentarily spent, she once again, tried to break free.

"Please, no," he said. He swallowed hard. "I don't . . . I don't ever want to let go," he whispered.

Fighting against herself not to return the embrace, not to breath in deeply of his warm scent, she leaned back and looked up at him. "It can't be, you know."

He didn't let go. "Just because you're an Oathtaker, that doesn't mean you've no life of your own."

A tear spilled down her cheek. "But it does, Dixon. You know it does. An Oathtaker cannot be unequally yoked. I've sworn a life oath."

"But—"

"Please, Dixon," she cried, "you're playing with fire here. It's like you've poured oil out around the both of us and you're asking me to light the flame." She wiped her tears away brusquely. "You know better, Dixon. You know . . ." She choked back a sob. "I owe my life to the girls. You know it's not possible."

"Mara—"

"Dixon, I'm begging you to stop!" Her voice fell to the softest of whispers as she fought to get her next words out. "I know you'd never ask me to break my oath. You of all people know its significance. And you know the danger of encouraging that from me. You'd forever after wonder when I'd break my word with you."

A long quiet moment passed.

"I'd be all wrong for you anyway," she whispered, as she finally broke his hold.

He turned to face her full on. "What are you talking about? I've spent how long with you now? I've watched you, worked with you, prayed with you, *fought* with you. I know you, Mara, and I know that—"

"You don't know me," she said between renewed sobs.

"Of course I do. You've a good and kind heart. You seek to do the right thing. You honor Ehyeh. You honor life!"

"Really, Dixon," she wept, "you don't know me. You don't know what a . . . fraud I am."

Reluctantly, he turned away, giving her some space. He leaned forward, clasped his hands and dropped them between his knees.

She turned forward as well. She took in a deep breath and looked out at the river.

"I'm sorry, Dixon. I'm sorry if I've not used the proper care where you're concerned. I guess when I found . . ." What was there to say? Wouldn't making admissions of her own weakness just make this all the worse? Wouldn't that be exactly the flame thrown to the oil she'd referenced? How could either of them rely on the strength of the other when both knew the weakness of the other? In that moment, she realized she'd been counting on Dixon's strength. Had she, in doing so, somehow absolved herself of the responsibility to avoid exactly this?

She struggled to hold back her own admission. *Don't. Admitting how you feel will only make this harder. Be strong.* "I'm just so, so sorry."

He sat up and stretched his shoulders back. He ground his teeth. "So what terrible thing is it that I don't know? What giant fraud have you committed that you think would change my mind about you?" He shook his head and then, hearing nothing, said, "You're wrong, you know. Nothing could be so bad. My mind won't be changed. I'll wait for you—however long it takes."

Once again, Mara's eyes welled with tears. *That would be quite a sacrifice! For me?* She grasped the edge of the bench and looked down. She sighed, then glanced out over the river. Starlight twinkled upon the waters.

It seemed he instinctively knew that he should remain silent, that he should give her room to think, time to speak.

"I find it nearly impossible to leave the girls," she finally said.

"You're their Oathtaker. That's not unexpected."

She shuffled her foot. "No, it's not that. Not *just* that anyway."

The musician's mournful music played on. Note by plaintive note, the discordant melody sang of sorrow felt, pain endured, love lost, youth spent.

"I don't know if I can leave a child again." She glanced his way, then looked out again. "I left a child once before, Dixon." She hesitated, but now that she'd started, she just wanted to unburden herself. "I was very young. That's not an excuse, it's an . . . explanation? I thought . . . Well, I guess it doesn't really matter what I thought."

"What are you talking about?"

"Some years ago, I met a man I thought I—a man I cared for deeply. But he, Jack, wasn't so . . . committed."

"You had his child?" Dixon asked. Whether it was judgment in his voice or disappointment, was hard to tell.

"Oh no! No . . . I thought he wanted to marry me. I thought he would . . . wait for me." She frowned. "But I found out that while I'd thought he understood my feelings and respected me for—you know, for waiting—that he was actually seeing my sister, Jo, behind my back.

"When Jo got pregnant, Jack refused to acknowledge the child as his own. He left our town. He never even said 'good-bye.' Jo had his son, Seth."

"I don't understand what this has to do with you."

"Jo left Seth with me. She demanded my promise to care for him, and then she simply . . . disappeared." Mara looked at Dixon. "I did. I told her I'd care for Seth, but . . ."

"But you didn't?"

"No, I didn't. I tried, but I could barely make ends meet. I even sought Jack out. I told him that we could try to make a family of our own with Seth. But he just . . . laughed at me."

She was quiet for some time, then turned and locked her gaze on Dixon. "I loved that child, Dixon, deeply." She wiped away a tear that slid down her cheek. "I was really more his mother than his aunt. I felt responsible. But in the end, I broke my word and . . . I failed."

"So what did you do?"

"Like I said, I tried to raise him on my own, to provide the necessary care for him. But sometime later, I . . ." She inhaled deeply. "You know, my grandmother told me that Jo got pregnant either because she didn't consider the consequences and was moved merely by her emotions or physical urgings—or a combination of them—or that she *did* consider the consequences and found them acceptable."

"So what happened?"

"Seth was not much older then than the girls are now. I was out with him one day, working at sanctuary, planting fall bulbs and preparing the grounds for the next spring." She shook her head. "Imagine my surprise to find Jo waiting for me at home when I returned."

"She came back?"

Mara grimaced. "Yes, she came back . . . pregnant." She looked out again. "I realized that what Grandmother had been telling me was right, that the consequences of Jo's behavior were consequences she might have found acceptable, but not me. I realized that whatever she'd done to Seth—to me—I had allowed. And I knew that when she bore her next child, she'd leave that one to me as well.

"So I packed our things. I walked out the front door and just . . . kept going. I never told my family what I was doing or where I was going . . . Mother would have just supported Jo at my expense anyway. She would have said that I should keep my word. But . . . I didn't. I didn't keep my word. I left. I took Seth away and I never went back."

She stood and paced, trying to hold her tears in check. Finally, she returned to Dixon's side.

"I knew by then that I couldn't meet Seth's needs myself. So with the assistance of a friend from the local sanctuary, I left him with a couple that had longed for a child for many years." Tears rolled down her cheeks. "I thought my heart would break." She sucked in a deep breath.

"Shortly after that, I joined the Oathtakers. I didn't want to think about families or children or risk ever having to lose someone, anyone, ever again.

"When I first became the girls' Oathtaker, I started thinking back to those days. I had stuffed my feelings of anger and betrayal and . . . failure and guilt, down, very deep, for a long time. I thought I had it all under control," she held back a cry, "until we left for Polesk and I had to leave the girls. And even then, I denied my feelings. But once we got back to the inn, back to them, I just . . ." She wept. "Well, the thought of leaving them again is like thinking about breathing in . . . mud.

"So you see, even if it could be—and you know it cannot—I wouldn't be worthy of you. I'm not someone whose word you can trust. I worry every day that I'll break the oath I swore to protect the twins, that I'll not live up to the demands, that I'm . . . unworthy of them."

He looked away.

"I'm sorry, Dixon. I should have been more careful. I shouldn't have chanced your coming with me from the beginning. This is all my fault."

He remained quiet for a long time, watching the starlight sparkle upon the water. Finally, he spoke. "So let me get this straight. Because you decided not to abide by a promise forced from you, you think your life is over. Because you were so horrible as to surrender a child to a better life, to parents who would love him and could care for him, you've no right to expect a future of your own. Because—"

"Don't, Dixon," she whispered. "It cannot be."

"Because you thought of someone else's needs over your own—"

"I said, '*Don't!*'"

"Wheewww! Don't you see? Everything you say confirms what I know and reveals what you're saying for the falsehood it is."

Her eyes flashed his way. "What do you mean?"

"Mara," he said quietly, "you think you broke an oath. All right, you feel guilty. I understand that. But I think you're wrong. Not only was the promise you gave forced from you—but you abided by it. You did care for Seth. You did the best thing for him that you could. But even if I'm wrong, even if you should shoulder some blame for what happened, it seems to me you're paying a heavier price than necessary. And who would I be to hold anything against you?" He caught her eye. "What? You think I've never done anything I was ashamed of or felt badly about? Shall we have a contest here? Let's see, there was the time—"

"Stop it, Dixon."

He looked down. "You're being too hard on yourself. Do you know anyone who's perfect? Anyone who's never made a mistake or questioned their own judgment about a decision they made? If you do, please, I beg of you, don't ever introduce him to me."

He watched a longboat float past. "You were taken advantage of and you did what you could to right the wrong. I can't help but think that both you and Seth are better off for what you did. Don't you think that one day you might have blamed him for your feeling so helpless?"

Glancing Mara's way again, he exhaled slowly. "From everything you just said, you did all you could to make things right."

"But I left him!" She jumped to her feet. "And after promising to care for him."

He reached up and grasped her hand. She tried to shake his grip loose, but he held on more tightly. "Sit," he commanded as he pulled her forward.

Reluctantly, she conceded.

"Hear me out. It's time you put this behind you. You were able to see that Jo used you, but you seem unable to understand that you're not to blame for that."

She looked away. A tear spilled.

"Mara, do you know how difficult it would have been to raise that child on your own? Have you any idea how much a child needs a family? You may think you broke a promise, one unfairly gained from you I might add, but you gave Seth the most and best you could. A real chance at a good life."

She bit her lip. "Somehow it all seems so clear when you say it that way."

"It is clear."

"So maybe Grandmother was right. Jo accepted the consequences but . . . I didn't. And I shouldn't have had to pay the price for her actions."

"It seems so."

She chuckled softly. "She was a good and most brilliant woman, my grandmother."

"And it seems you've followed in her footsteps."

"I don't know. I guess I'd like to think goodness could skip a generation and still re-appear."

"What do you mean?"

"Mother."

"What about her?"

"She's something else."

"Tell me about her."

Mara shook her head. "I guess to understand Mother is to understand Jo. I never really got that until . . . Jack."

Dixon listened quietly.

"Jo was—is still, I assume—difficult. No," she continued, holding her hand up as though physically arresting something, "wait a minute. That's too kind . . . and not altogether honest. Jo is willful, selfish, completely egocentric. She always got what she wanted, which was usually what I had, then she tossed it away like so much trash."

"And Mother?"

"Mother supported everything Jo did. If I did something wrong, Jo could hold it against me for an eternity. Mother would say we had to be understanding and patient. If Jo did something wrong, Mother said we had to be longsuffering and forgiving. If I held something against Jo, I was being judgmental. If Jo held something against me, she was simply misunderstood. We needed to give her time to get over her disappointments. 'Life had been hard on her,' Mother said."

Mara sighed. "Jo thought I was bitchy. I thought she was immature. Jo thought I was unforgiving. I thought she was unrepentant. Jo thought I was judgmental. I thought she was self-centered and completely thoughtless. Mother always backed her, making it a virtual certainty that she'd never grow up."

"Why do you suppose that was?"

"Ha! Why Mother always backed Jo? In short?" She glanced at Dixon. "Mother lived vicariously through Jo. I think on some level she admired that Jo did what Mother only longed to do. The more outrageous Jo's behavior, the more Mother backed her. There was no competing with that. And in the end, I'd never known such peace as I've known since I left home. I don't ever intend to go back."

The sounds of a boat floating down the canal drifted upward. The water splashed quietly as the oarsmen lifted and pushed, lifted and pushed.

Dixon patted out a rhythm on is thigh. "So this explains why you don't want to leave the girls."

She nodded. "I feel better about it now though." She looked at him, held his gaze. "I guess it did me good to talk about it. Thank you."

He smiled weakly. "So . . . where does this leave us?"

It was hard to tear her eyes away.

"Is Jack still in the picture?"

"Oh, no! But, Dixon, you know it's . . . not possible."

"I'll wait for you."

She looked away. "No," she sighed, "I couldn't ask that of you. And even if I could, you'd be in no place to make such a vow now to someone who can't return it, and at a time when you're still so vulnerable. You'd just be exchanging one sorrow for another."

"Vulnerable?"

"There's still Rowena."

"What? Rowena?"

"Rowena."

He pulled back. "I don't understand."

"Dixon, you're still in mourning. And you . . . loved her. You need time to get over her. It wouldn't be right to—"

His eyes opened wide. "You're wrong," he interrupted. "I loved her, yes, but not the way that you think. Oh, I'll admit that there was a time I was entirely smitten with her, but it was nothing more than youthful—I don't know. Inanity?

She never gave me reason to think my feelings were returned and, eventually, I came to understand that it was all . . . wrong. I was an Oathtaker. I'd sworn an oath. I wasn't available. She was my charge. She was married. She wasn't available. Talk about being unequally yoked!"

He stood for a moment, then sat back down. "But you know, even if none of that had been the case, Rowena would've been all wrong for me. Once I figured that out, I was free to care for her in a positive way."

"But when we first escaped with the girls. That night at the campfire. You remember. You told me that I was right."

"No, I told you that you were right 'about most things.' And yes, I remember. I remember perfectly." He paused. "I remember because, in that moment, I knew."

"You knew?"

"I knew what you thought. I let you think that. I *wanted* you to think that. The truth is that I knew the moment you told me to leave, that I could never be without you or the girls and . . . I hoped your believing that I loved Rowena would help to keep a distance between us."

Their eyes met.

He leaned in. "I remember because that was the moment I knew I was destined to love you."

For a moment, she was still, then she turned away. Her eyes welled with tears. "Stop it. I can't take any more."

"I told you. Truly, I'll wait for you. Unless of course, you don't find me . . . charming," he said, smirking, "in which case, I may have this all wrong."

"What?"

"It's a long standing family joke. My mother thought I was so difficult, that if I ever found a woman who found me charming, I would know I'd found the right one for me. She said that when I found her, I'd best hold on. But you said it yourself—tonight—at dinner. You said you were charmed." He smiled, his brow raised, looking long into her eyes.

She grinned. "And so I was."

"So, you see? There you have it. I knew it from that night and I know it now." Slowly he reached up and touched her cheek. "I love you," he whispered.

She closed her eyes. "Oh, gracious Ehyeh!" she exclaimed. "Dixon, this is all wrong. I can't break my oath and I can't ask you to wait for me. The girls are just infants! It'll be a lifetime before I'm free."

"Just for the moment, imagine you are."

She looked long in his eyes. "This is very dangerous, Dixon."

"Just for the moment, Mara. Just for *this* moment. What if you were free?"

She held her hand out. "Dixon, stop. I can't do this alone. You have to be strong for . . . You have to be strong . . . or I'll have to ask you to leave me . . . to leave the girls."

He looked away, then stood and paced, fueled by anger. He chewed his lip. A long minute passed. Finally, he sat back down and sighed.

She glanced his way.

"You're right."

She looked into his eyes smiling, sadly.

"You're right," he repeated.

She nodded and stood to go.

"Wait!" He reached for her. He intertwined his fingers with hers.

She glanced down at their hands. She considered how incredibly intimate was that gesture. It was as though it foretold of a further mingling. It charged her every nerve ending. She shook her head to dispel her thoughts.

"Please, Mara, please . . . just give me one thing to hold on to."

Her eyes held her question. What was he asking of her? She swallowed hard, not trusting herself to speak.

"Just for tonight let me hold you. Give me just that much. I . . . I won't ask again. I'll . . . I'll do my utmost never again to broach this subject." His eyes pleaded with her. "Truly, not another word. Not until you're free."

Her eyes filled with tears. *Just for tonight. Just for tonight he can love me. Just for tonight.* As though unable to restrain herself, she dropped back to her seat and leaned toward him.

He pulled her close and rested her head against his chest.

Just for tonight.

When a tear spilled down her cheek, he wiped it away gently.

Just for tonight.

They sat quietly. There was nothing more to say.

The musician changed tunes from his former plaintive notes to a melody that spoke of hope, trading bursts of mournful keys with occasional hints of joy. Mara wondered whether the fiddler had planned for the unburdening of the emotions, the secrets, she and Dixon shared. Or had his choice of tunes been in response to what transpired between the two of them? Or could it all have been merely . . . coincidental? Somehow that didn't seem likely.

After some time, they made their way back to the inn. Before they entered, Dixon tightened his grip on her hand.

She looked up at him. "We don't speak of this again. Agreed?"

He nodded.

Reluctantly, she released his hold.

They entered the inn.

"You kids have a good time?" Ezra spoke up from behind the bar, all the while watching Dixon closely.

Mara responded with a simple nod. She tried to smile, wondering if she'd ever do so again. Then she kissed his cheek. "Absolutely, Ezra."

They made their way back to their suite in silence.

"Good night," Mara said to Jules and Samuel, still standing guard.

"Good night," they responded in unison.

The Oathtakers entered. The room was empty; Basha and Therese had retired for the night.

Dixon approached the door to his room while Mara went to her own. They looked back at one another and nodded, then silently turned away.

"Mara?" Nina sat up. "Is that you?"

"It's me," she whispered as she kissed the girls.

"Good. I had a dream."

"Really!" Mara exclaimed, standing erect, suddenly attentive. "Anything I need to know?"

"Only that you'll be needing a wedding dress," Nina whispered as she fluffed her pillow and laid back her head.

Oh dear Good One. She doesn't know. She doesn't understand that it cannot be. Dear Ehyeh, will this pain ever cease?

CHAPTER THIRTY-FIVE

"Do you have everything?" Jules asked.

"Yes," Basha said.

"Where are Mara and Dixon?" Therese asked.

"They'll be right here. She wanted a moment with the girls."

The door to the suite opened. In came Mara holding Reigna, then came Dixon, who held Eden. Nina and Adele followed behind.

"Are you all ready to go, Basha?" Mara asked.

"Yes, whenever you are."

Mara turned to Therese. "Are you sure you don't mind my taking her?"

"I'll be fine. It's right for you to take her. Of course I'd like to travel with you myself. I understand it's quite extraordinary. But you're right that I shouldn't go back to the palace. Maybe I'll get a chance another time."

"I'd be happy to take you."

"Please just bring her back safely."

"Yes, and you bring Mara back safely," Dixon said to Basha. "The girls need her." He looked away.

Mara smiled, but it was a sad smile. She kissed Reigna and handed her to Nina, then turned to Dixon and Eden. She leaned down to kiss the infant, willing herself not to breathe in Dixon's scent.

"All right then," she said, momentarily gazing into his eyes, "we're on our way." She turned back to Basha. "Is there somewhere I should try to aim for? I'm not sure if it would be successful, but it might help to have a destination in mind."

"I think we should approach the palace from outside. It would raise fewer questions, don't you think?"

"That sounds good," Therese said. "I'd go for somewhere in Shimeron, then travel to the palace by carriage or on horseback."

"How about the meeting place of the Council when it's in residence near the palace?"

"I like it," Dixon agreed. "And you could walk to the palace from there. It's not far."

"Here we go then," Mara said, smiling weakly at him.

He winked in response. "We'll give you some privacy so you can concentrate."

"Thank you."

"Keep an eye on her, Basha," he said on his way out.

Basha smiled, then glanced at Mara, a question in her eyes. "I promise I will, Dixon."

Mara waved at him and watched him exit. "Well, you've done this before," she said, turning back, "so you know what to expect."

"Yes."

"Backpacks?"

"I've got mine and there's yours." Basha gestured to a pack on the floor.

Mara called her pack to herself by magic, then put it over her shoulder. She took Basha's hands, noting the woman's frown. "What? Is something wrong?" Try though she might, she could not hold back her grin.

Basha shook her head with a silent caution.

Mara closed her eyes and in an instant the colors of her traveling powers surrounded them.

Moments later, they stood at the top of a stairway to a large brick building. Mara didn't recognize her surroundings, but was grateful they'd traveled in the dark so they wouldn't garner any unwanted attention.

"Excellent! Right on target. This is the meeting place right here," Basha said.

A half dozen raucous men spilled out of a nearby pub door. Even from a distance, the Oathtakers could smell them, as their stench carried on the breeze. Weapons of various sorts hung from their belts. The hardware clanged and rattled, breaking the stillness of the night.

The men stumbled in their drunkenness. One reached for a knife, but his intended victim punched him in the face, knocking him to the ground. The pugilist stood over his fallen comrade, shaking his hand from the impact of his punch. He kicked the man, but got no response; his fist had finished off the work that the drink of spirits had begun. He grabbed the front of his jacket and dragged him along.

Basha pulled Mara deeper into the moon-cast shadows.

"Keep hold of me in case we need to make a quick exit," Mara said quietly.

"Hey!" one of the men shouted. "What say we have a little fun?" He teetered on his feet.

"What's that?" another asked.

"Let's go raise some trouble in the town hall there."

"Nah, we're on duty shortly. We'll barely make it back to the palace in time as it is."

"Duty at the palace?" Basha whispered.

Mara shrugged.

"Ahhh," the first soldier responded. He turned and followed the others out of town, dragging his drunken feet along.

"I've never heard of such a thing," Basha said. "I don't think they were locals or of the palace guard. Did you see them? They were filthy and . . . Ugghh!" She shuddered.

"They were dressed like the soldiers Dixon and I saw in Polesk. And that one said they were to be on duty at the palace. That means we can't just ride up without another whole level of danger. So now what do we do?"

"You could try to deliver us to the palace directly, but like we discussed, that could raise questions that we don't want to have to answer. Or we could arrive through the back way and no one in the palace would be surprised."

"What's this about a back way? You never mentioned that before."

"Sure I did. The palace has always had an alternative means of . . . escape. Remember? I'd hoped to get Dixon out that way when Lilith held him."

"Oh yes, I remember."

"No one has ever used it to break in. At least not to the best of my knowledge. But under the circumstances, I don't think anyone would be surprised to see me use it."

"Who knows about this . . . back way?"

"As far as I know, only the members of the first family and their Oathtakers."

Mara frowned. "So how would you explain disclosing the secret to me?"

"Hmmm," Basha thought. "Well, I could feign an injury and tell them I couldn't chance meeting up with those soldiers. The guards would forgive my disclosing the secret if I did it to protect myself. Especially if they know you're an Oathtaker yourself."

"All right, but what kind of injury would be sufficient not to raise too many questions, yet wouldn't have them wonder how it didn't keep you from being able to make the trip yourself?"

Basha pursed her lips, then tapped her finger against them. "A severe knee sprain. I had one in the past. I could use a fake crutch of sorts, a cane." She paused. "Yes, that'll work. Janine isn't likely to notice. She's . . . absent. And Sally's just . . . a moron."

Mara giggled. "You don't like this Sally much, do you?"

"Have you ever known someone so inept that she they left you wondering how her feet found their way to the floor in the morning?"

"No!" Mara feigned shock.

"Never mind. I just find her . . . Well, mostly I like not to think about her. Anyway, Lilith would be the one most likely to ask, and she's not there." Basha frowned. "Oh, poor Marshall. He really is such a good man. This all must be killing him."

"Marshall?"

"Lilith's Oathtaker."

"Oh, right. Well, it seems our only alternative is to use the back way then."

"Yes."

"So where to from here?"

Basha motioned for Mara to pull back against the wall as a lone figure exited the pub. After he passed and was some distance away, she started down the steps, then made her way to the back of the building. From there, she walked out until she came to an old well site. She took ten long strides, then got down on her hands and knees and felt around on the ground, moving rocks aside.

"What are we looking for?"

"There's a trap door here somewhere."

"But what if someone finds it after we go down? We can't cover it back up from down there."

"Yes, we can."

"We can?"

"Attendant magic."

Mara stopped, trying to figure out what Basha meant. "Oh, of course, we'll just move them."

"Yes, we'll move the rocks and things to cover the opening back up when we're safely inside." Basha hesitated. "Incidentally, this would be exactly the right time to use that particular attendant magic."

Mara grinned.

"Oh, here it is!"

They removed the obstacles to the opening and then, when through, Basha gestured for Mara to go down.

"There's no light down there."

Basha's brow furrowed. "Make a flare."

"A what?"

"A flare."

"What's a flare?"

Basha chuckled. "Oh, Mara, didn't you know?"

"Know what?"

"You can create a ball of light in your hand."

"What? How do you know?"

"All Oathtakers can."

"Seriously?" Mara held her hand out to give it a try.

"No," Basha cautioned, "not until we're both down there."

"Eeewwww. You mean I have to enter in the dark? I don't know if I can do that."

"Afraid of the dark, are you?"

Mara made a mock face.

"All right, I'll go first. See this handle here?" Basha asked as she guided Mara's hand. "Pull it closed behind you. Then I'll make a flare, and when you get down there, you can try making one."

Mara nodded her assent.

Basha stepped to the edge of the opening and turned around.

"Wait! How far down is it?"

"There's a ladder. It goes down about a dozen steep steps."

"All right." Mara waited a minute, then started down. She pulled on the latch to close the door. After a couple more steps, a light shone. When she reached the ground, she turned.

Basha stood with her hand held out. Hovering just above it was a ball of light about the size of a quail egg. It glowed more than burned, was more blue than yellow. "It's called a flare," she said.

"Is it hot?"

"Very."

"Then how long can you keep that up?"

"Without burning? A few minutes at a time."

"Huh. How is it I didn't know this?"

"Too busy with other things, I guess."

Mara looked around. Limestone, cave-like walls surrounded them. Water trickled down, while moss and mildew grew upward. There was a strong smell of dampness. She grimaced. "Gives me the creeps."

Basha laughed. "Here," she said, "hold your hand flat. If you curl your fingers, you increase the chance of burning yourself."

"All right." Nearly trembling, Mara concentrated on keeping her hand still as Basha poured her flare into it. "That's amazing!" She brought the flare close to her face.

"Careful. Don't start your hair on fire."

Mara's eyes flashed upward.

"Seriously. That's powerful magic you hold."

"What should I do then?"

"Just relax and keep your hand flat."

"What if I drop it?"

"It'll go out. It runs on magic. When it leaves your hand, it's done." Basha turned toward the ladder. "I'll go move things over the opening."

Moments later came sounds of moving rock.

When she was through, she made her way back down. "Is that getting too hot for you?"

"No, I don't feel it."

Basha's eyes narrowed. "At all?"

"Not at all." Mara moved her hand around.

"Hmmm. Give me that, then you try making one. Just hold your hand out and concentrate on creating a flare."

Mara did. In a flash, a light appeared. "Oh!" she exclaimed. Her flare was significantly larger and brighter than Basha's.

"Can you control its intensity?"

Mara concentrated. Moments later, the light decreased until it was barely more than a spark.

"Can you increase it?"

This time Mara made the flare so bright it was difficult to look at.

"Be careful. That light could blind you, not to mention burn you."

"It doesn't hurt at all." Mara reduced the light.

"How willing are you to experiment?"

Mara grinned. "How good are you at healing?"

"Huh! Not me, I'm afraid. That's part of your attendant magic, not mine."

"Never mind. What do you want me to do?"

Basha chewed on her lip. "I hesitate to ask this . . ."

"Ask away. I trust you. What should I do?"

"Close your hand."

Mara's eyes widened. "Can you do that? Without getting burned, I mean?"

"No, I can't. But I can feel the heat. You can't."

Mara closed her fingers over her flare. The light went out.

"Open your hand again."

"Oh!" There, in the palm of Mara's hand, sat a small, diamond-like crystal.

"Let me see that."

Mara pulled her hand back. "And if it burns you?"

"Then you'll have to heal me, of course."

"Oh, yes." Mara dropped the crystal into her companion's free hand. "Does it hurt?"

"Not in the least. It's pretty. I wonder what purpose this serves."

"Maybe it re-lights."

"Maybe."

"Let me try it again." Mara made another flare, then closed her hand over it. When she re-opened her hand, another crystal rested in her palm. She examined it. "They're really pretty."

"Yes, they are. But I can't imagine what use they would serve." Basha held out the crystal Mara had given her earlier.

"Try to light it," Mara said.

Basha tried. Nothing happened. "You try."

Mara tried. Again, nothing happened. "It's probably nothing," she said.

At that very moment, a mouse scurried at their feet. Basha, startled, bumped into Mara, causing the crystal to fly from her hand.

Booooom! A blast burst forth.

The Oathtakers reached up instinctively to cover their heads when the explosion sounded. As Basha did, she threw down her own flare, extinguishing it. Bits of rock and debris sprinkled down in the dark.

"What was that?" Basha cried.

"The crystal."

"You threw it?"

"No, it flew out of my hand when you bumped into me."

"Start a new flare."

Mara lit one.

"The crystal blew up? Where?"

"Here. Look." Mara pointed to where the crystal had landed. Streaks of soot marred the nearby walls.

"That's amazing! You know, you've spent a lot of time studying, but I think we've neglected what might be the most important thing—a full examination of your powers."

"You're probably right."

"You know, it might be wise to have a few of those made up in advance. They could make very valuable weapons."

"Agreed." Just then, Mara stumbled.

Basha grabbed her arm. "What is it?"

"Oh, it's nothing. I'm just, suddenly, very tired."

"We need to be careful of your magic output." Basha looked around for a place to sit. "There. Right there. Have a seat."

Mara sat down gingerly. "Can you take this?" she asked, reaching forward. Basha took her flare. Mara dropped her head into her hands.

"Are you all right?"

"I'm fine, I just need to catch my breath." After a few quiet minutes passed, she sat up straight. "There, I'm better now."

"Take your time. We don't need to hurry."

"No, I'm good now. As a matter of fact, I feel . . . rejuvenated." Mara stood. "I can take that now," she said pointing to the flare she'd given her friend. "It must be getting hot."

Basha's eyes narrowed. "Wait a minute."

"What?"

"It's not hot."

"What?"

"It's not hot!" Basha tilted her head one way, then the other, as she examined the flare. Slowly, she closed her fingers.

"Careful," Mara cautioned.

"It doesn't hurt." When the light expired, Basha lit a new one. "Check this out," she said, opening her fist. There, sat a crystal. "Oh, wait," she cried. She leaned hard against the rock wall. She grabbed Mara's hand and dropped her flare into it. Then she melted down until she sat.

"What is it?"

"Just exhausted suddenly." Basha breathed in and out slowly.

"Why does magic do that?"

"I don't know. It's rare I feel tired after using magic. But this is different. I feel like I've been up for days without rest."

"Well, I'm fine now." Mara sat and put Basha's head against her shoulder, "but you sound terrible." It was then she realized her fellow Oathtaker was already sound asleep.

While Basha slept, Mara experimented with her flares. She no longer tired after she turned one into a crystal, but she was careful not to drop any of them, for fear of another explosion. Upon hearing creaking sounds and the pitter-patter of falling rubble, she surmised the last one had caused some structural damage.

Finally, Basha awakened. "I feel marvelous!" she exclaimed, stretching her arms over her head.

"I'm glad you rested well, but I'm concerned about our safety here. We should go as soon as you're able."

"Sorry I fell asleep."

"Not a problem. I had a lot of company."

"Company?"

"Creepy crawly things. Ewww," Mara shuddered.

"Was I out long?"

"A few hours. I expect it's early morning now."

"Hmmm." Basha lit a flare, then started off.

"How long has this been here?" Mara asked as she bent away from the rounded limestone wall to her side.

"For as long as I've known." Basha came to a corner she couldn't see beyond. "Probably since the palace was built and that was hundreds of years ago, I guess." She reached her hand out to light up the space ahead and then suddenly, she stopped.

Mara almost ran into her, she'd been so busy looking about for lizards and spiders. "What is it? Is something wrong?"

Basha stood with her flare in her hand. She brought it toward her face.

"Careful. If it's too hot, you can put it out and I'll lead for a time."

"No, that's just it. It's not hot. My flares have always been hot. Everyone I know, except for you, creates flares that are hot. But after holding that one you created earlier and turning it into a crystal, my own isn't even warm." Basha rolled her flare from one hand to the other. "I wonder," she said as her eyes narrowed, "if . . ."

"If?"

"Well, since it's no longer hot, maybe . . ." Slowly, Basha closed her hand.

"Careful." Mara lit a new flare.

Basha's eyes flashed wide. She smiled, then slowly opened her hand. "Look!" She presented to Mara, a small blue crystal. "I wonder," she repeated as she looked around the cavern.

"No, don't! I'm afraid the walls might cave in."

"No, you're right, of course. I won't throw it in here. But still, it's something to think about. This is all so amazing. It's as though, somehow, your attendant magic changed mine."

"We'll need to test this, but not here and not now. Besides, look," Mara said as she pulled from her pocket, a handful of crystals.

"When did you do that?"

"While you slept."

"You need to be careful not to put too great a strain on your magic."

"That's the funny part. After I created those first ones, I had to rest. But none of these bothered me at all."

"Hmmm."

"You know, they remind me of something."

"What's that?"

"That's just it. I can't place it. But I think I've seen these before." A salamander, black with yellow spots, slithered at Mara's feet. "How long before we get out of here?"

Basha grinned. "Twenty—thirty minutes. Maybe a bit more."

"Let's get going then."

Some time later the Oathtakers passed a door, then another, and then another, all of thick, heavy wood slabs with handles of iron, each with a large skeleton key in its keyhole.

"This is where Lilith kept Dixon," Mara said quietly.

"That's right. In that room right there," Basha said, pointing.

"Why are these rooms here?"

"Originally the family stored foodstuffs here. You probably noticed we've been walking uphill and it's a bit drier here."

"Are they still used for food storage?"

"I don't really know."

"I want to see if there's anything left in them."

"Fine by me."

Mara approached the nearest door, grasped the key and turned it. The scraping sound of metal on metal filled the air. The door squeaked open. She stepped inside.

Large wooden shelves leaned-up against limestone walls. Upon the shelves sat lamps of exquisite silver with crackled glass hurricanes, tarnished candelabras, tea sets cracked and chipped, old framed paintings, and other assorted items. On the floor sat chests and trunks of exotic woods with metal corners and leather straps.

"I've never seen these things before," Basha said.

Mara opened the lid of a trunk. The ages old hinges initially protested, then succumbed. Dust dropped to the floor. She peered inside. "Books! Listen to these titles: *History of the First Family of the Select*; *Faith of our Forebears*; *The Great Crown, Sword and Scepter*; *Service to the Masses*; *The Significance of the Oath: Rules and Exclusions*; *What is to Come* . . . Basha, this is a veritable treasure!"

"Aren't there copies of those at sanctuary?"

"I've not seen any of these titles before. Who do these belong to?"

Basha grinned and whispered, as though she feared someone might hear her, "The girls."

"Do you think we could take them?"

"I don't know why not. It's not like anyone would miss them. You know, now that I think on it, Rowena kept these in her office."

"So it's likely Lilith put them here."

"I expect so."

"I can't carry them now, so we'll have to make our way back here before we leave."

"All right. Let's check the other rooms."

The remaining rooms were all empty, even the one in which Lilith had kept Dixon prisoner. When Mara looked around it, she shuddered. "It was horrible what she did."

"I know. "Do you still think you owe any duty to her? You know, since she's of the Select?"

"If there is any mercy in the Good One, any regard for truth and justice . . ."

"You know there is."

"Yes, I know there is. And that's why I will feel no compunction about doing anything to her," Mara said. "In fact, of all the studying I've been doing, it's the one conclusion I've drawn that I'm most sure of. As the girls' Oathtaker, I could take my place as head of the first family and of the Council. I could depose Lilith, denounce her and divulge all she's done. I could have her punished to the fullest extent—unto death. I believe anyone operating under my direction could do so as well, although I admit, I wouldn't want to risk someone else's eternity to test that. Still, so far as I'm concerned, she's lost her place. I owe her nothing but my contempt. If I ever get the chance, I'll . . ."

"Come on, let's go," Basha urged.

After they left the room, Mara returned to the door of the room that held the trunks and books. She removed the key. She caught her fellow Oathtaker's eye as she pocketed it.

"Taking no chances?"

"As few as possible."

Moments later, they came to a staircase.

Basha started up the steps.

"Stop. Wait!"

"What?"

"What about your injury? Our excuse for using this way to get into the palace?"

Mara looked around. There was an old straw broom standing in a corner, along with a shovel, a pickaxe, and other tools. She grasped the broom. "This will do." She brought it toward her flare, then rubbed her nose to rid it of the smell of the burned straw. She gave it to her companion. "From here," she said, looking to the top of the stairs, "I'll follow your lead."

Basha started back up the steps. As her makeshift cane hit each one along the way, it sounded out their presence.

When they reached the top step, the door swung open. There, stood a member of the palace guard. "Who goes there?"

"Not to worry. Not to worry. It's just me, Basha." She stepped closer. "Kennard, is that you?"

The guard pulled down his weapon. "Well, Basha, welcome home. But," he continued when he saw Mara at her back, "who's this and why have you come this way?" He looked accusatorially at the Oathtaker.

"I know. I know. I'm sorry, Kennard."

"You shouldn't use this way. You know that. The palace guard expects the cooperation of the Oathtakers—of all of you. How else are we to do our job?"

"I know. And we all appreciate everything you do. I just couldn't help it this time."

He glared.

"I was injured and my friend here . . . Mara come here. My friend and fellow Oathtaker agreed to assist me home. But we ran into soldiers of some kind. They weren't palace guard, Kennard."

He looked at Mara. "Oathtaker, huh?"

"That's right," she said.

"Very well. Welcome to the palace." His expression turned to one of worry.

"What is it, Kennard?" Basha asked.

"Trouble."

"I'll speak with Marshall to see what I can to do."

"Ahhhh, weeellll," he drawled, "Marshall's not here."

"Not here!" Basha sat on a nearby bench.

"What happened to you?"

"Oh, nothing serious, thank you. I took a nasty fall and sprained my knee—again. But Mara should be able to help with some healing." She massaged her faux injury. "Anyway, you were saying that Marshall is away. So where's Lilith?"

"Oh, he's not with Lilith."

Her eyes narrowed. "Not with her?"

"She released him."

"What?"

"Yes. And do you know? I think he was relieved."

"Relieved!"

"You saw the soldiers out there? Lilith brought them and more here, then left with some a while back on some 'mission.' She wouldn't tell anyone what she was doing and then, it was about the time they arrived . . ." He paused. "Yes, it was that very day, she released Marshall. No one knows what she's doing and she left without any protection."

"What have you heard from her?"

"Absolutely nothing, although I believe Janine and Sally have communicated with her."

"And Marshall? Where'd he go?"

"Don't know. Probably the City of Light to check in with the Council. It's a shame how she treated him. She made things nearly impossible for him."

"She can be difficult."

Kennard nodded. "So where'd you go anyway? We haven't seen you since—"

"Oh, you know me. I never stop anywhere for long."

"Yes, but to just up and disappear."

Basha's eyes flashed Mara's way. Kennard certainly had used the right word. She had disappeared—with Mara's help. "I just couldn't stand Lilith questioning Dixon. I had to leave."

"I understand." he commiserated.

"So that must be it. Lilith took Dixon to the Council."

"I don't think so."

"But that's what she said she was going to do when I was here last."

"That's right. But Dixon . . . Well actually, I don't know what happened to him."

"I don't understand."

Kennard's brow furrowed. "Lilith was keeping him for questioning. Course, you knew that. Then one day, she said he just . . . disappeared. She said Adele and some woman helped him to escape."

"Adele!"

"Yes, imagine that mousy little thing thwarting Lilith's wishes. Poor girl. It would have served Lilith right if Adele had acted against her interests. Still, what could she have done? But she did go missing at the same time as Dixon."

"So who was the other woman who helped him to escape?"

"I've no idea. Listen, Basha, I've got to get back to my duties. Can I get you anything?"

"No, thank you."

"You know your way around then. So I'll have to leave you and Mara to yourselves."

"Sure, Kennard, thank you."

"I'll send Bernard."

"That would be wonderful."

After Kennard walked away, Basha turned to Mara. She motioned that she should lock her lips.

Mara nodded her understanding. She was not to discuss anything questionable inside the palace. Lilith might have spies in her employ—spies with big ears.

Mara stood at the entrance to the dining room. She admired the majesty of the ages old home of the Select. Every detail was exquisite, every item in its place. Porcelain dishware glistened, crystal sparkled, and silver shined.

A woman looked up at the interruption. "Basha!" she exclaimed.

"Hello, Sally."

"When did you arrive?" asked another woman.

"Earlier today, Janine."

"And how long will you stay this time?" Janine's voice held a note of contempt. "You certainly . . . vanished rather unexpectedly the last time. Where did you go anyway? And what do you know of Dixon's disappearance?"

Basha and Mara sat down. Basha reached for a decanter of wine, filled Mara's glass, and then her own. "Questions, questions!" she said. "Well, I intend to stay only a short time. As to Dixon, what are you talking about?"

Janine's eyes narrowed. "You know Lilith held him for questioning."

"Yes, she was going to take him to the Council for a hearing."

"Well, it seems he suddenly . . . disappeared," Sally said.

"I don't understand. What happened?"

"You don't know?" Janine asked. "It seems you went missing at about the same time."

"I don't know anything about it. I just . . . I couldn't stand Lilith questioning him, so I left. Am I to check in and out with you whenever I come and go from now on? Is that it?"

Mara found both Sally and Janine very odd. Neither had any of Rowena or Therese's beauty. Indeed, they were rather frumpy. Sally's hair bow surprised her. On a little girl, it might be pretty. On Sally it looked . . . silly. Aside from that one small detail, the two women were entirely plain, dowdy even. They both had mousy yellow brown hair, and they dressed alike—in nondescript gray wool dresses.

"Don't be ridiculous," Janine said, scowling.

"Sally, Janine," Basha said, in an effort to change the subject, "I'd like to introduce you to Mara, a friend of mine."

The women glanced her way and nodded.

The hollowness of their eyes struck her. They were sad and tired—and pained.

"And this," Basha said as she turned her attention to Sally's left, "is Sally's Oathtaker, Ronald."

Mara nodded her greeting. There was absolutely nothing attractive or interesting about the man.

Finally, Basha introduced Janine's Oathtaker, Gisele.

"It's nice to meet you all," Mara said. "Thank you for having me."

Sally harrumphed; she didn't hide her displeasure.

"How long again did you say you'd be here, Basha?" Janine asked.

All tact these two, Mara thought.

"Not long. I was injured and needed a place to rest. Mara was with me and agreed to come along to assist me."

"So, you're an Oathtaker?" Janine asked.

"Yes, ma'am."

"You don't look hurt to me," Sally said, directing her comment to Basha, accusation in her voice.

My, but their social graces abound, Mara thought.

Basha sipped at her wine. She leaned back as one of the servers placed a salad down before her.

Mara, following suit, was delighted to find, when the server moved on, a crisp green salad, with slices of pear, blue cheese and candied walnuts.

"I'm better now, thank you," Basha said. *Twit*, she thought.

Mara's head jerked toward her fellow Oathtaker. She'd heard that. Surely Basha would not have said that out loud.

Basha smiled. *I can hear you too*, she thought. Then she added: *And you're right. They are both homely, both rude, and both socially inept.*

Mara's eyes lip up. They'd found the perfect way to communicate. She turned her attention back to her hosts, willing herself not to smile. Janine was asking Basha about her injury.

Their eyes are not right, Mara thought. *They look just like Lilith's when I saw her.*

Basha looked up. *You're right. Something's up.* "Oh, I injured my knee," she said in response to Janine's question. "You remember, after Therese dis-died, that I injured my knee? It seems I weakened it." *Goodness, I almost said 'disappeared' instead of 'died!'* "But Mara was good enough to do some healing and now," she rubbed her knee, "it seems quite good."

"You'll be on your way again soon then?" Sally asked.

Basha put her fork down. "Well of course, Sally, if I'm not welcome."

"No. No, it's not that. It's just that Lilith is away and . . . Well, as you know, we're very informal when the head of the family is not in residence."

"I see. Well actually, I hadn't meant to stay long. We have other plans."

Sally turned her attention to Mara. "I see you've no charge."

"There are so few Select left for us, you know. After losing one, it's unlikely a new assignment will come along." Mara had to account for attendant magic, her ability to heal. "It's frightful, really." *Was that believable Basha? I'm a horrible liar, may Ehyeh help me.*

Just take your time.

"Yes, it really is frightful," Ronald said.

The servers entered the room with the main course: pasta with grilled chicken in a creamy garlic sauce with coarsely chopped baby spinach greens, sprinkled with shredded cheese.

"Goodness!" Mara exclaimed. "Do you eat like this every day?" She grinned, trying to lighten the mood in the room. "And this is when you are being informal. Why, this is lovely."

"This is the palace of the Select," Sally said.

"Yes, of course. And it's quite beautiful." *These women are most disagreeable!*

"That's what Mara was telling me earlier," Basha said. "I told her I'd be delighted to show her around and that I was sure you wouldn't mind."

"No, of course not," Janine said, though her expression conveyed otherwise.

Liar! Mara thought.

"Certainly. Be our guest," Sally grunted.

"Thank you." Mara looked at Basha. "How long do you suppose it will take to make our way through the palace?"

"It depends on how many things you stop to admire. What do you say we begin this evening?"

"Perfect."

"So, Sally," Basha said, "what's going on with those soldiers outside?"

"The soldiers? Oh, I really don't know anything about them. It was all Lilith's doing."

"And you, Janine, do you know anything about them?"

"Not a thing." The woman never lifted her eyes from her plate. "Lilith asked us to ignore them, so we do."

"Well, I must confess, they give me the creeps."

"Me too," Mara said.

"You shouldn't venture out there," Gisele said. "It may not be safe."

"Yes, just ignore them," Sally quipped, "and you should be fine."

For once, the truth, Mara thought.

Chapter Thirty-Six

This is ridiculous. Where do you suppose Lilith put something as valuable as the scepter? We can't keep going through every room, every closet and drawer. Here it is—midnight—and we've only made it through a couple of rooms.

I know. There's got to be a better way. Basha slumped down into a sofa. Dust fluffed up into the air.

And how would we explain ourselves if someone saw us searching the place? Really! Mara threw up her hands and let them fall to her sides.

Basha pulled her fellow Oathtaker down to her side. *All right. What would be the most obvious places? Lilith's own quarters. Her office. Oddly enough, the rooms open to public view, as she may have put the scepter on display. Suppose we start with her office on the first floor, then go to her room. What do you think?*

I think you've been reading my mind.

Basha couldn't help herself. She laughed out loud, then covered her mouth to muffle the sound.

The two made their way to the first floor. The carpeted stair treads muffled the sounds of their steps. When they made it to the bottom of the stairs, footsteps from someone going down the hallway, sounded out.

Mara peeked around the corner. *It's Bernard.*

He went from door to door, jingling through his keys each time until he found the correct one, then locked the door. He walked past Lilith's office without stopping, then turned down the wicks of the lamps on the wall sconces. Once done, he took another set of stairs that led to the second floor and to his chambers.

Satisfied the coast was clear, the Oathtakers approached Lilith's office. The low lights from the sconces flickered, casting gargantuan shadows against the walls. All was quiet.

Mara reached for the doorknob. It wouldn't turn. *Now what? The door is locked.*

Basha grinned. *No problem. I'll move the tumblers until they fall into place.*

I never would have thought of that.

It may take a few minutes, but I can do it. Basha placed her hands on the doorknob and concentrated. The *click click* of tumblers falling into place disturbed the quiet hallway. Moments later, she turned the handle. With a minor squeak of protest, the door fell open before her.

The women entered.

Mara created a flare, keeping its light low. She picked it up with her fingers and made a dome over it with her other hand.

Basha watched, then replicated the procedure. Now that her flares were no longer hot, she also could hold them between her fingers. She smiled with satisfaction.

The room was spacious, completely decked out in the deep carmine red for which Lilith was so well known. The lights of the flares gave a sinister quality to the room, making the walls appear to ripple and move, almost as though blood covered them. Mara half expected to find a pool of it on the floor.

They made their way down the rich red carpet toward Lilith's desk.

Mara directed Basha to a bookcase near the back of the room, then turned her attention to the desk. She opened the drawers and removed the contents to examine them. She checked for possible secret compartments, got down on her knees to examine the inside portions, then ran her hands along the edges for possible keys or latches that might open to hidden treasure. She found none.

She examined Lilith's collection of quills, all made with black, likely crow, feathers. Then she moved ink jars, paperweights, and blotters, and rummaged through stacks of reports, personal correspondence, hand written lists, maps, and Council meeting notes. Finding nothing of interest, she held up her flare, seeking out other potential hiding places.

She examined the shelves upon the walls. When through, she returned to Basha's side.

Anything?

Basha shook her head. *These books are all trivial.*

Did you look behind them?

Yes. I even took the ones large enough for someone to hollow out down from the shelves to examine their insides. Nothing.

Well, this didn't take long. To Lilith's chambers?

Basha agreed.

They went to the door and put out their flares, each pocketing the crystal that came of doing so. Mara held her ear to the door, then grasped her companion's arm firmly, warning of footsteps in the hallway.

A palace guard, Basha commented. *He's probably just making his regular rounds.*

Mara waited a minute, then opened the door a few inches. She peeked out. Seeing nothing, she exited, Basha at her heels.

You'd best lock it.

Already done.

Basha led the way through the vestibule and up the side stairs to the family's quarters. Making her way down the second floor hallway, she scanned the paintings on the walls. She hesitated for a minute at an empty space.

What is it?

The painting of Mae, Rowena and Lilith's mother, is missing. Basha shrugged, then moved on.

When they came to Lilith's room, she grasped the door handle. *Locked.* She tried to unlock it.

A minute passed, then another.

A guard walked down the hall on the floor above. The sound of his footfalls kept a steady rhythm that sounded throughout the palace.

Another minute passed.

I'm having trouble here.

Let me try.

All right. Concentrate first on picturing the tumblers, then move them like you'd move anything else by magic. You should be able to hear them drop in place.

Mara placed her hand over the lock and concentrated. Within seconds, she could picture the tumblers and precisely how to move them. *Wait. What is that?* There was something in the way—a thread of sorts. She approached it from various angles. There was a knot in it. Was it magic? It held the tumblers solidly in place. She thought of how to remove it. Try to unknot it? It was very complicated. Try to remove it? Chop it in two?

Are you getting it?

What's this thread that's holding the tumblers in place?

Thread?

Here. Mara placed her fellow Oathtaker's hand back to the lock. *You feel it there?*

Basha nodded when she found the thread. She examined it from different directions, poked at it, prodded it, and even tried to pull it. *I didn't notice it before, but you know what it reminds me of?*

Mara's brow rose in question.

It's like the feel of a band. Remember the one Lilith used on Dixon? I couldn't remove it, but you could.

Mara smiled. *I remember. I just pulled.*

Try.

At just that moment, someone neared the top of the stairs at the end of the hall.

Quickly, Basha, do something to distract the guard!

The Oathtaker closed her eyes and concentrated on the objects she'd observed on their way to the family's quarters. Yes, there—just around the corner at the bottom of the stairs, is a vase. She jiggled the table upon which it sat. The delicate vessel fell over. A faint *clink* sounded out as it fell to its side, then came a crash as it met the floor, followed by the tinkling of shattering crystal.

The guard retreated back down the stairs.

In the meantime, Mara grasped the handle of the door, peered into the lock with her magic, grasped the thread, and then pulled.

The band released.

She concentrated on the tumblers. *Click, click, click,* they fell into place. She turned the handle and opened the door.

You did it!

In! Mara commanded.

Once inside, they lit flares and looked about. The deep carmine red walls answered back, once again causing them both to shiver.

Mara's mouth dropped open. Before her, and scattered about, lay a gallimaufry, a jumbled hodgepodge, of objects. Hair pieces hung over candelabras and lamps; clothing was piled in corners and strewn about; bottles and jars of creams and powders and perfumes and pastes seemed to jostle for position on the tables, some broken open and several having spilled forth their contents; books with torn pages laid open; hats and shoes and gloves and hair pins and jewelry were scattered and strewn about.

A large trunk, similar to those the Oathtakers had seen down in the tunnels, sat in the center of the room, nearly filled with papers and fabrics and a confused, mingled, scramble of objects. It appeared as though someone had thrown a tantrum within.

They looked at one another.

This will be difficult to do quietly, Mara said.

Just take your time. Basha wrinkled her nose. *Yikes! It smells like Lilith in here.*

You mean all rosewater and white lilies?

Uggh! It gives me a headache. I thought the Select were—

To smell like the throne of the Good One? Mara interrupted. *You're right. It's just further confirmation that she's lost her place. Look here,* she said, lifting a jar. *Essence of rose. She uses this stuff to make people think she's found favor with the Good One.*

I think you're right.

Mara looked around. *Where do we start?*

You take the table there. I'll start over there. Basha motioned toward the trunk.

The women moved things about, looking under, beneath, and around, the larger objects.

Dust from Lilith's perfumed powders rustled up into the air. Mara sneezed. She stifled the sound in the crook of her elbow. Then seeing something that roused her curiosity, she picked it up. It was a small jar of pink paint. She opened it and brushed some on her hand. *Basha!*

What?

Look at this.

What it is?

Mara made another mark on her hand.

Basha's brow furrowed. *What?*

Lilith is using this to make—

Something that looks like her sign of the Select!

Right.

They shook their heads.

She thought of everything, didn't she? Huh. Well, back to it. Mara set the item down. When she completed her search of the top of the dressing table, she bent down and looked beneath it. Something was lying in the back corner. She picked it up and brought it toward her flare. It was a book. "*Serving Daeva: The Power of the Great Under,*" she read the title aloud.

Basha's eyes flashed her way even as a voice sounded out, like nails scratching on slate.

"Looking for ssssomething?" The mirror above Lilith's dressing table burst into life.

The Oathtakers looked up. Within the looking glass, in flames of red, something took shape. In a flash, the outline filled in, revealing a skull. Flames flickered, grew, and lashed out at the women.

Mara sidestepped quickly, as fire rushed toward her.

"Well, well, well, who have we here?" the voice inquired.

Say nothing, Mara ordered her companion.

"Won't sssspeak to me, huh? Well, we'll ssssee about that." More fire burst forth.

Basha shrieked. The flames licked at her feet.

Mara rushed to her friend's side. She stood tall, staring at the countenance in the mirror.

"Well, well," the voice heckled, "if it isn't the great Oathtaker herself. At lasssst. At lasssst." The creature leaned back examining her. "So what are you made of?" it sneered as it shot out another burst of fire.

She stepped away from the flames, startled that though intensely hot, they consumed nothing in the room.

"It issss not here, you know," the creature said.

"Oh, really? What is it you think I seek, and why would you think I would trust you anyway, Daeva—lord of Sinespe?"

"Daeva!" Basha exclaimed.

"Ha ha ha ha ha. So you recognizzzze me? I am flattered." Daeva's hollow eyes bulged out of the sockets of his skull. "Well, you can trusssst me on thissss! Surely, Lilith would not leave such a ssssacred item out in the open. Particularly since she no longer has need of it. She hassss me!" He released another burst of flame. "She's packed up that old life, left it behind. She's mine now," he fairly whispered. "And in due time, so too will you be."

At that moment Mara knew where the scepter was hidden. Daeva had said too much. "Be gone!" she demanded.

"Ha ha ha ha ha."

"Mara, he's burning me!"

"Leave her be!" Mara cried.

"Oh, you like that heat?" Daeva heckled Basha. "Well then, here issss some more!"

Mara reached into her pocket to put the book she held in it for safekeeping. It was then she felt them—the crystals. She grasped one. Just as Daeva opened his mouth to laugh again, she threw it. When it hit, the mirror burst into millions of glass fragments that went cracking, shattering, clinking and tinkling down to the floor.

Daeva disappeared. With him every fragment of Lilith's looking glass vanished.

Mara gasped. It was so like the disappearance of a grut. "Are you all right?" she asked.

"I'm fine. His presence was just so . . . painful. I couldn't breathe. I felt my skin would go up in flames."

"Well, it seems you're all right now. And Basha!" Mara shook her fellow Oathtaker. "Basha, I think I know where it is!"

Footsteps came rushing toward the door.

"Let's go!" she cried. Then the two—disappeared.

Basha opened her eyes. They were back in the tunnels. Before she could open her mouth, Mara signaled that they should not speak, then approached the storage room they'd found earlier. She pulled the key from her pocket and unlocked the door. *Quickly. Before someone comes.*

Grab the books you want and let's go, Basha said.

No! I mean, yes, I'll grab the books. But didn't you hear what that evil thing said? Mara was loath to speak the name of the lord of Sinespe again.

Basha's eyes narrowed. *What?*

He said Lilith had 'packed up that old life.'

Packed up? You think it's here? In one of these trunks?

It's somewhere here. I know it! But we have to hurry. If the guards find us missing from our rooms, they may come here looking for us. Mara pointed out a trunk near the wall. *Check there. I'll start here.*

The women started searching through the trunks. Mara checked the title of each book she found, making a small stack of those she wanted to take along. She flinched at a spider, jumped at the occasional mouse, and started with each sound that seemed out of place. When through, she approached Basha's side. *Nothing?*

Nothing.

I don't understand. It has to be here. Mara remembered then how during training, her instructors played hiding games to hone their students' skills. They chose a place—it could be a single room or a town square. There they placed something for their students to discover.

She thought back to the advice they'd given the trainees. "If you look at groups, crowds, rooms, as a whole, you'll lose the pieces for the mass," cautioned one instructor. Another gave the advice: "If something looks out of place, it likely is." Finally, one who believed wholeheartedly in hiding things in plain sight, said he lived by the motto: "Don't ignore the obvious."

Mara gave the room a once over scan, then directed her attention to the shelves against the walls. She squinted as she looked from object to object.

She examined a brass candelabra that was beginning to rust, a heavy gray pottery bowl that showed signs of wear through its chips and cracks, an old sun faded and frayed lamp cover, outdated figurines and statues that didn't seem to go with the décor of any of the palace rooms she'd visited, a porcelain vase with nicks on its edges, a scratched jewelry box, an old tea server with only three cups, a spinning wheel with a missing bobbin and a splintered threading hook, a . . . She smiled.

Basha watched. *What?*

Mara walked up to the shelf and reached out. There was what appeared to be an oil lamp. Its base was a bowl. Inside sat the upright scepter, stuck into a block of wax. It glimmered in the faint light, even though someone had placed a dusty crackled glass hurricane over it.

She chuckled. The hiding place had fit all of the rules: it was one of the pieces of the mass, it looked out of place as it glimmered, though faintly, next to the items surrounding it, and it was in plain sight. She removed the hurricane glass and presented the scepter to Basha.

You did it! Oh, it's beautiful, isn't it?

Stunning. Now, let's get out of here. Mara dropped the scepter into her bag.

Can we travel from here?

Mara nodded, but then started to fall forward.

Are you all right?

Just a little tired.

Fending off that monster must have taken a great deal of power. Then you brought us here. And it seems you've used some kind of magic to locate that, Basha said pointing at the scepter. *Maybe we should leave the same way we came.*

Just give me a minute to rest.

We can't stop here. Come on! Basha grabbed the stack of books Mara had set aside and tucked them into her pack, then pulled her fellow Oathtaker out the door. She stopped to magically move the key back to the locked position.

Just let me rest. I won't be long.

Not yet. Not yet! Let's get as close to the exit as possible.

Mara allowed Basha to drag her like a rag doll. The minutes passed. Each step felt heavier, each corner proved more difficult to round. If she could just rest, just for a minute, she'd be all right.

Suddenly, Basha stopped.

Mara urged her eyes open. There before them, was a cave-in. Rock and debris covered the ground, cutting off their intended exit. Even in her exhaustion, she was able to put the pieces together: this had resulted from the crystal that had exploded.

"Here. Sit here." Basha pointed out a small hidden space amongst the debris. She placed her backpack beneath Mara's head. "You rest. I'll start moving these things."

Mara fell into a heap. She gave no further thought to creeping, crawling things.

A hand covered her mouth. She tried to resist.

Quiet, Basha communicated. *Don't move. Don't make a sound.*

It was then Mara heard voices.

"They must have come this way," a man said.

Is that Kennard?

Yes.

"How could they have gotten through that?" someone asked.

"Maybe Basha used her magic to cave the walls in once they were gone," Kennard said.

"I forgot she could do that."

Mara opened her eyes. It was dark as pitch. *Where are we?*

Still in the tunnel. I was waiting for you to awaken. But when I heard someone coming this way, I made us this little cove to hide in. If we're quiet, maybe they won't find us.

"Do we move these and make our way out the exit?" the person attending Kennard asked

That's Sergio, Basha answered Mara's unasked question. *He's Kennard's assistant. What would they do if they found us?*

Probably try to hold us for questioning. You must admit, this all looks a bit suspicious. Besides, they would find the scepter on us, which we would have a difficult time explaining, and that would just complicate things. It would be better if we simply disappeared.

"Well," Kennard said, "they must have come this way. There were footprints along the path here coming and going all the way to the palace. But they're long gone now. Let's go. We'll send someone into the village to see if anyone spotted them. I can't understand what Basha was doing, but I'd sure like some answers."

He kicked a rock. It fell to the ground, carrying bits of broken rubble with it. "This will need to get cleared out and I'll need to get the soundness of the structure checked. Arrange for a clean up detail down here right away."

"Right, sir."

The men's footsteps receded into the distance.

"Something's crawling on me!"

Basha lit a flare, then brushed debris from Mara's head. "Are you all right?"

"Yes."

"Do you think you could get us out of here now before the clean up detail arrives?"

Mara took a deep breath. "Where's the—?"

"Scepter? It's safe. Remember? You dropped it in your pack."

"And the—?"

"Books? Here. I've got them."

"Huh. You seem to be able to read my mind now before I even think something."

Basha giggled.

Mara looked overhead. Mere inches separated her from the roof of the cove. The closeness of the space unnerved her. "Yes, let's get out of here."

CHAPTER THIRTY-SEVEN

Leala sat up straight and groaned.

"What's on your mind, old woman?" Fidel asked.

"It's just that I'm not as young as I used to be."

"Do tell," he quipped.

She half sneered, half grinned, at him. "Well, junior, I've noticed you up and down regularly, stretching your legs. So in spite of your relative *youth*," she laughed, "you don't seem any better off than I."

Mara looked up from her book. "You two should take a break."

"No. No, if junior here can keep up with you, so can I," Leala said, leaning back over her book.

Mara grinned. She was grateful the two oldtimers somehow managed to keep her spirits light as she spent hour after hour, day after day, studying. "Which one are you reviewing now?"

The old woman slapped her book closed. She held it up. "One of the books from the palace. *History of the First Family of the Select.*"

"Anything new?"

"No." Leala stood and paced in her slow, old way.

"How about you, Fidel?"

"I've got *What is to Come* and *A History of Oosa.*"

"Need I ask?"

"There are some interesting things here in *A History of Oosa* that speak to some of your questions. I marked a page for you. But I can't seem to make heads or tails of this other one. It's as though it was written in some foreign language and someone then translated it to Oosian. It seems to be about the seventh seventh and she 'who is but is not,' but that's about all I can make out. Like, listen to this: *'Then shall they come through test and trial, once again revealing the flits,'*" he read.

"The what? The flits?" Mara asked.

"That's just it. It says 'the flits.' What's a flit?" He shook his head.

"Any idea, Leala?"

The woman screwed up her face, in thought. "You know, the trouble with age is that I've already forgotten more than I ever thought I could learn. The word is vaguely familiar, but . . ."

"What have you there?" Fidel asked Mara.

"I have *The Significance of the Oath: Rules and Exclusions*. Here, read this from the first chapter. Ahhh yes, here it is," she said, flipping pages. "It's called '*The Double Oath*.'" She turned her book toward him and waited as he read.

"Aha! That fits right in with the page I marked for you in this one," he exclaimed as he held up *A History of Oosa*.

Mara grabbed the book and turned to the marked page. She read for a couple of minutes, then put it down. "It answers a lot about having more than a single charge, doesn't it?"

He nodded. "Yes, it does."

"That's gratifying at least."

The three sat in one of Ezra's back rooms. Over the weeks they'd developed a pattern to their days. Whenever possible, they breakfasted as a group, spent the morning with their books, played with the twins over the lunch hour, took them out for some fresh air, and then resumed their studies until dinnertime. While they studied, Nina and Adele kept the twins in the adjoining room with Samuel and Jules in attendance.

Leala sighed. "When is Dixon due back?"

"He's with Ezra and his men that returned last night, debriefing them," Mara said.

"Maybe he knows what a flit is. He had a terrific, I'd call it a 'classic,' Oathtaker's education."

"Ezra too," Mara said. "Maybe one of them can make sense of it." She made her way to the end of the table where a pile of books sat, including some she'd taken from the palace. Time after time, she'd shuffled through the stack, picking one up, then putting it back down. The information seemed endless; her understanding, sadly, finite.

She placed *The Significance of the Oath: Rules and Exclusions* back on the pile. "I guess I'll send this one with the group that's going to Lucy's. I doubt there's anything more of importance in it. Maybe I'll get to finish reading it there."

Drawn once again to a small black leather-bound volume in the center of the stack, she moved some books aside and picked it up. "*Serving Daeva: The Power of the Great Under*," she read out loud. She slumped back down into a nearby chair. "I suppose I should try to tackle this one to get a better idea of Lilith, but I just can't bring myself to open it."

Leala reached forward with her cramped, arthritic fingers. "I'll try," she offered.

"No, thank you." Mara took in a deep breath and let it out slowly. "But I suppose it is long since time I tackled it."

Celestine entered, carrying a tray. "I thought you all could use some refreshments. I've got coffee, tea, and some sweets."

"Sounds good," Mara said. "Any word from Ezra and Dixon?"

"No, but Ezra is very thorough, you know. They'll probably be busy most of the day."

Nina and Adele entered. Mara's visage lightened as Reigna recognized and reached out for her. She took the infant, then leaned toward Eden to brush her cheek. "How are my little ones this morning, huh?" she asked. Her voice rose. "Are you well today?"

The girls cooed and jabbered and smiled.

"We thought you could use a break," Nina said, "and truth to tell, so could we."

"Have a seat. Celestine is just pouring the tea now."

"Great." Nina leaned back as the barmaid placed a cup down before her. "Coffee for me, please. Thank you, Celestine."

Mara sat with Reigna in her lap. She picked up the black book once again.

The child reached out and took it. Her eyes pooled with tears.

"What is it, little one?" Mara asked.

Reigna trembled as she tore the book open. Her body went momentarily rigid.

"What?" Mara asked again, looking into her eyes.

Reigna dropped the book on the table and cried.

"It's almost like she's trying to tell you something," Fidel offered.

"Yes."

The child slapped her hands on the opened book. Mara handed her back to Nina, then looked at the text, scowling.

"What is it?" Fidel asked.

"You thought your text was tough to make out. Look at this." She turned the book toward him.

He squinted. "What language *is* that?"

"Let me see," Leala said. She examined the text, then cocked her head right, then left. "I have no idea."

"May I see that?" Nina asked.

"Sure." Mara turned the book around.

"I think it's in Old Chiranian."

"What?"

"It's a dead language. That is, it *was* a dead language. It had been for centuries. But Zarek is bringing it back."

"Do you understand any of it?" Fidel asked.

"A few words."

Mara let out a long breath. "Well, enough of that then."

"No, let me try."

"It's odd the title is in Oosian, but the text is in Old Chiranian," Leala said.

"Makes me wonder if Lilith could read it at all," Mara said.

"Maybe she had a teacher," Nina suggested.

"A teacher?"

"She's working with soldiers from Chiran. Maybe she's had a longer connection with Chiran than anyone knew."

"Maybe. Are you willing to give it a try, Nina? Really?"

"Sure. Maybe I can make out enough that we can fill in the blanks."

"All right then. It's all yours."

"I'll do what I can, but you know . . ."

"What? What do you need?" Mara asked.

"Well, I know someone who might really be helpful with this."

"Who?"

"Erin."

"Oh?"

"That's right. I only learned some Old Chiranian from things like notices and invitations to Zarek's events."

"But?" Mara asked.

"But she ran a kitchen. She placed orders, dealt with vendors. She had to learn as much as she could as quickly as possible because Zarek was in the process of making Old Chiranian the official language of Chiran. She could be very helpful."

"It would mean another trip to Polesk. Still, I suppose after the others leave for Lucy's, you would appreciate the company."

"I'll see what I can do. For now, at a minimum, I could use some scratch paper."

"Done." Leala handed Nina paper and a quill.

"Is there anything that I can do?" Adele asked.

Mara grinned. "I can't tell you how much I appreciate the offer, but the most important thing you can do is to continue to help with the girls. Are you willing to do that?"

"Willing? I dare anyone to try to stop me!"

Chapter Thirty-Eight

The days moved slowly. The group spent a great deal of time studying and conducting experiments. Since they all knew the whereabouts of Lilith and her army from reports Ezra's men brought in, and since Lilith was still some distance away, they agreed they should stay in the City of Light for the present.

When not busy reading, Mara conducted exercises, trying to travel with multiple people, but whenever she did, she required a great deal of rest to recuperate. It didn't seem to matter with whom she chose to travel, the results were always the same—with one exception. She could travel with the twins without adverse effects.

Fidel and Leala pestered one another and argued betwixt themselves, with good humor, over history and prophecy. The only fact they agreed upon was with regards to a prophecy concerning the seventh seventh and "she who is but is not" entering the City of Light as young adults after years in exile.

Of late, the principle question they all pondered was how it was that Mara could pass her powers on to the other Oathtakers. They'd confirmed this fact when she passed to Dixon, and to Ezra, the ability to turn their flares to crystals, and with that, the ability to communicate with her by thought.

They were at first startled to find differences in the colors of their crystals. Mara's were like diamonds, clear and see-through, refracting light in a spectrum of color. Basha's were the soft azure of a summer sky. Dixon created crystals of a bright yellow-green, the color of a verdant spring pasture. Ezra added to the rainbow with crystals of the flammeous pink-orange of a splendid sunset.

The Oathtakers spent hours practicing and experimenting. They wanted to know how far apart they could be and still communicate with Mara by thought. With each person, the results differed, but in each case the distance and clarity of reception increased little by little, over time. Eventually, they discovered that the farthest possible distance was a city block or so.

Then one day they learned that, not only could they each communicate with Mara, but they each also could communicate with one another so long as they carried with them, a crystal created by the other person with whom they wished to communicate. Accordingly, they all kept pocketed, at all times, at least one crystal each of the others had created.

Leala found no historical accounts of Oathtakers transferring their powers to others. Fidel found a few weak prophetic references, but they were uncertain and open to various, sometimes contradictory, interpretation. Frequently frustrated, Mara felt she was left with continually more questions and continually fewer answers.

A small porcelain bowl sat in the center of a corner table in the group's common quarters. The Oathtakers, all of whom were fascinated with their ability to create crystals, did so regularly and repeatedly. Occasionally, they deposited them into the bowl.

Mara sat quietly, intensely focused on its contents sparkling in the early morning sunlight.

"What is it?" Dixon asked after watching her in silence for some time.

She tilted her head from one side to the other. "Hmmm, nothing." It was good to speak with him, though they both made efforts to keep distance between themselves. She took in a deep breath. "They . . . remind me of something."

His gaze followed hers. "You mean the crystals?"

"Mmhmmm."

"They're crystals. Maybe they remind you of, you know, something sparkly." He laughed.

Her eyes flashed his way. She smiled. "No, I mean, there's something about the colors of them, about their size and shape. They all are flat on one side and multi-faceted on the other. You know? And look at the way they refract light. It somehow differs from other crystals I've seen except . . ." Her eyes opened wide. "Oh, Dixon, I've got it!" She smiled. "Do you see it?"

He gazed at her for a long moment, drinking in the beauty of her smile. Finally, he looked back at the bowl. His eyes narrowed and then slowly, he shook his head. "Do I see what?"

"Do they remind you of anything?" She tapped on the bowl.

His brow furrowed as he concentrated. "I don't think so."

"Dixon, they're exactly like the crystals that make up the windows at sanctuary in Polesk! And look." She picked one up and allowed the light to shine through it. Then she pointed at the prism it created on the opposite wall. "Look."

Slowly, he smiled. "You're right."

She continued to study the crystals. "Wait a minute. Now that I think on it, I've seen these somewhere else as well. Wait right here."

She rushed out of the room and into the sleeping quarters she shared with the other women. A minute later she returned with one of her saddlebags. She held the flap open and rummaged inside of it.

"What are you looking for?"

She dug, then removed items one by one, emptying the bag. "It's here. I know it's here."

"What?"

"Oh, here it is!" She pulled something out of the bag. She held it in her closed fist, then put her hand out toward Dixon and opened it. There, in her palm, was the hairpin studded with crystals that she'd found among Rowena's things the day the girls were born.

"That was Rowena's."

"That's right. Look at it. Look at the crystals."

He picked up the object and examined it closely. "You're right. But what does it mean, do you think?"

Her shoulders slumped. Her smile fell. "I have no idea. Just one more question to answer, I guess." She got up to walk away.

He reached out, grabbed her hand, and pulled her toward himself.

She froze. His touch was intoxicating. She closed her eyes, willing herself to pull away.

He released his grip and took in a deep breath. "So what's one more question? With what seem to be hundreds already, what difference could one more make?" He smiled and winked at her. "Look, you need a change of scenery. Suppose we go out to the countryside today?"

"Leave the girls?" She sat at his side.

"No, of course not. We'll take the girls. We'll take everyone."

"Leave the city?" She squirmed in her excitement. Against her better judgment, she took in a deep breath, savoring his scent. She paused, then sat up straight, chiding herself for her weakness, determined to remain focused.

"We've planned to find a safe place to experiment with the crystals. Why not today?"

She leaned in, then pulled back suddenly. *Gracious Ehyeh!* It got harder all the time to stay away from him. She hadn't expected it would be so difficult. Keeping her distance was easier before she knew he returned her feelings. Even though they tried to respect each other's space as much as possible, the draw toward one another grew stronger every day—as did the pain that came of fighting it. Perhaps this was the reason Oathtakers were not to engage in such relationships, Mara thought, because they seem to shut out other things of importance—perhaps even oaths and duties.

She shook her head to clear her thoughts. "You always seem to know just what I need. A change of scenery. That's it. Let's do it."

The group spent the next hour preparing for their journey. A kind of holiday excitement reigned amongst them.

Ezra arranged for someone to watch over the inn during his absence and ordered the kitchen staff to prepare food for the journey. Samuel and Jules readied a carriage for the trip, filling it with blankets to keep the riders warm while en route. Finally, Therese and Basha packed necessities for the girls, as well as extra tools and weapons.

At last, everyone was ready. Mara grabbed the bowl of crystals on her way out. As a last thought she also brought the scepter out of hiding to take along. She didn't want to make the same mistake that Lilith had made when she'd left it behind at the palace.

* * *

Ezra rode ahead on horseback. Samuel and Jules took the reins of the coach, inside which rode Nina and Adele with the twins, along with Fidel and Leala. Mara and Dixon rode on either side of it. Finally, Therese and Basha brought up the rear.

They made their way through the city, taking in its sights and sounds, all in excitement over the long awaited change of scenery.

A couple hours later, they came to an old secluded farmstead Ezra used for his network. Nearby ran the river that cut through the city, some low rocky hills, and a glen of hardwood. The air was chilly. A shallow snow, covering the ground, glistened in the sunshine.

Dixon dismounted, then assisted Mara down from Cheryl while Ezra and Samuel entered the farmhouse to start a fire. Within moments the smell of woodsmoke filled the air.

When Dixon approached the carriage, Jules was already at its door. He reached up to assist Nina. Their eyes met for a moment, then they both turned away as though embarrassed they'd held their gaze for a fraction of a second longer than might have been anticipated. Mara, watching the exchange, smiled to herself as Dixon helped with Adele and Eden.

Dixon handed Eden to Therese. Basha made a snowball and held it out to the child, laughing as she reached for it and then promptly disposed of it with a howl. Once again, she reached toward the ground, begging for another chance.

Basha handed her another snowball. Eden held it and giggled, then sucked on it. The others watched on, all laughing, as she screwed up her face, then resumed her efforts.

After everyone was out of the carriage, Fidel offered his arm to Leala. "May I?"

She giggled like a schoolgirl and lifted her chin. "Why, certainly, young man."

Nina laughed. Just then, Jules approached her side. Like Fidel, he held his arm out. "May I?" he mimicked the old man.

She blushed and looked down.

"Go on, Nina, it's a party! Enjoy yourself," Mara urged.

"Yes, it's a party," Ezra chimed in as, having returned to the carriage, he reached behind the seat to remove a fiddle case that sported frayed, roughened edges.

"You play?" Mara asked. Her eyes were alight with pleasure.

He grinned. "The lady asked for a party and I intend to oblige." He made his way back to the house and moments later, the sound of music filled the air.

Dixon approached Mara after all the others had gone indoors. "You're putting on a good show." He looked down and shuffled his feet. "Are you all right, really?" He raised his head and glanced out across the countryside. "I should go in," he said a moment later. "It's . . . dangerous out here." He looked at her.

She held his gaze, but said nothing. As much as she appreciated his words, they also required that she exercise even greater restraint herself. She hoped, in her moments of weakness, that he would exercise for her, the same control. She glanced up as Nina walked out of the house and headed back to the wagon.

"Don't mind me," the young woman said as she retrieved the girls' packs. When she turned back, Dixon had gone inside. She approached Mara who'd watched him walk away. "Mara, may I speak with you?"

"Of course. What's on your mind?"

"Please don't be angry with me, but—"

"No, of course not. What is it?"

Nina hooked her arm through Mara's, then led her forward. "Just a minute ago, when Jules offered me his arm—"

"I know, Nina. I see the way the two of you look at one another. You have my blessing."

"Oh, no. No, that's not what I wanted to talk to you about."

"All right then, what's on your mind?"

Nina exhaled audibly.

"I won't be angry, I promise."

"It's just that . . . you love Dixon," the young woman said, looking Mara in the eye, "and he loves you. It's like everyone knows it but they pretend it's not so. And the two of you . . . You seem to avoid each other at every turn. You act as though—"

Mara held her hand up. "Stop, Nina."

"But—"

"No, stop." Mara looked away. She released Nina's hold on her arm and leaned against the railing. She looked out over the countryside. The bleakness of the snow-covered landscape seemed to mirror what she felt in her heart. "What do you know about Oathtakers?" she asked as she glanced back.

"Not much. Why?"

"An Oathtaker is not free."

"What do you mean?"

A tear spilled from Mara's eye. She wiped it away brusquely. "When I took my oath to protect the girls, I swore my life for their safety. How then could I swear myself to another?"

"But—"

"There are no 'buts.' I knew when I joined the Oathtakers that those were the conditions. I knew when I swore my oath that I was committing myself to abide by those conditions. If Dixon and I were to act on our feelings, I would be removed as the girls' Oathtaker." Mara bit her lip. "And . . . that is not an option."

"I don't understand. You swore an oath for both of the girls. Basha has Therese as her charge, yet she also swore an oath for their protection. Why then can you not commit to Dixon?"

Mara hung her head. "That's a good question. Interestingly, Fidel and I stumbled on some things the other day in our studies that helped to answer it." She hesitated. "You see, an Oathtaker does not swear an oath *to* their charge, they swear an oath *for* their charge."

"What difference does that make?"

"Well," Mara began, wondering how to relate what she'd learned, "in the early days, after Ehyeh commissioned the first of the Oathtakers, there were very few of them. So sometimes one would swear an oath to protect more than one person. Eventually, when the numbers of Oathtakers increased, it was possible for the Good One to assign each one to one of the Select. So it seems that it was not—is not—a problem to swear an oath to protect more than one person."

She sighed. "But entering into a relationship with someone—marriage," she said, choking down a sob, "is different. That sort of oath is an oath *to* someone. It is giving your word that you will become one with that person, and as a result, whatever you do affects them directly. How could you follow your oath to protect someone when it may be contrary to what your loved one desires, or what is good for them, or what is good for the two of you together? For that reason, an Oathtaker with a living charge may not commit to another. The two would be unequally yoked."

Nina was silent for a minute. "But why did you become an Oathtaker then?"

Mara huffed. "Well, funny thing, I thought there could be no one for me. Then, moments after I swore my oath, Dixon entered my life."

"So if you'd known him first, you wouldn't have done it?"

"I don't know. But I do know that if I hadn't been the right one for the girls, Ehyeh would never have called me to their aid. I don't know what the answer to this is, but—"

"But couldn't you just change your mind?" Nina interrupted.

"You mean about my oath for the girls' protection?"

"Yes."

"And then swear my life to a man who would always wonder if I'd change my mind about him? Ask someone, anyone, to take my word for something and expect they'd trust me because they knew I'd do whatever it took to abide by my word?"

Mara turned away. "Depending on the circumstances, I could be tried for treason. The penalty could be . . . Besides, what would happen with the girls? At a minimum, I'd be separated from them. And as hard as that would be for me, imagine how difficult it would be for them to suddenly be entrusted to the care of a . . . stranger." She turned back. "They aren't very old, but they know me. They know—us."

"But— Maybe—"

"No, Nina, it's not possible. I know it, and Dixon knows it. He swore a similar oath himself one day. He understood all of its implications. He wouldn't ask me to break my word, or to give up those girls, nor would he know what to make of it if I did."

"Oh, dear Good One! And I told you that you'd need a wedding dress!" Nina covered her face with her hands. "Why didn't you tell me then?" She uncovered her eyes and searched Mara's face.

The Oathtaker's eyes welled with tears. "I didn't have the heart to tell you. But now, you know. It simply cannot be."

When a tear spilled from Nina's eye, Mara wiped it away, smiling weakly. "I need you to be strong for me. Can you do that? There's no sense in our both being heartbroken."

Nina put her arms around Mara. "I'm so sorry."

"So am I, Nina, so am I." Mara grasped the young woman's forearms. "And yet, I know it was right to answer Ehyeh's call. I get to watch the girls grow. Since you asked, I suppose I'd have to say that, in the end, I wouldn't change anything."

She looked toward the cabin, taking in the sounds of music and laughter. "Are you ready to go in now? This is supposed to be a party, after all."

When they entered the farmhouse, Basha and Therese unpacked lunch amidst the exclamations from all around. They all beheld the beauty of the repast and their noses gloried in the smells that filled the cabin.

Everyone ate heartily of a fresh green salad, shallot and pancetta tarts kept warm in bundled woolen blankets during the trip, salty country ham and creamy brie sandwiches on flaky croissants, and sweet peaches drizzled with a light olive oil and sprinkled with cinnamon and sugar that they grilled at the hearth.

They talked and laughed and relaxed in a way they hadn't in weeks. Everyone vied for a chance to hold the infants, or to dance with them to Ezra's fiddling, or simply to watch their serene faces when they finally dropped to sleep in exhaustion.

The Oathtakers and the only Select of the group, Therese, gathered their things and stepped out of the hut, along with Samuel, who insisted on joining them. It was time for experiments. They made their way a short distance from the cabin, always keeping it within sight.

Mara carried the bowl of crystals. She grasped one of her own and turned it over in her fingers. "You know," she said to her friends, "I was telling Dixon this morning that these look just like the crystals that make up the windows at sanctuary in Polesk."

"That's what you must have been thinking when we were down in the tunnels of the palace," Basha said. "Remember? You said they reminded you of something. And you're right. I never noticed the likeness before." She picked one up, held it up to the light, and examined it closely.

"I don't know what it means," Mara said, smiling at Dixon in an effort to assure him that she was in good spirits, "but it is interesting." She looked out. "All right, as you know, the first time, when my crystal got bumped out of my hand, it blew up. Fortunately, harm did not come to Basha and me. But it might have. So let's all be careful. Who wants to go first?"

"Why don't you?" Basha suggested.

Mara watched for the consent of the others. "All right." She handed the bowl to her. "I'll throw it there." She pointed to an area filled with boulders and rocks.

She put out her free arm to caution the others to step back, then threw the crystal. When it hit the ground, it exploded. Smaller rocks flew into the air. Larger boulders rocked in place. One very large one split in two.

"Whoa!" Therese exclaimed.

Dixon stepped forward. "I wonder whether one of your crystals will explode for any of us."

"Good question. Here, you try." She handed him one of her crystals.

He confirmed the others were out of the way, then threw the crystal. Once again, an explosion rocked the area.

"You try, Basha," Mara said.

Basha followed suit, then Ezra. Each time, the crystal blew up.

Basha clapped in her excitement. "My turn! My turn!" she cried. "I want to try one of mine!"

Mara grinned at the woman's child-like enthusiasm. "All right."

"Wait!"

Everyone stopped and turned to Samuel. It was so unusual for him to speak.

"What is it?" Mara asked.

"May I try?"

"Yes, and me?" Therese added.

"Yes, they should try!" Dixon exclaimed.

"I quite agree." Mara gave each of them one of her crystals.

"You first," Samuel said.

Therese smiled, turned away, and then threw the crystal. It exploded on impact. "Now you, Samuel," she said.

He tossed the crystal. A moment passed. Nothing happened. Another second passed. Just as Mara turned his way, it exploded. She ducked and covered her head with her hands.

"That's interesting," Dixon said. "But I wonder. Did it work for Therese because she's Select? And did it work for Samuel even though he is neither Oathtaker nor Select because it would work for anyone? Or did it work for either or both of them because of something else like . . . Well, like the oaths they've sworn to protect the girls?"

For a moment Mara's shoulders slumped. "Always more questions."

"Yes, but we're getting answers too, don't forget," Therese said.

"Right you are." Mara's smile returned. Nothing was going to keep her from enjoying this outing.

Once again, Basha clapped her hands. "My turn! My turn!" she repeated her earlier demand.

As the others laughed at her, Dixon took the bowl of crystals. She extracted one of her blue ones. She cautioned the group to step back, then threw it. For a moment, nothing happened. Then they all exclaimed when frost covered all the trees and shrubs in the area.

"Interesting," Dixon commented. "Let me try." He chose another destination, one farther into the river where the current was sufficient to keep the water running. Within moments an ice patch formed. It was about the same distance across as Dixon was tall.

Once again, each of the others tried Basha's crystals, and each got the same result. This time Samuel's came with no delay.

Ezra was next. He tossed his orange-pink crystal. Moments later, flames shot out from the space where it landed, burning to soot, all the plant life within an area about six foot round. The others experimented with his crystals, and they all got the same results.

Finally, Dixon threw one of his green ones. A gust of wind mowed down to flat, everything in the area. Then, Mara tried one. She threw it at a sapling. A blast of wind blew it to the ground, root ball and all. Therese threw one at a larger tree. Its upper branches bent far down, though the trunk did not snap or break. As before, the others got similar results.

Satisfied with their experiments, Mara turned to the others. "Well, what do you say we get back to our party?"

"That sounds good," Basha said as she started toward the house. A moment later, she turned back. "You know, it took a couple of hours to get out here today and dusk does come on early this time of year. How long do you want to be?"

Mara looked skyward. The sun had visited them kindly this day, but soon would begin its short descent down for the night. "Another hour or so?"

"I suppose we'll have to pack up soon then. We'll let Ezra's music keep us company." Basha looked at him, smirking.

"Certainly," he responded.

"Why don't you all head in," Dixon said. "Mara and I will be there shortly."

She glanced at him, a question in her eyes, as their friends headed toward the cabin.

"Walk with me," he said.

She kept in step. "Something on your mind?"

"No, I just want to be near you."

"Oh, Dixon."

He turned toward her. A moment later, he grasped her arm and pulled her behind a nearby tree.

"Dixon!" she scolded.

"Shhh." He held a finger to his lips. He peeked around the tree, then pulled her forward. "See there?" he asked, pointing.

"Who is it, do you think?"

"It's a sentry. A scout. See his uniform?"

"He's dressed like the soldiers we saw in Polesk."

"Right."

"What do you think he's scouting?"

"Could be for us. Could just be for his dinner."

"But you think he's one of Lilith's men."

Dixon nodded.

"What do we do?"

The man turned toward a grove of trees and disappeared from view.

"If we talk to him, we have to kill him. Otherwise, he'd tell Lilith of our whereabouts."

Mara's jaw set. She thought about all she'd seen in Polesk. "Maybe we should just kill him anyway," she muttered. "It would be one less beast to prey upon the children of Oosa."

"And if he's not alone?"

"You think there are others?"

"I don't know. But for now, he hasn't seen us, so he can't report anything about us."

"So we should be on our way right away then?"

"I think so."

The sound of a breaking twig carried through the air. Mara reached for Spira and quickly turned toward it. There was Samuel, bringing things back to the carriage. She exhaled with relief as he returned to the cabin.

She looked back at Dixon. It was then that she saw him—another soldier— over Dixon's shoulder. He must have come up from behind when she and Dixon had taken cover. Standing not twenty feet away, he held a sword in his hand.

What? Dixon asked silently, apparently noticing her expression change.

Her eyes never left the stranger. She would throw Spira, but Dixon was in the way.

Slowly, he turned, simultaneously reaching for his blade.

The soldier stood nonchalantly. His head appeared upside down, as it's top was bald, while upon his face and throat a long, thick, grizzly black beard grew.

Dixon moved, revealing Mara's presence.

"I wouldn't if I were you," the man warned as he spat upon the ground. He tipped his head to the left.

The Oathtakers' eyes followed the gesture. There stood another man. They looked back to the first one. This time he tipped his head to the right. Again they followed his signal. There stood yet another.

"Like I was saying, I wouldn't make any fast moves."

"What are you doing here?" Mara asked.

He grinned. "I might ask you the same. There's been some commotion going on here."

"What do you want?"

He nodded to his cohorts. They both moved in closer.

Mara glanced at Dixon, then shifted her eyes toward the man at her side. *I'll take him.* Then she glanced at the man on Dixon's side. *You get him.*

With a lift of his chin, Dixon agreed to her proposal.

Their eyes met for a second and then in one quick move, they both turned and threw their blades.

Spira found its mark. The soldier's eyes opened wide. He sought to step forward, but before his foot came down, his body swayed, then crashed to the ground.

Mara rushed forward even as the man to Dixon's side fell. She crouched, rolled over the body of the one she'd killed, grasped Spira, and pulled her weapon from his chest.

The remaining soldier raised his sword. Everything had happened so quickly. He stood, as though in shock, his mouth open in surprise.

"What was that you were saying?" Mara quipped.

"Ah—I–"

Dixon stepped behind him, wrenched his sword away, then tossed it to the ground. "Are there more?"

He said nothing.

Dixon grasped him around the neck and pulled one of his arms behind his back. He twisted it up, up, up. "Are there more?" he asked between clenched teeth.

"Ahhhh! No!"

"Wrong answer." Dixon increased the tension.

Samuel, holding a sword, and Jules, with a dagger, ran up behind Mara.

The soldier groaned in pain. "I mean, yes. Yes!"

Dixon lessened the pressure for a moment. "Where?"

He shook his head.

"Where?" Dixon pulled his captive's arm up even tighter.

"Ahhhh!" the man cried. He tilted his head in the direction in which Mara and Dixon had seen the first of the scouts disappear in the trees.

"How many?" Mara asked.

"One. One!"

"You sure about that?" Dixon added more pressure.

"Yes!"

Dixon let up for a moment. The soldier gasped.

"Is he coming this way?" Mara asked.

The man clenched his jaw tight.

"You heard the lady," Dixon said. "Do I need to—"

"No! No, don't! There's only one more. Only one! He planned to meet us here soon, near the cabin." He gasped for breath.

Mara turned to Samuel and Jules and pointed toward the tree cover ahead. "We saw another one up there. Can you—"

"Consider it done," Samuel said between clenched teeth.

She turned her attention back. "What were you all doing out here?"

"We're just scouting out the area in advance—for our camp."

"Camp with Lilith?"

His eyes flashed upward. He said nothing, but his face revealed everything: they were part of Lilith's army.

"Why did Lilith send you this way?" Dixon asked as he shoved him to the ground.

"I can't say."

"What do you mean you 'can't say?'" Mara asked.

"Just kill me," he said between sobs. "Just kill me so that I don't have to die that horrible death."

Mara squinted in thought. She remembered how Udaye died when Basha and Therese questioned him. "You mean you don't want to burn up?"

"Just kill me," he repeated as his eyes settled on Spira, still in her hand.

Samuel and Jules came back into view.

"Done," Samuel said. "Done and good riddance."

She turned back toward the soldier and crouched down near him. "Ask me one more time," she taunted.

"Just kill me."

"For all the lives you've taken, for all the misery you've sown, I should be happy," she said as she leaned in closer, "to oblige." She spat on the ground as though ridding herself of a terrible taste. "But I don't feel anything about you or for you, but disgust."

She stood and turned away. She'd not taken more than two steps when Samuel cried, "Mara, look out!"

As she spun on her heel, the soldier grabbed her hand—the hand in which she held Spira. He latched hold just above her wrist. He pulled her closer, growling.

Her eyes locked on his. She tried to break free, but he was too strong.

Then his eyes bulged. He choked. His grasp loosened.

She drew back as he crumbled to the ground. His body shuddered, then went still. A sword stuck out from his back.

Mara looked up. There stood Samuel. "Oh, Samuel! Oh!" she exclaimed, a hand at her throat.

He pulled his sword free, wiped its blade in the snow, then nodded at her.

She feared she might collapse.

"I'm so sorry, Mara! You were in the way, so I couldn't use my blade," Dixon said.

She shook her head.

"I'm sorry your outing had to come to such a quick and difficult ending, but we'd best go."

She dropped her head in her free hand.

"Samuel, Jules," Dixon said, "ride out ahead while we pack things as quickly as possible. Scout the area, then get back here so we can be on our way."

The young men acknowledged their orders, then ran off.

Dixon approached Mara. He wrapped his arms around her. She still shook. "It's all right," he said. "Everything is all right."

"Oh, Dixon! I almost— He— If it weren't— If Samuel— If he'd turned my blade against me—"

"I know, I know," he said, trying to comfort her. When she calmed down some, he released her, took her by the hand, and then turned toward the cabin.

She walked quietly for a moment, then stopped in her tracks. She looked up. Tears welled in her eyes. "Dixon, sometimes it's all so overwhelming. Sometimes I wonder if I'm doing the right things."

"You are."

"How can you be so sure?"

"You do what you do because you love those girls. You love life and the one who gave it. Don't ever doubt yourself."

"But he could have—"

"Shhh. Shhh. Don't say it. I can't bear to think harm could come to you. You'll be even more careful next time, I'm sure."

She reached into her pocket and extracted a handful of crystals, sorted through them to find one of Ezra's pink-orange ones, then pocketed the remainder. She turned back toward the dead soldiers and tossed it. A moment later, they went up in a flash.

CHAPTER THIRTY-NINE

The day finally came. Mara could justify waiting no longer. It was time to send part of her group to Lucy's.

All were in a bustle. Backpacks and saddlebags sat near the door, stuffed nearly to overflowing with extra clothing, foodstuffs, candles, tools, herbal remedies, books, and weapons.

"When do you expect to follow us?" Adele stood at Mara's side, tears in her eyes, Reigna in her arms.

Mara leaned over the table, where sat Therese, Basha, Jules, and Dixon, all reviewing a map. She motioned to Adele to be patient. The compact, its existence and purpose long since disclosed to the others, sat open as the group discussed their plans with Lucy.

"Just there. Is that the place?" Mara asked, tapping on the map.

"That's it," Lucy said. "And by way of reminder, my people report finding men they assume are from Lilith's group in various places throughout Oosa. It seems they scout areas out well in advance of her moving her camp."

"Yes, Ezra's people are reporting the same thing." Mara looked at Basha, then Jules. "You'll have to be on high alert at all times," she cautioned. "All right, has everyone got the plan?"

"Got it," Jules said.

They'd mapped out every detail, right down to the camping places and inns that Ezra assured them would be safe to use. If necessary they could send messages back through the innkeeper's network.

"Thank you, Lucy. We'll be in touch soon," Mara said.

"Take care."

She closed the compact. As she pocketed it, she turned to Adele. Fear and uncertainty clouded the young woman's eyes. "It'll be all right. I need you to do this. We shouldn't be more than a month or so behind you. If we hear word of Lilith approaching the city before that, we'll leave even sooner."

Adele wiped at her eyes with the back of her hand. She grasped Reigna's tiny hand. The child's eyes seemed to acknowledge that something was amiss with one of her caretakers.

"I'll take the map," Jules said.

"Don't make any markings on it," Dixon cautioned. "We wouldn't want anyone to know where you were headed."

Nina sat down. "It seems like someone is always coming and going," she said as she glanced Jules's way.

"It can't be helped, Nina." Mara rolled up the map. "I want to get the scepter to safekeeping. I probably should have sent the group off sooner." She handed the scroll to Jules whose gaze rested on Nina.

His chair scraped against the floor as he pushed it back. "We can still get an early start—and we'll need to if we're to make it to Aventown before nightfall." He tucked the map under his arm. "I checked at the stables earlier. Our horses are saddled."

Adele groaned. Moody for days now, she'd intercepted Mara at every turn, each time with yet another argument for why she should stay behind. She'd even gone so far as to ask Mara to check with the oracle about whether to send her with the others, but the Oathtaker thought the idea preposterous. Why would the oracle bother over such a detail?

Bundled up in shawls and capes, they all made their way to the stables.

Dixon, late for an appointment with Ezra, clasped Jules's forearm, urged him to keep everyone safe, then returned to the inn.

Mara and Nina each held one of the twins as the travelers mounted. Mara grasped Eden's arm and raised it in a mock wave. Nina grinned, then followed suit, waving Reigna's hand at those departing.

As the riders left the courtyard, a man in black, on a large rust gelding, rushed toward the inn. He nearly collided with Adele. Mara winced at the encounter, glanced briefly at the newcomer, then turned her attention back to her departing friends.

Adele stretched so far back in her saddle, that for a minute it looked like she was riding backward. She appeared troubled.

"Poor Adele," Mara said as she, Nina, and Samuel, headed back to the inn.

Just then, the man in black nearly ran into them.

"Excuse *me*," Mara said as he jostled past.

He glanced at her briefly, then went inside.

She shook her head. Then, as she entered, Ezra and Dixon turned her way.

"Dixon!" the newcomer cried. "Dixon, it is you!"

Dixon's face broke into a big smile. His strong good looks caught Mara by surprise, as they often did. She tried to ignore his presence, but sometimes it was very difficult. This it seemed, was one of those times. She drank in the sight of him.

"Edmond! What are you doing here?" Dixon embraced his friend, clapping him on the back.

So this was Dixon's dear friend, Edmond. Mara was startled.

"Dixon!" Edmond exclaimed again. "I am so glad to see you. What are you doing here? How did you get here? I thought—"

"Oh, so many questions!" Dixon grasped his friend's arm and turned him toward Mara. "Here, I'd like to introduce you to someone."

"I believe we've already met," she said, not intending to hide her vexation.

Dixon looked puzzled. He turned back to his friend. "Edmond, I'd like to introduce you to Mara . . . and this is Nina," he continued, gesturing her way, "and Samuel," he added. "Everyone, this is my dear friend, Edmond. Edmond Chantry."

The newcomer looked down, shuffled his feet, then glanced back up. "Excuse me, ma'am. Seems we got off to a bad start."

Mara lifted her chin, and widened her eyes.

"Please forgive me."

She watched him closely. His mannerisms did not appear contrived, but rather, to display genuine repentance.

"You too?" Dixon clapped Edmond's back. "Well, my friend, you're in good company. I guess Mara has that effect."

"The only effect she has on me, is to shame me," Edmond said, tipping his head. "Had I known you were a friend of Dixon's—"

"You would have been polite? Whereas, if I was just some . . . unknown, it was acceptable for you to be rude and pushy?"

Dixon laughed. "See what I mean? Well, if it helps any, we had a similar beginning."

She looked at him, her eyes narrowed.

"Ah, come on, Mara, he's sorry. Can't you see that?" Dixon reached for Eden. Clearly, the infant was delighted when he took her into his arms. She touched his face and babbled at him.

"Truly, Mara, I beg your forgiveness."

She glanced at Dixon again. When he winked at her, she grinned. "Apology accepted." She shook Edmond's hand. "It's a pleasure to meet you. I've heard a great deal about you."

"The pleasure is all mine."

"How long will you be here?" Dixon asked.

"Well now, I don't know. I was just going to be passing through. I'm late for a meeting which accounts for my . . . well, my bad manners," Edmond said, glancing at Mara with a smile. "But after my business concludes, I'll know more. It would be great to have some time to catch up with you though, Dixon. I haven't seen you since—"

"I left the palace, yes."

"However did you—"

"Oh, later." Dixon turned to Mara. "You know, Edmond could have information about Lilith."

"Lilith? Yes, I've heard the occasional rumor."

"Have you seen her?"

"No, not since she left the palace and that was . . . months ago now."

"Well, have you got time after your meeting? This evening perhaps?"

"I'm free this evening."

"Mara?" Dixon asked.

"I just plan to study today and to help Nina. Without Adele, she'll need more help with the girls."

"Adele?" Edmond asked.

"You know Adele," Dixon said. "Lilith's former maid."

"Oh, sure. She's the one Rowena was so fond of, wasn't she? I thought the name sounded familiar." Edmond looked around. "She's here? However did you manage that?"

"No," Mara said, "she was here helping us, but she's gone now. That's what I was saying about Nina needing more help with the girls."

He cocked his head as he looked at the infants. "Twins?"

"Oh, Edmond, my friend," Dixon said, "you will never believe!"

"Since Edmond is running late for his meeting, what do you say we just plan for dinner this evening?" Mara asked.

Edmond smiled. "I wouldn't miss it."

"Great," Dixon said. He handed Eden off, then Samuel and Nina took the infants back to the group's quarters.

"I'll get checked in quickly and rush off to my meeting. Then I'll see you both here at . . . what time?"

"Doesn't matter. Just let someone know at the desk when you arrive and they'll get word to us," Dixon said.

"Perfect." Edmond waved and walked away.

Dixon turned to Mara. "Thank you. It means a lot to me."

"Say no more."

He smiled and started off.

She watched him. She never tired of his strong, certain presence. While she had transferred magic powers to the others, it was Dixon more than anyone, who had transferred confidence to her. He questioned her regularly, challenged her unapologetically, tested her and her limits without warning, but he also supported and trusted her decisions completely and wholeheartedly.

Great Ehyeh, how could this have happened?

Mara leaned back as the barmaid removed the dishes from their table. As usual, Celestine was dressed in a wholly pristine manner, yet every man in the pub seemed aware of her presence—Edmond not the least among them.

Having watched the woman for weeks, Mara had seen men make advances at her, fights break out over her, and contests declared for the rights to her favors. She recalled asking Celestine some days back whether it bothered her.

The barmaid had laughed. "See there," she said to Ezra, "I must be due a raise." She walked away.

Mara looked to Ezra, her eyes narrowed. "I don't understand."

The innkeeper chuckled. "Well you see, Mara, it's like this. A man who's busy watching a woman is not paying attention to business. For someone in the spy business like me, it helps to have the right women in place." He looked over the room. "Take Nancy there," he motioned her way. "She's a buxom young woman. Pretty, but not the same kind of—exotic beauty—Celestine is. She's got a great smile and a vivacious personality and she uses other . . . shall we say . . . tricks of the trade."

"You mean that low blouse she wears? She looks like she'll spill out of it."

"Exactly!" He laughed and slapped his knee. "Some men want to see the flesh. Others just want to imagine it. Together those two do more around here to move information than any of my spies. And they're paid well for it."

"That's awful."

"You think so?" He leaned closer as though preparing to tell her a secret. "Listen, Mara, I know my business and I know men. If you needed information and you thought placing the right beauties in a man's sight would help you, are you telling me that you wouldn't do just that?"

"Well—"

"You would. And what's more, you should. Just like you should be certain that those men upon whom you rely are well trained and disciplined, constantly aware of their own weaknesses and consistently fending them off.

"Men may be physically stronger than women—as a rule anyway—but they also have a . . . weakness that more than levels the playing field. The greatest losses I've witnessed in my time have not been losses due to a man's lack of physical strength or to bad tactical maneuvers. They've been brought about through the likes of women those men could not, or at least *did* not, ignore.

"The truth is, I employ many men, but if I ever caught one watching the women around him in a—well, you know in what way—while on duty, that would be the end of his engagement with me.

"You know, the Guild puts those who seek to be Oathtakers through enormous rigors to address the issue. Are you offended by the fact that they acknowledge such a . . . propensity, for lack of a better word, before a man can earn his credentials?"

"So, Nancy and Celestine are tools."

"If you like. But I don't ask them to do anything other than to be who and what they are. I would never attempt to sell their favors. Ever. I wouldn't have it. I respect them and rely upon them. I keep guards on site at all times, as you've seen. I do it to protect them. They are never in danger.

"I'm not sure I could say that I'd die for them. I understand the significance of such an oath. But I can say unreservedly that I'd kill for them, which, believe it or not, can be even more difficult. What's more, I have." He shuffled in his seat. "Why, they live right here on the premises so they don't have to leave here in the dead of night when they would be alone and vulnerable."

Mara turned her attention back to the present.

Edmond continued to study Celestine's every move. He was childlike in his attempts to get her attention. He grinned at her, raised his brow and puffed out his chest. To all appearances, the barmaid was uninterested, though Edmond's eyes moved from her face to her bosom. He reached out to touch her, but she, wholly aware, expertly moved away before he made contact.

"Still miss me, Celestine?"

She smiled. "Right, Edmond, I've been pining after you all these years."

"I know, I know. If it hadn't been for Dixon here, we'd have hooked up back when we were young."

"Hey, hey, enough of that, Edmond," Dixon said. "You know there was no truth to those rumors. Rumors *you* started. Besides, Celestine is family!"

"Ha ha ha," Edmond laughed. "Well," he leaned back, directing his comments to Celestine and further surveying the goods, "lucky for you, it's not too late."

"Right, Edmond." She stood tall. "But why bring Dixon into this? Clearly, you underestimate yourself." She looked to the bar where Ezra stood motioning for her, then back. "Fact is, I rejected you entirely on the basis of your own merits."

Dixon laughed and slapped his knee. "Oh, Edmond! She's always gotten the best of you."

Mara bit back her grin. She could see, even if Dixon could not, that Edmond was not amused. Actually, at this moment, she felt rather badly for him. "Thank you, Celestine," she said as the barmaid stepped away. She glanced toward Edmond, his eyes following the woman's every move, as she drank the last of her wine, savoring its fruity, smoky flavor.

"Here." Dixon took her glass. "Nancy and Celestine are both busy. I'll get you a fill."

"It's all right, I'll wait."

"No, really, it's my pleasure." He winked at her, then addressed his friend. "Can I get you anything?"

"No." Edmond glanced Mara's way. "I mean, yes. Yes, I'd like something stronger. Why don't you surprise me?"

"Be right back then." Dixon went to the bar. He stopped there to chat with Ezra while the staff went to get a new barrel of wine, having just emptied the old one.

"It's good to see Dixon has such a good friend in you."

Mara tore her gaze away from Dixon. She nodded.

"Well, unlike myself—witnessed by Celestine's behavior—Dixon does have a way with the women. Always did. Just never committed. Then of course, it was too late—after he accepted his charge." Edmond chuckled. "But you know, about Celestine? He never really had any interest in her. I just give him trouble now and then. They're cousins, you know."

"Yes, that's what I understand."

"Now Rowena. Rowena was a different story."

"Oh?"

"Oh!" Edmond swilled the last of his drink. "Dixon was completely taken with her. He took his Oathtaker's duty way beyond the limits. Never, and I mean *never ever*, left her side."

"Really?"

"Well of course, I don't expect he talks about her."

"I understand they were very close friends."

Edmond smirked. His brow rose. "Is that what he said?"

She looked away. Of course the man knew nothing of her relationship with Dixon. Surely he didn't intend to offend her. But his words did make her think about her own past experience. She hadn't done such a good job before in her judging of men. Jack had pulled the wool over her eyes. Was Dixon really different? *Of course. He's as different from Jack as night is from day.*

But maybe there had been more to his relationship with Rowena than he had let on. Surely she couldn't blame him for wanting to keep that from her. And Rowena would no longer be a challenge—even if Mara herself were free—which, she reminded herself yet again, she was not.

Edmond watched her closely. "Oh, I am sorry. I didn't . . . Well, that is, you should think nothing of it. I'm sure that's all changed."

"I don't know what you're talking about."

He looked away. "Well now, I am embarrassed. I didn't realize—"

"Embarrassed?"

He hung his head. "I should have realized, should have seen it. I'm really . . . Gosh, I'm sorry." He chewed on his lip. "You know, I bet Dixon would wait forever for you."

She shook her head. "Please, Edmond, change the subject."

He nodded and looked about. "Don't you find people just so amusing?"

"What do you mean?"

"Well . . . like look at that guy over there." Edmond gestured toward a nearby table. There sat a middle-aged man with a young woman. "See how he's trying to impress that girl?"

Mara looked. The sight was rather amusing. The man sat all puffed up, trying to look important as he rummaged through a handful of coins.

"She caught him looking at Celestine and now he's trying to make up ground. Ha ha ha. That reminds me of the funniest story."

Edmond's laughter was infectious. Mara grinned. "Oh?"

"Well see, I was watching this couple one night at a pub a lot like this." Edmond waved his hand. "This guy was trying to get some girl's attention. He told her how beautiful she was, how no one else in the room held a candle to her." He paused.

"And then?"

"So he says to her, he says, 'Why, look at you,' as he leers at her. She says, 'really, I'd prefer you didn't.' She was acting as though she wasn't interested, see?"

Mara smiled, caught up in Edmond's story.

"So he says, 'Well it can't be helped though, you know. Looking at you, I mean. Why, haven't you noticed all the men here ogling you?' Now the young woman says, 'Oh, I'm sure you're mistaken.' 'Mistaken!' he says as he slaps the table." Edmond slapped the table himself, to add to the telling of his story. "'Why I should say not. Why look around! Just look. Go on—look.'

"So the young woman—not wanting to appear rude—looks around, but she sees nothing. So she says, 'So?' as she turns back his way.

"Now by this time, don't you know, he'd drawn in so closely that the young woman nearly collided with him. So she pulls away and says, 'What is it I'm supposed to see?'"

Edmond chuckled. "Of course my curiosity got the best of me. I had to hear the rest of the story. So I leaned in. I could see the old guy leering at his intended . . . victim.

"So then he says, 'Why all of them! They're all looking at you. See that guy over there?' and he gestures toward some guy sitting near the door. 'He hasn't been able to take his eyes off of you.'"

Edmond stopped and laughed heartily. "Now this is where it gets really funny," he said as he pulled his chair in closer.

Mara anxiously awaited the punch line.

"So the young woman says, 'You mean that guy? Right there?' 'Yes,' the man says, 'that's the one.' 'Right there near the door?' 'That's the one,' he repeats. So she looks the old letch full on and says, 'He's a regular here.' 'So,' he says, 'he must watch you all the time.' 'No. No, I wouldn't say so.' 'You doubt me?' he asks her. She stares at him and says— You ready for this?" Edmond lifted a brow at Mara, in question.

She nodded.

"'Doug,' the young woman says, 'the man's blind.'"

Mara laughed. "That's very funny!"

Edmond chuckled. "Yeah, it reminds me of another conversation I overheard one night. This guy was harassing a young woman. Finally, she turned to him and said, 'Is it true that ignorance is bliss?'"

"No!"

"She did! But that wasn't the best part. He said . . . Oh, this is so funny. He said, 'What's bliss?' 'Never mind,' she told him, 'You just answered my question.'"

"Ha ha ha ha!" Mara laughed. She could see why Dixon enjoyed Edmond's company. "Where do you come up with these? Ha ha ha!"

He shrugged, still chuckling. "People watching."

"Here we are!" Dixon placed Mara's wine glass down before her, then set a drink at his friend's hand. "How are you two getting along?"

Mara opened her mouth to speak, but Edmond cut her off. "Famously! This is quite the remarkable woman here."

Dixon sat down. "Right you are." He turned back to business. "So you say the last you spoke to Lilith, she said she intended to make her way to the city to meet with the Council for the late-spring festival." He turned to Mara. "That still gives us plenty of time here to study."

She turned to Edmond, suddenly all business. "And when was that? When did you last speak with her?"

"Well . . . it was shortly after Dixon . . . disappeared. However did you manage to get away like that?"

"Mara here." Dixon jostled her elbow.

"Mara helped you to escape?"

"Yes, she—"

"Came in through the back way," she interrupted.

"The back way?"

Dixon frowned at her. She knew the tunnels were secret.

"I mean, I had the help of a palace insider and—"

"Well, doesn't matter. I'm just glad you're safe, Dixon."

"It's too bad you couldn't have done something to lend aid to him while he was at the palace, Edmond. You know? He was in terrible shape when I got to him."

Edmond blinked several times. "Well, I— That is, no one really knew what Lilith was up to. She's very secretive you know."

"I know, my friend. You were hardly in a position to circumvent her. Basha had the same problem," Dixon said.

"Oh, I didn't mean to imply anything!" Mara exclaimed.

Edmond looked away. His gaze rested on Celestine. With a seeming effort to pull his attention from the view, he turned back. "You know, Dixon, I would do whatever I could to help you, anytime."

"Of course I don't blame you. Lilith is quite a force."

"Yes, Dixon's right. It would be unfair to think otherwise," Mara said.

The three sat quietly for a minute.

"Wouldn't Lilith just cringe to learn of the girls though?" Edmond asked.

"Yes, but it could put them in grave danger," Dixon said.

"That's why we're so careful with the information," Mara added. "We plan to leave the city before she arrives."

"You're probably right to do so. Look, I could let the Council know I've been in touch with you, Dixon."

"No," Mara said, "I don't like the idea. It might not be safe for you, Edmond. I mean, what if they insist on knowing of his whereabouts? No, we can't chance it."

"Hmmm. Hadn't thought of that. So, you plan to just move on without checking in with the Council at all, Dixon? But really, don't you think they'd like to speak with you about Rowena? About her death?"

Dixon patted a rhythm out on his knee. "Well, we've been doing a lot of studying. Fact is, as Reigna and Eden's regent, Mara is the rightful leader of the Council. So, I think that so long as she's satisfied, I've met my duty. In short, that's good enough for me."

Edmond's eyes caressed Celestine who approached a nearby table. Finally, he turned back to Mara. "Then no one at the Council knows of you?"

"No. And that's the way I want to keep it."

"In that case, I'll say nothing."

"I appreciate it, my friend," Dixon said.

"Think nothing of it." Edmond downed the last of his drink. "Well, I should let you two alone. I think I'll call it a night." He stood to leave, somewhat off balance.

"Will we see you in the morning?" Dixon asked.

"Yes, but I'll need to be on my way then—for a few weeks at least. Maybe after that I can stop back and we can really catch up."

"Sounds good." Dixon stood and clapped his friend on the shoulder. "Since Lilith isn't due here until the late spring festival, that should work well."

"Excellent. Good night then, and good night, Mara. I really enjoyed the opportunity to get to know you."

"Good night, Edmond. Thank you."

As he walked away, he scanned the crowd for one final glimpse at Celestine.

Mara knew it would be unfair to leave Nina with the twins and without meaningful assistance or company. Thus, she decided to retrieve Erin from Polesk. Notwithstanding Dixon's initial objections, she convinced him she could travel solo, safely. Besides, she couldn't take him along and then return with both of them at the same time.

She traveled directly to sanctuary. Now, with Erin all packed and ready to go, she was saying her "good-byes," to her friends.

"Wouldn't you know, Hattie is at the library again," Faith said. "I would so like for you to meet her."

"Another time. Thank you—and you too, Ted—for caring for Erin. I promise we'll do our best for her as well."

"Does she know—" Ted began.

"No," Mara interrupted, her voice low. "I didn't tell her anything. I thought I'd let Nina do that. If Erin doesn't want to stay with us after she learns of the dangers, I'll bring her back here. In the meantime, the two of them will at least get to see one another."

"I understand."

"Well, Erin, are you ready to go?"

"I am."

Mara grasped the young woman's hands and in a flash, surrounded by clouds of color and light, the two disappeared. Moments later, they arrived back at the inn.

Erin stumbled as they came to a stop. "Oh!" she exclaimed. Her mouth was open, her eyes enlarged.

Mara chuckled. "Pretty amazing, isn't it?"

"Where's Nina?"

Mara released her hold, then looked up to find Edmond coming their way. "Oh, good morning," she offered with a smile.

"Great Good One! You just—" He stopped short, shaking his head. "You just came out of nowhere!"

"Ahhh . . . I'd rather hoped no one would see me."

"How did you do that?"

She chewed on her lip. "I suppose it's pretty obvious." There was no sense trying to convince him that he'd not seen what he most surely had seen. "Attendant magic."

"Why that's . . . wonderful! You can just come and go like that? And take people with you?"

She tipped her head right, then left. "It's not as easy as all that. There are limitations."

"Limitations?"

"Yes." She really did not want to discuss the matter and felt foolish for having taken the chance that someone might catch her. "I—"

"What kind of limitations?"

"Oh—"

"But you can take others with you! Is that how you came here? To the city? You brought the whole group by magic?"

"No," she said, grinning. She couldn't help herself. Edmond's enthusiasm was amusing and catchy. "I can't travel with more than a single person at a time—except for the girls."

"May I try? Would you take me somewhere?"

"Not just now, but maybe another time." She glanced at Erin, anxious to bring her conversation with Edmond to a close. "Is there anything else I can do for you though?"

"That is truly amazing!" he continued. "I didn't know you could do that."

"Yes, well, I don't like to attract attention with it. Appearing out of nowhere could prove difficult to explain."

"Right. Right."

"You're on your way then?"

"Yes, I just left Dixon and was on my way out," he said, pointing to the back door, "when I turned and saw you." Again he shook his head. "Well, I'm sorry to have interrupted, but I'm glad I had the opportunity to let you know how much I enjoyed dinner last night."

"Thank you. I did too. You take care and stay safe now."

"Sure thing. Well, my ride is saddled and ready to go, and my gear is all packed, so I'll see you." He started off.

"Don't run over anyone on your way out!" she teased.

He turned back, then smiled broadly. "No, I won't. I've learned my lesson."

"See you soon then, Edmond."

"So long!"

Mara reached for the door to their quarters just as someone opened it from the inside. Nina nearly collided into her.

"Erin!"

"Nina!"

Mara smiled as the two sisters greeted one another. "Where are the girls?"

"With Samuel and Dixon." Nina nodded toward the inner door. "I was just going for a walk while I awaited your return. I was too excited to sit still! Oh, thank you so much for bringing Erin to me." She took Mara's hands and held them tightly, then kissed her cheek.

"You're welcome, Nina. Now listen, I need you to tell Erin everything. Don't leave anything out. If she's not up to all this, then I'll bring her back to Ted and Faith. I just thought you should be the one to explain things to her."

"Is something wrong?" Erin asked.

"Oh, not really," Nina said. "I'll fill you in."

"You two discuss matters," Mara said. "You could sit in the front room. It's quiet there now. Just remember to keep your voices down."

"Oh, Erin, I can't wait for you to meet the twins." Nina led her sister away.

Mara stepped inside the suite and closed the door. Almost immediately, someone knocked. She answered it.

"Excuse me."

"Ezra! Good morning."

"One of my men returned this morning. He carried this message for you."

She took the envelope, broke the wax seal, then read the missive silently: *Mara. Had to write immediately. Thought I saw Edmond Chantry as we left the inn. He's trouble. Use care. We're all well.* It was signed: *Adele.* Mara bit her lip.

"Anything important?"

"I don't know. It's from Adele. I'll have to talk to Dixon about this." She refolded the note. "Thank you Ezra." She closed the door behind him, then turned as the door to Dixon's room opened.

He stepped out. "Oh, there you are, back already. You made good time."

"It was a quick and easy trip." She reopened Adele's note and handed it to him. "What do you make of this?"

"Something wrong?"

She shrugged. "Maybe I'm just jumpy. Edmond saw me reappear here, and that took some explaining, and then that note arrived."

Dixon read silently. He looked up.

"What do you suppose she means?"

He refolded the missive. "You know, when I was at the palace, I thought at first that Edmond seemed mighty chummy with Lilith. But then he'd catch my eye and shrug his shoulders or roll his eyes. I realized he was just putting on an act. It was his way of humoring her and keeping the peace."

"So you don't think there's anything to this? You know, sometimes I worry about so many people who know about all of this—about us—about the girls. And so many who've not sworn to protect them. Like— Well, like Edmond, and Ezra's men—"

"Ted and Faith," he added.

"Right." She exhaled slowly. "But you think there's nothing to this?" She sought his reassurance.

He shook his head. "Nah, Edmond is the quintessential politician. He knows that the best way to keep peace with Lilith is to make her the center of attention." He chuckled. "And boy does he! For a time there, it bothered me. But like I said, he just knows how to stroke her."

"That's certainly a relief."

Chapter Forty

The camp had been in turmoil all day, indeed since late the evening before when a visitor arrived unexpectedly. Velia wondered what all the fuss had to do with her. She looked out the back of her wagon at the guard who summoned her.

"In a minute," she said. She shivered as she contemplated what Lilith might want. She wrapped her cape over her shoulders and lifted the tarp.

In just the last week or ten days, winter had let up its hold. Icicles hanging from her wagon melted as it basked in the warm sun. Puddles and mud replaced most of the former snow cover. But with all that, the air remained quite cool.

"Don't keep her waiting," the guard chided.

She scowled, felt for her Oathtaker's blade just to reassure herself it was in its sheath, then started down the steps. He reached out to help her, but she brushed his hand away. "What does she want?"

"No idea." He walked toward Lilith's wagon, Velia in his wake. "Your guest!" he called upon their arrival.

Lilith lifted the tarp at the back of her wagon. "That will be all, Freeman," she said. "In," she commanded with a wave of her hand.

Velia climbed up and entered.

A man sat in a chair next to Lilith's rumpled bed. He was slim, dressed all in black.

So, this must be the visitor that set the camp into such an uproar. She sat, then took down the hood of her cape. She found the wagon unexpectedly warm and that it smelled, sickeningly, of roses, lilies—and wine.

"Ma'am?"

Lilith, dressed only in a robe and looking disheveled, wore an expression like a beast that had cornered its prey. "I have someone I'd like you to meet," she said, "and then I have a request to make of you."

"Certainly," Velia replied. Inwardly, she cursed. She couldn't wait to get away from this monster, but she needed more information.

Lilith sat on the edge of her bed and leaned down on one arm. The front of her robe draped open toward the man in black. The Oathtaker looked his direction, then stifled a grin as she saw his eyes on the prize.

"This is Edmond."

For the first time, the man glanced Velia's way. His eyes slowly ran over her.

She glanced at Lilith, wondering how the woman would react to his leering, but she appeared ignorant of what had transpired. "Edmond," Velia said with a nod. She despised him already.

Lilith grasped a curl of her golden locks and wrapped it around her fingers. "Edmond has just brought me the most wonderful news."

"And what news is that?"

"You remember I told you about an imposter child?"

"You mean the child someone is trying to pawn off as a seventh seventh?"

"That's the one," Edmond said.

Lilith frowned at him, then turned back to Velia. "That's the one," she said.

"What of this child?"

"Well, as I mentioned before, we cannot allow such a trick to be played out on the people."

"But surely the child is innocent."

The woman glared. "Well yes, of course the *child* is innocent, and no harm will come to her. But those responsible for this must be stopped."

Liar! You do mean her harm! "Of course. What can I do?"

"I need for you to accompany me."

The Oathtaker smiled inwardly. "When do we leave?"

"Oh, you darling!" Lilith purred. "Didn't I tell you, Edmond, that she is a darling?"

"Yes," he said, his eyes returning to take in another dose of Velia's beauty.

She shifted uncomfortably under his stare, then cringed when he licked his lips at her. "Well of course, Lilith, I'm happy to assist you. When do we leave?"

"First thing tomorrow morning."

"But won't it take longer than that for all of the—men—to break camp?"

Lilith pointed to a bottle of wine and some glasses. "Edmond, do be a dear and do the honors."

"Certainly."

"Yes, I'm sure it would take the men longer than that to break camp," she said, "but they're not going."

Edmond poured the wine, then handed a glass to each of the women.

Velia resisted cringing when her hand inadvertently touched his. "Not going?"

"No. There will be the three of us and one additional guard."

"You think that's safe?"

"Safe? Why, that's why you're going to accompany me." Lilith put her glass down.

"But I'm not your Oathtaker. If anyone should recognize you as one of the Select—"

"No, you're not my Oathtaker, but as I told you earlier, that's neither here nor there. The point is, your presence will keep anyone from trying to harm me if they do recognize me as one of the Select. What's more, people aren't accustomed to seeing an unattended Select, so it will help to keep questions at a minimum." Lilith rolled her eyes. "I simply abhor questions."

Velia set her glass down. "I'll be ready."

"Fortunately, you haven't got much to take. We'll need to keep it light. We won't be taking a wagon."

"I'm a good rider."

"I knew you would be. You may see yourself out now."

The Oathtaker turned to go as Lilith whispered to Edmond. "Well now, where were we?"

He chuckled meaningfully in response.

Velia motioned to the guard to see her to her wagon. Once there, she found her backpack and put her few things inside it. She stopped to thank the Good One that she would accompany Lilith on the trip. Now all she had to do was find out who and where the child was. With that information, she could give the infant's caretakers sufficient warning.

On further reflection, that was rather a tall order.

Morning arrived with a steady rain. At a shout from Freeman, Velia rolled out of bed. She stretched and changed into her day clothes, then pulled on her boots. Quickly she combed through her hair and ran a brush over her teeth. She unsnapped the leather strap holding an extra weapon inside her boot so she could retrieve it quickly if need be, grasped her cloak, wrapped it over her shoulders, and then made her way out of her wagon.

The rain slapped down. She followed Freeman to Lilith's wagon, doing her best to avoid puddles. Most of the camp still slept. Campfires sizzled and smoked in the rain.

"Your guest!" Freeman called.

Edmond stuck his head out. "Wait there."

"I see you've been replaced," Velia whispered to her guard.

"Not for long."

"Really," she taunted.

"I'm going to kill him," he muttered through his teeth and under his breath.

"You'll have to get in line," she quipped.

Lilith emerged from the wagon, dressed in black. It was the first time Velia had seen her in anything other than red. She was surprised the woman could stay warm in such a light dress and one with such a plunging neckline. She didn't know Lilith kept warm with the burning heat of Daeva.

When Lilith's feet touched the ground she turned toward Freeman, his arms around her, her face just inches from his. She hesitated for a moment as though lost in thought, then thrust her pelvis forward and tossed her head to the side, leaving a long expanse of décolletage and cleavage for his eyes. A long moment passed.

"You can let go now," she whispered.

Edmond made his way to the ground, Pooch in one arm.

"Don't forget to keep an eye on Pooch when I'm gone," Lilith said to Freeman as she took her pet.

"I won't forget."

"Are our horses ready?"

"As you ordered."

"Lead the way then." She grasped his arm.

The foursome made their way through the main camp. It was the first time Velia had been through the area. She fought with herself to keep from showing her disgust. The tents were in shambles, the thoroughfare spotted with refuse, dog dung, and rotting food scraps that even the hounds would not eat.

Outside one tent, a woman sat near what had been a campfire. Her long hair, wet from the rain, hung down over her shoulders and bruised face. Blood from a long jagged laceration across her cheek ran in the rainwater down her face and neck. Velia fought to tear her eyes from the woman's gaze.

Lilith marched on by as though nothing was out of the ordinary or worthy of note.

The Oathtaker tried to keep her eyes forward so she wouldn't see the misery around her, but some of the sights pulled her attention against her will. A young woman held her own clearly broken forearm in her other hand. In apparent shock, she swayed back and forth, lost in some other place. Though her mouth was open, no sound escaped her lips.

Another victim, barely more than a child, kneeled in the mud. She keened as she pulled at her shift upon which was a large spot of blood. It screamed out in the gray morning surroundings. A dead woman was on the ground near her. Her limbs were twisted, her chest motionless, her eyes open, as though she'd watched her spirit set out on its journey into eternity.

After several minutes of passing by more similar scenes, Velia let go of her tears, relieved that the rain hid them.

Finally, they arrived at the stables. Two men stood holding the reins of four horses.

Freeman assisted Lilith to mount. "'At's Bob, ya got," he said.

When the guard tried to assist Velia, she held her hand out to stop him, then hung her backpack on the saddle and swung into place. The guard turned away.

"Wait. What's her name?"

"Victory."

She patted the horse's neck. "Good, Victory." She hoped her mount's name was an omen of good things to come.

"Careful with that one," the guard cautioned as Edmond approached his mount.

"Why is that?"

"His name is Donagh. He's fast and he's strong."

Edmond pulled on the reins. Donagh bucked and screamed.

"Whoa! Whoa!" the guard scolded. He didn't hide his disdain.

Edmond scowled at the guard, but let up on the reins. Moments later, the animal quieted, though its eyes remained afire.

Finally, the guard who'd cautioned Edmond and who it turned out would accompany the group, mounted his horse, a large gray gelding. Well over six foot tall, he wore little against the cold: light linen pants and a sleeveless vest that exaggerated his biceps and abdominal muscles. From his belt hung numerous knives, an axe, a weapon with a long curved blade, and one that consisted of a chain on each end of which hung metal balls with protruding spikes. At his side he carried a sword and from his knee-high boots hung more knives. Tattoos of serpents with their mouths open and fangs exposed, decorated his shaved head and body.

Lilith introduced the guard as "Jabari."

He didn't acknowledge her traveling companions. He simply awaited her orders.

They started out. A flock of crows lifted into the air around them like an escort. Velia had noticed more of the vagrants around the camp in the past day or so. She cringed at the volume of their collective caw and settled in for a long day.

The countryside passed by. A few patches of snow remained on the sides of rocks and hills that, throughout the long winter, had been shaded from direct sunlight.

The escort of crows circled over the group. From time to time one dropped down to peck at some refuse or carrion along the way. They cawed and swore at one another to Velia's utter frustration and Lilith's apparent delight.

After several hours, the sun made its way through the blanket of cloud cover and feebly began warming the air. Even so, as her clothing was damp from the cold rain, Velia shivered constantly. She wrapped her cloak more tightly around herself. Were it not for Victory's body heat, she thought her teeth would chatter.

Late in the day, the travelers stopped at a small country inn. The guard, who ate and slept in the stables, kept his distance at all times. Velia had hoped she might get more information about where they were headed from him, but it seemed that at least for now, her hope had been in vain.

CHAPTER FORTY-ONE

The days wore on, their pattern never changing: riding, eating, waiting, sleeping, riding, eating, waiting, sleeping. Velia grew tired of the monotony and more and more concerned with the passing time, that Lilith and Edmond would never discuss what she wished to know.

Finally, on the fifth evening, after making their way through a particularly desolate area, the travelers came upon an inn, the first they'd seen for hours. Little more than a shack, it sported a weathered sign that read *The Resting Place* in flaking blue and orange paint along with a depiction of what might once have been a setting sun.

Gray and dilapidated, the place boasted cracked windows with missing shutters. Crows alighted upon the building's roof, weathervane, and chimney top, from whence they maintained a constant cawing conversation.

Lilith and Edmond entered while Velia waited outside with Jabari, who paid her no attention. Minutes later Lilith emerged after arranging for their rooms.

The wooden steps leading to the front door, weak with age, threatened to collapse at any moment under an unsuspecting visitor's weight. The Oathtaker held her breath in anticipation of the worst when she stepped on the first tread, then cautiously made her way up.

The moment she entered the rickety inn, the odor of decay assaulted her. A cat, rat, mouse, mole, or other creature, left the odor behind as its only lasting hold to the world of the living. Likely the varmint had died somewhere within the inn's walls.

As she stepped through the dust and old dead bugs littering the floor, a sudden urge to wash her hands overcame her. Fearing the infestation of lice or other unwanted visitors upon her person, Velia pulled her cloak tightly around herself. She imagined her skin crawling with vermin.

The proprietor's clothing was filthy, pestiferous. Velia cringed upon the sight of his bare feet with toenails, long and dirty, and his few remaining teeth, crooked and decayed. He showed the travelers to their rooms.

Sick to her stomach, Velia passed on dinner, informing Lilith she'd be in her room.

On each of the last evenings, Lilith had stayed in a room across or down the hall from the Oathtaker, but this time the only two rooms available were next to one another on the same side of the hallway.

Velia entered the one appointed her. Inside she found a single cot, a small table upon which sat a lamp low on oil, and a wooden chair. An aged and threadbare quilt covered the bed. She pulled the blanket back. Sheets, clearly unwashed for some time, greeted her. She fought back a gag reflex. Grimacing, she stepped away.

Better I should sleep in the stables with the horses. They're cleaner and smell better.

Hoping the squalor surrounding her would at least present her with an opportunity to get information, she surveyed, inch by inch, the wall separating her room from Lilith's. She looked for any weakness in it through which she might hear something.

There!

She ran her fingers over a knothole. She had to be sure that Lilith wouldn't notice the opening, or she'd censure her speech.

What would give away its presence? Light. Sound.

Quickly, before the woman returned to her room, Velia placed a chair near the opening in the wall. Then she turned out her light, vowing she'd wait in that same exact place and position all night if she had to. She offered a quick prayer for strength, and then sat.

Blast!

The chair squeaked. She got back up and moved it out of the way. Then she placed a small blanket from her pack on the floor and sat back down. She groaned. The place reeked. She covered her face with her sleeve to shut out the worst of the smell and prepared for her vigil.

Tired, she closed her eyes. Her head sprang up when someone knocked on her door.

"Velia?" Lilith called.

The Oathtaker didn't answer, didn't move.

Another knock sounded out. "Velia?" This time it was Edmond.

She sat quietly watching shadows at the crack beneath her door.

"Must be sleeping," Lilith said.

The shadows retreated. Fully awake now, the Oathtaker leaned gently against the wall. She heard the door to the next room open.

"You can go now, Edmond."

"But—"

"Really, Edmond, I'm tired."

"Not tired of me, I hope."

There was no sound for a moment. "You?" The hesitation in Lilith's response lent a lack of credibility to her words. "No, of course not. How could I be when you've nearly delivered them to me."

Them?

"Just a short time now to go. A week or so," he said.

Lilith moaned. "Mmmmm, yes. I can almost feel the satisfaction already."

"What do you think will be the best part?" Edmond's voice was muffled, lost in what Velia surmised was Lilith's breast.

Sounds of shuffling made their way through the wall, cutting off the next few words. Then came the end of Lilith's comments, ". . . and of course, the children."

Children? I thought she was looking for a single child.

"Astounding, isn't it?"

"One would have been enough. But two? Isn't it just like Rowena to pull a stunt like this!"

Two children? Rowena's? She bore twins? *But the Select never had twins!*

There were more unintelligible sounds, then Lilith said, "And that woman. She'll pay."

"He seems entirely smitten with her."

Who? Who's 'she?' Who's 'he?' With whom is 'he' smitten?

All was silent for a minute. "I'll kill him," Lilith then said, her words as clear as though she stood right next to Velia. "I'll kill them all."

The Oathtaker nearly gasped, the voice sounded so close. She willed herself to remain still. She wondered if Lilith had discovered the knothole. Then the voice quieted again. "Really, Edmond, I'm tired."

Velia thought about what she'd heard and what it all meant. So Rowena had born twins. But who was the woman to whom they referred? And where were they all going anyway?

Dear Ehyeh, tell me more. Use me. Guide me. Help me!

The day dawned with a weak sun that crept in through the dirty window. A few of the first birds of spring called out to one another, breaking the silence of the countryside, but the crows' screeching on the grounds of, and in the air around the inn, quickly drowned them out.

Velia continued to find it odd that wherever Lilith went, the scavengers followed and even seemed to multiply. Did the woman do something purposefully to attract them? Or did they simply follow her of their own accord? Crows had always reminded the Oathtaker of darkness and evil. Now that feeling intensified.

She ached all over. Her head hurt from the stink of the inn. Her knees rebelled from her nightlong position. Her back cramped as though someone had locked her inside a box for days.

She tried to stretch out her kinks and pains, but her efforts were to little avail. She held her head between her hands for a moment. It throbbed to the beat of her heart. Today would be difficult riding, but she couldn't let on that she'd not slept or Lilith might grow suspicious.

She listened for sounds from the next room. When it was clear that Lilith had awakened and was preparing to leave, Velia collected her things. After what seemed an eternity, a knock came at her door.

"Are you ready?" Lilith asked.

"Certainly." Velia followed Lilith and Edmond down the stairs. She couldn't wait to take in a breath of fresh air.

When she stepped outside, she breathed in deeply. Unfortunately, the stink of the place seemed stuck in her nostrils. She found a hankie in her pack and blew her nose. It didn't help. She tried again.

"Something wrong?"

Velia looked at Lilith. "Oh, no. Why?"

"You sick or something?"

"No, just trying to clear my nose of the smell of the place."

Lilith's brow furrowed. "The smell of the place?" She looked back at the inn. "What smell?"

The Oathtaker, shocked to realize that the woman had been unaware of the stench of death permeating The Resting Place, glanced at the inn, then turned her gaze back. For a moment her mouth hung open. "Oh," she finally said, "I just meant that it was dusty in there."

Lilith raised her head. Her chin jutted forward. "Let's go."

They met up with Jabari who'd already prepared their horses, then set out with him in the lead.

Velia rode behind Lilith and Edmond, hoping they might pick up their conversation from the night before. Finally, a few relevant words floated back her way including "City of Light." She surmised that they might be headed there.

When the day wound to a close, they again found refuge. Fortunately, the accommodations were better than the night before. Unfortunately, Velia's room was across the hall from Lilith's.

After dinner, the Oathtaker excused herself and made her way up the stairs. For a moment, she stood outside her door. The innkeeper's wife, a short plump woman with manly features and mannerisms, passed behind.

"Excuse me, ma'am?"

"Yes?"

"Is that room taken?" Velia pointed to a room diagonal to her own.

"Is there something wrong with your room?"

"Oh, no, thank you for asking. I was just . . . curious."

"Do you want me to change your accommodations? No one is checked in there yet."

"No, but thank you." The Oathtaker went into her room, waited for a minute, then re-opened her door a crack and peeked into the hall as the innkeeper's wife descended the stairs.

Velia darted across the hall and tried the door handle. It turned. She stepped inside, shut the door, then approached the wall separating the room from Lilith's.

A built-in closet occupied one corner. She entered it, closed the door, then allowed her eyes to adjust to the darkness. With her hands, she examined the wall. She found an opening, though it was very small. She might be able to hear if she had her ear right to it. She retraced her steps back to her own room, then waited.

A short time later, Lilith and Edmond made their way up the stairs. When a knock came at her door, Velia opened it.

"We'll leave at first light," Lilith said cryptically.

"I'll be ready. Is that all?"

"That's all."

Lilith entered her room. Edmond, behind her, turned Velia's way. His eyes ran up and down her form. Carrying a bottle of wine and two glasses, he motioned to her, suggesting he'd be willing to share with her rather than with Lilith. The Oathtaker stood firm at his effrontery, but she certainly hoped the alcohol would loosen his lips. She closed her door and paced.

The minutes dragged. She pulled her hair back and tied it up. She cracked open her door. The hallway was empty. She crossed the hall and then, upon hearing someone at the bottom of the stairs, quickly entered the room next to Lilith's. She tiptoed to the closet, stepped inside, dropped down to the floor, then pressed her ear to the wall.

"But you can't do anything at sanctuary," came Edmond's voice.

"Of course I can."

"But—"

"Oh, Edmond, the only sanctuary I need fear is the one in Polesk."

"I don't understand."

"It was built with magic."

"Really?" He sounded surprised.

"Yes. The windows were made from the magic of Oathtakers. I could not, now that I serve Daeva, do anything there."

Daeva! Lilith serves Daeva? Oh, she must be stopped!

"But I thought that was true of all sanctuaries."

"No, it's a myth—that all sanctuaries were built with magic—that the Select perpetuated. It serves them well."

"So you think—"

Velia could not hear the rest of Edmond's question.

The cork of the wine bottle popped.

"Well of course we can't stay at the—what was the name of that place?"

Edmond's response was too quiet to hear.

"Yes, well we can hardly go riding up to the door there, Edmond, and ask for them. But—"

This time it was Lilith's words that Velia could not make out.

"Maybe," Edmond said.

"You said Dixon trusted you—that you won Mara over."

"He does, and I did. But Dixon is just so . . . insufferable. There's definitely something going on between those two."

"But you could get them to go where you direct?"

"I think so."

"We have to take them by surprise, you know."

"Yes, I know. From what Dixon says, Mara takes her position as Oathtaker to the girls very seriously. He says she studies all the time, that she's consumed with issues like what she's to do if the interests of the girls are at odds—things like that."

"Well I intend to put her to the test."

"I wonder whose interests she'd put first if *Dixon's* were at odds with those of the girls."

"Oh, Edmond, that *is* a delicious thought!"

He laughed. "I understand her magic is very strong—but there are limits. She can't travel with the girls and Dixon at the same time."

Travel? What does that mean?

"How do you intend to take her down anyway?" Edmond asked.

"What? She's not vulnerable to a good old-fashioned stabbing? The point of an arrow? Or have you forgotten this?"

What is 'this?' Velia tried to peek through the hole in the wall, but the opening was too small to see anything.

"You intend to use that?"

"Why not?" Lilith quipped. "It would serve all those do-gooders right to—"

The rest was unintelligible.

Edmond laughed. Glasses clinked.

Velia gasped as the door to the room in which she was in, opened. From outside the closet door came voices.

"Will this do?" the innkeeper asked. "There's a place for your things, water, soap, and towels." A second passed in silence. "The dining room is still open. Or we can bring your dinner here if you like."

"Yes, that would be good. Thank you."

Velia's heart beat wildly. She could be stuck here all night. There would be trouble if Lilith looked for her later.

"On second thought, no. No, thank you. I'll get settled in and then be down for dinner shortly."

Slowly, Velia exhaled. She listened as the innkeeper left the room, then rose to her feet. She stood behind the door, in the event it opened. Just as she made her way there, it did. She tightened up against the wall. The pattern of light on the floor grew. Then it stopped and the door closed again.

Her heart still pounding, she listened for more. Something dropped on the floor, then water splashed. Minutes later, the door to the room opened and closed. She waited. Might he return? Did she dare stay to hear more? No, she couldn't risk someone finding her in a stranger's room.

She peeked out. The room was empty. She made her way to the door that exited into the hallway. Placing her ear to it, she listened. She heard nothing. *Wait* . . . Someone knocked on a door, once, then twice. Apparently, no one answered. Were they knocking on *her* door? More seconds passed, then someone went down the stairs.

Again the Oathtaker peeked out. Finding the way clear, she dashed across the hall and opened her door. She stepped inside and turned to close it, just as Lilith's door opened.

"Going somewhere?"

"Lilith, did you knock?" Velia's breath came heavy in her fear and surprise. "I'm sorry, I must have dropped off."

"No, I didn't knock."

"Oh, all right then. I thought I heard someone knocking at my door. I guess it awakened me, but it must have been for someone else."

Lilith smiled weakly. Her eyes narrowed. "Velia, I'd like for you to ride next to me tomorrow."

"Me! But I thought you preferred Edmond's company."

"I just think it would be good to get to know you a bit better."

"Well, I'd be . . . honored. Good night, ma'am."

Lilith said nothing.

Velia closed her door. She leaned her back against it and exhaled slowly. That was a close call, but she'd learned so much. Now she could make her way to the City of Light to find Dixon and this—Mara, warn them of the danger they were in, and tell them how Lilith intended to trap them and to harm the girls.

Did she dare leave tonight? No, she'd best get some sleep first. If she was to make her way to the city before Lilith, it was essential she first see to that detail.

CHAPTER FORTY-TWO

They traveled over rocky terrain cut through by the river that ran north to south across Oosa and that wound its way through the City of Light. It was evidence they neared their destination.

Lilith insisted that Velia ride near her and behaved as though she didn't want the Oathtaker out of her sight. For the past two nights she'd even arranged for them to room together. Knowing Lilith observed her carefully, Velia felt more and more like a prisoner with each passing moment.

She led Victory into the stables when Lilith went inside to arrange for their rooms. Edmond, awaiting Jabari's assistance with Bob and Donagh, eyed her closely—and much to her chagrin. She longed for a moment alone, a moment to give thought to how she might escape Lilith's clutches. She started removing Victory's saddle.

"I've got it," Jabari said, startling her out of her reverie.

"No, really, I'd like to groom her myself this time."

He shrugged and walked away.

Moments later, Lilith returned. "Your room is ready, Velia."

The Oathtaker looked up. "I'd like to see to Victory myself this evening."

Lilith sighed. "Very well, but I'll expect you in for dinner soon." She turned to Jabari. "The staff will deliver yours here," she said, then headed back to the inn with Edmond.

Currycombs and brushes hung from rusty nails on the wall. Velia started in with her task. Stopping to offer Victory a handful of grain, she smiled at the whisper soft feel of the equine's muzzle. She patted her neck. "Good girl."

"She's not going to let you out of her sight, you know," came a voice just above a whisper.

Velia turned at the sound. Jabari stood just feet away from her. She stepped back and instinctively reached for her blade.

"You won't be needing your blade," he said as he hefted Bob's saddle off the beast. He turned away to place it over a sawhorse. What would have been a burden to the average person appeared of little difficulty to the brawny man.

Velia's eyes followed his every move. "What are you talking about?"

He looked toward the inn, then back at her. "Something roused her suspicions. What'd you do?"

Her eyes narrowed. "Nothing."

"Well if you're going to get away from her, which it appears to me—and apparently to her, as well—has been your objective for days now, you're going to need my help." He removed Donagh's saddle.

"And why would I accept help from you?"

"Because," he stood unwavering, "Lilith is an evil woman and she must be stopped."

"Wh—ah—" She stuttered. "What are you talking about? You—one of her hired thugs?"

"Wasn't hired." He set the saddle down and started grooming Bob's coat.

Velia turned back to brush Victory. "You weren't hired? What? You joined Lilith's campaign of death for the fun of it?" She glanced at Jabari. "You're despicable."

He stepped toward her. "I wasn't hired, I'm not one of her 'thugs,' and I have no part in her plans."

She bit the inside of her cheek and looked him over carefully. "You certainly look like one of them."

"Well then, I guess my disguise has served its intended purpose." He stepped away, then resumed grooming Bob.

Velia watched him for a long moment. "Well, you're certainly a man of few words. So, are you just going to leave me in suspense here? What's this all about?"

He turned toward her and reached back. When he brought his hand forward, he held what was unmistakably an Oathtaker's blade.

Her mouth dropped open. Her eyes narrowed. "I don't understand."

He put his finger to his lips and looked toward the inn where someone had just stepped out. Seconds later, the smell of burning pipe tobacco wafted through the air. When it reached the inside of the stables, Victory stomped a foot and snorted. Velia patted the animal's back, hip, then rump, as she made her way around to the other side.

"Tell me more, Jabari."

"Name's not Jabari."

She sighed. "You know, Lilith is likely to come out here, or to send someone to check on me, any minute now. Do you think you could dispense with the 'strong and silent' image long enough to just fill me in? What are you doing with her? Why didn't you tell me earlier that you're an Oathtaker? Why haven't you tried to stop her?"

She checked herself, realizing that her voice had risen. "I don't understand," she said, dropping to a whisper.

Jabari glanced at her. "Keep your voice down. Keep busy there, and listen up.

My name is Jerrett. I lived in one of the towns Lilith passed through on her campaign shortly before you showed up. When I saw what was happening, I knew I had to learn more. Who'd believe any of what we've seen?"

He brushed Bob. "I dressed myself as close to the look of Lilith's men as I could so I would fit in. Fortunately I have some leftover tattoos from my young and restless days. They don't know who's who anyway." He put the brush down. "As to doing something to stop Lilith, I might ask you the same thing."

She pursed her lips. "Go on."

"That's pretty much it. I infiltrated. Later, I offered to accompany Lilith on this mission. None of the others wanted to go anyway, so that part was easy. That's all."

He moved Bob back and brought Donagh forth. "Quiet down. Quiet down," he said to the animal, stroking its neck gently. As though by magic, the horse shook its head and dropped it in submission.

"You have a way with him."

"He's mine. We're closely connected by attendant magic."

"Why aren't you riding him yourself? Why have Edmond ride him?"

"Like I said, we're closely connected by attendant magic."

"So—what? He talks to you?"

"Not exactly."

"What then?"

"Sometimes he acts as my ears."

"Any other powers?"

Jerrett shrugged. "Mostly just powers related to hearing. You know, like the ability to hear at considerable distances, that sort of thing."

"Why didn't you say something earlier?"

His face registered no emotion. "Because I thought you might be helping Lilith."

"And now you don't?"

He smirked and shook his head. "Here's a little advice. Don't look so anxious to get away from her. Smother her with your presence, your willingness to be of service. When she's convinced of your loyalty, she'll grow tired of you and give you some space."

Velia turned back to her task and finished grooming Victory, then brushed her cheek against the animal's neck. She turned back to Jerrett. "So did you choose Victory for me?"

"Mmhmmm."

"Thank you. She's been great."

"Mmhmmm."

"I guess I'd best get back. Put your proposal into effect. Thank you, Jerrett."

He stared hard at her. "Name's Jabari."

"Right. Jabari. I won't forget. Thank you—Jerrett. You give me hope."

Velia walked back to the inn, dodging the crows that flew near, stifling her smile.

Velia put Jerrett's advice into effect immediately, offering to see to Lilith's every need, to assist her in every way possible. Gradually, the woman seemed to relax. Velia knew she'd won her over when Lilith again started, a couple days later, to share her room with Edmond.

Finishing off her cup of tea, the Oathtaker shook off the irritation she felt when she found Edmond's eyes upon her. Turning toward Lilith, she asked if there was anything more she could do.

"No, but I'd like to get an early start in the morning. I believe we'll arrive in the city sometime tomorrow."

"Very well. If you don't mind then, I think I'll call it a night."

Lilith handed over a key. "Your room is the last one on the left at the top of the stairs. I'll be just across the hall."

"Thank you."

"I'll awaken you at first light."

The Oathtaker headed up the stairs. She so wanted to speak more with Jerrett. Now that she'd regained Lilith's trust, she might be able to get away and make her way to the city. She could go tonight. Would he help her?

For a change, their accommodations were impeccable. Velia dropped her cloak over a chair and cleaned up, grateful for the fresh water, the soap, and the clean towels in her room. Wiping her face dry, inhaling deeply of the scent of lavender, she went to the window and looked out.

All three moons were in different stages of waning, so there was little light. Every time she witnessed the phenomenon, she recollected the prophecies that told of dark events that would transpire when all three moons were new, the sky left void of moonlight. It was an enormously rare event, only happening once every few hundred years. A shiver ran down her spine as she contemplated what dark things such days—or *nights* as the case may be—might bring.

Glancing toward the stables, she spotted Jerrett scanning the exterior of the inn. She opened her window, letting in the crisp early nighttime air of late winter, early spring. It invigorated her. She leaned out a few inches.

When Jerrett saw her, he tilted his head downwards, silently entreating her to meet him at the stables. She nodded her agreement, but she couldn't leave until Lilith and Edmond were down for the night, so she held up a finger, indicating that he should wait.

He sat on a bench outside the stables and slid his legs out long before him, as though at rest.

She paced, waiting for Lilith to retire. Finally came the sound of footsteps down the hall. Velia listened at her door as Lilith and Edmond entered their room. She would wait a bit longer.

Time seemed to drag. She paced, occasionally stopping to glance out her window. Jerrett didn't move.

Finally, the Oathtaker opened her door. She glanced up and down the hall. Light peeked out from below some of the doors, but not from the one across the hall. She drew closer and placed her ear to it. Silence responded. She closed her own door, leaving it unlocked for easy and quiet access upon her return, then made her way down the stairs.

At a small table in the entrance to the inn sat a lamp, its wick turned down low. Velia's eyes darted around the room. No one manned the reception desk. She exited the inn and walked to the stables, offering a silent prayer of gratitude that the crows had quieted for the night.

Jerrett was gone. Just as she was about to step inside the barn to find him, someone grabbed her from behind and put a hand over her mouth. Startled, she tried to pull away.

"Shhh, it's me."

When she relaxed, Jerrett removed his hand.

She turned around as he held a finger to his lips and tipped his head to the side. Her eyes followed the gesture. There, just inside the barn, a stable boy leaned against a bale of hay, apparently asleep.

"You frightened me," she whispered.

Jerrett grasped her arm. He was gentle, notwithstanding his enormous size and strength. He led her around the back of the building. Carefully, they stepped around an old broken cart, shovels and rakes, and an upside down wheelbarrow. Then, he directed her to a bench under the roof of a defunct lean-to.

The night insects stilled. Even the lightflies went momentarily dark.

Velia reached out to test the bench's integrity. Satisfied it was safe, she sat. Jerrett followed suit.

The music of the insects, the glimmer of the lightflies, resumed.

"I was hoping to have an opportunity to speak with you," she said.

"I take it things are going better with Lilith?"

"Yes, thank you for your insight and your suggestions. They worked."

"Don't mention it."

She leaned forward. "I need to get away. I need to warn someone. You'll help me, won't you?"

"No."

"No!"

He put his hand out to silence her. "No, I don't think that's the right plan."

"Excuse me?"

"I've listened in on Lilith and Edmond."

"Listened in? You mean, with Donagh's assistance?"

Jerrett chuckled. "That's right."

"What did you hear?"

"Something about a child, or children, I couldn't make that part out for sure."

"Children. Two. Rowena's seventh born."

His eyes widened. "There *is* a new seventh seventh then."

Velia tucked some of her hair back behind her ear. "Sort of. Well, that is, in part." She hesitated. "You recall ever hearing about a seventh seventh 'who is but is not?'"

"Sounds vaguely familiar."

"I think that's what we're dealing with here. A seventh seventh and her *twin*. It seems an interesting way to describe a child of a seventh pregnancy who isn't seventh born."

"I think you're right."

"I had an instructor once," Velia said as she batted a moth away, "who was fascinated with prophecy. He used to talk about that one in particular. It stumped him. He couldn't figure it out, but I think I could tell him now."

Jerrett nodded, contemplating. "What made you decide to go along with Lilith?" he finally asked.

"I knew she lied. That's how I discovered the facts about the children."

"How did you know that?"

"Attendant magic."

"Discernment of truth and falsehood?"

"That's right."

"So you didn't just overhear their conversations while we've been traveling?"

"Some, but not much. Lilith has been very careful." Again, Velia's hair fell forward. She untied it completely, then pulled it all up and retied it. "Lilith told me one day that someone was trying to pawn off an imposter child as a seventh seventh. I knew she lied. I kept asking questions, trying to get more information. She's been pretty close-mouthed, but I did manage to learn of the child, and I believe that Lilith intends to kill her.

"She went on her murderous campaign hoping that someone would give the child up to her. It wasn't until Edmond came to camp that she discovered Rowena had born *two* children. Now, I wonder, am I to report her to the Council? She's not the legitimate head of the first family."

"Let me think." Jerrett rubbed his head. "Who's this 'Dixon' she and Edmond keep discussing?"

"I don't know what Edmond's relationship to Dixon is, but it seems quite personal. From what I've been able to pick up, Dixon thinks they're great friends. According to Edmond, the man trusts him implicitly—so much so that Edmond believes he can deliver Dixon to Lilith. But Edmond is obsessed with getting even with him for something."

"Do you know anything about this—Dixon?"

"All I know for sure is that he was Rowena's Oathtaker."

"Oh, of course, Dixon Townsend."

"You know him?"

"No. I knew his brothers. I met one of them during my training and the other when I traveled back home with him to the hinterlands for a summer." Jerrett stood. "Now, who's this 'Mara' person they've mentioned?"

"The girls' Oathtaker. Dixon is with her. I understand they're somewhere in the city. I want to go find them and warn them."

"You'd never find them. Not in a city that size. And even if you could, why would Dixon believe you? If what you say is true, he wouldn't believe that Edmond would betray him. No, it would be better for him to confront Edmond directly."

"But that could put the children in grave danger!" Velia got to her feet. She seemed miniature compared to Jerrett's immense stature and bulk.

"I just don't see how it's possible."

Her shoulders sagged. "You're probably right. I wouldn't even know where to start."

The Oathtakers started back around the building. As they rounded the corner, Velia saw someone walking to the stable. She turned toward Jerrett and threw her arms around his neck. She drew him forward and then, as he started pulling away, got up on her tiptoes, leaned in, and whispered, "Someone's coming!"

"There you are."

Velia released Jerrett quickly, in feigned embarrassment. There was no mistaking that voice. "Lilith," she said.

The woman's eyes, discernable by the lamplight coming from the stable, scanned up and down Jerrett. "Interesting choice in men, Velia."

"I'm sorry, Lilith." The Oathtaker frowned at Jerrett. "We didn't hear you coming," she said, her accusation not lost on him. Where had his attendant magic been when they'd needed it? *Increased powers of hearing indeed!*

Lilith lifted her chin. "Do I need to be concerned about this?"

Velia shuffled her feet. "No, ma'am, it won't happen again."

Lilith's gaze turned to Jerrett. "And what about you? I can't have her hanging out here in the stables. I need her assistance."

"Sorry, ma'am, it won't happen again."

"That's what I thought."

Velia went to Lilith's side. "Was there something you needed?"

"Me? No, I just couldn't sleep. I saw the light under your door and thought you might share a nightcap with me."

Velia cursed herself for leaving her lamp burning and her door unlocked, and cursed Jerrett for failing to hear Lilith's approach. "I'd like that, Lilith," she said. Inwardly, she groaned.

Chapter Forty-Three

Making their way through the streets and byways of the City of Light, the travelers slowed their pace as they neared sanctuary. Crowds meandered from one street vendor's stall to another, all the while trying to steer clear of the thousands of crows that had descended upon the city.

Food smells, both savory and sweet, filled the air: roasting lamb, fresh bread, cinnamon sprinkled almonds, sweet fruits, and fresh herbs.

Lilith and Edmond rode ahead, seemingly oblivious to the black varmints flying overhead. Velia frowned at the flock. It seemed to grow by the minute. It called to her mind an old childhood verse:

Black and loud
Like a cloud,
Come the crows
Murdering rogues.

Occasionally one swooped down to snatch food from the hands of a babe, or pecked someone who tried to keep his food away from the winged thief so hard, that the person's hands bled from the assault.

Lilith glanced at the crowds. Dressed in nondescript brown, and with her hood up, no one recognized her. She motioned for Velia to pull up.

"Where to?" the Oathtaker asked.

"Just there." Lilith designated with a nod, an inn situated on a corner. *The Home Place,* read its welcome sign. Already crows lined the ridge of the roof and sat on the veranda's railings that ran the full length of the building.

When she lifted her arm, one of the flock landed on it. The creature looked her full in the eye. She stroked the animal, then raised her arm into the air to push it off again. With a caw sounding distinctly like a scream, the vagrant flew away. It landed, seconds later, at the apex of the building.

The travelers reached the reception desk as a hotel guest complained that the crows' presence forced him indoors. "I'll not stay here another minute!" he exclaimed to the clerk's disappointment.

"I am sorry sir, but I'm afraid there's nothing we can do. The fliers report that the birds overtook the city today."

"Then we'll leave the city."

"But, Harry," whined the woman at his side, "we planned this trip for so long."

"We'll not stay, I say!" He slammed his fist on the desk. "First thing tomorrow, we leave this place!" He turned on his heel and walked away. His disappointed family followed behind.

"Two rooms, please," Lilith requested as she stepped forward.

The clerk looked up. "The crows haven't scared you off?"

"Not at all."

He glanced at his book, then grabbed two keys from a wall hook and handed them over. "You're just down the hall there," he directed.

"Can you arrange for baths to be delivered to our rooms?"

"Certainly, ma'am, we'll have them sent over immediately."

"Very well. Also, I'll need dinner sent out to our guide in the stables."

"Yes, ma'am."

When the travelers arrived outside their rooms, Lilith handed Edmond a key. "You'll stay here with me," she then said to Velia as she opened the door to a room.

After Lilith chose one of the beds, the Oathtaker sat on the other. She bent down to remove her boots. "Is everything all right?"

"Fine. Just fine. I just wanted to be certain you didn't repeat your former transgression and return to Jabari in the stables. I need you with me to see to my safety. I've much to attend to."

Velia said nothing; responding would serve no purpose.

A knock came at the door. She answered it. Outside stood two young men. They entered, pulling on the handle of a cart upon which a metal tub sat. Behind them followed two women carrying large pitchers of steaming water.

The men stepped behind a room divider arranged to offer privacy for dressers and bathers. They pulled on levers that locked the cart's wheels in place. Once done, the women poured their pitchers of hot water into the tub. Then they all left.

Lilith bathed first. When through, she ordered a second tub for Velia.

The Oathtaker stepped behind the divider, undressed, and got into the tub. Since Lilith was quiet, she felt no need to keep up a conversation. She washed her hair, scrubbed her skin with a luffa until it glowed pink, then leaned back and closed her eyes. She was surprised to find she'd fallen asleep when, suddenly, she awakened with a start.

The water swished.

"She'll be right back."

Velia sprang forward. Water sloshed around her, then ran over the tub's edge and onto the floor. "Edmond! What are you doing here?" She grabbed a nearby towel and held it against herself.

"Like I said, Lilith will be right back. She asked me to keep an eye on you." He cocked a brow. "Not a difficult duty."

"Get. Out."

He smirked. "Don't act so 'holier than thou.' Lilith told me all about your late night rendezvous with Jabari." He swished the bath water again. "Lovely," he said, as though to himself.

"Get out!"

"Or what? Or you'll use your blade on me and risk Lilith's ire? I don't think so."

Velia hated Edmond, but she didn't fear him, and she didn't care if her feelings showed. "Where is she?"

"Don't know. Maybe she thought to check in with Jabari herself."

"Get out of here, Edmond."

The sound of the door opening interrupted any further conversation. Edmond sprang to the other side of the divider as Lilith made her way in. "She awake?"

"Don't know. She hasn't said anything."

Velia sighed. Who would have thought she'd feel relief because of Lilith's presence? "I'm nearly through here," she called out. She stepped out of the tub, dried herself briskly, then dressed.

"Dinner is ready," Lilith said.

"I'll be ready in a minute." Velia retrieved her backpack, then found refuge again behind the divider. She rummaged for a comb. As she groomed her hair, she listened.

"This came for you," Lilith said.

"That was quick." Paper rustled. "They're still there," Edmond said.

"Why don't you send another message? Ask them to meet tomorrow at sanctuary." For a moment, no one spoke. "Are you about through?" Lilith asked, her voice raised.

"Yes." Velia finished tying up her hair.

On their way to dinner, Edmond stopped at the reception desk to arrange to send another message. Then the three ate, their conversation stilted. From time to time, Velia felt Edmond's eyes burning into her. When that happened, she sat up even straighter and glared back at him in response. He was a weasel. She wasn't going to let him intimidate or frighten her.

"For you, sir," said a waiter, leaning over to deliver a note.

Edmond opened the missive, perused it, then smiled. He nodded at Lilith.

"We've scheduled a meeting for tomorrow at sanctuary," Lilith said to Velia.

"Oh? Who'll we be seeing?"

"Just some friends of Edmond's."

"And then?"

"Then we'll likely leave the city."

"So soon? I thought you had so much to do here."

Lilith smiled insincerely. "Oh, well, I've changed my plans some. As to where we go next, I'm not sure yet. In any case, it's nothing to bother yourself about."

The Oathtaker pursed her lips in thought. "All right. I guess I'll head off to bed then."

"Good night. I'll be up shortly."

"If you don't mind, I need a change of clothing from my saddle bag. I forgot it there."

Lilith leaned back. "Mind? Why, you're not a prisoner, Velia. Of course I don't mind."

"Very well. I'll be back in a minute."

"Yes, I know you will. I warned Jabari to stay away from you."

Edmond smirked.

Velia opened her mouth to speak, but then thought better of it, not wanting to make Lilith angry or suspicious.

She walked out the front door. She had to hurry if she wanted to speak with Jerrett at all.

As she stepped off the veranda, a crow chased at her heels. She danced around it. When she couldn't get free of the beast, she kicked it with all her might, finding intense satisfaction when it hit the side of the building and fell to the ground. She hoped it never moved again.

She rushed to the stables as more birds darted at her. "Jabari? Jabari?"

He stepped into view.

She looked around the stables. They were alone. "Jerrett," she whispered, "they've arranged for a meeting at sanctuary tomorrow. I think it's with Mara and Dixon. Lilith means to trap them there with the girls. I just know it. Oh, Jerrett, we have to warn them!"

"Sanctuary!" he exclaimed. "But she can't do anything against the interests of the Select there."

"But she can! I heard her myself. She told Edmond that the only sanctuary she needed to fear was the one in Polesk because it was made with magic."

He scowled. "I'd do what I could to intercept them, but I don't know what they look like."

"Neither do I. Look, I have to hurry." Velia reached for a blade hanging from his belt. "May I have this?"

"Sure."

She dropped the blade into her boot. Evidently while bathing, Lilith, or perhaps Edmond, found and removed the extra knife she usually kept there. Now, with this one, along with her Oathtaker's blade, she carried two weapons. She smiled weakly. Two was just the right number: one for Lilith, and one for Edmond. Oh, if only she really could take Lilith down. She rushed to her saddlebag and pulled out her nightclothes.

"Oh, Jerrett, what'll we do?"

"Keep your eyes and ears open. When you can, whatever the cost, disclose Edmond for what he is."

She turned away, then glanced back at him, worry in her eyes.

"Stay safe," he called out as she dashed back to the inn, dodging crows along the way.

CHAPTER FORTY-FOUR

"Dinner is served!" exclaimed Celestine as she and Nancy slapped plates on the table. The appetite inducing smells of pork loin stuffed with rosemary and garlic, buttery mashed potatoes, and warm fresh garden peas, filled the air.

Mara and Dixon each held one of the twins. The girls had become difficult at mealtimes, as they demanded to taste the savory offerings. Mara laughed as she scooped up a spoonful of mashed potatoes, blew on it to cool, then offered it to Eden. The child's eyes lit up. She grasped the edge of the table and pulled forward, begging for more.

After weeks of study, they would leave for Lucy's first thing in the morning. Mara believed it the right course of action, as the oracle, which she checked almost daily, once again displayed the message "Go." Tonight they celebrated with Ezra, Fidel, and Leala.

Taking a seat, the innkeeper handed Dixon a note.

"What's this?"

"I believe it's a follow up message from Edmond."

Dixon handed Reigna to Nina, then opened the note. After scanning it over quickly, he read out loud:

> *So glad I got back before you left. Unfortunately, I have to stay elsewhere, as I've much business to attend to and should remain singularly focused. However, I implore you and Mara to meet me tomorrow at sanctuary. The place is crawling with visitors, but I've got crucial information to share about the person we previously discussed. I've taken the liberty of reserving the room on the top floor facing the compound, for midday. Please, please come.*

"That's it?" Mara asked.

"I thought you didn't want to go to sanctuary," Ezra said to Dixon, "that you were concerned someone might recognize you."

"He could wear a disguise," Leala suggested.

Dixon turned to Mara. "I suppose I could. What do you think?"

"Yes, that should work." She didn't want to miss out on any information about

Lilith. Dreams had troubled her sleep the past few nights—dreams that started when the oracle once again provided its message. They made her anxious to get out of the city.

"I suppose I could meet Edmond alone, but I'd prefer having you there. I'd rather not travel by magic though because . . . Well, I don't want to chance someone catching me again, and it sounds like sanctuary is very busy just now." She hesitated. "So it seems if we don't go by magic, it would be quicker if I leave the girls here. And really, if I did go by magic, I couldn't take you and the girls all at the same time anyway."

"Just the two of you will go then?" the innkeeper asked.

"Would you be willing, Ezra, to help keep an eye out here with Samuel?"

"Sure. But what of your plans to leave the city?"

"I guess we'll have to wait until first thing the next morning then." Mara fed Eden another spoonful of mashed potatoes. "What time did Edmond say?"

"Midday."

Ezra answered a knock at the door. "What is it?" he asked his man, Arne.

"A report from Jamison."

"He's back?"

"Just arrived."

The innkeeper turned to Dixon and Mara. "Do you mind?"

Mara had come to trust Ezra's men. They were instrumental in keeping her informed of Lilith's whereabouts. Moreover, it appeared the woman had followed, at least to some extent, the false information they'd passed out. They had led her to remote, unpopulated areas once they discovered what she was doing.

"Not at all."

Arne walked away, only to return minutes later with Jamison, a young man, clean and dressed simply. His blonde hair hung to his shoulders. His blue eyes darted around the room as he took a quick inventory of those in attendance. He'd met the group weeks ago, before his last venture out.

"Have a chair," Ezra said as he directed the young man to a nearby seat. "What's the news? You hungry?" he added as an afterthought.

"No, thank you."

"So what's the news?" the innkeeper repeated.

"The army hasn't moved. It's been stationed at the same place for a couple weeks or so now."

Ezra stopped, his fork halfway to his mouth. "That's odd. Lilith generally hasn't stayed long in any one place."

"That's what I thought. But as usual we couldn't get very close to her camp."

"At least they're not coming this way," Mara said.

"I must say, I'm surprised you're still here."

"They had planned to leave tomorrow," Ezra said.

"Overmorrow, now," Dixon offered.

"Their plans just got delayed," the innkeeper explained. "So, that's it then?" he asked the young man.

"That's it. I left when Carlyle arrived to relieve me. He'll remain there until I go back in another week or so."

"Are you sure you don't want something to eat?" Mara asked.

"No, but thank you." He paused. "Could I be of any help to you tomorrow? I'll be around all day and have no other plans."

"Well," Dixon said, "since you're offering, perhaps you could help Samuel keep an eye on things for a time so that Ezra would be free to see to his business. Mara and I have a meeting to attend."

"I'd be happy to." Jamison reached into his pack and pulled out two small balls. He offered one to each of the girls. They both promptly took the toys to their mouths. Then he got up to leave. "Say, I'm curious, have the crows been over this way?"

"Crows?" Ezra asked.

"Yes, it's the strangest thing. A murder of them invaded the city earlier today. I saw them causing no end of problems in the main square when I made my way through there a short time ago."

"Now that you mention it, I saw a few earlier today."

"I hate those birds," Nina said.

"Me too," Erin agreed.

"Well . . . use care when they're around," Jamison cautioned. "They've attacked a number of people in the city. It might just have been rumor, but I heard that one guy lost an eye."

Mara shuddered. "Thank you, Jamison." She turned to Dixon. "Good thing we're not taking the girls with us tomorrow."

"I'll see you later then," Jamison said.

After dinner, Mara offered small tokens of her appreciation to Fidel, Leala, and Ezra. Later she urged Ezra to play his fiddle for them. Laughing and visiting, they whiled away the hours, trying to keep away any sadness over their separation soon to come.

Chapter Forty-Five

Lilith rode, Jabari at her side. She thought about Velia who'd served her purpose getting her to the City of Light without questions. She smiled. Yes, the Oathtaker had served an important purpose—and the most important was yet to come.

Now, to get those children, she thought. She wished she could just dispose of them on the spot, but she sought the immortality Daeva promised her if only she sacrificed them on a sanctuary altar.

"Out of the way!" she shouted at a passerby who stepped out in front of Bob. Then she sat back and rode on silently, a scowl on her face.

"Excuse me, ma'am?" Jabari interrupted her reverie.

Startled, she looked at him. He'd never initiated a conversation with her in the past. "Yes?"

"Do you mind my asking where we're heading?"

"As a matter of fact, I do."

"Are Edmond and Velia to meet us there?"

She shook her head. "It's none of your concern."

He shrugged in apparent disinterest.

"Why do you ask?"

"Just curious. I thought Velia was your Oathtaker."

"No, she wasn't—she isn't."

"Isn't that rather odd?"

"What? Not to have an Oathtaker?" Lilith eyed her guard. "I don't want one and I don't need one. What would you know of Oathtakers anyway?"

He said no more. He simply watched ahead as the crows seemed to open a way for them. Earlier, when Lilith had informed him that they were going somewhere without Edmond and Velia, he'd decided to take Donagh for himself. Now he coaxed the animal to stay calm in the midst of the beasts.

Lilith turned to the right, off the main thoroughfare, and then continued until she came to a small but busy inn. She pulled up to the stables. "This is it."

"We're stopping here?"

"Yes."

"But—"

Her eyes darted his way. "Excuse me?"

"Nothing."

She instructed him to keep the horses saddled so that she could come and go at will. Then she pulled her hood up closer around her face and made her way inside.

She looked for the hallway that Edmond had told her led to Dixon and Mara's suite. She wanted a room as near to their quarters as possible.

She approached the reception desk. "I need a single room for the night," she said to Ezra, who she recognized from Edmond's description of the man.

"Are you new to the city?" The innkeeper rubbed his hand under his scruffy chin.

"Just visiting."

"I have a room for you right down that hall." He pointed, then placed a key on the counter.

The room was down the wrong wing of the building. "Pardon me, but I'd prefer a room near the back door to the stables."

Ezra looked up, though he couldn't see his newest visitor's face, as she wore her hood too far forward. "Very well," he said. He retrieved another key, then handed it over. "Second on the left down that hall," he indicated with a nod.

She turned away.

"Have you anything you need brought to your room?"

"No, thank you, I just need lunch delivered to my assistant in the stables. My things will arrive before long."

"Anything for you? For lunch, I mean?"

"Nothing, thank you."

"We'll see to your assistant."

Lilith found her room. Midday was still some time off, but likely Dixon and Mara would leave soon. Then so much depended on Edmond. He needed to stretch his meeting with them out for as long as possible.

This was the moment she'd waited for, worked for, longed for. She sat at the dressing table. It was time to connect with Daeva. She placed her hands in her lap, closed her eyes, and then called on the power of Sinespe.

Her skin started to burn. The heat went deeper and deeper. Soon she felt as though she'd melt. She glanced into the looking glass, surprised at how red the whites of her eyes had become. Steam drifted up.

"Daeva!"

A face formed in the mirror. The underlord grinned maliciously. "It'ssss about time, Lilith. What kept you?"

She gasped for air. "You know well, Daeva, that I've seen to the commission you set before me." She looked into his cadaverous eyes. "They're here. The time is now! I've arranged for their Oathtaker to be called away. She and Dixon will leave soon."

"Did you know that thissss Oathtaker was at the palacccce? Ssssearching? No doubt looking for the sssscepter?"

Her expression fell.

"I thought not."

"Not to worry, Daeva. She could never have found it."

"Well, we'll discussss this later. For now, what issss your plan, my pet?"

"Once they leave, I'll take the children, return to sanctuary, and then sacrifice them there myself. Just as you commanded."

"That eassssy?"

"No. Too many people roam the streets. The crows have turned back only a small number of them."

"What issss that to me?"

"I need more of them. I need the people off the streets."

"Very well. More crowssss you shall have." He tilted his head back. "And then?"

She closed her eyes. "Please, turn down the heat. I'll be consumed if you do not."

"Lilith, my pet. Need I remind you? I have already conssssumed you. There issss no turning back for you." He increased the burning. Satisfied when she cried out, he turned it back down again. "Have you what you need to ssssee to this?"

"Right here." She patted at her belt.

"And she is alive?"

"She's still breathing—for the moment. But she won't be for long."

"Procccceed," he ordered. Then slowly, his visage faded away.

The heat of Daeva's presence lingered. Finally, when reduced to the point familiar to Lilith, she went to an end table upon which sat a glass and a decanter of water. Her hands still shaking, she filled the glass and drank it, then filled it again.

When her tremors subsided, she took in a deep breath. Time marched forward. She'd best watch for Dixon and Mara, as she needed every second she could get.

She glanced out the window. *Oh! There he is now and . . . So, that's the great Oathtaker.* Lilith got her first good look at Mara. *They're alone, just as Edmond predicted.* Her plan would work. The girls were without sufficient protection.

It was time.

CHAPTER FORTY-SIX

Mara patted Cheryl's neck. She'd not ridden regularly for some time and had missed the good company of her faithful assistant. Fortunately, Ezra's people had taken good care of the mare.

While preparing to leave for sanctuary, they'd found it difficult to disguise Dixon. His height and bearing, his air of confidence, made him all too recognizable. In the end, they'd settled on simple garb intended to secret his strength: an eye patch and a long, ragged, hooded cloak. Though he mocked the idea of carrying a tin cup for alms, his friends outvoted him.

They planned that upon arriving at sanctuary, Fidel and Leala would meet Dixon at the stables. From there, the oldtimers would guide him to the upper chambers through seldom-used back hallways. Meanwhile, Mara would make her way to the meeting place solo, through the public walkways.

The Oathtakers chose not to ride side-by-side so that if someone should recognize Dixon and take him into custody, Mara could still meet with Edmond.

People bustled through the streets. Wagons, buggies, vendors' carts, and carriages, hurried toward their destinations. Now and again a brazen child darted across the roadway, zigzagging between the traffic.

The criers called out to the crowds: "Crows invade!" "A murder of crows attacks!"

As the minutes passed, more and more of the winged thieves swept through the air and darted at the crowd. One swooped down and plucked a treat from a child who cried, then turned his empty uplifted hands to his caregiver.

Momentarily distracted by the sight, Mara almost didn't see another as it neared her. It came in with its legs stretched out, its feet extended like claws. Instinctively, she steered Cheryl to the right. Then she lashed out to scare the beast away, but the action served instead to encourage another attack. This time, the bird flew straight toward her face. She swatted at it with all her force. Stunned, it landed on the street at her feet. Cheryl stopped, then stamped her hooves to crush the dazed creature.

Are you all right? Dixon asked.

Yes. She pulled her hood up for added protection.

In the center of the city, the vendors remained on alert. Many in the crowd carried things overhead to keep the crows from their faces. Mara couldn't recall ever having seen the creatures behave quite so aggressively before, but she felt she had a new understanding for why a group of them was known as a *murder*.

As the Oathtakers turned the corner toward the sanctuary stables, a trio of the birds dashed towards Mara. When one pierced Cheryl's neck with its beak, the mare bucked. Then, another grabbed Mara's hood and pulled it down. The third rushed toward her face. Quickly, she pulled her arms up and leaned forward. The crow missed her by mere inches.

She urged Cheryl into the stables. Once under its roof, she quickly dismounted and checked on her ride. "Easy girl, easy. It's all right, Cheryl. Everything is all right." She stroked the equine's neck.

When Dixon rode up seconds later, she glanced his way to confirm that he was well and safe.

Blood ran down the back of his hand. *Is everything all right?* he asked.

Fine. They missed me. You?

Blasted things. One of them pecked my hand.

Yes, I see. Is it bad?

It's fine.

What do you suppose is causing this—with the crows, I mean?

I have no idea. Let's just get inside quickly. Oh, here Fidel and Leala are now. I'll find you in the upper chambers.

Mara handed Cheryl's reins to the attendant and then dropped a coin in his hand. "Thank you. Would you kindly tend to her wound?"

"Certainly ma'am."

"I shouldn't be long."

"I saw those crows come at you. They've pestered people since yesterday, but not as aggressively as when they came after you."

"Have you ever seen anything like this before?"

"Never. I hope they move on, but there seem to be more all the time. They're a real safety hazard. I heard that earlier today, a large group attacked a child and pecked unrelentingly. Finally, sanctuary guards scared them away, then got medical attention for the little one. So be careful out there."

"Yes, thank you, I will."

Not many people were assembled on sanctuary grounds where clusters of crows filled the trees, lined up on the backs of benches and railings, and congregated over planters and statuary.

Mara kept her head down and rushed to the main building. Several birds came at her, but through deft maneuverings, she evaded them all. Once inside, she took her hood down.

People stood in groups, watching from the windows while sanctuary personnel lent first aid to guests who'd been pecked by the beasts.

"Are you all right?"

She turned to the voice. A young Oathtaker watched her, his eyes filled with concern.

"I'm fine, thank you."

"A whole group of them came at you! They're getting more combative and hostile by the minute."

"Yes."

"Thank the Good One, you're safe. Is there anything I can do for you?"

"Oh, no, thank you. I just have a meeting to attend."

She started through the main vestibule. The crowds inside were more dense than usual, just as the crowds outside were less so.

After swerving through the masses and making her way to the back of the building, she approached a staircase leading to the upper floor. She grasped the railing, then began her ascent.

CHAPTER FORTY-SEVEN

A fog hovered over her thoughts. She couldn't seem to fight her way through it. Then came the same sound again that had stirred her just moments before. She willed herself to consciousness, fought to awaken, then opened her eyes. It felt like someone had attached lead weights to her lids. They closed again, heavily.

"Oh, excuse me, ma'am, I'd forgotten you were in here."

Velia dragged her eyes open. The door was closing. She pulled on all of her reserves. "Wait," she managed to say. Her voice was weak, barely more than a whisper.

"Excuse me?"

"Wait. Help me."

The maid approached.

"You were told to stay away from that room!" came a voice from the hall.

She looked up to the doorway where the hotel proprietor stood. "I'm sorry, I—"

"It's all right," Velia said.

"I gave you strict instructions to leave that young woman until she awakened. She's ill."

"I'm sorry, I . . . forgot."

The Oathtaker struggled to her elbows. "No, I'm not . . . I'm not ill."

The proprietor looked in at her, then scowled.

"Please," Velia said. "I need her help."

He shook his head and moved on.

"Here," the maid said, placing a hand behind Velia's shoulder and pushing her forward.

"What time is it?"

"Nearly midday now."

"Help me up."

"I don't know, ma'am, I don't think you'd be safe on your feet."

"Ohhhh . . . I think I've been drugged. Have you any coffee?"

"I'll get it."

"Be quick," Velia pleaded. She leaned back, willing herself not to fall asleep again. Her eyes wanted to remain closed. Her head throbbed. Her body begged to return to slumber. Summoning all her strength, she pulled her legs to the side of the bed.

The door opened. "Here you go." The maid rushed to the bedside. She placed a tray on the end table, then poured a cup of coffee.

Velia inhaled deeply. She felt some small bit of life returning.

"Careful, it's hot."

"What's your name?"

"Charlotte."

"Charlotte, thank you. Have you any cold water?"

"Right here." She pointed to a carafe.

Velia reached for it. Her hand shook violently.

"I've got it." Charlotte poured some cold water into Velia's cup.

"Nearly midday, did you say?"

"That's right."

"Are the rest of my party up?"

"Oh, miss, they all left some time ago. The woman checked out for you. That's why I'd forgotten your room wasn't empty. I thought I needed to clean it."

Velia downed her drink quickly, then held her cup out for a refill. Flashes of memories from the previous night came to her recollection. She struggled to grasp the images as she drank.

"Thank you." She took in a deep cleansing breath. "I need your help."

"Certainly, ma'am."

"I need my horse readied."

"Very well, ma'am, I'll make the arrangements."

"Did the woman say where she was going?"

"No. Well, that is, she mentioned something about sanctuary."

Suddenly, Velia recollected all. They were in the City of Light where Lilith intended to trap Mara, Dixon, and the infant twins. She jumped to her feet, but found herself unsteady.

The maid assisted her. "Careful, ma'am, not too fast."

"Charlotte, are you a believer?"

"Yeeesss. Why do you ask?"

"Because I need your prayers right now. Prayers for strength and speed. Please, will you help me to get dressed? I've got to get out of here—quickly!"

"Certainly. Shall I order your horse prepared for you first?"

"Yes, do! Then come back right away. Please?"

She turned away.

"And Charlotte, hurry. Hurry! Lives are at stake. Time is of the essence!"

After she rushed out the door, Velia stumbled to the dressing table. She splashed her face repeatedly with water from the washbasin. Resting her hands on the sides of the bowl, she leaned forward. Little by little, she became more awake.

She had to hurry to sanctuary. She had to warn Mara and Dixon. She splashed water over her face once again.

Charlotte returned. "They're getting your horse ready now."

"Please, help me get dressed."

By the time the Oathtaker was clothed, her thoughts came clearer. She downed another cup of coffee, then grabbed her backpack and opened it. "Where is it?"

"Where is what?"

Velia ran to the dressing table and brushed aside the items there. They clattered to the floor. Then she ransacked the night table. "Oh no! Oh, dear Good One. Great Ehyeh!"

"What is it, ma'am?"

"Oh, Charlotte, she took it. My Oathtaker's blade!" Velia slumped down on the edge of the bed and rubbed her head. "Oh!" Anger consumed her.

She pulled herself back to her feet, set her jaw, and then rushed to the door. "I need a cloak."

"It's right there." The maid pointed to a garment hanging against the wall.

"No! I need one she won't recognize."

"Follow me."

Charlotte hurried down the stairs, Velia at her heels.

When they reached the front door, she took a moss colored wool cloak from a nearby hook. "Here," she said, "take mine."

"Oh, bless you!" Velia donned it, then opened the door.

"There's the groomsman at the stable door with your horse now."

She ran for the stables.

"Watch out for the crows!" Charlotte called out.

The groomsman handed over Victory's reins.

Velia jumped up into the saddle.

"Careful," he cautioned.

She leaned forward, dug in her heels, and rode away.

CHAPTER FORTY-EIGHT

Lilith pulled from her bag, one of her signature red dresses. Red always made her feel better. It brought out her deepest emotions. Yes, she mused, she would be seeing red soon.

Once changed, she slipped her cape over her shoulders, then took from her pocket, a slip of brown wrinkled paper. On it, Edmond had drawn a map to Dixon and Mara's quarters. She reviewed it to get her bearings. So much rode on her success. She held her head high, pulled up her hood, and then opened the door.

The hallway was empty. She noted which direction led to the front of the inn, then turned the other way. When she came to the end of the hall, she glanced around the corner. The suite Mara and her cohorts occupied was the only one down that way. Outside stood a single man. He was no Oathtaker, of that Lilith was certain. Still, he seemed alert.

She turned the corner and marched forward.

He adjusted his stance.

She drew nearer.

"Excuse me, ma'am, may I help you?"

She stared straight ahead.

"Ma'am, this hall is not open. You'll have to turn back now. You'll have to go back the way you came."

She looked him in the eyes and then reached out and turned on the heat.

"Ma'am," he choked out, "you have to turn back."

Standing just steps from him, she pulled her hood down. "Or what?"

He choked and gasped, and then, overcome with pain, slumped against the wall. He reached for the door handle, but before he could turn it, Lilith stepped forward, a knife in hand. She plunged it into his belly.

His eyes widened. He reached down, then brought his hand back up. It dripped blood. "Turn back," he managed to say before falling to the floor.

Someone opened the door from inside. There, stood a young woman. She cried out, "Samuel!"

"What is it?" came a voice from an inner room.

"Samuel! Jamison's dead!" She looked up. "And—oh gracious Ehyeh, she's found us. It's her! It's Lilith!"

Lilith shoved the young woman to the floor. When Samuel entered, she thrust out her fist and twisted it, turning on the heat.

He fell to his knees.

"So this is the protection the great Oathtaker leaves for her charges?"

"Get out," Samuel said through clenched teeth.

Lilith grabbed the young woman's hair and pulled her to her feet. "Come here. Help me move this body."

"Oh, Jamison!"

"Shut up. Take his arms there. I've got his legs. Drag him in. Now!"

When through, Lilith closed the door. Then she pulled the woman's hair again, yanking her head back. "What's your name?"

"Erin. I'm Erin."

Lilith looked closely. Her eyes narrowed. "Do I know you?"

"I was with your camp."

"Well after today, Erin, you're going to wish you'd never left. Now where are they?"

"Get out!"

Lilith didn't want to kill Erin. Someone had to help her to get the infants back to sanctuary. She looked around the room. There it was—the door that Edmond said led to the inner chambers where the infants spent much of their time.

Erin struggled to her feet.

Once again, Lilith grabbed her arm, turned her around, and then pushed her toward the door. "Open it," she ordered, her voice just a whisper, her lips to her captive's ear, her teeth clenched.

"No!" Erin fumbled with something at her waist. A moment later, she held a knife. She broke Lilith's hold and brandished her blade.

"Ha! You've got no chance against me. Do you want some of that?" Lilith pointed at Samuel. Then, with Erin's attention on him, she grabbed her wrist and wrenched it. When Erin's knife fell to the floor, Lilith pushed her toward the door. "Now open it."

"I can't. I won't!"

Lilith reached for the handle, opened the door and pushed her inside. A moment later, Erin fell to the ground.

Lilith looked up. There stood another young woman, a knife in her hand, blood dripping from its blade. Her eyes were wide in horror and her hand shook.

"Oh, Erin! Erin, I didn't know it was you. No!" She crouched down.

Lilith grabbed her arm and squeezed. The knife fell.

"Who are you?"

"I'm Nina," she said, disgust and violence in her voice.

Lilith spun Nina around and pulled her arm up tightly behind her back. Then she looked around the room.

There they are. The infants. Oh, Daeva, we've done it!

"Here's what we're going to do. If you don't want to see anyone else hurt, you will do exactly as I say."

"I won't help you."

"You will. I'm taking those girls to sanctuary, and you're going to help me."

"Sanctuary!"

"Yes. Whatever they told you about me was a lie. I mean the children no harm. I'm just trying to do right by them."

"I don't believe you."

"You can't afford not to, or I'll leave you right here next to her." Lilith tilted her head toward Erin. "Then how much good could you do for them?"

"All right, all right. What do you want me to do?"

"I'm going to release you now. Then you're going to pick up the children and walk out of here ahead of me without any show of resistance or fear. If you don't, I'll take them anyway. I'll just leave you behind . . . dead," Lilith added after a pause for effect. "And perhaps others as well. So, have I got your agreement?"

Nina nodded.

Lilith released her hold. "Get them."

Nina turned toward the sleeping twins. Gently, she picked up one, then the other. "Now what?"

Lilith took a cloak hanging near the door and placed it over Nina's shoulders, hiding the infants beneath. "Now lead the way to the stables."

Nina nearly stumbled over Erin's body. Tears welled in her eyes, but she kept going. She made her way out to the shared common area and past where Jamison was, clearly dead.

Samuel groaned. He held his head in his hands. Steam rose up from his body.

"Leave him be. He can't hurt you now."

"Move!"

When they approached the door to the hallway, Lilith opened it. "Walk straight forward. Speak to no one."

Nina exited, walked down the hall, and then headed out the back door.

When they arrived at the stables, Lilith smiled at the swarm of crows in the air. "Jabari!" she called.

He stepped forward.

"Help her into that saddle." Lilith pointed to Donagh. "You'll have to pick her up."

He followed her orders.

Lilith mounted up, then ordered him to hand Bob and Donagh's reins over.

"Hang on, Nina. Hang on tight. We're wasting no time." She moved out into the swarm of crows.

Jabari waited a minute, then grabbed the reins of a nearby horse. He jumped into the saddle and followed.

Chapter Forty-Nine

Edmond watched the grounds below. The squawking, rushing, murderous crows, mesmerized him. He held back a smile as sanctuary guests scurried from one building to another trying to avoid the raucous birds.

He felt immensely satisfied. He'd waited for this day for a very long time. He thought back to when he was just a child, to when the Council pronounced his father's sentence. His father exacted a promise from him that very day, a promise to vindicate him. "But don't forget," he had said, "a man who seeks his revenge before forty years has passed, has acted in haste."

Well, forty years had not yet passed, but more than twenty had. Ever since Dixon's father prosecuted the case against Madden Chantray, Edmond had waited. Over the years, the idea of getting back at Dixon changed from one of vindication to one of simple personal revenge.

The time was now. The day had arrived—and it had not come in haste. Edmond had felt every long minute. In this moment, he could barely contain his mirth. For once, Dixon would not come out the victor; for once, he would be under Edmond's foot.

It was nearly midday. He waited with baited breath. Soon Dixon and Mara would arrive.

The sounds of sanctuary guests rushing through the halls made their way to him. He started as footsteps stopped at the door. A quiet moment passed, then they moved on.

"Patience," he muttered aloud to himself. "Just have patience." He turned back to the window and recommenced his reverie.

A sound came from the door. Slowly, it opened. In walked a hooded beggar, his back bent and his feet shuffling as he stepped inside.

"Out! You're not allowed in here!"

The beggar closed the door behind himself, then reached for his hood. He turned it down as he stood to his full height.

"Dixon!" Edmond cried, reminding himself to keep his emotions disciplined, his expressions under control. He should be pleased to see his old friend. He smiled. Though it was not genuine, Dixon didn't seem to notice. "A disguise, huh?" He approached.

Dixon removed the eye patch he wore, then shook his friend's hand and smiled weakly. "Just a precaution."

"You're still concerned about being recognized?"

"A lot of people in the city know me. If someone informed— Well, it would be difficult to have to explain things to the Council while Lilith remains out and about."

"You know I still don't understand why Mara doesn't just tell the Council about the girls—claim her rightful position."

"Well yes, it may seem odd that she keeps this to herself, but she feels very strongly that she shouldn't expose the girls when she doesn't know the Council members. And of course, to bring accusation against Lilith would require that she spend enormous time and attention to make her case. Meanwhile, who would protect the twins?"

"So, where is she?"

"She should be here any minute. We arrived together but made our way up here separately."

"And the girls?"

"Mara considered bringing them along, but with the invasion of the crows, it seemed best not to take them out."

"I understand." Edmond walked back to the window.

"What's this all about?"

Edmond was in no hurry. He wanted the minutes to drag and to multiply. He took a deep breath. "We should wait until Mara arrives, so I can answer your questions and hers at the same time."

"Very well."

"Dixon, what do you make of the all the crows?"

Dixon made his way to the window. He looked out just as a bird swooped down on a group of sanctuary guests trying to make their way to the main building. "I've no idea. It's strange, don't you think?"

"Yes, it's almost like an evil presence." There was an odd quality to Edmond's voice.

"That's a terrible thought."

"Yes, it is. You're right."

A knock came at the door. Edmond went to it slowly, reminding himself that every minute counted. Lilith depended on him. He opened it. "Mara," he said, "it's good to see you."

Her eyes quickly darted around the room. When she saw Dixon, she visibly relaxed. "Thank you, Edmond, and you. I hope your trip went well."

"Yes, it did. Come in. Come in."

"Is everything all right?" she asked Dixon.

"All is well. You? It took you a while to get here."

"Sorry. The hallways are filled with people escaping from the crows. But yes, all is well." Then she became all business. "So, Edmond, what can you tell us?"

He directed his guests to chairs. Though Dixon sat, Mara remained standing.

"I was just asking Dixon about the crows. Have you ever seen anything like this?"

"No. They're very aggressive."

"Well, I'm glad you got here safely. Can I get you anything?"

"No, thank you."

"If you don't mind, I think I'll order up some refreshments anyway."

"Fine with me, Edmond, but let's try to wrap this up quickly. I really don't like to be away from—well, you know."

He smiled. "Sure." Taking his time, he picked up a tablet of forms left in the room for sanctuary guests to place orders from the kitchens. Slowly he filled one out, then sauntered to the door to place it on a corkboard on the wall just outside. When sanctuary staff came by, they would pick up the order and fill it in due course. He closed the door.

Dixon tapped on his thigh as he often did when nervous.

Mara paced.

Edmond needed to keep them calm and occupied. "Are the girls well, Mara?"

"Yes, thank you."

"Well, have a seat," he said, again motioning toward a chair.

"What's this all about, Edmond?" she asked as she sat down. "What have you learned about Lilith?"

He turned once again toward the windows and watched below as a young woman, covered in a moss green cape, dashed toward the stables. A crow rushed toward her, then another, and then another. Her horse reared, nearly unseating her.

He could just see inside the stables where she dismounted. Her movements seemed familiar. Who did she remind him of? *Oh yes, Velia.* He smiled. He needn't worry about her. She barely breathed anymore. He'd tried to encourage Lilith to kill her outright, but the woman insisted Velia had to remain alive for a time. In the end, he'd watched Lilith lace the young Oathtaker's bedtime tea with drugs enough to kill her . . . eventually.

He turned back toward Mara and Dixon.

Velia made her way to sanctuary as quickly as possible. When a crow rushed toward her, she pulled sideways. It missed her. Another rushed in. Again she turned away, just before it struck. For the third time, a crow attacked, but this time it aimed for Victory. The horse pulled sideways and reared, nearly unseating her. She held the reins tightly and tried to calm her mount just as another crow flew at her. With the stables just ahead, she leaned forward, urging Victory onward. Moments later, they dashed inside.

She halted, then talked to the animal with quiet words, but due to her own frenzy, it remained skittish. When one of the attendants neared her, she requested his assistance.

"I'll be back shortly!" she called out.

She ran for the main building, dodging crows along her way.

Once inside, she looked around the crowded lobby. Where should she go now? Where were they supposed to meet? She wracked her memory for any clue as to where Lilith and Edmond might be, but she got nothing. They'd never said where they were going to meet.

"Excuse me," the Oathtaker said as she made her way through the crowd. "Excuse me. Excuse me." Trying to be polite, trying not to offend those around her, she advanced.

"May I help you, ma'am?"

She surmised that the inquiry was directed her way. She turned to find an attendant. "I don't know. I'm looking for someone."

"You appear to be in some hurry."

"Yes, I'm looking for . . ." She paused. Lilith hadn't worn her signature red for weeks. Now Velia knew why. The woman wasn't about to enter sanctuary without taking on some sort of disguise. So now no one would recognize her, and thus, no one could help Velia to find her. Her shoulders sagged. She didn't know where to begin.

"Ma'am?" the attendant interrupted her reverie.

"Oh, sorry, I just . . ." She looked around the massive place yet again. The guests numbered in the hundreds. She felt completely overwhelmed. "I just don't know where to begin."

He raised a brow. "Perhaps you might start in the inner sanctuary, the prayer room."

"Excuse me?"

He smiled. "When all else would fail us, the Good One would not. Ehyeh, the Great Provider, will hear your prayer."

She was accustomed to solving problems on her own. Still, she had no idea where else to go, so she had nothing to lose in taking his advice. "Perhaps you're right."

"Right this way," he said.

Velia followed him through the crowds and to the door of the inner sanctuary. She nodded her thanks, then entered.

A few elderly people strolled about. She listened as they lifted their cries and prayers upward and then made her way to the front altar. When she arrived, she collapsed to her knees.

"Dear Good One!" she cried, "Ehyeh, Great Provider, help me. Help me!" She leaned forward and put her hands on the floor, nearly prostrate.

"Are you all right?"

She pulled back up. She wanted to cry, but that would serve no purpose. She looked at the old woman who'd addressed her. "I'm . . . fine," she said, her voice faltering.

"You don't look fine."

Velia looked away. "It's just that someone is in great need of help—of warning. And I don't know where to begin! I feel helpless."

"Who are you looking for?"

The Oathtaker sighed. "No one can help. I'm afraid all is lost."

"Try me." The woman reached a tired arthritic hand out to her.

Velia sat back on her heels. "I'm trying to find two Oathtakers—to warn them."

"Do these Oathtakers have names?" Her gray eyes looked on, comfortingly.

Velia smirked, then her expression fell. "Yes, they've got names. I was hoping to warn them . . . but I don't know where they are."

"Maybe I can help." Smiling, she patted Velia's hand. "My name is Leala."

The Oathtaker surmised there was nothing the woman could do for her. She shook her head. "You wouldn't happen to know anyone by the name of Mara? Or Dixon?" she asked, frowning.

Leala's smile fell.

Velia jumped to her feet. "You do! You do know them. You do. I can see it. Help me, please. I have to warn them!"

"Warn them?"

"I know this sounds—preposterous—but they're in grave danger, as are the girls!"

Leala grabbed Velia's arm and pulled her to the side. "What do you know of the girls?"

"I know Lilith plans to harm them. Here. Today!"

"Oh, dear Good One! Come. Come with me."

As they made their way to the back of the room, an old man approached them. He bowed low. His cloak fell forward, draping at his sides.

"Get out of the way, Junior!" Leala cried.

"What's going on, Leala?"

"We've got to warn them, Fidel!" She rushed toward the door, dragging Velia behind.

Fidel caught up to them. "What's going on?" he asked again as he grasped Leala's wrist firmly. When she tried to pull away, he held on tighter.

"Please, sir, we've got to warn them!" Velia pleaded.

Fidel refused to release Leala. "What's going on?"

"Sir, we haven't time! Dixon and Mara are in great danger. Lilith is here. She came here to harm them!"

He looked closely at Velia. In that moment, he took her measure. "This way," he said as he made his way swiftly through the crowd to a back staircase.

—————

Edmond needed to stall. Lilith required more time. "Did the two of you travel by magic?"

"No," said Dixon.

"As you know, it would have been difficult to arrive that way without attracting unwanted attention," Mara added, her voice clipped.

"Yes, that's right." Edmond knew how uncomfortable she'd been when he discovered her power to travel. He'd counted on it. "And then of course, there are the crows, so the two of you came alone."

"Those birds are a nuisance. No, I take that back. They're a danger." Mara looked back at Dixon. "How's your hand?"

He waved it. "Fine."

"You were attacked?" Edmond asked.

"It's nothing."

"We could get someone to take a look."

"No, Edmond. My hand is fine."

"Well, what did you learn about Lilith?" Mara asked.

"Not much, I'm sorry to say." Edmond sat down.

"So, you don't know where she is now?"

"No."

"We heard she's been stationed in one place with her army for some time now," Dixon said.

"Is that right?"

"Look, Edmond, I don't mean to be rude, but—"

"No, Mara, I quite understand. It's just that . . ." He sat forward on his chair. "Well, this is it, Mara. I really think you should go to the Council and I'm hoping I can convince you to do that," he said hurriedly. "We could make arrangements right now. Today. I could help to speak for you."

"No," she said without hesitation.

"Mara, you don't know the Council, but I do. I've been an advisor to the Council for years. They'll believe you."

"No, Edmond." She stood. "So is that all we came for? You don't have any more information for us?"

"Hear me out." He turned to Dixon. "Dixon, try to get her to listen, to see reason."

Dixon grinned and shook his head. "Look, this is Mara's call. I've already told you her reasoning and I find no fault with it. If she says 'no' then—"

"But, Dixon," Edmond interrupted, "I have good reason to suggest this." Lilith needed more time. He couldn't let them leave yet. "Look, I think there are some who already suspect the truth, and if they just met Mara, that might be enough." He turned back her way. "You could take your rightful place as the girls' regent to lead the Council."

"No. I don't care about leading the Council right now. I care about keeping the girls safe."

"What about you, Dixon? Don't you care that the Council doubts your faithfulness, your innocence? Don't you think she," he said, motioning towards Mara, "owes you at least that much? At least the opportunity to clear your name?" He fought to keep his voice from becoming shrill or accusatory.

Dixon leaned in. "You don't seem to understand. I told you before. So long as I've got Mara's back and she's got mine, I don't care what the Council thinks."

"But—"

"If that's all Edmond, we're leaving." Mara said. "Actually, I wish you hadn't wasted our time."

"But, Mara—"

"This is not up for discussion, Edmond. There will be no debate. I've made up my mind." She turned toward the door, then flew back as it burst open before her. In stumbled Leala, Fidel, and a young woman. "What's this?"

The young woman's eyes shot around the room before coming to rest on Edmond. "Where is she?"

"Where is who?" Mara asked. "And who are you?" She looked at the oldtimers. "What's the meaning of this Leala? Fidel?"

"Hear her out," Leala said, struggling to catch her breath.

Mara turned to the young woman. "Who are you?"

"Where is she, Edmond?" the woman asked again as she stepped closer to him.

"Where is who? And . . . and . . . who are you?" he asked.

"Where is Lilith?"

Mara, still near the door, tried to close it just as a member of the sanctuary staff sought to enter. He carried a tray with a pot and cups. "Go away!" she shouted at him.

"But—"

"We don't want it! Send it back!" She closed the door in his face, then turned back to the others. She glared at the young woman. "What is the meaning of this? Who are you? What do you want? And what's this about Lilith?"

She bowed. Her hair fell forward. She stood up and tucked it behind her ears. "You must be Mara."

Mara's eyes narrowed. "Who are you?"

"Listen to me. You're in great danger."

"Who are you?" Mara cried, Dixon now at her side.

"My name is Velia. I've been traveling with Lilith and Edmond." Her eyes darted his way, then turned back. "I've come to warn you."

"What's she talking about, Edmond?" Mara asked.

His mouth dropped open, his eyes went wide. "I have absolutely no idea what she's talking about. I've never seen this woman before."

"Liar!" Velia snapped at him. She looked back at Mara. "Edmond has been traveling with Lilith, making plans for your demise. She intends to harm the girls. She and Edmond arranged to meet you here today so that she could do just that."

Mara watched Velia closely. The woman seemed to be telling the truth. She looked back at Edmond.

He stepped forward. "Listen, I don't know her. I've no idea who she is or what she's up to."

"What are you talking about? You mentioned 'the girls,' Velia. Who do you mean?" Dixon asked.

"Rowena's girls! The seventh seventh and 'she who is but is not.' Look Mara, Dixon, I know you don't know me, but Lilith is here. She came to kill you. I'm an Oathtaker. I found out that she was lying about— She said someone was trying to pawn off an imposter child as a seventh seventh. But she lied. I know it! Please, you've got to believe me. Lilith is probably making her way to this room even as we speak."

Mara looked at Edmond.

"She's lying," he said. "I don't know her, I tell you. I don't know what she's talking about. She's probably trying to lay a trap of her own."

Velia stepped toward him. She hauled back and slapped him with all her might.

His head snapped to the side. Slowly, he turned back, his lip curled in a sneer. "You're a liar. If you're an Oathtaker as you say, then prove it."

She reached back for her blade, then turned to Mara, her hand empty. "She took it. They took it! Lilith and Edmond stole my blade!"

"It doesn't make any sense, Mara," Dixon said. "Edmond wouldn't harm me."

"He would!" Velia cried. "He wants revenge!"

"Revenge! Revenge for what? No," Dixon said to Mara, "she must be a—an imposter. She hasn't got a blade. What she says makes no sense. There's no reason to believe any of it. Word must have gotten out somehow—about our being here, I mean."

Velia's shoulders slumped. "How can I convince you? What can I say? They want to harm the girls. There's no time to lose!"

Mara eyes narrowed. "There is one way to know for sure," she said.

"What are you talking about?" Dixon asked.

She held his gaze for a long moment before turning away. "Edmond," she said, "this is really very simple. Just assure me that you wouldn't harm the girls. Assure me that—"

"What?" he interrupted. "Assure you of what? You want me to swear to you that I wouldn't harm the girls? That I'd do whatever I could to protect them?" He scowled, then looked at Dixon accusatorially. "I can't believe you'd even allow her to ask me this. I suppose you doubt me too."

"Just do as she says, Edmond. Just . . . do as she says."

"Well," Edmond said, his voice dripping with anger, "since you seem to feel the need to hear me say it, in the face of this—this unfounded accusation, by someone who can't even prove she is what she claims to be!" He shook his finger at Velia. "Mara, trust me. I don't know what she's talking about. I've had nothing to do with Lilith. Why," he paused, "I swear I'd . . . I'd . . . I'd protect those girls with my very life!"

A moment passed.

Nothing happened.

Mara looked to Dixon, then to Leala, and then to Fidel. The truth was not lost on any of them. The earth had not moved. Edmond's oath was not sincere. He had betrayed them.

"Oh, gracious Ehyeh!" she exclaimed, a cry in her voice, a hand to her throat. "Oh, Dixon, Lilith must have gone to the inn!" She grabbed his arm as she sucked in a breath.

Edmond, a knife in his hand, lunged.

Velia rushed him from behind.

Before Mara could exhale, she and Dixon vanished.

CHAPTER FIFTY

Mara came to a quick stop, her legs buckling beneath her. Dixon pulled her up. She looked at him, her eyes wide with fear. They stood just outside their quarters. She opened the door and stepped inside, then nearly tripped over something. When Dixon grabbed her arm, she firmed her stance and looked down.

"Oh, it's Jamison!" She reached down. "No. No!" she cried. "He's dead!"

"Mara," Dixon rushed past her, "here's Samuel." He reached down to the young man, and then felt for his pulse. Quickly he got back to his feet and pulled out his blade. Mara followed suit.

They stepped toward the inner room and then opened the door.

Utter silence greeted them.

"They're gone! Oh, Dixon, where could she have taken them?"

A single bloody body lay on the floor. She had to know: was it Nina or Erin? She crouched down and rolled the body over. *Erin.* Blood covered her. Mara felt for a pulse. It was very weak. She wanted to heal her, but she knew she couldn't. Time wasn't on her side.

Where had Lilith gone? Where had she taken the girls? Where was Nina? Her mind raced. Filled suddenly with an intense anger, all she could think was to hurry.

Dixon's bent down. "She looks bad." Then he returned to Samuel's side, Mara in his wake. "Samuel. Samuel!" He shook him.

The man trembled. His eyes rolled back up into his head.

"Samuel!"

Mara grabbed his hands.

"No, Mara, you can't afford to use your magic. We need you," Dixon cautioned.

"But we have to know where Lilith took them. Don't you see? It's our only chance."

"Please, Mara."

"Dixon, he's our only chance. We might still have time, but we have to know where she took them."

"Just use a minimum of magic then. You need to keep up your strength."

"I understand. I'll do my best."

She pushed a faint stream of magic healing into Samuel. She felt him react ever so slightly. *It isn't enough. It isn't enough!* She increased the flow.

Dixon shook the man. "Where did they go, Samuel? Samuel!"

Exasperated, Mara again increased the stream of magic.

Samuel coughed and sputtered.

She turned his face toward herself. "We'll send help as soon as possible, but you have to tell us where Lilith went."

His lips moved, but no sound came.

She took his hands again, sending yet another stream of magic into him.

His eyes opened slowly, then just as slowly, closed again.

"Samuel!" Dixon cried. "Where did Lilith go? Where did she take them?"

The man was silent.

"It's no use, Mara. You've got to stop."

Hot tears stung her eyes. She fought them back and pleaded, "Please Ehyeh, help us, please!"

Samuel's head moved. A faint sound escaped his lips.

Mara's eyes opened wide. "What did you say? Where are they?"

His lips moved again.

"I think he's trying to say 'sanctuary.'" She shook him. "Did you say 'sanctuary?' Is that where Lilith went?"

He groaned.

"Can you open your eyes? Just open your eyes. Please. Did you say 'sanctuary?'"

Slowly his eyes opened. He nodded ever so faintly.

"Sanctuary. They went to sanctuary. Is that right?" Dixon asked.

Samuel nodded again, then passed out.

Mara jumped to her feet. "Let's go!"

"Can we get Ezra to help him?"

Her tears fell. "We can't. Every second counts!"

"You're right, of course." Dixon stood. "Wait. If Ezra's in the inn and carrying a crystal, we can—"

"Do it. Quickly!"

Directing his thoughts, he shouted. *Ezra, help! Lilith took the girls! Mara and I are going back to sanctuary where she headed, but Samuel and Erin need your help. Hurry. Hurry!*

"I'm going to kill her," Mara said, her jaw tight, her eyes hard.

Dixon held her forearms. "Let's go!"

She spun her magic.

Seconds later, they landed in the sanctuary stables. She sneezed from the hay dust, then pulled Dixon through a crowd of stable hands, all of whom stared at them.

"Did you see that?" one exclaimed.

"Who are they?"

"I think I'm seeing things!"

Mara rushed away, ignoring their stares and exclamations.

"Where are we going?" Dixon asked.

"I don't know!"

"Wait, Mara!"

She stopped at the stable doors. "We have to keep moving." She looked out at the crows. "Cover your head!" she exclaimed. Then she grabbed his hand, ran out, and headed toward the main building.

A dozen crows rushed them. One clawed at her shoulder, another grabbed her hood. When she reached up to slap the beast away, yet another pecked at her hand, piercing it deeply. Dixon also fought off the savage birds.

Several leaps later, the Oathtakers arrived at the main building. When someone opened the door for them, they hurried inside.

Mara stopped. Crowds of people watched her and Dixon.

"Are you all right?" someone asked.

She looked toward the voice. It was a young Oathtaker. "I'm fine." She fought for breath.

Dixon stood at her side. "Where are we going?"

"I don't know. I don't know!" She looked at the thick crowd.

Wait. What is that—that smell?

"Oh!" she gasped as she bent over, her hand to her mouth.

"What? What is it? Are you hurt?"

"I can . . . smell her. I can— Oh!" She coughed and gagged.

"What? You smell her rosewater? What?"

"No." She coughed again. "Can't you smell that? Oh, and it tastes horrible!"

"What?"

"Lilith." Mara swallowed hard. "I think I'm going to throw up!" she exclaimed as she turned away, covering her mouth.

"What do you smell? Taste?"

Her saliva ran fast and thin. She swallowed and swallowed, again and again.

"What do you smell? What?"

"Red." She coughed. "It's like my mouth is full of blood." She turned aside and leaned over. Her stomach lurched. She feared she'd retch. She tried to hold back her nausea with a hand over her mouth.

When she gained control over herself, she grabbed Dixon's hand. "This way!" she cried.

Following her nose, she rushed past sanctuary visitors and headed toward the main prayer room. She smelled Lilith. She tasted the red of the woman's clothing, heavy and thick. Periodically she coughed or gagged.

As they pushed through the crowd, the smell increased. Then, just as Mara had to stop again to fight back her nausea, the ground erupted before where she and Dixon stood. Fragments of foundation and flooring burst into the air. They covered their heads as debris crashed down and bodies flew out in every direction.

A pack of grut shrieked outward.

Instinctively, Mara confirmed that she wore her protection from them. "You wearing your tooth?" she asked Dixon over the gruts' screeching.

"Yes. Look, they're attacking people in the crowd!"

"Come on, let's go!"

One of the beasts bounded toward them.

The Oathtakers stopped in their tracks. Though the smell of death filled their nostrils, though the beast exuded evil intent, they stood defiant. It could do nothing to them.

Mara grabbed the handle of a knife at her belt, pulled it from its sheath, and then threw it.

Whoosh! The grut went up in flames.

As she reached for another knife, Dixon threw a weapon. Another blast of heat and flame burst out when it found its target.

Frenzied, they watched as the grut attacked sanctuary guests, leaving in their wake, bodies strewn about and blood splattered on the walls and floor.

From off to one side, several Oathtakers threw knives and shot arrows.

The gruts' screams drowned out those from the crowd who sought to escape the melee.

Another grut burst into flame.

Mara couldn't tell where the blade that killed the creature had come from. "Come on, Dixon," she urged, pulling him. She hoped no one's weapon hit them in error.

A moment later they stopped when another grut tried to intercept them. The beast's red eyes shone. As though it knew it could not attack, but was confused as to why, it studied them, screaming all the while.

Dixon drew another blade. He threw it. His aim was true. The beast burst into flame, then disappeared.

Yet another approached. Mara froze. She had no more knives and needed her blade to take out Lilith. Then she thought of something.

She reached into her pocket. "Where are they? Where are they?" she cried. Her hands shook.

There. There! She pulled out some crystals. Confirming there was no one close to the beast before her, she threw one.

The beast went up in flame.

An Oathtaker rushed by. Mara grabbed his arm. "Here!" she cried. She pulled his fist open and deposited some crystals in his hand. "Be very careful with those. Throw them at the grut. But be careful!"

Once done, she and Dixon continued through the mayhem. They jumped over fallen debris and the bodies of the gruts' victims as they neared the door to the inner sanctuary. A crowd surrounded it. Mara pushed through and then reached for the door handle.

"Don't!" someone shouted.

"Stand back!" Dixon ordered.

Whoosh! Another grut burned away.

Mara felt the heat. She pulled her arms up to protect her face. Then she reached for the handle again.

"No," a man at the door cried, "don't go in there! Some crazy woman just dragged someone in there and then ordered everyone else out."

"Mara, it's got to be Lilith—and Nina," Dixon said.

"I know. It is Lilith. I can smell her!" Unable to control herself, she gagged. Then, she turned back to the door. Again, she reached for the handle.

Just then, someone hit another of the beasts. A blast of heat burst forth.

"Mara!" came a cry from the crowd.

She turned to the voice. Velia pushed through to her.

"Velia, get out of here. It's not safe!"

"But Mara—"

"Get out. Get out! The grut!"

Another grut went up in a flash.

Velia shielded her face with her forearm, then turned to Mara. "Lilith's in there."

"I know!"

"Velia!" someone cried.

A man headed their way. Mara had seen him in the crowd earlier, fighting the grut.

"That's Jerrett," Velia said. "He's an Oathtaker. He'll help."

Again, Mara pulled at the door.

Velia stood against it, holding it closed.

"Velia, move aside!"

"No, Mara, Lilith is in there."

"She has the girls."

Velia's mouth fell open. "Oh, gracious Ehyeh. And she's got my blade."

Mara's heart sank. She hadn't thought about the significance of that before. Lilith could cut off Rowena's entire line if she killed the girls with an Oathtaker's blade. With newfound strength, she pulled at the door again.

This time Jerrett held it closed.

"Get *out* of my way!" she ordered.

He put one hand out. "There's a back way into that room. Lilith will expect you to come barging in from here. Let someone distract her while you make your way to the other entrance."

"Don't any of you hear me? She has the twins! There's no time to lose!"

"I'll take you the other way. Let the others distract Lilith from here."

She glanced at Dixon.

"Go!" he urged. "I'll distract Lilith from here. Hurry!"

"But, Dixon, she'll kill you!" Tears sprang to her eyes.

He held her gaze for a moment. "Go," he repeated.

"Mara," Velia said, "you're the only one who can—"

"Kill her," Mara said, her jaw set.

"Right. Now, go! I'll help Dixon to distract Lilith."

Mara turned to Jerrett. "Go!" she ordered.

As Mara and Jerrett disappeared around the corner, Dixon opened the door and stepped inside. Velia followed immediately behind. She dropped down to the floor to make her way forward unseen.

It was quieter inside the inner sanctuary than without. Its thick walls muffled the sounds of the shouting crowd and screaming grut. Lilith had turned out all the candles except for those immediately around the altar at the front of the room.

Dixon allowed his eyes a moment to adjust to the low light.

"I said, 'get out!'"

There was no mistaking that voice.

He started toward the altar where Lilith stood, an Oathtaker's blade in her hand. Nina was on its other side, holding the infants under her cloak.

"Out!" Lilith demanded.

As he stepped into the area the candlelight embraced, Velia crawled forward in the surrounding darkness.

"Well, well, Dixon," Lilith said when she turned his way. She smiled grotesquely. "So you made it back. I had rather hoped you wouldn't be too late. I'm looking forward to sharing all of this with you." She turned away.

Nina stepped back.

"Stay there," Lilith ordered her. "So you've come to see me enter immortality," she then said, turning back to Dixon. "You know," she added, lifting her brow, "you could join me."

"What are you talking about?" He needed to keep her talking, distracted.

Her head tilted. "So, Dixon, where is this lady love of yours, this Oathtaker you've taken such a fancy to? Mousy little thing from what I could see. What's her name?" She hesitated, playacting. "Oh, yes. Yes, Mara." She smiled condescendingly. "Did my grut do their job? Good thing I had this little thing with me." She pulled out from where it was nestled between her breasts, a grut call. "That was a special touch, don't you agree?"

Dixon snatched up the idea that she'd unwittingly given him. If Lilith thought

Mara had fallen victim to the grut, then she wouldn't expect her to show up.

"That's right, Lilith." He took another step forward. "So you called the grut up? Well they've certainly done their damage. But it doesn't matter now what happened to Mara. It's still not too late for you. Lilith, you must stop this—now."

"No. I've worked for this moment for a very long time—for nearly as long as Edmond has sought his revenge on you." She paused. "How does it feel, Dixon, to have your friend betray you? Because, you know, that's just how I feel about you."

"What are you talking about?"

"You served Rowena. Enough said. So now you can watch me take her place— circumvent her plans—once and for all. Just watch, and then you can be the first to feel the—warmth, shall we say—of my wrath." She smiled, cheerlessly. "Yes, that sounds right. As soon as I'm through here. I look forward to it," she added, her voice barely above a whisper.

He watched her every move. *Hurry, Mara! Lilith is in front of the altar with Velia's blade. Nina is just behind it. She's hiding the girls under her cloak.*

"So, what is it you intend to do, Lilith?" he asked, seeking to buy time.

I'm nearly there, Mara said.

"You don't have to do this, Lilith," he pleaded.

"Stay away," she warned.

I'm here, Mara said. *Blast! The door is locked. Oh, wait, I know how to do this.*

You know how to do what?

Unlock the door. I'll move the tumblers.

Hurry!

Oh great Ehyeh. She's jammed this one up with magic.

Can you do it?

Just—give me a minute.

Hurry. Hurry!

Dixon took another step. Lilith didn't seem the least bit concerned by his advances.

I did it. I'm coming.

He willed himself not to glance toward the faint outline of movement that appeared seconds later in the darkness behind Lilith.

Keep her talking. I'm going to change places with Nina.

"Lilith, what possible good can this do you?"

"Good?" she spat. "Why, Dixon, I don't intend to do any *good*." She started to turn away.

"Lilith!" he cried. "Why don't you just leave the girls be? They're just infants. They can't harm you."

She faced him full on, scowling. "You've always been incredibly naive, Dixon. Of course the girls can't 'harm' me. That's not the point. If they die, their power will just go up their line. No, this is the surest way for me to acquire the power for myself."

He saw, out of the corner of his eye, Velia crouched behind a pillar within steps of where Lilith stood.

"Stop this, please," he said, as Mara suddenly came into view. She stood, her finger to her lips, at Nina's side. He willed himself not to turn his eyes toward her.

Again, Lilith started to turn around.

"Lilith!" he called.

Just then, Velia rushed out from behind the pillar. She grabbed at Lilith's legs, trying to upset her balance. She couldn't kill the traitor, but she could distract her— maybe disarm her. And if Lilith did use Velia's own blade against her, then its magic would die. Clearly, it was a sacrifice the Oathtaker was willing to make, a price she was willing to pay.

Lilith held her blade to strike Velia, but then stopped, her arm mid-air. "Velia?" She grabbed the altar to maintain her balance. She needed the blade's magic, so she needed the Oathtaker alive—at least for now. Screeching with frustration, she threw a stream of magic out at her.

Velia gasped and choked. Seconds later, she fell back with a scream, hitting her head on the pillar. Down, down, her body sank slowly to the floor.

Dixon looked up. Velia had created the distraction that Mara needed. When Nina's eyes opened wide at the sight of her, Mara pushed her toward the back door, then stood where she'd been a moment before, her hood pulled up to conceal her identity.

Slowly, Velia made it back to her feet.

Lilith threw more magic at her.

The impact, when it made contact, sent the Oathtaker back to her knees. She cried out.

"You bore me," Lilith said. "I'd kill you right now if I didn't need your blade." She started turning back toward the altar.

"Wait, Lilith!" Dixon cried. "What's the point of all this? Turn back from this. Please, Lilith."

She shook her head. "The point," she said with a sneer, "is that after I sacrifice those girls," she continued as she pointed to where Mara stood, "on this altar," she went on as she slapped the altar behind her, "with this blade," she said as she brandished Velia's blade, "then Rowena's line will be over and Ehyeh's reign will cease. *I'll* have all the power. And I'll be immortal!" She laughed. "Come here, Nina. Now. Or you'll suffer a terrible death as well."

"It's not too late, Lilith. Turn back."

"You're pathetic, Dixon." She sent a burst of magic at him.

His skin burned. He choked. Reaching up to loosen his cloak, he gasped for air.

She increased the magic.

"Stop!" Mara cried.

Lilith turned and looked up at Mara who'd removed her hood so as to reveal her true identity.

"You! How did you get here?" Once again she flung her arm out toward Dixon, throwing yet another stream of her evil magic his way.

He dropped to his knees, then started falling forward.

"Aren't you going to try to save him, Oathtaker?"

Mara reached back and grasped Spira.

"You can't harm me," Lilith sneered.

Mara's eyes darted to Dixon, then quickly back to Lilith. She'd seen enough.

"Then I guess you won't feel *this!*" With a flick of her wrist, she released her blade. It flew through the air and found its target.

"Ahhhh!" Lilith screamed. Her hands trembled as she reached for the weapon which had entered her chest full to its hilt. "Ahhhh!"

"Who's pathetic now, Lilith?"

She sank slowly to her knees.

"You were given every chance to turn back, but you wouldn't."

Blood ran from Lilith's wound. Her face turned ashen.

Mara stepped forward. "But you know what your biggest mistake was?" she asked as she advanced. "Your biggest mistake was in not taking your opportunity to kill the girls the first chance you got. It seems every wrong turn you made came about because you wanted more." She leaned in. "Well, Lilith, I didn't make that mistake. I took my first chance." She paused. "Turns out it was the only one I needed," she added as she reached out and pushed the traitor.

Lilith fell back, choking. Blood spilled from her lips. She gasped for air, but could get none. Her eyes widened. Her head dropped back and then, in a flash, she disappeared in a burst of fire.

Mara sprang back, away from the heat and flames. The moment they dissipated, she rushed to Dixon's side.

"I'm sorry, Dixon. I should have done it sooner. I'm so sorry." She dropped down at his side. She put his head in her lap and sent a stream of magic healing into him. "I'm sorry. I'm so, so, so sorry. I thought she should have the one last chance you tried to give her. Oh, Dixon, forgive me."

He gasped for air, then smiled weakly. "You were perfect."

She stroked his cheek. "I'm so sorry."

He tried to sit up, but couldn't. "Is Velia all right? Where are the girls?"

"The girls are fine. They're with Nina and Jerrett in the hallway. Are you all right?"

"Mmmm." He rubbed his head. "Check on Velia." Slowly, he made his way to his knees.

Reluctantly, she went to Velia's side. Blood trickled down the woman's face. Mara poured a stream of magic healing into her. Fortunately Lilith had used a minimum of her evil magic on the Oathtaker, as she had needed her alive.

Velia coughed and sputtered.

"Are you all right?"

"Uhhhh . . . I'm fine." She pulled herself up.

"Don't move too fast."

"No, I'm fine. She didn't use much magic on me. Mostly, it's just my head that hurts," Velia said, rubbing it, "and that from hitting the pillar."

"You sure?"

When she nodded, Mara helped her to her feet. Once done, she returned to Dixon's side.

Standing, though unsteadily, he reached out and put his hand under Mara's chin, cupping her face. Tenderly, he wiped a tear from her cheek with his thumb. "Did I ever tell you how much I love your freckles?"

Her brow rose.

"Like this one here," he said as he touched her forehead, "and this one here," he continued as he brushed her cheek, "and this one . . . right here," he said as he gently ran his finger over her lips.

"That's not a freckle."

"Well, I love it anyway."

Hot, salty tears sprang to her eyes. How cruel it seemed that the Good One would bring Dixon, the man she'd come to love, into her life just moments too late—just moments after she'd sworn her oath. She tried to move away. "Dixon—"

"This is just too cruel . . ." He hung his head. "There has got to be an answer to this dilemma." He pulled her into his arms.

For a moment, she sank into his embrace. Then with tears spilling freely, she broke free and looked deeply into his eyes. Yes, there was an answer, and in that moment, she knew what she must do.

"Come," she said. "Can you walk?"

He nodded, then dropped his head and shook it. "I'm sorry. I'm so sorry. I know—I promised you. I forgot myself."

She smiled weakly. "Don't be sorry." Then, looking away so that he couldn't see her pain, she grasped his hand. "Come on, it's over. Let's go."

CHAPTER FIFTY-ONE

The room sported marble walls, and floors, and pillars so large it would take several men to wrap their arms around any one of them. Paintings with gold gilded frames hung on the walls. A ceiling mural depicted stories from *The Book of the Blood*. Mara identified some of them: the Select breaking their chains of slavery; the Good One bestowing magical power to Patience, the first leader of the Select; and the Good One commissioning the first Oathtakers.

She marveled at the beauty of the artists' renderings. She took in a deep breath, then glanced at Dixon, who winked at her.

She smiled sadly, looked away, and sighed. She would not give in to her emotions. With his help, she'd kept the girls safe thus far, but now it was time to resolve her dilemma. She loved Dixon, of that she was certain. But she couldn't go on like this. She could no longer bear having him so near, yet so completely out of her reach. Her oath made it impossible for her to be with him, to love him, to commit to him. And so it was decided: when this was all over, she would ask him to leave her. She choked back a sob as her being was awash with the pain of a loss she had yet to experience fully.

Once again the giant oak door opened and closed. Yet another Council member had arrived. Now four sat waiting; only two had yet to arrive. Mara watched as the newest attendee sat. In spite of her heavy emotions, she had to stifle a snicker. The man's face was round and rough and hairy. He looked like a porcupine. His wide eyes seemed to peek out between his frosty, unruly eyebrows and beard. What little hair remained on his head poked out in every direction.

Skylar, Dixon said by magic. *Skylar Hadwin. He's the most renowned teacher and historian in Oosa.*

He looks like a scholar.

To Skylar's left and nearer Mara, sat a woman of advanced years, who presented herself with ageless class. She sat ramrod straight. With her hair in a bun at the crown of her head, she appeared quite tall. Lines of age criss-crossed her skin, yet it maintained a sort of luminescence, a freshness that spoke of good care. Looking at her papers, she scribbled something. The feather of her quill, obviously from some grand, exotic bird, danced.

That's Harper Larkspur, he said.

What do you know of her?

Very little. Her expertise is the law. She replaced a woman by the name of Mabel Marcel shortly before Rowena's death. I only met her once.

At whose suggestion did she replace Mabel? Lilith's?

Sorry, no idea.

Mara went back to her review of the Council members. To Harper's left, and nearest Mara on one side of the table, sat another woman, this one of fewer years. Likely in her forth decade or so, her dark hair, with one streak of white at her temple, shone. Her harsh gaze glanced about. Her jaw was set.

And she is?

Mildred Crane.

One of Lilith's supporters?

When no answer came, Mara glanced at Dixon. He smirked.

Not one of Lilith's supporters?

Mildred is as bendable as a blade of grass. She tries to portray strength, but in fact she's quite mild. She supports whoever is in charge.

What's her specialty?

Health and healing.

Mara continued her survey. Across the table from Mildred sat a man whose demeanor exuded power. His gray hair sparkled in the light. His features looked as though someone had chiseled them from stone, but also as though the sculptor had been called away too soon, leaving rough patches in his work. The man's dark eyes bore into whatever they settled on.

Piers Hamilton.

What of him?

Business. Economics.

Hmmm.

Some have said he and Lilith were 'romantically' involved—but then, with whom wasn't Lilith rumored to have been involved? He was the most vocal dissenter of Rowena's causes, verbalizing his opposition to whatever measures she suggested.

Because he genuinely disagreed? Or because he's confrontational by nature?

Dixon snickered. The Counsel members all looked his way. He brought his grin under control. *I guess we'll find out.*

The great oak door opened again. In scurried a frazzled looking man. His eyes darted about. He headed toward the nearest empty seat, across the table from Harper and to Piers's left. He caught the eye of each of the other members before taking his seat.

Eben, Dixon said. *Eben Taft.*

What should I know of him?

He's a scientist. He's frayed at the edges, but he's a rock.

Is that good or bad?

Dixon smiled. *It's good. He didn't like Lilith. He thought she was too power hungry. He regularly cautioned Rowena not to give her sister any leeway. He got that right, huh?*

One more time, the great oak door opened and closed. Mara glanced up. The last Council member to arrive was a woman who appeared to be in her late twenties or early thirties. Her face was round—some might say *cherubic*. Her light blue eyes danced, as might those of a child full of mischief. Her cheeks were rosy. Her short curly hair glistened under the lights as she seemed to bounce forward to claim the last remaining chair. She sat at Eben's left.

Mara's brow furrowed. Her eyes darted toward Dixon.

Don't be angry, he said.

Angry! Are you serious? Why didn't you tell me?

I couldn't.

Couldn't!

He looked down.

But it's—it's Lucy!

He looked back up. *I couldn't.*

Why? Because Rowena ordered you not to? What? She directs you from the grave? Mara glanced at Lucy who smiled in response. She didn't acknowledge the greeting. She looked back to Dixon and glared. *You should have told me. I might have called this meeting long ago.*

You had to do this your own way. Besides, I thought you were right not to expose the girls when we couldn't be sure what Lilith might do.

But why didn't you tell me?

I couldn't. Mara, only those who meet with the Council know who the members are.

That makes no sense.

It makes perfect sense and you know it. The rules are set up so that people cannot unfairly direct the members' attention to any cause. They keep their identity secret. If one was found out, he or she would be removed from the Council immediately. So they tell no one.

Are you telling me that if someone meets with the Council and discovers who the members are, that the information remains secret? That's crazy. People talk all the time.

Yes, but most people who meet the Council never see their faces.

Mara set her jaw. *And I'm the exception?*

Yes.

Why?

Because you called this meeting to claim your rightful place as the Council's leader. It's like I told you before—if what you said turned out to be false, the punishment would be death. You'd never have an opportunity to disclose the identity of any of the members to anyone else.

And how is it that you know who they are?

As Oathtaker to Rowena, I attended all of the Council meetings with her.

Mara huffed. *And what of their advisors? Like Edmond?*

They never meet face to face. That is, the Council sees the faces of the advisors, but not the other way around. The Council needs to be able to read the advisors' expressions and body language. In that way they can best ascertain the veracity of what the advisors tell them and can judge the power of their convictions. But the advisors do not know the identity of the Council members. It's not intended that they should read the members' faces, fashion their arguments, or create facts according to what they think someone may want to hear.

See there? They use that room there, Dixon continued as he nodded toward the back of the room, *so this is made possible. You see the window there?*

Yes.

From the other side, it's a mirror. We'll present one witness at a time. The Council will see them, but the witnesses won't see the Council.

Mara turned back to find that all of the Council members looked her way. The smile on Lucy's face seemed pasted on.

Relax, Mara, it had to be this way. Lucy's on your side. And you can prove Reigna and Eden are what you say they are. For now, that's all that matters.

I can't believe you kept this from me. All this time!

I told you. An oath bound me. I could not.

She shook her head, then slowly exhaled, as the Council members continued to stare at her.

Piers took in a deep breath and leaned forward. "Very well then," he said, "let's get started."

"Has the witness been instructed as to the penalty for telling falsehoods to this body?" asked Harper Larkspur, her legal mind ever at work.

"She has," Dixon said.

"And she was informed prior to being directed here?"

"She was."

"And she was given the option to have the ear of this Council in a closed meeting? Without benefit of attendance before us?"

"She was."

"And I understand," Harper said as she glanced down at her paperwork, "that she's been sworn in. Is that right?"

"That is correct."

"Kindly state your understanding of these legalities," Lucy said, directing her comments to Mara.

Mara stood tall. "I understand that if I give false witness about my own identity or regarding a member of the Select, if my facts and accusations are not truthful, the penalty would be death."

"Very well."

The other Council members all nodded. They wore grave expressions.

"Perhaps you'd introduce yourself," Piers said. "This is, after all, a highly unusual request—one I cannot say I support. You put us all in a very precarious position with your request and, I don't mind saying, I do not like it." He paused for effect. "Nevertheless, as you know the consequences—"

"I am Mara, rightful head of this Council by virtue of my oath taken for Rowena Vala's last born daughters, and therefore their regent," she interrupted.

Piers frowned. "I am not accustomed to being interrupted, young lady."

She smiled at him. "Pardon me, Mr.—"

"Hamilton," he filled in.

"Yes, of course, Mr. Hamilton." She glanced at the other members, all of whom, with the exception of Lucy, looked most serious. "I am Mara Richmond."

"And you have called us here because?" he asked, looking down his nose at her.

"I've called you here to introduce you to Rowena's daughters, to whom I am Oathtaker."

"I hear you refer to the first of them as the seventh seventh and the other as 'she who is but is not,' of prophetic fame," said Skylar.

"That's correct."

He smiled at her. "Tell us more." He unapologetically displayed his curious scholarly interests.

As Piers sighed, Mara pulled out her chair. "May I?" she asked. Hearing no objection, she sat. She placed her arms on the table before her. "I was called to Rowena's side as she was giving birth to the twins. I took my oath then and there. Rowena released her power with her dying breath."

"And you received a confirmation?" Skylar asked.

"I did."

"And their names are?" Mildred asked.

"Stop!" Piers ordered.

"Piers, get off your high horse," Lucy said.

His eyes flashed her way.

A stifled snicker sounded out. From whom it came, Mara could not tell. For her part, she maintained a stoic expression.

"I just want to be certain we're not misled," he said. "After all, this woman," he pointed, "is responsible for Lilith's death. It's unheard of for an Oathtaker to take the life of one of the Select."

"No, it's not," Skylar said.

All eyes turned to him. "History has some, not many, but some, examples of this. It's allowed for the ranking Select to take the life of another who tries to usurp her place."

"But she is not Select," Piers said.

"No, but an Oathtaker may act with the full authority and power of her charge. Moreover, an Oathtaker may act when the life of her charge is in imminent danger."

"Still," Piers went on, "she murdered Lilith."

"She did not murder her," Lucy said. "She pronounced and carried out the appropriate sentence—a sentence which, may I remind you, she was entirely within her rights to render, given her position as Oathtaker to the rightful ranking member."

"And how do you know it was appropriate?" Piers asked. "We haven't even determined yet whether she is the rightful head of this Council. Isn't that what this hearing is all about? Moreover, she may have misunderstood what Lilith was doing. Perhaps—" He visibly choked off his next words. Then, after a long pause, he said, "I'd like to hear the testimony of the witnesses that Miss—Miss—"

"Richmond," Mara filled in for him.

"Yes, of course, Miss . . . Richmond." He looked down his nose. "Would you be so kind as to call your first witness? I for one, do not intend to take your word alone for what has transpired. I take it your witnesses have been sworn in?" he added as an afterthought.

"They have," Dixon said.

Piers waved his hand in a circle, a gesture intended to convey that they should get on with things.

"Very well," Mara said. She turned to Dixon. "Please call Velia."

He left the room for a moment to put Velia in the witness room. Once done, he returned.

"Can you hear me, Velia?" Mara asked.

The young woman's eyes darted around the room. She saw no one, but she recognized Mara's voice. She sat forward on the edge of her chair. "I can hear you."

"Kindly tell the Council what transpired when you were with Lilith."

"Well," Velia said as she pulled in a deep breath and pulled her hair back, "Lilith traveled through the countryside with a band of thugs. There were hundreds—no, *thousands* of them. I later discovered they came from Chiran. They entered the town where I resided and they engaged in despicable behavior."

She closed her eyes as though reliving the scenes in her memory, then relayed how the soldiers entered her village and how she'd allowed them to capture her so that she could get more information about what was happening.

"You willingly went along?" Harper asked.

"That's right."

"And then?" Lucy asked.

"After I made it to their camp, I was forced to defend myself against the monsters. That's when Lilith found me. She told me she had no Oathtaker and asked if I would accompany her."

"And you agreed?" Piers asked. "If what you say about what you witnessed is true, whyever would you have agreed to accompany her?"

The witness sat up straighter and stared forward. "Because I knew she was up to no good. No Select would allow the things I saw to happen. And I knew she lied."

"How did you know that?"

"Attendant magic."

"What did you expect to learn by accompanying her?" Harper asked.

"I sought information to bring here, to this Council."

"Knowing that bearing false witness against a member of the Select carries a sentence of death?" Lucy inquired.

"Exactly. The Good One didn't call me to be Lilith's Oathtaker and fortunately, she never asked me to take an oath for her benefit. I couldn't have done so, given what I knew. She said she needed me to accompany her so that people wouldn't question the unusual circumstances of her traveling without an Oathtaker."

"Velia, what did you learn about Lilith's intentions?" Mara asked.

"I learned from her conversations with Edmond, that she intended to kill them—Rowena's girls."

"Edmond Chantray?" Lucy asked.

"That's right."

"That's what she said? That she was going to kill them?" Piers asked.

"Yes. Lilith said 'I'm going to kill him,' meaning Dixon, and then she said 'I'm going to kill them all,' meaning Dixon, Mara, and the twins."

"And there was no mistaking of whom she spoke?" Mildred inquired.

"None whatsoever. What's more, when I was with Dixon in the inner sanctuary, trying to distract Lilith, she clearly said that she was going to kill the girls."

"Is that true, Dixon?" Skylar asked.

"It is."

"What else happened?" Mildred asked.

"Well, she stole my Oathtaker's blade the day before."

Several of the Council members gasped.

"You let her take your blade?" Piers asked.

"No, I did not *let* her take my blade. She drugged me, then stole it. She needed an Oathtaker's blade to bring an end to the chain of rightful leadership through Rowena's line when she killed the girls."

"She said that?" Lucy asked.

"Yes. She said she'd only kept me alive because she needed my blade."

"And where is it now?" Eben asked.

"Right here." The witness pulled it forward. "I retrieved it when Lilith died."

"Tell us about Edmond's part in all this," Lucy said.

Velia relayed how he'd told Lilith of Mara and Dixon's whereabouts, and about the girls.

"I understand you confronted him with your accusations," Lucy said. "You did so in Dixon and Mara's presence. Is that right?"

"That is correct."

Piers directed his next question to Mara. "And Edmond denied it?"

"That's right."

He squinted his eyes. "How did you know he lied, Miss Richmond?"

"I have some ability to discern truthtelling, but that was not how I knew he lied." She explained the phenomenon that occurred when someone swore to protect the girls. "It was then we knew that Edmond was assisting Lilith. Ehyeh didn't confirm his oath."

"Miss—what's her name?" Piers asked, directing his question to Mara and gesturing toward Velia in the witness room.

"Bettina. Velia Bettina."

"Right," Piers said. "Miss Bettina, what happened with Edmond?"

"When Mara and Dixon learned of his treachery, they prepared to leave sanctuary immediately to try to stop Lilith. Edmond rushed them. He pulled a weapon. It was clear he intended to hurt one or both of them, so I grabbed a knife from my belt and stopped him in his tracks. Then I bound him and ordered a guard over him until I returned."

"Where is he now?" Mildred asked.

"He is here," Mara said.

The room quieted.

"Are there more questions for Miss Bettina?" Hearing nothing, Mara asked Dixon to get the next witness. Meanwhile, she addressed the Council. "My next witness is Jerrett Creed."

When Dixon returned, she said, "Jerrett, please tell of your time with Lilith."

"Lilith and her murderous cohorts came through my town. I learned later she'd told the soldiers that someone was trying to pawn off an imposter as a seventh seventh and that she, Lilith, would kill all the infant girls she could find—unless or until someone brought forth the child she sought. Then she hunted out all the infant girls and had them killed.

"I wanted more information to bring to this Council, so I disguised myself and joined her forces—in appearance only. When she left her camp to travel to the City of Light, none of the others wanted to accompany her. As I hoped to get more information against her anyway, I agreed to go along."

"What happened during your travels?" Lucy asked.

"I thought Velia—who I knew was an Oathtaker—assisted Lilith, but I later discovered that she also sought information and evidence against her."

"What did you discover of Lilith's plans?" Mildred asked.

"Very little. Over time I learned only that she looked for Dixon and Mara, and a child, or children."

"How did you come by this information?" Eben asked.

"Attendant magic."

"Of what form?"

"I picked up fragments of Lilith's conversation with Edmond through Donagh, my horse."

"Interesting talent," Harper commented.

As there was no question there, Jerrett said nothing.

"Anything else to add?" Mildred questioned.

"Only that Lilith did as no Select ought. Clearly, she acted with evil, wicked intent. She used terrible magic to burn people to death from the inside out and the things her men did were unspeakable."

"That will do, Jerrett, thank you," Piers finally said after a long silent moment. "Your next witness?" he asked Mara.

Dixon placed Nina in the witness room. She introduced herself, then told of how she'd joined Mara and Dixon, and how they all learned about Lilith's venture after Mara and Dixon traveled by magic to Polesk.

"Traveled by magic?" Piers inquired.

Mara explained her attendant power, then turned to her witness. "What happened when Lilith was at The Clandest Inn?"

Nina took in a deep breath. "I just remember hearing commotion in the outer room. Then I heard someone say 'Lilith.' I stood at the door to the room where I had the girls. I held a knife." She shuddered. "But the first one to enter was, I learned too late, my sister, Erin."

"What happened to her?"

"I stabbed her, thinking she was Lilith."

"And she died?" Mildred interrupted. "How awful!"

"No, she lives, thank the Good One. Someone arrived to render healing in the nick of time. She's still recovering, but she lives."

"What happened next?" Lucy asked.

"Lilith insisted that I accompany her and that we take the girls with us. She told me we were going to sanctuary."

"And you agreed to go?" Mara asked.

"What choice did I have? If I had not, she might have killed me on the spot."

"So your only concern was for your own safety," Piers said.

"No! Oh, no, I would die for those girls! I just knew that every minute I bought was one more in which Mara might discover what had happened so that she could rescue the girls."

"Then what?" Lucy asked.

Nina told the Council what transpired after she and Lilith arrived at sanctuary, how Lilith forced her into the inner room and then demanded that everyone else leave, and how Mara later rescued her and the twins.

"So you don't really know what Lilith's plans were," Piers said. "She may have meant to dedicate the children as she said, to bestow a blessing upon them."

"Oh, no. That's what she said when she took me from the inn, but when Dixon arrived, she told him she was going to take Rowena's place. It was clear she intended to kill the girls."

"Anything more?" Lucy asked.

Hearing nothing, Mara asked Dixon to prepare the next witness.

"Wait!" Nina exclaimed.

"Yes?" Piers asked, disdain in his voice. Clearly, he was not accustomed to taking orders from anyone.

"I don't know what this means, but I thought you should know that . . ." She paused. "I haven't even discussed this with Mara, as yet." She picked at her fingernail as she collected her thoughts.

"Yes?" Piers urged.

"Well . . . I was a slave in Chiran. I worked in Zarek's palace. I didn't know until Lilith came to the inn that day who she was, but I'd met her several times before."

"What's this?" Lucy sat up straighter.

"About five, maybe six years ago, she spent a good deal of time in Chiran. She accompanied Zarek wherever he went. But there, she went by a different name."

"What name was that?" Piers asked.

"Semira."

Semira? Nighttime companion? Mara said to Dixon magically. *She chose the name 'nighttime companion?'*

I wonder if she was.

"Nina," Mara said, "what was Lilith-Semira doing in Chiran?"

"Like I said, she accompanied Zarek everywhere. She acted as his consort, I guess you'd say. And at his gatherings, she played hostess."

"How long was she there?"

"I'm not sure. I saw her regularly at events for—I don't know. I guess about a year or so."

"Have you any idea why she left?"

"No." Nina shifted in her chair. "Well, that is, I can't say for certain. But it was widely believed she was pregnant at the time."

"Pregnant!" Lucy exclaimed.

"Yes, that's right. Of course she rarely spoke to us slaves directly, but I did hear that rumor."

Lucy let out a slow breath.

Mara watched her, then glanced at Dixon.

The timing is right. That child is almost certainly the one Rowena took from Lilith—the one with Lucy now.

Mara's eyes opened wide. *Great Ehyeh!* The more things seemed resolved, the more questions she found raised. She turned back to Nina.

"Did you meet Marshall? When Lilith was in Chiran, I mean?"

"Oh, no. Lilith was alone with Zarek."

Mara looked at Dixon, a question in her eyes.

It was one of Marshall's great complaints about Lilith. Occasionally, she just disappeared . . . and sometimes for long periods. At times he seemed frustrated that his bond to her didn't disclose her whereabouts to him, but as I think on it, I suppose it may have been severed when she first turned from Ehyeh and was no longer worthy of an Oathtaker's protection.

Hmmm. Makes sense. Mara thanked Nina, then asked Dixon to prepare their next witness. He did, then returned to her side.

"It's Marshall!" Mildred whispered.

"Marshall, we thank you for coming today," Mara said.

"My pleasure. I appreciate the opportunity to restore my good name."

"What do you know about all that transpired with Lilith?" Piers inquired.

"I know it was Lilith who sent assassins after Rowena."

"Are you sure about that?" Eben asked.

"As sure as I can be. Rowena heard rumors of the danger she was in at the palace, so she and Dixon left. Lilith was furious. Months later, we—that is, Lilith and I—came across Dixon in Polesk. He told Lilith about Rowena's death.

"Now, I'd been with Lilith for years and always found her to be . . . difficult, but she showed absolutely no sign of surprise or sorrow at the news of her sister's death.

"Shortly afterward, she commissioned a group of soldiers from Chiran. I saw horrible things happen between her and those . . . dogs—and that was just within the first few minutes after their arrival." He sat up straight and took in a deep breath. "That was when she released me."

"And you had committed no crime? Engaged in no behavior unbecoming?" Eben pursued.

"None whatsoever."

"How did you happen to meet up with Mara and Dixon in the city here?" Piers asked.

"I saw them at sanctuary just moments after Lilith's death."

Mara turned to the Council members. "Have you any more questions for Marshall?"

"None," Piers answered.

"Just one," Eben said.

"Go ahead," she urged.

"Marshall, would we be correct in understanding that you would like for us to restore your credentials?"

The witness looked down. He said nothing for a long moment. "Yes, but I intend to take only one oath after this."

"And that would be?"

Marshall looked straight ahead. "I intend to swear an oath to protect Rowena's girls, the rightful ranking Select."

"Is there any more testimony?" Piers inquired.

"I have three more witnesses," Mara said.

"Please proceed." He waved his hand.

Dixon set Samuel up in the witness chamber.

"Samuel, can you tell us what happened at the inn when Lilith arrived?" Mara asked.

"Mara?" he responded as he sat forward in his chair, his gaze flitting about.

"Yes."

"Is that you?"

The Council members laughed lightly.

"Yes, Samuel. I know you can't see me, but can you hear me all right?"

He nodded, but his eyes continued to dart about.

"It's all right, Samuel. Just answer the questions honestly."

"All right."

"Please tell us what happened at the inn when Lilith arrived."

"Yes," he said as he slowly relaxed. "Ahhh . . . right. Ahhh, Lilith killed Jamison who guarded the outer door. When she got inside, she used some awful magic on me. I tried to use some of our magic crystals to stop her, but I couldn't get to them in time."

"Magic crystals!" Lucy exclaimed.

Mara grinned. "Another story for another time." She turned her attention back to her witness. "Then what happened?"

"She pushed Erin into the inner room."

Mara was momentarily startled as she realized that she'd never before heard Samuel say so much at any one time. "Did Lilith say anything?"

"Yes. She said she'd kill Nina if she didn't help. I wanted to lend aid, but . . ."

"What happened when Dixon and I arrived?"

"I was in a bad state." He told how Mara healed him enough so that he could tell her where Lilith had gone. "Ezra arrived minutes later. He helped Erin and then me. Had he not, we might both be dead now."

"Thank you, Samuel."

Mara looked at the Council members one by one, inquiring with her raised brow whether they had any more questions. Confirming they did not, she asked Dixon to prepare the next witness.

"My next witness is Ezra," she said to the Council. "Thank you, Ezra, for attending today."

"Think nothing of it." He brushed the beard below his chin with the back of his hand.

"What can you tell us about Lilith's visit to the inn?"

"Not much. She— Well, I feel terrible I didn't recognize her. But all our evidence indicated that she camped with her army miles from the city." He hesitated. "She wasn't dressed in her usual manner when she arrived and she kept her face from view."

"And you never suspected it was Lilith?"

He shook his head. "Never. As I said, we thought she was elsewhere and . . . and it is not, after all, unusual for people to show up at the Clandest Inn for, shall we say, their own private affairs."

"The Clandest Inn?" Harper said. If anything, she sat up even straighter.

Ezra grinned. "That's right."

"And you are an Oathtaker yourself, are you not?" Mildred inquired. There was a note of severe disapproval in her voice.

"That's right."

"Rather unusual occupation for an Oathtaker, wouldn't you say?" Harper asked.

Ezra coughed to suppress a smile. "You might say. But when it comes to gathering necessary information, it can't be beat."

"Have you a charge?" Piers asked.

"Nope. Did have. Died of old age."

"Very well then," Mara said. "When Dixon called you by magic to assist with Samuel—"

"Called by magic?" Eben interrupted.

Mara grinned. "Yes. Again, that's another topic for another time. I'll happily fill you in." She turned back to her witness. "So you helped to heal Samuel and Erin, is that right?"

"That's right."

"Have you anything further to add?"

"Only that they both identified Lilith as the person responsible for their injuries when they still thought they might die."

"Death bed statements," Harper muttered, her legal mind never resting.

"Any further questions for Ezra?" Mara asked.

"None," several of the Council members responded together.

"Thank you, Ezra." She turned to the Council. "We have one final witness—a hostile witness."

"Edmond?" Lucy asked.

"That's right."

Dixon put Edmond in the witness room. The man sat haughtily, though his hands were tied behind his back. In addition to his standard solid black attire, he wore a sneer.

"May I?" Dixon asked Mara.

"Please, do," she said, with an uplifted hand.

"Edmond," he said, "you traveled with Lilith. Is that right?"

The witness made a face. "Yes."

"And you told her of the whereabouts of Mara and the twins?"

"If you say so."

"Velia testified that you intended to get even with me, that you wanted revenge. Please tell the Council why you sought revenge."

Edmond's lip curled. "What's the point, Dixon? They'll believe anything you say, just as the Council believed everything your father said about mine. Your father's lies were the reason mine was sentenced to death."

Dixon looked to the Council. "Have you any further questions for this witness?"

"Yes," Lucy said quietly, then raised her voice so Edmond could hear her. "Ahhh, Edmond," she began slowly, "you were with Dixon when Judith died. What do you know of her death?"

Dixon's eyes opened wide.

"Judith? Dixon's first charge? The first one he allowed to die?" Edmond responded mockingly.

"The very one."

He shrugged. His sneer became more intense.

"Did you have anything to do with her death?"

He smiled. "Of course not."

"He's lying," Mara said. She'd been unable to read through Edmond before. Gratified she could now, she picked up the questioning. "Edmond, did Lilith use some magic on you to disguise your true intentions from us?"

He said nothing. He closed his eyes and sighed deeply as though bored with the goings on.

All went silent.

"Any other questions for Edmond?" Dixon finally asked.

"None," the members responded collectively.

Dixon escorted Edmond out from the witness room, then returned.

Mara faced the Council. "That was our last witness."

Not surprisingly, Piers spoke first. He took in a deep breath and leaned forward. "Are you so sure Lilith did not serve the Good One? That you did not misunderstand something?"

"There was no misunderstanding," Dixon stated emphatically.

Piers stared at him. "You're so certain? Sometimes things are not what they seem."

Dixon drummed a rhythm on his thigh. "Have you ever seen a grut when it's killed?"

Piers pulled back. "I don't see what that has to do with anything."

"It has everything to do with it," Mara said. "If you ever saw a grut die, then you know it goes up in a burst of flame as it's returned to Sinespe."

"That's right."

"And that's exactly what happened when Lilith died," she said.

He pursed his lips. "She went up in a burst of fire?"

"She did."

"Very well," he said, smiling weakly. He paused, tapping on the table. "So you say Lilith went up in flames because she tried to usurp the girls' position?"

"No," Mara responded without hesitation, "she went up in flames because she swore to serve Daeva."

"That is as would be expected under such circumstances," Skylar, always the scholar, offered.

"Well," Eben finally spoke, "I am convinced. Does anyone have any remaining questions?"

No one said anything.

"Very well then," he said, "let's see a show of hands of those who agree Mara is who she claims to be, and that her part in Lilith's death was justified."

One by one, the Council members raised their hands, Piers the last of them.

Mara bowed slightly to the group, then tapped on the edge of the table. "If there's nothing more, I'm prepared to introduce Rowena's girls to you."

"Yes, I believe you were going to tell us their names," Mildred said as her eyes shot toward Piers.

Mara grinned. "Reigna is the firstborn. Eden is her twin."

"And you can prove their identities?" Harper inquired.

"I can. They still bear the signs of their birth."

"Well, I'd like to see them," Lucy said. "Would you bring them in?" she asked Dixon.

He walked out. Moments later he returned, carrying the girls in his arms. He approached Mara.

She took Reigna from him, then smiled as the infant placed her little hands upon her caregiver's cheeks.

"Here, baby," she said, "let's show them your sign." She moved Reigna's hair to reveal her birthmark.

"Oh!" Mildred exclaimed.

"Ah!" "Skylar added.

Dixon showed them Eden's sign. Once again, exclamations came from around the table. After everyone took a good look, Skylar asked to hold Eden. Dixon passed her to him.

"Well, I have never seen the like!" the scholar exclaimed, unable to take his eyes from the child's most unusual birth sign.

"And your plans at this stage are?" Mildred asked.

Mara glanced at Lucy. "I'm concerned about raising the girls in the city. I feel led to remove them."

"But what of your Council duties?" Harper asked as she reached for Reigna who went to her without complaint.

"I'll travel as need be."

"May we inquire where you'll take the girls?" Piers asked.

"You may," she said, looking him in the eyes, "but I will not say."

One by one the Council members nodded their understanding and consent.

"Have you any further questions then? Mara asked.

No one spoke.

"There being no further business then, we will—

"Wait!"

Mara looked up. It was Lucy who'd spoken.

"There is one more item of business."

"Very well."

Lucy leaned forward. She hesitated for a long moment. "I have had the . . . opportunity . . . to spend some time with some people who traveled with you during these past months."

"Yes, Rowena's sister, Therese, and her Oathtaker, Basha, among others."

"Therese!" exclaimed Harper.

"That's right, she lives," Mara said.

"Why, that's amazing!"

"It is so," Lucy said, smiling. Then her expression turned serious. "They tell me that . . . Well, I understand this may seem a private matter to you, but it is an appropriate one for this Council."

Mara gulped. She feared she knew what was coming. "Yes?"

Lucy's eyes darted to Dixon, then back to Mara. "I understand that you and Dixon—"

"Say no more," Mara interrupted, lifting her hand to stop Lucy mid-sentence. She looked at Dixon. Her eyes filled with tears. Turning her attention back to the Council, she swallowed hard, trying to hold her tears at bay. "Dixon will be moving on after this meeting," she finally said, her voice barely above a whisper.

Chapter Fifty-Two

Dixon sat up straight. "What? No! No, Mara!"

She refused to meet his eyes. She looked around the table. "Rest assured, we did not intend it, but . . . but Dixon and I—" She choked back a sob. "The truth is that . . ." Finally, she looked again at him. A tear spilled. She wiped it away roughly.

"You love him," Lucy said.

Mara looked down. "Yes," she finally acknowledged, turning her gaze back up. "And you, Dixon?"

His eyes hadn't moved from Mara. He looked as though he wanted to reach out, to hold her, to wipe her tears away. "Yes, I love her. But we . . . understand. It is not possible for us to . . . That is, an Oathtaker may not be committed—does not marry."

Mara fought to hold back her tears. He'd never said the word *marry* before. Somehow it made the whole thing even more painful.

"And why is that?" Lucy asked.

Mara lifted her head high. "An Oathtaker may not marry so long as his or her charge lives."

"Yes, but why?"

"Because an Oathtaker may not be unequally yoked."

"Do you know what that means?"

"Yes. That's why I'm asking Dixon to . . . leave me." Mara glanced his way, but he looked only at the floor.

The room went quiet. Moments later, someone chuckled. Mara looked around. It was Lucy. How could she take something so serious, so painful, as a joke? *How cruel!*

Lucy stifled her smile. "I *am* sorry. I just—" She put on a serious expression. "Mara, Dixon," she said as her gaze shifted from one to the other, "do you know what it means to be unequally yoked? Why it's not allowed?"

Dixon beat a rhythm on his knee. "Yes, we do," he said as he went still. Clearly, he was angry at the woman for her apparent lack of feeling.

"I don't think so."

He looked up and glared at her. "What do you mean?"

"An Oathtaker takes an oath unto death to protect his or her charge. Correct?"

"Correct," Mara and Dixon responded together.

"If an Oathtaker has a charge, that Oathtaker cannot also swear his life to another in marriage because that other person would not be subject to the same oath. It would be like yoking a—an oxen and a horse together. They don't proceed at the same pace, move with the same gait, or seek the same destination.

"Even the Oathtaker's own charge couldn't take the same oath in an effort to try to be equally yoked with his Oathtaker because it would mean taking an oath to himself. And even if that was possible—and it is not, it would cause an . . . imbalance between them. The relationship would be entirely one-sided, lopsided. They would be unequally yoked. Correct?"

"Correct," Mara and Dixon again replied in unison.

"But you two have both taken the same oath."

Mara's eyes opened wide. "Wh—what?"

"Unless I got the news wrong, both you and Dixon swore to protect those girls with your life and Ehyeh confirmed both of your oaths." Lucy looked from one to the other. "Do I understand this correctly or did I get this all wrong?"

"No! I mean yes. I mean, no you didn't get it wrong!" Mara exclaimed.

"So then, you are equally yoked." Lucy leaned back and shook her head. "I can't believe you didn't know this." She paused. "Did you even bother to read this— this—" She patted at her pockets, then pulled out a book. "Here it is. *The Significance of the Oath: Rules and Exclusions*," she read from the cover. "You sent it with Basha and Therese. Did you read it?"

"I—ahhh," Mara stuttered. She recognized the book as the one from which she learned that an Oathtaker could swear to protect more than one of the Select.

"Well, *I* did," Lucy said, "and I've discussed what it says with Skylar. There is no mistake. It clearly provides that if two people swear a life oath for the benefit of the *same* of the Select and if both of those Oathtakers receive a confirmation of that oath, then—"

"Do you mean to say—" Dixon interrupted.

"I do."

"But what if—" Mara began.

"It's true," Skylar cut her off. "Really, you young people should read more," he said, shaking his head.

Mara's mouth dropped open and her eyes widened as she stared at the scholar. If he knew how much they'd read and studied over the past months, he would never have said such a thing.

Dixon jumped to his feet. He paced. Then he turned back to Mara, dropped to his knees and took her hand.

She put her finger on his lips, then smiled and shook her head. "You don't even have to ask!"

The room erupted in laughter and applause.

He rose, pulled her up, and wrapped his arms around her. He leaned in and lingered, his lips almost touching hers. Finally, he kissed her softly, sweetly.

"Well," she said as she looked out at the others, "as I was saying earlier, if there's no further business . . ." Tears glistened in her eyes.

"None!" the Council members exclaimed in unison.

"Then we are adjourned!" she said over her shoulder before kissing Dixon again.

The Counsel members all offered Mara and Dixon their congratulations. Skylar bounced Eden on his knee. Harper and Mildred took turns holding Reigna.

"I'm happy the days of Lilith are over," Eben said to Mara as he stood at her side.

She laughed. "So am I, Mr. Taft."

"Eben."

"Eben," she repeated. She looked back at Dixon who stood behind her with his arms around her. He and Piers talked.

Piers looked at Reigna with a broad smile. He stepped toward the infant, whom Mildred held, and reached for her. Reigna went to him without hesitation. Then she leaned forward, her mouth full open, to kiss him in the manner that infants do.

He wiped the slobber off his cheek. Mara, expecting him to scowl, was surprised when instead, he laughed. He turned to her. "They are beautiful, healthy girls."

She was taken aback. She expected him to be distant and argumentative. "Thank you."

"Listen." He leaned in. "The truth is, I'm a softie. Especially for children . . . and beautiful young women."

Her brow shot up.

"Hey, hey, hey!" Dixon said.

"Not to worry. I've no unseemly intentions. Just know that I'm on your side—though I do have a reputation to protect," Piers added, his voice lowered. "And remember this: someone has to ask the hard questions. Someone has to resist what's easy." He grinned and raised a brow.

Mara smiled back. "You're right. Thank you, Mr. Hamilton."

"Piers. It's Piers to you."

"Piers," she repeated. "Thank you."

Some minutes later, the Council members all made their way out through the secret passages and tunnels connected to their offices. Mara marveled at the planning that had gone into the building to accommodate for such a group. She had so much to learn. Now holding Reigna on one hip, she turned to Dixon who held Eden in a similar manner.

"Oh, how I love you!" he exclaimed. He looked down and shuffled his feet. "I told you before that I thought I loved you from the moment you tried to send me away, but . . ." He looked back up. "But I wonder. Maybe I really loved you from the moment I first set eyes on you."

He put his hand under her chin and kissed her. Then he leaned back and studied her closely. "And you? When did my charm get the better of you?" he asked, smiling.

She took in a deep breath. "I never thought it was possible . . . But from the moment you tried to kill me—"

"What? I never!"

"You most certainly did!" she exclaimed. "When you burst into that hut, I thought I'd never laid eyes on anyone so—so fearsome! And then you tried to kill me. I guess I just couldn't help myself. I mean, really, how could I not love that?"

They laughed together. Then Dixon put his arm around her and kissed her again. His gaze softened.

"Well, my future Mrs. Townsend," he said, smiling. "You will be my Mrs. Townsend, won't you?" He tilted his head in question.

"I will," she said, "provided—"

"Provided!" His brow furrowed.

"Provided you don't try to kill me again."

"I never!"

"You did!" she exclaimed, laughing all the while.

Dixon winked at her. "Are you ready to go then?"

"So long as you go with me."

Keep reading for a sneak peek at Select: The Oathtaker Series, Volume Two

Excerpt

Select: The Oathtaker Series, Volume Two

Chapter One

Hurry. Hurry!

Stop. Come this way.

Do you see him there? There, to your left. See? Right there!

I've got him. I've got him!

Stop. No, don't go. This way. This way! Come with me.

Watch out! There's one behind you.

The shouts and exclamations the Oathtakers communicated to one another magically, and therefore silently, continued as the group that had left their home base earlier to search for a missing compound member, sought to respond to an invasion of their place of refuge. After moving to the camp nearly two decades earlier, the Oathtakers had used magic crystals to fortify most of its perimeter against incursions from the curious and the threatening. But a recent vicious storm knocked down portions of those protections in the surrounding hills and across the wide river that separated one side of their retreat from the outside world. Consequently, encroachments across its borders had increased over the past months, and in recent weeks, had become incrementally more frequent and dangerous.

I've got it, Dixon, Mara said, after peeking around the boulder behind which the two of them hid.

She pulled a poison-tipped arrow from her quiver, stood, quickly took aim, and then released her shot. Moving easily in her standard Oathtakers' garb, a half dozen knives hung from sheaths about her waist and boots, and resting in its holder at the back of her neck, ready to be used with the flick of her wrist, she carried Spira, her Oathtaker's blade, a magic weapon that would never miss its mark.

Dixon crouched down. His back to Mara, he turned her way, caught her eye momentarily, and then winked. She was the love of his life, and he of hers. It was only due to a unique magic exception that the two had been able to commit to one another even though Mara had a living charge—or charges, as it happened—the twins, Reigna and Eden, the current ranking members of the Select.

"Charmer," she whispered, grinning.

Got you! Ha!

She spun around to find Velia, who smiled with satisfaction as she sprang out from her place of concealment. Seconds later, her latest target grunted and then fell to the earth.

Good work, Velia, Basha complimented her cohort.

Mara offered a silent prayer of gratitude for her friends. Over time, she'd discovered that each of the other Oathtakers and Select who'd sworn a life oath to protect her charges, enjoyed as did she, *continued youth* from the moment he pledged his vow. None knew if he'd ever age again. Indeed, they preferred not to know, as they surmised that they'd learn the answer to their question only after the death of one, or of both, of the twins. Even so, the phenomenon meant that each remained every bit as strong and vital as he'd been on the day he'd first given his oath. Better yet, as time progressed, each became fortified with the wisdom that came with age, experience, and a continuously improving understanding and appreciation of the Good One's principles.

She glanced briefly at her longtime friends, Basha and Velia, then at the two additional Oathtakers who rounded out her troop. She'd chosen Kayson to accompany her on her mission, since his attendant magic included, as did her own, the power to heal. She'd also selected Raman, whose temperament she particularly enjoyed. Since nothing brought the man's spirits down, he wore a nearly constant smile.

She peeked around the edge of the boulder. Waves of heat hung in the air, making things in the distance appear distorted. For a moment, she recollected a long ago similarly sweltering day—the day she'd been called to the side of Rowena, the former ranking member of the first family of the Select as she labored to birth her twins.

She inched closer to Dixon.

Turning to her, he raised five fingers to designate the number remaining.

"Ready?" Velia whispered as she sidled nearer.

When Mara stepped back to make room for her, Dixon restrained her, as from there the ground quickly dropped off.

Looking down at the treacherous area below, littered with sharp rocks that fell away at a steep slant, Mara nodded her understanding. Then she gestured for the group to divide their attentions. She and Dixon would direct theirs to the left, while Basha, Velia, Kayson, and Raman, would remain focused to the right.

After retrieving a clear magic crystal from her pocket, she peeked out again.

Just then, the enemy, apparently also recognizing the Oathtakers' vulnerable position, advanced in a rush.

"They're coming!" she cried.

Dixon sprang out from the left, with a knife in each hand.

Kayson, similarly armed, ran out from the right. Basha followed at his heels, holding a bow with an arrow nocked. Behind her came Velia, sporting her Oathtaker's blade, Justise, at the ready. Finally, Raman headed out, wielding a sword.

Mara jumped up. She pulled her arm back, preparing to throw her crystal. She needed to toss it sufficiently far that it wouldn't harm her cohorts when it landed and then exploded.

At precisely that moment, one of the enemy forces, hidden in a tree, shot an arrow that rushed in at Mara from high on her left side. She tossed her crystal a mere heartbeat in time before the trespasser's arrow pierced her shoulder.

Startled, she stepped back, catching her foot on the edge of the drop off. Then, in the space of a single breath, she experienced the shock of finding no earth beneath her.

Tumbling backward, she fell down . . . down . . . down . . .

The crystal that Mara threw, blew up, killing three of the remaining trespassers. Then Dixon and the other Oathtakers defeated the last of the intruders.

Dixon turned back. "Where's Mara?" he asked.

"She probably traveled magically to come in at the enemy from its other side," Basha said.

The Oathtakers waited for a time, but when Mara didn't reappear, spread out to scout the area.

Minutes later, Dixon found scuffmarks at the edge of the precipice behind the boulder. He looked down to find her below, unmoving, just as Basha approached his side.

"Move. Move!" he ordered.

"Oh, dear Ehyeh!" Basha exclaimed, her eyes following his gaze.

He brushed past her, then started down the drop-off. A rock loosened beneath his step. Pebbles scattered before him. Not wanting to cause an avalanche of rock, he focused more carefully.

She has to be all right—she just has to be.

His foot slipped. He readjusted his weight, found new purchase with his next step, and then continued. The minutes seemed interminably long.

Finally, just a few feet from where Mara rested, he jumped to the ground and rushed to her side.

"Is she all right?" Velia cried from above.

Ignoring her query, he fought to still the rising panic that bubbled up in his stomach.

He removed brush from over her, careful not to touch the arrow that protruded from her shoulder. He didn't remove it, reasoning that so long as it remained imbedded, she wouldn't bleed severely.

He checked her pulse. *She lives!*

Leaning in closer, he whispered, "Mara. Mara, are you all right?" Gently, he turned her face toward himself. He felt blood from a gash decorating the side of her head, warm and sticky against his skin.

"Is she all right?" Velia called out again, her voice worry-laden.

He looked up and, swallowing hard, nodded.

He contemplated how he'd return to the others. He couldn't carry her back up the rocky wall, but the ground below leveled off before meandering toward the nearby river.

"I'll take her that way," he said, gesturing to his right.

He put one arm behind Mara's neck, the other beneath her knees, and then gently lifted her. Her weight was nothing compared to the heaviness of his worry and guilt. He scolded himself for having let her join him in such a precarious place, for not having protected her.

"Mara," he whispered, "are you all right? Can you hear me?"

She remained silent, unmoving.

He fought his way through the rock and brush that lead to the river. When he arrived at its edge, Basha made her way toward him. Shaking with worry, he pulled Mara closer, then kissed her forehead.

Basha moved Mara's hair to the side to reveal the cut on her head. "Put her down, Dixon. Kayson can heal her."

Tears misted his eyes. "The cut is not the worst of it," he said. "It bleeds, but not all that badly. For that matter, her shoulder wound doesn't seem the primary concern. I'm afraid she's suffered a concussion. She hasn't responded to anything. I think we should just hurry back to the compound and then see to healing her there. You know Mara," he added, then swallowed hard, holding his emotions in check, "if she regains consciousness now, she'll insist on making her own way back home."

Basha watched her fellow Oathtaker closely. Having believed some years past that she'd lost her charge, Therese, when she fell from a cliff during an assassination attempt, she wordlessly conveyed her understanding and sympathy.

Kayson and Raman drew near.

"How is she?" Kayson asked.

Basha glanced his way, then turned back to Dixon. "Why don't you at least let Kayson remove the arrow and stem the bleeding?"

Nodding, Dixon dropped to his knees. He placed Mara on the ground.

Velia stepped up to his side. "Is she all right?"

"The gash on her head is . . . Well, I've seen worse," Dixon said, through gritted teeth. "Kayson's going to remove the arrow now, and then I'll carry her back to the compound. He can see to her other injuries there."

"That sounds good."

"I'll keep an eye out," Raman offered. Contrary to his usual demeanor, he was not smiling.

Kayson knelt at Mara's side. He examined her wounds. The arrow hadn't gone quite through her back. After snapping off the fletching end, he turned her on her side. Then, while Dixon and Basha held her still, he forced the point through. Once done, he slipped out the remaining shaft.

Blood poured.

Placing his hands over the wound, Kayson peered into it with his attendant magic and then sent forth a healing stream.

A long minute passed in silence as Mara's bleeding slowed. Then, after what seemed an eternity to Dixon, it stopped altogether.

He glanced at each of his friends in turn, his heart in his eyes, his hands shaking.

"Dixon, she's going to be fine," Velia said, stroking his arm.

"Let me see to the wound on her head," Kayson offered.

"No, it's not bleeding now," Dixon said. "Let's get going." He took Mara back into his arms.

"Careful," Basha cautioned, "her shoulder wound could easily re-open."

"Why don't you let us help carry her at least, Dixon? We could make a stretcher," Velia suggested.

He pulled his beloved closer. "No, I've got her."

"But, Dixon, we're quite a distance from the compound center."

"I've got her," he repeated, his voice soft but emphatic. He would not release his hold.

"All right then," Basha said, "we're through here. Let's go."

Just then, an arrow came flying in. The leaves of the trees overhead rustled as the projectile flew past the Oathtakers.

"Down!" Kayson cried.

They dropped to the ground. Dixon gently covered Mara's body with his own.

Another arrow came forth, this time just missing Velia.

Basha looked up. "There!" she shouted, pointing.

A man, grinning, stood at the top of the crag.

Her jaw set. Then, as the intruder reached for another arrow, so too did she. She moved so quickly that hers reached the intruder's chest before he could loose his own.

The man swayed, then tumbled down.

"Leave him," Dixon ordered as he got to his feet and marched off.

With the river to his right, Velia rushed up to his left. Kayson and Raman took the lead, and Basha, the rear.

Then they all, but for Dixon, continually scanned the area for possible additional attacks. He, fully intent on his mission, kept his eyes fixed firmly forward.

Although Kayson and Raman repeatedly asked Dixon if they could carry Mara for a time, he refused any offer of assistance. Rather, each time they approached him, he tightened his hold. All the while, she remained as silent as death in his arms.

Hours later, the group arrived back at the central compound. When they finally made it to the innermost area, Basha's charge, Therese, with a handful of guards following, ran out to meet them.

"I can help," offered one of the newcomers.

Dixon shook his head "no." His arms suffered from the weight he'd carried for so long, but he refused any assistance.

"Dixon! Dixon!" a woman shouted.

He looked up.

Lucy rushed toward him. Her light blue eyes, usually dancing with mischief, portrayed only seriousness now, as they darted from one member of the incoming group, to another.

"Is she all right?" she cried.

Basha grabbed her arm and pulled her along. "She'll be fine," she said. "She took an arrow in her shoulder and fell, and it seems she's suffered a concussion."

Lucy tapped on Kayson's shoulder from behind. "Why didn't you see to her injuries immediately?"

"Because," Dixon interrupted, his voice hard, "we didn't want her insisting on making her own way back."

"You were right, Dixon, of course."

Lucy first established the camp when Rowena still carried Reigna and Eden. Over the years, the compound residents developed it into a place that met nearly all the needs of the numerous Select, along with their Oathtakers, who resided there. In addition, the camp was home to Oathtakers who were trained, but didn't currently have charges of their own. Most of the residents had sworn life oaths to protect Reigna and Eden.

The compound afforded the community with their own sanctuary for prayer, separate family living quarters, a common meeting area, a library and place for study, an infirmary, and training grounds. Largely self sufficient, living off the land, hunting the surrounding forest and fishing from the nearby river, the camp residents also kept gardens, tended orchards, and grew their own herbs for both culinary and medicinal purposes.

Dixon strode past several buildings and gardens, down the center thoroughfare.

"Make sure a unit is sent out to that section," he said to no one in particular, "and make sure they're well armed and relieved regularly."

"It's already been done, Dixon," Velia said.

"I don't know how a group that large made it through all of our sentries before we noticed," he muttered.

"We're looking into it now, Dixon," said Lucy, the unofficial leader at the compound—in her own eyes, if not in the eyes of the others. Looking just older than Mara, with curly hair and rosy cheeks, she was actually centuries old. She'd been Oathtaker to the last two known female sevenths before Rowena. Years later, she worked with Rowena, planning and orchestrating for her coming children—girl children—down to her seventh pregnancy. The two hoped that the child Rowena bore would be the seventh seventh foretold of in prophecy—the one who might help to usher in a new age.

Reigna was Rowena's seventh-born child—a seventh daughter of a seventh daughter. But to the amazement of all, Rowena also bore Reigna's identical twin, Eden. Until that day, no Select had ever before born more than a single child at a time. Thus, it was not until after the twins' birth, that Lucy and the others finally made sense of prophecies that theretofore went beyond their understanding. The scripts told of a seventh seventh and of "she who is, but is not." Eden, born of a seventh pregnancy, was not a seventh-born child. Her birth fulfilled those prophecies.

When Dixon reached the infirmary, Basha jumped before him to open the door.

He stepped inside.

"Dixon. Dixon!" someone called.

"Oh Dixon, what happened?" another cried.

He looked up. Tears welled in his eyes, as Reigna and Eden rushed toward him. The girls, actually young women now, could always soften his brashness.

His eyes darted from one of the beauties to the other. Whenever he looked at one of them, he felt he saw their mother once again, though whereas Rowena had sported brilliant green eyes, the twins' eyes were light brown, and whereas Rowena's hair had been auburn, the girls had lighter tresses that glistened with copper highlights. Aside from those differences, the two had grown into Rowena's spitting image, with her high cheekbones, and with the same flawless skin—skin that gave them an almost unearthly quality. But while so identical in sight as to be difficult to differentiate from one another, their likenesses ended there. They differed profoundly in personality. Reigna was loud, Eden, quiet; Reigna, a speaker, Eden, a listener; Reigna, a doer, Eden, a thinker; Reigna, an instigator, Eden, a responder. They balanced one another perfectly, and each idolized the other.

Gently, Dixon laid Mara on a nearby cot. "She'll be all right. She'll be all right," he said.

The door opened to more visitors. In walked Nina and Jules, each of whom wore a grim expression.

"Did you find her?" Nina asked, tears in her eyes.

Basha neared her. "No, I'm sorry, we found no sign of Carlie."

"What could have happened, do you think?"

"I don't know, but we'll keep looking. She's been trained to survive in the wilderness, don't forget."

Nina held Jules's hand. Together, they approached Dixon.

"We're so sorry about Mara," Nina said to him. A petite woman, with raven hair and coffee colored skin, she wiped the tears from her deep, dark eyes. Having escaped her homeland, Chiran, as a young woman, losing her child along the way, she'd met Mara and Dixon when the twins were just days old. She agreed to join them to help mother the twins, and had been with them since.

Jules stood at her side. He and his cousin, Samuel, had also joined Mara and Dixon years ago. To Mara's delight, he and Nina fell in love, and married. Their three children brought great joy to everyone at the compound, along with some recent sadness, as their eldest, Carlie, had been missing now for days.

Dixon turned their way. "Yes, well, like Basha said, we didn't find Carlie."

"Yes, we know." Nina swallowed hard. "Will Mara be all right, do you think? Is there anything we can do?"

"What happened?" Reigna asked, as she and her sister sidled up to Dixon.

His eyes flickered toward the young women for an instant and then, just as quickly, he averted his gaze.

Basha stepped up. She put an arm around each of the twins. "She'll be fine. Now, why don't you two leave us to see to her needs?"

"We want to help," Eden said.

"There's really nothing you can do."

"Can't someone heal her?"

"Of course. We just didn't want her to try to do too much, too soon. So we brought her back here right away." Basha squeezed them closer for a moment. "Really, she's going to be fine. Kayson already healed her shoulder. So, you two go on then, and I'll let you know when we're through here."

Reigna pulled away. "Goodness, we're not children, you know."

The remark startling her, Basha blinked repeatedly. "Of course not. I know that. We just need some space, that's all. You'd be of most help if you left us to this."

"I'm not leaving."

Letting her breath out slowly, Basha glanced at her, then at her sister.

"Neither am I," Eden said.

All eyes turned her way. It was so unlike Eden not to act as the peacemaker.

"All right, then," Basha said, "but you'll have to stay out of the way and allow

Kayson some quiet so that he can concentrate."

Reigna pulled out two chairs. She pointed to one, directing with a nod at Eden that it was meant for her. Then she sat in the other.

Dixon watched them. He couldn't recall that they'd ever before asserted their will over that of their elders. But just now, they refused to be ignored. He knew that when a young person came of age, she often had to demand her place amongst the adults in just such a manner. He also knew that her doing so, even just once, was usually sufficient. Too often the young person who lacked the wherewithal to do so, never fully grew up. In that moment, he knew that he and Mara had done a fine job raising the twins, of preparing them for independence. Perhaps they'd soon be ready to take their rightful places and to lead the Select. The thought both satisfied and alarmed him.

"Isn't there something we can do to help?" Reigna asked.

Basha smiled weakly. "Not just now. But your being here is sure to help Mara when she comes to."

She brought another chair to the bedside and then motioned to Kayson that it was for him. Once done, she turned to the rest of the company. "You all should go now," she said.

"I'm staying," Dixon said.

"Of course you are, Dixon. As to the rest of you though . . ." She gestured toward the door.

Slowly, Lucy, Therese, Nina, and Jules, made their way toward it.

"Keep us posted," Lucy said, stepping out.

After they left, Basha got chairs for herself and Dixon. As she sat down, she turned to Kayson. It was time to begin.

He moved Mara's hair to inspect the wound on her head. Then he placed his hands to each side of her face, concentrating, calling forth his magic.

Dixon paced back and forth, back and forth.

"Dixon, sit down," Basha ordered without looking his way.

He sat. Within moments, he started tapping a beat with his hand to his thigh. It was a mannerism he often acted out when concerned or in deep thought.

"Dixon," Basha said, glancing his way.

"What?" He sprang to his feet.

"Stop it," she ordered, looking at his hand when he resumed patting to an unheard beat.

He held her gaze, exhaling slowly, audibly. He sat back down, folded his hands, and then dropped them between his knees. He leaned forward and looked down. With his toes to the floor and heels raised, he bounced one leg up and down.

The twins watched him for a moment. Then Eden took his hand. She smiled softly when their eyes met. With her other hand, she reached for her sister. The three exchanged glances and then collectively, turned back to Kayson.

With Dixon momentarily quieted, Basha nodded at the healer, signaling for him to continue.

After shaking his head to clear his thoughts, Kayson peered inside to get a firm idea of the extent of Mara's injuries. Then he sent a stream of magic into his patient. With both his physical eyes, and his eyes of magic, he watched as the gash to her head healed. Within minutes, only a thin pink line remained of the wound.

He increased his magic stream as he surveyed her other injuries. The fall had jarred her shoulder. He concentrated on putting it in place and then added a cushion of comfort around it while removing some excess inflammation.

Continuing on, he followed his attendant power to her head. He poured out more magic.

The minutes seemed to drag on in the silent room.

Finally, when his energy waned, Kayson glanced up at Basha and nodded.

She turned to Dixon and the twins. "Now, we wait," she said.

About the Author

Patricia Reding leads a double life. By day, she practices law. By night, she reads, reviews a wide variety of works, and writes fantasy. She lives on an island on the Mississippi with her husband and youngest daughter (her son and oldest daughter having already flown the nest), and Flynn Rider, an English Cream Golden Retriever. From there, she seeks to create a world in which she can be in two places at once. She took up *Oathtaker* as a challenge, and re-discovered along the way, the joy of storytelling.

Oathtaker, is Volume One of *The Oathtaker Series*. *Select*, is Volume Two of *The Oathtaker Series*. *Ephemeral and Fleeting*, is Volume Three of *The Oathtaker Series*.

For more information, join the author at www.PatriciaReding.com. Also, you may like her at her Amazon page and at www.Facebook.com/PatriciaRedingAuthor, fan and follow her at www.Goodreads.com, and follow her at www.PatriciaReding.BookLikes.com.

NOTE FROM THE AUTHOR

Thank you for your kind attention to *Oathtaker*, and now to *Select*. I hope you've enjoyed the journey. I would very much appreciate if you'd take a minute to leave a review at (any or all of) Amazon, Barnes and Noble, Goodreads, Booklikes, Readers Favorite, or elsewhere. Also, please take a minute to add your name to my mailing list at www.PatriciaReding.com. Thank you, again.

AWARDS

Oathtaker was a GOLD medal winner in the Literary Classics International Book Award contest, was an award-winner in the Readers' Favorite International Book Award contest, and was a Finalist in the Beverly Hills International Book Award Contest. Find out more at www.LiteraryClassics.org, www.ReadersFavorite.com, and at www.BeverlyHillsBookAwards.com.

Select was a SILVER medal winner in the Literary Classics International Book Award contest, and was awarded a Finalist in the Readers' Favorite International Book Award Contest.

Both *Oathtaker* and *Select* have earned the Literary Classics Seal of Approval and the Readers' Favorite Five-Star Seal.